PENGUIN BOOKS

OUT TO CANAAN

Jan Karon writes "to give readers an extended family and to applaud the extraordinary beauty of ordinary people living ordinary lives." Other bestselling novels in the Mitford Years series are *At Home in Mitford; A Light in the Window; These High, Green Hills; A New Song; A Common Life: The Wedding Story;* and *In This Mountain.* Her children's books include *Miss Fannie's Hat* and *Jeremy: The Tale of an Honest Bunny.*

Now you can visit Mitford online at
www.penguinputnam.com/mitford or
www.mitfordbooks.com

Enjoy the latest news from the little town with the big heart including a complete archive of the *More from Mitford* newsletters, the Mitford Years Readers Guide, and much more.

The Mitford Years

Out to Canaan

JAN KARON

PENGUIN BOOKS

PENGUIN BOOKS
Published by the Penguin Group
Penguin Putnam Inc., 375 Hudson Street,
New York, New York 10014, U.S.A.
Penguin Books Ltd, 27 Wrights Lane, London W8 5TZ, England
Penguin Books Australia Ltd, Ringwood, Victoria, Australia
Penguin Books Canada Ltd, 10 Alcorn Avenue,
Toronto, Ontario, Canada M4V 3B2
Penguin Books (N.Z.) Ltd, 182–190 Wairau Road,
Auckland 10, New Zealand

Penguin Books Ltd, Registered Offices:
Harmondsworth, Middlesex, England

First published in the United States of America by Viking Penguin,
a division of Penguin Books USA Inc. 1997
Published in Penguin Books 1998

19 20 18

PUBLISHER'S NOTE
This is a work of fiction. Names, characters, places, and incidents either are the
product of the author's imagination or are used fictitiously, and any resemblance
to actual persons, living or dead, events, or locales is entirely coincidental.

THE LIBRARY OF CONGRESS HAS CATALOGUED THE HARDCOVER AS FOLLOWS:
Karon, Jan, date.
Out to Canaan / Jan Karon.
p.   cm.—(The Mitford years)
ISBN 0-670-87485-X (hc.)
ISBN 0 14 02 6568 6 (pbk.)
I. Title.   II. Series: Karon, Jan, date.   Mitford years.
PS3561.A678078   1997
813'.54—dc21   97–5867

Printed in the United States of America
Set in Adobe Garamond
Designed by Francesca Belanger

Illustrations by Hal Just
Town map by Donna Kae Nelson

For all families
who struggle to forgive
and be forgiven

*"I will restore unto you
the days the locusts
have eaten . . ."*

Joel 2:25

ACKNOWLEDGMENTS

My warmest thanks to:

Candace Freeland; Barry Setzer; Joe Edmisten; Carolyn McNeely; Dr. Margaret Federhart; Fr. Scott Oxford; Jerry Walsh; Blowing Rock BP; Crystal Coffey; Mary Lentz; Jane Hodges; Jim Atkinson; Derald West; Loonis McGlohan; Laura Watts; David Watts; Rev. Gale Cooper and my friends at St. John's; Rev. Jim Trollinger and my friends at Jamestown United Methodist; Fr. Russell Johnson and my friends at St. Paul's; Roald and Marjorie Carlson; W. David Holden; Alex Gabbard; Kay O'Neill; Dr. Richard Chestnutt; Everett Barrineau and all my friends on the Viking Penguin sales force; Aunt Wilma Argo; The Fellowship of Christ, The Saviour; Charles Davant, III; Posie Dauphine; Chuck Meltsner; Kenny Johnson; Fr. Richard Bass; Rev. Richard Holshouser; Christine Hillis; Danilo Ragogna; Dr. Rosemary Horowitz; Helen Horowitz; Susan Weinberg; Sarah Cole; and Tim Knight.

Special thanks to Judy Burns; Jerry Torchia; Dan Blair, a national umpire staff member of the Amateur Softball Association; Flyin' George Ronan of Free Spirit Aviation; Dr. Bunky Davant, Mitford's attending physician; Tony diSanti, Mitford's legal counsel; Alex Hallmark, Mitford's tireless realtor; and all the wonderful readers and booksellers who are helping put the little town with the big heart on the map.

Contents

Out to Canaan

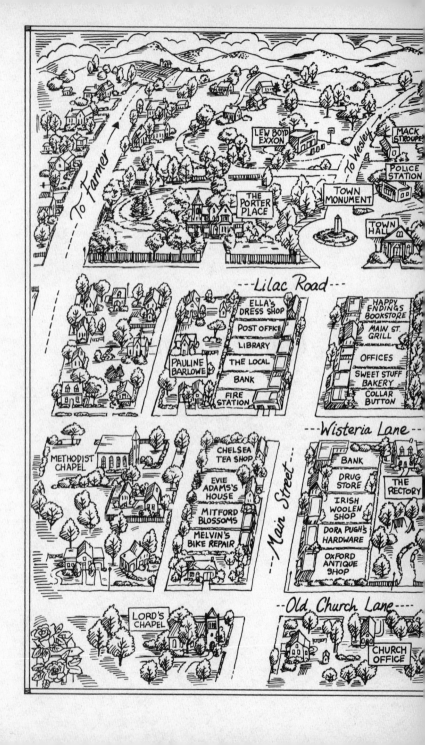

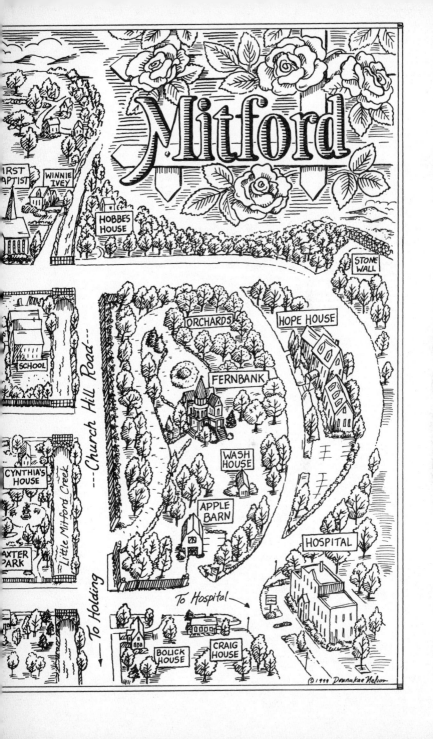

CHAPTER ONE

A Tea and a Half

The indoor plants were among the first to venture outside and breathe the fresh, cold air of Mitford's early spring.

Eager for a dapple of sunlight, starved for the revival of mountain breezes, dozens of begonias and ferns, Easter lilies and Wandering Jews were set out, pot-bound and listless, on porches throughout the village.

As the temperature soared into the low fifties, Winnie Ivey thumped three begonias, a sullen gloxinia, and a Boston fern onto the back steps of the house on Lilac Road, where she was now living. Remembering the shamrock, which was covered with aphids, she fetched it from the kitchen and set it on the railing.

"There!" she said, collecting a lungful of the sharp, pure air. "That ought to fix th' lot of you."

When she opened the back door the following morning, she was stricken at the sight. The carefully wintered plants had been turned to mush by a stark raving freeze and minor snow that also wrenched any notion of early bloom from the lilac bushes.

It was that blasted puzzle she'd worked until one o'clock in the morning, which caused her to forget last night's weather news. There she'd sat like a moron, her feet turning to ice as the temperature plummeted, trying to figure out five letters across for a grove of trees.

Racked with guilt, she consoled herself with the fact that it had, at least, been a chemical-free way to get rid of aphids.

At the hardware, Dora Pugh shook her head and sighed. Betrayed by yesterday's dazzling sunshine, she had done display windows with live baby chicks, wire garden fencing, seeds, and watering cans. Now she might as well haul the snow shovels back and do a final clearance on salt for driveways.

Coot Hendrick collected his bet of five dollars and an RC Cola from Lew Boyd. "Ain't th' first time and won't be th' last you'll see snow in May," he said, grinning. Lew Boyd hated it when Coot grinned, showing his stubs for teeth. He mostly hated it that, concerning weather in Mitford, the skeptics, cynics, and pessimists were usually right.

"Rats!" said Cynthia Kavanagh, who had left a wet scatter rug hanging over the rectory porch rail. Lifting it off the rail, she found it frozen as a popsicle and able to stand perfectly upright.

Father Timothy Kavanagh, rector at the Chapel of our Lord and Savior, had never heard such moaning and groaning about spring's tedious delay, and encountered it even in Happy Endings Bookstore, where, on yet another cold, overcast morning, he picked up a volume entitled *Hummingbirds in the Garden*.

"Hummingbirds?" wailed young Hope Winchester, ringing the sale. "*What* hummingbirds? I suppose you think a hummingbird would dare stick its beak into this arctic tundra, this endless twilight, this . . . this *villatic barbican*?"

"Villatic barbican" was a phrase she had learned only yesterday from a book, and wanted to use it before she forgot it. She knew the rector from Lord's Chapel was somebody she could use such words with—he hadn't flinched when she said "empirical" only last week, and seemed to know exactly what she was talking about.

While everyone else offered lamentations exceeding those of the prophet Jeremiah, the rector felt smugly indifferent to complaints that spring would never come. He had to admit, however, that last

Sunday was one of the few times he'd conducted an Easter service in long johns and ski socks.

Turning up his collar, he leaned into a driving wind and headed toward the office.

Hadn't winter dumped ice, snow, sleet, hail, and rainstorms on the village since late October? Hadn't they been blanketed by fog so thick you could cut it with a dull knife, time and time again?

With all that moisture seeping into the ground for so many long months, didn't this foretell the most glorious springtime in years? And wasn't that, after all, worth the endless assault?

"Absolutely!" he proclaimed aloud, trucking past the Irish Woolen Shop. "No doubt about it!"

"See there?" said Hessie Mayhew, peering out the store window. "It's got Father Tim talking to himself, it's that bad." She sighed. "They say if sunlight doesn't get to your pineal glands for months on end, your sex drive quits."

Minnie Lomax, who was writing sale tags for boiled wool sweaters, looked up and blinked. "What do you know about pineal glands?" She was afraid to ask what Hessie might know about sex drive.

"What does anybody know about pineal glands?" asked Hessie, looking gloomy.

Uncle Billy Watson opened his back door and, without leaving the threshold, lifted the hanging basket off the nail and hauled it inside.

"Look what you've gone and done to that geranium!" snapped his wife of nearly fifty years. "I've petted that thing the winter long, and now it's dead as a doornail."

The old man looked guilt-stricken. "B'fore I hung it out there, hit was already gone south!"

"Shut my mouth? Did you say shut my mouth?" Miss Rose, who refused to wear hearing aids, glared at him.

"I said *gone south*! Dead! Yeller leaves!"

He went to the kitchen radiator and thumped the hanging basket on top. "There!" he said, disgusted with trying to have a garden in a climate like this. "That'll fire it up again."

The rector noted the spears of hosta that had congregated in beds outside the church office. Now, there, as far as spring was concerned, was something you could count on. Hosta was as sturdy a plant as you could put in the ground. Like the postman, neither sleet nor snow could drive it back. Once out of the ground, up it came, fiercely defiant—only, of course, to have its broad leaves shredded like so much Swiss cheese by Mitford's summer hail.

"It's a jungle out there," he sighed, unlocking his office door.

§

After the snow flurry and freeze came a day of rain followed by a sudden storm of sleet that pecked against the windows like a flock of house sparrows.

His wife, he noted, looked pale. She was sitting at the study window, staring at the infernal weather and chewing her bottom lip. She was also biting the cuticle of her thumb, wrapping a strand of hair around one finger, tapping her foot, and generally amusing herself. He, meanwhile, was reading yet another new book and doing something productive.

A low fire crackled on the hearth.

"Amazing!" he said. "You'd never guess one of the things that attracts butterflies."

"I don't have a clue," said Cynthia, appearing not to want one, either. The sleet gusted against the windowpanes.

"Birdbaths!" he exclaimed. No response. "Ditto with honeysuckle!"

He tried again. "Thinking about the Primrose Tea, are you?"

The second edition of his wife's famous parish-wide tea was coming in less than two weeks. Last year at this time, she was living on a stepladder, frantically repainting the kitchen and dining room, removing his octogenarian drapes, and knocking holes in the plaster to affect an "old Italian villa" look. Now here she was, staring out the window without any visible concern for the countless lemon squares, miniature quiches, vegetable sandwiches, and other items she'd need to feed a hundred and twenty-five women, nearly all of whom would look upon the tea as lunch.

His dog, Barnabas, ambled in and crashed by the hearth, as if drugged.

Cynthia tapped her foot and drummed her fingers on the chair arm. "Hmmm," she said.

"Hmmm what?"

She looked at him. "T.D.A."

"T.D.A.?"

"The Dreaded Armoire, dearest."

His heart pounded. Please, no. Not the armoire. "What about it?" he asked, fearing the answer.

"It's time to move it into our bedroom from the guest room. Remember? We said we were going to do it in the spring!" She smiled at him suddenly, as she was wont to do, and her sapphire-colored eyes gleamed. After a year and a half of marriage, how was it that a certain look from her still made him weak in the knees?

"Aha."

"So!" she said, lifting her hands and looking earnest.

"So? So, it's not spring!" He got up from the sofa and pointed toward the window. "See that? You call that spring? This, Kavanagh, is as far from spring as . . . as . . . ."

"As Trieste is from Wesley," she said, helping out, "or the Red Sea from Mitford Creek." He could never get over the way her mind worked. "But do not look at the weather, Timothy, look at the calendar! May third!"

Last fall, they had hauled the enormous armoire down her stairs, down her back steps, through the hedge, up his back steps, along the hall, and finally up the staircase to the guest room, where he had wanted nothing more than to fall prostrate on the rug.

Had she liked it in the guest room, after all that? No, indeed. She had despised the very sight of it sitting there, and instantly came up with a further plan, to be executed in the spring—all of which meant more unloading of drawers and shelves, more lashing the doors closed with a rope, and more hauling—this time across the landing to their bedroom, where, he was convinced, it would tower over them in the night like a five-story parking garage.

"What are you going to do about the tea?" he asked, hoping to distract her.

"Not much at all 'til we get the armoire moved. You know how they are, Timothy, they want to poke into every nook and cranny.

Last year, Hessie Mayhew was down on her very hands and knees, peering into the laundry chute, I saw her with my own eyes. And Georgia Moore opened every cabinet door in the kitchen, she said she was looking for a water glass, when I know for a fact she was seeing if the dishes were stacked to her liking. So, I certainly can't have the armoire standing on that wall in the guest room where it is clearly . . ." she paused and looked at him, "*clearly* out of place."

He was in for it.

§

He had managed to hold off the move for a full week, but in return for the delay was required to make four pans of brownies (a specialty since seminary), clean out the fireplace, black the andirons, and prune the overgrown forsythia at the dining room windows.

Not bad, considering.

On Saturday morning before the big event the following Friday, he rose early, prayed, studied Paul's first letter to the Corinthians, and sat with his sermon notes; then he ran two miles with Barnabas on his red leash, and returned home fit for anything.

His heart still pounding from the final sprint across Baxter Park, he burst into the kitchen, which smelled of lemons, cinnamon, and freshly brewed coffee. "Let's do it!" he cried.

And get it over with, he thought.

§

The drawers were out, the shelves were emptied, the doors were lashed shut with a rope. This time, they were dragging it across the floor on a chenille bedspread, left behind by a former rector.

"*. . . a better way of life!*"

Cynthia looked up. "What did you say, dearest?"

"I didn't say anything."

"*Mack Stroupe will bring improvement, not change . . .*"

They stepped to the open window of the stair landing and looked down to the street. A new blue pickup truck with a public address system was slowly cruising along Wisteria Lane, hauling a sign in the bed. *Mack for Mitford*, it read, *Mitford for Mack*.

"*. . . improvement, not change. So, think about it, friends and neigh-*

bors. *And remember—here in Mitford, we already have the good life.
With Mack as Mayor, we'll all have a better life!*" A loud blast of country music followed: *"If you don't stand for something, you'll fall for anything. . . ."*

She looked at her husband. "Mack Stroupe! Please, no."

He wrinkled his brow and frowned. "This is May. Elections aren't
'til November."

"Starting a mite early."

"I'll say," he agreed, feeling distinctly uneasy.

§

"He's done broke th' noise ordinance," said Chief Rodney Underwood, hitching up his gun belt.

Rodney had stepped to the back of the Main Street Grill to say
hello to the early morning regulars in the rear booth. "Chapter five,
section five-two in the Mitford Code of Ordinance lays it out. No PA
systems for such a thing as political campaigns."

"Startin' off his public career as a pure criminal," said Mule Skinner.

"Which is th' dadgum law of the land for politicians!" *Mitford
Muse* editor J. C. Hogan mopped his brow with a handkerchief.

"Well, no harm done. I slapped a warning on 'im, that ordinance
is kind of new. Used to, politicians was haulin' a PA up and down th'
street, ever' whichaway."

"What about that truck with the sign?" asked Father Tim.

"He can haul th' sign around all he wants to, but th' truck has to
keep movin'. If he parks it on town property, I got 'im. I can run 'im
in and he can go to readin' *Southern Livin'*." The local jail was the
only detention center the rector ever heard of that kept neat stacks of
Southern Living magazine in the cells.

"I hate to see a feller make a fool of hisself," said Rodney. "Ain't
*no*body can whip Esther Cunningham—an' if you say I said that, I'll
say you lied."

"Right," agreed Mule.

"Course, she *has* told it around that one of these days, her an' Ray
are takin' off in th' RV and leave th' mayorin' to somebody else."

Mule shook his head. "Fifteen years is a long time to be hog-tied
to a thankless job, all right."

"Is that Mack's new truck?" asked Father Tim. As far he knew, Mack never had two cents to rub together, as his hotdog stand across from the gas station didn't seem to rake in much business.

"I don't know whose truck it is, it sure couldn't be Mack's. Well, I ain't got all day to loaf, like you boys." Rodney headed for the register to pick up his breakfast order. "See you in th' funny papers."

J.C. scowled. "I don't know that I'd say nobody can whip Esther. Mack's for improvement, and we're due for a little improvement around here, if you ask me."

"Nobody asked you," said Mule.

Father Tim dialed the number from his office. "Mayor!"

"So it's the preacher, is it? I've been lookin' for you."

"What's going on?"

"If that low-down scum thinks he can run me out of office, he's got another think coming."

"Does this mean you're not going to quit and take off with Ray in the RV?"

"Shoot! That's what I say just to hear my head roar. Listen—you don't think the bum has a chance, do you?"

"To tell the truth, Esther, I believe he does have a chance. . . ."

Esther's voice lowered. "You do?"

"About the same chance as a snowball in July."

She laughed uproariously and then sobered. "Of course, there is *one* way that Mack Stroupe could come in here and sit behind th' mayor's desk."

He was alarmed. "Really?"

"But only one. And that's over my dead body."

Something new was going on at home nearly every day.

On Tuesday evening, he found a large, framed watercolor hanging in the rectory's once-gloomy hallway. It was of Violet, Cynthia's white cat and the heroine of the award-winning children's books created by his unstoppable wife. Violet sat on a brocade cloth, peering into a vase filled with nasturtiums and a single, wide-eyed goldfish.

"Stunning!" he said. "Quite a change."

"Call it an *improvement*," she said, pleased.

On Wednesday, he found new chintz draperies in the dining room and parlor, which gave the place a dazzling elegance that fairly bowled him over. But—hadn't they agreed that neither would spend more than a hundred bucks without the other's consent?

She read his mind. "So, the draperies cost five hundred, but since the watercolor is worth that and more on the current market, it's a wash."

"Aha."

"I'm also doing one of Barnabas, for your study. Which means," she said, "that the family coffers will respond by allotting new draperies for our bedroom."

"You're a bookkeeping whiz, Kavanagh. But why new draperies when we're retiring in eighteen months?"

"I've had them made so they can go anywhere and fit any kind of windows. If worse comes to worst, I'll remake them into summer dresses, and vestments for my clergyman."

"That's the spirit!"

Why did he feel his wife could get away with anything where he was concerned? Was it because he'd waited sixty-two years, like a stalled ox, to fall in love and marry?

§

If he and Cynthia had written a detailed petition on a piece of paper and sent it heavenward, the weather couldn't have been more glorious on the day of the talked-about tea.

Much to everyone's relief, the primroses actually bloomed. However, no sooner had the eager blossoms appeared than Hessie Mayhew bore down on them with a vengeance, in yards and hidden nooks everywhere. She knew precisely the location of every cluster of primroses in the village, not to mention the exact whereabouts of each woods violet, lilac bush, and pussy willow.

"It's Hessie!" warned an innocent bystander on Hessie's early morning run the day of the tea. "Stand back!"

Armed with a collection of baskets that she wore on her arms like so many bracelets, Hessie did not allow help from the Episcopal

Church Women, nor any of her own presbyters. She worked alone, she worked fast, and she worked smart.

After going at a trot through neighborhood gardens, huffing up Old Church Lane to a secluded bower of early-blooming shrubs, and combing four miles of country roadside, she showed up at the back door of the rectory at precisely eleven a.m., looking triumphant.

Sodden with morning dew and black dirt, she delivered a vast quantity of flowers, moss, and grapevine into the hands of the rector's house help, Puny Guthrie, then flew home to bathe, dress, and put antibiotic cream on her knees, which were skinned when she leaned over to pick a wild trillium and fell sprawling.

The Episcopal Church Women, who had arrived as one body at ten-thirty, flew into the business of arranging "Hessie's truck," as they called it, while Barnabas snored in the garage and Violet paced in her carrier.

"Are you off?" asked Cynthia, as the rector came at a trot through the hectic kitchen.

"Off and running. I finished polishing the mail slot, tidying the slipcover on the sofa, and trimming the lavender by the front walk. I also beat the sofa pillows for any incipient dust and coughed for a full five minutes."

"Well done!" she said cheerily, giving him a hug.

"I'll be home at one-thirty to help the husbands park cars."

Help the husbands park cars? he thought as he sprinted toward the office. He was a *husband*! After all these months, the thought still occasionally slammed him in the solar plexus and took his breath away.

§

Nine elderly guests, including the Kavanaghs' friend Louella, arrived in the van from Hope House and were personally escorted up the steps of the rectory and into the hands of the Altar Guild.

Up and down Wisteria Lane, men with armbands stitched with primroses and a Jerusalem cross directed traffic, which quickly grew snarled. At one point, the rector leaped into a stalled Chevrolet and managed to roll it to the curb. Women came in car pools, husbands dropped off spouses, daughters delivered mothers, and all in all, the narrow street was as congested as a carnival in Rio.

"This is th' biggest thing to hit Mitford since th' blizzard two years ago," said Mule Skinner, who was a Baptist, but offered to help out, anyway.

The rector laughed. "That's one way to look at it." Didn't anybody ever *walk* in this town?

"Look here!"

It was Mack Stroupe in that blasted pickup truck, carting his sign around in their tea traffic. Mack rolled by, chewing on a toothpick and looking straight ahead.

"You comin' to the Primrose Tea?" snapped Mule. "If not, get this vehicle out of here, we're tryin' to conduct a church function!"

Four choir members, consisting of a lyric soprano, a mezzo soprano, and two altos, arrived in a convertible, looking windblown and holding on to their hats.

"Hats is a big thing this year," observed Uncle Billy Watson, who stood at the curb with Miss Rose and watched the proceedings. Uncle Billy was the only man who showed up at last year's tea, and now considered his presence at the event to be a tradition.

Uncle Billy walked out to the street with the help of his cane and tapped Father Tim on the shoulder. "Hit's like a Chiney puzzle, don't you know. If you 'uns'd move that'n off to th' side and git that'n to th' curb, hit'd be done with."

"No more parking on Wisteria," Ron Malcolm reported to the rector. "We'll direct the rest of the crowd to the church lot and shoot 'em back here in the Hope House van."

A UPS driver, who had clearly made an unwise turn onto Wisteria, sat in his truck in front of the rectory, stunned by the sight of so much traffic on the usually uneventful Holding/Mitford/Wesley run.

"Hit's what you call a standstill," Uncle Billy told J. C. Hogan, who showed up with his Nikon and six rolls of Tri-X.

As traffic started to flow again, the rector saw Mack Stroupe turn onto Wisteria Lane from Church Hill. Clearly, he was circling the block.

"I'd like to whop him upside th' head with a two-by-four," said

Mule. He glared at Mack, who was reared back in the seat with both windows down, listening to a country music station. Mack waved to several women, who immediately turned their heads.

Mule snorted. "Th' dumb so-and-so! How would you like to have that peckerwood for mayor?"

The rector wiped his perspiring forehead. "Watch your blood pressure, buddyroe."

"He says he's goin' to campaign straight through spring and summer, right up to election in November. Kind of like bein' tortured by a drippin' faucet."

As the truck passed, Emma Newland stomped over. "I ought to climb in that truck and slap his jaws. What's he doin', anyway, trying to sway church people to his way of thinkin'?"

"Let him be," Father Tim cautioned his secretary and on-line computer whiz. After all, give Mack enough rope and . . .

§

Cynthia was lying in bed, moaning, as he came out of the shower. He went into the bedroom, hastily drying off.

"Why are you moaning?" he asked, alarmed.

"Because it helps relieve exhaustion. I hope the windows are closed so the neighbors can't hear."

"The only neighbor close enough to hear is no longer living in the little yellow house next door. She is, in fact, lying right here, doing the moaning."

She moaned again. "Moaning is good," she told him, her face mashed into the pillow. "You should try it."

"I don't think so," he said.

Warm as a steamed clam from the shower, he put on his pajamas and sat on the side of the bed. "I'm proud of you," he said, rubbing her back. "That was a tea-and-a-half! The best! In fact, words fail. You'll have a time topping that one."

"Don't tell me I'm supposed to *top* it!"

"Yes, well, not to worry. Next year, we can have Omer Cunningham and his pilot buddies do a flyover. That'll give the ladies something to talk about." He'd certainly given all of Mitford something to talk about last May when he flew to Virginia with Omer in his rag-wing taildragger. Four hours in Omer's little plane had gained him more credibility than thirty-six years in the pulpit.

"A little farther down," his wife implored. "Ugh. My lower back is killing me from all the standing and baking."

"I got the reviews as your guests left."

"Only tell me the good ones. I don't want to hear about the cheese straws, which were as limp as linguine."

"'Perfect' was a word they bandied around quite a bit, and the lemon squares, of course, got their usual share of raves. Some wanted me to know how charming they think you are, and others made lavish remarks about your youth and beauty."

He leaned down and kissed her shoulder, inhaling the faintest scent of wisteria. "You are beautiful, Kavanagh."

"Thanks."

"I don't suppose there are any special thanks you'd like to offer the poor rube who helped unsnarl four thousand three hundred and seventy-nine cars, trucks, and vans?"

She rolled over and looked at him, smiling. Then she held her head to one side in that way he couldn't resist, and pulled him to her and kissed him tenderly.

"Now you're talking," he said.

The phone rang.

"Hello?"

"Hey."

Dooley! "Hey, yourself, buddy."

"Is Cynthia sending me a box of stuff she made for that tea? I can't talk long."

"Two boxes. Went off today."

"Man! Thanks!"

"You're welcome. How's school?"

"Great."

Great? Dooley Barlowe was not one to use superlatives. "No kidding?"

"You're going to like my grades."

Was this the little guy he'd struggled to raise for nearly three years?

The Dooley who always shot himself in the foot? The self-assured sound of the boy's voice made his hair fairly stand on end.

"We're going to like you coming home, even better. In just six or seven weeks, you'll be here. . . ."

Silence. Was Dooley dreading to tell him he wanted to spend the summer at Meadowgate Farm? The boy's decision to do that last year had nearly broken his heart, not to mention Cynthia's. They had, of course, gotten over it, as they watched the boy doing what he loved best—learning more about veterinary medicine at the country practice of Hal Owen.

"Of course," said the rector, pushing on, "we want you to go out to Meadowgate, if that's what you'd like to do." He swallowed. This year, he was stronger, he could let go.

"OK," said Dooley, "that's what I'd like to do."

"Fine. No problem. I'll call you tomorrow for our usual phone visit. We love you."

"I love you back."

"Here's Cynthia."

"Hey," she said.

"Hey, yourself." It was their family greeting.

"So, you big galoot, we sent a box for you and one to share with your friends."

"What's in it?"

"Lemon squares."

"I like lemon squares."

"Plus raspberry tarts, pecan truffles, and brownies made by the preacher."

"Thanks."

"Are you OK?"

"Yes."

"No kidding?"

"Yep."

"Good!" said Cynthia. "Lace Turner asked about you the other day."

"That dumb girl that dresses like a guy?"

"She doesn't dress like a guy anymore. Oh, and your friend Jenny was asking about you, too."

"How's Tommy?"

"Missing you. Just as we do. So hurry home, even if you are going to spend the summer at Meadowgate, you big creep."

Dooley cackled.

"We love you."

"I love you back."

Cynthia placed the receiver on the hook, smiling happily.

"Now, you poor rube," she said, "where were we?"

He sat on the study sofa and took the rubber band off the *Mitford Muse.*

Good grief! There he was on the front page, standing bewildered in front of the UPS truck with his nose looking, as usual, like a turnip or a tulip bulb. Why did J. C. Hogan run this odious picture, when he might have photographed his hardworking, good-looking, and thoroughly deserving wife?

Primrose Tee Draws
Stand-Out Crowd

Clearly, Hessie had not written this story, which on first glance appeared to be about golf, but had given her notes to J.C., who forged ahead without checking his spelling.

Good time had by all . . . same time next year . . . a hundred and thirty guests . . . nine gallons of tea, ten dozen lemon squares, eight dozen raspberry tarts . . . traffic jam . . .

The phone gave a sharp blast.

"Hello?"

"Timothy . . ."

"Hal! I've just been thinking of you and Marge."

"Good. And we of you. I've got some . . . hard news, and wanted you to know."

Hal and Marge Owen were two of his closest, most valued friends. He was afraid to know.

"I've just hired a full-time assistant."

"That's the bad news? It sounds good to me, you work like a Trojan."

"Yes, but . . . we won't be able to have Dooley this summer. My assistant is a young fellow, just starting out, and I'll have to give him a lot of time and attention. Also, we're putting him up in Dooley's room until he gets established." Hal sighed.

"But that's terrific. We know Dooley looked forward to being at Meadowgate—however, circumstances alter cases, as my Mississippi kin used to say."

"There's a large riding stable coming in about a mile down the road, they've asked me to vet the horses. That could be a full-time job right there."

"I understand. Of course. Your practice is growing."

"We'll miss the boy, Tim, you know how we feel about him, how Rebecca Jane loves him. But look, we'll have him out to stay the first two weeks he's home from school—if that works for you."

"Absolutely."

"Oh, and Tim . . ."

"Yes?"

"Will you tell him?"

"I will. I'll talk to him about it, get him thinking of what to do this summer. Be good for him."

"So why don't you and Cynthia plan to spend the day when you bring him out? Bring Barnabas, too. Marge will make your favorite."

Deep-dish chicken pie, with a crust like French pastry. "We'll be there!" he said, meaning it.

§

"Will you tell him?" he asked Cynthia.

"No way," she said.

Nobody wanted to tell Dooley Barlowe that he couldn't spend the summer doing what he loved more than anything on earth.

§

She opened her eyes and rolled over to find him sitting up in bed. "Oh, my dear! Oh, my goodness! What happened?"

He loved the look on his wife's face; he wanted to savor it. "It's already turned a few colors," he said, removing his hand from his right temple.

She peered at him as if he were a butterfly on a pin. "Yes! Black . . . and blue and . . . the tiniest bit of yellow."

"My old school colors," he said.

"But what happened?" He never heard such *tsk*ing and gasping.

"T.D.A.," he replied.

"The Dreaded Armoire? What do you mean?"

"I mean that I got up in the middle of the night, in the dark, and went out to the landing and opened the windows to give Barnabas a cool breeze. As I careened through the bedroom on my way to the bathroom, I slammed into the blasted thing."

"Oh, no! Oh, heavens. What can I do? And tomorrow's Sunday!"

"Spousal abuse," he muttered. "In today's TV news climate, my congregation will pick up on it immediately."

"Timothy, dearest, I'm so sorry. I'll get something for you, I don't know what, but something. Just stay right there and don't move."

She put on her slippers and robe and flew downstairs, Barnabas barking at her heels.

T.D.A. might stand for "The *Dreaded* Armoire" as far as his wife was concerned. As far as he was concerned, it stood for something else entirely.

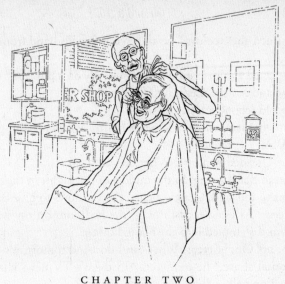

CHAPTER TWO

Step by Step

He was missing her.

How many times had he gone to the phone to call, only to realize she wasn't there to answer?

When Sadie Baxter died last year at the age of ninety, he felt the very rug yanked from under him. She'd been family to him, and a companionable friend; his sister in Christ, and favorite parishioner. In addition, she was Dooley's benefactor and, for more than half a century, the most generous donor in the parish. Not only had she given Hope House, the new five-million-dollar nursing home at the top of Old Church Lane, she had faithfully kept a roof on Lord's Chapel while her own roof went begging.

Sadie Baxter was warbling with the angels, he thought, chuckling at the image. But not because of the money she'd given, no, indeed. Good works, the Scriptures plainly stated, were no passport to heaven. "For by grace are you saved through faith," Paul wrote in his letter to the Ephesians, "and that not of yourselves, it is the gift of God—not of works, lest any man should boast."

The issue of works versus grace was about as popular as the issue of sin. Nonetheless, he was set to preach on Paul's remarks, and soon. The whole works ideology was as insidious as so many termites going after the stairs to the altar.

Emma blew in, literally. As she opened the office door, a gust of cold spring wind snatched it from her hand and sent it crashing against the wall.

"Lord have mercy!" she shouted, trying to snatch it back against a gale that sent his papers flying. She slammed the door and stood panting in front of it, her glasses crooked on her nose.

"Have you *ever*?" she demanded.

"Ever what?"

"Seen a winter that lasted nine months goin' on ten? I said, Harold, why don't we move to Florida? I never thought I'd live to hear such words come out of my mouth."

"And what did Harold say?" he asked, trying to reassemble his papers.

"You know Baptists," she replied, hanging up her coat. "They don't move to Florida; they don't want to be warm! They want to freeze to death on th' way to prayer meetin' and shoot right up to th' pearly gates and get it over with."

The Genghis Khan of church secretaries wagged her finger at him. "It's enough to make me go back to bein' Episcopalian."

"What's Harold done now?"

"Made Snickers sleep in the garage. Can you believe it? Country people don't like dogs in the house, you know."

"I thought Snickers was sleeping in the house."

"He was, 'til he ate a steak off Harold's plate."

"Aha."

"Down th' hatch, neat as a pin. But then, guess what?"

"I can't guess."

"He threw it all up in the closet, on Harold's shoes."

"I can see Harold's point."

"You would," she said stiffly, sitting at her desk.

"I would?"

"Yes. You're a man," she announced, glaring at him. "By the way . . ."

"By the way what?"

"That bump on your head is the worst-lookin' mess I ever saw. Can't you get Cynthia to do somethin' about it?"

Then again, maybe works *could* have an influence. Exercising the patience of a saint while putting up with Emma Newland for fifteen years should be enough to blast him heavenward like a rocket, with no stops along the way.

Emma booted her computer and peered at the screen.

"I nearly ran over Mack Stroupe comin' in this morning, he crossed th' street without lookin'. I didn't know whether to hit th' brakes or the accelerator. You know that hotdog stand of his? He's turnin' it into his campaign headquarters! Campaign headquarters, can you believe it? Who does he think he is, Ross Perot?"

The rector sighed.

"You know that mud slick in front that he called a parkin' lot?" She clicked her mouse. "Well, he's having it paved, the asphalt trucks are all over it like flies. Asphalt!" she muttered. "I hate asphalt. Give me cement, any day."

Yes, indeed. Straight up, right into a personal and highly favorable audience with St. Peter.

§

"Something has to be done," he said.

"Yes, but what?"

"Blast if I know. If we don't get a new roof on it soon, who can guess what the interior damage might be?"

Father Tim and Cynthia sat at the kitchen table, discussing his second most worrisome problem—what to do with the rambling, three-story Victorian mansion known as Fernbank, and its endless, overgrown grounds.

When Miss Sadie died last year, she left Fernbank to the church, "to cover any future needs of Hope House," and there it sat—buffeted by hilltop winds and scoured by driving hailstorms, with no one even to sweep dead bees from the windowsills.

In Miss Sadie's mind, Fernbank had been a gift; to him, it was an albatross. After all, she had clearly made him responsible for doing the best thing by her aging homeplace.

There had been talk of leasing it to a private school or institution, a notion that lay snarled somewhere in diocesan red tape. On the other hand, should they sell it and invest the money? If so, should they sell it as is, or bite the bullet and repair it at horrendous cost to a parish almost certainly unwilling to gamble in real estate?

"We just got an estimate on the roof," he said.

"How much?"

"Thirty, maybe thirty-five thousand."

"Good heavens!"

They sat in silence, reflecting.

"Poor Fernbank," she said. "Who would buy it, anyway? Certainly no one in Mitford can afford it."

He refilled his coffee cup. Even if they were onto a sour subject, he was happy to be hanging out with his wife. Besides, Cynthia Kavanagh was known for stumbling onto serendipitous solutions for all sorts of woes and tribulations.

"Worse than that," she said, "who could afford to fix it up, assuming they could buy it in the first place?"

"There's the rub."

After staring at the tablecloth for a moment, she looked up. "Then again, why worry about it at all? Miss Sadie didn't give it to *you* . . ."

So why had he worn the thing around his neck for more than ten months?

". . . she gave it to the church. Which, in case you've momentarily forgotten, belongs to God. So, let Him handle it, for Pete's sake."

He could feel the grin spreading across his face. Right! Of course! He felt a weight fly off, if only temporarily. "Who's the preacher around here, anyway?"

"Sometimes you go on sabbatical, dearest."

He stood and cranked open the kitchen window. "When are we going up there and pick out the token or two that Miss Sadie offered us in the letter?"

She sighed. "We don't have a nook, much less a cranny that isn't already stuffed with *things*. My house next door is full, the rectory is brimming, and we're retiring."

She was right. It was a time to be subtracting, not adding.

"What have the others taken?" she wondered.

"Louella took the brooch Miss Sadie's mother painted, and Olivia only wanted a walnut chest and the photographs of Miss Sadie's mother and Willard Porter. The place is virtually untouched."

"Did anyone go sneezing through the attic?"

"Not a soul."

"I absolutely love sneezing through attics! Attics are full of mystery and intrigue. So, yes, let's do it! Let's go up! Besides, we don't have to shop, we can *browse*!"

Her eyes suddenly looked bluer, as they always did when she was excited.

"I love it when you talk like this," he said, relieved.

At least one of the obligations surrounding Fernbank would be settled.

§

Fernbank was only his second most nagging worry.

What to do about Dooley's scattered siblings had moved to the head of the line.

Over the last few years, Dooley's mother, Pauline Barlowe, had let her children go like so many kittens scattered from a box.

How could he hope to collect what had been blown upon the wind during Pauline's devastating bouts with alcohol? The last that Pauline had heard, her son Kenny was somewhere in Oregon, little Jessie's whereabouts were unknown, and Sammy . . . he didn't want to think about it.

Last year, the rector had gone with Lace Turner into the drug-infested Creek community and brought Dooley's nine-year-old brother out. Poobaw was now living in Betty Craig's cottage with his recovering mother and disabled grandfather, and doing well in Mitford School.

A miracle. But in this case, miracles, like peanuts, were addictive. One would definitely not be enough.

§

"This news just hit the street," said Mule, sliding into the booth with a cup of coffee. "I got it before J.C."

"Aha," said the rector, trying to decide whether to butter his roll or eat it dry.

"Joe Ivey's hangin' it up."

"No!"

"Goin' to Tennessee to live with his kin, and Winnie Ivey cryin' her eyes out, he's all the family she's got in Mitford."

"Why is he hanging it up?"

"Kidneys."

Velma appeared with her order pad. "We don't have kidneys n'more. We tried kidneys last year and nobody ordered 'em."

"Meat loaf sandwich, then," said Mule. "Wait a minute. What's the Father having?"

"Chicken salad."

"I pass. Make it a BLT on whole wheat."

"Kidneys?" asked the rector as Velma left.

"I don't have to tell you Joe likes a little shooter now and again."

"Umm."

"Lately, he's been drinkin' peach brandy, made fresh weekly in Knox County. The other thing is, varicose veins. Forty-five years of standing on his feet barbering, his legs look like a Georgia road map." Mule blew on his coffee. "He showed 'em to me."

Except for a couple of visits to Fancy Skinner's Hair House, Joe Ivey had been his barber since he came to Mitford. "I hate to hear this."

"We all hate to hear it."

There was a long silence. The rector buttered his roll.

"I despise change," said Mule, looking grim.

"You and me both."

"That's why Mack won't call it change, he calls it improvement. But you and I know exactly what it is. . . ."

"Change," said Father Tim.

"Right. And if Mack has anything to do with it, it won't be change for the better."

What the heck, he opened the container of blackberry jam left from the breakfast crowd and spread that on, too. With diabetes, life may not be long, he thought, but the diet they put you on sure makes it seem that way.

"Have you thought of the bright side of Joe getting out of the business?" asked Father Tim.

"The bright side?"

"All Joe's customers will be running to your wife."

Mule's face lit up. "I'll be dadgum. That's right."

"That ought to amount to, oh, forty people, easy. With haircuts at ten bucks a head these days, you and Fancy can go on that cruise you've been talking about, no problem."

Mule looked grim again. "Yeah, but then Fancy'll be gettin' varicose veins."

"Every calling has an occupational hazard," said the rector. "Look at yours—a real estate market that's traditionally volatile, you never know how much bread you can put on the table, or when."

J.C. threw his bulging briefcase onto the bench and slid into the booth.

"Did you hear what Adele did last night?"

"What?" the realtor and the rector asked in unison.

The editor looked like he'd just won the lottery. "She busted a guy for attempted robbery and probably saved Dot Hamby's life." Adele was not only a Mitford police officer, but J.C.'s wife.

"Your buttons are poppin' off in my coffee," said Mule.

"Where did it happen?"

"Down at the Shoe Barn. She parked her patrol car in back, went in the side door, and was over behind one of the shoe racks, tryin' to find a pair of pumps. Meanwhile, this idiot walks in the front door and asks Dot to change a ten, and when Dot opens the cash register, he whips out a gun and shoves it in her face. Adele heard what was going on, so she slipped up behind the sucker, barefooted, and buried a nine-millimeter in his ribs."

"What did she say?" asked Mule.

"She said what you're supposed to say in a case like that. She said, 'Drop it.'"

Mule raised his eyebrows. "Man!"

J.C. wiped his face with a handkerchief. "His butt is in jail as we speak."

"Readin' casserole recipes out of *Southern Living*," said Mule. "It's too good for th' low-down snake."

"It's nice to see where my recyclin' is ending up," said the editor, staring at Mule.

"What's that supposed to mean?"

"I just read it takes twenty-six plastic soda bottles to make a polyester suit like that."

"Waste not, want not," said Mule.

J.C. looked for Velma. "You see what Mack's doing up the street?"

"We did."

"A real improvement, he says he's throwing a barbecue soon as the parking lot hardens off. Live music, the whole nine yards. I might give that a front page."

Mule appeared frozen.

"What's the deal with you not liking Mack Stroupe?" asked J.C. "The least you can do is listen to what he has to say."

"I don't listen to double-dealin' cheats," snapped Mule. "They don't have anything to say that I want to hear."

"Come on, that incident was years ago."

"He won't get my vote, let me put it that way."

J.C.'s face flushed. "You want to stick your head in the sand like half the people in this town, go ahead. For my money, it's time we had something new and different around here, a few new businesses, a decent housing development.

"When they staffed Hope House, they hired twenty-seven people from outside Mitford, and where do you think they're living? Wesley! Holding! Working here, but pumping up somebody else's economy, building somebody else's town parks, paying somebody else's taxes."

The rector noticed that Mule's hand was shaking when he picked up his coffee cup. "I'd rather see Mitford throw tax money down a rat hole than put a mealymouthed lowlife in Esther's job."

"For one thing," growled J.C., "you'd better get over the idea it's *Esther's* job."

The regulars in the back booth had disagreed before, but this was disturbingly different.

The roll the rector had eaten suddenly became a rock.

❦

"Just a little off the sides," he said.

"Sides? What sides? Since you slipped off and let Fancy Skinner do your barberin', you ain't got any sides."

What could he say? "We'll miss you around here, Joe. I hate like the dickens to see you go."

"I hate like the dickens to go. But I'm too old to be doin' this."

"How old?"

"Sixty-four."

Good Lord! He was hovering around that age himself. He instantly felt depressed. "That's not old!" he said.

"For this callin', it is. I've tore my legs up over it, and that's enough for me."

"Where are you moving in Tennessee?"

"Memphis. Might do a little part-time security at Graceland, with my cousin. I'll be stayin' with my baby sister—Winnie's th' oldest, you know, we want her to move up, too."

Winnie gone from the Sweet Stuff Bakery? Two familiar faces missing from Mitford, all at once? He didn't like the sound of it, not a bit.

"Here," said Joe, handing him a bottle with an aftershave label. "Take you a little pull on this. It might be your last chance."

"What is it?"

"Homemade peach brandy, you'll never taste better. Go on and take you a snort, I won't tell nobody."

For fifteen years, his barber had offered him a nip of this, a shooter of that, and he had always refused. The rector had preached him a sermon a time or two, years ago, but Joe had told him to mind his own business. Without even thinking, he unscrewed the cap, turned the bottle up, and took a swig. *Holy smoke.*

He passed it back, nearly unable to speak. "That'll do it for me."

"I might have a little taste myself." Joe upended the bottle and polished off half the contents.

"Are you sure you poured out the aftershave before you poured in the brandy?"

Joe cackled. "Listen here," he said, brushing his customer's neck, "don't be lettin' Mack Stroupe run Esther off."

"I'll do my best."

"Look after Winnie 'til she can sell her bake shop and get up to Memphis."

"I will. She's a good one."

"And take good care of that boy, keep him in a straight line. I never had nobody to keep me in a straight line."

"You've done all right, Joe. You've been a good friend to us, and you'll be missed." He might have been trying to swallow down a golf ball. He hated goodbyes.

He got out of the chair and reached for his wallet. "I want you to take care of yourself, and let us hear from you."

Tears stood in Joe's eyes. "Put that back in your pocket. I've barbered you for fifteen years, and this one's on me."

He'd never noticed that Joe Ivey seemed so frail-looking and pallid—defenseless, somehow. The rector threw his arms around him in a wordless hug. Then he walked down the stairs to Main Street, his breath smelling like lighter fluid, bawling like a baby.

§

The date for the Bane and Blessing sale was official, and the annual moaning began.

No show of lilacs, no breathtaking display of dogwoods could alleviate the woe.

Three ECW members suddenly developed chronic back trouble, and an Altar Guild member made reservations to visit her sister in Toledo during the week of the sale. Two Sunday School teachers who had, in a weak moment, volunteered to help trooped up the aisle after Wednesday Eucharist to pray at the altar.

After Esther Bolick agreed to chair the historic church event, she went home and asked her husband, Gene, to have her committed. The Bane and Blessing was known, over the years, for having put two women flat on their backs in bed, nearly broken up a marriage, and chased three families to the Lutherans in Wesley.

Besides, hadn't she virtually retired from years and years of churchwork, trying to focus, instead, on cake baking? Wasn't baking a ministry in its own right? And didn't she bake an orange marmalade cake at least twice a week for some poor soul who was down and out?

In the first place, she couldn't remember saying she'd *do* the Bane. She had been totally dumbfounded when the meeting ended and everybody rushed over to hug and thank her and tell her how wonderful she was.

In the end, she sighed, determined that it should be done "as unto the Lord and not unto men."

"That's the spirit!" said her rector, doling out a much-needed hug. He wouldn't have traded places with Esther Bolick for all the tea in China. Esther, however, would do an outstanding job, and no doubt put an unprecedented amount of money in the missions till.

Because it was the most successful fund-raising event in the entire diocese, the women who pulled it off usually got enough local recognition to last a lifetime, or, at the very least, a couple of months.

"October fourth," Esther told Gene.

"Eat your Wheaties," Gene told Esther.

He'd rather be shot. But somebody had to do it.

"Hey," said Dooley, knowing who was on the phone.

"Hey, yourself. What's going on up there?"

"Chorus trip to Washington this weekend. We're singing in a church and a bunch of senators and stuff will be there. I bought a new blazer, my old one got ripped on a nail. How's ol' Barnabas?"

"Sitting right here, licking my shoe, I think I dropped jam on it this morning. There's something I need to talk with you about."

Silence.

"Hal Owen hired an assistant."

He may as well have put a knife in the boy, so keenly could he feel his disappointment.

"That means he'll have help this summer, and the fellow will be . . ."—he especially hated this part—"be staying in your room until he gets situated."

"Fine," said Dooley, his voice cold.

"Hal had to do it, he's been asked to vet a riding stable that's moving in up the road. He's got his hands full and then some."

He couldn't bear Dooley Barlowe's silences; they seemed as deep as wells, as black as mines.

"Hal and Marge want you to come out for two weeks when you get home from school. They'll . . . miss having you for the summer."

"OK."

"You might want to think about a job."

More silence.

"Tommy's going to have a job."

"Where?"

"Pumping gas at Lew's. He'll probably have a uniform with his name on it." It was a weak ploy, but all he could come up with. He pushed on. "Summer will give you time with your brother. Poobaw would like that. And so would your granpaw."

Give him time to think it over. "Listen, buddy. You're going to have a great summer, you'll see. And we love you. Never forget that."

"I don't."

Good! "Good. I'll talk with you Saturday."

"Hey, listen . . ." said Dooley.

"Yes?"

"Nothin'."

"OK. God be with you, son."

He took out his handkerchief and wiped his forehead.

"He who is not impatient is not in love," said an old Italian proverb.

Well, that proved it right there, he thought, leaving his office and hurrying up Main Street toward home.

Why did he feel such excitement about seeing his wife, when he had seen her only this morning? She had brought them coffee in bed at an inhuman hour, and they'd sat up, drinking it, laughing and talking as if it were high noon.

A woman who would get up at five o'clock in order to visit with her husband before his prayer and study time was a saint. Of course, he admitted, she didn't make a habit of it. And didn't that make it all the more welcome?

Cynthia, Cynthia! he thought, looking at the pink dogwood in the yard of the tea room across the street. Like great pink canopies, the trees spread their lacy shade over emerald grass and beds of yellow tulips.

Dear Lord! It was nearly more than a man could bear—spring coming on like thunder, and a woman who had kissed him only hours ago, in a way he'd never, in his bachelor days, had the wits to imagine.

It wouldn't take more than a very short memory to recall the women who'd figured in his life.

Peggy Cramer. That had taught him a thing or two. And when the engagement broke off while he was in seminary, he'd known that it was a good thing.

Then there was Becky. How his parish had worked to pull that one off! She was the woman who thought Wordsworth was a Dallas department store. He hoofed it past Dora Pugh's hardware, laughing out loud.

Ah, but he felt an immense gratitude for his wife's spontaneous laughter, her wisdom, and even her infernal stubbornness. He snapped a branch of white lilac from the bush at the corner of the rectory yard.

He raced up his front steps, threw open the door, and bounded down the hall.

"Cynthia!"

As if he had punched a button, a clamor went up. Puny Guthrie's red-haired twins, Sissy and Sassy, began squalling as one.

"Now see what you've done!" said Puny, standing at the ironing board in the kitchen.

"I didn't know you'd still be here," he said lamely.

"An' I just rocked 'em off to sleep! Look, girls, here's your granpaw!"

His house help, for whom he would be eternally grateful, was determined that he be a granpaw to her infants, whether he liked it or not.

"So, looky here, you hold Sissy and I'll jiggle Sassy, I've got another hour to finish all this ironin' from th' tea."

He took Sissy and, as instantly as Sissy had started crying, she stopped and gazed up at him.

"Hey, there," he said, gazing back.

"See? She likes you! She loves 'er granpaw, don't she?"

He could not take his eyes off the wonder in his arms. Because Puny was often gone by the time he arrived home, or was next door at the little yellow house, he hadn't seen much of the twins over the winter. And now here they were, nearly a full year old, and one of them reaching up to pull his lower lip down to his collar.

Puny put Sassy on her hip and jiggled her. "If you'd jis' walk Sissy around or somethin', I'd 'preciate it. Lord, look at th' ironin' that come off of that tea, and all of it antique somethin' or other from a bishop or a pope. . . ."

"Where's Cynthia?"

"I've not seen 'er since lunch. She might be over at her house, workin' on a book."

As far as he knew, his industrious wife was not working on a book these days. She'd decided to take a sabbatical since last year's book on bluebirds.

"I'll just take Sissy and go looking," he said.

"If she cries, jiggle 'er!"

Wanting to be proactive, he started jiggling at once.

He walked through the backyard, ignoring the dandelions that lighted his lawn like so many small, yellow fires. No, indeed, he would not get obsessive over the dandelions this spring, he would not dig them out one by one, as he had done in former years. Dandelions come and dandelions go, and there you have it, he thought, jiggling. Wasn't he a man heading into retirement? Wasn't he a man learning to loosen up and live a little?

Sissy gurgled and squirmed in his arms.

"Timothy!"

It was his wife, trotting through the hedge and looking like a girl. "You'll never guess what!"

"I can't guess," he said, leaning over to kiss her. He tucked the branch of lilac in her shirt pocket as Sissy socked him on the chin.

"Thank you, dearest! Mule just called to say someone's interested in Fernbank! He tried to ring you at the office, but you'd left. Can you imagine? It's someone from out of town, he said, a corporation or something. Run and call him, and I'll take Sissy!"

Why didn't he feel joyful as he went to the phone in his study? He didn't feel joyful at all. Instead, he felt a strange sense of foreboding.

§

He lay on his side, propped up on his elbow. "I thought about you today," he said, shy about telling her this simple thing.

She traced his nose and chin with her forefinger. "How very odd! I thought about you today."

"It was the five o'clock coffee that did it," he said, kissing her.

"Is that what it was?" she murmured, kissing him in return.

Perhaps almost anyone could love, he thought; it was the loving back that seemed to count for everything.

§

He tossed the thing onto a growing pile.

A man who had time to dig dandelions was a man with time to waste, he thought.

While he had no time at all to do something so trivial, he found he couldn't help himself. He'd been lured into the yard like a miner lured to veins of gold.

There were, needless to say, a hundred other things that needed doing more:

The visit to Fernbank's attic, and get cracking now that a possible buyer was on the scene.

Fertilize the roses.

Mulch the beds.

Get up to Hope House and talk to Scott Murphy. . . .

Scott was the young, on-fire chaplain that he and Miss Sadie had hired last year. Ever since he'd come last September, they'd tried to find time to run together, but so far, it hadn't worked. Scott was like the tigers in a favorite childhood story—he was racing around the tree so fast, he was turning into butter.

The new chaplain not only held services every morning, but was making personal rounds to every one of the forty residents, every day.

"It's what I was hired to do," he said, grinning.

In addition, he'd gotten the once-controversial kennel program up and running. In this deal, a Hope House resident could "rent" a cat or a dog for up to two hours a day, simply by placing an advance order for Hector, Barney, Muffin, Lucky, etc. As the rector had seen on his visits to Hope House, this program doled out its own kind of medicine.

Evie Adams's mother, Miss Pattie, who had been literally out of her mind for a decade, had taken a shine to Baxter, a cheerful dachshund, and was, on certain days, nearly lucid.

Every afternoon, the pet wagon rolled along the halls at Hope House, and residents who weren't bedridden got to amuse, and be amused by, their four-legged visitors. There were goldfish for those who couldn't handle the responsibility of a cat or dog, and, for everyone in general, Mitford School kept the walls supplied with bright posters.

"I'll be dadgum if I wouldn't like to move in there," said several villagers who were perfectly able-bodied.

He sat back on his heels and dropped the weed-puller. What about the Creek community? Hadn't he and Scott talked last year about doing something, anything, to bring some healing to that place? It was overwhelming even to think about it, and yet, he constantly thought about it.

And Sammy and Kenny and Jessie . . . there was that other overwhelming, and even more urgent issue, and he had no idea where to begin.

He dug out a burdock and tossed it on the pile.

And now this. A corporation? That didn't sound good. Mule hadn't known any details, he had merely talked on the phone with a real estate company who was making general inquiries about Fernbank.

"Take no thought for the morrow . . ." he muttered, quoting Matthew.

"Don't worry about anything . . ." he said aloud, quoting his all-time standby verse in the fourth chapter of Philippians, "but in everything, by prayer and supplication with thanksgiving, make your requests known unto God, and the peace that passes all understanding will fill your hearts and minds through Christ Jesus."

He'd been doing it all wrong. As usual, he was trying to focus on the big picture.

He glanced at the stepping-stones he and Cynthia had laid together last year, making a path through the hedge. There! Right under his nose.

Step by step. That was the answer.

CHAPTER THREE

Eden

"You know how some people think all we have to do in Mitford is watch paint peel?"

"I do."

Emma snorted with disgust. "Mack Stroupe's house could've held us spellbound for th' last fifteen years."

"I haven't driven by there in a while."

"Looked like a shack on th' Creek 'til guess what?"

"I can't guess."

"Four pickups hauled in there this mornin' with men and step-ladders. Th' first coat was on by noon, I saw it myself when I went to Hessie's for lunch."

"Aha."

"They painted it blue. I hate blue on a house. Somebody said blue is the color of authority—which is why police officers are th' men in blue. They say it's a color that makes you look like you *are* some-body!"

"Well, well . . ."

"An' take pink. What do you think happened when a sheriff in Texas painted his jail cells pink? The men calmed down, no more violence, can you beat that?"

"Hard to beat," he said, gluing the wooden base back onto the bookend. "And Texas, of all places."

"Where do you think Mack Stroupe gets his money?"

"What money?"

"To buy a new truck, to paint his house. I even heard he had a manicure at Fancy Skinner's place."

"A manicure? Mack?"

"A manicure," she said icily.

"Good heavens." This was serious. "He didn't get a mask, too, did he?"

"A mask? Why would he need a mask when he can lie, cheat, and steal without one?"

"Now, Emma, I don't know about the stealing."

"Maybe you don't, but I do." She looked imperious.

Run from gossip! the Scriptures said. It would be hard to put it more plainly than that.

"I'm going up the street a few minutes. It looks like rain, better close the windows before you leave. Give Harold my congratulations on being moved off the route and into sorting."

"Sorting *and* working the window," she said proudly.

§

"Winnie!" he called, as the bell jingled on the bakeshop door.

Blast if he didn't love the smell of this place. What would happen if the bakery was sold? Anybody could move in here, hawking any manner of goods and wares. Could cards and stationery smell this wonderful, or piece goods, or kitchen wares?

Five years before he arrived on the scene, Winnie had scraped together the money for this storefront, painted it inside and out, installed ovens and secondhand display cases, stenciled *Sweet Stuff Bakery* on the window, and settled into twenty years of unflagging hard work.

Her winning smile and generous spirit had been a hallmark of this street. Hadn't she faithfully fed Miss Rose and Uncle Billy when the old couple tottered by for their daily handout? Yes, and sent something home for the birds, into the bargain.

He found her in the kitchen, sitting on a stool and scribbling on a piece of paper. "Winnie, there you are!"

She beamed at the sight of her visitor. "Have an oatmeal cookie," she said, passing him a tray. "Low-fat."

He was suddenly as happy as a child. "Well, in that case . . ."

He sat on the other stool and munched his cookie. "You know, Winnie, I've been thinking . . ."

Winnie's broad face sobered. She had never known what preachers thought.

"Sweet Stuff isn't a bakery."

"It's not?"

"It's an *institution*! Do you have to go to Tennessee? Can't we keep you?"

"I might be here 'til kingdom come, the way things are lookin'. Not one soul has asked about buyin' it."

"They will, mark my words. God's timing is perfect, even in real estate."

"If I didn't believe that, I'd jump out th' window."

"Wouldn't have far to jump," he said, eyeing the sidewalk through the curtains.

Winnie laughed. He loved it when Winnie laughed. The sound of it had rung in this place far more often than the cash register, but she had done all right, she had come through.

"I'm goin' home in a little bit," she sighed. "I'm not as young as I used to be."

"Who is? I'll be pushing off soon myself, I just came to say hello. How do you like living on Lilac Road?"

"I miss my little cottage by the creek, but that young preacher from Hope House takes good care of it."

"Scott Murphy . . ."

"He washed the windows! Those windows have never been washed! My house sittin' right on th' street and all keeps 'em dirty."

"Well, never much traffic by there to notice."

They sat in silence as he finished his cookie.

"Have another one," she said, wanting him to.

He did. It was soft and chewy, just as he liked cookies to be, and low-fat into the bargain. This was definitely his day. "What do you hear from Joe?"

"Homesick."

"But Tennessee is home."

"Yes, but Mitford's more like home; he's been away from Tennessee fifty years. To tell th' truth, Father, I don't much want to go up there, but here I am with no family left in Mitford, and it seems right for me to go."

Sometimes, what seemed right wasn't so right, after all, but who was he to say?

"Look here," she said, picking up the sheet of paper she'd been scribbling on. "I'm enterin' this contest that's twenty-five words or less. You're educated, would you mind seein' if th' spelling is right?"

He took the paper.

I use Golden Band flour because it's light and easy to work. Also because my mother and grandmother used it. Golden Band! Generation after generation it's the best.

"They sure don't give you much room to rave," he said. "And it looks like you've got twenty-eight words here."

"Oh, law! I counted wrong. What do you think should come out?"

"Let's see. You could take out 'my' and say, 'because Mother and Grandmother used it.'"

"Good! Two to go," she said, sitting on the edge of her stool.

"You could take out 'flour' in the first sentence, since they know it's flour."

"Good! One more to go!"

"This is hard," he said.

"I know it. I been writin' on that thing for four days. But look, they give you a cruise if you win! To the Caribbean! Have you ever been there?"

"Never have."

"Only thing is, it's for two. Who would I go with?"

"Cross that bridge when you get to it," he said. "OK, how about this? 'Generation after generation, Golden Band is best.'"

"How many words?" she asked, holding her breath.

"Twenty-five, right on the money!" He cleared his throat and read aloud. "I use Golden Band because it's light and easy to work. Also because Mother and Grandmother used it. Generation after generation, Golden Band is best."

"Ooh, that sounds good when you read it!" Winnie beamed. "Read it again!"

He read it again, using his pulpit voice. He thought the town's prize baker would fall off the stool with excitement. Why couldn't his congregation be more like Winnie Ivey, for Pete's sake?

As he left the bakery, he saw Mitford's Baptist preacher, Bill Sprouse, coming toward him at a trot.

"Workin' the street, are you?" asked the jovial clergyman, shaking hands.

"And a good day for it!"

"Amen! Wish I could work the south end and we'd meet in the middle for a cup of coffee, but I've got a funeral to preach."

"I, on the other hand, had a baptism this morning."

Bill adjusted the white rose in his lapel. "Coming and going! That's what it's all about in our business!"

"See you at the monument!" said the rector. Since spring arrived, they'd often ended up at the monument at the same time, with their dogs in tow for the evening walk.

He ducked into Happy Endings to see if his order had arrived.

"How do you like your new butterfly book?" asked Hope Winchester, looking fetching, he thought, with her long, chestnut hair pulled back.

"Just the ticket!" he said. "You ought to review it for the *Muse* and first thing you know, half of Mitford would be attracting butterflies."

"That," she said, "is a *very* preponderant idea!"

"Thank you."

"The Butterfly Town! It would bring people from all over."

"I don't think the mayor would much take to that. Unless, of course, they all went home at night."

"Well, Father, progress is going to happen in Mitford, whether our mayor likes it or not. We can't sit here idly, not growing and adapting to the times! And just think. People who like butterflies would be people who like books!"

"Aha. Well, you certainly have a point there."

"Sometimes our mayor can be a bit overweening."

He grinned. "Can't we all? Did my book come in?"

"Let's see," she said, "that was the etymological smorgasbord, I believe."

"'Amo, Amas, Amat,'" he said, nodding.

"I declare!" sniffed Helen Huffman, who owned the place. "Why don't y'all learn to speak English?"

§

"Father, is this a good time?"

He heard the urgency in Olivia Harper's voice when she rang him at the office.

"It's always a good time for you," he said, meaning it.

"Lace went to the Creek to see her friend Harley. I implored her not to go, Father, I know how dangerous it could be. But she went, and now she's home saying that Harley's sick and she's going back to nurse him. Hoppy's in surgery, and I don't . . . Please. She's packing her things. You're so good at this."

"I'll be right there," he said.

Barnabas leapt into the passenger seat of his Buick and they raced up Old Church Lane.

No, he was not good at this. He was not good at this at all. His years with Dooley Barlowe had been some of the hardest of his life; it had all been done with desperate prayer, flying by the seat of his pants. Who was good at knowing the right parameters for wounded kids? Yet, blast it, it was his job to know about parameters. Being a clergyman, being a Christian, had a great deal to do with parameters, which is why the world often mocked and despised both.

He felt the anxiety of this thing. Lace Turner was a passionately determined girl who had suffered unutterable agony in her thirteen years at the Creek—a bedridden mother whom she had faithfully nursed since early childhood, and a brutalizing father suffering the cumulative effects of drugs, alcohol, and regular unemployment.

Through it all, the toothless, kindhearted Harley Welch had looked after Lace Turner's welfare, shielding her whenever he could from harm. It was Harley's truck that Lace had used to transport Dooley's mother, then another Creek resident, to the hospital last summer.

He shuddered at the memory of Pauline Barlowe, who, burned horribly by a man known as LM, had not only endured the agony of skin grafting and the loss of an ear, but had to live with the bitter truth that she'd given away four of her five children.

Though Lace's father and older brother disappeared last year, no one knew when Cate Turner might return to the Creek, nor what he might do if he found his daughter there.

He made a right turn into the nearly hidden driveway of the Harper's rambling mountain lodge. With its weathered shingles, twin stone chimneys, and broad front porch, it was a welcome sight.

Barnabas leapt out, barking with abandon at the sudden alarm of countless squirrels in the overhead network of trees.

Thanks be to God, Lace was now in the care of the Harpers and doing surprisingly well at Mitford School. Naturally, she continued to use her native dialect, but she had dazzled them all with her reading skills and quick intelligence. He was even more taken, however, by the extraordinary depth of her character.

Another Dooley Barlowe, in a sense—with all of Dooley's hard and thorny spirit, and then some.

He put the leash on his dog and left him secured to the porch railing, then opened the screen door and called. Olivia rushed down the hall and gave him a hug.

"Father, you're always there for us."

"And you for us," he said, hugging back.

"She's in her room, packing. I'm sorry to be so . . . so inept. . . ."

"You're not inept. You're trying to raise a teenager and deal with a broken spirit. Let's pray," he said. He looked into her violet eyes, which he always found remarkable, and saw her frantic concern.

He took Olivia's hands. "Father, this is serious business. Give us your wisdom, we pray, to do what is just, what is healing, what is needed. Give us discernment, also, by the power of your Holy Spirit, and soften our hearts toward one another and toward you. In Jesus' name."

"Amen!" she said.

"Shall we talk to her together?"

"I've said it all, she's heard enough from me, I think. Would you . . . ?"

He found Lace in her room, wearing the filthy hat from her days at the Creek, and zipping up a duffel bag.

She turned and glared at him. "I knowed you'd come. You cain't stop me. Harley's sick and I'm goin'."

"What's the matter with Harley?"

"Pukin' blood. Blood in 'is dump. Cain't eat, got bad cramps, and so weak he cain't git up. But they's somethin' worser."

"What?"

"Somebody stoled 'is dogs."

"Why is that worse?" He'd try to stall her until he collected his wits.

"His dogs bein' gone means anybody could go in there and take th' money he's saved back in 'is bed pillers. I've got t' drive 'is truck out, too, or they'll be stealin' that."

"What do you think the sickness might be?"

"I ain't no doctor!" she said, angry.

"It could be something contagious."

"So? Harley done it f'r me time an' again. I was sick nearly t' dyin' an' he waited on me, even went an' fed my mam when my pap was gone workin'."

She picked up the bag and shoved the hat farther down on her head, and walked to the door.

"I'll go with you," he said. Was he crazy? It was broad daylight. He had gone into the drug-infested Creek with her once before, to bring out Poobaw Barlowe—but that had been under cover of darkness and he'd never felt so terrified in his life.

"You ain't goin' in there with me in th' daylight, a preacher wouldn't be nothin' but trouble. Besides, you couldn't hardly git up th' bank that time, you like t' killed y'rself."

She was right about that. He'd taken one step up and two back, all the way to the top. "What kind of medicine have you got?"

She stopped and looked at him.

"Why go in empty-handed? What can you do, not knowing? Come with me to the hospital, we'll talk to a nurse."

"I ain't goin' t' no hospital.

"Lace. Get smart. You can't do this without help. Drive to the hospital with me, I'll get Nurse Kennedy to come out to the car, if necessary. Tell her what you know, see what she thinks."

Lace looked at the floor, then at him. "Don't try t' trick me," she said.

"I don't think you'd be easy to trick."

God in heaven, he didn't have a clue where this was leading.

§

Nurse Kennedy leaned down and talked to Lace through the open car window. Lace sat stoically, clutching the duffel bag in her lap.

"It could be a bleeding ulcer," said Kennedy. "Does Harley drink?"

"Harley was bad to drink f'r a long time, but he's sober now."

"Any diarrhea?"

"An awful lot, an' passin' blood in it."

"How's his color?"

"Real white. White as a sheet."

The nurse looked thoughtful. "Vomiting blood, passing blood, pale, weak, cramps, diarrhea. All symptoms of a bleeding ulcer."

At least whatever it was wasn't contagious, thought the rector, feeling relieved. And it was curable.

"What's the prognosis?" he asked.

"I could be wrong of course, but I don't think so. If it's a bleeding ulcer, it can be treated with antibiotics. Diet plays a part, too. The main thing is, he'll need treatment. His hemoglobin will be low, and that's serious."

"We can't thank you enough."

As they drove down the hill, he still didn't know where he was headed or how this would unfold.

He pulled the car to the curb in front of Andrew Gregory's Oxford Antique Shop. "Let's stop and think this through. If you go to the Creek, there's nothing you can do. You heard the nurse, he's got to have treatment. Let me get Chief Underwood to drive us in there, we'll bring Harley out, money, truck, and all."

"Where would you take 'im to? He ain't goin' t' no hospital."

"I don't know. Let me think." Not Betty Craig's, that was for certain. Betty's little house was stuffed to the gills with Russell Jacks, Dooley's disabled grandfather; Dooley's mother, Pauline Barlowe, who was looking for work; and her son, Poobaw. There wasn't a bed available at Hope House, even if Harley could qualify, and the red tape for the county home would be a yard long.

"Blast!" he said.

"Is that some kind of cussin'?" asked Lace.

"In a manner of speaking," he replied.

§

He was running late for dinner, and he had no idea how he would explain it all to his wife.

Of course, she was vastly understanding about most things, he had to hand her that. So far, she hadn't run him out of the house with a broom or made him sleep in the study.

This, however, could definitely turn the tide in that direction.

She was standing at the back door, looking for him, when he walked up to the stoop with Lace Turner and a weak and failing Harley Welch.

She said only "Good Lord!" and came out to help him.

§

Hoppy Harper was on his way, possibly the last of that sterling breed of doctors who made house calls.

Heaving Harley up the stairs to the guest room was worse than hauling any armoire along the same route. Though shockingly frail, Harley's limp body seemed to have the weight of a small elephant. It took three of them to get Harley on the bed, where the rector undressed him and bathed him with a cloth, which he dipped in a pan of soapy water.

Harley looked comic in the rector's pajamas, which had to be changed immediately, given Harley's inability to make it to the adjoining bathroom on time. "I didn't go t' do that," said Harley, whose flush of embarrassment returned a bit of color to his face.

What had he gotten into? Father Tim wondered. He didn't know. But when Harley Welch looked at him and smiled weakly, the rector felt the absolute wisdom of this impulsive decision, and smiled back.

§

He went to bed, exhausted. Lace had gained permission to stay over, sleeping in Dooley's room next to Harley's, and keeping watch.

He reached for his wife, and she took his hand. "Am I dead meat around here?" he asked.

She rolled toward him and kissed him softly on the nearly bare top of his head.

"I married a preacher," she said. "Not a banker, not an exporter, not an industrialist. A preacher. This is what preachers do—if they do it right."

§

Nobody on the vestry had heard a word from the real estate company that had made inquiries around town.

Oh, well, they'd thrown out the line and there would be another bite at another time. But had they made the bait attractive enough? They couldn't worry about that. They couldn't install additional bathrooms in the hope that Fernbank would lure a bed and breakfast. They couldn't cut up the ground floor into classrooms in the hope it would lure an academy. In the end, they couldn't even afford to paint and roof it, hoping to lure anyone at all.

At eight in the morning he dropped by Town Hall and sat in a Danish modern chair that once occupied the mayor's own family room. He declined the weak coffee in a Styrofoam cup.

"Barbecue?" growled the mayor. "Barbecue? Two can play that game. Ray Cunningham makes the best barbecue in the country—outside the state of Texas, of course."

"I don't know if I'd fight barbecue with barbecue," he said. "I hear Mack's planning to have these things right up 'til election day."

The mayor was just finishing her fast-food sausage biscuit. "Why do anything at all, is what I'd like to know! I don't see how that snake could oust me, even if I was the most triflin' mayor ever put in office."

"Any town in the country would be thrilled to have you running things, Esther. Look at the merchant gardens up and down Main Street, look at our town festival that raised more money than any event in our history. Look at Rose Day, and how you put your shoulder to the wheel and helped turn the old Porter place into a town museum! Look how you rounded up a crew and painted and improved Sophia's little house. . . . The list is endless."

"And look how I don't take any malarkey off the council. You know we've got at least two so-and-sos who'd as soon put a paper plant and a landfill in here as walk up th' street."

"You've never taken your eyes off the target, I'll hand you that."

"So what do you think?" asked Esther, leaning forward. The rector saw that she'd broken out in red splotches, which usually indicated her enthusiasm for a good fight.

"I think I'd wait a while and see how things go in the other camp."

"That's what Ray said."

"In the meantime, I hope you'll have a presence at the town festival. I hear Mack's setting up quite a booth."

"You can count on it! Last year I kissed a pig, this year I'll be kissin' babies. And one of these days, I want to do somethin' for the town, thanking them for their support all these years. Lord, I hope talkin' to you doesn't infringe on any laws of church and state!"

He laughed. "I don't think so. By the way—how about laying off the sausage biscuits for a while? I'd like to see you make it through another couple of terms."

She wadded up the biscuit wrapper and lobbed it into the wastebasket. "You're off duty," she said. "So I'll thank you not to preach."

School would be out in two weeks and Dooley would be home.

Where in the dickens would he find the boy a job, or where would Dooley find one for himself? It would have to be in Mitford, which was no employment capital. He'd talk to Lew Boyd when he filled up his tank, or maybe the fellow who was looking after the church grounds could use a helper. . . .

Another thing. Maybe he and Cynthia could do something he'd never done in his life: take a week at the beach, rent a cottage—his wife would know how to do that. As for their mutual dislike of sand and too much sun, weren't there endless compensations—like time to read, the roar of the ocean, and seafood fresh from the boat?

Dooley would like that, and he could take Tommy. They'd load the car and head out right after Dooley's two weeks at Meadowgate Farm.

A vacation! For a man renowned for his stick-in-the-mudness, this was a great advance.

Whistling, he headed toward home.

§

Lace Turner was still wearing the battered hat. But her life with the Harpers had revealed a certain beauty. Her once-tangled hair was neatly pulled away from her face, dramatizing the burning determination in her eyes.

"He ain't doin' too good," she said, indicating the pale, small man who lay in the guest room bed.

For someone devoid of a single tooth, Harley Welch's smile was infectious, the rector thought. "I am, too, Rev'rend, don't listen to 'er. She's makin' me walk a chalk line."

"He ain't eat nothin' but baby puddin'."

"Cain't have no black pepper, no red pepper, no coffee, and no choc'late candy," said Harley. "They say it makes you gastric. Without a little taste of candy, I'd as soon be dead."

"You nearly was dead!" said Lace.

"How's your setup?" asked the rector. "Do you have everything you need?"

"Everything a man could want, plus Lace an' your missus an' Puny to look after me. But I feel it's my bounden duty t' tell you I run liquor most of my early days, and I been worryin' whether th' Lord would want me layin' in this bed."

"Seems to me the Lord put you in this bed," said the rector.

Harley's birdlike hands clutched the blanket. "I've not always lived right," he announced, looking the rector in the eye.

"Who has?" asked Father Tim, looking back.

"I pulled y'r shades down," Lace said, "'cause he cain't have no sunshine, he's on this tetra . . . cyline stuff four times a day f'r three weeks. He's got t' take all that's in this other bottle, too, an' look here—Pepto-Bismol he's got t' swaller twice a day."

"I ain't never lived as bad as all that," said Harley.

Father Tim sat on the side of the bed. "Dr. Harper says you're going to be all right. I want you to know we're glad to have you and want you to get strong."

"He has t' eat six times a day. It ain't easy f'r me'n Cynthia t' figure out six snacks f'r somebody with no teeth."

"Teeth never give me nothin' but trouble," said Harley, grinning weakly. "Some rotted out, some was pulled out, and th' rest was knocked out. I've got used t' things th' way they are. Teeth'd just take up a whole lot of room in there."

"I'm comin' after school an' stayin' nights," Lace announced. "Olivia and Cynthia said I could."

"Good, Lace. Glad to have you around. You've got a fine friend, Harley."

Harley grinned. "She's a good 'un, all right. But awful mean to sick people."

"Well, you're lying on your money and your truck's over at Lew Boyd's getting the oil change you mentioned, so you can rest easy."

"I hate that I've let my oil go, but here lately, I've had t' let ever'thing go. I didn't mean f'r you t' do that, Rev'rend, I'm goin' t' do somethin' for you an' th' missus, soon as I'm up an' about."

"Oh, but I wasn't saying—"

"I know you wasn't, but I'm goin' t' do it, I'm layin' here thinkin' about it. Lace tol' me you got a Buick with some age on it, I might like t' overhaul your engine."

Father Tim laughed heartily. "Overhaul my engine?"

"After my liquor days, I was in car racin'."

Was he imagining that good color suddenly returned to Harley Welch's cheeks? "You were a driver?"

"Nossir, I was crew chief f'r Junior Watson."

"Junior Watson! Well, I'll say!"

Harley's grin grew even broader. He didn't think preachers knew about such as that.

That explains it, mused the rector, going downstairs. Yesterday, he had headed Harley's old truck onto Main Street, thinking he'd have to nurse it to Lew Boyd's two blocks away. When he hammered down on the accelerator, he saw he had another think coming. He had roared by Rodney Underwood's patrol car in a blur, as if he'd been shot from a cannon.

He had never gone from Wisteria Lane to the town monument in such record time, except on those occasions when Barnabas felt partial to relieving himself on a favorite monument boxwood.

"Landscaping," announced Emma, her mouth set like the closing on a Ziploc bag.

"Landscaping?" he asked.

"Mack Stroupe."

"Mack Stroupe?"

"Hedges. Shrubs. Bushes." In her fury, his secretary had resorted to telegraphic communications. *"Grass,"* she said with loathing.

He didn't recall ever seeing grass in Mack's yard. Dandelions, maybe . . .

"Plus . . ."

"Plus what?"

Emma looked at him over her half-glasses. "Lucy Stroupe is getting her hair dyed today!"

Manicures, landscaping, dyed hair. He didn't know when his mind had been so boggled by political events, local or otherwise.

He thought he'd never seen his garden look more beautiful. It filled him with an odd sense of longing and joy, all at once.

Surely there had been other times, now forgotten, when the beauty and mystery of this small place, enclosed by house and hedges, had moved him like this. . . .

The morning mist rose from the warm ground and trailed across the garden like a vapor from the moors. Under the transparent wash of gray lay the vibrant emerald of new-mown grass, and the unfurled leaves of the hosta. Over there, in the bed of exuberant astilbe, crept new tendrils of the strawberry plants whose blossoms glowed in the mist like pink fires.

It was a moment of perfection that he would probably not find again this year, and he sat without moving, almost without breathing. There was the upside of a garden, when one was digging and planting, heaving and hauling, and then the downside, when it was all weeding and grooming and watering and sweating. One had to be fleet to catch the moment in the middle, the mountaintop, when perfection was as brief as the visit of a butterfly to an outstretched palm.

For this one rare moment, their garden was all gardens, the finest of gardens, as the wild blackberry he'd found last year had been the finest of blackberries.

He remembered it distinctly, remembered looking at its unusual elongated form, and putting it in his mouth. The blackberry burst with flavor that transported him instantly to his childhood, to his age of innocence and bare feet and chiggers and freedom. The blackberry that fired his mouth with sweetness and his heart with memory was all the blackberry he would need for a very long time, it had done the work of hundreds of summer blackberries.

He gazed at the canopy of pink dogwoods he had planted years ago, at the rhododendron buds, which were as large as old-fashioned Christmas tree lights, and at the canes of his French roses, which were the circumference of his index finger.

Better still, every bed had been dressed with the richest, blackest compost he could find. He had driven to the country where the classic makers of fertilizer resided, and happened upon a farmer who agreed to deliver a truckload of rotted manure to his very door. He'd rather have it than bricks of gold. . . .

He took a deep draught of the clean mountain air, and shut his eyes. Beauty had its limits with him, he could never gaze upon great beauty for long stretches; he had to take rest stops, as in music.

"Praying, are you, dearest?"

His wife appeared and sat beside him, slipping her arm around his waist.

He nuzzled her hair. "There you are."

"I've never seen it so lovely," she whispered.

A chickadee dived into the bushes. A junco flew out.

"Who loves a garden still his Eden keeps," she said, quoting Bronson Alcott.

He had looked upon this Eden, quite alone, for years. The old adage that having someone to love doubles our joy and divides our sorrow was, like most adages, full of plain truth.

He wanted to say something to her, something to let her know that having her beside him meant the world to him, meant everything.

"I'm going to buy us a new frying pan today," he said.

She drew away and looked at him. Then she burst into laughter, which caused the birds to start from the hedge like cannon shots.

He hadn't meant to say that. He hadn't meant to say that at all!

A Full House

He put two pounds of livermush and a pack of Kit Kats in a paper sack, and set out walking to Betty Craig's.

Thank heaven his wife wasn't currently working on a book—they'd sat up talking like teenagers until midnight, feeling conspiratorial behind their closed bedroom door, and coming at last to the issue of Dooley's siblings.

"I don't know, Timothy," she said, looking dejected. "I don't know how to find lost children."

Why did he always think his wife had the answers to tough questions? Even he had the sense to believe that milk cartons, though a noble gesture on someone's part, probably weren't the answer.

"You must press Pauline for details," Cynthia told him. "She says she can't remember certain things, but that's because the memories are so painful—she has shut that part of herself down." His wife leaned her head to one side. "I wouldn't have your job, dearest."

People were always telling him that.

He peered through Betty Craig's screen door and called out.

"It's th' Father!" Betty exclaimed, hurrying to let him in.

He gave her a hug and handed over the bag. "The usual," he said, laughing.

"Little Poobaw's taken after livermush like his granpaw! This won't go far," she said, peering at the contents.

Russell Jacks shuffled into the kitchen with a smiling face. "It's th' Father, Pauline! Come an' see!" The old sexton had run down considerably, but there would never be a finer gardener than this one, thought the rector. A regular Capability Brown. . . .

The two men embraced.

"He's buildin' me a little storage cupboard, go and look!" said Betty Craig, pulling at his sleeve.

"I know you b'lieve if a man can build a cupboard, he can keep th' church gardens," said Russell, "but I've not got th' lung power t' plant an' rake an' dig an' all." He looked abashed.

"I understand, I know. And the leaf mold, that's not good for your lungs."

Russell looked relieved as they walked out to the back porch. "See this here? That was a wood box, I'm turnin' it into a cupboard for waterin' cans an' bird seed an' all. Puttin' some handles on it that we took off th' toolshed doors. If I was stout enough to do it, I'd pull that shed down before it falls down."

"Dooley and I might give you a hand with it this summer. He'll be home in two weeks, you know."

"Yessir, and it'll do his mama a world of good. She's not found a job of work nowhere, it's got to 'er a good bit."

"I understand. But something will come through, mark my words."

"Oh, an' I do mark y'r words, Father. I been markin' y'r words a good while, now. About fifteen year, t' be exact."

Poobaw came to the screen door and peered out shyly, his mother standing behind him. "Father?" she said. Tears sprang to her eyes at once and began coursing down her cheeks.

"Oh, law," sighed Russell, looking at the porch floor.

"I don't know," Pauline said. "I don't remember."

Her storm of weeping had passed and she sat quietly with him in the small rear bedroom of Betty Craig's house.

"You've got to remember."

He noticed the patch of skin on the left side of her face, only one of the places where grafting had been done—it was a slightly different color, with a scar running along its boundaries like pale stitching on a quilt. Her long brown hair, tinged with red, covered her missing left ear and hid most of the grafting on her neck. A miracle that she was sitting here. . . .

They sat for a time, wordless. He wouldn't try to chink the cracks of silence with chitchat. He would force her, if he could, to do what she dreaded. But he dreaded it more. He didn't want to force anyone into sorrow. Yet, without this, he couldn't help her do the thing he'd promised when she lay mute and devastated from the horrific burns.

"Holding," she said, turning away from him.

"You were living in Holding?"

"Yes. Mama's second cousin, Rhody, she came and took Jessie. I never told Daddy who done it." She continued to look away from him. "I remember missin' Jessie th' next morning, and there was a note. Rhody said she was taking Jessie for life and for me not to look for her." There was a long silence and Pauline bent her head. "I didn't look. By then, things were so bad . . ."

She was suffering, but without tears.

He waited.

". . . I knew I couldn't take care of her, I might hurt her, I used to lose my temper and throw things. I remember hitting Dooley, it was Christmas. . . ."

She put her head in her hands.

"He'd rode down the mountain on his new bicycle to see me, he was living with you then. I hurt him awful bad when I hit him, and he never said a word back. . . ."

Dooley! He wanted to get in the car and drive to Virginia and find him in his classroom and bring him home and love him, take him fishing, though he didn't have a clue how to fish. He remembered seeing the abandoned boy in overalls for the first time, and his eager, freckled face. . . .

"I remember he rode off on his bicycle and I thought . . . I'll kill myself, I don't deserve to live. And I tried to, Father, I did. I tried to kill myself with drinkin'."

He prayed for her silently.

"I don't know where Rhody is, I wisht I could say she's a good person, but . . . she's not. I think she was glad to see me go down, glad to run off with one of my kids." Pauline took a deep breath. "I've tried to forgive her. Sometimes I can, sometimes I can't. But . . . maybe Jessie was lucky that someone took her."

One thing at a time, his heart seemed to say. This wasn't the day to talk about Sammy and Kenny.

§

They walked around the sagging toolshed, checking it out.

Why beat around the bush? "Russell, tell me about your wife's cousin Rhody."

The old man looked at him somberly.

"Double-talkin' is what I say. Two-faced. I ain't seed much of 'er since Ida passed."

"How can I find her?"

"Be jinged if I know. Her man run out on 'er, he used t' work at th' post office in Holding, but I don't know what come of 'im. Her mama died, I guess they won't much left in Holding to keep 'er. Seems like th' last I heard, she was off in Florida som'ers."

"Any recollection of where in Florida?"

"Law, I cain't recollect. Seem like it started with a *L*. Los Angelees, maybe."

"Aha," he said.

§

When he retired from Lord's Chapel and moved out of the rectory, the yellow house next door would be home. And not enough room inside those four walls to skin a cat.

It was time, and then some, he reasoned, to get an architect to tell them how to add a sunroom and study, enlarge the downstairs bath and Cynthia's garage.

Speaking of expansion projects, it was also time to call the president of Buck Leeper's company, the people who'd done such a shining job of constructing Hope House, and see whether he could get in line for Buck as superintendent of the church attic project.

That, and find Dooley a job. And go through Miss Sadie's attic. And figure out what to do with Fernbank before it ran down so badly there'd be nothing to do with it, period.

It was no surprise that he'd never made it up the ladder to bishop; it was all he could do to say grace over being a country parson.

§

He was hoofing it toward home when Avis Packard stepped out of The Local, wearing his green apron. The screen door slapped shut behind him.

"I don't reckon you'd be havin' a boy who'd like to bag groceries this summer?"

Bingo!

§

It was different having a full house.

Olivia was in and out, helping Cynthia with the responsibility of a man who wasn't yet able to help himself. Lace arrived after school and did her homework in Harley's room, where she was clearly good medicine for what ailed him.

Violet was spending more time at the rectory, since her mistress wasn't often at the little yellow house, and Barnabas lay in wait for the glorious opportunity of finding Violet on the floor instead of the top of the refrigerator, which she had claimed as permanent headquarters with a potted gloxinia.

"Perfect!" said Cynthia, who set Violet's food up there as nonchalantly as if all cats lived on refrigerators.

With the increased workload of the household, Puny was sometimes still there with the twins when he came home.

Five o'clock in the afternoon might have been ten in the morning, for all he could see. It was not unusual for the washing machine to be running, the vacuum cleaner roaring, the blender turning out nutrition for the toothless and infirm, and the twins jiggling in their canvas seats suspended in the kitchen doorway.

During all this, Barnabas sat patiently in front of the refrigerator, blocking traffic and gazing dolefully at Violet, who scorned his every move.

A madhouse! he thought, grinning. Blast if it wouldn't run most men into the piney woods. But after more than sixty years of being an only child and a bachelor into the bargain, the whole thing seemed marvelous, a veritable circus of laughing and slamming and banging and wailing. He wouldn't wish it on his worst enemy, but for himself, he liked the novelty of it.

"Come in, Rev'rend!" Harley was sitting up in bed, having one of his multiple snacks.

"How're you?" Lace asked, without taking her eyes off the patient.

A civil greeting! Olivia was making headway with her indomitable thirteen-year-old charge. "I'm fine. How about you?"

"I'm OK. Harley, if you hide that banana bread an' don't eat it, I'll knock you in th' head."

Harley grinned. "See there? A feller don't have a chance, she's like a revenue agent lookin' f'r liquor cars, got eyes in th' back of 'er head."

"You're stronger today."

"Yessir, I am. I ain't never laid up in such style as this in m' life, we had it hard when I was comin' up in Wilkes County. We was s' poor, all we had t' play with was a rubber ball, an' th' dog eat half of that."

"Kind of hard to judge which way it would bounce," said the rector.

"Shoot, we was s' poor, I went t' school one time, I was wearin' one shoe. Th' teacher said 'Harley, have you lost a shoe?' an' I said, 'No, ma'm, I found one.'"

"Don't lie," said Lace. "It ain't right."

Harley looked doleful. "I ain't lyin'! Another thing, Rev'rend, I'm gittin' out of this bed tomorrow, sure as you're born. I looked out that back winder and seen y'r yard, you need some rakin' around that hedge."

Lace glared at Harley from beneath her hat brim. "You ain't movin' 'til Doc Harper gives you th' green light."

"Lord have mercy! Git that girl a job of work t' do."

The rector laughed. "She's got a job of work to do! And you leave my hedge alone, buddyroe."

"I hate t' be hangin' on you an' th' missus like a calf on a tit."

"I don't want to hear about it. Eat your banana bread."

"Law, now they's two of 'em," said Harley, taking a bite.

"An' drop y'r crumbs on y'r napkin," said Lace.

"Lace has real beauty."

"But she hides it with that dreadful hat. We let her wear it in the house, of course, but never to school or church."

"Sounds fair," he said.

Cynthia had gone next door for a cake pan, and Olivia was finishing a cup of tea with him.

"It represents something to her," said Olivia. "It's a defense of who she is, I think, of something she doesn't want us to change."

"You're doing a grand job, you and Hoppy, we're seeing a difference."

"We love her. She's quite extraordinary." Olivia stirred her tea, thoughtful. "Perhaps what we want more than anything . . . is for Lace to be able to cry."

"What I wanted more than anything was for Dooley to be able to laugh."

Olivia smiled. "The two things aren't so different, perhaps. Laughter, tears . . . it's all a way of letting something out, letting something go. Forgiveness . . . somehow, I think that's the answer. Did I tell you she's making straight A's?"

"Amazing!"

"She hasn't had much schooling, really, yet she loves to learn, it comes naturally to her. She keeps her nose in a book, with the radio tuned to a country music station."

They sipped their tea.

"She adores Hoppy, of course," Olivia said.

"I'm sure she cares for you, too."

"I don't know. She . . . fights me."

"Ah, well. I know about that."

"I take her to see her mother twice a week."

"What's her mother like?"

Olivia shook her head slowly. "Hard and unkind. I hoped she'd be different. Lace has taken care of her mother all her life, Lila Turner has been ill since Lace was a toddler. I think the only person who ever really cared about Lace, who loved her, is Harley."

"Was Harley ever married? Any children of his own?"

"His wife died years ago, he loved her deeply and never quite got over her death. There weren't any children." Olivia finished her tea. "Well, on to brighter things," she said, smiling. "Our school is out in two weeks. When is Dooley coming home?"

"Next Friday," he said. "He'll come in with a friend's parents. Avis wants him at The Local for the summer."

"Lovely! How does he feel about Meadowgate not being there for him?"

"He'll tough it out. After a couple of weeks at The Local, and hanging around with Tommy, and a few days at the beach . . ." He shrugged, hopeful.

"All the best," she said, her violet eyes bright with feeling.

"All the best to you," he replied, meaning it.

Avis wanted Dooley ASAP, which could mean three days at the farm and four at the beach. Or no days at the beach and a week at the farm. Another thought: Maybe Dooley would like to take Poobaw to the beach and let Tommy fill in for him at The Local before Tommy went to work at Lew Boyd's.

Why did something so simple boggle his mind? Should he call Dooley and tell him he had a job that would place some constraints on the farm? Should he even mention the beach? Should he just wait 'til Dooley came home and deal with it then?

"Lord . . ." he sighed, lifting his hands.

"A billboard," said Emma.

"A billboard?"

"Mack Stroupe."

Mack on a billboard? Is that why Mack had gotten a manicure? He didn't know how these things worked.

"On the highway after you pass Hattie Cloer's market. Right in your face. It's enough to make you jump out of your skin, that thing loomin' up on you. You talk about ugly, his nose takes up half th' board. And those bushy eyebrows, and that egg-suckin' grin . . .'" Emma shivered.

"What does it say?"

"It says *Mack for Mitford, Mitford for Mack, Vote Stroupe for Mayor.* I told Harold to stop the car while I puked."

"A billboard. Amazing." Who was repackaging Mack Stroupe?

"Have you seen Lucy since she got her hair dyed? Blond! Can you believe it? Her hair's been the color of a church mouse for a hundred years. You know Mack made her do it. Lucy Stroupe would no more think of dyin' her hair blond than I'd think of runnin' a marathon. But—do you think blond hair will keep Mack Stroupe from cheatin' on his wife with that black-headed hussy in Wesley? I don't think so."

Emma glowered at him as if he were personally responsible for the whole affair. "Are you goin' to his barbecue on Saturday?"

"Dooley's coming in Friday, and we'll be spending the day at Meadowgate on Saturday."

"Good! I hope th' whole town stays away in droves."

"Unfortunately, a lot of people love barbecue."

"You can bet your boots that Harold and I won't be staying more than fifteen minutes."

"You're *going*?"

"Of course we're going, I want to see what the lowlife has to say. How can you knock the opposition when you don't know what they stand for?"

"Aha," he said.

§

Dooley was home and Barnabas was wild with excitement. The rector wondered if the joy that people seemed so expert at containing somehow transferred to their dogs, who had nothing at all to hide.

"Hey, Barn! Hey, buddy!"

Barnabas licked Dooley on every exposed area with special attention to his left ear. "Say a Scripture!" he yelled.

The rector laughed. "You say a Scripture!"

"Ah . . . the Lord is my shepherd, I shall not want!" Dooley thundered.

Barnabas crashed to the floor and sighed.

"A miracle, if I ever saw it," said Cynthia, of the only dog anyone had ever known whose behavior could be controlled by Scripture recitation.

"Well, you've had your bath," said the rector, putting his arms around the boy in the navy school blazer. "Welcome home!"

"Welcome home, you big lug!" said Cynthia, giving him a warm embrace. "Good heavens, you're tall! You're positively towering!"

"I'm the same as when you saw me the last time," said Dooley.

"Then I guess I've gotten shorter!"

Father Tim hoisted two duffel bags. "I'll help carry your things up. There's someone we'd like you to meet. We have a guest in the guest room."

"Who?"

"Harley Welch," said Cynthia. "He hasn't been well, so he'll be recuperating with us. Put on some old clothes and get comfortable. Dinner will be ready soon. Are you hungry?"

"I'm starved!" said Dooley, meaning it.

§

Dooley came into the kitchen, glaring at them. "Some girl's stuff is in my room," he said curtly.

Cynthia was taking a roast from the oven. "What kind of stuff?"

"A jacket. A hairbrush. Some . . . hair clips or somethin'."

"Lace Turner has been staying in your room and helping nurse Harley."

He glared at Cynthia. "That's what I thought. My room smells different. She better not come in there again . . . and I mean it!" he said, raising his voice.

Cynthia set the roast on the stove top and took a deep breath. "For the moment, this is a happy, busy, contented household. That is a precious thing for any household to be, and each of us must work to keep it that way.

"It was important for Lace to help with Harley, as I could not do it all myself. She is now out of your room, and you are in it. I will expect you to treat her civilly when you see her, and I expect to be treated civilly, as well. Dinner is nearly ready, it is everything you like best. If your stomach is upset by this incident, which I expect it may be, go to your room and pray about it, then come down and eat like a horse.

"You have," she said, looking at him steadily, "ten minutes."

Dooley stood for a moment, then turned and stomped upstairs.

The rector placed forks, knives, and spoons on the table, trying to be quiet about it. With his wife and Lace Turner running things around here, he and Dooley might be heading for the piney woods, after all.

§

Dooley Barlowe was indeed taller and, if possible, thinner. For twenty thousand bucks a year, didn't those people at school put food on the table?

And where were his freckles?

"Waiting for the sun to get to them!" exclaimed Cynthia.

What about his cowlick, then? Would they never see that again?

"Not in this lifetime," his wife said.

And his grades—how about those grades? Not bad! Not bad at all! He owed the boy a small fortune. A couple of twenties, at least.

"Would you tell him?" he asked her after dinner.

"What do you think?"

"I think you won't do it," he said, striding into the study and trying to appear casual.

Dooley was waiting for Tommy to come over and fooling with the electric train they kept in the corner by the windows.

"Buddy, I've got good news!" He sounded as phony as a three-dollar bill. "You've got a job for the summer . . . which means, of course, that—"

"I know," said Dooley, looking up.

"You do?"

"Avis told Tommy and Tommy called me up. Avis is hiring Tommy, too."

"I thought Tommy was going to work for Lew Boyd."

"He was, but Lew's nephew turned up for the job. We start Monday."

"Really?"

"Eight o'clock sharp, Avis said."

"Ah, well. We were going to take you to the beach for a few days with Tommy or Poobaw. Stay in a cottage. Swim. Like that." Swim? He couldn't swim a stroke, but Cynthia was a fish. "Eat seafood." Dooley was fooling with the train again. "Have . . . you know, *fun*."

Dooley looked up and suddenly grinned at him. "That's OK. You do stuff for me all the time. It'll be fun working. Me'n Tommy will have a blast."

"Right. Well. Congratulations! We can go out to Meadowgate on Saturday, then. For the day. How's that?"

"Great."

"There!" Cynthia said when he came back to the kitchen. "See how easy it was?"

Easy? Except for the relief of Dooley's grin, he hadn't found it easy at all.

There was, of course, an unexpected compensation.

Now they wouldn't have to get in the car and drive five long hours to the beach. He could stay right here in Mitford like the stick-in-the-mud he was known to be.

§

Meadowgate.

The very name soothed him, and was, in fact, an apt description.

A broad, green meadow ran for nearly a mile along the front of the Owens' property, sliced in half by a country lane that led through an open farm gate.

He had found solace in this place time and time again over the years, first as a new priest with a brand-new parish.

It had taken months, perhaps even a couple of years, to come to terms with the fact that he'd followed in the footsteps of a canonized saint. Father Townsend had been tall, dynamic, handsome, and at Lord's Chapel for nearly twenty years. Though the parish had called

Timothy Kavanagh after a tough and discriminating search, it had taken all his resources to wean them, at last, from the charismatic Henry Townsend.

He thought back on the pain he'd felt through much of that time, glad, indeed, that he could now laugh about it.

"Dearest, you're laughing!"

"Darn right!" he said, feeling the happiness of driving along a beckoning lane with a comfortable wife, a happy boy, and a dog the size of a haymow.

"Let me drive the rest of the way." Dooley was suddenly breathing on the back of his neck.

"I don't think so."

"Tommy's dad lets him drive. Jack, this guy at school, his dad lets him drive his four-wheel all the time—"

"You can drive when you're sixteen—and believe me, you won't have long to wait."

"You could just let me drive to the house. I know how."

"Since when?"

"Since I went home with Jack and his dad let me drive."

"Aha."

The house came into view and, failing any more intelligent response, he stepped on the accelerator. He'd completely forgotten about the torrid romance between boys and cars.

§

Marge Owen's French grandmother's chicken pie recipe was a study in contrasts. Its forthright and honest filling, which combined large chunks of white and dark meat, coarsely cut carrots, green peas, celery, and whole shallots, was laced with a dollop of sauterne and crowned by a pastry so light and flaky, it might have won the favor of Louis XIV.

"Bravo!" exclaimed the rector.

"Man!" said Dooley.

"I unashamedly beg you for this recipe," crowed Cynthia.

The new assistant, Blake Eddistoe, scraped his plate with his spoon. "Wonderful, ma'am!"

Hardly anyone ever cooked for diabetes, thought the rector as they trooped out to eat cake in the shade of the pin oak. Apparently it was a disease so innocuous, so bland, and so boring to anyone other than its unwilling victims that it was blithely dismissed by the cooks of the land.

He eyed the chocolate mocha cake that Marge was slicing at the table under the tree. Wasn't that her well-known raspberry filling? From here, it certainly looked like it. . . .

Ah, well. The whole awful business of saying no, which he roundly despised, was left to him. Maybe just a thin slice, however . . . something you could see through. . . .

"He can't have any," said Cynthia.

"I can't believe I forgot!" said Marge, looking stricken. "I'm sorry, Tim! Of course, we have homemade gingersnaps, I know you like those. Rebecca Jane, please fetch the gingersnaps for Father Tim, they're on the bottom shelf."

The four-year-old toddled off, happy with her mission.

Chocolate mocha cake with raspberry filling versus gingersnaps from the bottom shelf. . . .

Clearly, the much-discussed and controversial affliction from which St. Paul had prayed thrice to be delivered had been diabetes.

§

They were sitting on the porch, working up the energy to pile into the Buick and head back to Mitford.

When in Mitford, it seemed only the small, unhurried village that one loved it for being, with a populace of barely more than a thousand. From out here, however, Mitford seemed a regular metropolis, with traffic, political billboards, and barbecue events staged on slabs of asphalt.

Dooley had been to his room and silently carried out a box of his things.

Thump, thump, thump, thump . . . One of the farm dogs scratched himself vigorously, then licked the irritated flesh.

"Oh, dear," said Marge. "Here we go! It's skin allergy season for Bonemeal."

Hal took his pipe from his pocket. "Every year, he has a hot spot on his right rear flank, where he chews and scratches the skin."

"I can give him a shot of Depo-Medrol," said Blake. He turned to the Kavanaghs. "A long-acting steroid. Goes into the system and lasts up to three months. He'll stop scratching in a couple of hours."

Dooley looked up from the box he was holding between his legs. "I wouldn't do that."

There was a brief silence.

Blake looked awkward. "What would you do?"

"Use a short-acting cortisone, which is easier on his system, and follow it up with tablets and a change of diet . . . medicate his shampoos."

"This is a country practice," said Hal Owen, tamping the tobacco in his pipe. "Not much time to fool with new diets and fancy shampoos."

Dooley stood up with his box. "Right," he said.

They were silent on the way home to Mitford. Maybe it was because of the late afternoon meal and the fresh country air.

§

"Is Dooley home from school yet?"

It was Jenny, the girl who lived down the street in the house with the red roof. She had shown up at their door, off and on, for the last couple of years, and he knew for a fact that Dooley had once spent hard-earned money on a coffee-table horse book for this girl.

"He is! Won't you come in?"

She came in, looking only slightly less shy than last year.

Barnabas skidded up, wagging his tail and barking. But there was no need to shout a Scripture verse. Jenny looked his dog in the eye and began scratching behind his ears.

He dashed upstairs to Dooley's bedroom, feeling some odd excitement in the air. "There's someone here to see you."

"Who?"

"Jenny."

Aha. He couldn't help but see Dooley's face turning red.

§

"You missed it," she said archly.

Why did he ever part with fifty cents for a newspaper, when all the news that was fit to print poured unhindered from his secretary?

"Say on."

"You know th' big wooded area behind the Shoe Barn?"

"I do."

"When Mack is elected, that whole sorry-looking scrub pine deal will be a fancy new development called Mitford Woods."

"Mitford Woods?"

"Plus, he said he personally knows of big-money interest in Miss Sadie's old house, which will be revealed shortly."

"Aha." If there was nothing to worry about as far as Mack Stroupe's mayoral win was concerned, why did he feel as if someone had punched him in the solar plexus? "So how was the barbecue?"

"Great. None of that vinegary stuff you sometimes get with politics. Plus, he had a whole raft of country musicians that got half th' crowd to clogging."

He looked at her, but she avoided his eyes. "Hmmm. So what do you think about Mack?"

"Oh . . . time will tell," she said, clicking on her menu. Was this the woman who, barely forty-eight hours ago, had labeled the candidate low-down scum?

"Esther Cunningham has been a great mayor for this town," she said, "but . . ."

He hated to hear it.

". . . but there's always room for improvement."

§

At the light on Main Street, Rodney Underwood yelled from his patrol car.

"What do you think this is? *Talladega*?"

Could he help it if Harley's truck blew past Rodney like he was standing still? Besides, what business did Rodney have being on Main Street every time he tried to do somebody a favor and take care of their vehicle?

Rodney winked at him. "Don't let it happen ag'in, buddyroe."

He felt the heat above his collar as the truck lunged away from the light and roared south on Main Street.

§

"What have you got under the hood of that '72 Ford? You nearly got me nailed twice in a row."

The rector thought Harley's toothless grin might meet at the back of his head.

"Lord, I was hopin' you'd ask. Here's what I done. I got rid of th' Ford engine and transmission, took out th' drive train an' rear end, an' dropped a '64 Jagwar XKE engine and transmission in there. Then I bolted in a Jagwar rear end and hooked it up to a new drive shaft. Three hundred and twenty horses! Course, that's all a man needs on a public highway."

He didn't understand a word Harley said, but he knew one thing: He was leaving that truck alone.

"I messed with flathead V-8s most of my life, 'til one day I looked under th' hood of a Jag and seen a steel crank case, twin alumium valve covers, an' a alumium head. Now, you take Junior, he didn't like nothin' foreign, but t' me, hit was th' prettiest thing I ever seen. Well, Rev'rend, when I left th' business, I fell away from flatheads an' ain't never looked back."

"Aha."

"You got t' handle it gentle or it'll jump over th' moon."

Father Tim laid the keys on the dresser. "Tell me about it. I sucked the awnings off every storefront on Main Street."

Harley hooted and cackled 'til the tears streamed from his eyes. If laughter was the medicine the Bible claimed it to be, Harley Welch was a well man.

The patient wiped his eyes on his pajama sleeve. "I thank you ag'in f'r all you an' th' missus do f'r me. Ain't nobody ever treated me s' good, an' I'm goin' t' make it up to you. Doc Harper lets me up to-morrow, said take it easy a day or two an' first thing you know, I'll be ol' Harley ag'in. I'll git me some new dogs an' go back t' my little setup on th' Creek. But not before I do somethin' t' repay y'uns."

"Don't think about it, my friend. Do you have a job to go back to?"

"I had one, but it give out th' same time as I did. I ain't worked in a good while, what with my stomach s' bad off. But I'll git back, I ain't lazy—I like a good job of work."

"We'll see how it goes," said Father Tim. "Has our boy been around this afternoon'

"Heard 'im come in, heard 'im go out is all."

"This was his first day at the store. Where's Lace?"

"After her school lets out tomorrow, she'll be here t' he'p me git up, take me out in th' fresh air an' all."

"Good! I want you to take it easy."

"Yessir, Rev'rend, I will. I want t' be feelin' strong when I go t' work on y'r car engine."

The rector laughed. "You leave my car engine alone," he said, meaning it.

CHAPTER FIVE

Out to Canaan

He peered into the vegetable crisper and took out three zucchini, a yellow onion, two red potatoes, and a few stalks of celery.

Somewhere in here was a beef bone he'd picked up at The Local. Aha. Wrapped in foil, behind the low-fat mayonnaise which he wouldn't touch with a ten-foot pole . . .

He put it all in a brown paper bag with a can of beef broth and a pound of coffee, and set out to Scott Murphy's house next to the bridge over Little Mitford Creek.

They walked along the path by the creek, with Luke and Lizzie straining ahead on their leashes.

It was hot for a June afternoon in the mountains, and he and Scott Murphy were going at a trot. The rector moved the grocery bag to his other arm and took out his handkerchief and wiped his face.

"Father, about your concern for having a Creek ministry . . ."

"Yes?"

"It occurs to me that you have one."

The rector looked at him, puzzled.

"You brought Dooley's kid brother out of there, who's living in the first real home he ever had. You're also providing a home for their mother. . . ."

"But—"

"And look at Lace Turner—last year she was living in the dirt under her house, trying to keep away from an abusive father. Now she's living with one of the most privileged families in town and making straight A's in school."

"Aha."

"And Harley Welch, your race car mechanic . . . you and Mrs. Kavanagh have taken him in, nursed him, maybe even saved his life."

"Yes, well . . ."

Luke stopped to lift his leg at a tree.

"I think we're always looking for the big things," Scott mused. "The big calling, the big challenge. Seems like Bonhoeffer had something to say about that."

"He did," said the rector. "Something like, 'We think we dare not be satisfied with the small measure of spiritual knowledge, experience and love that has been given to us, and that we must constantly be looking forward eagerly for the highest good.'"

"Yes, and I like that he talks about being grateful even where there's no great experience and no discoverable riches, but much weakness, small faith, and difficulty."

The two men pondered this as they walked. It was good to talk shop on a spring day, on a wooded path beside a bold creek.

"Before I came here," said Scott, "I told you I'd go in there and see what can be done. I'm sticking to it."

"Good fellow."

"I've been meaning to tell you we got the garden in at Hope House, fourteen of the residents are able to plant and hoe a little, we have peas coming up."

"You're everything Miss Sadie wanted," said the rector. "You're making Hope House live up to its name."

"Thank you, sir. Mitford is definitely home to me. Maybe I can buy Miss Ivey's little cottage when she sells the bakery and moves to Tennessee—I don't know, I'm praying about it."

They rounded the bend in the footpath and saw Homeless Hobbes sitting on the front step of his small, tidy house, a colorful wash hanging on the line.

"Lord have mercy, if it ain't town people!" Homeless got up and limped toward them on his crutch, laughing his rasping laugh. His mute, brown-and-white spotted dog crouched by the step and snapped its jaws, but no sound escaped. Luke and Lizzie barked furiously.

"Homeless!" The rector was thrilled to see his old friend, the man who'd given up a fast-lane advertising career, returned to his boyhood home, and gone back to "talkin'" like he was raised."

"I'm about half wore out lookin' for company! I told Barkless a while ago, I said somebody's comin', my nose is itchin', so I put somethin' extra in th' soup pot!"

The rector embraced Homeless and handed over the bag. "For the pot. And this is Scott Murphy, the chaplain at Hope House. He works sixteen hours a day and still has time to meddle in Creek business."

Homeless looked at the tall, lanky chaplain approvingly. "We need meddlin' in here," he said.

§

"I'd like to see th' dozers push th' whole caboodle off th' bank, and good riddance!"

Homeless had brought out two aluminum folding chairs that had seen better days, and set them up for his guests. He sat on the step, and the dogs lay panting in a patch of grass.

"They say th' whole thing'll be a shoppin' center in a couple of years. Where all them trailers is parked—Wal-Mart! Where all them burned-out houses is settin'—Lowe's Hardware! Where you could once go in and get shot in th' head, you'll be able t' go in an' get you a flush toilet.

"Still an' all, two years is a good bit of time, and you could do a good bit of work on the Creek, if you handle it right. Now, you take ol' Absalom Greer, he come in here and preached up a storm and some folks got saved and a good many lives were turned around, but Absalom was native and he was old, and they let him be.

"They won't take kindly to a young feller like yourself if you don't give 'em plenty of time to warm up.

"What I think you ought to do is come to my place on Wednesday night when I make soup for whoever shows up, and just set an' talk an' be patient, an' let th' good Lord do a work."

"I'll be here," said Scott.

Homeless grinned. "I wouldn't bring them dogs if I was you. Jack Russells are a mite fancy for my crowd."

§

"We lost our dining room manager last week," Scott said on the walk back home. "A family problem. Everybody's been pitching in, it's kind of a scramble."

"I like scrambles," said the rector, who was currently living in one.

§

Sometimes, a thought lodged somewhere in the back of his mind and he couldn't get it out, like a sesame seed stuck between his teeth.

Walking down Old Church Lane the following day, his jacket slung over his shoulder, he tried to focus on the place—was it in his brain?—that had something to tell him, some hidden thing to reveal.

Blast! He hated this. It was like Emma's aggravating game, Three Guesses. He couldn't even begin to guess. . . .

A job. Why did he think it had to do with a job?

We lost our dining room manager last week, Scott had said.

Yes!

Pauline!

Hanging on to his jacket, he started running. He could go to the office and call from there, but no, he'd run across Baxter Park, through his own backyard, and then up the hill and over to Betty Craig's house. Why waste a minute? Jobs were scarce.

He was panting and streaked with sweat when he hit the sidewalk in front of Betty's trim cottage. He stopped for a moment to wipe his face with a handkerchief when Dooley blew by him on his red bicycle.

"Hey!" shouted Dooley.

"Hey, yourself!" he shouted back.

He saw the boy throw the bicycle down by Betty's front steps, fling his helmet in the grass, and race to the door.

"Mama! Mama!" he called through the screen door.

Pauline appeared at the door and let him in as the rector walked up to the porch.

"Mama, there's a job at Hope House! Something in the dining room! I heard it at the store, they need somebody right now."

"Oh." Pauline grew pale and put her hand to the left side of her face. "I . . . don't know."

"You've waited tables, Mama, you can do it! You can do it!"

He saw the look on Dooley's face, and tried to swallow down a knot in his throat. In only a few years, this boy on a bicycle would be worth over a million dollars, maybe two million if the market stayed strong. Dooley wouldn't know this until he was twenty-one, but the rector could see that Sadie Baxter had known exactly what she was doing when she drew up her will.

"Come on, Mama, get dressed and go up there, I've got to get back to The Local or Avis'll kill me, I got five deliveries."

"I'll take you," the rector told Pauline. "I'll go home and get the car, won't be a minute." Hang the meeting in the parish hall at two o'clock.

Pauline looked at him through the screen door, keeping her hand over the left side of her face. "Oh, but . . . I don't have anything to . . . I don't know . . ."

"Don't be afraid," he said.

Tears suddenly filled Pauline's eyes, but she managed to smile. "OK," she said, turning to look at her son. "I can do it."

"Right!" said Dooley. He charged through the door and raced down the steps and was away on his red bicycle, but not before the rector saw the flush of unguarded hope on his face.

"I'll be back," said Father Tim. "Wear that blue skirt and white blouse, why don't you? I thought you looked very . . ."—he wasn't terribly good at this; he searched for a word—"nice . . . in that."

She gazed at him for a long moment, almost smiling, and disappeared down the hall.

An attractive woman, he thought, tall and slender and surprisingly poised, somehow. Her old life was written on her face, as all our lives are written, but something shone through that and transformed it.

§

In his opinion, Hope House might have done a notch better on their personnel director, Lida Willis.

"How long have you been sober?" asked the stern-looking woman, eyeing Pauline.

"A year and a half."

"What happened to turn you around?"

"I prayed a prayer," said Pauline, looking fully into the director's cool gaze.

"You prayed a prayer?"

Though he sat well across the room, feigning interest in a magazine, Father Tim felt the tension of this encounter. God was calling Pauline Barlowe to come up higher.

"Yes, ma'am."

"Are you in AA?"

"No, ma'am."

"Why not?"

"I don't know. I . . . feel like God has healed me of drinkin'. I don't crave it no more."

"Shoney's fired you for drinking on the job?"

"Yes. But they said that . . . when I was sober, I was the best they ever had."

"Miss Barlowe, what makes you think you might be right for this job?"

"I understand being around food, I get along real well with people, and I'm not afraid of hard work."

The director sat back in her chair and looked at Pauline, but said nothing.

"I need this job and would be really thankful to get it. I know if you call Sam Ward at Sam and Peg's Ham House in Holding, he'll tell you I do good work, I never missed a day at th' Ham House, my station was fourteen tables."

"Were you drinking when you worked there?"

Pauline looked down for a moment, then looked straight at Lida Willis. "Not as bad as . . . later."

"Has your personal injury handicapped you in any way?"

"Sometimes I don't hear as good out of my left ear, but that's all. My arm works wonderful, it's a miracle."

"I appreciate your honesty, Miss Barlowe." She stood up. "Please don't call us. We'll be in touch."

Pauline stood, also. "Yes, ma'am."

Dear God, he wanted this job for Pauline. No, wrong. He wanted this job for Dooley.

He saw Scott Murphy in the hall. "If there's anything you can do," he said under his breath as Pauline drank at the water fountain. "Your dining room manager's job . . ." He never begged anyone for anything, but this was different and he didn't care.

Scott looked at him, knowing.

"She can do it," he told the chaplain.

§

He was looking something up in his study when he heard a noise in the garage. It sounded like his car engine revving.

Surely Harley wasn't already working on . . .

He went through the kitchen, carrying J. W. Stevenson's rare volume on his ministry in the Scottish highlands.

Dooley was sitting in the Buick, gunning the motor. Barnabas sat on the passenger side, looking straight ahead.

"What's going on?" Father Tim asked through the open car window.

"Nothin'."

"Nothing, is it? Looks like you're gunning that motor pretty good."

"I'm checking it out for Harley."

"Really?"

"He didn't ask me to, but I thought it would help him to know how it sounds."

"Right. Well, you're out of there, buddy. Come on."

Dooley gave him an aloof stare. "Jack's dad lets him—"

"Look. What Jack's dad does is beside the point." Was it, really?

He didn't have a clue. Why would people let fourteen-year-old kids drive a car, two years before they could get a license? Or was that the going thing and he was a stick-in-the mud? "Maybe one day we can drive out to Farmer. . . ."

Dooley turned off the ignition: "Cool," he said. "Your engine's got a knock in it."

At six-thirty, Barnabas was finishing up last week's meat loaf, Violet was sneering down from the refrigerator, Cynthia was running a garlic clove around the salad bowl, Dooley was taking one of his endless showers, and Lace was stuffing a snack down a reluctant Harley Welch.

Father Tim still couldn't get over the fact that only three or four years ago, the rectory had been quiet as a tomb. No dog, no boy, no wife in an apron, no red-haired babies, and hardly ever a soul in the guest room, with the agonizing exception, of course, of his phony Irish cousin and an occasional overnight visit by Stuart Cullen, his seminary friend and current bishop.

"Can I talk t' you som'ers?" Lace wanted to know.

Harley was sitting on the side of the bed, fully dressed, but looking weak. He scraped the last bite from a cup of peach yogurt and wiped his mouth with his sleeve.

"Rev'rend, Lace has got a notion I cain't argue 'er out of. Don't pay no attention to 'er if she talks foolish."

"I don't believe I've ever heard Lace talk foolish," he said. "You look a little peaked today, Harley. How're you feeling?"

"Wore out. We was up an' down an' aroun' ever' whichaway, th' doc said I needed exercise. I been eatin' like a boar hog an' layin' up in this bed 'til I was runnin' t' fat."

"We could go down t' y'r basement," said Lace, tugging at her hat brim.

"My basement?"

"I hate like th' dickens I couldn't talk 'er out of this," said Harley. "She's pigheaded as a mule, always has been since I knowed 'er as a baby."

"What's the deal?" he asked as they trooped down the basement stairs.

"You'll see," she said.

The musty smell of earth came to him, and he remembered the cave he and Cynthia had been lost in only last year. They had wandered in circles for fourteen agonizing hours, until the local police, led by Barnabas, brought them out.

He shuddered and flipped the switch that lit the dark hallway.

There was the bathroom that hadn't been used since he moved here fifteen years ago, and the two bedrooms and the little kitchen—which had served, during the tenures of various rectors, as a mother-in-law apartment, a facility for runaways and later for elderly widows, a home office, an adult Sunday School, a church nursery, and storage space for the detritus of nearly a century of clergy families.

Lace folded her arms across her chest. "This is what I think."

"Shoot."

"When me'n Harley was ramblin' around today outside, we seen y'r basement door. F'r somethin' t' do, I tried t' git th' door open and had t' nearly bust it in."

"Really?"

"But it ain't broke, it was just stuck."

"Good!"

"So we seen how this is a place t' live, with a toilet an' kitchen an' all. An' I got to thinkin' how if Harley goes back to th' Creek, how he ain't goin' t' take care of hisself, an' besides, somethin' bad could happen to 'im."

"Aha."

"So I thought if you was to like th' idea, Harley could live down here and go t' work f'r you an' Cynthia."

He pulled at his chin.

"Harley can work, you ain't never seen 'im work, you just seen 'im laid up sick. Harley can rake, he can saw, he can hammer, he can paint."

"I'll be darned."

"An' he wouldn't charge you a cent to keep you an' Cynthia's cars worked on."

She looked at him steadily under the dim glow of the bulb.

"Well, I don't know. I'd have to think about it, talk to Cynthia about it."

"He wouldn't be no trouble. They wouldn't be no cookin' or nothin' to do for 'im, he could take care of hisself. He could paint this place for you, fix it up, I'd help 'im."

She paused, then said: "You ought t' do it, it'd be good for ever'-body."

Lace Turner had made her case, and rested it.

§

"Can he draw cats?" asked Cynthia. "He could do my next book."

Uh-oh. "Your next book?"

"I've been meaning to tell you, dearest. I'm starting a new book. You know how I said I'd never do another Violet book?"

"You definitely said that. Several times."

"I lied."

"Aha."

"You won't believe the advance they'll give me to do another Violet book."

It was true. When she told him, he didn't believe it. "Come on. That's four times what they gave you for the bluebird book."

"Well, you see, I refused so fiercely to do another Violet book, they had to make me an offer I couldn't resist."

"You're tough, Kavanagh."

"So kiss me!" she said, laughing.

He kissed her, inhaling the elusive scent of wisteria. "Congratulations! We can build a boat and retire to the Caribbean and spend our lives cruising and fishing."

"Where did you get an idea like that?"

"From Mike Jones at Incarnation in Highlands. He said that's what he wants to do when he retires—the only problem is, he's never mentioned it to his wife."

"The only problem is," she said, "we'll need gobs of money to en-large my little yellow house to contain a man, an ocean of books, and a dog the size of Esther Bolick's Westinghouse freezer."

"Well, then. What do you think?"

"I think we should let him have the basement and fix it up. I love Harley. He's funny and good-hearted and earnest. And it would be wonderful to have some more help around here. For openers, your garage could use a cleanup and my Mazda needs a new alternator."

"What do you know about alternators?"

"Absolutely nothing. Which means it would be nice to have Harley living in the basement. We'll buy the paint and I'll make his kitchen curtains."

"Done!" he said.

A new book? He knew what that meant. It meant his wife would be working eight hours a day or more, complaining of a chronically stiff neck, staring out the window without speaking, getting headaches from eye strain, and crashing into bed at night as lifeless as a swamp log.

Oh, well. He sighed, trudging up the stairs with his dog to tell Harley the news.

§

"Goodnight, buddy."

He had left Harley's room and stepped down the hall to sit on the side of Dooley's bed.

"'Night."

"We're praying that your mother gets the job."

"Me, too."

"How about your job? You like it all right?"

"It's neat. But I'm about give out."

When Dooley was tired or angry, Father Tim noted, he often lapsed into the vernacular. He grinned. That prep school varnish hadn't covered the boy's grain entirely. "Are you going to run a booth at the town festival?"

"Yep. Avis wants Tommy and me to do it. Avis'll be the bigwig and take the money."

"Sounds good. What will you do?"

"We'll sell corn and stuff from the valley. Avis has buckets of blackberries and strawberries comin' in from Florida, and peaches from Georgia and syrup from Vermont and all. He's calling it 'A Taste of America.'"

"Great idea! That Avis . . ."

"I'm about half killed."

"Well . . . see you at breakfast."

"What were you doing up at Mama's today? Taking livermush to Granpaw?"

"Just dropped by to say hello, that's all, and check on Poobaw."

"He likes to be called Poo now."

"I'll remember that. I'm glad you heard about the job at Hope House and didn't waste any time."

"Me, too. 'Night."

"Goodnight."

He went downstairs with a heart nearly full to bursting. To borrow a phrase from Dooley's granpaw, blast if he didn't love that boy better than snuff.

§

In less than a week, the bishop would arrive at Lord's Chapel on his annual confirmation pilgrimage. This year, however, he also had a dirty job to do. It had fallen on him to break the news of Timothy Kavanagh's retirement, just eighteen months away.

Stuart Cullen did not look forward to this bitter task. The parish wouldn't like the news, not even a little. In fact, he was prepared to duck after divulging this woe. Unless he and Martha got out of there immediately after the service, he was in for a virtual cantata of moaning and groaning, not to mention wailing and gnashing.

All that, he knew, would be followed by a series of outraged letters and phone calls to diocesan headquarters, and possibly a small, self-appointed group who would show up on his doorstep, begging him to force Father Tim to remain at Lord's Chapel until he was on a walker or, worse yet, senile and unable to commandeer the pulpit.

The rector, in the meantime, was trying to get himself in shape for an occasion that seemed variously akin to a wedding and then a funeral. His feelings rose and plummeted sharply. Bottom line, he couldn't dismiss the fact that once the words left Stuart's mouth, the deed was done, it was writ on a tablet, he was out of there.

His wife had certainly done everything in her power to help, though nothing seemed to calm his nerves. Certainly not the new suit she ordered from New York and which, he was aghast to find, was double-breasted. Would he look like some Mafia don at the parish brunch, as he struggled to give his stunned parish a look of innocent piety?

And so what if he'd managed to lose a full four pounds six ounces and appear positively trim? The downside was, his stomach stayed so infernally upset, he couldn't eat.

For years, he had feared this whole retirement issue. Even Stuart confessed to dreading it, and had once called retirement "a kind of death."

For himself, however, he had made peace with his fear last year in the cave. He had been able, finally, to forgive his father, to find healing and go on.

In some way he would never fully understand, he'd thought that by preaching into infinity, he could make up for having been unable to save his father's soul. Not that he could have saved it, personally— that was God's job. But he had somehow failed to soften his father's heart or give him ears to hear, and had believed he could never make up for that failing, except to preach until he fell.

Now he knew otherwise, and felt a tremulous excitement about stepping out on faith and finding his Canaan, wherever it may be. Indeed, the fear he now wrestled with was the fear of the unfamiliar. Hadn't he been wrapped in a cocoon for the last sixteen years, the very roof over his head provided?

"By faith, Abraham went out," he often quoted to himself from Hebrews, "not knowing where. . . ."

He knew one thing—he didn't want to leave the priesthood. He was willing to supply other pulpits here, there, anywhere, as an interim. Wouldn't that be an adventure, after all? Cynthia Kavanagh certainly thought so. He suspected she had already packed a bag and stashed it in the closet.

There were only a couple of things left to be done prior to Sunday. One, attend the closed vestry meeting on Friday night and tell them the news before it hit the pulpit. He dreaded it like a toothache. As far as he knew, they didn't have a clue what was coming, and they'd be shocked, stunned. He could stay and take it like a man, or duck out the back door while Buddy Benfield gave the closing prayer.

The list was all downhill from there. Two, book Stuart and Martha's lodging in Wesley, and three, get a haircut.

But hadn't he just had a haircut?

His hair was growing fast, Cynthia said, because of the olive oil in his diet.

Emma said he looked shaggy because Joe Ivey had gotten slack toward the end and hadn't given him his money's worth.

Somebody else declared it was the time of year when hair had a growth spurt like everything else, from ragweed to burdock.

He called Fancy Skinner for an appointment. Today, if possible, and get it over with.

"Oh, law, I don't have an openin' 'til kingdom come! Ever' since Joe Ivey went to Tennessee, I've gone like a house afire! The haircuts he's let loose around here gives me th' shivers, you can spot a Joe Ivey cut a mile away, it's always these little pooches of hair over th' ears, it'll take me a year to get rid of that chipmunk look in this town.

"Let's see . . . Ruth Wallace at eleven for acrylic nails, J. C. Hogan at noon, that's a cut, Beth Lawrence for a perm at twelve-thirty, that'll take two hours, you should see her hair, she calls it fine, I say she's goin' bald. Do you know her, she always wears a hat—if you ask me, wearin' a hat will make you bald, and oh, Lord, look here, at three o'clock I've got Helen Nelson, she will gnaw your ear off talkin', you can't get a word in edgewise, on and on and on, about every old thing from her husband growin' a mustache and how it scratches when he kisses, to th' pig they bought to keep as a house pet. Have you ever heard of keepin' a pig as a house pet? They say they trained it to a litter box!

"I'd rather have a dog any day, which reminds me, did you know one of my poodles ran away and Rodney Underwood found her under the bridge and brought her home in the front seat of his patrol car? Mule took a picture, you should ask to see it.

"How's your wife, how come she don't let me highlight her hair sometime? Does she do it herself? It looks like she does it herself. I bet she uses a cap—honey, foil works better, but don't tell her I said so.

"Let's see, four o'clock, oh, Lord, look here. I've got Marge Beatty's three kids, all at the same time, I should get a war medal. Then at five,

I'm doin' a mask—which reminds me, have I told you about my new product line called Fancy's Face Food? What it is, your face desperately needs nourishment just like your body, did you know that? Most people don't know that.

"First, I do th' Vitamin E Deluxe Re-Charge and Hydration Mask, which is the entrée, followed by a Cucumber Apricot Sesame Soother, which is the dessert, and honey, I'm tellin' you, you will walk out of here lookin' ten years younger, some say fifteen, but I try not to stretch the truth.

"The mask I'm doin' at five takes an hour, so the answer is, no, I couldn't take you today if my life depended on it, how about next Wednesday at ten o'clock?"

§

Harley removed two twenty-dollar bills from under the guest room mattress and was on his way to the Shoe Barn for new work shoes.

"Harley, be careful. Rodney Underwood has it in for that truck."

"Don't you worry," said Harley. "I'd never let them horses loose in town."

"I don't want to have to haul you out of jail."

"Nossir, Rev'rend, you won't."

So why did he watch that truck like a hawk, all the way to the end of Wisteria, 'til it turned north on Main?

§

"Miami," said Emma, looking curious.

He lifted the receiver from the phone on his desk.

"Hello?"

"Father, this is Ingrid Swenson with Miami Development Group. I'd like to talk with you about the old Fernbank property, which we understand is owned by your church."

"That's right."

"We're very interested, Father, in viewing this property next week, if that would be convenient."

"Well . . ."

"It is our intention, if everything looks as good as we hope it might, to develop this property as a world-class spa."

"A spa."

"Yes. We've developed similar properties around the country that have gained international clientele."

"Aha."

"How does next Wednesday look to you? Say, around eleven?"

"Ah, well, fine, I think. Yes. I'll have to gather up some of the vestry, and our realtor."

"Good. There'll be two of us."

"We're at the corner of Old Church Lane and Main Street, just as you come into town. Very easy to find."

"You may like to know that Mr. Mack Stroupe has highly recommended this property to us."

"I see."

"We're very grateful for such valued assistance in locating a property as special as Fernbank promises to be. We're told it has seventeen rooms."

"Twenty-one."

"Marvelous!"

"Yes. Well. We'll be looking for you, Miss Swenson."

"Ingrid, Father. And thank you for your time."

He put the phone on the hook.

"You don't look so good," said Emma.

Strange. He didn't feel so good, either. That phone call should have him dancing in the streets, shouting from the rooftops.

If Fernbank was such an albatross, why did he suddenly know he didn't want to lose it?

§

His heart hadn't pounded like this, even on the day of his ordination. It had pounded, yes, when he preached his first sermon to his first parish in his first small church. But he couldn't remember anything like this. He was glad he was sitting down, and glad he'd been able to persuade Cynthia to trim his hair.

He looked for his lifeline, which was the third pew, gospel side, where his wife sat scratching her nose. That was her signal for "Smile!"

Sitting next to her was Pauline Barlowe, then Poobaw, who was gazing at the ceiling, and Dooley. Russell Jacks anchored the pew at the opposite end.

"I have some good news and some bad news," Stuart told the congregation at the eight o'clock.

Did he have to put it that way? The rector shifted in the carved chair. This was the dress rehearsal for the more formal, well-attended eleven o'clock; whatever happened now would also happen then— except worse. Much worse.

"The good news," said Stuart, smiling the smile that had undoubtedly helped him rise in his calling, "is that Timothy Kavanagh, your beloved priest, generous counselor, and trusted friend . . ."

Get it over with, he thought, gripping the chair arms and closing his eyes. This was like flying with Omer Cunningham in his ragwing taildragger. . . .

". . . is getting ready to . . . *go out to Canaan!*"

How odd that Stuart would have had the same thought, found the same analogy! He noted that most of his congregation didn't seem to know anything about Canaan. Where was Canaan? He saw Esther Bolick glance at Gene and shrug her shoulders. Maybe it was overseas. Or maybe somewhere in Wilkes County, where they had that cheese factory.

"We're told in Genesis that Abram took Sarai his wife, and Lot his brother's son, and all their substance that they had gathered, and they went forth into the land of Canaan . . . a strange land, an alien land.

"God was sending Abram, whom He would later call Abraham, on the greatest journey, the grandest mission, of his life. But what would Canaan be like? Some said giants inhabited the land, and I recall what Billy Sunday once said, 'He said if you want milk and honey on your bread, you must be willing to go into the land of giants!'"

Father Tim felt his hair standing up on his head.

"What," asked Stuart, looking resplendent in embroidered brocade, "did Abraham *feel* when he was called by God to go out into this unfamiliar land, hundreds of miles from home?"

The rector believed he clearly heard the thoughts of half the crowd: *Beats me!*

In fact, Abraham hadn't even made an appearance in this morning's Old Testament reading. Oh, well. Bishops could do whatever they darn well pleased.

Stuart leaned over the pulpit and peered at the assembly, most of whom were admiring his satin mitre.

"Did he, like your faithful friend and priest, feel fearful of this journey into the unknown? Of course! Did he feel sorrow for leaving the familiar behind? Almost certainly! But"—and here Stuart drew himself up to his full height of six feet plus—"given what God had in store for him, didn't he also feel hope and excitement and expectation and *joy*?"

None of the above, thought the rector. What he felt was sheer, holy terror.

§

With no small amount of admiration, he observed Stuart Cullen getting exactly what he wanted from the congregation, rather like a conductor extracting a great symphony from an orchestra.

Where Stuart wanted tears, he got unashamed tears.

Where he wanted riotous laughter, there it came, pouring forth like a mighty ocean.

By the end of the service, nearly everyone felt as if they'd been called out to a Canaan of their own; that life itself was a type of Canaan.

The rector left the eleven o'clock on legs that felt like cooked macaroni, clinging to the arm of his wife, who was beaming.

"There, now, dearest, this is not a lynching, after all! Cheer up!"

He couldn't believe that his congregation had kissed him, hugged him, pounded him on the back, congratulated him, and wished him well.

Where he had expected faces streaming with tears, he saw only lively concern for his future. Where he had feared stern looks of indignation, he received smiles and laughter and the assurance they'd always love him.

Didn't they *care*?

"Don't kid yourself," said Stuart, as he and Martha dove into the car after the parish hall brunch. "The backlash is yet to come."

As Stuart gunned the Toyota Camry away from the curb, the rector felt brighter. So, maybe his parishioners really would hate to see him go! Right now they were just having a good time—after all, the bishop's visit was always a festive occasion.

CHAPTER SIX

A Small Boom

Emma was right. The billboard of Mack Stroupe's face seemed to loom over the highway. And whoever was responsible for the photo didn't appear to think much of retouching.

Zooming past it in his Buick, he wondered at his feelings about the new candidate, and determined, once and for all, to think the thing through and come to a conclusion he could live with. He was tired of the whole issue crawling around in the back of his mind like so many ants over a sugar bowl.

Why did he feel queasy and uncomfortable about Mack Stroupe being his mayor? J.C. was right—the mayorship wasn't Esther's job, it was the job of anybody who qualified to make the most of the office. But—did Mack qualify?

He couldn't think of a single reason why he should. Was it mere gossip that Mack had carried on a long-term extramarital relationship with a woman in Wesley? People were notorious for giving clergy all manner of information, and apparently the affair wasn't rumor at all, but fact.

While that sort of behavior may be acceptable to some, for him, it wouldn't fly. The whole business spoke of treachery and betrayal, however admissible it might be in the world's view.

He thought of Esther's plank, so well known by everyone in Mitford that first graders could recite it: Mitford Takes Care of Its Own.

Esther had carried out that philosophy in every particular, never wavering.

Wasn't it true that when you take care of what you have, healthy growth follows? Hadn't his trilliums, planted under all the right conditions, spread until they formed a grove? And the lily of the valley, established in the rich, dark soil behind his study, had become a virtual kingdom from only three small plants.

Actually, there had been growth in Mitford; it was no bucolic backwater. The little tea shop next to Mitford Blossoms was flourishing. They were still limited to cakes, cookies, tea, and coffee, but as everyone agreed, you have to crawl before you walk.

Recently, Jena Ivey, their florist, had been forced to add a room to her shop. And take the Irish Woolen Shop. Now, there was a flexible endeavor. In late spring and summer, when temperatures soared, Minnie Lomax removed the word *Woolen* from the store sign, thereby assuring a brisk, year-round trade.

Avis Packard was another example. Avis was a small-town grocer who had done such a terrific job of providing world-class provender that people came from surrounding counties to fill up his rear parking lot and jam the streets, especially when the Silver Queen corn rolled in.

And Happy Endings. When he first came here, there was no such thing as a bookstore; he'd been forced to drive to Wesley and spend his money in another tax jurisdiction. Last summer, there had actually been a queue in front of Happy Endings—he had seen it with his own eyes—when the newest Grisham book arrived by UPS. The UPS man had been astounded when he pulled to the curb and everybody cheered.

Mitford was making it, and without neon signs and factory smoke. So, yes, maybe some well-planned growth would be good, but face it, they were doing something right, and he didn't want to see that mind-set replaced by a mind-set that was only for development and change, whatever the cost.

Another thing. It boggled his mind that Mack Stroupe knew anyone outside the confines of Wesley and Holding. How had Mack engineered contact with what sounded like a large Florida development firm? And this thing about Mitford Woods, and Mack being the ringleader . . .

In the end, what about Mack's platform?

Was Mack really for Mitford?

Or was Mack for Mack?

§

He found his breakfast cereal tasting exactly like oil-based latex.

Every window was up, three fans were running wide open, and Violet sprawled as if drugged on the top of the refrigerator. Even the gloxinia seemed oppressed by the noxious fumes rising from the basement.

"Let's move!" said Cynthia, meaning it.

"Where?" he asked, liking the idea.

"The little yellow house! I don't even know some of the people I'm meeting in my own hallway!"

"You know Tommy," he said. "He only spent three nights."

"Yes, but—"

"And Harley's friend Cotton, didn't he tell great stories?"

"Of course, but—"

"And certainly Olivia was well meaning when she came down with the women from the hospital auxiliary to bring pots and pans and scatter rugs for Harley's kitchen. I'm sure they didn't mind that you still had curlers in your hair."

"I married a bachelor who led the quietest of lives, and now look!" she exclaimed, eyeing a kitchen sink that contained a roller pan, rollers, and a bevy of brushes.

"The plumbing repairs in the basement," he said lamely, "will be finished tomorrow, and they can wash the brushes down there."

"A likely story!"

"You're beautiful when you're mad," he said.

"I read that line in a pulp novel thirty years ago!"

"So sue me."

She came around the breakfast table and sat in his lap. "I love you, you big lug."

"I love you more," he said, pulling her to him and kissing her hair. "Have you started your book?"

She laughed gaily. "Of course I've started my book! None of this would have happened if I hadn't started my book!"

⸙

These days, clergy seldom liked living in rectories. Because they generally preferred to own their own homes, and because the upkeep of the rectory had been considerable over the years, the vestry had long ago voted to sell the old house at the end of his tenure. What with the recent improvement below, the rector suspected they'd get a much better price for it.

Who would have dreamed he'd ever see the grim downstairs hall-way come alive under a coat of Peach Soufflé, or a kitchen transformed by Piña Colada and his wife's bright curtains fluttering at the window?

Harley Welch would be living high in this basement.

⸙

Before the Miami contingent arrived the following day, he cleaned up some matters at his desk.

Emil Kettner, head honcho of the construction company that built Hope House, regretted that Buck Leeper would be tied up for two years on a project in Virginia.

Perhaps after that, Kettner said, they could send Buck to Mitford for six months, which ought to be enough time to overhaul the church attic. His company never sent Buck on small jobs, but in this case, they'd try to make an exception. Could they wait?

Their Sunday School wasn't yet overflowing, said the rector, but they were getting there.

The conclusion was, Lord's Chapel was willing to wait, as they really wanted Buck for the job.

"He's doing better, I thought you'd like to know that," said Emil.

"A few weekend benders here and there, but nothing daily like it was for years. What happened in Mitford, Father?"

"Buck got rid of something old, so something new could come in."

"You have my personal thanks."

"No thanks to me," said the rector. "Thanks be to God!"

§

Lace Turner met him at the foot of the basement steps.

"He's done eat a whole bag of choc'late candy!" she said.

Harley, who was a ghastly color, was sitting on the floor of the hallway, clutching his stomach. "Don't be tattlin' on me like I was some young 'un!"

"You act like a young 'un!" said Lace. "That choc'late'll git your ulcer goin' again, just when you was gettin' better!"

"Rev'rend, hit was all that baby puddin' that made me do it. A man needs somethin' he can get 'is teeth into, you might say. But oh, law, I repent, I do, I'm sorry I ever bought that bag of candy, I'll never take another bite long as I live! Nossir!"

"Forty-two pieces, I counted 'em," said Lace. "He wadded up th' wrappers and stuck ever' one under 'is mattress."

"You cain't git by with a thing around this 'un, she's th' worst ol' *po*lice I ever seen." Harley stood up suddenly, looking distraught. "Oh, law! You 'uns better leave!"

He headed for the bathroom at a trot.

What timing. The basement plumbing had been completed barely an hour ago.

§

He squirmed in his office chair and looked at his watch.

In thirty minutes, he and Ron Malcolm and several others on the vestry were squiring strangers around Sadie Baxter's homeplace. He hated the thought, but he despised himself more for his wishy-washy attitude about the whole situation.

They needed desperately to sell it, get it off the shoulders of the parish; yet, here was a golden opportunity driving up the mountain in a rented car, and he wanted to run in the opposite direction.

Surely it was as simple as his dread of letting Sadie Baxter go entirely. Surely he was trying to hold on to what was vanished and gone, to another way of life that had been vibrantly preserved in Miss Sadie's engrossing stories.

When Fernbank was sold, all that would be left of the old Mitford was three original storefronts on Main Street, Lord's Chapel and the church office, the town library, and the Porter mansion–cum–town museum where Uncle Billy and Miss Rose lived in the little apartment.

Blast! he exhorted himself. Stop being a hick and move on. This is today, this is now!

He glanced at Emma, who was staring at her computer screen. What did people find to stare at on computer screens, anyway? Nothing moved on the screen, yet she was transfixed, as if hearing voices from a heavenly realm.

"I'll be darned," she muttered, clicking her mouse.

He sighed.

"Look here," she said, not taking her eyes off the screen.

He got up and went to her desk and looked.

"What? It looks like a list."

"It is a list. It's a list of everybody in the whole United States, and their addresses. Our computer man sent it to us. See there?"

She moved her pointer to a name. "Albert Wilcox!" he exclaimed. "Good heavens, do you suppose . . ."

"We've been lookin' for Albert Wilcox for how long?"

"Ten years, anyway! Do you think it's *our* Albert Wilcox?"

"We heard he'd moved to Seattle," she said, "and we tried to find him in the phone book, but we never did. This town is somewhere close to Seattle, it's called Oak Harbor."

"Well done! Let's write this Albert Wilcox and see if he's the one whose grandmother's hand-illuminated prayer book turned up in the parish hall storage closet."

"A miracle!" she said. "I remember the day we found it—right behind the plastic poinsettias that had been there a hundred years. How in th' dickens it ended up *there* . . ."

"That book could be worth a fortune. Every page is done in calligraphy and watercolor illustrations—by his own grandfather. When it disappeared out of the exhibition we did for a Bane and Blessing, it broke Albert's heart."

"It was only Rite One, remember, not th' whole thing!"

"Nonetheless . . ."

"And don't forget he was goin' to sue the church 'til Miss Sadie talked him out of it."

Well, that, too.

§

Ingrid Swenson was fashionably thin, deeply tanned, and expensively dressed.

"Arresting!" she said, as they drove along Fernbank's proud but neglected driveway.

Tendrils of grapevine leapt across the drive and entwined among a row of hemlocks on the other side. To their right, a gigantic mock orange faded from bloom in a tangled thicket of wisteria, star magnolia, and rhododendron.

The house didn't reveal its dilapidation at once, and for that he was relieved. In fact, it stood more grandly than he remembered from his caretaker's visit in March.

He was touched to recall that exactly two years ago there had been the finest of fetes at this house.

On the lawn, young people in tuxedos had served champagne and cups of punch on silver trays, as lively strains of Mozart poured through the tall windows. Inside, the ballroom had been filled with heartfelt joy for Olivia and Hoppy Harper, the glamorous bride and groom, and with awe for the hand-painted ceiling above their heads, which was newly restored to its former glory.

Roberto had flown from Italy to surprise Miss Sadie, and Esther Bolick's orange marmalade cake had stood three tiers high, each tier supported by Corinthian columns of marzipan bedecked with imported calla lilies. It had been, without doubt, the swellest affair since President Woodrow Wilson had attended a ball at Fernbank and given little Sadie Baxter a hard candy wrapped in silver paper.

The man who came with Ingrid Swenson seemed interested only

in biting his nails, speaking in monosyllables, and exploring Fernbank quite on his own. The rector saw him peering into the washhouse and wandering into the orchards, taking notes.

"A little over twelve acres," said Ron Malcolm, a longtime member of Lord's Chapel who kept his broker's license current.

"Excellent," said Ingrid, who took no notes at all. "Twelve acres translates to twenty-four cottages. Town water, I presume?"

"On a well."

"Town sewer, of course. . . ."

"Afraid not," said Ron. "And I must tell you in all fairness that the cost to connect this property to town services will run well above a hundred thousand. The connection is a half mile down the hill and the right-of-ways pose some real problems."

Ingrid looked at him archly. "It could behoove you to make that investment and offer your buyer an upgraded property."

"It behooves us even more," said Ron, "to avoid putting a burden of debt on the parish."

She smiled vaguely. "That is, in any case, a trifle, Mr. Malcolm. But let's consider an issue which is the polar opposite of a trifle, and that's the number of jobs such a facility would bring to your village. An upscale property of twenty-one rooms and twenty-four cottages, including a state-of-the-art health center, would employ well over a hundred people, many of them coming from Europe and the British Isles and requiring satisfactory housing. This, gentlemen, could create a small boom." She paused for effect. "A small boom for a small town!" she said, laughing.

"Yes ma'am," said Ron Malcolm.

"But we'll get to all that later. Now I'd like to start in the attic and work down to the basement."

"Consider it done," said the rector, wanting the whole thing behind them.

§

She would talk it over with her associates, Ingrid told them in the church office. They wouldn't buy an option—they'd take a risk on the property still being available when they returned with an offer in thirty to sixty days.

"Risk," she said, toying with the paperweight on his desk, "has a certain adrenaline, after all."

Their lawyer would begin the title search immediately, and a full topo would be done by a surveyor from Holding. No, they didn't want the window treatments or furnishings, with the possible exception of Miss Sadie's bed, which Ingrid concluded was French, a loveseat and secretary that were almost certainly George II, and a china cabinet that appeared to be made by a native craftsman.

Her people wanted to talk with the town engineer again, and expressed regret that the heating system appeared defunct and the plumbing would have to be completely modernized.

Before leaving, she mentioned the seriousness of the water damage due to years of leakage through a patched roof, and frowned when the subject of the well and sewer emerged again.

He tried to be elated, but was merely thankful that the first phase was over and done with. He made a note to get up to Fernbank with Cynthia and go through the attic, pronto.

§

Pauline Barlowe had the job and was to report to work on Monday morning at six-thirty.

He called Scott Murphy at once.

"Thank you!" he said. "I can't thank you enough."

"What for, sir?"

"Why, for . . . saying anything that might have helped Pauline Barlowe get the job in your dining room."

"I didn't say a word."

"You didn't?"

"Not a peep out of me. That was our personnel director's idea. She said she knew she might be taking a chance, but she wanted to do it and came to talk to me about it. Lida Willis is tough, she'll watch Mrs. Barlowe like a hawk, but Lida has a soft center; she wants this to work."

"We're thrilled around our place. This means a lot to Dooley as well as his mother. When will you come for dinner? We've got a regular corn shucking going at the rectory; it's just the thing to liven up a bachelor."

"Name the time!" said the chaplain.

"I'll call you," said the rector.

§

"We're giving a party," announced his wife, flushed with excitement.

"We are?"

"Friday night. In the basement, a housewarming! I'm baking cookies and making a pudding cake for Harley, and Lace is doing the lemonade. I've invited Olivia, Hoppy has a meeting, and oh, I've asked Dooley, but he's not keen on the idea. Who else?"

"Ummm. Scott Murphy!" he wondered

"Perfect. Who else?"

"Tommy. But wait, I think Dooley mentioned that Tommy has a family thing on Friday, and Dooley's going over there later to watch a video."

"OK, that's seven. Terrific! They finished painting today, the place looks wonderful, and it's all aired out and Harley is excited as anything. He raked tons of leaves from under the back hedge, and in the next couple of days he's replacing my alternator."

"Wonderful!" he said

"Harley's so happy, he can't stop grinning, and Lace—she doesn't say so, but she's thrilled by all this."

"It was her idea, and she was bold enough to step forward and ask for it."

"Let us come *boldly* to the throne of grace . . ." said his wife, quoting one of their favorite verses from Hebrews.

". . . that we may obtain mercy and find grace to help in time of need!" he replied.

"Amen!" they cried in unison, laughing.

He frankly relished it when they burst into a chorus of Scripture together. As a boy in his mother's Baptist church, he'd been thumpingly drilled to memorize Scripture verses, which sprang more quickly to memory than something he'd studied yesterday.

"One of the finest exhortations ever delivered, in my opinion," he said. "Well, now, what may I do to help out with the party?"

"Help me move that old sofa from the garage to Harley's parlor, I don't think he's strong enough, then we'll shift that maple wardrobe from the furnace room to his bedroom."

Was there no balm in Gilead?

"Oh, and another thing," she said, smiling innocently. "We need to haul that huge box of books from his parlor to the furnace room."

For his wife's birthday in July, she was getting a back brace whether she wanted it or not. In fact, he'd get one for himself while he was at it.

§

On his way to Hope House, he stopped at the Sweet Stuff Bakery to buy a treat for Louella.

Winnie Ivey looked at him and burst into tears.

"Winnie! What is it?"

"I heard you're leaving," she said, wiping her eyes with her apron.

"Yes, but not for a year and a half."

"We'll miss you somethin' awful."

"But you'll probably be gone before I will."

"Oh," she said. "I keep forgetting I'm going."

"Besides, we'll still be living in Mitford, in the house next door to the rectory."

"Good!" she said, sniffing. "That's better. Here, have a napoleon, I know you're not supposed to, but . . ."

What the heck, he thought, taking it. At least one person was sorry to hear he was retiring. . . .

§

When he left the bakery, he looked up the street and saw Uncle Billy sitting in a dinette chair on the grounds of the town museum, watching traffic flow around the monument.

He walked up and joined him. "Uncle Billy! I'm half starved for a joke."

"I cain't git a new joke t' save m' life," said the old man, looking forlorn.

"If you can't get a joke, nobody can."

"My jokes ain't workin' too good. I cain't git Rose t' laugh f'r nothin'."

"Aha."

"See, I test m' jokes on Rose, that's how I know what t' tell an' what t' leave off."

"Try one on me and see what happens."

"Well, sir, two ladies was talkin' about what they'd wear to th' Legion Hall dance, don't you know, an' one said, 'We're supposed t' wear somethin' t' match our husband's hair, so I'll wear black, what'll you wear?' an' th' other one sorta turned pale, don't you know, an' said, 'I don't reckon I'll go.'"

"Aha," said Father Tim.

"See, th' feller married t' that woman that won't goin' was *bald,* don't you know."

The rector grinned.

"It don't work too good, does it?" said Uncle Billy. "How about this 'un? Little Sonny's mama hollered at 'im, said, 'Sonny, did you fall down with y'r new pants on?' An' Sonny said, 'Yes 'um, they won't time t' take 'em off.'"

The rector laughed heartily. "Not bad. Not half bad!"

"See, if I can hear a laugh or two, it gits me goin'."

"About like preaching, if you ask me."

"Speakin' of preachin', me 'n Rose ain't a bit glad about th' news on Sunday. We come home feelin' s' low, we could've crawled under a snake's belly with a hat on. It don't seem right f'r you t' go off like that."

"I'll be living right down the street, same as always. We'll be settling in the yellow house next door to the rectory."

"Me 'n Rose'll try t' git over it, but . . ." Uncle Billy sighed.

Father Tim couldn't remember seeing Bill Watson without a big smile on his face and his gold tooth gleaming.

"See, what Rose 'n me don't like is, when you leave they'll send us somebody we don't know."

"That's the way it usually works."

"I figure by th' time we git t' know th' new man, we'll be dead as doornails, so it ain't no use to take th' trouble, we'll just go back to th' Presbyterians."

"Now, Uncle Billy . . ."

"I hate t' say it, Preacher, but me 'n Rose think you could've waited on this."

The rector made his way down Main Street, staring at the sidewalk. It was the only time in his life he hadn't come away from Bill Watson feeling better than when he went.

§

At the corner of Main and Wisteria, he saw Gene Bolick coming toward him, and threw up his hand in greeting. It appeared that Gene saw him, but looked away and jaywalked to the other side.

§

June.

Something about June . . .

What else was happening this month? His birthday!

Dadgum it, he'd just had one.

In fact, the memory of his last birthday rushed back to him with dark force. His wife had brought him coffee in bed and wished him happy birthday, then the phone had rung and he'd raced to the hospital and discovered that a woman who would be irrevocably fixed in his life had been horribly burned by a madman.

He sat back in his swivel chair and closed his eyes. Wrenching, that whole saga of pain and desperation. And days afterward, only doors down the hall from Pauline, Miss Sadie had died.

No wonder he'd come close to forgetting his birthday. When was it, anyway? He looked at the calendar. Blast. Straight ahead.

How old would he be this year? He could never remember.

He called Cynthia at home. "How old will I be this year?"

"Let's see. You're six years older than I am, and I'm fifty-seven. No, fifty-six. So you're sixty-two."

"I can't be sixty-two. I've already been sixty-two, I remember it distinctly."

"Darn!" she said. "Then you're sixty-three?"

"Well, surely I'm not sixty-five, because I'm retiring at sixty-five."

"So you must be sixty-three. Which makes me fifty-seven. Rats."

He realized as he hung up that they could have used their birth years to calculate the answer. What a pair they made! He hoped nobody had tapped his phone line and overheard such nonsense.

§

"I've been thinking," said Emma.

Please, no.

"I might as well retire when you retire."

"Well!" He was relieved. "Sounds good!"

She looked at him over her half-glasses. "But I wasn't expecting you to give up so soon."

"Give up?"

"I guess you can't take it anymore, the pressure and all—two services every Sunday, the sick and dying . . ."

"It has nothing to do with pressure, and certainly not with the sick and dying. As you know, I've committed to supply pulpits from here to the Azores."

"Yes, well, that's vacation stuff, anybody can go supply somewhere and not get involved."

He felt suddenly furious. Thank God he couldn't speak; he couldn't open his mouth. His face burning, he got up from his desk and left the office, closing the door behind him with some force.

There! he thought. Right there is reason enough to retire.

He deserved a medal for putting up with Emma Newland all these years—which, he realized only this morning, would be a full sixteen in September.

Sixteen years in an office the size of a cigar box, with a woman who made Attila the Hun look sensitive and nurturing?

"A medal!" he exclaimed aloud, going at full trot past the Irish Shop.

"There he goes again, talking to himself," said Hessie Mayhew, who had dropped in to share a bag of caramels with Minnie Lomax.

"What do you think it is?" asked Minnie, who hoped the caramels wouldn't stick to her upper plate.

"Age. Diabetes. And *guilt*," she announced darkly.

"Guilt?"

"Yes, for leaving those poor people in the lurch who've looked after him all these years."

"My goodness," said Minnie, "we don't look after our preacher at all. He looks after himself."

"Yes, but you've got a Baptist preacher. They've been *raised* to look after themselves."

"I declare," said Minnie, who had never considered this possibility.

§

At The Local, he saw Sophia Burton, who wasn't even a member of Lord's Chapel, and was flabbergasted when she burst into tears by the butcher case.

"I'm sorry," she told him.

"Don't be sorry!" he implored, not knowing what else to say.

"It's just that . . . it's just that you've been so good to us, and . . . and we're *used* to you!"

Didn't he despise change? Didn't he hate it? And here he was, inflicting it on everyone else. If his wife wasn't so excited about the whole adventure of being free, he'd call Stuart up, and . . . no, he wouldn't do any such thing. Actually, he was excited, himself.

"I'm . . . pretty excited, myself," he muttered weakly.

"That's easy for you to say!" Mona Gragg, a former Lord's Chapel Sunday School teacher, strode up to him, clutching a sack of corn and tomatoes. For some reason, Mona looked ten feet tall; she was also mad as a wet hen.

"When I heard that mess on Sunday, I just boiled. Here we've all gotten along just fine all these years, *plus* . . . you're still plenty young, and no reason in the *world* to retire. Did Grandma Moses quit when *she* was sixty-five? Certainly not! She hadn't even gotten *started*! And Abraham, which Bishop Cullen was so quick to yammer about on Sunday . . . he moved to a whole new *country* when he was way up in his *seventies* and didn't even have that *kid* 'til he was a *hundred*!"

Mona stomped away, furious.

"One of my ah, parishioners," he said, flushing.

Sophia wiped her eyes and smiled. "Father, now I can see why you're retiring."

He checked out, liking the sight of Dooley bagging groceries at one of Avis's two counters.

"How's it going, buddy?"

Dooley grinned. "Great! Except for people raisin' heck about you retiring."

"Ah, well." For some reason he didn't completely understand, Dooley seemed to approve of his plans. It wasn't the first time Dooley had stood up for him. A year or so ago, when Buster Austin had called the rector a nerd, Dooley had proceeded to beat the tar out of him.

As he left The Local, he saw Jenny parking her blue bicycle at the lamppost.

§

He left one end of Main Street feeling like a million bucks, and reached the other end feeling like two cents with a hole in it.

Up and down the street, he was besieged by people who had heard the news and didn't like it, or, on the rarest of occasions, proffered him their sincere best wishes.

Rodney Underwood was shocked and, it seemed, personally insulted.

Lew Boyd shook his head and wouldn't make eye contact. Why in heaven's name his *car mechanic* was piqued was beyond him.

The owner of the Collar Button rushed into the street and extended his deepest regrets. "What a loss!" he muttered darkly, sounding like a delegate from a funeral parlor.

A vestry member called him at the rectory. "This," she announced, "is the worst news since they found somethin' in Lloyd's limp nodes."

He phoned Stuart Cullen.

"Gene Bolick crossed to the other side of the street!" he said, feeling like a ten-year-old whining to a parent.

"Denial! If he doesn't have to talk to you, he doesn't have to acknowledge the truth. He'll get over it. It takes time."

"And some people are mad because I'm retiring so early! I feel like a heel, like I'm running out on them."

"Let them squawk!" Stuart exclaimed. "When people don't express their anger, it turns into depression. So, better this than a parish riddled by resentment and low morale."

"Then," Father Tim said miserably, "there are those who feel it's merely a blasted inconvenience."

"They're right about that," said Stuart. "By the way, your Search Committee is already up and running, but it'll be a long process. So hang in there."

His bishop hadn't been any help at all.

❧

The hasty trim he'd gotten from his reluctant wife had carried him through Stuart's visit, but wouldn't carry him a step further. And blast if Fancy Skinner wasn't booked. That was the way with those unisex shops, he thought, darkly. He made an appointment for a month away, and deceived himself that he could talk Cynthia into an interim deal.

"No, a thousand times no. I can't cut hair! Go to Wesley, where they have the kind of barbershop you like, where men talk trout fishing and politics!"

"I know zero about trout fishing, and even less about politics," he said. "Where did you get that idea?"

"Oh, phoo, darling!" she said, waving him away.

"I'll trim you up!" said Harley, who was getting ready for the party in his basement.

"Oh, I don't—"

"Law, Rev'rend, I've cut hair from here t' west Texas, they ain't nothin' to it, it jis' takes a sharp pair of scissors. Now, th' right scissors is ever'thing. I've cut with a razor, I've cut with a pocketknife, but I like scissors th' best. I ain't got a pair, but I got a good rock I use t' sharpen m' knife, so you git me some scissors, an' we're set. What're you lookin' for—mostly t' git it off y'r collar, I reckon."

"I don't know about this, Harley."

Harley looked at him soberly. "You ought t' let me do it f'r you, Rev'rend. I don't want th' Lord sayin' 'What did you do f'r th' Rev'rend?' an' me have t' tell 'im, 'Nothin', he wouldn't let me do nothin'!' I know what th' Lord'll say, he'll say, 'Harley, that ain't no excuse, you jis' git on down them steps over yonder, I know hit's burnin' hot, but . . .'"

"Oh, for Pete's sake," said the rector. "I'll get the scissors."

There went Harley's grin, meeting behind his head again.

§

"Ummm," said Cynthia, looking at him as he dressed for Harley's housewarming party.

"Ummm, what?"

"Your hair . . ."

"What about it?"

"It's sort of scalloped in the back."

"Scalloped?"

"Well, yes, up, down, up, down. What did Harley use—pinking shears?"

"Scissors!"

"Not those scissors I cut up chickens with, I fondly hope."

"Absolutely not. He used the scissors from my chest of drawers, which I keep well sharpened."

"You would," she said, looking at him as if he were a beetle on a pin. "Why don't you sit on the commode seat and let me sort of . . . shape it up? You know I hate doing this, but you can't go around with that scalloped look."

Certainly not. He sat on the commode seat, draped with a bath towel, glad he'd soon have the whole dismal business behind him.

§

Cynthia had done the deed and dashed downstairs. He was putting on a clean shirt when Dooley wandered into the bedroom.

He looked at the boy, fresh from a day's work, and now fresh from the shower. Clean T-shirt, clean jeans; hair combed, shoe laces tied. Upstanding! Getting to look more like a millionaire every day!

The rector might have been a statue in a park, the way Dooley walked around him, staring.

"Man . . ." said Dooley.

"What are you looking at?"

"Your hair."

"What about my hair?" He was beginning to feel positively churlish at any mention of his hair.

"It's cut in a kind of V in the back. I've never seen that before."

"A V? What do you mean, a *V*?"

He stomped to his dresser and, with his wife's hand mirror, looked at the back of his neck in the trifold mirror. It wasn't a V, exactly, it was more like a U. What was the matter with people around here, anyway?

"I'll trim it up for you," said Dooley, "if you'll let me drive your car Saturday."

"Dooley . . ."

"You can drive as far as Farmer, and I can take over at the cutoff."

"This is no time—"

"Anyway, you better let me fix your hair. I know how to do it."

"You're kidding me."

"I'm not kidding you. I've cut Tommy's hair bunches of times."

"A likely story."

"I swear on a stack of Bibles."

"I wouldn't do that. The Bibles you so casually stacked up ask us not to swear."

"That V is hanging down over your collar."

He would drive to Memphis next week, it was only nine or ten hours one way, and see Joe. While he was there, maybe Joe would give him a tour of Graceland. . . .

He sighed deeply. For the third time that day, he got his scissors out of his dresser drawer and handed them over. This time, however, he had the good sense to pray about it.

CHAPTER SEVEN

Housewarming

The showy pudding cake had been reduced to crumbs, the fruit bowl ransacked, the cookies demolished. All that remained in the glass pitcher were two circles of lemon and a few seeds.

In the freshly painted sitting room, Harley opened the last of his housewarming presents.

"Oh, law!" he said, holding up the framed picture of Jesus carrying a sheep. "Hit's th' Lord an' Master, ain't it?"

"Bingo!" said Cynthia, who had given him the print to go over his bed.

"That sheep was lost," Dooley announced. "Tell about it," he said, looking at the rector.

"Why don't you tell about it?"

Dooley scratched his head. "Well, see, it's like . . . if you had a hundred sheep and one of 'em ran off and got lost, you'd go after it, you'd go to the mountains and all, looking for it. And like, when you found it, it would make you feel really good, I mean better than you even feel about the ninety-nine that didn't run off."

"By jing!" said Harley.

Lace sat forward in the chair. "What th' story's about," she said, "is when somebody's lost and Jesus finds 'em an' they give their heart to 'im, it makes 'im feel happier than He feels about all them other'ns that wadn't lost."

Dooley looked at her coldly.

"I reckon that's what th' Lord done with me," said Harley. "Searched through th' mountains lookin' t' find me, an' brought me here." He grinned. "And I ain't lost n'more."

The rector was captivated by an odd confidence—a new maturity, perhaps—in Lace Turner.

"Well, now, I want t' thank ever' one of you'ns," said Harley, tears coming to his eyes. "I ain't never had a Bible with m' name on it, I ain't never had a 'lectric fan that moves to th' left an' right . . ."

He took a paper napkin from his pocket and blew his nose.

". . . I ain't never had a picture t' hang on m' wall 'cept of m' mama as a little young 'un . . . an' Lord *knows,* I ain't never had a . . ." Harley patted Scott's gift, which lay beside him on the sofa. "What d'you call this what you give me?"

"That's an afghan," said the chaplain, grinning. "One of our residents crochets those. They're a big hit on the hill."

"What exactly is it f'r, did you say?"

"It's to keep you warm in winter when you lie on the sofa and watch TV."

"I'll use it, yes, sir, I will, and I thank you, but I ain't goin' t' be layin' on no sofa watchin' TV, I'm goin' t' be workin'."

"Harley's going to change my alternator!" announced Cynthia.

"I'd sure appreciate it if you'd take a look at my brakes," said Scott. "They're sticking."

"Might be y'r calibers."

"I'll pay the going rate."

"Th' only rate goin' for you 'uns is no rate," Harley declared.

Scott Murphy glanced at his watch and stood. "I've got to look in on my folks before they get to sleep. Thanks for inviting me, sir . . . Mrs. Kavanagh—"

"Cynthia!" said Mrs. Kavanagh.

"Cynthia! I had a really good time. Harley, come up and see me at Hope House. And let me know when you can look at my brakes."

Scott left by the basement door, as the rest of the party said their goodbyes to Harley, then trooped up the stairs to the rectory kitchen and along the hall to the front stoop.

"Soon as I get my stuff, I'm going to Tommy's house!" Dooley raced up the steps to his room, Barnabas at his heels. "His dad's waitin' for me, we're going to Wesley to rent a video."

The rector stood on the front walk and talked with Cynthia and Olivia as Lace searched under the bench on the stoop. Then she came down the steps to the yard and peered into the boxwoods near the steps.

"Lace—what is it?" asked Olivia.

"Somebody's stoled my hat," she said. "My hat ain't where I left it at."

"Where did you leave it?" wondered Cynthia.

"I asked her to leave it on the bench," Olivia confessed, looking concerned.

"I'll have a look with you," said the rector, going to the boxwoods. "It probably fell . . ."

"It didn't fall nowhere!" Lace shouted. "It's gone!"

The screen door slammed and Dooley ran down the steps.

"It was you that stoled my hat, won't it? I ought t' bash y'r head in!"

She lunged toward Dooley, and Olivia moved almost as quickly, catching Lace's jumper. There was a ripping sound as the skirt tore from part of the bodice.

"Look what you done t' my new outfit!" Lace struggled to free herself from Olivia. "Let me go, I'm goin' t' knock his head off—"

"Lace! Don't." Cynthia caught her wrist.

"I ought t' kill you, you sorry, redheaded son of a—"

Dooley's face was crimson. "Why would I steal your dirty, stinking, stupid, beat-up hat?"

The rector put his hand on the boy's shoulder. "Easy, son."

"Well, why would I?" he yelled.

"You better give it back and give it back now!" Lace trembled with rage, her own face ashen.

"What would anybody want with your dumb, stupid hat that makes you look so stupid everybody laughs behind your back? Who would even touch your stupid, snotty, dirty hat?"

Lace wrenched away from Cynthia and Olivia and flew at Dooley, who threw his arm in front of his face. She slammed her fist into his left rib, which sent him reeling backward toward the stoop.

Barnabas barked furiously as the rector grabbed Lace by the shoulders. "Stop it *now*," he said.

Dooley regained his balance and stood without a word. He straightened his shirt. "I've got to go," he said, tight-lipped. "Tommy's dad is waiting for me."

"Go," the rector said quietly.

"If you done it," Lace shouted after Dooley, "I'll stomp your butt 'til you're flatter'n a cow dab."

Cynthia and Olivia walked with Lace to the blue Volvo at the curb, as the rector sat wearily on the top step. Barnabas crashed beside him. He felt shaken by the intensity of Lace Turner's sudden and virulent outburst.

If Dooley Barlowe were, indeed, the culprit, he'd do well to hide in the piney woods 'til this thing blew over.

§

He sat in the chair next to Dooley's desk, reading the Thirty-seventh Psalm, the first two words of which he considered an entire sermon.

He looked up as Dooley raced into the room on the stroke of his curfew.

"Did you do it?"

Dooley stood in the doorway, panting. He hesitated for a moment, peering at his shoes, then faced the rector and said, "Yes, sir."

"Why did you lie about it?"

"I didn't lie. I never told her I didn't do it."

That was true. Dooley had responded to her questions with questions. "Where is it?"

"In my closet."

"Take it to her in the morning and apologize. To Lace *and* Olivia." He would also call Olivia in the morning.

"Do I have to?"

"What do you think?"

Dooley went to the closet and opened the door. He lifted the hat off the floor as if it were something Barnabas had deposited in the backyard. "Man, I hate this stupid hat."

"So do I," said the rector.

"You do?"

"I do. But that hat belongs to someone else, and you were wrong to steal it."

"Yeah." Dooley looked at the hat for a moment, then looked the rector in the eye.

"I'm sorry," he said.

A genuine apology! If this is what that fancy prep school had accomplished, he should be forking over an extra twenty thousand a year, out of the mere goodness of his heart.

"You'll also apologize to Cynthia."

"What for?"

"Helping put a bitter end to Harley's party."

"Lace Turner makes me puke. I could've knocked her stupid head off."

"But you didn't, and I commend you for it."

Dooley sat on the bed, holding his left side. "She'll kill me," he said.

"You might want to apologize to Lace while Olivia is in the room—then run for it."

There was a long silence. A moth beat around the lamp bulb.

"Do something like this again," the rector said, "and I'll . . ." What he needed in closing was a good, hair-raising threat, something like taking the car keys away for a couple of weeks—but Dooley didn't drive.

"And I'll . . ." he said.

Blast. He realized he couldn't come up with a decent threat if his life depended on it.

§

The mayor asked him to trot to her office—and be quick about it, according to the tone in her voice.

When Esther Cunningham pulled the string, he, like most people, jumped. He hated that about himself, but why not? Esther had kept an unflagging vigil over Mitford, sacrificing years of her time and even her health to keep things on the up and up. They hadn't even had a tax hike in her long tenure. So yes, he came when she called, and glad to do it.

She leaned across the desk, the splotches on her face and neck looking redder than ever.

"Guess what th' low-down jackleg has done now."

"I can't guess."

"He's throwin' one of his free barbecues next Friday—th' very day of the town festival." She looked at him darkly. "See th' strategy?"

He didn't.

"That'll siphon th' crowd down to his place and leave us sittin' under those shade trees at th' town museum like a bunch of flour sacks."

"Aha." The cheese was getting binding.

"Here's what I want you to do," she said, looking at the door and lowering her voice.

He was in for it.

"Sittin' in a booth draped with th' flag won't cut it this election. Times are changin.' I want you to go home and pray about it and come up with somethin'."

"But the town festival is only four days away."

"Somethin'," she said, "that'll blow Mack Stroupe and his barbecue deal clear to Holding."

"You want *me* to do that?"

"And be quick about it," she said, scratching a splotch.

Hadn't his wife arranged countless retreats to help him relax, and cooked dinner on evenings when he wasn't up to the task?

Hadn't she prayed for him faithfully, and overhauled the rectory, and given him a complete set of Charles Dickens, not to mention a lighted world globe?

And wasn't she working on a book nearly eight hours a day?

He would do what the Russians do. Though it was his very own birthday, he would be the host, he would give the dinner.

It would be just the two of them, and afterward, they would dance. He'd put on the CD of the rhumba—or was it the tango she liked?—and positively whirl her around the study. His blood was getting up for it.

And champagne! That was the ticket. Something expensive, of course, that wouldn't give you a blinding headache even as it went down your gullet. Avis would know which label, and didn't Avis mention that a shipment of fresh lamb was expected any day?

Furthermore, weren't his antique French roses blooming like he'd never seen, drenching the air with their intoxicating scent?

By jing!

He examined the back of his head in the mirror again. He'd been fairly butchered in the privacy of his own home.

Best to nip out and get the matter settled, once and for all.

A decent haircut, the new blue sport coat Cynthia had found on sale, dancing with his wife on his birthday—what else could a man want or imagine?

Suddenly he didn't feel a hundred years old in the shade, he was feeling more like—why not say it?—seventeen.

As he looked up Fancy's number, he had to admit he missed Joe Ivey. So what if Joe had never gone to hair conventions to learn the latest thing? Joe was eminently companionable, and never talked your ear off while he barbered your head.

Another thing—Joe hadn't been shy about slapping on the Sea Breeze, an all-time favorite treat for the way it made the scalp tingle. Fancy Skinner, on the other hand, considered the use of Sea Breeze beneath her station.

Ah, well. He sighed, dialing 555-HAIR. Fancy Skinner was the only game in town, and he hoped she could work him in.

"Th' shop's closed today, I'm here givin' Mama a rinse. Mama, she lives in Spruce Pine, but I'm from Newland. If you get over here quick, I'll trim you up because it's you. You might be th' only one I'd do this for, I'm not sure I'd do it for my own preacher, did you see what his wife did to him, it looked like she put a soup bowl on his head and hacked around it with a steak knife. How he had th' nerve to preach a revival lookin' like that is beyond me.

"Oh, Lord, I just remembered, would you mind stoppin' by Th' Local and gettin' me some sugarless gum, I'll pay you th' minute you get here or take it off your bill, either one, I like to have gum in th' shop, I do my best work if I have somethin' in my mouth, at least it's not a cigarette, law, I used to suck down two packs a day, unfiltered, can you believe it?

"Well, if you're comin', come on, tomorrow'll be a zoo, everybody's gettin' ready for the town festival, why anybody would want highlights to eat barbecue in a parkin' lot is beyond me, and if you could pick up a sack of peppermint while you're at it, that'd be great, I like to have it for people with onion breath, doin' hair is close work."

§

As Fancy draped him with the pink shawl, he sighed resignedly and closed his eyes.

"Prayin', are you? You ought to know by now I won't cut your ear off or poke a hole in your head. Law, I've had too much coffee this mornin', you know I can't drink but two cups or I'm over the moon, how about you, can you still drink caffeine, or are you too old? Course, your wife is young, she probably can do it, I used to drink five or six cups a day . . . and smoke, oh, law, I smoked like a stack! But not anymore, did you know it makes you wrinkle faster? I hate those little lines around my mouth worse than anything, but that wadn't coffee, that was sun, honey, I used to lay out and bake like a chicken.

"Look at this trim! Who did this? I thought Joe Ivey was workin' at Graceland. Mama, come and look at this, this is what I have to put up with. Father, this is Mama, Mama, he's a friend of Mule's, he got married a while back for the first time.

"He preaches at that rock church down the street where they use incense, I declare, Mule and I passed by your church one Sunday, you could smell it comin' out of th' chimney! Lord, my allergies flare up somethin' awful when I smell that stuff, I thought incense was Catholic, anyway, do y'all talk Latin? I had a girlfriend one time, I went to church with her, I couldn't understand a word they said.

"Your hair's growin' like a weed. I hear if you eat a lot of grease, it'll make your hair grow, you shouldn't eat grease, anyway, you've got diabetes.

"Mama! Did you know th' Father has diabetes? My daddy had diabetes. Is that what killed him, Mama, or was it smokin'? Maybe both.

"Look at that! Whoever trimmed your hair, you tell 'em to leave your hair alone. You can call me anytime, I'll work you in. I'm sorry I couldn't take you—when was it?—I think your pope was here, I guess he don't always stay at the Vatican, have you ever been to the Vatican? Law, I haven't even been to Israel, everybody's been to Israel, our preacher is takin' a whole group next year, but I'd rather go on a cruise, do you think that's sacrilegious?

"You ought to let me give you a mask with Fancy's Face Food while we're at it, especially with your wife havin' a birthday, or is it you that's havin' one? Either way, my mask is about as good as a face-lift, not to mention four thousand dollars cheaper. No, I mean it, I'll do it for you, it won't take but an hour. Just *name* a better birthday present than lookin' fifteen years younger, which is more in your *wife's* age group, if I'm not mistaken. OK, lay back, you're stiff as a board, I'm not goin' to claw your eyes out, men are babies, aren't they, Mama? She can't hear for beans, bein' under th' dryer an' all.

"Now, don't try to talk while I'm puttin' this on your face, OK? It'll get hard and you have to lay like this for thirty minutes without sayin' a word or th' whole thing'll crack off and fall on th' floor and that's forty bucks down the tubes. You ought to see this nice green color, it's got mint in it, and cucumber, and I don't know what all, I think there's spinach in here, too, and burdock—my granmaw used to dig burdock for whoopin' cough medicine!

"Don't that feel good, don't you just feel your skin releasin' all those toxins? And those wrinkles on your forehead, I bet you pucker your forehead when you think, you seem like th' type that thinks, well, you can kiss your wrinkles goodbye, honey, 'cause I'm talkin' sayonara, adios, outta here. . . ."

❧

Lying in Fancy's chair had given him a headache, not to mention a crick in his neck that seemed to extend to his upper shoulders and into most of his spinal column. Oh, well. A small price to pay for looking forty-eight on his sixty-third birthday.

Fancy had urged him not to look in the mirror at Hair House. "Why look in the mirror," she asked in what he considered a marvelous burst of philosophy, "when you can see th' real difference by lookin' in her eyes?" She winked at him hugely and blew a bubble, which wasn't easy to do with sugarless spearmint gum.

Not wanting to seem ungrateful, he tipped her five dollars, noting that she hadn't offered a discount for clergy on this particular deal.

He couldn't help himself. The minute he came in the back door, he turned and looked in the mirror.

Good Lord!

His face was . . . *green.*

Unbelievable! Surely not. Was it the dim natural light in the kitchen? He switched on the overhead fixture, fogged his glasses, and looked again.

It wasn't the light.

He dialed 555-HAIR from the kitchen phone, his heart beating dully. No answer.

He raced up the stairs to the bedroom and looked in the mirror he was accustomed to using.

Green.

His watch said five p.m. He'd invited Cynthia to come over at seven.

The birthday dinner, the champagne, the roses . . . the whole deal dashed. Blown on the wind.

He went to the bathroom and lathered his hands with soap and warm water and scrubbed his face.

Who would want to dance the tango with someone whose face was green? And how could he possibly confess that he'd had a facial, something which no other man in the village of Mitford would ever do in a hundred—no, a million—years?

He splashed his face and dried it and looked in the medicine cabinet mirror, which was topped by a 150-watt bulb that never lied.

Green. No two ways about it.

He stood gazing into the mirror, stunned. That's what he got for being a weak-minded sap, unable to say no to a woman in a pair of Capri pants so tight they looked as if they'd been robbed from a toddler.

He wanted to dig a hole and crawl in it.

§

They had dined, they had danced, they had remarked upon the extraordinary fragrance of the roses. She had raved about his cooking, she had sung a rousing "Happy Birthday," and she'd given him a book about himself and the parish of Mitford, which she had written and illustrated.

He was visibly moved and completely delighted. To have a book in which he saw himself walking down Main Street and standing on the church lawn in his vestments . . . Now he knew how Violet must feel.

He thought it immensely good of her not to comment on anything unusual in his appearance, though he was certain that he saw her staring a time or two, once with her mouth open.

He poured a final glass of champagne.

"This is like . . . like a date!" she said, flushed and happy.

"Which we never had, except for that movie where you ate all my Milk Duds."

"I detest dating!" she said. "I think it should be reserved for marriage."

"Amen!"

He served the poached pears he'd served the first time she came for dinner, drizzling hers with chocolate sauce.

"Dearest," she said, as they lolled on the study sofa, "there's something I've been wanting to say. . . ."

Here it comes, he thought, his heart sinking.

"You aren't looking well at all. You seem . . . a little green around the gills. I'm worried about you, Timothy."

"Aha." He had paid good money to look fifteen years younger, and wound up looking sick and infirm. He would never step foot in

Fancy Skinner's place again, not as long as he lived, so what if the round-trip to Memphis would take eighteen hours' hard driving?

"All that business about your retirement and the worry over Fernbank, and whatever this new, urgent project is for the mayor . . . I think it's time for a retreat."

His wife specialized, actually, in the domestic retreat. It was, to a worn-out clergyman, what retreads were to a tire. Once they'd had a picnic in Baxter Park, once a picnic overlooking the Land of Counterpane, and once she'd carried him off to the little yellow house where they had reclined on her king-size bed like two dissolute Romans, drinking lemonade and listening to the rain.

"Right," he said. "A retreat."

She peered at him again, her brow furrowed.

"Definitely!" she said, looking concerned.

While they partied in the study, Barnabas had stood up to the kitchen counter like a man and polished off what was left of the lamb. He also helped himself to two dinner rolls, half a stick of butter, a bowl of wild rice, and all the mint jelly he could lick off a spoon in the dishwasher.

At two in the morning, the rector felt a large paw on his shoulder. This was major, and no doubt about it.

He hastily pulled on his pants and a shirt, slipped his feet into his loafers, and thumped downstairs behind his desperate dog.

He barely got the leash on before Barnabas was out the back door and across to the hedge.

Barnabas sniffed his turf. Possums, raccoons, hedgehogs, squirrels, and cats had passed this way, not to mention the rector's least favorite of all creatures great and small, the mole. The place was a veritable smorgasbord of smells, apparently causing his dog to forget entirely why he had barreled outside in the middle of the night, dragging his master behind like a ball on a chain.

"Sometime in this century, pal?"

More sniffing.

Suddenly Barnabas had the urge to go around the house . . . then across the yard . . . then out to the sidewalk . . . then up the street.

"Not the monument!" he groaned.

Barnabas strained forward with the muscle and determination of a team of yoked oxen. They were going to the monument.

He trotted behind his dog, noting the peace of their village when no cars were on the street. There seemed an uncommon dignity in the glow of the streetlights tonight and the baskets brimming with flowers that hung from every lamppost.

They had a good life in Mitford, no doubt about it. Visitors were often amazed at its seeming charm and simplicity, wanting it for themselves, seeing in it, perhaps, the life they'd once had, or had missed entirely.

Yet there were Mitfords everywhere. He'd lived in them, preached in them, they were still out there, away from the fray, still containing something of innocence and dreaming, something of the past that other towns had freely let go, or allowed to be taken from them.

How much longer could the Esther Cunninghams of the world hold on? How much longer could common, decent, kind regard hold out against utter disregard?

Like the rest of us, he thought, *the mayor may have her blind spots, but I'll take my chances with Esther any day.*

He'd almost forgotten what he'd come out here for; he'd been walking as in a dream. Then, thanks be to God, his dog found a spot behind the hedge surrounding the monument.

He stood there as Barnabas did his business, and looked at the summer sky. Cassiopeia . . . the Three Sisters . . . the Bear . . .

He nearly missed seeing the car as it went around the monument and headed down Lilac Road.

Lincoln. New. Black. Quiet.

He felt alarmed, but couldn't figure why. The car seemed to remind him of something or someone. . . .

He had the strange thought that it didn't seem right for a car to be so quiet—it was oddly chilling.

§

"What's the scoop?" he asked Scott Murphy.

"Interesting. I can't figure it out exactly. When they come to see

Homeless on Wednesday night, they don't have much to say, but they seem to sense something special about being there, as if they're . . . waiting for something."

They are, he thought, suddenly moved. They are.

"I hate to tell you this," he said, glancing at his wife as they weeded the perennial bed next to her garage. The town festival was tomorrow, and all of Mitford was scurrying to look tidy and presentable. Certainly he was looking more presentable. The greenish cast to his skin had disappeared altogether.

A long silence ensued as he pulled knotgrass from among the foxgloves.

"Well? Spit it out, Timothy!"

"I did some simple arithmetic . . ."

"So?"

". . . and I was sixty-four yesterday."

"No!"

"Yes."

"I thought you were sixty-three! This means I'll be fifty-eight, not fifty-seven. Oh, *please*!"

Her moan might have ricocheted off the roof of the town museum two blocks away.

"The neighbors . . ." he said.

"We don't *have* any, remember? Since I moved to the rectory, we don't *have* any neighbors, which means I can wail as loud as I want to."

"Good thinking, Kavanagh."

Sixty-four! He felt like letting go with a lamentation of his own.

"Th' volts was down t' ten," said Harley, wiping his hands on a rag. "Hit was runnin' off the battery. Why don't you take it out and spin it around, I tuned it up some while I was at it."

"We thank you, Harley. This is terrific."

"Hit ought t' go like a scalded dog."

The rector opened the door and Barnabas jumped into the passenger seat, then he got in and backed his wife's Mazda out of the garage.

What a day! he thought as he drove up Main Street, glad to see the bustle of commerce. In a day of shopping malls on bypasses, not every town could boast of a lively business center.

He saw Dooley pedal out of The Local alleyway on his bicycle, wearing his helmet and hauling a full delivery basket. He honked the horn. Dooley grinned and waved.

There was Winnie, putting a tray of something sinful in the window of the Sweet Stuff, and he honked again but was gone before Winnie looked up.

As he approached the monument, he saw Uncle Billy and Miss Rose, stationed in their chrome dinette chairs on the lawn of the town museum, where everybody and his brother had gathered to put up tents, booths, flags, tables, umbrellas, hand-lettered signs, and the much-needed port-a-john, which this year, he observed, appeared to lean to the right instead of the left.

He honked and waved as Uncle Billy waved back and Miss Rose looked scornful.

How in the dickens he could have lived in this town for over fifteen years and still get a kick out of driving up Main Street was beyond him. He'd liked living in his little parish by the sea, too, but the main street hadn't been much to look at, and often, during the hurricane season, their few storefronts had stayed boarded up.

Count your blessings, his grandmother had told him. Count your blessings, his mother had often said.

He eased around the monument and headed west on Lilac Road.

Did anyone really count their blessings, anymore? There was, according to the world's dictum, no time to smell the roses, no time to count blessings. But how much time did it take to recognize that he was, in a sense, driving one around? Hadn't Harley Welch just saved them a hundred bucks, right in his own backyard?

Besides, if there were no time in Mitford, where would there ever be time?

"Ah, Barnabas," he said, reaching over to scratch his dog's ear.

Barnabas stared straight ahead, a behavior he'd always considered appropriate to riding in a car.

He turned on the radio and heard Mozart straining to come across the mountains from the tower in Asheville, and fiddled with the dial until he got a weather report. Sunshine all weekend. Hallelujah!

He realized he was grinning from ear to ear.

How often did he feel as if he didn't have a care in the world? Not often. He'd been equipped, after all, with a nature that could run to the melancholy if he didn't watch it.

"Serious-minded!" a neighbor had said of him as a child, putting on his glasses to get a better look at the tyke who stood before him with a large book under his skinny arm.

He thought of last night, of his vibrant and unstoppable wife sitting up in bed, reading to him, knowing how he loved this simple sacrifice of time and effort. He had put his head in her lap and reached down and held the warm calf of her leg, knowing with all that was in him how extraordinarily rich he was.

He had heard Dooley come in, racing up the stairs on the dot of his curfew, and afterward, the sound of his dog snoring in the hall. . . .

He thought of the old needlepoint sampler his grandmother had done, framed and hanging in the rectory kitchen. He had passed it so often over the years, he had quit seeing it. The patient stitching, embellished with faded cabbage roses, quoted a verse from the Sixty-eighth Psalm.

"Blessed be the Lord," it read, "who daily loadeth us with benefits."

"Loadeth!" he exclaimed aloud. "Daily!"

The car was running like a top, thanks to his live-in mechanic, but he didn't want to turn around and go home; he had a sudden taste for a view of the late-June countryside, maybe a little run out to Farmer, four miles away, then back to help Cynthia bake for the church booth tomorrow.

And while he did the run to Farmer, he would do a seemingly childish thing—he would count his blessings as far as he could.

Quite possibly the list could go on until Wednesday, for he knew a thing or two about blessings and how they were, even in the worst of times, inexhaustible.

It came to him that Patrick Henry Reardon had indirectly spoken of something like this. He had copied it into his sermon notebook only days ago.

"Suppose for a moment," Reardon had said, "that God began taking from us the many things for which we have failed to give thanks. Which of our limbs and faculties would be left? Would I still have my hands and my mind? And what about loved ones? If God were to take from me all those persons and things for which I have not given thanks, who or what would be left of me?"

What would be left of me, indeed? he wondered. The very thought struck him with a force he hadn't recognized when he copied it into his notebook.

He put his hand on his dog's head and hoarsely whispered the beginning of his list:

"Barnabas . . ."

§

He saw her standing at the corner of Main Street and Wisteria, looking toward the rectory. He had never seen her before in his life, but he knew exactly, precisely, who she was.

He felt himself loving her at once, as she held out her arms and smiled and started running toward him. He tried to run, also, to meet her, but found he moved as if through sand or deep water, and was dumbstruck, unable to call her name.

His wife was shaking him. "Wake up, dearest!"

"What . . . what . . . ?"

"You were dreaming."

He sat up with a pounding heart.

"We have to find Jessie," he said.

CHAPTER EIGHT

Political Barbecue

There was plenty of talk on the street. As early as seven-thirty on the morning of the festival, he couldn't walk from the south end to the north without picking up new funds of information.

Dora Pugh, who was setting flats of borage, chives, and rosemary outside the hardware door, asked if he'd seen the billboards on the highway. They must have been put up in the middle of the night, she said, because when she drove home yesterday, she certainly hadn't noticed Mack Stroupe's ugly mug plastered on three new boards, all the way from Hattie Cloer's market to the Shoe Barn.

"That," she snorted, "is three times more of that cracker than I ever wanted to see." Dora once lived in Georgia, where "cracker" had nothing to do with party snacks.

At the Sweet Stuff, Winnie Ivey hailed him in.

"I'm experimenting," she said, tucking a strand of graying hair under her bandanna. "My license says people can sit down, so I thought I should try fixin' things to where people don't have to stand at th' shelf."

The shelf along the wall had come down, replaced by posters of mountain scenery, and in the long-empty space in front of her display cases stood three tables and a dozen chairs.

"I'm tryin' to do all I can to bring in business. If I'm goin' to sell out, I want my ledgers lookin' good," she said.

"I'm proud of you, Winnie! And to think you've done all this by yourself!"

"I have to do whatever it takes, Father! Of course, it's just coffee and sweets, as usual, except now you get a chair to sit in—but I might add sandwiches next week. And soup in the winter. What do you think?"

"I think you should!"

She brightened. "It helps to have advice."

"Don't I know it!" Weren't his parishioners full of it?

"My husband, Johnny, used to know what to do about things, but he died so many years ago, I can hardly remember his face. Do you think that's bad?"

He could seldom recall his father's face. "No," he said, "it can happen like that. . . ."

"You know, sometimes I . . ." Winnie blushed.

"Sometimes you . . . ?"

"You wouldn't tell this?"

"You have my word."

"Sometimes I think of a man standin' beside me in th' kitchen back there, I don't know who it is because I can't exactly see his face, but it seems like he's tall and dark-headed, and I can tell he has a big heart." She paused, looking shy. "He bakes all th' cakes, and he's always laughin' and sayin' nice things, like how good my cream horns are, and how pretty I glazed the fruit tarts."

He nodded.

"He always has flour on his apron."

"He would."

"It would be nice. . . ." she said, looking at him.

"I know," he said, looking back.

"It might not be right to pray for such as that. . . ."

"I think it would be wrong if we didn't," he said.

❧

Apparently, all of merchantdom was up and at it, a full two hours before the festival opened.

The Collar Button man was sweeping the sidewalk, with a sprinkler turned on the handkerchief-sized garden next to his store.

"Good morning, Father! How're you liking the jacket your wife selected for your birthday?"

"Immensely! It brings out the blue of her eyes. How's business?"

"Couldn't be better!" said the Collar Button man, going full tilt with his broom.

When he reached the Grill, he stopped and sniffed the balmy air. The smell of roasting pork drifted on the breeze from Mack Stroupe's campaign headquarters near the monument.

Then he squinted up at the sky.

Blue. Here and there, a few billowing clouds.

Perfect.

§

He slid into the booth with a mug of coffee

"Where's J.C.?"

"Went upstairs to get film out of his refrigerator," said Mule.

"Film was all he had in his refrigerator 'til he married Adele. What's going on with you?"

"Feelin' like somethin' the cat covered up. I can't half sleep 'til Fancy gets to bed, and she was going like a circle saw 'til two o'clock this morning."

"Doing what?"

"Doin' hair."

"Who in the dickens would get their hair done at two o'clock in the morning?"

"You'd be surprised."

"That's true, I would."

"How's your new boarder?" asked the realtor.

"Working on my Buick. I pay for the parts, he insists on doing the labor. He was under the hood at seven o'clock this morning."

J.C. slung his briefcase into the corner and slid in.

"I looked out th' upstairs window and dadgum if th' street ain't *jumpin'*." The editor rubbed his hands together briskly. This was front-page stuff, everything from llamas and political barbecue to a clogging contest and tourists out the kazoo.

"Let me guess," said Velma, arriving at the rear booth in an unusually cheerful frame of mind. "Poached for th' preacher, scrambled for th' realtor—"

"Fried for th' editor," said J.C. "And don't be bringin' me any yogurt or all-bran."

Velma looked him over as if he were a boiled ham. "You're pickin' up weight again."

"I've picked up worse," said J.C.

Mule stirred his coffee. "Just dry toast with mine."

"No grits?" she asked, personally offended.

"Not today."

"What's the matter with Percy's grits?"

"Oh, well, all right. But no butter."

"Grits without butter?" What was wrong with these people?

"Lord, help," sighed Mule. "Just bring me whatever."

"I'll have mine all the way," said J.C., who had lately thrown caution to the wind. "Biscuits, grits, sausage, bacon, and give me a little mustard on the side."

"I'll have the usual," said Father Tim.

Mule looked approving. "That's what I need to do—figure out one thing and stick with it. Same thing every morning, and you don't have to mess with it again."

"Right," said the rector.

"Have you seen Mack's new boards?" asked J.C.

They hadn't.

"They rhyme like those Burma-Shave signs. First one says, *'If Mitford's economy is going to move'* . . . th' second one says, *'we've got to improve.'* Last one says, *'Mack for Mitford, Mack for Mayor.'*"

"Gag me with a forklift," said Mule.

"Esther Cunningham better get off her rear end, because like it or not, Mack Stroupe's eatin' her lunch. She's been lollin' around like this election was some kind of tea party. You're so all-fired thick with the mayor," J.C. said to the rector, "you ought to tell her the facts of life, and the fact is, she's lookin' dead in the water."

"Aha. I thought we agreed not to talk politics."

"Right," said Mule, whose escalating blood pressure had suddenly turned his face beet red.

J.C. looked bored. "So what else is new? Let's see, I was over at the town museum 'til midnight watchin' those turkeys get ready for the festival. Omer Cunningham was draping th' flag on Esther's booth and fell off the ladder and busted his foot."

"Busted his foot?" the rector blurted. "Good Lord! Can he fly?"

"Can he fly? I don't know as he could, with a busted foot."

Mule cackled. "He sure couldn't fly any crazier than when his foot's *not* busted."

"Toast!" said Velma, sliding two orders onto the table.

The rector felt his stomach wrench.

"Biscuits!" said Velma, handing off a plate to J.C.

"May I use your phone?" asked Father Tim.

"You can, if you stay out of Percy's way, you know where it's at."

He went to the red wall phone and dialed, knowing the number by heart. Hadn't he called it two dozen times in the last few days?

No answer.

He hung up and stood by the grill, dazed, his mouth as dry as cotton.

"I just busted th' yolk in one of y'r eggs," said Percy, who despised poaching.

So? Busted feet, busted yolks, busted plans.

He might possibly be looking at the worst day of his life.

§

His palms were damp, something he'd never appreciated in clergy. Also, his collar felt tight, even though he'd snapped the Velcro at the loosest point.

When he and Cynthia arrived on the lawn of the town museum at 9:35, they had to elbow their way to the Lord's Chapel booth, which was situated, this year, directly across from the llamas and the petting zoo.

"Excellent location!" said his wife, who was known to rely on animals as a drawing card.

They thumped down their cardboard box filled with the results of last night's bake-a-thon in the rectory kitchen. Three Lord's Chapel volunteers, dressed in aprons that said, *Have you hugged an Episco-palian today?* briskly set about unpacking the contents and displaying them in a case cooled by a generator humming at the rear of the tent.

Though the festival didn't officially open until ten o'clock, the yard of the Porter mansion–cum–town museum was jammed with villagers, tourists, and the contents of three buses from neighboring communities. The rear end of a church van from Tennessee displayed a sign, *Mitford or Bust.*

The Presbyterian brass band was already in full throttle on the museum porch, and the sixth grade of Mitford School was marching around the statue of Willard Porter, builder of the impressive Victorian home, with tambourines, drums, and maracas painted in their school colors.

Why was he surprised to see posters on every pole and tree, promoting Mack Stroupe's free barbecue at his campaign headquarters up the street?

His eyes searched the crowd for the mayor, who said she'd be under the elm tree this year, the one that had miraculously escaped the blight.

"I'll be back," he told Cynthia, who was giving him that concerned look. The way things were going, he'd need more than a domestic retreat, he'd need a set of pallbearers.

He saw Uncle Billy next to the lilac bushes, sitting in a hardback chair with a bottomless chair in front of him and a bucket of water at his feet.

"Stop in, Preacher! I'll be a-canin' chairs, don't you know, hit's a demonstration of th' old ways, and I've set out a few of m' birdhouses f'r sale."

"How's your arthur?" asked the rector, concerned.

"Well, sir, last night, I slapped it and said, 'Git on out of there, I ain't havin' nothin' t' do with you!' And m' hands are feelin' some better this mornin', don't you know." He wiggled a couple of fingers to prove his point.

"Where's Miss Rose?"

"She ain't a-comin' out this year, says she don't like s' many people ramblin' around on 'er property."

"Hold that green birdhouse for me, I'll be back!"

He spotted Esther and her husband, Ray, shaking hands by a booth draped with an American flag and a banner hand-lettered with the mayor's longtime political slogan.

"Mayor! Where's Omer?"

"Where's Omer? I thought you'd know where Omer is."

"What about his foot?"

"Broken in two places."

"Right, but what about . . . can he *fly?*"

She glared at him in a way that made Emma Newland look like a vestal virgin. "That's your business," she said, and turned back to the people she'd been shaking hands with.

He headed to the Lord's Chapel booth, his heart hammering. He was afraid to let his wife see his face, since she could obviously read it like a book—but where else could he go?

Dooley! Of course! A Taste of America!

He hung a hard left in the direction of Avis Packard's tent, cutting through the queue to the cotton candy truck, and ran slam into Omer Cunningham on a crutch.

"Good heavens! *Omer!*" He threw his arms around Esther Cunningham's strapping brother-in-law and could easily have kissed his ring, or even his plaster cast.

Heads turned. People stared. He wished he weren't wearing his collar.

Omer's big grin displayed teeth the size of keys on a spinet piano. "We're smokin'," he said, giving a thumbs-up to the rector, who, overcome with joyful relief, thumped down on a folding chair at the Baptists' display of tea towels, aprons, and oven mitts.

§

"Father!"

It was Andrew Gregory, the tall, handsome proprietor of Oxford Antiques, calling from his booth next to the statue of Willard Porter.

The rector could honestly say he felt a warm affection for the man who once courted Cynthia, escorting her hither and yon in his gray Mercedes, while Father Tim moped at the upstairs window of the rectory. Andrew might be six-four with a closetful of cashmere jackets, but hadn't the five-nine, less stylish country parson won Cynthia?

By jing!

He felt positively lighthearted as he stepped up to the booth and shook hands with the antique dealer, who looked elegant in a linen shirt and trousers.

"Great to see you, my friend!"

"How is it," asked Andrew, "that we seldom meet, though our doors are directly across the street from one another?"

"We've mused on that before," said the rector, "and always to no avail. I've missed you. How are you?"

"Off next week to Italy, to my mother's birthplace, a little town called Lucera."

"I've often visited Italy. . . ."

"You have?"

"In my imagination," confessed the rector.

Andrew smiled. "I'm afraid I've cultivated my paternal English side to the vast neglect of my Italian side. I'll do like you did a couple of years ago—go searching for my roots, sample the local wines, visit cousins."

"Good for the soul! You're selling your fine lemon oil, I see."

"Makes all the difference. Look at this eighteenth-century chest." One side of the late-Georgian walnut chest appeared dark and sullen. The other side shone, revealing the life of the wood.

"I'll take three bottles!" the rector announced.

"I've been wondering," said Andrew, as he bagged the lemon oil, "whether I might give you a price on the contents of Fernbank. If you're interested, I'd like to take a look before I chase off to the old country."

"Well! That's a thought. Let me run it by the vestry." He had certainly dragged his feet on emptying Miss Sadie's house in advance of the possible sale to Miami Development. Why had he tried to put the whole Fernbank issue out of his mind when it clearly needed to be handled—and pronto?

Walking away with his package under his arm, he also questioned why on earth he'd bought three bottles of lemon oil when he hardly had a stick of furniture to call his own. Living in partially furnished rectories since the age of twenty-eight had had its bright side, but it wasn't all it was cracked up to be.

"Father Tim!"

It was Margaret Ann Larkin with five-year old Amy, waving at him from the petting zoo.

He pushed through the crowd.

"Father, we've been looking all over for you. Amy wants to pet the animals, but she's afraid to do it. She wondered if . . . I know this is a strange request, but she wants you to do it for her."

"Aha."

Margaret Ann looked imploring. "She doesn't want me to do it."

Amy handed him a dollar. "You pet," she said soberly.

He knelt beside her, clutching his package. "You could walk inside the fence with me."

"You pet," she said.

He turned his lemon oil over to Margaret Ann and went through the gate, relinquishing the dollar to Jake Greer, a farmer from the valley.

"Pet the goat first," said Amy, looking through the fence.

"Please," instructed Margaret Ann.

"Please!" urged Amy.

He petted the goat, which trotted to the other side of the pen, clearly disgusted.

"Now pet the lamb, please."

He petted the lamb. What a black nose! What soulful eyes!

"Now pet the chickens."

A Dominecker rooster and two Leghorn hens squawked and scattered.

He turned and smiled at Amy. "Now what?"

"Pet the pony!"

He petted the pony, who nuzzled his arm and bared its teeth and flared its nostrils, giving him his money's worth. Having petted the entire assembly, including a small pig named Barney, he withdrew through the gate, laughing.

"That was . . . fun," he said, meaning it.

"Was you afraid?" asked Amy.

"Not a bit. I liked it."

"Was the lamb soft?"

"Very soft."

"Amy, honey, what do you say?"

Amy broke into a dazzling smile. "Thank you!" she said, patting him on the leg.

§

His wife peered at him again in that odd way. "You look like *you're* having a good time!"

"You mean you're not?" he asked.

"Not since Gene stepped in Esther's cake."

"No!"

"She came in and set the box behind the table, and when Gene came in, he stumbled over it . . ."

"Uh-oh."

". . . then fell on top of it."

"Good grief."

"Mashed flat," she said.

"Orange marmalade?"

"You got it."

"How's Gene?" he inquired, sounding like an undertaker.

"Unhurt but terrified."

"How's Esther?"

"Three guesses."

"That cake was worth some bucks for the Children's Home."

"I think we could still auction it."

"Mashed flat, we could auction it?"

"There was a top on the box when he fell on it. I mean, it's still Esther's orange marmalade cake—some people would be thrilled to eat it out of the box with a *spoon*."

"If you'll auction it, I'll start the bidding," he said, feeling expansive.

§

He had stopped to pass the time of day with the llamas, who looked at him peaceably through veils of sweeping lashes.

He'd bought a tea towel from the Baptists, a sack of tattered volumes from the Library Ladies, a cookbook from the Presbyterians, and was on his way to see Dooley Barlowe in action.

He paused to check the sky. As he started to look at his watch, he spied them through the queue for popcorn and ducked across.

Olivia kissed him on the cheek. Lace stood looking into the crowd.

He put his arm around Lace's shoulders and found them unyielding. "You ladies are looking lovely—a credit to the town!"

Lace nodded vaguely. "I got to go over yonder a minute."

"Go," said Olivia. "I'll meet you at the llamas in half an hour."

They sat on one of the town museum benches.

"Father, I've had time to think it through and I wanted to say I admire Dooley for the way he handled Lace's outburst. He might have . . . knocked her head off when she attacked him."

"He was asking for it."

"He did a fine job of delivering his apologies. He has character, your boy."

"So does Lace. But character often takes time to show itself. They've both come out of violence and neglect, a matched set. How are you holding up?"

"Better, I think. We're still visiting her mother every week, but it's never a happy visit—her mother is demanding and cold, and her health is deteriorating. Hoppy looked in on her; we're not encouraged."

"We keep you faithfully in our prayers. We're all flying by the seat of our pants." Who would have dreamed he'd be raising a boy? The challenge of it was breathtaking.

"I've read how Lindbergh often flew with the windshield iced over. It's rather like that, don't you think?"

"Indeed. Is she making any friends?"

"Mitford's children have been warned all their lives to avoid anyone from the Creek, so that is very much against her. Then she's smart and she's pretty. Some don't like that, either. They really don't know what to make of her."

"Lord bless you."

"And you, Father."

As they walked away from each other, he turned around and called, "Olivia! Philippians Four-thirteen, for Pete's sake!"

She threw up her hand, smiling at this reminder of the Scripture verse she claimed as a pivot for her life.

It was good to have a comrade in arms, he thought, trotting off to A Taste of America.

Avis Packard's booth was swamped with buyers, eager to tote home sacks of preserves, honey, pies, cakes, and bread from the valley kitchens, not to mention strawberries from California, corn from Georgia, and syrup from Vermont.

Avis stepped out of the booth for a break, while Tommy and Dooley bagged and made change. "I've about bit off more'n I can chew," said Avis, lighting up a Salem. "I've still got a load of new potatoes comin' from Georgia, and lookin' for a crate of asparagus from Florida. Thing is, I don't hardly see how a truck can get down th' street."

"I didn't know you smoked," said the rector, checking his watch.

Avis inhaled deeply. "I don't. I quit two or three years ago. I bummed this offa somebody."

The imported strawberries were selling at a pace, and Avis stepped to the booth and brought back a handful.

"Try one," he said, as proudly as if they'd come from his own patch. "You know how some taste more like straw than berry? Well, sir, these are the finest you'll ever put in your mouth. Juicy, sweet, full of sunshine. What you'd want to do is eat 'em right off th' stem, or slice 'em, marinate in a little sugar and brandy—you don't want to use th' cheap stuff—and serve with cream from the valley, whipped with a hint of fresh ginger."

Avis Packard was a regular poet laureate of grocery fare.

"Is that legal?" asked the rector.

He watched as Dooley passed a bag over the table to a customer. "Hope you like those strawberries!"

He was thrilled to see Dooley Barlowe excited about his work. His freckles, which he and Cynthia had earlier reported missing, seemed to be back with a vengeance.

Avis laughed. "Ain't he a deal?"

"Is he doing right by you?"

"That and then some!"

He noticed Jenny and her mother queuing up at A Taste of America, and saw Dooley glance up at them. Uh-oh. That look on Dooley's face . . .

Was this something he ought to discuss with him, man to man? The very thought made his heart pound.

Ben Sawyer hauled past, carrying a sack of tasseled corn in each arm. "That's a fine boy you got there, Preacher!"

He felt a foolish grin spread across his face, and didn't try to hold it back.

§

He noticed the crowd was starting to thin out, following the aroma of political barbecue.

In his mind, he saw it on the plate, thickly sliced and served with a dollop of hot sauce, nestled beside a mound of cole slaw and a half dozen hot, crisp hushpuppies. . . .

He shook himself and ate four raisins that had rolled around in his coat pocket since the last committee meeting on evangelism.

§

At eleven forty-five, Ray and Esther Cunningham strode up to the Lord's Chapel booth with all five of their beautiful daughters, who had populated half of Mitford with Sunday School teachers, deacons, police officers, garbage collectors, tax accountants, secretaries, retail clerks, and UPS drivers.

"Well?" said Esther. The rector thought she would have made an excellent Mafia don.

"Coming right up!" he exclaimed, checking his watch and looking pale.

Cynthia eyed him again. Mood swings, she thought. That seemed to be the key! Definitely a domestic retreat, and definitely soon.

And since the entire town seemed so demanding of her husband, definitely not in Mitford.

§

Nobody paid much attention to the airplane until it started smoking.

"Look!" somebody yelled. "That plane's on f'ar!"

He was sitting on the rock wall when Omer thumped down beside him. "Right on time!" said the mayor's brother-in-law. "All my flyin' buddies from here t' yonder have jumped on this." The rector thought somebody could have played "Moonlight Sonata" on Omer's ear-to-ear grin.

"OK, that's y'r basic Steerman, got a four-fifty horsepower engine in there. Luke Teeter's flyin' 'er, he's about as good as you can get, now watch this . . ."

The blue and orange airplane roared straight up into the fathomless blue sky, leaving a plume of smoke in its wake. Then it turned sharply and pitched downward at an angle.

"Wow!" somebody said, forgetting to close his mouth.

The plane did another climb into the blue.

Omer punched him in the ribs with an elbow. "She's got a tank in there pumpin' Corvis oil th'ough 'er exhaust system . . . ain't she a sight?"

"Looks like an *N*!" said a boy whose chocolate popsicle was melting down his arm.

The plane plummeted toward the rooftops again, smoke billowing from its exhaust.

"*M!*" shouted half the festivalgoers, as one.

Esther and Ray and their daughters were joined by assorted grandchildren, great-grandchildren, and in-laws, who formed an impenetrable mass in front of the church booth.

Gene Bolick limped over from the llamas as the perfect *I* appeared above them.

"*M . . . I!*" shouted the crowd.

"Lookit this!" said Omer, propping his crutch against the stone wall. "Man, oh, man!"

The bolt of blue and orange gunned straight up, leaving a vertical trail, then shut off the exhaust, veered right, and thundered across the top of the trail, forming a straight and unwavering line of smoke.

"*M . . . I . . . T!*"

The *M* was fading, the *I* was lingering, the *T* was perfect against the sapphire sky.

The crowd thickened again, racing back from Mack Stroupe's campaign headquarters, which was largely overhung by trees, racing back to the grounds of the town museum where the view was open, unobscured, and breathtaking, where something more than barbecue was going on.

"They won't be goin' back to Mack's place anytime soon," said Omer. "Ol' Mack's crowd has done eat an' run!"

"*F!*" they spelled in unison, and then, "... *O* ... *R* ... *D!*"

Even the tourists were cheering.

J. C. Hogan sank to the ground, rolled over on his back, pointed his Nikon at the sky, and fired off a roll of Tri-X. The *M* and the *I* were fading fast.

Uncle Billy hobbled up and spit into the bushes. "I bet them boys is glad this town ain't called Minneapolis."

"Now, look," said Omer, slapping his knee.

Slowly, but surely, the Steerman's exhaust trail wrote the next word. *T* ... *A* ... *K* ... *E* ... *S* ... , the smoke said.

Cheers. Hoots. Whistles.

"Lord, my neck's about give out," said Uncle Billy.

"Mine's about broke," said a bystander.

C ... *A* ... *R* ... *E* ...

"Mitford takes care of its own!" shouted the villagers. The sixth grade trooped around the statue, beating on tambourines, shaking maracas, and chanting something they'd been taught since first grade.

> *Mitford takes care of its own, its own,*
> *Mitford takes care of its own!*

Over the village rooftops, the plane spelled out the rest of the message.

O ... *F* ... *I* ... *T* ... *S* ... *O* ... *W* ... *N* ...

TAKES soon faded into puffs of smoke that looked like stray summer clouds. *CARE OF* was on its way out, but *ITS OWN* stood proudly in the sky, seeming to linger.

"If that don't beat all!" exclaimed a woman from Tennessee, who had stood in one spot the entire time, holding a sleep-drugged baby on her hip.

Dogs barked and chickens squawked as people clapped and started drifting away.

Just then, a few festivalgoers saw them coming, the sun glinting on their wings.

They roared in from the east, in formation, two by two.

Red and yellow. Green and blue.

"Four little home-built Pitts specials," said Omer, as proudly as if he'd built them himself. "Two of 'em's from Fayetteville, got one out of Roanoke, and the other one's from Albany, New York. Not much power in y'r little ragwings, they're nice and light, about a hundred and eighty horses, and handle like a dream."

He looked at the sky as if it contained the most beautiful sight he had ever seen, and so did the rector.

"I was goin' to head th' formation, but a man can't fly with a busted foot."

The crowd started lying on the grass. They lay down along the rock wall. They climbed up on the statue of Willard Porter, transfixed, and a young father set a toddler on Willard's left knee.

People pulled chairs out of their booths and sat down, looking up. All commerce ceased.

The little yellow Pitts special rolled over and dived straight for the monument.

"Ahhhhhh!" said the crowd.

As the yellow plane straightened out and up, the blue plane nose-dived and rolled over.

"They're like little young 'uns a-playin'," said Uncle Billy, enthralled.

Miss Rose came out and stood on the back stoop in her frayed chenille robe and looked up, tears coursing down her cheeks for her long-dead brother, Captain Willard Porter, who had flown planes and been killed in the war in France and buried over there, with hardly anything sent home but his medals and a gold ring with the initials SEB and a few faded snapshots from his pockets.

The little planes romped and rolled and soared and glided, like so many bright crayons on a palette of blue, then vanished toward the west, the sun on their wings.

Here and there, a festivalgoer tried getting up from the grass or a chair or the wall, but couldn't. They felt mesmerized, intoxicated. "Blowed away!" someone said.

"OK, buddy, here you go," Omer whispered.

They heard a heavy-duty engine throbbing in the distance and knew at once this was serious business, this was what everyone had been waiting for without even knowing it.

The Cunningham daughters hugged their children, kissed their mother and daddy, wept unashamedly, and hooted and hollered like banshees, but not a soul looked their way, for the crowd was intent on not missing a lick, on seeing it all, and taking the whole thing, blow by blow, home to Johnson City and Elizabethton and Wesley and Holding and Aho and Farmer and Price and Todd and Hemingway and Morristown. . . .

"Got y'r high roller comin' in, now," said Omer. The rector could feel the mayor's brother-in-law shaking like a leaf from pure excitement. "You've had y'r basic smoke writin' and stunt flyin,' now here comes y'r banner towin'!"

A red Piper Super Cub blasted over the treetops from the direction of the highway, shaking drifts of clouds from its path, trembling the heavens in its wake, and towing a banner that streamed across the open sky:

ESTHER . . . RIGHT FOR MITFORD, RIGHT FOR MAYOR.

The Presbyterian brass band hammered down on their horns until the windows of the Porter mansion rattled and shook.

As the plane passed over, a wave of adrenaline shot through the festival grounds like so much electricity and, almost to a man, the crowd scrambled to its feet and shouted and cheered and whistled and whooped and applauded.

A few also waved and jumped up and down, and nearly all of them remembered what Esther had done, after all, putting the roof on old man Mueller's house, and turning the dilapidated wooden bridge over Mitford Creek into one that was safe and good to look at, and sending Ray in their RV to take old people to the grocery store, and jacking up Sophia's house and helping her kids, and making sure they had decent school buses to haul their own kids around in bad weather, and creating that thing at the hospital where you went and held and loved a new baby if its mama from the Creek was on drugs, and never one time raising taxes, and always being there when they had a problem, and actually listening when they talked, and . . .

. . . and taking care of them.

Some who had planned to vote for Mack Stroupe changed their minds, and came over and shook Esther's hand, and the brass band nearly busted a gut to be heard over the commotion.

Right! That was the ticket. Esther was *right* for Mitford. Mack Stroupe might be for change, but Esther would always be for the things that really counted.

Besides—and they'd tried to put it out of their minds time and time again—hadn't Mack Stroupe been known to beat his wife, who was quiet as a mouse and didn't deserve it, and hadn't he slithered over to that woman in Wesley for years, like a common, low-down snake in the grass?

"Law, do y'all vote in th' *summer*?" wondered a visitor. "We vote sometime in th' fall. I can't remember when, exactly, but I nearly always have to wear a coat to the polls."

Omer looked at the rector. The rector looked at Omer.

They shook hands.

It was done.

CHAPTER NINE

Life in the Fast Lane

"What I done was give you thirty more horses under y'r hood."

"Did I *need* thirty more horses?" He had to admit that stomping his gas pedal had been about as exciting as stepping on a fried pie. However . . .

Harley gave him a philosophical look, born from experience. "Rev'rend, I'd hate f'r you t' need 'em and not have 'em."

What could he say?

On Monday morning, he roared to the office, screeching to a halt at the intersection of Old Church Lane, where he let northbound traffic pass, then made a left turn, virtually catapulting into the parking lot.

Holy smoke! Had Harley dropped a Jag engine in his Buick?

Filled with curiosity, he got out and looked under the hood, but realized he wouldn't know a Jag engine from a Mazda alternator.

"Can you believe it?" asked Emma, tight-lipped.

He knew exactly what she was talking about. "Not really."

For a while, he thought they'd lost his secretary's vote to Esther Cunningham's competition. Last week, however, had turned the tide; she'd heard that Mack Stroupe had bought two little houses on the edge of town and jacked up the rent on a widow and a single mother.

"Sittin' in church like he owned th' place, is what I hear. Why th' roof didn't fall in on th' lot of you is beyond me."

"Umm."

"Church!" she snorted. "Is that some kind of new campaign trick, goin' to *church*?"

He believed that particular strategy had been used a time or two, but he didn't comment.

"The next thing you know, he'll be wantin' to *join*. If I were you, I'd run his hide up th' road to th' Presbyterians."

He laughed. "Emma, you're beautiful when you're mad."

She beamed. "Really?"

"Well . . ."

"So, what did he *do,* anyway? Did he kneel? Did he stand? Did he *sing*? Can you imagine a peckerwood like Mack Stroupe singin' those hymns from five hundred years ago, maybe a thousand? Lord, it was all *I* could do to sing th' dern things, which is *one* reason I went back to bein' a Baptist."

She booted her computer, furious.

"I heard Lucy was with him, wouldn't you know it, but that's the way they do, they trot their family out for all the world to see. Was she still blond? What was she wearin'? Esther Bolick said it was a sight the way the crowd ganged up at the museum watchin' the air show, and that barbecue sittin' down the street like so much chicken mash."

She peered intently at her screen.

"Well," she said, clicking her mouse, "has the cat got your tongue? Tell me somethin', *anything*! Were you floored when he showed up at Lord's Chapel, or what?"

"I was. Of course, there's always the possibility that he wants to turn over a new leaf. . . ."

"Right," she said, arching an eyebrow, "and Elvis is livin' at th' Wesley hotel."

§

As much as he liked mail, and the surprise it was capable of bringing, he let the pile sit on Emma's desk until she came back from lunch.

"No way! I can't believe it!" She held up an envelope, grinning proudly. "Albert Wilcox!"

She opened it. "Listen to this!

"'Dear one and all, it was a real treat to hear from you after so many years. My grandmother's prayer book that gave us such pain— and delight—sits on my desk as I write to you, waiting to be handed over to the museum in Seattle, which is near my home in Oak Harbor. . . .'"

She read the entire letter, which also contained a great deal of information about Albert's knee replacement, and his felicitations to the rector for having married.

"Have you ever? And all because of modern technology! OK, as soon as I open this other envelope, I've got a little surprise for you. Close your eyes."

He closed his eyes.

"Face the bookcase!" she said.

He faced the bookcase.

He heard fumbling and clicking. Then he heard Beethoven.

The opening strains of the Pastorale fairly lifted him out of his chair.

"OK! You can turn around!"

He didn't see anything unusual, but was swept away by the music, which seemed to come from nowhere, transforming the room.

"CD-ROM!" announced his resident computer expert, as if she'd just hung the moon.

§

He went home and jiggled Sassy and burped Sissy, as Puny collected an ocean of infant paraphernalia into something the size of a leaf bag.

After a quick trot through the hedge to say hello to his hardworking wife, he and Dooley changed into their old clothes. They were going to tear down Betty Craig's shed and stack the wood. He felt fit for anything.

"Let's see those muscles," he challenged Dooley, who flexed his arm. "Well done!" He wished he had some to show, himself, but thinking and preaching had never been ways to develop muscles.

What with a good job, plenty of sun, and a reasonable amount of home cooking, Dooley Barlowe was looking good. In fact, Dooley Barlowe was getting to be downright handsome, he mused, and tall into the bargain.

Dooley stood against the doorframe as the rector made a mark, then measured. Good heavens!

"I'll be et for a tater if you ain't growed a foot!" he exclaimed in Uncle Billy's vernacular.

Soon, he'd be looking up to the boy who had come to him in dirty overalls, searching for a place to "take a dump."

§

They were greeted in the backyard by Russell Jacks and Dooley's young brother.

"I've leaned th' ladder ag'inst th' shed for you," said Russell.

"Half done, then!" The rector was happy to see his old sexton.

Poo Barlowe looked up at him. "Hey!"

"Hey, yourself!" he replied, tousling the boy's red hair. "Where were you on Saturday? We missed you at the town festival."

"Mama took me to buy some new clothes." The boy glanced down at his tennis shoes, hoping the rector would notice.

"Man alive! Look at those shoes! Made for leaping tall buildings, it appears."

Poo grinned.

"Want to help us pull that shed down?"

"It ain't hardly worth pullin' down," said Poo, "bein' ready t' fall down."

"Don't say ain't," commanded his older brother.

"Why not?"

" 'Cause it ain't good English!" Realizing what he'd just said, Dooley colored furiously.

Father Tim laughed. He'd corrected Dooley's English for three long years. "You're sounding a lot like me, buddy. You might want to watch that."

Betty Craig ran down the back steps.

"Father! Law, this is good of you. I've been standin' at my kitchen window for years, lookin' at that old shed lean to the south. It's aggravated me to death."

"A good kick might be all it takes."

"Pauline's late comin' home, she called to say she'd be right here. Can I fix you and Dooley some lemonade? It's hot as August."

"We'll wait 'til our work is done."

"Let's get going," said Dooley.

Father Tim opened the toolbox and took out a clawhammer and put on his heavy work gloves. He'd never done this sort of thing before. He felt at once fierce and manly, and then again, completely uncertain how to begin.

"What're we going to do?" asked Dooley, pulling on his own pair of gloves.

He looked at the shed. Blast if it wasn't bigger than he'd thought. "We're going to start at the top," he said, as if he knew what he was talking about.

§

He had removed the rolled asphalt with a clawhammer, pulled off the roofboards, dismantled the rafters, torn off the sideboards with Dooley's help, then pulled nails from the corners of the rotten framework, and shoved what was left into the grass.

Running with sweat, he and Dooley had taken turns driving the rusty nails back and pulling them out of every stick and board so they could be used for winter firewood.

Dooley dropped the nails into a bucket.

"Wouldn't want t' be steppin' on one of them," said Russell, who was supervising.

They paused only briefly, to sit on the porch and devour a steaming portion of chicken pie, hot from Betty's oven, and guzzle a quart of tea that was sweet enough to send him to the emergency room.

Betty apologized. "Hot as it is, your supper ought to be somethin' cold, like chicken salad, but you men are workin' hard, and chicken salad won't stick to your ribs."

"Amen!"

"I want you to come and get your kindlin' off that pile all winter long, you hear?"

"I'll do it."

After they ate, he and Dooley and Poo carried and stacked and heaved and hauled, until it was nearly nine o'clock, and dark setting in.

"You've about killed me," grumbled Dooley.

"I've done sweated a bucket," said Poo.

"I'm give out jis' watchin'," sighed Russell.

As for himself, the rector felt oddly liberated. All that pulling up and yanking off and tearing down and pushing over had been good for him, somehow, creating an exhaustion completely different from the labors surrounding his life as a cleric.

And what better reward than to sit and look across the twilit yard at the mound of wood neatly stacked along the fence, with two boys beside him who had helped make it happen?

❧

Dooley was inspecting Poo's new, if used, bicycle, Russell had shuffled off to bed, and Betty had gone in to watch TV. He sat alone with Pauline.

He didn't see any reason to beat around the bush. "We need to talk about Jessie."

There was a long silence.

"I can do it," she said.

"I need to know everything you can possibly tell me, and the name of the cousin who took her and where you think they might be, and the names of any of your cousin's relatives—everything."

He heard the absolute firmness in his voice and knew this was how it would have to be.

As she talked, he took notes on a piece of paper he had folded and put in his shirt pocket. Afterward, he sat back in the rocker.

"If we find Jessie, can you take care of her?"

"Yes!" she said, and now he heard the firmness in her own voice. "I think about it all the time, how I want to rent a little house and have a tree at Christmas. We never had a tree at Christmas . . . maybe once."

His mind went instantly to all that furniture collecting dust at Fernbank. He and Dooley would load up a truck and . . . But he was putting the cart before the horse.

"There's something we need to look at, Pauline."

"Is it about the drinking?"

"Yes."

"I don't crave it anymore."

"Alcohol is a tough call. Very tough. Do you want help?"

"No," she said. "I want to do this myself. With God's help."

"If you ever want or need help, you've got to have the guts to ask for it. For your sake, for the kids' sake. Can you do that?"

Betty switched the porch light on, and he saw Pauline's face as she turned and looked at him. "Yes," she said.

"Didn't want y'all to be setting out there in the dark," said Betty, going back to her room.

They were silent again. He heard Poo laughing, and faint snatches of music and applause from Betty's TV.

"There's something you need to know," she told him.

He waited.

"I won't make trouble, I won't try to make Dooley come and live with us. He's doing so well . . . you've done so much . . .

"If he wants to, he can come and stay with us anytime he's home, but I want you to be the one who . . . the one who watches over him."

She was giving her boy away again. But this time, he fervently hoped and prayed, it was for all the right reasons.

§

He kissed her on the cheek as he came into the bedroom.

"Kavanagh . . ." he said, feeling spent.

"Hello, dearest," she said, looking worn.

After he showered, they crawled into bed on their respective sides and were snoring in tandem by ten o'clock.

§

"Emma, that program on your computer, that thing that helped you find Albert Wilcox . . ."

"What about it?"

"I'd like you to search for these names. I've written down the states I think they could be in."

"Hah!" she said, looking smug. "I knew you'd get to liking computers sooner or later."

§

Some days were like this. One phone call after another, nonstop.

"Father? Emil Kettner. We met when Buck Leeper—"

"Of course, Emil. Great to hear your voice." Emil Kettner owned the construction company that employed Buck Leeper as their star superintendent.

"I have good news for you, I think, if the timing works for Lord's Chapel."

"Shoot."

"The big job we thought we had fell through, and to tell the truth, I think it's for the best—as far as Buck's concerned. He needs a break, but he'd want to be working, all the same. I wondered if we could send him out to you for the attic job."

He was floored. This was the best news he'd had since . . .

"The way he described it, it sounds like six months, tops. I hate to send him on a job that small, I know you understand, but it's the kind of job he'd find . . . reviving, though he'd never admit it."

"We'd be thrilled to have Buck back in Mitford. We'll look after him, I promise."

"You looked after him before, and it worked wonders. There's been a real change in him, but he still works too hard, too fast, and too much. You won't hear many bosses complaining about that."

They laughed.

"The money's in place if we can keep on budget," said the rector.

"That's what Buck's all about, if you remember."

"I do! Well, I can't say enough for your timing, Emil. Our Sunday

School enrollment is mushrooming, I've had three baptisms this month, and the month's hardly begun. When can we expect to see Buck?"

"A week, maybe ten days. And we can't give him much support on this project, he'll be rounding up locals to do the job. How does that sound?"

"Terrific. The carved millwork in the Hope House chapel is locally done. We've got good people in the area."

"Well, then, Father, I'll be looking in on the project like I did last time. Until then."

"Emil. Thanks."

He'd asked for Buck Leeper to do the attic job, never really believing it could happen, only hoping.

And—bingo.

"Father? Buck Leeper."

"Buck!"

He heard Buck take a drag on his cigarette. "You talked to Emil."

"I did, and we're thrilled."

"You reckon I could get that cottage again?"

That dark, brooding cottage under the trees, where the finest construction superintendent on the East Coast had thrown furniture against the wall and smashed vodka bottles into the fireplace? He didn't think so.

"Let me look around. We'll take care of you."

"Thanks," Buck said, his voice sounding gruff.

And yet, there was something else in his voice, something just under the surface that the rector knew and understood. It was a kind of hope.

"Father. Ingrid Swenson."

Dadgum it, and just when he was having a great day.

"Ingrid."

"We're very close to getting everything in order. I'd like to person-

ally make a proposal to you and your committee on the fifteenth. I'm
sure the timing will be good for Lord's Chapel."

He didn't especially care for her almighty presumption about the
timing.

"Let me get back to you," he said.

"Father, it's Esther." Esther Bolick didn't sound like herself. "This
is th' most awful thing I ever got myself into. . . ."

"What do you mean?"

"I mean I've never heard such bawlin' and squallin' and snipin'
and fussin' in my life! I'm about sick of workin' with women, and
church women in particular!"

"Aha."

"Why I said I'd do it, I don't know. Th' *Bane*! Of all things to take
on, and me sixty-seven my next birthday, can you believe it?" She
sighed deeply. "I ought to be sent to Broughton."

"Don't beat yourself up."

"I don't have to, a whole gang of so-called church workers is
thrilled to do it for me!"

"You want to come for a cup of coffee? Emma's home today. I'd
love to hear more."

"I don't have time to come for a cup of coffee, I don't have time to
pee, excuse me, and Gene hadn't had a hot meal in I don't know
when!"

Esther Bolick sounded close to tears. "So even if I can't come for a
cup of coffee, I wish you'd do your good deed for the day and pray for
me. . . ."

"I will. I pray for you, anyway."

You *do*?"

"Of course. The Bane is a cornerstone event for Lord's Chapel,
and you've taken on a big job. But you've got a big spirit, Esther, and
you can do it. I know it's easy for me to say, but maybe you could stop
looking at the big picture, which is always overwhelming, and just
take it day by day."

"Day by day is th' problem! Nearly every day, somebody dumps something else in our garage, and mainly it's the worst old clothes and mildewed shoes you ever saw! Mitch Lewis backed his truck up to th' garage, *raked* out whatever it was in th' bed, and drove off. Gene said to me, he said, 'Esther, what's that mound of *stuff* layin' in th' garage?' We couldn't even *identify* it.

"We need *toaster ovens,* we need *framed prints* and *floor lamps* and *plant stands* and such! This sale's got a *reputation* to maintain, but so far, I never saw so much polyester in my *life,* it looks like we'll *never* get rid of polyester, they won't even take it at th' *landfill!*"

He wished he could offer some of the contents of Fernbank, but Miss Sadie hadn't wanted her possessions picked over. One thing was for certain, he wouldn't donate those mildewed loafers from the back of his closet. . . .

"You know the good stuff always comes in," he said, trying to sound upbeat. "It never fails."

"There's always a first time!" she said darkly.

"Let me ask you—are you praying about this, about the goods rolling in and your strength holding out?"

"I hope you don't think th' *Lord* would mess with the *Bane?*"

"I hope you don't think He wouldn't! Tell me again where the funds from the Bane will go."

"Mission fields, as you well know, including a few in our own backyard."

"Exactly! Some of the money will fly medical supplies to a village where people are dying of cholera. Do you think the Lord would mess with that?"

"Well . . ."

"Then there's the four-wheel drive ambulance they need in Landon," he said. "Remember the blizzard we had three years ago?"

"That's when I had to call an ambulance for Gene, who nearly killed himself shoveling snow! I shouted for joy when I saw it turn the corner. If it hadn't been for that ambulance . . ."

"That winter, two children died of burns because nobody could get a vehicle into the coves around Landon."

"I think I know where you're headed with this," she said.

"I don't believe He'll let Esther Bolick—or the Bane—fail."

"Maybe I could ask Hessie Mayhew to help me out, even if she is Presbyterian!" Esther was sounding more like herself.

"I believe it's going to be the best Bane yet. Now, about your volunteers—my guess is, they're moaning and groaning because they need strong leadership, which is why they elected you in the first place! Look," he said, "I have an idea. Why don't I pray for you? Right now."

"On the *phone?*"

"It's as good a place as any. Try taking a deep breath."

"Lately, it's all I can do to get a deep breath."

"I understand."

"You do?"

"I do."

"I didn't know men ever had trouble gettin' their breath."

"Are you sitting down?"

"Standin' up at the kitchen phone, which is where I've been ever since I let myself get roped into this."

"Could you get a chair?"

He heard her drag a kitchen chair from the table, and sit down.

"OK," she said, feeling brighter. "But don't go on and on 'til th' cows come home."

§

"Fernbank or bust!" cried Cynthia, huffing up Old Church Lane.

"It's only taken us a full year to do this."

"And it's all sitting right there, just as you left it."

He realized why he had put this off, over and over again. He had ducked into Fernbank a few times to check the roof leaks, and ducked out again as if pursued. To see those empty, silent rooms meant she was gone, utterly and eternally, and even now he could hardly bear the fact of it.

"This must be a hard time for Louella, the anniversary of—"

"I'll see her tomorrow," he said, doing some huffing of his own. "Let's have her down to dinner."

"I love that idea. Maybe sometime next week? Oh, for a taste of her fried chicken!"

"We'll have to settle for a taste of my meat loaf. . . ."

They were up to the brow of the hill and turning into the driveway, which was overhung by a thicket of grapevines gone wild. Though Fernbank hadn't been well groomed since the forties, it had still looked imposing and proud during Miss Sadie's lifetime. Now . . .

He saw the house, surrounded by a neglected lawn, and felt the dull beating of his heart.

"Let's buy it!" he croaked. Good Lord! What had he said?

She looked astounded. "Timothy, you don't need a domestic retreat, you need 911. How could you even *think* such a thing?"

And why couldn't he think such a thing? Didn't a man have a right to his own mind?

He felt suddenly peevish and disgruntled and wanted to turn around and run home, but he remembered Andrew Gregory was meeting them on the porch in ten minutes.

§

Andrew stood in the middle of the parlor and looked up.

That's what everyone did, thought the rector—they stared at the water stains like they were some kind of ominous cloud above their heads. Why couldn't people see the dentil molding, the millwork . . .

"Beautiful millwork!" said Andrew. "I've been here only once before, the day of the wedding reception. I was enchanted by the attention to detail. It's a privilege to see Fernbank again."

"Would you like to see it, stem to stern?"

"Stem to stern!" said Andrew, looking enthused.

§

Two hours later, they were close to a deal.

"The development firm has unfortunately asked for several of the finest pieces," said Andrew. He referred to notes that he had hastily jotted as they toured the house.

"Nonetheless, I'd be interested in the Federal loveseat in Miss Sadie's bedroom, the Georgian chest of drawers in her dressing room, the three leather trunks in the attic, the chaise in the storage room, which I believe is Louis XIV, the English china dresser, and all the beds in the house, which are exceedingly fine walnut . . . now, let's see . . . the six framed oils we discussed, which appear to be French . . . and the pine farm table in that wonderful kitchen! It must have been made by a local craftsman around the turn of the century."

"Anything else?" asked the rector, feeling like a traitor, a grave robber.

"In truth, I'd like the dining room suite, but it's Victorian, and I never fare well with Victorian. There are two chairs on the landing, however—I'm not certain of their origins, but they're charming. I'll have those chairs, into the bargain . . . and oh, yes, the contents of the linen drawers. I have a customer in Richmond who fancies brocade napery."

"Hardly used!" said Father Tim, knowing that Miss Sadie had certainly never trotted it out for him.

Cynthia roamed around, sounding like a squirrel in the attic, as he went through the miserable ordeal of dismantling someone's life, someone's history.

Miss Sadie's long letter, which was delivered to him after her death, gave very clear instructions: "Do not offer anything for view at a yard sale, or let people pick over the remains. I know you will understand."

Was Andrew picking over the remains? He didn't think so, he was being a four-square gentleman about the whole thing. Besides, something had to be done with the contents of twenty-one rooms and the detritus of nearly a century.

"How about the silver hollowware?" asked the rector. He felt like Avis Packard who, after selling and bagging a dozen ears of corn, was trying to get rid of last week's broccoli. "The, ah, flatware, perhaps?"

"Well, and why not?" agreed Andrew, looking jaunty. "Who cares if it's all monogrammed with *B*, I think I'll have it for my own!"

The rector drew a deep breath. This wasn't so hard.

"The rugs! How about the rugs?" After all, every cent he raised would go into the Hope House till. . . .

Andrew smiled gently. "I don't think Miss Sadie's father did his homework on the rugs." He jotted some more and offered a price that nearly floored the rector.

"Done!" he exclaimed.

Feeling vastly relieved, he shook Andrew's hand with undeniable vigor.

§

"While you and Andrew toured around like big shots, eyeing major pieces, I was burrowing into minor pieces. Look what I found!"

His wife's face was positively beaming.

"An easel! Hand-carved! Isn't it wonderful? And look at this—an ancient wooden box of watercolors, two whole compartments full! The cakes are dried and cracked, of course, but they'll spring back to life in no time at all, with—guess what?—water!"

He hadn't seen Christmas make her so jubilant.

"And look! A boxful of needlepoint chair covers, worked with roses and hydrangeas and pansies, in all my favorite colors! Perfect for our dining room! Oh, Timothy, how could we have neglected this treasure trove for a full year? It's as if we stayed away from a gold mine, content with digging ore!"

She held up a chair cover for him to admire.

"Now it's your turn to find something for yourself, like Miss Sadie asked you to do. She said 'Take anything you like,' those were her very words."

He stood frozen to the spot, suddenly feeling as if he'd burst into tears.

Cynthia quietly put the chair cover down, and came to him and held him.

§

He found it in the dimly lit attic.

Though the box appeared to be of no special consequence, he felt drawn to it, somehow, and knelt to remove the lid and unwrap the heavy object within.

The figure had the weight of a stone, but a certain lightness about its form, which rested on a sizeable chunk of marble.

Back at the rectory, he set the bronze angel on the living room mantel and stood looking at it.

It was enough. He wanted nothing more.

§

"Mule! What have you got in a little rental house, maybe two bedrooms, something bright and sunny, something spacious and open—and oh, yes, low-maintenance, in a nice part of Mitford, maybe with a fireplace and a washing machine, not too much money, and—"

"Hold it!" exclaimed Mule. "Are you kidding me? You're talkin' like a crazy person. Think about it. If I *had* anything like that, would it be *available*?"

He thought about it. "Guess not," he said.

§

Cynthia's interest was growing. "Let's invite Pauline and Poo!"

They sat in the kitchen, planning the dinner party while their own supper roasted in the oven.

"Terrific idea. Louella, Pauline, Dooley, Poo, Harley, you, and me. Meat loaf for seven!"

"Better make it for ten. Dooley has the appetite of a baseball team."

"Right! Ten, then."

"I'll make lemonade and tea and bake a cobbler," she said.

"Deal."

"In the meantime, dearest, I've planned our retreat."

"Really?"

"Really. Next week, I'm taking you away for two days."

"But Cynthia, I can't go away for two days. I have things to *do*."

"Darling, that's exactly why I'm taking you away!"

"But there's an important vestry meeting, and—"

"Poop on the vestry meeting. Since when does the rector have to attend every vestry meeting as if it were the Nicene Council?"

"Cynthia, Cynthia . . ."

"Timothy, Timothy. Let me remind you of all you've recently done—you've had three baptisms, a death at the hospital, you're working on that project with the bishop which keeps you talking on the phone like schoolgirls, you do two services every Sunday, Holy Eucharist every Wednesday, not to mention your weekly Bible class. *Plus*—"

"There's no way—"

"Plus your hospital visits every morning, and pulling together that huge thing for the mayor, and working on the benefit for the Children's Hospital, and tearing down Betty's shed—not to mention that on your birthday you made a wonderful evening for *me*!"

She took a deep breath. "*Plus*—"

Not that again. "But you see—"

"Plus you still think you haven't done enough."

What was enough? He'd never been able to figure it out.

"Well, dearest, I can see you have no intention of listening to reason, so . . . I shall be forced do what women have been forced to do for millennia."

She marched around the kitchen table and thumped down in his lap. Then she mussed what was left of his hair and kissed him on the top of his head. Next she gave him a lingering kiss on the mouth, and unsnapped his collar, and whispered in his ear.

He blushed. "OK," he said. "I'll do it."

§

While Cynthia scraped and stacked the dishes, he sat in the kitchen, awaiting his cue to wash, and read the *Muse.*

Violet was perched by the gloxinia, purring; Barnabas lay under the table, snoring.

Four Convicted in Wesley Drug Burst

He roared with laughter. This was one for his cousin Walter, all right! He got up and pulled the scissors from the kitchen drawer and clipped the story. Walter liked nothing better than a few choice headlines from the type fonts of J. C. Hogan.

"Who discovered America?" He heard Lace Turner's voice drifting up the stairs through the open basement door.

"Christopher Columbus!" said Harley.

"Who was America named for?"

"Amerigo Vespucci! Looks like it ought've been named f'r Mr. Columbus, don't it? But see, that's th' way of th' world, you discover somethin' and they don't even notice you f'r doin' it."

Cynthia whispered, "She's been coming over and teaching him for several nights, you've been too busy to notice."

"Who was th' king of England when North Carolina became a royal colony?" Lace Turner sounded emphatic.

"George th' Second!"

"When was th' French and Indian War?"

"Lord, Lace, as long as I've lived, ain't never a soul come up t' me and said, 'Harley, when was th' French and Injun war?'"

"Harley . . ."

"They ain't a bit of use f'r me t' know that, I done told you who discovered America."

"Who defeated George Washington at Great Meadows?"

"Th' dern French."

"Who was th' first state to urge independence from Great Britian?"

"North Carolina!" Harley's voice had a proud ring.

"See, you learn stuff real good, you just act like you don't."

"But you don't teach me nothin' worth knowin'. If we got t' do this aggravation, why don't you read me one of them riddles out of y'r number book?"

"OK, but listen good, Harley, this stuff is hard. You borrow five hundred dollars for one year. Th' rate is twenty percent per year. How much do you pay back by th' end of th' year?"

There was a long silence in the basement.

The rector put his arm around his wife, who had come to sit with him on the top basement step. They looked at each other, wordless.

"Six hundred dollars!" exclaimed Harley.

"Real good!"

"I done that in m' noggin."

"OK, here's another'n—"

"I ain't goin' t' do no more. You git on back home and worry y'r own head."

She pressed forward. "A recipe suggests two an' a half to three pounds of chicken t' serve four people. Karen bought nine-point-five pounds of chicken. Is this enough t' serve twelve people?"

"I told you I ain't goin' t' do it," said Harley. "Let Karen fig'r it out!"

The rector looked at Cynthia, who got up and fled the room, shaking with laughter.

He went to his study and took pen and paper from the desk drawer. Let's see, he thought, if the recipe calls for two and a half to three pounds of chicken to serve four people . . .

CHAPTER TEN

Those Who Are Able

He was changing shirts for a seven p.m. meeting when he heard
Harley's truck pull into the driveway. Almost immediately he heard
Harley's truck pull out of the driveway.

Harley must have forgotten something, he mused, buttoning a
cuff.

When he heard the truck roll into the driveway again, he looked
out his bathroom window and saw it backing toward the street. From
this vantage point, he could also see through the windshield.

Clearly, it wasn't Harley who was driving Harley's truck.

It was Dooley.

He stood at the bathroom window, buttoning the other cuff,
watching. In, out, in, out.

He didn't have five spare minutes to deal with it; he was already
cutting the time close since he was the speaker. He'd have to talk to
Dooley and Harley about this.

Dadgum it, he thought. He had a car-crazed boy living down the hall and a race-car mechanic in the basement. Was this a good combination? He didn't think so. . . .

§

Emma looked up from her computer, where she was keying in copy for the pew bulletin.

"I know I'm a Baptist and it's none of my business . . ."

You can take *that* to the bank, he thought.

" . . . but it seems to me that people who can't stand shouldn't have to."

"What do you mean?"

"I mean all those people you get in th' summer who don't know an Episcopal service from a hole in the ground, and think they have to do all th' stuff th' pew bulletin tells 'em to do. I mean, some of those people are old as the hills, and what does th' bulletin say? Stand, kneel, sit, stand, bow, stand, kneel, whatever! It's a workout."

"True."

"So why don't we do what they do at this Presbyterian church I heard about?"

"And what's that?" He noticed that his teeth were clenched.

"Put a little line at the bottom of the bulletin that says, 'Those who are *able,* please stand.'"

Who needed the assistance of a curate or a deacon when they had Emma Newland to think through the gritty issues facing the church today?

§

As he left the office for Mitford Blossoms, Andrew Gregory hailed him from his shop across the street.

"We go three months without laying eyes on each other," said the genteel Andrew, "and now—twice in a row!"

"I prefer this arrangement!"

"Before pushing off to Italy, I have something for your Bane and Blessing. I'll be back in only a month, but what with making room for the Fernbank pieces, I find I've got to move other pieces out. Would you mind having my contribution a dash early?"

"Mind? I should say not. Thrilled would be more like it." He could imagine Esther Bolick's face when she heard she was getting antiques from Andrew Gregory.

Talk about an answer to prayer. . . .

§

He climbed the hill, slightly out of breath, carrying the purple gloxinia, and stood for a moment gazing at the impressive structure they had named Hope House.

But for Sadie Baxter's generosity, this would be little more than the forlorn site of the original Lord's Chapel, which had long ago burned to the ground. Now that Miss Sadie was gone, he was the only living soul who knew what had happened the night of that terrible fire.

Ah, well. He could muddle on about the fire, or he could look at what had risen from the ashes. Wasn't that the gist of life, after all, making the everyday choice between fire and phoenix?

Louella sat by her sunny window, with its broad sill filled with gloxinias, begonias, philodendron, ivy, and a dozen other plants, including a bewildered amaryllis from Christmas.

Dressed to the nines, she opened her brown arms wide as he came in. "Law, honey! You lookin' like somebody on TV in that blue coat."

He leaned eagerly into her warm hug and returned it with one of his own.

"Have you got room for another gloxinia?"

"This make three gloxinias you done brought me!"

That's what he always took people; he couldn't help it.

"But I ain't never had purple, an' ain't it beautiful! You're good as gold an' that's th' truth!"

He set it on the windowsill and thumped down on the footstool by her chair. "How are you? Are they still treating you right?"

"Treatin' me *right*? They like to worry me to death treatin' me right. Have a stick of candy, eat a little ice cream wit' yo' apple pie, let me turn yo' bed down, slip on these socks to keep yo' feet toasty . . ." She shook her head and laughed in the dark chocolate voice that always made a difference in the singing at Lord's Chapel.

"You're rotten, then," he said, grinning.

"Rotten, honey, and no way 'round it. That little chaplain, too, ain't he a case with them dogs runnin' behind 'im ever' whichaway?"

"Are you still getting Taco every week?"

"Taco done got mange on 'is hip and they tryin' to fix it."

"You could have a cat or something 'til Taco gets fixed."

"A cat? You ain't never seen Louella messin' wit' a *cat*."

"Are you working in the new garden?"

"You ain't seen me messin' wit' a hoe, neither. Nossir, I done my duty, I sets right here, watches TV, and acts like somebody."

"Well, I've got a question," he said.

Louella, whose salt-and-pepper hair had turned snow-white in the past year, peered at him.

"Will you come to dinner at the rectory next Thursday? Say yes!"

"You talkin' 'bout dinner or supper?"

"Dinner!" he said. "Like in the evening." Louella, he remembered, called lunch "dinner," and the evening meal "supper."

"I doan hardly know 'bout goin' out at *night*," she said, looking perplexed. "What wit' my other knee needin' t' be operated on . . ."

"I'll hold on to you good and tight," he said, eager for her to accept.

"I doan know, honey. . . ."

"Please," he said.

"Let 'Amazin' Grace' be one of th' hymns this Sunday and I'll do it," she said, grinning. "We ain't sung that in a *month* of Sundays, an' a 'piscopal preacher *wrote* it!"

"Done!" he said, relieved and happy. He had always felt ten years old around Miss Sadie and Louella.

He took the stairs to the second floor to see Lida Willis.

He didn't have to tell her why he'd come.

Lida tapped her desk with a ballpoint pen, still looking stern. "She's doing well. Very well. We couldn't ask for better."

"Glad to hear it," he said, meaning it.

He found Pauline in the dining room, setting tables with the dishes Miss Sadie had paid to have monogrammed with HH. A lifelong miser where her own needs were concerned, she had spared no expense on Hope House.

"Pauline, you look . . . wonderful," he said.

"It's a new apron."

"I believe it's a new Pauline."

She laughed. He didn't think he'd heard her laugh before.

"I have a proposal."

She smiled at him, listening.

"Will you come to dinner next Thursday night and bring Poo? Dooley will be with us, and Harley and Louella."

He could see her pleasure in being asked and her hesitation in accepting.

"Please say yes," he requested. "It's just family, no airs to put on, and we'll all be wearing something comfortable."

"Yes, then. Yes! Thank you. . . ."

"Great!" he said. "Terrific!"

He'd heard people ask, "If you could have anyone, living or dead, come to dinner, who would it be?" Shakespeare's name usually came up at once; he'd also heard Mother Teresa, the Pope, St. Augustine, Thomas Jefferson, Pavarotti, Bach, Charles Schultz . . .

For his money, he couldn't think of anyone he'd rather be having for dinner than the very ones who were coming.

§

He found Scott Murphy at the kennels.

"That's Harry," said Scott, pointing to a doleful beagle. "He's new."

"Looks like an old bishop I once had."

"That's Taco over there."

"How's his mange?"

"You know everything!"

"I wish."

"I've been thinking," said the chaplain. "I'd like to get my crowd out of here, take them to—I don't know, a baseball game, a softball game, something out in the fresh air where they can hoot and holler and—"

"Eat hotdogs!"

"Right!"

"Great idea. I don't know who's playing around town these days. . . ."

"Maybe you and I could get up our own game? Sometime in August?"

"Well, sure! Before Dooley goes back to school."

"I'll start looking for players."

"Me, too," said the rector.

A softball game!

He felt like tossing his hat in the air. If he had a hat.

§

"Bingo!" said Emma, handing him the computer printout of names and addresses.

§

The vestry had said what he thought they'd say, virtually in unison: "Let's get on with it!"

Yes, they wanted Ingrid Swenson and her crew to come on the fifteenth. It was unspoken, but the message was clear—let's unload that white elephant before the roof caves in and we have to get a bank loan to pick up the tab.

He asked Ron Malcolm to call her immediately after the meeting.

§

There were quite a few R. Davises in the state of Florida, according to the printout, but Lakeland was the only town or city with a Rhody Davis. "Starts with a *L*," Russell Jacks had said of Rhody's dimly recalled whereabouts in Florida.

He was disappointed, but not surprised, that Rhody Davis had an unlisted phone number.

He called Stuart Cullen.

"Who do you know in Lakeland, Florida? Clergy, preferably."

"Let me get back to you."

By noon, he was talking to the rector at a church in Lakeland's inner city. It was an odd request, granted, but the rector said he'd find someone to do it.

The next morning, he got the report.

"Our junior warden drove by at nine o'clock in the morning, and a car was parked by the house. Same at three in the afternoon, and again at eight in the evening. Lights were on in the evening, but no other signs of anyone being around. Maybe this will help—there was a tricycle in the front yard. I used what clout my collar can summon, but no way to get the phone number."

"Ever make it up to our mountains?" asked Father Tim.

"No, but my wife and I have been wanting to. A few of my parish go every summer."

"We've got a guest room. Consider it yours when you come this way."

It was a long shot, but he knew what had to be done.

"I don't want t' worry you, Rev'rend, that's th' last thing I'd want t' do, but th' boy ragged me nearly t' death, an' I done like you'd want me to and told 'im no, then dern if I didn't leave m' key in th' ignition, an' since all he done was back it out and pull it in, I hope you won't lick 'im f'r it, hit's th' way a boy does at his age, hit's natural. . . ."

Harley looked devastated; the rector felt like a heel.

"Maybe you ought t' let me take 'im out to th' country an' put 'im behind th' wheel. In two years, he's goin' t' be runnin' up an' down th' road, anyhow, hit'd be good trainin'. I'd watch 'im like a hawk, Rev'rend, you couldn't git a better trainer than this ol' liquor hauler."

"I don't know, Harley. Let me think on it."

"What's it all about?" he asked his wife, sighing.

"Hormones!" she exclaimed.

Mitford, he noted, was becoming a veritable chatterbox of words and slogans wherever the eye landed.

The mayoral incumbent and her opponent had certainly done their part to litter the front lawns and telephone poles with signage, while the ECW had plastered hand-lettered signs in the churchyard and posters in every shop window.

Even the Library Ladies were putting in their two cents' worth.

14th annual Library Sale
10–4, July 28
Book It!

You Don't Want It? <u>We Do!</u>
34th Annual Bane and Blessing

MACK STROUPE:
Mack For Mitford,
Mack For Mayor

Esther Cunningham:
Right For Mitford
Right For Mayor

Clean Out Attics In Mitford
Help Dig Wells
In Africa!

Cunningham Cares.
Vote Esther Cunningham
For Mayor

YOUR BANE IS OUR BLESSING.
Lord's Chapel, October 4

Mack Stroupe:
I'll Make What's
Good Even Better

He thought he'd seen enough of Mack Stroupe's face to last a lifetime, since it was plastered nearly everywhere he looked. Worse than that, he was struggling with how he felt about seeing Mack's face in his congregation every Sunday morning.

§

When he dropped by her office at seven o'clock, the mayor was eating her customary sausage biscuit. It wasn't a pretty sight.

Three bites, max, and that sausage biscuit was out of here. But who was he to preach or pontificate? Hadn't he wolfed down a slab of cheesecake last night, looking over his shoulder like a chicken poacher lest his wife catch him in the act?

Oh, well, die young and make a good-looking corpse, his friend Tommy Noles always said.

"If Mack Stroupe's getting money under the table," he said, "isn't there some way—"

"What do you mean *if*? He *is* gettin' money under the table. I checked what it would cost to put up those billboards and—get this—four thousand bucks. I called th' barbecue place in Wesley that helps him commit his little Saturday afternoon crimes—six hundred smackers to run over here and set up and cook from eleven to three. Pitch in a new truck at twenty-five thousand, considering it's got a CD player and leather seats, and what do *you* think's goin' on?"

"Isn't he supposed to fill out a form that tells where his contributions come from? Somebody said that even the media can take a look at that form."

She wadded up the biscuit wrapper and lobbed it into the wastebasket. "You know what I always tell Ray? Preachers are the most innocent critters I've ever known! Do you think th' triflin' scum is goin' to *report* the money he's gettin' under th' table?"

"Maybe he's actually getting enough thousand-dollar contributions legally to pull all this together. It wouldn't hurt to ask."

She scratched a splotch on her neck and leaned toward him. "Who's going to ask?"

"Not me," he said, meaning it.

❧

The screen door of the Grill slapped behind him. "What's going on?" the rector asked Percy.

"All I lack of bein' dead is th' news gettin' out."

"What's the trouble?"

"Velma."

"Aha."

"Wants to drag me off on another cruise. I said we done been on a cruise, and if you've seen one, you've seen 'em all—drink somethin' with a little umbrella in it, dance th' hula, make a fool of yourself, and come home. I ain't goin' again. But she's nagged me 'til I'm blue in th' face."

" 'Til she's blue in the face."

"Whatever."

Velma, who had heard everything, walked over, looking disgusted.

"I hope you've told th' Father that th' cruise you took me on was paid for by our children, and I hope you mentioned that it's the only vacation I've had since I married you forty-three years ago, except for that run over to Wilkes County in th' car durin' which I threw up the entire time, bein' pregnant."

Velma took a deep breath and launched another volley. "And did you tell him about th' varicose veins I've got from stompin' around in this Grill since Teddy Roosevelt was president? Now you take the Father here, I'm sure he's carried *his* wife on *several* nice trips since *he* got married."

Velma tossed her order pad on the counter, stomped off to the toilet, and slammed the door.

Percy looked pained.

The rector looked pained.

If Velma only knew.

§

She would be let down, he thought, maybe even ticked off—and for good reason. After all, she had worked hard to plan something special.

"Listen to me, please," he said. "I can't go on our retreat."

She gazed at him, unwavering, knowing that he meant it.

"I've got to go and look for Jessie Barlowe."

"I'll go with you," she said.

He sat heavily on the side of the bed where she was propped against the pillows with a book. "It's in Florida, a long drive, and I don't know what we'll run into. I also need Pauline to come along. Since she's the birth mother and no papers were signed for Jessie to live with Rhody Davis, Pauline has custody. She can take Jessie legally."

"Would you need . . . police to go in with you? A social worker?"

"It's not required. Only if it looks like a bad situation."

"Does it look bad?"

"I don't know. There's no way to know."

"Do you think you should investigate further, I mean . . ."

"I feel we need to act on this now."

"Will we be back for our dinner next Thursday?"

"Yes," he said.

She leaned against him, and they sat together, silent for a time.

"We need to pray the prayer that never fails."

"Yes," he said again.

§

He pled Pauline's case with Lida Willis, who gave her dining room manager two days off.

"She'll make it up over Thanksgiving," said Lida. That was when families of Hope House residents would pour into Mitford, straining the reserves of the dining room.

He was vague with Dooley about what was going on and said nothing at all to Emma. He didn't want anyone getting their hopes up. As far as everyone was concerned, he was taking his wife on a small excursion, and Pauline was riding with them to South Carolina and visiting a great aunt. He regretted saying anything to anybody about Florida.

"Florida in July?" asked his secretary, aghast.

"Lord at th' salt they got down there!" said Harley. "Hit'll rust y'r fenders plumb off. Let me git m' stuff together and I'll give you a good wax job."

"You don't have to do that, Harley. Besides, we're leaving early in the morning."

"I'll git to it right now, Rev'rend, don't you worry 'bout a thing. And I'll sweep you out good, too."

It was all coming together so fast, it made his head swim.

"Look after Dooley," he told his resident mechanic as they loaded the car, "and hide your truck keys. Dooley will walk and feed Barnabas, Puny will be in tomorrow, help yourself to the pasta salad in the refrigerator, the car looks terrific, a thousand thanks, we'll bring you something."

Harley grinned. "Somethin' with Mickey on it, Rev'rend! I'd be much obliged."

$\oint$

Hot. He didn't remember being so hot in years, not since his parish by the sea.

And the colors in this part of the world—so vivid, so bright, so . . . different. In the mountains, in his high, green hills, he felt embraced, protected—consoled, somehow.

Here, it was all openness and blue sky and flat land and palm trees. He never ceased to be astonished by the palm tree, which was a staple of the biblical landscape. How did the same One who designed the mighty oak and the gentle mimosa come up with the totally fantastic concept of a palm tree? Extraordinary!

He chuckled.

"Why are you laughing, dearest?"

"I'm laughing at palm trees."

There went that puckered brow and concerned look again. Soon, he really would have to go on a retreat with his wife and act relaxed, so she'd stop looking at him like this.

$\oint$

"You're flying," announced Cynthia, craning her neck to see the speedometer.

Good Lord! Ninety! They'd be arriving in Lakeland in half the anticipated time.

He could feel the toll of the 670-mile one-way trip already grinding on him as they zoomed past Daytona and looped onto the Orlando exit.

The engine might be working in spades, and the wax job glittering like something off the showroom floor, but the air-conditioning performed only slightly better than a church fan at a tent meeting.

He hadn't noticed it at home where the elevation was a lofty five thousand feet, but here, where the sun blazed unhindered, they were all feeling the dismally weak effort of the a/c.

He peered into the rearview mirror, checking on Pauline. She had ridden for hours looking out the window.

He would let Cynthia drive when they got to the rest station in Providence, and once in Lakeland, they'd take a motel and rest before looking for Rhody Davis on Palm Court Way. In order to get Pauline back in time to keep Lida Willis satisfied, they would have only a few short hours to look for Jessie before they hauled back to Mitford on another ten-hour drive.

Maybe he'd been a fool to risk so much on this one grueling trip. But if not now, when?

§

He parked the car under a tree by the sidewalk, where the early morning shade still held what fleeting cooler temperature had come in the night.

"That's Rhody's car in the driveway," said Pauline.

"Sit here," he said, "while I check this out. I'll leave the engine running, so you can stay cool."

"Cool!" said his wife. "Ha and double ha. Can't I come with you, Timothy?"

"No," he said.

He had worn his collar, but only after thinking it through. He always wore his collar, he reasoned—why should he not?

His eyes made a quick reconnaissance.

The small yard was nearly barren of grass. Plastic grocery bags were snared in the yucca plants bordering the unsheltered porch. The car was probably twenty years old, a huge thing, the hood almost completely bleached of its original color. A weather-beaten plastic tricycle lay by the steps. No curtains at the windows.

He rang the doorbell, but failed to hear a resulting blast inside, and knocked loudly on the frame of the screen door.

Hearing nothing, he knocked again, louder than before.

Already the perspiration was beginning a slow trickle under his shirt. He might have been a piece of flounder beneath a broiler, and it wasn't even nine a.m.

Had they come so far to find no one home?

He glanced at the bare windows again and saw her face pressed against the glass.

His heart pounded; he might have leaped for joy.

She looked at him soberly, and he looked at her, seeing the reddish blond hair damp against her cheeks, as if she'd been swimming. There was no doubt that this was five-year-old Jessie Barlowe; the resemblance to her brothers was startling.

Not knowing what else to do, he waved.

She lifted a small hand and waved back, eyeing him intently.

He gestured toward the door. "May I come in?" he said, mouthing the words.

She disappeared from the window, and he heard her running across a bare floor.

He knocked again.

This time, she appeared at the window on the left side of the door. She pressed her nose against the glass and stared at him. Perhaps she was in there alone, he thought with some alarm.

She vanished from the window.

Suddenly the door opened a few inches and she peered at him through the screen.

"Who is it?" she asked, frowning. She was barefoot and wearing a pair of filthy shorts. Her toenails were painted bright pink.

"It's Timothy Kavanagh."

"Rhody can't come!" she said, closing the door with force.

He was baking, he was frying, he was grilling.

He mopped his face with a handkerchief and looked toward the street, seeing only the rear end of his Buick sitting in the vanishing point of shade.

"Jessie!" he yelled, pounding again. "Jessie!"

He heard her running across the floor.

She opened the door again, this time wider. "Rhody can't come!" she said, looking stern.

He tried the screen door. It wasn't locked.

He opened it quickly and stepped across the threshold, feeling like a criminal, driven by his need.

The intense and suffocating heat of the small house hit him like a wall. And the smell. Good Lord! His stomach rolled.

He saw a nearly bare living room opening onto a dining area that was randomly filled with half-opened boxes and clothing scattered across the floor

"You ain't 'posed to come in," she said, backing away. "I ain't 'posed to talk to strangers."

"Where is Rhody?"

"Her foot's hurt, she done stepped on a nail." She wiped the sweat from her face with a dirty hand, and put her thumb in her mouth.

"Is she here?"

Jessie glanced down the hall.

"I'd like to talk with her, if I may."

"Rhody talks crazy."

"Can you take me to her?"

She looked at him with that sober expression, and turned and walked into the hall. "Come on!" she said.

The smell. What was it? It intensified as he followed her down the long, dark hallway to the bed where Rhody Davis lay in a nearly empty room. A baby crib stood by the window, containing a bare mattress and a rumpled sheet; a sea of garbage was strewn around the floor.

The woman was close to his own age, naked to the waist, a bulk of a woman with wispy hair and desperate eyes, and he saw instantly what created the odor. Her right foot, which was nearly black, had swollen grotesquely, and streaks of red advanced upward along her bloated leg. The abscesses in the foot were draining freely on the bedclothes.

Her head rolled toward him on the pillow.

"Daddy? Daddy, is that you?" Sweat glistened on her body and poured onto the soaked sheets.

"Rhody—"

"You ain't got no business comin' here lookin' for Thelma."

"What—"

"Thelma's long gone, Daddy, long gone." She moaned and cursed and tossed her head and looked at him again, pleading. "Why'd you bring that dog in here? Git that dog out of here, it'll bite th' baby. . . ." She tried to raise herself, but fell back against the sodden pillow.

"Do you have a phone?" he asked Jessie. He was faint from the heat and the stench and the suffering.

Jessie sucked her thumb and pointed.

It was sitting on the floor by an empty saltine cracker box and a glass of spoiled milk. He tried to open the windows in the room, but found them nailed shut.

Then he dialed the number everyone was taught to dial and went through the agonizing process of giving the name, phone number, street address, and the particular brand of catastrophe.

"Gangrene," he said, knowing.

At the hospital, he got the payoff for wearing his collar. The emergency room doctor not only took time to examine Rhody Davis within an hour of their arrival, but was willing to talk about what he found.

"There was definitely a puncture to the sole of the foot. Blood poisoning resulted in a massive infection, and that led to gangrene."

"Bottom line?" asked the rector.

"There could be a need to amputate—we don't know yet. In the meantime, we're putting her on massive doses of antibiotics."

"What follows?"

"Based on what you've told me, our department of social services will plug her into the system."

"She'll be taken care of?" asked Cynthia.

The amiable doctor chuckled. "Our social services department loves to get their teeth into a tough case. This one looks like it fills that bill, hands down."

"I'll check on her," said Cynthia. "I'm his deacon."

He should have been exhausted, with one long trip behind him and another one ahead. But he wasn't exhausted, he was energized. They all were.

Cynthia chattered, fanning herself with one of the coloring books she'd been optimistic enough to bring. Pauline talked more freely, telling them Miss Pattie stories from Hope House, and holding Jessie on her lap.

Jessie alternately ate cookies, broke in a new box of crayons, and asked questions. What was that white thing around his neck? What was their dog's name? Where were they going? What was wrong with Rhody? Could they get some more french fries? Did they put her monkey in the trunk with her tricycle? Why didn't Cynthia paint her toenails? Why did the skin on Pauline's arm look funny? Could they stop so she could pee again?

Sitting behind the wheel on the first leg of the journey, he glanced often into the rearview mirror.

He saw Jessie touching her mother's face, though the concept of having a mother was not clear to her. "You're pretty," said the child.

"Thank you."

"You don't got no ear."

"It was . . . burned off."

"How'd you burn it off? Did you cry?"

"I'll tell you about it one day. That's why my arm looks funny. It was burned, too."

"Are we goin' back to get Rhody? Are you Rhody's friend?"

"I'm your mother."

Stick in there, he thought, feeling the pain as if part of it belonged to him. He looked at his wife. He knew when she was praying, because she often moved her lips, silently, like a child absorbed in the reading of a book.

As soon as they got around Daytona, they all played cow poker with enthusiasm, using truck-stop diners in place of the nearly nonexistent cows.

໖

He felt as if he'd been hit by a truck, but thanks be to God, he hadn't.

They rolled into Mitford at midnight, dropped Pauline and Jessie at Betty Craig's, and went home and found Dooley's note that said he was spending the night at Tommy's. Crawling into bed on the stroke of one, he looked forward to sleeping in, until Cynthia told him she'd asked Pauline to leave Jessie with them on her way to work. Betty Craig was spending a rare day away from home with a sister, and did it make sense to leave Jessie with her elderly grandfather, who was a total stranger?

He slept until seven, when he heard Jessie come in, shrieking with either delight or fear upon encountering Barnabas. He woke again at eight, when he heard Puny, Sissy, Sassy, and the overloaded red wagon bound over the threshold and clatter down the hall like so much field artillery.

He burrowed under the covers, feeling the guilt of lying abed while the whole household erupted below him.

Someone was bounding up the stairs, and it definitely wasn't his wife.

"Wake up, Mr. Tim!"

Jessie Barlowe, freshly scrubbed, with her hair in a pony tail, trotted into the room. As he opened his eyes, she scrambled onto the bed and peered down at him.

"Time to put your collar on and get my tricycle out of your car!"

Actually, it was more like he'd gone a few rounds with Mike Tyson.

Standing helplessly by the coffeepot, he'd fallen prey to Puny's plea that he "watch" the twins while she did the floors upstairs. Cynthia and Jessie had gone next door, out of the fray, and here he was, drinking strong coffee in the study behind closed doors, as Sassy bolted back and forth from the bookcase to the desk, laughing hysterically, and Sissy lurched around the sofa with a string of quacking ducks, occasionally falling over and bawling. Barnabas crawled beneath the leather wing chair, trying desperately to hide.

"Ba!" said Sissy, abandoning the ducks and taking a fancy to him. "Ba!"

"Ba, yourself!" he said.

With the vacuum cleaner roaring above his head on bare hardwood, and Sissy banging his left knee with a rattle, he read Oswald Chambers.

"All your circumstances are in the hand of God," Chambers wrote, "so never think it strange concerning the circumstances you're in."

The fact that this piece of wisdom was the absolute gospel truth did not stop him from laughing out loud.

CHAPTER ELEVEN

Amazing Grace

Pauline and Jessie were sitting at the kitchen table as he cooked dinner.

They heard Dooley coming down the hall.

"It's Dooley," said Pauline, gently pushing Jessie toward her brother as he walked into the kitchen.

Dooley was suddenly pale under his summer tan.

"Jess?"

It had been three years, the rector thought, and for a five-year-old, three years is a long time.

"Jess?" Dooley said again, sinking to his knees on the kitchen floor.

Jessie looked at him soberly. Then, standing only a couple of feet away, she slowly lifted her hand and waved at her brother.

"Hey, Jess."

"Hey," she murmured, beginning to smile.

It came to him during the night.

At seven o'clock on Sunday morning he called Hope House,

knowing she would be sitting by the window, dressed for church and reading her Bible.

"Will you do it?" he asked

"Law, mercy . . . " she said, pondering.

"For Miss Sadie? For all of us?"

Louella took a deep breath. "I'll do it for Jesus!" she said.

Harley Welch was dressed in a dark blue jacket and pants, a dress shirt that Cynthia had plucked out of Bane contributions and washed and ironed, and a tie of his own. It was, in fact, his only tie, worn to his wife's funeral thirteen years ago, and never worn since.

"You look terrific!" exclaimed Cynthia.

"Yeah!" agreed Dooley.

"Here!" said the rector.

Harley took the box and opened what had been hastily purchased at a truck stop in South Carolina.

"Th' law, if it ain't a Mickey watch! I've always wanted a Mickey watch! Rev'rend, if you ain't th' beat!"

There went Harley's grin. . . .

Driving his crew to Lord's Chapel, he thought how it was Harley who was the beat. Harley Welch all rigged up for church and wearing a Mickey Mouse watch was still another amazing grace from an endlessly flowing fountain.

He stood in the pulpit and spoke the simple but profound words with which he always opened the sermon.

"In the name of the Father, and of the Son, and of the Holy Spirit, amen."

Then, he walked over and sat in the chair next to the chalice bearer, leaving the congregation wondering. This morning, someone else would preach the top part of the sermon—an English clergyman, long dead, and one of his own parishioners, very much alive.

In the middle of the nave, on the gospel side, Louella Baxter Marshall rose from her pew and, uttering a silent prayer of supplication, raised the palms of her hands heavenward and began to sing, alone and unaccompanied.

> *Amazing grace! how sweet the sound*
> *that saved a wretch like me!*
> *I once was lost but now am found*
> *was blind, but now I see.*

The power of her bronze voice lifted the hymn of the Reverend John Newton, a converted slave trader, to the rafters.

> *'Twas grace that taught my heart to fear,*
> *and grace my fears relieved;*
> *how precious did that grace appear*
> *the hour I first believed!*
>
> *The Lord has promised good to me,*
> *his word my hope secures;*
> *he will my shield and portion be*
> *as long as life endures.*

The words filled and somehow enlarged the nave, like yeast rising in a warm place. In more than one pew, hearts swelled with a message they had long known, but had somehow forgotten.

For those who had never known it at all, there was a yearning to know it, an urgent, beating desire to claim a shield and portion for their own lives, to be delivered out of loss into gain.

The rector's eyes roamed his congregation. This is for you, Dooley. And for you, Poo and Jessie, and for you, Pauline, whom the hound of heaven pursued and won. This is for you, Harley, and you, Lace Turner, and even for you, Cynthia, who was given to me so late, yet right on time. . . .

> *Through many dangers, toils, and snares,*
> *I have already come;*
> *'tis grace that brought me safe thus far,*
> *and grace will lead me home. . . .*

❧

Today was the day. He was ready.

Ron Malcolm, who had priced Fernbank at three hundred and fifty thousand, suggested they accept an offer of no less than two ninety-five. Fernbank was not only an architecturally valuable structure, even with its flaws, but the acreage was sizable, chiefly flat, and eminently suited for development. At two hundred and ninety-five thousand, give or take a few dollars, it would be a smart buy as well as a smart sell.

The rector looked toward Fernbank as he walked to the Grill. He couldn't see the house, but he could see the upper portion of the fern-massed bank, and the great grove of trees.

A spa?

As hard as he tried, he couldn't even begin to imagine it.

§

"Softball?" said Percy. "Are you kiddin' me?"

"I am not kidding you. August tenth, be there or be square."

"Me'n Velma will do hotdogs, but I ain't runnin' around to any bases, I got enough bases to cover in th' food business."

"Fine. You're in. Expect twenty-five from Hope House, twenty or so players . . . and who knows how many in the bleachers?"

Percy scribbled on the back of an order pad. "That's a hundred and fifty beef dogs, max, plus all th' trimmin's, includin' Velma's chili—"

"Wrong!" said Velma. "I'm not standin' over a hot stove stirrin' chili another day of my life! I've decided to go with canned from here out."

"Canned chili?" Percy was unbelieving.

"And how long has it been since you peeled spuds for french fries? Years, that's how long. They come in here frozen as a rock, like they do everywhere else that people don't want to kill theirselves workin'."

"Yeah, but frozen fries is one thing, canned chili is another."

"To you, maybe. But not to me."

Velma stalked away. Percy sighed deeply.

The rector didn't say anything, but he knew darn well their conversation wasn't about chili.

It was about a cruise.

§

He turned into Happy Endings to see if the rare book search had yielded the John Buchan volume.

Hope Winchester shook her head. "Totally chimerical thus far."

"So be it," he said. "Oh. Know anybody who plays softball?"

§

Ingrid Swenson was, if possible, more deeply tanned than before. He didn't believe he'd ever seen so much gold jewelry on one person, as his wealthy seasonal parishioners tended to be fairly low-key while summering in Mitford.

She read from the offer-to-purchase document as if, being children, they couldn't read it for themselves. Every word seemed weighted with a kind of doom he couldn't explain, though he noted how happy, even ecstatic, his vestry appeared to be.

"Miami Development, as Buyer, hereby offers to purchase, and The Chapel of Our Lord and Savior, as Seller, upon acceptance of said offer, agrees to sell and convey—all of that plot, piece or parcel of land described below . . . "

While some appeared to savor every word as they would a first course leading to the entrée, he wanted to skip straight to the price and the conditions.

In the interim, they dealt with, and once again agreed upon, the pieces of personal property to be included in the contract.

"The purchase price," she said at last, looking around the table, "is one hundred and ninety-eight thousand dollars, and shall be paid as follows—twenty thousand in earnest money—"

"Excuse me," he said.

She glanced up.

"I don't think I heard the offer correctly."

"One hundred and ninety-eight thousand dollars." He noted the obvious edge of impatience in her voice.

"Thank you," he said, betraying an edge in his own.

§

Buddy Benfield made coffee, which they all trooped into the kitchen to pour for themselves. Ron brought Ingrid Swenson a china cup, not Styrofoam.

"You do realize," she said, smiling, "that the electrical system violates all state and local ordinances."

Had they realized that?

She withdrew a sheaf of papers from her briefcase. "Let's look at the numbers, which is always an informative place to look.

"The new roof, as you know, is coming in at around forty-five thousand. The plumbing as it stands is corroded cast-iron pipe, all of which must be removed and replaced with copper." She sipped her coffee. "Twenty thousand, minimum. Then, of course, there's the waste-lines replacement and the hookup to city water and sewage at a hundred thousand plus.

"As to the heating system, it is, as you're aware, an oil-fired furnace added several decades ago. Our inspection shows that the firebox is burned through." She sat back in her chair. "I'm sure I needn't remind you how lethal this can be. Estimates, then, for the installation of a forced warm-air system with new returns and ductwork is in excess of ten thousand."

Would this never end?

"Now, before we move to far brighter issues, let's revisit the electrical system."

There was a general shifting around in chairs, accompanied by discreet coughing.

"As you no doubt realize, Mr. Malcolm, Father—the attic has parallel wiring, which fails to pass inspection not merely because it is dangerous, but because it is . . . "—the agent for Miami Development Company gazed around the table—"illegal. Throughout the structure, there is exposed wiring not in conduit, all of which, to make a very long story conveniently shorter, is sufficient to have the structure condemned."

His heart pounded. Condemned.

Ron Malcolm sat forward in his chair. "Miss Swenson, have you stated your case?"

"Not completely, Mr. Malcolm. There are two remarks I'd like to make in closing. One is that the property improvements so far noted will cost the buyer in excess of two hundred and twenty thousand dollars. With that in mind, I believe you'll see the wisdom of selling your . . . distressed property . . . at the very fair price which we're offering.

"Now, to address the brighter side. What we propose to do will bring a vital new economy to Mitford. It will strengthen your tax base by, among other things, raising the value of every property in your village. Mr. Malcolm, I believe that you, for one, live on property contiguous to Fernbank. I don't have to tell you just how great an advantage this will be to your personal assets.

"Surely, all of you realize that nobody in Mitford could afford to take this uninhabitable property off your hands, and I know how grateful you must be to your own Mr. Stroupe for bringing our two parties together. Lacking the local means to reclaim this property, it would be tragic, would it not, to stand by helplessly while Fernbank, the very crown of your village, is torn down?"

The agony he felt was nearly unbearable. He wanted desperately to turn the clock back and have things as they were. He fought an urge to flee the smothering confines of this nightmarish meeting and run into the street.

"In closing, then," she said, looking into the faces of everyone assembled, "we're asking that you respond today, or within a maximum of seven days, to our offer—an offer that is as much designed for the good of Mitford as it is designed to accommodate the interests of Miami Development."

The rector stood, hearing the legs of his chair grate against the bare floor, against the overwhelmed silence of the vestry members.

"We will consider your offer for thirty days," he said evenly.

She paused, but was unruffled. "Thirty days, Father? I assume you understand that, in the volatile business of real estate, seven days is generous."

He saw his vestry's surprised alarm that he'd seized control of a sensitive issue. However, they silently reasoned, he'd been the liaison with Miss Sadie all these years. They probably wouldn't have the property at all if it weren't for the Father.

"And you do realize," Ingrid Swenson continued, "that our legal right to withdraw the offer in view of such a delay puts the sale of your property greatly at risk."

He said to her what she had said to him only weeks before. "Risk, Miss Swenson, has a certain adrenaline, after all."

§

She kissed his face tenderly—both cheeks, his forehead, his temples, the bridge of his nose. "There," she said, and trotted off to fetch him a glass of sherry.

He couldn't recall feeling so weary. Somehow, the road miles to Florida and back were still lurking in him, and the meeting . . . he felt as if it had delivered a blow to his very gut.

Ron Malcolm had argued that Miami Development was placing far too much emphasis on the flaws of the structure, and far too little on the valuable and outstanding piece of land that went with it. Though Ron made his case convincingly, even eloquently, Ingrid Swenson was not only unmoved, but in a big hurry to get out of there.

The rector couldn't dismiss some deeply intuitive sense that the whole thing was . . . he couldn't put his finger on what it was. But every time he denied his intuitions, trouble followed. He hadn't turned sixty-three—or was it sixty-four?—without learning a few things, and paying attention to his instincts was one of the precious few things he'd learned.

But how could he reasonably argue for holding on to a property that may, indeed, end up under the wrecking ball? His vestry hadn't said it in so many words, but they wanted the blasted thing behind them—their hands washed, and money in the till.

He put one of the old needlepoint pillows under his head and lay back on the study sofa. His dog sprawled on the rug beside him and licked his hand.

Dear God! If not for this consolation of home and all that now came with it, where or what would he be?

Wandering the waysides, a raving maniac. . . .

§

"Now that you've rested, dearest . . . "

He knew that look. He knew that look as well as his own face in the mirror.

She leaned her head to one side in the way he'd never been able to resist. "You have rested, haven't you?"

"Well . . . " He didn't know which way to step.

"So here's my idea. You know how formal the dining room is."

"Formal?" The dining room she'd painted that wild, heedless pumpkin color?

"I mean, with the carved walnut highboy from one of the Georges, and those stately chairs with the brocade cushions—"

"Spit it out, Kavanagh."

"I want to move the dining table into the kitchen."

"Are you mad?" he blurted.

"Only for Thursday night," she said, cool as a cucumber. "You see, Pauline and Harley aren't dining room people, and neither is Louella, they'd be stiff as boards in that setting. They know our kitchen, it's like home to them, it's . . . "

He couldn't believe his ears.

" . . . it's what we have to *do*," she said, looking him in the eye. "Pumpkin walls notwithstanding, the dining room seems filled with the presence of . . . old bishops!"

He had definitely, absolutely heard it all.

§

Dooley Barlowe was nowhere to be found, and Harley's strengths lay in other areas of endeavor. It was fish or cut bait.

They turned the mahogany table on its side and, by careful engineering, managed to get it through the kitchen door without slashing the inlaid medallion in the center.

He was certain this was a dream; convinced of it, actually.

That there was hardly room to stand at the stove and cook, once the table was in and upright, was no surprise at all. Could he open the oven door?

"Perfect!" she said, obviously elated. "We'll just use that plaid damask cloth of your mother's."

"That old cloth is worn as thin as a moth's wing. Hardly suitable," he said, feeling distinctly grumpy.

"I love old tablecloths!" she exclaimed.

He sighed. "What don't you love?"

"Grits without butter. Dust balls on ceiling fans. Grumpy husbands."

"Aha," he said, going down on his hands and knees to put a matchbook under a table leg.

§

At breakfast the next morning, he found the much-larger table with the worn cloth looking wonderful in the light that streamed through the open windows. She had filled a basket with roses from the side garden and wrapped the basket with tendrils of ivy. Her cranberry-colored glasses, already set out for the evening meal, caught the light and poured ribbons of warm color across the damask.

Lovely! he mused, careful not to say it aloud.

§

Finding Jessie had been uncannily simple, he thought, walking to the office with Barnabas on his red leash. He had given thanks for this miracle over and over again. The chase, after all, might have led anywhere—or nowhere. But they'd gone straight to the door and knocked, and she had answered.

He would thank Emma Newland from his very heart, he would do something special for her, but what? Emma loved earrings, the bigger, the better. He would buy her a pair of earrings to end all earrings! No fit compensation for what she had done, but a token, nonetheless, of their appreciation for her inspired and creative thinking.

He pushed open the office door as Snickers rushed past him, snarled hideously into his own dog's face, barked at an octave that could puncture eardrums, and peed on the front step—seemingly all at once.

Barnabas dug in and barked back, grievously insulted and totally astounded. From her desk, Emma shouted over the uproar, "I wouldn't bring him in here if I were you!"

The rector saw that urging his dog over the threshold would result in a savage engagement with this desperately overwrought creature, an engagement in which someone, possibly even himself, could be injured.

Furious, he turned on his heel and stomped toward the Grill, dragging his even more furious dog behind.

He blew past the windows of the Irish Shop, as Minnie Lomax finished dressing a mannequin whose arms, years earlier, had been mistakenly carted off with the trash.

"Can't even get in my own office!" he snorted. "Earrings, indeed!"

"Not again," sighed Minnie, watching him disappear up the street.

§

Passing the Collar Button, he was hailed by one of his parishioners, one who hadn't been even remotely amused by the announcement that he was going out to Canaan—or anywhere else.

"Father! You're looking well!"

Things were on an even keel again, thanks be to God. After all that uproar, most people seemed to have forgotten he was retiring, and it was business as usual.

He saw Dooley wheel out of the alley across the street and stop, looking both ways. As he glanced toward the monument, Jenny ran down the library steps, carrying a backpack. She saw Dooley and waved, and he pedaled toward her.

He didn't mean to stand there and watch, but he couldn't seem to turn away. Although Dooley's back was to him, he could see Jenny's face very clearly.

She was looking at The Local's summer help as if he had hung the moon.

§

"It's big doin's," Mule was saying to J.C. as the rector slid into the booth.

"What is?" he asked.

"Th' real estate market in this town. There's Lord's Chapel with that fancy outfit tryin' to hook Fernbank, Edith Mallory's Shoe Barn just went on the block, and I hear major money's lookin' at Sweet Stuff."

"Whose major money?"

"I don't know, Winnie's trying to sell it herself to save the commission, so I don't have a clue who th' prospect is. Meantime, some realtor from Lord knows where is handlin' th' Shoe Barn, Ron Malcolm's brokerin' for Lord's Chapel, and as for yours truly, I can't get a lead, much less a listin'."

"Water, water everywhere, and not a drop to drink," said J.C., hammering down on a vegetable plate with a side of country-style steak.

"Speakin' of th' Shoe Barn, what ever became of that witch on a broom?" asked Mule.

The rector's stomach churned at the mention of Edith Mallory, who owned the large Shoe Barn property. Her focused, unrelenting pursuit of him before he married Cynthia was something he'd finally managed to put out of his mind.

"You're ruinin' his appetite," said Percy, pulling up a stool. Percy had fought his own battle with the woman, who also owned the roof under which they were sitting—she'd tried to jack up the rent and blow him off before his lease expired. That's when the rector discovered that the floor beams of the Grill were rotten and nearly ready to bring the whole building down. Bottom line, Percy walked off with a new lease—on his terms, not hers.

Percy grinned at the rector. "Boys howdy, you fixed her good, you put her high-and-mighty butt through th' *grinder*."

"Watch your language," said Velma, passing with a tray of ham sandwiches.

"And she ain't been back, neither! No, sirree bob! Hadn't had th' guts to show her face in this town since th' night you whittled her down to size."

J.C. used his favorite epithet for Percy's lessor.

"So when are you closing the deal on Fernbank?" asked Mule.

"I don't know. We'll consider their offer for thirty days."

Mule gave him an astounded look. "You want to sit around for thirty days with that white elephant eatin' out of your pocket?"

He felt suddenly angry, impelled to get up and leave. Chill, he told himself, using advice learned from Dooley Barlowe.

"Do you play softball?" he asked the *Muse* editor, who was busy chewing a mouthful.

"Prezure fum dinnity monce."

"Right. So how about you?" he asked Mule. "Scott Murphy wants to get up a game for the residents at Hope House. August tenth. We need players."

"I ain't too bad a catcher."

"You're on," he said. "Percy, I wouldn't mind having a cheeseburger all the way. With fries!"

Percy scratched his head. "Man! In sixteen years, you prob'ly ordered a cheeseburger twice. And never all the way."

"Life is short," he said, still feeling ticked. "And put a strip of bacon on it."

§

"How's it coming, buddy?"

"I got Tommy and his dad and Avis. Ol' Avis says he can hit a ball off th' field and clean over our house."

"No kidding? What do you think about Harley? Think he could do it?"

"Harley, don't . . . doesn't have any teeth."

"What do teeth have to do with playing softball?"

Dooley grinned. "We could see if he wants to."

They were setting the table as Cynthia busied herself at the stove. He was leaving in five minutes to pick up Pauline and the kids, and run up the hill for Louella.

He liked setting the table with Dooley. Bit by bit, little by little, Dooley was coming into his own, something was easier in his spirit. Pauline had been part of it, and Poo, and now Jessie. Each brought with them a portion of the healing that was making Dooley whole. He watched the boy place the knife on the left side of the plate, look at it for a moment, then remove it and place it on the right. Good fellow! He saw, too, the smile playing at the corners of Dooley's mouth, as if he were thinking of something that pleased him.

Dooley looked up and caught the rector's gaze. "What are you staring at?"

"You. I'm looking at how you've grown, and taking into account the fine job you're doing for Avis—and feeling how good it is to have you home."

Dooley colored slightly. He thought for a moment, then said, "So let me drive your car this weekend."

Blast if it didn't fly out of his mouth. "Consider it done!"

§

"Low-fat meat loaf, hot from the oven!" he announced, setting the sizzling platter on the table.

Louella wrinkled her nose. "Low-fat? Pass it on by, honey, you can *skip* this chile!"

"Don't skip this 'un," said Harley.

"He was only kidding," Cynthia declared. "In truth, it contains everything our doctors ever warned us about."

He saw the light in Pauline's face, the softness of expression as she looked upon her scrubbed and freckled children. Thanks be to God! Three out of five. . . .

He sat down, feeling expansive, and shook out one of the linen napkins left behind, he was amused to recall, by an old bishop who once lived here.

He waited until all hands were clasped, linking them together in a circle.

"Our God and our Father, we thank You!" he began.

"Thank You, Jesus!" boomed Louella in happy accord.

"We thank You with full hearts for this family gathered here tonight, and ask Your mercy and blessings upon all those who hunger, not only for sustenance, but for the joy, the peace, and the one true salvation which You, through Your Son, freely offer. . . . "

They had just said "Amen!" when the doorbell rang.

"I'll get it! And for heaven's sake, don't wait for me. Who on earth . . . " Cynthia trotted down the hall to the door.

Father Tim passed the platter to Louella and was starting the potatoes around when he heard Cynthia coming back to the kitchen, a heavy tread in her wake.

"You'll never guess who's here!" said his wife.

Buck Leeper stepped awkwardly into the doorway. In the small, close kitchen, his considerable presence was arresting.

Good Lord! Finding Buck a place to stay had gone completely out of his head. It hadn't entered his mind again since he called Mule. He was mortified.

He stood up, nearly knocking his chair to the floor.

"Good timing, Buck! We'll set another plate, there's more than plenty. Good to see you!" He pumped Buck's large, callused hand. "You remember Louella, Miss Sadie's friend and companion. And Dooley, you remember Dooley."

Buck nodded. "Dooley . . . "

"Hey."

"And this is Harley Welch, Harley lives with us, and there's Pauline, Dooley's mother—as I recall, you brought her a rose when she was in the hospital."

Buck flushed and glanced at the floor.

Rats. He shouldn't have said that. "This is Dooley's brother Poo, and this is Jessie, his sister."

Poobaw grinned at Buck.

"I'm hungry!" said Jessie.

"This is Buck Leeper, everybody, the man who did such a splendid job at Hope House. Can you believe he was born just up the road from me in Mississippi? Keep the potatoes passing, Dooley, there's the gravy. Ah, I see we forgot to set out the butter for the rolls! Buck, I hope you're hungry, we've got enough for an army. Here, take this chair, we're glad to have you back in Mitford! Louella, have you got room over there? Dooley, scoot closer to your sister. . . . "

What a workout. He was exhausted.

"Please sit down, Mr. Leeper," said his smiling wife, taking over.

§

Dooley had taken Poo and Jessie to his room; Cynthia, Louella, and Pauline were making tea and coffee; and the men had gone into the study.

"What it was," said Harley, "Junior liked t' run on dirt better'n asphalt, which is why they called 'im th' Mud Dobber. One ol' boy said how th' law was tryin' t' jump Junior, said Junior cut out th'ough a cornfield in a '58 Pontiac with th' winders down, said he plowed th'ough about a ten-acre stand of corn 'til he come out th' other side an' looked around an' 'is whole backseat was full of roastin' ears."

Buck laughed the laugh that sounded, to the rector, like a kettle boiling.

"Harley, you ought to tell Buck about your services as a mechanic. There'll be a lot of vehicles on the Lord's Chapel job."

"Yes, sir, I work on most anything with wheels, but I don't touch earth-movin' equipment. Course, I'm goin' t' be tied up pretty good, I'm cleanin' out 'is missus's basement and garage, then startin' on th' attic up yonder." Harley pointed to the ceiling. "Hit ain't been touched since one of them old bishops lived here."

Pauline came to the door of the study. Jessie was right, thought the rector, she's pretty.

"Excuse me . . . "

"Are you ready for us?" he asked.

She smiled. "Yes, sir. Cynthia said please come in."

Buck stood up from the wing chair, gazing at Pauline.

Father Tim saw that he appeared, for a moment, as eager and expectant as a boy.

§

"I couldn't do that," said Buck.

"Well, you see . . . the truth is, you have to. I looked for a place for you to live and ran into a dead end, and, well, first thing you know, I forgot to keep looking, and there you have it, you're stuck with us—the sheets are clean and the toilet flushes."

Buck laughed. At least he was laughing. . . .

He showed Buck to the guest room at the top of the stairs, where the superintendent's size somehow made the space much smaller. Buck chewed a toothpick, and carefully scanned the room and its adjoining bath.

"I believe you'll be comfortable, and don't worry about a thing. We'll have you out of here in no time, into a place of your own."

"If you're sure . . . "

"More than sure! Oh. By the way—do you play softball?"

Buck took the toothpick out of his mouth. "I've kicked more tail on a softball field than I ever kicked on a construction site. Before I hired on with Emil, I coached softball for a construction outfit in Tucson. The last couple of years I was there, we won every game, two seasons in a row."

Dooley suddenly appeared at the guest room door.

"I'm on his team," he said.

§

Buck offered to deliver Pauline and the children, while he took Louella to Hope House.

"I had a big time," said Louella, looking misty-eyed. "You and Miss Cynthia, you're family."

"Always will be," he said, meaning it.

At the door of Room Number One, he kissed her goodnight, loving the vaguely cinnamon smell of her cheek that had something of home in it.

§

Emma looked at him over her half-glasses.

"I guess you're hot about Snickers runnin' you off the other day."

"You might say that."

"How did I know you'd bring Barnabas to work? You never do, anymore. And besides, Snickers has never been here but twice, it seems like he *deserved* a turn. . . . "

"Ummm."

"Emily Hastings called, she said she has an axe to pick with you."

An axe to grind, a bone to pick, what difference did it make?

"Esther Bolick called, said things are looking up, Hessie Mayhew's th' biggest help since Santa's elves."

"Good."

"Hal Owen called, said it's time for Barnabas to get his shots."

"Right."

"Evie Adams called, guess what Miss Pattie's done now?"

"Can't guess," he said curtly, taking the cover off his Royal manual.

"She goes up and down the halls at Hope House, stealing the Jell-O off everybody's trays."

"That's a lot of Jell-O."

"Don't you care?"

"About what?"

"Stealing from old people."

"Miss Pattie is old people."

"So?"

He would like nothing better than to knock his secretary in the head. "So they have a staff of forty-plus at Hope House, I'm sure they can come up with some kind of curtailment of her behavior."

"Some kind of what?"

He didn't answer.

"How can you *use* that old thing?" she asked, glaring at his Royal manual.

He refused to respond.

There was a long silence as she peered at her computer monitor, and he rolled a sheet of paper into the carriage of his machine.

"So when are you going to give me some more names to find?" she inquired at last, trying to make up.

CHAPTER TWELVE

Waiting

"Will you do it?" he asked his wife.

"Of course I won't do it! It's not my job to do it."

"Deacons," he reminded her, "are supposed to do the dirty work."

"You amaze me, Timothy. You bury the dead, counsel the raving, and heedlessly pry into people's souls, yet when it comes to this . . ."

"I can't do it," he said.

"You have to do it."

Of course he had to do it. He knew that all along. He was only seeing how far he could get her to bend.

Not far.

§

"Dooley . . ."

He picked a piece of lint from his trousers. He stared at his right loafer, which appeared to have been licked by his dog, or possibly the twins, and after he had polished it only yesterday. . . .

"Yessir?"

Barnabas collapsed at his feet and yawned hugely, indicating his extreme boredom. Not a good sign.

"Well, Dooley . . . "

Dooley looked him squarely in the eye.

"It's about Jenny. I mean, it's not about Jenny, *exactly*. It's more indirectly than directly about Jenny, although we could leave her out of it altogether, actually. . . . "

"What about Jenny?"

"Like I said, it's not exactly about Jenny. It's more about . . . "

"About what?"

Had he seen this scenario in a movie? In a cartoon? He was old, he was retiring, he was out of here. He rose from the chair, then forced himself to sit again.

"It's about sex!" Good Lord, had he shouted?

"Sex?" Dooley's eyes were perfectly innocent. They might have been discussing Egyptology.

"Sex. Yes. You know." Hal Owen would have done this for him, Hal had raised a boy, why hadn't he thought of that before?

Dooley looked as if he might go to sleep on the footstool where he was sitting. "What about sex?"

"Well, for openers, what do you *know* about it? If you know anything at all, do you know what you *need* to know? And how do you *know* if you know what you need to know, that is to say, you can never be too *sure* that you know what you need to know, until—"

He actually felt a light spray as Dooley erupted with laughter in his very face. The boy grabbed his sides and threw back his head and hooted. Following that, he fell from the footstool onto the floor, where he rolled around in the fetal position, still clutching his sides and cackling like a hyena.

Father Tim had prayed for years to see Dooley Barlowe break down and really laugh. But this was ridiculous.

"When you're over your hysteria," he said, "we'll continue our discussion."

Not knowing what else to do, he examined his fingernails and tried to retain whatever dignity he'd come in here with.

❦

"Good heavens, Timothy. You look awful! Is it done?"

"It's done."

"What did you tell him?"

"It's more like . . . what he told me."

"Really?" she said, amused. "And what did he tell you?"

"He knows it all."

"Most teenagers do. Figuratively speaking."

"And there's nothing to worry about, he's not even interested in *kissing* a girl."

Cynthia smiled patiently. "Right, darling," she said.

He wouldn't say a word to anybody about the two-thousand-dollar check Mack Stroupe had put in the collection plate on Sunday. He only hoped Emma would keep quiet about it.

On that score, at least, she was pretty dependable, though she'd been the one to tell him about the check. From the beginning, his instructions were, "Don't talk to me about the money, I don't need to know." As he'd often said, he didn't want to look into the faces of his parishioners and see dollar signs.

"Harley, ever played any softball?"

"No, sir, Rev'rend, I ain't been one t' play sports."

"Ah, well."

"I can run as good as th' next 'un, but hittin' and catchin' ain't my call."

The rector was peering into the tank of Harley's toilet, which had lately developed a tendency to run.

"I thank you f'r lookin' into my toilet, hit's bad t' keep me awake at night, settin' on th' other side of th' wall from m' head."

"It's old as Methuselah, but I think I can fix it."

"I want you t' let me fix somethin' f'r you, now, Rev'rend, I'm runnin' behind on that."

"Can't think of anything that needs it," he said, taking a wrench out of his tool kit.

"Maybe it's somethin' that don't need fixin', jis' tendin' to."

"Well, now." Wouldn't Dooley rather get his driving lesson from a bona fide race car mechanic than a preacher? He was sure Harley could make the lesson far more interesting, and even teach Dooley some professional safety tips from the track. Besides, even with the new torque in the Buick, Harley's truck would be a much more compelling vehicle to a fourteen-year-old boy.

"There is something you could do," he said, "if you're going to be around Saturday afternoon."

§

He could feel the bat in his hands. How many years had it been since he'd slammed a ball over the fence? Too many! He'd better get in shape, he thought, huffing up Old Church Lane in his running gear. Barnabas bounded along in front on the red leash.

Cooler today, but humid. Overcast skies, rain predicted. And didn't the garden need it? He'd worn a hood, just in case.

He wished he could get his wife to run with him, but no way. She was a slave to her drawing board, and lately looking the worse for it. The unofficial job of deacon, the job of organizing their jam-packed household, and the job of children's author/illustrator were wearing on her. And hadn't he helped put another portion on her already full plate by stowing Buck in the guest room?

He was frankly stumped about how to find housing for the superintendent, and with the attic job gearing up, Buck hardly had time to look around for himself. Maybe Scott Murphy would take in a boarder. . . .

He ran up to the low stone wall overlooking what he called the Land of Counterpane, and thumped down with Barnabas, panting.

There was the view that Louella and all the other residents farther along the hill could wake up and see every day of their lives. A feast for the eyes! He didn't get up here much, but when he did . . .

It was here, sitting on this wall, that he had known, at last, he *could* marry her, *must* marry her, and experienced the terrible anxiety of what it could mean to lose her. And it was here that he and Cynthia decided they both wanted to stay in Mitford when he retired.

Was he on time for the train? He looked at his watch. Another few minutes. Perhaps he would wait. Was life so all-fired urgent that he couldn't find five minutes to see a sight that always blessed and de-lighted him?

He was utterly alone in this place where, for all its singular beauty, few people ever came. It was set steeply above the village, it was off the beaten path, it was . . .

He heard the car below him, on the gravel road that ran along the side of the gorge and was seldom used except by a few local families.

He peered down and saw the black car pull to the shoulder of the road and stop. A man opened the driver's door and leaned out, looking around, then closed the door again. He was wearing a hat, a cap of some kind.

Mighty fine car to be out on Tucker's Mill Road, he thought, glancing again at his watch. Maybe the train would be early.

The pickup truck didn't move so slowly. He saw the plume of dust through the trees, then saw the blue truck screech to a stop beside the black car. A man jumped out, walked around the front of the truck, and stood for a moment by the car. It appeared that he was handed something through the car window.

The driver quickly got back in the truck, gunned the motor, and drove away, leaving a cloud of dust to settle over everything in its wake.

He watched as the car backed onto a narrow turnout, reversed direction, and rolled almost silently along Tucker's Mill.

By George, there was the train; he heard its horn faintly in the distance. Around the track it came, breaking through the trees by the red barn . . .

That scene he had just witnessed—had there been something strangely unsettling about it?

. . . then it huffed along the side of the open fields by the row of tiny houses and disappeared behind the trees.

He hadn't been able to tell from this vantage point what kind of car it was, but then, what difference did it make, anyway?

"Enough!" he said to his dog, and they bounded down the slope toward Baxter Park in the first drops of a misting rain.

❦

Instead of turning into the park, he decided to run to the bottom of the hill and pop into Oxford Antiques. He'd inquire about Andrew and look for a present for Cynthia's birthday. He was barely getting in under the wire, considering that July 20 was two days hence.

Marcie Guthrie, Puny's mother-in-law and one of the mayor's five good-looking deluxe-size daughters, was reading a romance novel behind the cash register. "Father! Bring your dog in, but tell him to watch his tail!"

He tethered Barnabas to the leg of a heavy table. "Marcie, give me a few ideas for my wife's birthday, and I'll give you my eternal thanks."

"Well! Goodness! Let's see."

Cynthia was nearly as simple in her wants as he, thanks be to God. And she always seemed touchingly grateful when he gave her a gift.

"It must be something . . . wonderful," he said.

"I've got it!" she exclaimed. "The very thing! Come over here."

He trotted behind her to a gigantic walnut secretary with beveled glass doors. "There!" she said.

"Oh, no. That's far too large!"

"Not the secretary. The lap desk!"

Aha! Sitting next to the secretary on a Georgian buffet was a lap desk of exquisite proportions. That was it, all right, he knew it at once. A small lap desk with a pen drawer, a built-in inkstand, and a leather writing surface. Perfect!

He was afraid to ask.

"Four hundred and seventy-nine dollars!" she informed him. "It's not that old, just turn-of-the-century."

"Ummm."

"But for you, only four hundred. Andrew said whenever you come in to buy, to give you a special discount."

"Done!" he said, feeling a combination of vast relief, excitement over such a find, and momentary guilt for shelling out four hundred bucks. "I'll bring you a check in the morning. Will you wrap it?"

"Of course, and look at this little drawer. Lined with old Chinese tea paper, and here's one of the original pen nibs."

His guilt vanished at once.

"Have you heard about Andrew?" she asked.

"How is he, when is he coming home?"

"He doesn't know. It all sounds mysterious to me. He usually never stays away so long. But of course, it is his mama's hometown and he's probably visitin' cousins an' all. . . . "

"Probably. I seldom see him, but when he's not here, I miss him."

"He's called twice to see how business is. He sounds . . . different."

"Oh? How do you mean, different?"

"I mean, well, really *happy* or somethin'."

"Cousins can do that for you," he said, grinning. He suddenly realized he missed his own cousin, the only blood kin he had on the face of the earth. He'd call Walter tonight.

He put his hood up and sprinted along Main Street with his dog. May as well make one more stop, then head for home.

"Winnie?"

He parked Barnabas by the door and peered over the bakery counter.

"I'm comin'!" she said, breezing through the curtains that hid the bakery kitchen. "Father, I'm glad it's you!"

"I hear you got a bite!"

"Maybe a nibble, I don't know."

"What's the scoop?"

"Well, this real estate agency wants to know everything, so I sent 'em all the information, but nobody's turned up to see it yet."

"Terrific!" He didn't really think it was terrific, but what else could he say? "Who's the realtor?"

"Somebody named H. Tide Realty from—I forget, maybe Florida."

Florida again. "How do you feel about it?"

"After waitin' for somebody to be interested, when this finally happened, it kind of . . . "

"Kind of what?"

"Made me sick."

"I understand."

"You do?"

"Definitely."

She looked uncertain.

"You know we want you to stay. But if you decide to go, remember we'll stand behind that, too."

Winnie looked relieved. "Good! I don't know why, but I always feel better when I talk to you."

"Maybe it's the collar."

"Have a napoleon!" she urged, in her usual burst of generosity.

"Get thee behind me, absolutely not. But tell you what—I've got a houseful, so bag me a dozen donuts, Dooley will love that, and Harley, too, and let's see, a dozen oatmeal cookies . . . "

"Low-fat!" she said.

"Great. Now, what about that pie on the right? The one with the lattice top?"

"Cherry!"

"My favorite. Box it up!" Spending four hundred dollars had made him feel so good, he was trying to do it all over again.

§

Rhody Davis's leg was being amputated today.

He was praying for her this morning at first light, soon after reading Blaise Pascal. A young man who lived in the seventeenth century knew what Rhody Davis and several others on his current prayer list needed more than anything else.

"There is a God-shaped vacuum in the heart of every person," Pascal wrote. "And it can never be filled by any created thing. It can only be filled by God, made known through Jesus Christ."

Pascal had dazzled Europe with his sophisticated mathematical equations when he was only sixteen, and written about the God-shaped vacuum when he wasn't much older.

Nearly every day of his priesthood, Father Tim had seen what happened when people tried filling that vacuum with any created thing. Pauline had tried to fill it with alcohol. Rhody Davis had tried to fill it with someone else's child. . . .

He closed his eyes and prayed for all those who turn to the created thing, expecting much and receiving nothing.

The talk on the street was that Mack Stroupe was responsible for hooking the Fernbank sale, which would do wonders for Mitford's economy. Not only would such an enterprise draw people from other parts of the country, maybe even the world, but a major part of the staff would be locals. All that landscaping, all that maintenance, all that ocean of roofing and plumbing—and all that money flowing into Mitford pockets.

According to several reports, Fernbank was already sold, it was a done deal.

Mack Stroupe was looking good.

He called the mayor's office.

"She's not in," said the painfully shy Ernestine Ivory, who gave the mayor a hand two days a week.

"May I ask where she is?"

"Down at the school. She's doing a special program for the children."

"Children can't vote," he said.

"Yes, Father, that's true. But their parents can."

Bingo. "Tell her I called."

Harley nodded, looking sober.

"Don't let him talk you into anything you don't think is right . . . "

"Yes, sir."

" . . . or safe. Especially safe!"

"No, sir, I wouldn't."

The rector sighed and moved closer to Harley's oscillating fan.

"Now, don't you worry, Rev'rend. I'll watch after 'im like m' own young 'un."

"I know you will."

"Hit'll work some of th' juice out of 'im."

"Right."

"While I've got a educated man settin' here, I'd be beholden if you'd give me a little help with m' homework an' all."

"Your homework?"

"Lace has it in 'er head t' educate me, she's givin' me a test in a day or two."

"How do you feel about getting educated?"

"I've a good mind t' quit, but she's got 'er heart set on learnin' me somethin'. Lace has had a good bit of hard knocks, I don't want t' let 'er down."

"That's right. How can I help you?"

"Well, looky here. Sixty seventh-grade students toured th' Statue of Liberty in New York City. Two-thirds of 'em climbed to th' halfway point, and one-fourth of 'em was able t' climb all th' way to th' top. Now, th' remainin' group, they stayed down on th' base of th' pedestal, it says here. How many students didn't climb th' steps? I can't figger it t' save m' neck."

The rector mopped his brow. "Oh, boy."

"Here's another'n, this 'uns easier. The torch of th' Statue of Liberty is three hundred an' five foot from th' bottom of th' base. If th' pedestal on which th' statue rests is eighty-nine foot high, how high is th' base?"

"Let me go get a drink of water and I'll come back and see what I can do."

As he drank a glass of water at Harley's kitchen sink, he heard him muttering in the next room, "Elton washes winders at a office buildin'. Some offices has four winders and some has six . . ."

How did he get himself into these scrapes, anyway?

He kissed the nape of her neck, just under the ponytail she'd lately taken to sporting.

"Is there anything special you'd like to do for your birthday?" Please, Lord, don't let her say a domestic retreat. I don't have time, she doesn't have time, it can't happen.

She sighed. "We're both exhausted, dearest. Let's don't do any fancy dinners or tangos, let's get Chinese take-out from Wesley, lock our bedroom door, and just *be*."

And what would their teeming household think about such a thing? Oh, well.

"I can handle that," he said, drawing her close.

§

"Ron, was there ever any discussion with Miami Development about Fernbank's apple orchard? There are a hundred and sixty-two trees up there, and all are still bearing."

"She mentioned the orchard the first time she was here. They'd tear it out. That's where most of the cottages will be built."

A small point, but it stung him. Those trees had dropped their fruit into any hand that passed, for years. They had filled Mitford's freezers with pies and cobblers, and crowded endless pantry shelves with sauce and jelly.

An even smaller point, perhaps, but he noticed that Ron had said "*will* be built."

§

A new day-care program was getting under way at Lord's Chapel as Buck Leeper's crew began their invasion of the attic.

Given that the only access to the attic was through the trapdoor over the pulpit, merely getting into the attic was a project.

Under Buck's supervision, the crew removed stones from the east wall, cut through studs, sheeting, and insulation, installed a new header and a sill, and created a double-door entrance. Until the outside steps could be built, ladders and scaffolding permitted the crew to haul up endless feet of lumber for classroom partitions and a restroom.

It was all going forward exactly as he expected: his very hair, what was left of it, was filled with a fine dust, as were the pews and all that lay below. Kneelers got their share, so that when parishioners wearing black arose from prayer, the fronts of skirts and trousers displayed a clear mark of piety.

Anybody else, he thought, would have retired and left the attic project to the next poor fellow, but he had celebrated and preached beneath the vast, empty loft for sixteen years, dreaming of the day they could fill it with children.

Yes, there'd be the patter of little feet above the heads of the congregation, though measures would be taken to muffle the sound considerably. In any case, it was a sound he'd be glad to hear.

§

Puny met him at the front door with Sissy on one hip and Sassy on the other.

"Father, I jis' don't think I can keep bringin' th' girls to work with me, even though I know how much it means to you to have 'em here." She looked unusually distressed.

He took Sissy and walked down the hall behind his house help.

"Ba!" said the happy twin, bashing him on the head with a plastic frying pan. "Ba!"

"That's what she calls you, did you know that?"

"Really?"

"That's your name. When I show her your wedding picture at home, she always says Ba!"

He felt honored. Ba! He'd never had another name before, except Father.

He sat down at the kitchen table and took a twin on either knee, which he immediately geared to the jiggling mode. "I know it's hard for you trying to work with two little ones. . . ."

"I cain't hardly get my work done anymore, but I hated to put 'em out to day care, they'll only be babies once, and I didn't want . . ." Puny looked close to tears. "I didn't want to miss that!"

"Of course not! I know it's a strain for you, but we'll work with you on it. We're pleased with all you do, Puny. You're the best, and always have been."

Her face brightened. He loved the look of the red-haired, freckle-faced Puny Guthrie, who was like blood kin, the closest thing to a daughter he'd ever have. Besides, who else would clean the mildew off his shoes, wipe *behind* the picture frames, mend his shirts, bake cornbread deserving of a blue ribbon, and keep the clothes closets looking like racks at a department store? What she was able to do, even with two toddlers in tow, was more than anyone else *would* do, he was sure of it.

"The church day care will be open next week. Hang on, and if you'd like to put them in for a day or two to see how it goes, well . . . "

"Thank you, Father! You're a wonderful granpaw. Would you mind holdin' 'em a minute while I run up and bring th' laundry down?"

"Mama, Mama!" yelled Sassy.

"Ba!" sighed Sissy, snuggling against him.

He nuzzled the two heads of tousled hair and thought that, all things considered, he was a very fortunate man. He needed challenges in his life . . . But wait a minute, did he need that warm, wet feeling spreading over his left knee?

He had showered, she had bathed in a tubful of scented bubbles; she had laid out his clean robe, he had plumped up the pillows behind her head; they had devoured their chicken with almonds, shrimp with lobster sauce, and two spring rolls.

"What's your fortune?" she asked, looking discontented with her own.

"I will uncover a surprise and receive great recognition."

"Poop, darling, you're always receiving great recognition. Everyone loves you, it's like being married to the Pope. Here's mine. 'Prepare for victory ahead!' Who writes this stuff?"

"Now," he urged.

"OK!"

"Close your eyes."

"I love this part," she said, putting her hands over her eyes. "Don't you want me to guess?"

"Absolutely not. We're going straight to the punch line."

He trotted to the closet, retrieved the box which Marcie had wrapped in the signature brown paper of Oxford Antiques, and thumped it on the bed next to his wife.

"OK. You can look."

"A box! I love boxes!"

"Heave to, Kavanagh."

She tore the raffia bow off, and the paper, and pulled back the tape on top of the box.

He helped remove the writing desk and set it on her lap.

"Timothy!" she whispered, unbelieving.

"Happy birthday, my love."

No two ways about it, he had hit a home run.

§

They lay in bed, holding each other, the room warmed by the glow of her bedside lamp.

"You're wonderful," he said, meaning it.

She smiled. "But I'm old!"

"Old? You? Never!"

"Just look at these crow's feet. . . . "

"I don't see any crow's feet," he said, kissing her crow's feet.

§

"Father, this is Lottie Greer."

Lottie Greer—the spinster sister of Absalom Greer, the elderly revival preacher who had loved Sadie Baxter . . .

"It's Absalom." He heard the fear in her voice.

"What is it?"

"It's pneumonia. He wants you to pray."

"I will, Miss Lottie, and others with me. Shall I come?"

"He said to just pray. There's fluid in his lungs."

He told her he was available anytime, that she should let him know what he could do. Then he called Cynthia and the all-church prayer chain.

He had come to love Absalom Greer. The eloquent, unschooled preacher had been a force in his life and those of countless others, including Pauline and Lace. He was among the last of the old warriors who fearlessly confronted the issue of sin, preached repentence and salvation, and pulled no punches when it came to the Gospel of Jesus Christ.

Bottom line, the old man was his brother. He would go out on Sunday.

§

What was he waiting for?

The question was unspoken, but every time he ran into a member of the vestry, he felt the weight of it. Thirty days? For what? Ingrid Swenson didn't look like somebody who could be bluffed into coughing up two ninety-five after she offered one ninety-eight. But the point was, the property was fully worth two ninety-five, and in his opinion, Miami Development was trying to steal it. To be bluffed themselves was a humiliation not to be suffered lightly.

The answer was, he didn't know what he was waiting for. He only knew that selling Fernbank to Miami Development was something that didn't feel right. Maybe it would feel right later—then again, later could be too late.

He hated this, he hated it.

§

He tried to act nonchalant by puttering in the side garden as they backed out of the driveway. Dooley was lit up like downtown Holding at Christmas, and Harley was generating a few kilowatts himself.

He looked up and waved, and they waved back.

Four-thirty. Dooley had left work a half hour early, and they had promised to be back at the rectory around six.

He looked through the hedge to the little yellow house. A window box needed fixing, the bolt had come loose and the box was hanging whomper-jawed under the studio window.

Too bad that little house didn't get more use. But one day . . .

He'd better get cracking and have Buck look it over, tell them what to do, help them get started with the additions and renovations. If there was ever a perfect opportunity to get top-drawer input, Buck Leeper was providing it.

He turned to go inside, then stopped and looked at the yellow house again.

By jing!

§

"But he'll never be there when you're there, because when you're working, he'll be working."

"That great big man in work boots and chinos stomping around and picking his teeth? In my *house*? Goodness, Timothy . . . "

"His company will pay the rent."

"Do you really think it would be all right?"

"Of course it would be all right. With Buck living there, he'd get to know exactly what we need and how to pull it off, and we wouldn't have to hire an architect, he can draw it up—*and* hire the crew."

She wrinkled her brow. "I don't know. . . . "

"It's a great opportunity."

"Consider it done, then," she said, quoting her priest.

§

At a quarter 'til six, he was standing at the front door, searching the street. Then he walked out and sat on the top step of the front porch.

"Come out with me," he called to Cynthia.

She came and sat with him and took his hand.

"I've been thinking," she said.

"Uh-oh."

"I want to play in that softball game."

"You do?"

"Yes. I can hit a ball. I can run. I can—"

"You can whistle."

She put her fingers to her mouth and blew out the windows.

"You're good, Kavanagh."

"So hire me."

"You're the only female."

"So far," she said. "I hear Adele Hogan wants to play."

"The police officer? J.C.'s wife?"

"She's the baddest softball player you ever want to see. At least, that's what she said."

"J.C. didn't mention that."

"He probably thought it was a guy's game."

"Well," he said, "it was. . . . "

§

At seven o'clock, he was ready to make a search of Farmer, which he and Harley had judged a perfect location for the driving lesson.

But maybe he should call the hospital first. He went to the study to find his cordless.

Cynthia wasn't worried at all. "Give them another fifteen minutes. It's a beautiful summer evening. . . . "

"Yes, but Harley knew the curfew, he wouldn't do this. I'm calling the police."

Barnabas let out a loud series of barks. As the rector raced up the front hall, he saw Harley standing on the porch. He looked like he'd gone a few rounds with a grizzly.

"Now, Rev'rend, I wouldn't want you t' worry. . . . "

He pushed open the screen door. "Where's Dooley? What happened?"

"Th' last thing I'd want t' do is cause you an' th' missus t' worry. . . . "

"Tell me, Harley."

"No, sir, worry's not what I'd ever want to' bring in y'r house. . . . "

"Dadgum it, Harley, I am worried, and will be 'til you tell me what the dickens went on."

"Well, sir, y'r boy's fine."

"Thank God."

"We crashed m' truck."

"No!"

"We did."

"Who did?"

"Now, I don't want you t' worry. . . . "

"Harley . . . "

"Y'r boy did."

"Good Lord!"

"But hit 'us my fault."

"You're sure he wasn't hurt? Where is he?"

"No, sir, he won't hurt, but m' truck was."

"How bad?"

"Tore up th' front an' all."

"Any damage to your engine?"

"Good as new."

"How'd you get home?"

"You mean after we hauled it out'n th' ditch?"

"Yes."

"You mean after we hauled it out'n th' ditch an' had t' help th' farmer chase 'is cow back to th' pasture?"

"What about a cow?"

"That's what come high-tailin' 'cross th' road an' made th' boy hit 'is brakes an' land in th' ditch."

"I see."

The rector glanced toward the driveway and saw Dooley peering at him around a bush.

"I'd sure hate f'r you t' worry. . . . "

Ha. Worry had just become his middle name—at least until Dooley Barlowe went back to school where somebody else could do the worrying.

CHAPTER THIRTEEN

The Fields Are White

He unlocked the office and went in, feeling an odd foreboding as he raised the windows and turned on the fan. Today's temperature was nearly what they'd had in Florida.

He heard the bathroom door creak on its hinges and wheeled around. Edith Mallory was standing there in something like a bathrobe.

"Edith . . ."

She smiled and moved toward him, smelling of the dark cigarettes she smoked, untying the sash. . . .

"*Timothy!*"

He opened his eyes and looked into the face of his anxious wife. "Thank God!" he said, sitting up.

"These dreams you've been having . . . it's scary. What was it this time?"

"I can't remember," he lied. Bathed with perspiration, he reached to the bedside table and turned the fan on high.

"That's better," she said. "Are you all right?"

"Yes. Sorry I woke you."

"Don't be. I remember the times I used to wake in the night with bad dreams and there was no one to turn to."

She switched off her bedside lamp and rolled over to him and held his hand.

Soon she was sleeping again, but he was not.

This wasn't the first dream he'd had of Edith Mallory. He distinctly remembered the one in which he was locked with her in the parish hall coat closet, pounding on the door for help.

While he was in Ireland a couple of years ago, her husband, Pat, had died of a heart attack. When the rector returned home, she had tried every strategy imaginable to seduce and dominate him. Always seeking to entice, always looking at him in a way that made him want to run for the hills, once detaining him overnight at Clear Day, her house on the highest ridge above Mitford.

He recalled the visit to Children's Hospital, where she gave $15,000 as imperiously as if it were a quarter million, and afterward being trapped in the backseat of her car while she stroked his leg. He had demanded that Ed Coffey, her chauffeur, stop the car, and had jumped from the Lincoln while it was still rolling.

After the miserable wrestling match over the Grill, which she had thumpingly lost, she had gone to Spain and, as far as he knew, hadn't returned—nor had she sent her annual contribution to Lord's Chapel. Fine. So be it. It was money he didn't want, though the finance chairman was certainly anxious about it.

He'd been able to put her out of his mind until someone at the Grill had brought up her name.

Suddenly he was feeling the old contamination he'd felt for years as her eyes roved over him in the pulpit. . . .

Blast.

He rolled on his side and tried to imagine the breeze from the fan was an island trade wind somewhere in the Indian Ocean.

"My wife's house is nonsmoking. Will that be a problem?" Buck Leeper was known for sucking down two packs of unfiltered Lucky Strikes a day.

"No problem. I've cut back, anyhow."

They walked into Cynthia's kitchen, where a faint breeze stirred through the open windows.

"The house is small, but—"

"There's something I've been wanting to tell you," said the super-intendent.

There was a brief silence while Buck looked at his work boots, then directly at Father Tim.

"I appreciate what you did for me."

The rector nodded, silent.

"I could have killed you, slingin' th' furniture around like that."

He remembered Buck's drunken violence at Tanner Cottage during the construction of Hope House. Unable to flee, he had sat, praying, as Buck's torrential anger poured forth for hours.

"Sorry," Buck said, hoarse with feeling.

"Don't even think about it." He hadn't expected an apology for that long-ago night, but it felt better to have it, somehow. He knew instinctively that Buck didn't want to say anything more.

"Well . . . you can see how cramped the house is. Built for one, really."

"What are you lookin' to do?"

"We'd like to knock out this rear wall and add a large studio with a bank of windows, maybe French doors leading to a patio, perhaps connecting with a two-car garage and extra storage. I know you can help us figure it out.

"Also, we thought it would be good to have a fireplace at that end, possibly of native stone, with bookshelves on either side. Oh, and hardwood floors, of course, with another bathroom adjoining the studio. The only bathroom is upstairs, which reminds me . . . "

This was exciting. His blood was up for it.

" . . . we're thinking of widening the stairway, if possible, and building storage closets on the landing, but I'm getting ahead of my-self. Since we're in the kitchen, what would you think about a cooking island, and bay windows looking out to the hedge?"

Buck took the toothpick from his mouth and stared around the small room. "You want to live in it a year from now?"

"Right!"

"You'll have to haul ass," he said.

§

Mack Struope
Already Working For
Improved Economy

"I'm not going to wait til I'm elected to work hard for Mitford," says mahoral candidate MackStrouope at his downtown campaign headquarters. "I'm already working hard to bring in new growth and development.

"For example, I recommended the fine property of Sweet Stuff Bakery to one real estate company, and was able to get another realtor to look at Fernbank. When the Fernbank deal goes through, it will put big dollars in everybody's pockets.

"I'm not one to say if it ain't broke, don't fix it. I say let's make a good thing better."

Strouple is running against mayoral incumbent, Esther Cunninghanm, who has seen eight terms in local office, with three of those terms unopposed.

Stroupe's free Saturday barbecues will be held until election week at his campaign headquarters on Main Street.

ThisSaturdzy will feature the live country music of everybody's favorit, the Wesley Washtub Band. All are invited.

He hadn't missed Mack's terminology, "*when* the Fernbank deal goes through . . . "

Part of Miss Sadie's letter had been running through his mind like a chanted refrain.

"I leave Fernbank to supply any requirements of Hope House," she had written. "Do with it what you will, but please treat it kindly."

Treat it kindly.

Was selling it for half its worth treating it kindly? All her adult life, Sadie Baxter had done without, so that her mother's and father's money could be invested wisely. Hadn't her penury and smart management provided a five-million-dollar budget for Hope House, and a home for forty people who needed one?

Who was he to swallow down an arrogant offer that robbed the coffers of a deserving institution?

But then, what was the alternative?

Back and forth, back and forth—always the same questions, and never any answers. At least, not as far as he was concerned.

He couldn't deal with this any longer.

He got up from the sofa and knelt by his desk in the quiet study.

"Lord, Miss Sadie's house belongs to You, she told me that several times. You know I've got a real problem here."

He paused. "Actually, You've got it, because I'm giving it to You right now, free and clear. I'll do my part, just show me what it is. In Jesus' name, amen."

"Poached, whole wheat, no grits," he told Velma, as he walked to the rear booth and slid in.

"J.C., I've got a story idea for you."

"Don't give me any small-town, feel-good stuff," snapped the editor. "I've had enough of that to choke a horse."

"I hear political candidates have to fill out a form that discloses the amount of a campaign contribution and who made it. I'm also told that anyone, including media, can ask to see that form."

He could tell J.C. was getting the message, and didn't particularly like it, either. "So why don't you get Mack to show it to you?" asked the editor.

"So why don't *you*?" asked the rector.

"Father?"

It was Lottie Greer. Years of experience told him all he needed to know.

"I'm on my way," he said.

He parked behind a long line of cars and pickup trucks on the country road, and walked to Greer's Store.

Men were congregated on the porch, dressed in overalls and work clothes; many were smoking, and all talked in undertones.

They nodded to him as he came up the steps. He heard the faint singing inside.

"How is he?" he asked an elderly man sitting on a bench.

"Bad off, Preacher."

He opened the fragile screen door that had slapped behind him on happier occasions, and entered the store that resembled a room in a Rembrandt canvas. The aged floors and burnished wood, the low wattage in the bulbs, the fading afternoon light through the windows—it was beautiful; saintly, somehow, more a church than a store. But then, hadn't Absalom Greer preached the gospel in this place for nearly seventy years?

Several women sat around the cold summer stove, talking in low voices. One sang softly with the chorus inside. "*. . . that calls me from a world of care, and bids me at my Father's throne, make all my wants and wishes known . . .* "

Three men in ill-fitting dark suits met him at the door of the rooms where Absalom lived with his sister, Lottie. All were clutching Bibles, and all spoke or nodded as if they knew him.

Lottie Greer sat in the chair by the fireplace, where she always implored him to sit when he visited.

"Miss Lottie . . . "

She looked up, gaunt and shockingly frail, her cane across her knees. "He said yesterday he wanted to see you, Father. He asked to die at home, the old way."

He put his hand on her shoulder.

"He's lingered on," she murmured, lowering her head. "It's been hard."

"Yes," he said. "I understand." And he did. His mother had lingered, fighting the good fight.

Seven or eight men were gathered outside Absalom's open bedroom door, and quietly, but forcefully, singing the old hymn the rector had known since a child.

"He wanted us to sing his favorites," said one of the men with a Bible. "Join in, if you take a notion. Th' doctor's with 'im right now, looks like he's in an' out of knowin' where he's at."

"Lena, get the Father something," said Lottie.

"I've just poured him a glass of tea, Miss Lottie. I hope you like it sweet," she said, placing the icy glass in his hand.

"Oh, I do. Thank you."

"And some cake, you'll want some cake," she said, eager to please.

"Thank you, not now."

"You help yourself, then, anytime," she said, pointing to the kitchen table, which was laden with food. "It's to eat, not throw out." She colored slightly, and made a faint curtsy. "I hope you'll try my pineapple upside down, it's over by the sink."

"Sing up!" said one of the chorus. "Brother Greer likes it loud."

"Jesus, lover of my soul . . . " they began, limning the words of Charles Wesley.

He joined in.

> *. . . Let me to Thy bosom fly,*
> *While the nearer waters roll,*
> *While the tempest still is high:*
> *Hide me, O my Savior hide,*
> *Till the storm of life is past;*
> *Safe into the haven guide,*
> *O receive my soul at last.*
>
> *Other refuge have I none;*
> *Hangs my helpless soul on Thee;*
> *Leave, O leave me not alone,*
> *Still support and comfort me . . .*

He felt as if he were a child again, in his mother's Mississippi Baptist church, where his own grandfather once preached. A kind of joy was rising in him, but how could it not? Absalom Greer would soon pass safely into the haven. . . .

Someone who appeared to be the doctor stepped out of Absalom's room. "Go in, Father," he said. "He's asked for you."

The bed on the other side of the spartan room seemed far away. It was as if he treaded water to reach it.

He heard the dense rattle in Absalom's chest.

"Brother Timothy, is that you?" The old man kept his filmy blue eyes fixed on the ceiling.

"It is."

"I've been lookin' for you."

Over the years, he'd seen it—as death drew near, the skin had a way of connecting with the bones, of fusing into a kind of cold marble that was at once terrible and beautiful.

"The Lord's given me a truth for you," said Absalom. It was as if each word were delicately formed, so it would move through the maze of the rattle and come forth whole and lucid.

Father Tim bent closer. "I'm listening, my Brother."

"The fields are white. . . . "

Jesus had said it to the disciples. . . .

Then Absalom turned his head and looked past him, his face growing suffused with a kind of joy. "Glory, glory . . . there they are . . . I knew they'd come again. . . . "

The rector's heart raced with feeling—he knew instinctively that Absalom Greer was seeing the angels, the angels he'd once seen as a young boy, swarming around his mother and baby sister in the next room.

The old preacher lifted his trembling hands above the coverlet, issuing a last pastoral command.

The men stopped singing. The talking in the kitchen ceased.

Lottie came into the room, leaning on her cane. "Is it his angels?" she whispered.

"I believe so," he said.

§

He took the back roads, wanting to see pastures and open fields, wanting a span of silence between dying and living.

Perhaps Sadie Baxter had been among the first to greet Absalom, to bestow some heavenly welcome upon one to whom God would surely say, "Well done, good and faithful servant."

He would miss Absalom Greer. It had been a privilege to know him. He was the last of a breed, willing, like Saint Paul, to be "a fool for Christ."

In the fields, Queen of the Meadow towered over goldenrod and fleabane, over milkweed and wild blue aster. Beautiful, but dry. They needed rain. He wished he had his dog with him, licking up the windows to a fare-thee-well.

He made a turn onto the state highway and spoke it aloud: "The fields are white. . . . "

"Lift up your eyes, and look on the fields," Jesus had said to his disciples, "for they are white already to harvest."

The standing fields were the legions who hadn't filled their God-vacuum with the One who was born to fill it; the standing fields were those who waited for someone to reach out and speak the truth, and tell them how they might be saved.

He had received Absalom's message as a reminder, and did not take it lightly.

He glanced at the gas gauge. Nearly empty.

There was a little grocery store and service station up the road. He'd once stopped there for a pack of Nabs and a Cheerwine.

It came up sooner than he expected. He wheeled in and parked beside the building, then got the key from the store owner and walked around and unlocked the restroom. First things first.

Coming out of the restroom, he saw the black Lincoln pull off the road and ease past the gas pumps.

He stepped back instinctively, and watched Ed Coffey get out of the Lincoln and go into the station.

Ed Coffey. Edith Mallory's chauffeur. The one who was driving when he leaped from the moving car in the Shoe Barn parking lot, the one who'd driven him home after the gruesome, rain-drenched night at Clear Day.

Ed wasn't wearing his uniform. The rector didn't think he'd ever seen Ed out of uniform since Pat Mallory died.

He stood by the building, wondering why he didn't step forward and speak to the man, a Mitford native who had always seemed a decent fellow, though clearly snared by the lure of Mallory money. Hadn't Ed looked at him a couple of times as if to say, I don't want to do this, I know better, but it's too late?

Ed left the station with a bulging paper sack in his arm, which he put in the trunk. Then he got in the car and quietly pulled onto the road, headed south.

A new Lincoln, clearly, not the old model Edith had kept around after Pat's death. And this one had dark windows. He despised dark windows in a car. . . .

So Edith was back in Mitford. He could probably expect to see her at Lord's Chapel. Edith on the gospel side, Mack Stroupe on the epistle side.

What happened when clergy looked into their congregations, only to see a growing number of people whose motives they distrusted, and whose spirits made their own feel anxious and uneasy?

§

He noticed that a new battery of yard signs had gone up, along with the general clutter.

We're stickin' with Esther
BILL AND ARLENE

We're stickin' with Esther
Ralph And Fay Lewis

OUR BANE WILL
BE YOUR BLESSING
Best Sale Ever!
Oct. 4, from 10 a.m.
After Work Supper
6:00 p.m.

MACK MEANS
MONEY IN
MITFORD POCKETS.
$Mack for Mayor$

VOTE YOUR VALUES
Esther for Mayor

Play Ball!
Come one, come all
Baxter Field, August 10
HOTDOGS $1

❦

"Seventy-five bucks from the glove factory, a thousand from Lee-land Mining Company—which should be no surprise, that's his fourth cousin. Five hundred from the canning plant, who'd also like to see some more development in these parts, ten bucks from Lew Boyd's cousin, fifteen from Henry Watts, blah, blah, blah—exactly what you'd expect." J.C. looked pleased with himself. "You can get off your high horse, buddyroe."

Why pursue it? "So, tell me, have you seen Ed Coffey around lately?"

"Ed Coffey? If he's around, so's your old girlfriend."

He felt as if he'd been dashed with cold water. "You might rephrase that," he said.

"You're plenty touchy," snapped the editor.

"I learned it from you," he replied.

❦

Lace Turner was visiting Harley and had come up to the kitchen to have a piece of cake with Cynthia. He was taking the pitcher of tea out of the refrigerator when they heard a light knock at the door.

Jenny stood outside, peering through the screen. "Hello! Is Dooley home?"

Barnabas skidded into the kitchen, barking.

"He ain't here!" Lace said.

"Why, Lace!" said Cynthia. "He *is* here. Won't you come in, Jenny?"

"No ma'am. I just brought Dooley this."

Cynthia opened the screen door and took the parcel. "We're having cake, it's chocolate—"

"No, ma'am, I can't. Thank you." She ran down the steps and across the yard.

Cynthia looked at Lace. "Why did you lie?"

"I didn't know he was here."

"But you did. You saw him come in ten minutes ago. So, that's two lies." His wife never pulled punches.

Lace shrugged.

"I'm not going to preach you a sermon," said Cynthia, "but I want you to know something. I'm disappointed that you'd lie to her and to me. You're better than that."

Lace stared at the half-eaten cake on her plate. "I hate that girl."

"Why?"

"She thinks she's so smart, so pretty, so . . . *fine*." Lace spit the word.

"Lace, look at me, please." Lace looked at her. "You're smart. You're pretty. You're—"

"I ain't! I ain't nothin'!" She stood up from the table, weeping, and ran down the basement stairs.

"So," said his wife, looking grim. "She's crying—it's what Olivia's been hoping for."

"That's good news," he said, putting his arm around her shoulders.

She smiled weakly. "Yes, but sometimes even good news feels bad."

§

Esther Bolick picked up on the first ring.

"So, Esther, how's it coming?"

"You'll never believe it—we got an armoire from Marie Sanders!"

If he had anything to do with it, Esther would have two armoires. "How's Hessie working out for you?"

"A saint, Hessie's a saint. She's heading up the After Work Sale, includin' th' supper."

"Wow."

"Did you know Hessie and I are wearin' beepers? I feel like Dick Tracy."

"I've heard everything."

"Course, th' polyester and double-knit is still pourin' in."

"Find me an orange leisure suit with stitched lapels, I'll pay big money."

"Too late, Mule Skinner already spoke for it."

"Oh, well."

"But the quality's picking up, we just got a Hoover vacuum cleaner and a whole set of Hummel figurines. Oh, and a mink jacket, th' hole's where you can't even see it."

"How's Gene?"

"Suing for divorce."

"It could be worse," he said.

Esther laughed heartily. How he loved hearing a Bane chairperson laugh. A minor miracle!

He was putting the receiver on the hook when it came to him out of left field.

Land of Counterpane. Black car, blue pickup.

Surely not . . .

And the black car that had eased around the monument at two in the morning, so quiet he scarcely heard the engine . . .

But that was weeks ago. That was the evening of his birthday, which was well over a month back, maybe five or six weeks. If Edith was around, why hadn't anyone seen her?

Was Ed Coffey steering clear of Mitford, buying their groceries at country stores, keeping to the back roads, going ununiformed to attract less attention?

He'd drive by Clear Day and see what was going on, but there wasn't any way to spot the house, since it sat a half mile beyond a locked electronic gate. That gate had been locked even on evenings when Edith invited the vestry to meet at her house. Guests were required to punch a password into a black box at the entrance.

There was a churning sensation in his stomach.

Not knowing what else to do, he went into the office bathroom and stuck his finger for a glucometer check. In his opinion, the glucometer was a decided improvement over peeing on a strip to check his sugar.

One twenty-four. Not bad.

§

He made a call from the office, still knowing the number by heart, and went home and got his old gardening hat from the closet shelf.

Rifling through the chest of drawers, he found the sunglasses he seldom wore because someone said they made him look like a housefly.

He put on the hat and glasses as he went down the stairs, thinking he'd check himself out in the kitchen mirror.

"Lord God!" shrieked Puny, standing frozen at the foot of the stairs. "You like to scared me to death!"

Hearing their mother's alarm, both babies set up an earsplitting wail in the kitchen.

He tried bouncing their car seats, squeaking a rubber duck, making a face, and barking like a dog, but they were inconsolable, and he was out of there.

"This Cessna 152 don't make as much noise as m' little ragwing," shouted Omer.

The rector was holding up pretty well, all things considered. He had skipped lunch, knowing he'd be airborne, had driven twenty-five miles to the airstrip, and here he was, skimming above the treetops with the mayor's brother-in-law in a borrowed plane, wearing a decrepit garden hat and shades.

Father Roland, who occasionally wrote from the wilds of Canada, was totally wrong to think he was having all the fun, celebrating the Eucharist in crude forest huts and being chased by a bull moose. Mitford had its grand adventures, too. You just had to go looking for—

"Holy smoke, Omer!"

Omer flashed his piano-key grin at the rector, who was only momentarily hanging upside down.

"That's what you call a one-G maneuver."

"No more, thanks!" His face had been green twice in only a few weeks.

"OK, I'll fly steady," yelled his pilot. "How low d'you think you'll want to go?"

"Low enough to see what's going on."

"I can take you down to two hundred feet, how's that?"

He swallowed hard. "Fine."

"You sure don't look like yourself in that getup," Omer shouted.

"Good!" he shouted back.

They saw the ridge looming ahead, the ridge from which Clear Day could see forever, but could not be seen.

"Here she comes!" Omer said. Father Tim pulled the brim of the hat farther down and adjusted the glasses.

What could have been a small landing strip emerged from the trees. It was the shake roof that covered the much-talked-about eight thousand square feet of living space, with its vast expanse of driveway and parking area to the left.

Bingo.

A blue pickup truck was parked next to a black car. And there, on the uncovered terrace, standing by the striped umbrellas, were two people.

"Circle back!" he shouted to his pilot.

He wanted to be dead sure.

Omer circled back and buzzed the house. The man and woman on the terrace looked up angrily as he looked down.

Then the blue Cessna roared over the quaking treetops and across the gorge.

Omer glanced at him and winked.

Edith Mallory was not touring Spain or France or Malaysia or any of her other haunts, and neither was she living in her sprawling home in Florida.

She was living in Mitford, at Clear Day, and masterminding the political career of Mack Stroupe.

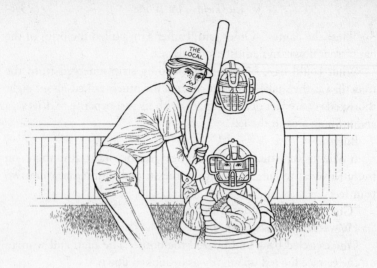

CHAPTER FOURTEEN

Play Ball

On the morning of the game at Baxter Field, Velma Mosely had a change of heart and started chopping onions.

This, she told herself, would absolutely, positively be her last pot of homemade chili.

§

"Listen up!"

Buck Leeper looked ten feet tall as he stood in the dugout before the Mitford Reds.

"We're not here to fool around," said the team manager, "we're here to win. Got it?"

"Got it!" said his players, who were wearing red-dyed T-shirts and ball caps advertising The Local.

It was twenty minutes before game time, and the rector felt his adrenaline pumping like oil through a Texas derrick.

"Father, you're th' team captain, and I'm lookin' to you to be th' coach on th' field. Keep 'em pepped up and give 'em advice when they need it—your job is to call the shots." Buck looked him in the eye. "I know you can do it."

Could he do it? He had prayed about this softball game as if it were life or death, instead of good, clean fun on a Saturday afternoon. Surely the three practice games, which had gone pretty well, would count for something.

Buck took a Lucky Strike out of his shirt pocket and paced in front of them. "Dooley, you're my first batter. I've watched you get ready for today's game, and you're always hustlin', always quick on your feet. I want you to wait on the pitch that's yours, got it?"

"Got it," said Dooley.

"We want you on that base."

"Yes, sir."

"Adele, you're plenty quick and sure-handed, you'll play first base. I'm hittin' you in th' second slot. When Dooley gets on, advance th' runner at any cost. We've got to get somebody in scoring position."

Adele socked her right fist into her glove.

Buck laughed his water-boiling-in-a-kettle laugh. "We want those turkeys to play with their backs to the wall. Right?"

"Right!" said his team.

"Avis, you're my first power hitter. I want you to slam it clear to Wesley. Father, you're my cleanup batter—stay strong and quick, and remember to keep your shoulders straight."

Buck might have been commandeering a crew of backhoe operators in a thirty-foot excavation.

"Mrs. Kavanagh—"

"Cynthia," she said.

"Cynthia, you're battin' in my number five spot. I want you to dig in and crush that ball. As the catcher, I want you to call our pitches—look at how they're standin', check out their feet. Bottom line, be alert at all times."

"You got it, Coach."

Buck completed the lineup with Hal Owen as second baseman and Mule Skinner, Jena Ivey, Pauline Barlowe, and Lew Boyd in the outfield.

"I've been watchin' th' other team," said Buck, "and we're better than they are. We can do the job. I want you to give it a hundred percent, understand? Not eighty-five, not ninety-five—a *hundred*."

He looked at every earnest face, rolling the unlit cigarette between his fingers. "Father, you want to pray?"

"He wants to!" said Dooley.

After the prayer, they scrambled to their feet and trooped past the concession stand. At that moment, the rector was certain he experienced a brief out-of-body reverie. He saw their team charging out on the field, and there he was in the middle of the fray, wearing, for Pete's sake, his green Pentecost vestments.

§

"Man!" exclaimed Dooley.

The stands were full, people were sitting on the grass, and the smell of hotdogs and chili wafted through the humid summer air.

Tommy's dad, who was the plate umpire, looked at the coin he'd just flipped. The Mitford Reds were the home team.

The rector scanned the crowd, just as he always did at Lord's Chapel.

The residents of Hope House were lined up in wheelchairs and seated on the front bleachers, looking expectant.

There was Mack Stroupe, standing with one foot on a bleacher and a cigarette in his mouth, and over to the right, Harley and Lace. He spotted Fancy Skinner and Uncle Billy and Miss Rose and Coot and Omer, and about midway up, Tommy, who had hurt his leg and couldn't play. He noted that quite a few sported a strawberry sucker stuck in their jaw, evidence that the mayor had doled out her customary campaign favors.

From the front row, where she sat with Russell Jacks and Betty Craig, Jessie waved to the field with both hands.

"Ladies and gentlemen," announced town councilman, Linder Hayes, "it is my immense privilege to introduce Esther Cunningham, our beloved mayor, who for sixteen years and eight great terms in office has diligently helped Mitford take care of its own! Your Honor, you are hereby officially invited to . . . *throw out the first ball*."

"Burn it in, Esther!" somebody yelled.

The other umpire ran a ball to the mayor, who stood proudly in the dignitaries section, cheek by jowl with the county sheriff.

At this, the *Muse* editor bounded from the concession stand to the bleachers and skidded to a stop about a yard from the mayor. He dropped to his knees and pointed the Nikon upward.

"Dadgum it," hissed the mayor, "don't shoot from down there, it gives me three double chins!"

"And behind the plate," boomed Linder Hayes, "our esteemed police chief and vigilant overseer of law and order, Mr. Rodney Underwood!"

Applause. Hoots. Whistles. Rodney adjusted his holster belt and waved to the crowd with a gloved hand.

"Hey, Esther, smoke it in there!"

The mayor threw back her head, circled her arm like a prop on a P-51, and let the ball fly.

"*Stee-rike* one!" said the umpire.

"Oh, *please*," said Cynthia, who was perspiring from infield practice.

"What is it?" whispered the rector.

"I have to use the port-a-john."

"It's your nerves," declared her husband, who appeared to know.

"Take the field!" yelled Buck.

The players sprinted to their positions. Then, the home-plate ump took a deep breath, pointed at the pitcher, and shouted what they'd all been waiting to hear.

"*Play ball!*"

§

The Reds' batboy, Poo Barlowe, passed his brother a bat which he had personally inscribed with the name *Dools* and a zigzag flash of lightning. He had rendered this personal I.D. with a red ballpoint pen, bearing down hard and repeatedly until it appeared etched into the wood.

Dooley took a couple of warm-up swings, then stepped into the batter's box. He gripped the bat, positioned his feet, and waited for the pitch.

A high, looping pitch barely missed the strike zone.

"Ball one!"

The second pitch came in chest-high, as Dooley tightened his grip, took a hefty swing, and connected. *Crack!* It was the first ball hitting the bat for the newly formed Mitford Reds; the sound seemed to reverberate into the stands.

"Go, buddy!"

Dooley streaked to first base, his long legs eating the distance, and blew past it to second as the crowd cheered. He slid into second a heartbeat ahead of the ball that socked into Scott Murphy's glove.

"Ride 'em, cowboy!" warbled Miss Pattie, who believed herself to be at a rodeo.

The game was definitely off to a good start.

§

"Mama!"

Fancy Skinner waved to her mother, who was shading her eyes and peering into the stands. "I'm up here!"

Fancy was wearing shocking pink tights and a matching tunic, and stood out so vividly from the crowd that her mother recognized her at once and made the climb to the fifth row, carrying a knitting bag with the beginnings of an afghan.

"I declare," said Fancy, "I hardly knew that was you, don't you just love bein' blond, didn't I tell you it would be more fun? I mean, look at you, out at a softball game instead of sittin' home watchin' th' Wheel or whatever. And oh, my lord, what're you wearin', I can't believe it, a Dale Jarrett T-shirt, aren't you th' cat's pajamas, you look a hundred years younger!

"Next, you might want to lose some weight, if you don't mind my sayin' so, around forty pounds seems right to me, it would take a strain off your heart. Lord have mercy, would you look at that, he backed th' right fielder clean to th' fence. *Hey, ump, open your eyes, I thought only horses went to sleep standin' up!*

"Oh, shoot, I forgot about your hearin' aid bein' so sensitive, was that me that made it go off? It sounds like a burglar alarm, I thought th' old one was better, here, have some gum, it's sugarless. Look! There he is, there's Mule, mama, see? Th' one in the grass over yonder, idn't he cute, *Mule, honey, we're up here, look up here, sweetie,* oh mercy, the ball like to knocked his head off. *Pay attention to what you're doin', Mule!*

"Mama, you want a hotdog? I'll get us one at th' end of fifth innin', Velma made th' chili. I didn't say it's chilly, I said Velma— mama, are you sure that hearin' aid works right, it seems like th' old one did better, and look at what you paid for it, an arm and a leg, you want relish? I can't hardly eat relish, it gives me sour stomach.

"How in th' world you can knit and watch a ballgame is beyond me, I have to concentrate. See there, that's th' preacher Mule hangs out with at the Grill, th' one I gave a mask to th' day you got a perm, you remember, I can't tell whether he tries to hit a ball or club it to death. That's his wife on third base, I think she bleaches with a cap, I never heard of a preacher's wife playin' softball, times sure have changed, our preacher's wife leads th' choir and volunteers at th' hospital.

"Go get 'em, Avis! Hit it outta there! I wonder why Avis idn't married, I think he likes summer squash better than women, but it's important to really like your work. Lord, he sent that ball to th' moon! Look, Mama, right over yonder, see that man eyeballin' you? So what if he's younger, that's th' goin' thing these days, I told you blondes have more fun. Whoa, did you see that, he winked at you, well, maybe he got somethin' in his eye. *Hey, ump, pitcher's off th' plate, how thick are your glasses?*

"That red-headed kid, that's Dooley, he's sort of th' preacher's boy, he's a real slugger and he can run, too. Was that a spitball, Mama, did it look like a spitball to you? *Spitball! Spitball!* Who is that umpire, anyway, he's blind as a bat and deaf as a tater, oops, I better go down an' get in line, did you say you want relish?"

§

Ben Isaac Berman, whose family had brought him to Hope House all the way from Decatur, Illinois, was liking this ball game better than anything he'd done since coming to Mitford in July.

He liked the fresh air, the shouting, the tumult—even the heat was a *makhyeh*—though he didn't like the way his hotdog had landed in his lap, requiring two Hope House attendants to clean it up. What he couldn't figure was how chili had somehow made its way into one of his pants cuffs.

He felt like a *shlimazel* for not having better control of his limbs. But then, there was Miss Pattie sitting right next to him, who couldn't control a thought in her head, God forbid it should happen to him.

He also liked the game because it reminded him of his boyhood, which was as vivid in his recall as if he had lived it last week.

Take that boy at second base, that red-haired kid who could run like the wind. That was the kind of kid he'd been, that was the kind of kid he still was, deep down where nobody else had ever seen or ever would, not even his wife, blessed be her memory. Even he forgot about the kid living inside him, until he came out to a game like this and smelled the mountain air and heard the crack of the bat—that was when he began to feel his own legs churning, flying around to the bases and tearing up the dirt as he slid into home. . . .

§

At the bottom of the seventh inning, the score was 10–10.

"It's our bat and we've got three outs," said the rector. "We don't want any extra innings, so let's finish now and go home winners."

His shirt was sticking to him. He felt like he'd been rode hard and put up wet, as Tommy Noles used to say.

He watched as Mule Skinner stepped up to bat.

The ball came in high.

"Ball one!"

Mule swung at the next pitch and cracked it over second base into center field. The rector was amazed at Mule's speed as he sprinted to first. This game would be fodder for the Grill regulars 'til kingdom come.

After Jena Ivey made the first out of the inning, it was Pauline Barlowe's turn to bat.

She looked confident, he thought. In fact, she'd made a pretty good showing all afternoon, but had a tendency to waffle, to be strong one minute and lose it the next.

She took a couple of pitches, and slammed a hit to second base. Dadgum, a double play! But the second baseman kicked the ball, and all runners were safe.

"Time out!" yelled Buck, striding onto the field.

"OK, Pitch," he said to Lew Boyd, "you've been a defensive star all day, I want you to use that bat and get the big hit. Or give me a fly ball to the outfield to advance the runners."

"I'm gonna give you premium unleaded on this 'un."

The first pitch came down the middle.

"Strike one!"

Lew hit the next pitch into right field, where the outfielder nailed it and threw it to third. The runners held.

Two outs.

Dooley hurried into the batter's box and scratched the loose dirt to get a strong foothold.

Buck yelled, "You've got to get on base. Can you do it?"

"I can do it!"

Poobaw Barlowe squeezed his eyes shut and prayed, *Jesus, God, and ever'body . . .*

The rector was holding his breath. Dooley had been on base every time he came to bat today. He saw the determined look on the boy's face as he waited for the pitch.

Realizing her feet were swelling, Fancy Skinner removed her high heel shoes and put them in her mother's knitting bag.

Coot Hendrick hoped to the good Lord he would not lose the twenty-five dollars he had bet on the Reds. He had borrowed it out of the sugar bowl, leaving only a few packages of NutraSweet and three dimes. He squirmed with anxiety. His mama might be old, but she could still whip his head.

Crack!

Dooley connected on a line shot into the outfield, which was hit so sharply that Father Tim stopped Mule at third.

"Way to go, buddy, way to do it, great job!" he yelled.

Dooley punched his fist into the air and pumped it, as the crowd hooted and cheered.

With two outs and the bases loaded, it was Adele Hogan's turn at bat.

"OK, Adele, let's get 'em, let's go, you can do it!" For tomorrow's services, he would sound like a bullfrog with laryngitis.

"Ball one!"

The second ball came in on the outside.

"Ball two!"

She swung at the next pitch.

"Strike one!"

The stands were going crazy. "Hey, ump," somebody yelled. "Wake up, you're missin' a great game!"

The ball came down the middle.

"Strike two!"

Two balls, two strikes. Adele stooped down, grabbed some dirt and rubbed it in her hands, then took the bat and gripped it hard. The rector thought he could see white knuckles as she rocked slightly on her feet and watched the pitch.

She caught the ball on the inside of her bat, away from the heavy part, sending it into short left center field.

Nobody called for the ball.

The outfielders all moved at once, collided, and stumbled over each other as the ball fell in. Adele Hogan ran for her life and reached first base as Mule scored.

The game was over.

The crowd was wild.

The score was 11–10.

Ray Cunningham huffed to the field with the mayor's ball and asked Adele to sign it. Unable to restrain himself, he pounded her on the back and gave her a big hug, wondering how in the world J. C. Hogan had ever gotten so lucky.

Ben Isaac Berman pulled himself up on his aluminum walker and waved to the red-haired kid on the field. He squinted into the sun, almost certain that the boy waved back.

The *Muse* editor, who had been sitting under a shade tree, panted to first base and cranked off a roll of Tri-X. All the frames featured his wife, who, as far as he was concerned, looked dynamite even with sweat running down her face. He wondered something that had never occurred to him before; he wondered how he'd ever gotten so lucky, and decided he would tell her that very thing—tonight.

Well, maybe tomorrow.

Soon, anyway.

CHAPTER FIFTEEN

Day into Night

"You know how I respect your judgment, I don't fight you on much."

"That's true, you don't."

Ron Malcolm had come to the rectory, and they'd taken refuge behind the closed door of the study.

His senior warden looked pained, but firm. "The time to sit on this thing is over. We've got to make a decision, and the only decision to make is to sell it to Miami Development. You know why, I know why. We can't afford to do otherwise."

Father Tim sat back in the chair. He was exhausted from the ordeal of it, from the conflict between hard-nosed reality and his own intuitions, however vague. He had prayed, he had stalled, he had wrestled, he had hoped—all the avenues open to most mortals—and like it or not, there was nothing else he could do.

"All right," he said.

At the front door, they shook hands on what had been agreed, and Ron went down the walk to his car.

The rector stood there, looking through the screen into the dusk. Treat it kindly. . . .

"Now, Miss Sadie," he said aloud, "don't be wagging your cane at me. I did the best I could."

He was running late for the meeting, having just fled one at First Baptist, and stopped at the water fountain in the parish hall corridor.

Around the bend to the right, he heard footsteps on the tile floor, and someone talking.

"The old woman was lucky to die a natural death, the furnace in that dump could have blown her head off."

Ingrid Swenson. Then he heard the murmured assent of her nail-biting crony, and their mutual laughter as they passed through the door into the parish hall.

The voices around the table droned on. He tried to pay attention, but couldn't. It was all done but the signing of the contract. There was hardly any reason for him to be here.

His gaze roamed the assembly. Buddy Benfield was grinning from ear to ear. Ron Malcolm was facing down Ingrid Swenson in a last contest of wills concerning the crumbling pavement of the Fernbank driveway. Mamie Gordon, who had a new job at the Collar Button, was looking anxiously at her watch. Sandra Harris was trying to figure how she could pop outside for a smoke. Clarence Daly was trooping in with a tray of cups and a pot of coffee.

The phone rang in the parish kitchen, but no one moved to answer it.

Sandra drummed her nails on the table, impatient. "We look forward to seeing Fernbank turned into a spa," she said to Ingrid, "but I hope you don't try to push body wraps and mud, I don't think anybody around here would go for that."

The phone continued to ring.

"So," said Ron, "even though our attorneys have gone over the contract thoroughly, let's take one last look before we sign, to the advantage of all concerned."

"I can't imagine what purpose that will serve."

Ron smiled. "Won't take but a couple of minutes."

The phone persisted.

"Here you go," said Clarence, setting cups before Ingrid and her associate. "Fresh out of th' pot."

"Oh, for Pete's *sake*," said Sandra, "why doesn't somebody answer the phone?"

Nobody moved.

"Who would let a phone ring like that, anyway?" Scowling, she marched to the kitchen.

Ron glanced at Ingrid. "I've struck through and initialed your clause about the driveway repairs being a responsibility of Lord's Chapel."

She gave him a cold look and pushed the coffee away.

"Father! It's Andrew Gregory on the phone!"

"Tell him—"

"He's calling all the way from Italy. Says it's *important*!"

"Excuse me," he said, leaving the table.

Sandra handed him the receiver with a look of rekindled interest in the morning's proceedings. The most exotic call she'd ever had was from Billings, Montana.

"Andrew?"

"Father, Emma told me I could find you in the parish hall. Sorry to disturb you, but something . . . terribly important has just happened. Is the Fernbank property still available?"

"Well . . . " For about five minutes, maximum.

"I'd like to make an offer. I'll wire earnest money at once."

Had he heard right? Was he dreaming this?

"Two hundred and ninety-five thousand, Father." Andrew took a deep breath. "As is."

He felt a sudden, intense warmth throughout his body, as if he were melting in a spring thaw.

"Andrew?"

"Yes?"

"Consider it done!"

§

He didn't think he'd ever confess to anyone, not even his wife, how thrilled he'd been to see the look on Ingrid Swenson's face.

No. *Ecstatic* was the word. He'd been forced to restrain himself from leaping into the air, clicking his heels together, and whooping.

Upon being told that Fernbank would in fact be sold, but not to Miami Development, Ingrid Swenson had used language that, as far as he knew, had never been spoken on the grounds of Lord's Chapel. Mamie Gordon had actually put her hands over her ears, her mouth forming a perfect O.

When he saw Andrew, he would kiss his ring, the very cuff of his trousers! He would sweep his chimney, wash his windows, put him at the head of the Christmas parade in Tommy Ledbetter's yellow Mustang convertible . . . the possibilities for thanking Andrew Gregory were unlimited.

Hallelujah!

"I'm jealous," said his wife, rejoicing with him.

"Whatever for?"

"You weren't this happy on our wedding day!"

"How quickly you forget. Let's dance!"

"But there's no music."

"No problem!" he said, doing a jig step. "I'll hum!"

Happy Endings was having a twenty-percent-off sale on any book title starting with A, to commemorate August.

"What about Jane Austen, can I get twenty percent off?" asked Hessie Mayhew, who didn't have time to read a book in the first place.

"Sorry, no authors starting with A, just book titles," said Hope Winchester.

He staggered to the counter with *A Guide to Fragrance in the Garden, Andersonville: Men and Myth* (Walter's Christmas present), *A Reunion of Trees, A Grief Observed, Alone* by Admiral Byrd, *Anchor Book of Latin Quotations,* and *A Child's Garden of Verses.*

"A very perspicacious selection!" said Hope.

"Thank you. My wife will not be thrilled, however, as we have no place to put them."

"As long as you have any floor space at all, you have room for books! Just make two stacks of books the same height, place them

three or four feet apart, lay a board across them, and repeat. Violà!
Bookshelves!"

"I'll be darned."

He nearly always learned something new on Main Street.

The nave of Lord's Chapel became a deep chiaroscuro shadow as
dusk settled over Mitford. Candles burned on the sills of the stained-
glass windows to light the way of the remnant who came for the
evening worship on Thursday, scheduled unexpectedly by the rector.

Winnie Ivey had donated tarts and cookies for a bit of refreshment afterward, and the rector's wife had made pitchers of lemonade from scratch, not frozen. Hearing of this, Uncle Billy and Miss
Rose Watson, not much used to being out after dark, arrived in good
spirits.

Esther Bolick, weary in every bone, trudged down the aisle with
Gene to what had long ago become their pew on the gospel side. Several Bane volunteers, already feeling the numbing effects of pulling
together the largest fund-raiser in the diocese, slipped in quietly, glad
for the peace, for the sweetness of every shadow, and for the familiar,
mingled smells of incense and flowers, lemon wax and burning wick.

Most of the vestry turned out, some with the lingering apprehen-
sion that they'd robbed Mitford of a thriving new business, others
completely satisfied with a job well done.

Hope Winchester, invited by the rector and deeply relieved that
the A sale was successful, stood inside the door and looked around
awkwardly. She found it daunting to be here, since she hadn't been
raised in church, but Father Tim was one of their good customers and
never pushy about God, so she figured she had nothing to lose.

She slid into the rear pew, in case she needed to make a quick exit,
and lowered her head at once. It was a perfect time to think about the
S sale, coming in September, and how they ought to feature *Sea of
Grass* by Conrad Richter, which nobody ever seemed to know about,
but certainly should.

The *Muse* editor and his wife, Adele, slid into the rear pew across
the aisle, and wondered what they would do when everybody got
down on their knees. They both had Baptist backgrounds and felt

deeply that kneeling in public, even if it was in church, was too in-your-face, like those people who prayed loud enough for everybody in the temple to hear.

Sophia Burton, who had seen the rector on the street that morning, had been glad to come and bring Liza, glad to get away from the little house with the TV set she knew she should turn off sometimes, but couldn't, glad to get away from thinking about her job at the canning plant, and the supervisor who made her do things nobody else had to do. Not wanting her own church, which was First Baptist, to think she was defecting, she had invited a member of her Sunday School class so it would look more like a social outing than something religious.

Farther forward on the gospel side, Lace Turner sat with Olivia and Hoppy Harper, and Nurse Kennedy, who had been at the hospital long before Dr. Harper arrived and was known to be the glue that held the place together.

And there, noted the rector, as he stood waiting at the rear of the nave, were his own, Cynthia and Dooley, and next to them, Pauline and Jessie and Poo and . . . amazing! Buck Leeper.

The rector might have come to the church alone and given thanks on his knees in the empty nave. But he'd delighted in inviting one and all to a service that would express his own private thanksgiving—for the outcome of Fernbank, for Jessie, for this life, for so much.

He came briskly down the aisle in his robe, and, in front of the steps to the altar, turned eagerly to face his people.

"Grace to you and peace from God our Father and from the Lord Jesus Christ!" he quoted from Philippians.

"I will bless the Lord who gives me counsel," he said with the psalmist, "my heart teaches me, night after night. I have set the Lord always before me; because He is at my right hand, I shall not fall."

He spoke the ancient words of the sheep farmer, Amos: "Seek Him who made the Pleiades and Orion, and turns deep darkness into the morning, and darkens the day into night; who calls for the waters of the sea and pours them out upon the surface of the earth: the Lord is His name!"

There it was, the smile he was seeking from his wife. And lo, not one but two, because Dooley was giving him a grin into the bargain.

"Dear friends in Christ, here in the presence of Almighty God, let us kneel in silence, and with patient and obedient hearts confess our sins, so that we may obtain forgiveness by His infinite goodness and mercy."

Here it comes, thought Adele Hogan, who, astonishing herself, slid off the worn oak pew onto the kneeler.

Hope Winchester couldn't do it; she was as frozen as a mullet, and felt her heart pounding like she'd drunk a gallon of coffee. Her mouth felt dry, too. Maybe she'd leave, who would notice anyway, with their heads bowed, but the thing was, there was always somebody who probably wasn't keeping his eyes closed, and would see her dart away like a convict. . . .

"Most merciful God," Esther Bolick prayed aloud and in unison with the others from the Book of Common Prayer, "we confess that we have sinned against You in thought, word, and deed . . . "

She felt the words enter her aching bones like balm.

" . . . by what we have done," prayed Gene, "and by what we have left undone."

"We have not loved You with our whole heart," intoned Uncle Billy Watson, squinting through a magnifying glass to see the words in the prayer book, "we have not loved our neighbors as ourselves."

He found the words of the prayer beautiful. They made him feel hopeful and closer to the Lord, and maybe it was true that he hadn't always done right by his neighbors, but he would try to do better, he would start before he hit the street this very night. He quickly offered a silent thanks that somebody would be driving them home afterward, since it was pitch-dark out there, and still hot as a depot stove into the bargain.

"We are truly sorry and we humbly repent," prayed Pauline Barlowe, unable to keep the tears back, not wanting to look at the big, powerful man beside her. Though plainly reluctant to be there, he nonetheless held the hand of her daughter, who was sucking her thumb and gazing at the motion of the ceiling fans.

"For the sake of Your Son Jesus Christ, have mercy on us and forgive us," prayed Cynthia Kavanagh, amazed all over again at how she'd come to be kneeling in this place, and hoping that the stress she'd recently seen in her husband was past, and that this service would mark the beginning of renewal and refreshment.

" . . . that we may delight in Your will, and walk in Your ways," prayed Sophia Burton, wishing with all her heart that she could do that very thing every day of her life, really do it and not just pray it— but then, maybe she could, she was beginning to feel like she could . . . maybe.

" . . . to the glory of Your Name!" prayed the rector, feeling his spirit moved toward all who had gathered in this place.

"Amen!" they said in unison.

It wasn't that it didn't trouble him; in fact, it made him a little crazy whenever the thought crossed his mind. But what could he do? What could he prove?

He couldn't talk about it around town—it would seem like the worst sort of rumor-mongering and political meddling; he certainly wouldn't mention it at the Grill, and didn't think it wise to tell his wife, either. The new Violet book was wearing on her, and why clutter her mind with what appeared to be a very nasty piece of business?

Omer had sworn he'd keep quiet, at least for the time being. What could talk like that do, after all, except give his sister-in-law a stroke? And who could prove anything, anyway?

The rector took some comfort in the fact that election day was more than a couple of months away. Surely by that time Mack would show his hand, somebody would stumble, something . . .

The attic job was the current local recreation for those who had nothing better to do. Uncle Billy shambled down the street on his cane and gave all manner of directions to the crew, occasionally sharing the lunches they carried in bags from home or raced to the highway to pick up from Hardee's. So far, he had wheedled french fries from two stonecutters and a joiner.

Coot Hendrick pulled his rusted pickup truck to the curb every morning around eleven, scooted over to the passenger side, rolled the window down, and watched the whole show in the privacy and comfort of his vehicle. While the crew mixed mortar, sawed lumber, and in general tore up large expanses of grass and two perennial beds, he ate Nabs, shucked peanuts, and drank Cheerwine until three o'clock. He then drove to Lew Boyd's Esso, where he played checkers until five, after which he went home to his elderly mother and fixed her supper, usually a small cake of cornbread accompanied by a bowl of lettuce and onions, which he wilted with a blast of sizzling bacon grease and cider vinegar.

Beneath the attic, yet another church project was going at a trot.

While the preschool crowd gave new life to the old verger's quarters, the kindergarten had stationed itself in the largest of the Sunday School rooms, where all manner of shrieking, cackling, giggling, and wailing could be heard emanating from its walls.

The rector loved walking into a room that was completely alien to the adult world—filled with fat plastic tricycles and huge vinyl balls that could be knocked around without smashing the windows. He especially liked the rocking horses, which, upon each visit, were going at a frantic pace with astonished babies hanging on for dear life.

Sissy and Sassy had taken to the fray like fish to water. After a full day of howling for their mother, they had settled down to a new life and hardly noticed the guilt-stricken Puny when he went with her to see them at lunchtime.

"Sassy, it's Mama, come to Mama, *please*!" Sassy turned her head and chewed on a string of rubber clowns, recently chewed by a toddler who had poured a cup of juice on his head.

Sissy pulled up on a wooden table and tottered toward him at full throttle. "Ba!" she shouted. "Ba!"

"Ba, yourself!" He fell to his knees and held out his arms. "Come to granpaw, you little punkinhead!"

"I didn't know he was a granpaw," said Marsha Hunt, who was in charge of the mayhem.

Puny looked suddenly cheerful. "Oh, yes!" she declared. "And it's the best thing that ever happened to him!"

After the eleven o'clock, Mack Stroupe positioned himself a couple of yards to the left of the rector and pumped hands enthusiastically as the crowd flowed through the door. Anyone driving by, thought Father Tim, wouldn't have known which was the priest if one of them hadn't worn vestments.

As she tallied the collection on Monday morning, Emma couldn't wait to tell him:

Mack Stroupe had dropped a thousand bucks in the plate.

§

Rain. Torrents of rain. Rain that washed driveways, devastated what was left of the gardens, and hammered its way through roofs all over Mitford. The little yellow house had its first known leak, which Buck fixed by climbing around on the slate in a late afternoon downpour.

The rector drove up to check the leak problem at Fernbank and arrived in the nick of time. The turkey roaster and other assorted pots and pans were only moments before overflowing. He dutifully dumped each potful down the toilet, giving Fernbank a free flush, an economy which Miss Sadie had often employed.

He had tried to be completely candid with Andrew in a subsequent phone conversation, giving him the hair-raising truth about everything from roof to furnace. Oddly, Andrew had seemed jubilant about the whole prospect.

The wire for the earnest money had arrived at the bank and was deposited, the papers were being drawn up, and all was on go. Andrew would return to Mitford in a few weeks, anxious to begin work on the house before winter.

Father Tim stood in the vast, empty kitchen, looking out to sheets of rain lashing the windows. Even on a day like this, he hadn't felt so good about Fernbank in a very long time.

§

Everywhere he went, he made known that he was on the incumbent's side—without, he hoped, seeming preachy. Local politics was a fine line to walk for anybody, much less clergy.

What else could he do?

"You've already *done*!" said Cynthia. "An air show with banners and barrel rolls!"

"Yesterday's barrel rolls can't compete with today's barbecue."

"You've got a point there," she said.

He watched as his wife furrowed her brow, looking thoughtful. Maybe *she'd* be able to come up with something.

❦

"Tell me how things are, Betty."

He'd gone to sit on the porch with Betty Craig, who heaved a sigh at his question.

"Well, Father, Jessie wets the bed and has awful bad dreams."

"I'm sorry, but not surprised."

"And poor Pauline, she's just tryin' ever' whichaway to be a good mama, but I don't think anybody ever showed her how."

"I'm hoping preschool will help Jessie. I doubt if she's been with other children very much."

"She came home cryin' her heart out yesterday, sayin' she didn't want to go back. But of course she seemed all right about it this morning when I took her to day care at Lord's Chapel. I take her, you know, because Pauline goes to work so early."

"Can you handle all this crowd in your house?"

"Oh, yes! It's good to have a crowd, but I don't think we could stuff another one in, unless they set on their fist and lean back on their thumb. You won't be . . . sendin' any more?"

"I believe Pauline will be looking for a little house soon."

Betty was quiet, rocking. "You know, Mr. Leeper's coming around."

"What do you think of that?" he asked, trusting her judgment.

"Oh, I like Mr. Leeper, and he's good to th' children, too. But with her tryin' to stay off alcohol . . . and I hear he's still drinkin' some . . . I don't know if it's the best thing."

He'd thought the same, but hadn't wanted to admit it to himself.

❦

"I'd like to see," he said, feeling shy as a schoolboy.

"Are you sure?" she asked.

"Of course! I've been wanting to do it for weeks."

They trooped through the hedge to her workroom, where she showed him the growing stack of large watercolor illustrations for *Violet Goes Back to School.* He sat on her minuscule love seat and she displayed the results of her labors, revealing at the same time a shyness of her own.

He was dazzled by his wife's gift. It knocked his socks off. "It's wonderful, absolutely wonderful. The best yet!"

"Thank you! That means so much."

"And Violet—in this one, she looks so, what shall I say? Happy!"

"Yes! You see, Violet likes going to school."

"Aha."

"Which reminds me—I've been wanting to tell you something, dearest."

"Tell me," he said, loving the earnest look of her in a bandanna and denim jumper.

"I'll be traveling for several weeks after the book is released, going to schools and libraries. I know how you feel about that."

He hated it, actually. He remembered how pathetically lost he felt when she traveled a couple of times last year. Worse, he'd gotten the most bizarre notions—that she might miss the bridge and drive into the river, or be mugged in the school parking lot, or that her crankcase was leaking oil. And what if she were stranded on the side of the road? Did she realize that people had been murdered doing that very thing?

He said what he always said. "Do you have to?"

And she said what she always said. "Yes."

§

Ron removed his cap and jacket and shook the rain onto the rug at the office door.

"Feast or famine," he said. "Drought or flood."

"Are you talking about life or the weather?" queried Father Tim.

"Life *and* the weather," said Ron. "We're currently seeing a flood of real estate activity."

"Now what?" He was sick of real estate activity.

"We've got a prospective buyer for the rectory."

His blood chilled. "Already?"

Ron sat on the visitor's bench. "They're very interested, and said they'd like to see it next week."

"Who is they?" Why did he feel so defensive, even angry?

"H. Tide. Out of Orlando."

"That's who's looking at Sweet Stuff." And if that's who's looking at Sweet Stuff, then Mack Stroupe was involved. Hadn't Mack taken credit in the newspaper article for sending Winnie a realtor who was, in fact, H. Tide?

He'd never been able to bear the brunt of bad news in his head, in his intellect; he felt it instead in his body—in his chest, in his stomach, in his throat.

"Sorry," said Ron, seeing the look on his face. "If they want it right away, we'll do all we can to help you find whatever situation you need. Ideally, we'll try to work something out that lets you stay in the rectory 'til you retire."

"You'll *try* to work something out?"

"Well . . . " Ron looked embarrassed and uneasy.

"Keep me posted," he said, hearing the cold anger in his voice. He hadn't meant to sound that way, but he couldn't help it, couldn't mask it.

He felt strangely frightened and alone.

᛭

Walking home, he concluded that he wouldn't mention this to Cynthia, not until he had to. After all, nothing was written in stone.

Here was yet another circumstance he'd be withholding from his wife, and he knew instinctively this wasn't a good tactic—the most fundamental counseling book would tell him that.

Disrupting the household . . . where would they go? Buck had a crew starting next door in September, in only a couple of weeks, and Cynthia would be moving her drawing board and library into his study. He had never liked change, and here he was, facing the biggest change of his life, combined with a possible change of address at the most inconvenient time imaginable.

His retirement had all looked so smooth, so easy, so . . . reviving when he made the decision last year. Now it looked as if he could be set out on the sidewalk like so much rubbish.

But he was being hasty. Premature. He was overreacting.

He sucked in a draught of fresh air and turned the corner onto Wisteria. He dreaded facing Cynthia Kavanagh, who could look in his eyes and know instantly that something was wrong.

For two cents, he'd get in the car and drive.

And keep going.

CHAPTER SIXTEEN

Bookends

Going at a clip toward the Grill, they met Uncle Billy tottering homeward from the construction site at Lord's Chapel.

"I'll be et f'r a tater if y'r boy ain't growed a foot!"

Dooley cackled, looking at his feet. "Where's it at?"

The rector noted that Dooley was slipping back into the vernacular, which, frankly, he had rather missed. Any wild departure from the King's English, of course, would be remedied just ten days hence. Blast, he hated the thought of driving Dooley to Virginia and depositing him in that place, even if it was helping him learn and grow and expand his horizons.

Percy turned from the grill and beamed. "Lookit th' big ball player. You ought t' be traded to th' Yankees and that's a fact."

"Dodgers," said Dooley, laughing again.

The rector had seen more laughter in his boy this summer than ever before. And why not? He had a steady paycheck, a girl who was crazy about him, a best friend, a family that was pulling itself together, and, generally, a swarm of people who loved him. Not to mention, of course, an education that was annually the cost of a new car—with leather and airbags.

"Hey, buddyroe," said J.C., cracking one of his biennial grins.

"Hey," said Dooley, sliding into the rear booth. This was his first time hanging with these old guys, and he wasn't too sure about it. He could have been scarfing down a pizza with Tommy over on the highway.

"Hey, slugger!" said Mule. "Let's see that arm!"

Dooley flexed the muscle in his upper right arm, and everybody helped themselves to squeezing it.

"A rock," said J.C., approving.

Mule nodded soberly.

"Killer!" said the rector.

J.C. pulled out a handkerchief and mopped his face. "I'll treat!"

"There it is again," said Mule. "The feelin' I'm goin' deaf as a doorknob."

"I mean I'll treat Dooley, not th' whole bloomin' booth."

"You better have some deep pockets if you're feeding Dooley Bar-lowe," said Father Tim, as proud as if the boy had an appetite for Aristotle.

"I'll have a large Coke, large fries, and two hotdogs all th' way," announced the editor's guest.

"All th' way?" Mule raised his eyebrows. "I thought you had a girl-friend, you don't want to be eatin' onions."

"Don't listen to these turkeys," said J.C., "they tried to run my . . . my, ah . . . thing with Adele and like to ruined my life. Anything you want to know about women, you ask me."

Mule nearly fell out of the booth laughing.

"What's goin' on over here?" asked Velma, who couldn't bear to hear laughter unless she knew what it was about.

"You don't want to know," said Father Tim.

"I certainly do want to know!" She put her hands on her hips and squinted at them over her glasses.

"Oh, shoot," said Mule. "Can't a bunch of men have a little joke without women wantin' to know what it's about?"

"No," said Velma. "So what's it about?"

"We're teachin' Dooley about the opposite sex," said Mule.

"Oh, Lord, help!" Velma looked thoroughly disgusted.

"I wish y'all would quit," said Dooley. "I don't need to know anything about girls, I already know it."

"See?" said Velma. "Now, let 'im alone. Dooley, if you ever want to know anything about th' opposite sex, you come and ask me or Percy, you hear? We'll tell you th' blessed truth."

"Dadgum!" Mule covered his face with his hands. "He'll be glad to get back to school after listenin' to this mess. . . . "

"Right!" said Dooley.

§

Ron Malcolm called to say that he'd be at the rectory Wednesday at noon, with the people from H. Tide.

Father Tim decided he'd be in the piney woods, as far from that miserable experience as he could get.

When he finally got the nerve to tell Cynthia, she looked at him blankly.

"Why are they showing it now if they're not going to sell it until we move?"

"The truth is, if they get the right offer and the buyer's anxious to move in, they'll sell it now and find us something. . . . "

He could tell she didn't believe her ears. "Find us something . . . ?"

He looked away. "The real estate scene in Mitford, as you know, is historically sluggish. The vestry feels they can't afford to pass up the offer, if it's right. People have known for two or three years that it would be on the market, and nobody's spoken up for it."

"The real estate market is historically sluggish because development in Mitford goes at a snail's pace." She turned away, and he saw a muscle moving in her cheek. "It's almost enough to make me vote for Mack Stroupe."

"I can't believe you said that."

"I was only kidding, for Pete's sake, you don't have to bite my head off."

"I didn't bite your head off."

"You most certainly did. And furthermore, your nerves stay absolutely frazzled these days. You tote every barge and lift every bale in Mitford, with nothing left over for yourself. And now you tell me we could be run out of our home, thanks to a parish you have faithfully served for sixteen years? If that's the way your vestry thinks, Timothy, then I would ask you to do me the favor of lining them up, one by one, and enjoining them to bend over. I will then go down the row and give every distinguished member exactly what they deserve, which is, need I say it, a good, swift kick!"

She turned and left the study, and he heard her charging up the stairs. Their bedroom door, which was rarely closed, slammed.

He felt as if he'd been dashed with ice water. All the feelings he'd lately had, the heaviness on his chest, the pounding of blood in his temples, the wrenching in his stomach . . . all rushed in again, except worse.

He sat at the kitchen table, stricken. They'd never before had words like that. They were both overworked, overstressed, and who wanted to be told they might be dumped on the street?

He was grieved that this was even a consideration by his own church officers.

Also, he was humiliated for Ron Malcolm, one of the finest men he'd ever known, and a personal friend into the bargain. Ron Malcolm was behaving like . . . like Ed Coffey, doing whatever it took, and all because of money.

Money!

He was glad he didn't have enough money to matter, glad he'd given most of it away in this fleeting life. Dear God, to see what some people would do for a dollar was enough to make him call his broker and have the whole lot transferred to the coffers of Children's Hospital.

What was the amount, anyway, that was left of his mother's estate? A hundred and forty thousand or so, which he'd been growing for years. Even though he'd dipped into it heavily every time the Children's Hospital had a need, smart investing had maintained most of the original two hundred thousand.

Actually, it hadn't been smart investing, it had been safe investing. He was as timid as a hare when it came to flinging assets around. He wished he'd asked Miss Sadie her investing strategies. There were a thousand things he'd thought of asking after she died, and now it was too late to find out how she'd come up with more than a million bucks for Dooley, even after spending five million on Hope House.

Should he go upstairs and talk to Cynthia? What would he say?

He couldn't remember feeling so weary, so . . . He searched for the word that would express how he felt, but couldn't find it.

He didn't have the energy to say he was sorry. Actually, he didn't know if he was sorry. What had he said, after all? He couldn't remember, but it all had something to do with Mack Stroupe.

Blast Mack Stroupe to the lowest regions of the earth. He was sick of Mack Stroupe.

§

So what if he shouldn't have a napoleon? Hadn't he waited more than a decade to eat a measly cheeseburger the other day?

He was no ascetic living in the desert, he was a busy, active clergyman in need of proper nourishment.

He did the glucometer check and marched to Winnie Ivey's, blowing past several people who greeted him, but to whom he merely lifted a hand. They stared after him, dumbfounded. They'd never seen the local priest scowling like that. It was completely unlike him.

The bell on the Sweet Stuff door jingled, which turned the heads of four customers sitting at a table. It was fifth- and sixth-grade teachers from Mitford School, having tea. He could tell at once they wanted to talk, and he turned to leave.

"Father?" said Winnie, coming through the curtains behind the bake cases. "Can you stay a minute?"

Good heavens, Winnie Ivey looked as glum and pressed to the wall as he felt. What was wrong with people these days?

She set out another pot of hot water for the teachers, who were peering at him oddly, and caught his sleeve. "I need to talk to you about something," she said, whispering.

They went to the kitchen, which, as always, smelled like a child's version of paradise—cinnamon, rising dough, baking cookies. Somebody should put the aroma in an aerosol container. It was so soothing that he immediately felt more relaxed.

"You look terrible," she said.

"Oh, well." If Winnie Ivey didn't tell him so, Emma Newland certainly would, or, for that matter, any number of others.

"Father, the most awful thing . . . "

If it wasn't one awful thing these days, it was two.

"That real estate company wants to buy my business."

"They do?"

"And I can't get a minute's peace about selling it. After runnin' ads and prayin' my head off, here's my big chance and I feel awful about it."

"If you've prayed and there's no peace about a decision, then wait. That's one rule I stick with."

"But they want to buy it right away."

"Will they give you your asking price?"

"Not exactly. Mr. Skinner believes it's worth seventy-five thousand, but I'm asking sixty, and they want to give me forty-five."

"Forty-five thousand for twenty years' work," he said, musing. "That's not much more than two thousand a year."

"Oh," she said, stricken.

He was feeling worse by the minute. Any longing for a napoleon had flown out the window.

"I'd really like your advice, Father, I trust what you say."

He didn't like being anyone's Providence, but she'd asked for help and he'd give her his best shot. He said what he was becoming known for saying in all real estate matters these days.

"Tell them you'd like to think about it for thirty days."

She looked alarmed. "I don't believe they'd like that."

"They probably wouldn't. That's true."

"And I might not get another offer."

"That's true, too. However, consider this: You're the only game in town. There's not another business currently for sale on Main Street, and this is highly desirable property. I think you're holding the ace."

She hugged herself, furrowing her brow and thinking. "Well, I *might* do that. But . . . it's risky."

He wouldn't tell her that risk had a certain adrenaline.

§

Didn't he have a bishop? An advocate? He wasn't hanging out there in space, all alone. Stuart Cullen would go to bat for him. That's what bishops were for, wasn't it?

But Stuart wasn't in the office and wouldn't be in for two long weeks, as his wife, according to Stuart's secretary, had forced the bishop to go away to—she wasn't sure where, but she thought it was southern France, or at least someplace where they spoke another language and wore bikinis on the beach.

§

Dooley, whose job had ended day before yesterday, showed up at the church office with a letter in his hand.

He sat on the visitor's bench and examined his tennis shoes, whistled, jiggled his leg, and stared into space while the rector opened it and read:

My dearest husband,

I regret that I snapped at you this morning. You snapped, I snapped. And for what? As you left, looking hurt, I wanted to run after you and hold you, but I could not move. I stood upstairs on the landing and moped at the window like a schoolgirl, watching as you went along the sidewalk.

I saw you stop for a moment and look around, as if you wanted to turn back. You seemed forlorn, and I was overcome with sorrow for anything I might ever do to give you pain. My darling Timothy, who means all the world to me—forgive me.

It was the slightest thing between us, something that would hardly matter to anyone else, I think. We are both so sensitive, so alike in that region of the heart which fears rejection and resists chastisement.

As I looked down upon you, I received your hurt as my own, and so have had a double measure all these hours.

Hurry home, dearest husband!

Come and kiss me and let us hold one another in that way which God has set aside for us. You are precious to me, more than breath.

Ever thine,
Cynthia
(still your bookend?)

*PS I know it is a pitiable gesture, but I shall roast something
savoury for your supper and make your favorite oven-browned
potatoes.*

Truce?

Dooley looked at the ceiling, got up, peered out the window, sat
down again, then found some gum on the sole of his left shoe and
painstakingly peeled it off. "You an' Cynthia had a fuss?"

"Yes."

"I understand."

"You do?" He was thrilled to hear those words out of Dooley Barlowe. *I understand.* A mature thing for anyone, much less a fourteen-
year-old boy, to utter.

"Jenny and I had a fuss. She blamed me for somethin' I didn't do."

"Aha."

"She said I paid too much attention to Lace Turner the other day."

"No kidding. . . . "

"I didn't."

"I'm sure."

"Lace wanted to talk about American history, is all, and I talked
back." He shrugged.

"Right. What did you talk about—I mean, concerning American
history?"

"About going west in a wagon train. I'd like to do that. Lace said
she'd like to." His freckles were showing. "That's all."

"I'm amazed every day," said the rector, "how people can misun-
derstand each other about the simplest things."

"Lace is writing a story about going west on a wagon train from
Springfield, Illinois, where the Donner party started out. In her story,
the leader gets killed and a woman has to lead the train."

"Wow."

"She got A's for her stories last year."

"Well done."

"She quit wearin' that stupid hat."

"I noticed."

"So, look, I don't have all day. Are you goin' to write Cynthia
back?"

"You bet."

"I've got to go see Poo and Jessie. You goin' to type or write by hand?"

"Type. I'll hurry."

He took the cover off the Royal manual and rolled in a sheet of paper.

Bookend—

dooley has delivered your letter and is waiting for me to respond. ii have suffered, you have suffered.

Enough!

You are dear to me beyond measure. That God allowed us to have thiis union at all stuns me daily/

"Bright star, would I were stedfast as thou art—"

love, timothy—who, barely two years ago, you may recall, vowed to cherish you always, no matter what

Truce.

ps. ii will gladly wash the dishes and barnabas will dry.

He had to do something for Esther.

More billboards on the highway wouldn't cut it. Esther's campaign needed one-on-one, it needed looking into people's eyes and talking about her record. It needed . . . a coffee in someone's home.

But not in his home. No, indeed. For a priest to dip his spoon into mayoral coffee was not politically correct. He would have to talk someone else into doing it.

Esther Bolick laughed in his face. "Are you kidding me?" she said. He should have known better than to call Esther. What a dumb notion; he felt like an idiot. So why did he pick up the phone and call Hessie?

"You must have the wrong number," said Hessie Mayhew, and hung up.

He called the president of ECW, thinking she might be interested in having the mayor do a program at the next monthly meeting.

"She did a program last year," said Erlene Douglas, "and we never repeat a speaker unless it's the bishop or a bigwig."

"Put a sign in your window," he implored Percy, "one of those that says, 'We're stickin' with Esther.'"

"No way," said Percy. "I run a business. I'm not campaignin' for anybody. Let 'em tough it out whichever way they can."

"Olivia," he said in his best pulpit voice, "I was wondering if . . . "

But Olivia, Hoppy, and Lace were going to the coast for the last couple of days before school started, which, except for their honeymoon, would be the first vacation her husband had had in ten years.

He sat staring at his office bookshelves, drumming his fingers on the desk. Maybe Esther could visit the police station and hand around donuts one morning. Better still, what about giving out balloons at Hattie Cloer's market on the highway? He was running on fumes with this thing.

He called Esther's office, noting that she sounded depressed.

"I don't know," she said, sighing heavily. "Who needs this aggravation? Th' low-down egg sucker has been campaignin' practically since Easter, it's more politics than I can stomach."

"But you can't give up now!"

"Who says I can't?" demanded the mayor.

§

"Mr. Tim!"

On his livermush delivery to Betty Craig's, Jessie met him at the door, carrying a coloring book. "Look!" she said, holding it up for his close inspection.

"Outstanding!" he said squatting down.

"Them's camels. Camels stores water in their humps."

"Right. Amazing!"

"Can I sit on your lap?"

"Absolutely."

He set the bag of livermush down and sought out the slipcovered armchair in the living room. Jessie crawled into his lap and clung to him, sucking her thumb.

"I thought you were going to try and quit sucking your thumb," he said, cradling her in his arm.

"Betty put pepper on it, but I washed it off."

He didn't know much about thumb-sucking, but he knew the cure. It was the thing that cured every other ill in this world, and of which there was far too little in general supply.

§

After talking with Pauline, he put another list, however brief, on Emma's desk.

But this time, Emma found nothing. Nothing at all.

§

The realtors from Orlando had made an offer. A hundred and five thousand, cash. Which was, to a penny, the asking price.

He hadn't heard of anybody meeting an asking price lately.

When he spoke to Ron about it, he felt as if his jaws were frozen, or partially wired shut. "When do they want occupancy?"

"October fifteenth."

"Who's buying it?"

"They didn't specify. Whoever it is may be renting it."

"I'd like you to wait on this."

"They made it clear they don't want to drag their feet. They were ready to shell out the cash today, but I won't sign anything of course, 'til I run all this by the vestry."

"I'm going to ask you to do something."

"You know I want to help, Father."

Did he know that? "I want you to wait on this for ten days. Don't do anything for ten days." He didn't think his now-customary thirty days would wash, but he had to have some time to adjust to this. The thought of the deal being done immediately made him feel trapped, helpless.

Ron pulled at his chin. "They've already said they want me to get back to them by the end of the week. If we make them wait, they could withdraw the offer."

"Look. If you think we feel good about being swept out of our house like this, you've got another think coming. I've got to tell you that I don't appreciate it, and if you have in mind some early retirement plan I don't know about, then let's lay the cards on the table."

His heart wasn't pounding, his brow wasn't perspiring. He was as cool as a cucumber.

Ron tried to smile, but couldn't. "Early retirement? Father, we'd keep you forever, if you'd let us. Retirement wasn't our idea, it was yours."

"And it's my idea to have ten days to digest all this. Sixteen years in this parish has earned me ten days." Period.

He wasn't taking no for an answer, and Ron knew it.

§

"Father! Stop! Wait!"

It was Winnie Ivey in her apron, running up Main Street behind him.

"I saw you pass, but I was on th' phone. Oh, you won't believe this! You won't believe it!"

"I'll believe it!" he said, laughing at her excitement.

"I won that cruise! I won it! A cruise to a whole bunch of islands!"

"Hallelujah!" he said, taking her hands as she jumped up and down. Her bandanna slipped back from her forehead, and graying curls sprung loose.

"I've never won anything, not even a stuffed animal in a shootin' gallery!"

"First time for everything!" he said, rejoicing with her.

"Golden Band said I could go anytime, starting in October! They were the nicest people, they said my entry was just perfect, they said it hit th' nail on th' head! I thank you for helpin' me with it, Father, stop by for a napoleon anytime! Well, gosh, I better get back, I've got two customers havin' donuts and coffee."

He watched her dash down the street, thinking he might see her leap off the pavement and fly.

§

In two short days, Harley had hauled away three barrows of trash from Cynthia's garage, washed and waxed her car, mowed the grass at both houses, removed the dead and dying stems of the hosta, and weeded the flower beds.

"Harley, you'd better slow down," said the rector, taking a turn at the weeding himself.

"No, sir, I ain't goin' to, I'm glad t' be workin', it's th' best fix I've been in and I thank th' Lord 'n Master f'r it."

Right there, he thought, was another consideration. Any interim living arrangement the vestry might provide may not accommodate Harley Welch.

Father Tim squatted by the perennial bed and watched the dappled light play over the grass. He and Cynthia had prayed the prayer that never fails, and besides that, what else could they do?

He pondered the sudden, unexpected idea he'd had this morning as he ran. It had come to him out of the blue and slowed him to a walk. Of course, he'd never done anything like that before. But was that any reason not to do it now? Cynthia would know the answer.

The rotten thing about this new development with the rectory was that every time he turned around these days, he was standing under an ax waiting to fall. Thirty days here, ten days there, it seemed endless.

There was an upside, however. Going out to Canaan didn't look so ominous anymore. It looked like a blasted good way to introduce a little peace into his life.

§

He thought they might have to talk about it until the wee hours. But it was coming together very quickly.

"I think we should do it," he told his wife.

"I think we should, too," she said, looking intrigued.

She reached out to him, put her warm palm to his cheek, and smiled. "It would solve everything," she said.

CHAPTER SEVENTEEN

Deep Blue Sea

The following morning, he reached the office earlier than usual and found a message on his machine.

"Father? Ron here. I talked with H. Tide and they want to do the deal now—or never." Ron cleared his throat. "Ah, also, they're saying they don't want to rent to us, they'd like to take possession by October fifteenth."

There was a moment of uneven breathing. "Don't worry about a thing, Father, we'll take care of you."

Wilma Malcolm's voice sounded in the background. "The Randall house!"

"Wilma heard the Randall house is available, and I'm sure we could work something out. Well, listen, we're headed to see the grandkids for a couple of days, I'll get back to you." The machine clicked, whirred, and clicked again.

He sat at his desk, frozen.

In all his years as a priest. . . .

He didn't move for what seemed a long time.

Then he got up, hit the erase button on the machine, and walked out the door.

§

He went home to oversee Dooley's packing for the trip to Virginia in the morning.

He didn't know how he could face anybody right now, much less Dooley Barlowe. Would he break down and bawl like a baby? Or worse, reach for some heavy object and slam it through a window?

He made an effort to remember how Ron had stood by him the night they faced down Edith Mallory. It had happened a few years ago at Clear Day.

After confronting her with the rotten floor beams that they discovered under the Grill, Edith was persuaded to repair the damage and extend Percy's lease for five years, at a fraction of the rent hike she'd originally hit him with—the rent hike that had, in fact, been designed to put the Grill out of business.

Edith Mallory hated his guts, no two ways about it. She had revealed her rage toward him that night in a way he didn't care to recall.

He and Ron had left Clear Day, triumphant and ecstatic, brothers in a victory that had less to do with winning than with maintaining something central to the core and spirit of the village. While the sense of connectedness was vanishing in small towns everywhere, he and Ron had fought for something vital, and won.

Before he let this thing with the rectory eat him alive, he'd better forgive Ron Malcolm. By God's grace, maybe he could actually do it. So what if he might have to start all over again every five minutes?

The point was to start.

"You home?" yelled Dooley from the landing.

"I'm home. Give me a half hour." He stopped in the kitchen to drink a glass of ice water.

Cynthia was shopping in Wesley, and Lace, who was leaving for the beach tomorrow, was baking cookies in Harley's kitchen. The fragrance drifted up the stairs like a sylph.

He went to his bedroom with Barnabas at his heels and sat in the wing chair, taking a few deep breaths to quiet the turmoil that had moved from his head and invaded his heart.

He and Cynthia had already prayed the prayer that never fails regarding the rectory, but he felt the need to pray it again.

Barnabas laid his head on his master's foot.

"Ah, fella," he sighed, nudging his good dog's neck with the toe of his loafer.

§

The sound came through the open bedroom windows—a terrible screeching noise, a loud thud, the high-pitched yelping of a dog. Dooley was shouting.

He bolted to the front window and looked down on Wisteria Lane.

Good God! Barnabas lay in the street with Dooley bending over him.

He didn't remember racing down the stairs, but seemed to be instantly in the street with Dooley, crouching over Barnabas, hearing the horrific sound that welled up from his own gut like a long moan.

Blood ran from his dog's chest, staining the asphalt, and he reached out. . . .

"Don't touch 'im!" shouted Dooley. "He'll bite. We got t' muzzle 'im! Git Lace! Git Lace!"

The rector was on his feet and running for the house, calling, shouting. "And git me some towels!" yelled Dooley. "He's got a flail chest, I got t' have towels!"

His heart was pounding into his throat. Dear God, don't take my dog, don't take this good creature, have mercy!

Lace flew through the door. "Help Dooley!" he said, running toward the guest bathroom, where he picked up an armload of towels, then turned and sprinted up the hall and down the steps and into the street in a nightmarish eternity of slow motion.

"Give me that thing on your head," Dooley told Lace, "and help me hold 'im! We got to muzzle 'im or he'll bite, look, do it this way, hold 'im right here."

Father Tim could hardly bear the look of his dog, suffering, whimpering, thrashing on the asphalt, as fresh blood poured from the wound in his chest.

Dooley tied the bandanna around the dog's nose and mouth, and knotted it. "Okay," he said, taking off his T-shirt. "Don't look, you can see 'is lungs workin' in there." He pressed the balled-up shirt partially into the gaping wound; immediately, the dark stain of blood seeped into the white cotton.

"Give me a towel," Dooley said, clenching his jaw. He took the towel and wrapped the heaving chest, making a bandage. "Another one," said Dooley, working quickly. "And git me a blanket, we got t' git 'im to Doc Owen. He could die."

The rector ran into the house, praying, sweat streaming from him, and opened the storage closet in the hall. No blankets. The armoire! *He could die.*

Christ, have mercy. He dashed up the stairs and flung open the door of the armoire and grabbed two blankets and ran down again, breathless, swept out of himself with fear.

Cynthia, come home . . . *he could die.*

"Spread 'em down right there," Dooley told the rector. "Help 'im," he said to Lace.

They spread the blankets, one on top of the other, next to Barnabas, as a car slowed down and stopped. "Can we help?" someone called.

"You can pray!" shouted Lace, waving the car around them.

Together, they managed to move Barnabas onto the blankets. "Careful," said Dooley, "careful. He's in awful pain, and his leg's broke, too, but they ain't nothin' I can do about it now, we got to hurry. Where's Harley?"

"He walked t' town," said Lace, her face white.

"Git his keys, they're hangin' on th' nail. Back 'is truck out here, we'll put Barnabas in th' back, an' you'n me'll ride with 'im."

She raced to the house as Dooley, naked to the waist, crouched over Barnabas and put his hand on the dog's head. "It's OK, boy, it's OK, you're goin' t' be fine."

"Thank You, Jesus, for Your presence in this," the rector prayed. "Give us your healing hands. . . . "

They heard Lace gun the truck motor and back out of the driveway. She hauled up beside them and screeched to a stop, the motor running.

"Let down th' tailgate," said Dooley. Lace jumped out of the truck and let it down.

"Grab this corner of th' blanket with me," he said to Lace. "Dad, you haul up that end. Take it easy. Easy!"

The dog's weight seemed enormous as they lifted him into the truck bed. "OK, boy, we're layin' you down, now."

Lace and Dooley climbed up with Barnabas and gently positioned the whimpering dog in the center of the bed. Then Dooley slammed the tailgate and looked at the rector.

"Hurry," he said.

They blew past Harley, who was walking home on Main Street. He turned to look after them, bewildered.

In twenty-five minutes, Barnabas was on the table at Meadowgate, and Hal Owen and Blake Eddistoe were at work. "You'd better not come in," said Dooley, closing the door to the surgery.

The rector sat with Lace in the small waiting room. A fan droned overhead. The front door stood open to a yard where four chickens scratched in the grass.

His legs had turned to rubber when he got out of the truck a few minutes ago. He had driven like the wind, praying without ceasing, making the half-hour run in twenty minutes. Twice, he glanced behind him, through the window of the cab, to see Dooley give him the high sign.

Lace looked firm. "I believe he's goin' to make it."

"I believe that with you," he said, taking her hand. "You were wonderful."

"I like your dog," she said.

Barnabas would stay at Meadowgate for a couple of weeks, recovering. The leg would mend; it was a clean break. But the chest wound, apparently caused by the violent assault of the chassis when the vehicle ran over him, would take longer, and could even open the door to pneumonia.

Bottom line, it would be a while before Barnabas would go jogging with his master.

The rector went into the surgery, where Hal had made a comfortable bed on the floor, and looked at Barnabas sleeping, his chest swaddled in bandages, his left leg stiff in the splint. He watched for his breathing, then knelt and put his hand on his forepaws, which were curled together peacefully.

He wept, tasting the salt in his mouth.

Afterward, they sat in Hal's office, drinking Marge Owen's iced tea, trying to reconstruct the chain of events.

He supposed he had fallen asleep in the chair in the bedroom, with Barnabas lying at his feet. When Barnabas heard Dooley go downstairs, he followed, and at the moment Dooley opened the front door to look for Tommy, Barnabas saw a squirrel on the lawn.

"I didn't even know he was standin' there," said Dooley, "and then he was through the door so fast I couldn't have stopped him." Dooley, sitting bare-chested in his jeans and tennis shoes, dropped his head.

"Don't blame yourself," said Father Tim. "A dog is a dog. He saw the squirrel and did what dogs do. It could have happened with me just as easily."

"Right," said Hal. "The issue isn't that you opened the door, it's that you saved his life."

"I agree," said Lace, her amber eyes intense.

"I don't want to go back to school," said Dooley. "I want to stay here and look after Barn."

Hal leaned against the wall, lighting his pipe. "You can trust me to do that, pal. I'll even give you a report once a week. How's that?"

"No kidding? You will?"

"You bet. Leave me your new phone number at school. Just write it on the wall over there, everybody else does."

"What I don't understand," said Lace, "is why the person who hit 'im didn't stop."

Dooley shrugged. "It happened so fast. . . . I saw Barnabas run after the squirrel, and then the car . . . I don't know what kind of car it was. Maybe brown, I think it was brown."

Father Tim phoned Cynthia, who was frantic. A neighbor across the street told her Barnabas had been hurt and the preacher had taken him to the hospital. Harley reported he'd seen his truck roaring up Main Street, but didn't have any idea what was going on.

"He's going to be fine, Timothy," said Hal. "I'll watch him carefully for any signs of pneumonia. You know we love Barnabas like family. We won't let him suffer."

Marge nodded. "It's true, Tim. And Blake and Rebecca and I will also look after him."

Still, he felt like a heel for leaving his dog.

Blake Eddistoe walked into the yard with them and shook hands with Dooley. "Well done," he said.

At the truck, Dooley suddenly turned and said, "You ought to let me drive."

When it came to persistence, the kid was a regular Churchill. He tossed him the keys.

Dooley's eyes grew bigger. "You mean it?"

"All the way to the highway."

Dooley, now wearing one of Hal's shirts, opened the driver's door. "Get in," he said to Lace. "You can ride in th' middle."

He was glad the Meadowgate road to the highway seemed a little longer than he remembered, glad for the boy's sake. He wished the road could go all the way to Canada before it reached the highway.

He was home and in the shower before it hit him.

Today, for the first time, Dooley Barlowe had called him "Dad."

Driving to Virginia, part of Miss Sadie's letter ran through his mind.

> *. . . the money is his when he reaches the age of twenty-one. (I am old-fashioned and believe that eighteen is far too young to receive an inheritance.)*
>
> *I have put one and a quarter million dollars where it will grow,*

and have made provisions to complete his preparatory education.
When he is eighteen, the income from the trust will help send him
through college.

   I am depending on you never to mention this to him until he is old
enough to bear it with dignity. I am also depending on you to stick
with him, Father, through thick and thin, just as you've done all along.

The question of sticking with Dooley had been answered nearly
four years ago; he was in for the long haul. The question of when the
boy might bear such information with dignity was another matter.

In truth, if he'd ever seen dignity, he'd seen it yesterday in the
street. Dooley had acted with the utmost precision, wisdom, and
grace.

Even so, something cautioned him about speaking of the inheritance. Soon before they reached the school, he knew the answer, and
the answer was, "Wait."

"Buddy?"

"Yes, sir?"

"When you come home at Christmas, I'll loan you the keys to the
Buick."

Ah, the bright hope that leapt into the boy's face. . . .

"There's only one problem."

The bright hope dimmed.

"You'll have to do your driving on back roads, and I'll have to ride
in the backseat."

Dooley munched one of the cookies Lace had sent along. "OK,"
he said, grinning, "but try and hunker down so nobody can see you."

§

He rang Buddy Benfield to ask when the contract would be
signed. "Whenever Ron gets back," said the junior warden, clearly
uncomfortable to be talking to a man who would soon be evicted.

"Timothy."

His wife was sitting on the back stoop, having her morning coffee
and looking determined about something.

"I want you to call Father Douglas to lead the service for you on
Sunday."

"Whatever for?" he asked.

"Because you're exhausted."

She didn't argue, she didn't nag. She just stated the fact, and looked at him with her cornflower-blue eyes, meaning business.

"All right," he said.

She was clearly surprised. "I suppose I should quit while I'm ahead . . ."

"Probably."

" . . . but I'd also like you to plan to sleep late on Sunday morning. None of that padding around in your slippers at five a.m., like a Christmas elf."

"Keep talking," he said.

"You mean you'll actually *do* it?"

"Whatever you say," he assured her. "Just don't ask me to go to any beaches wearing a bikini."

§

What had Velma done to herself? She was sporting some gaudy garland of colored paper around her neck, and earrings that appeared to be small bananas. He wouldn't say so, but it looked like she'd dressed herself out of Emma Newland's closet.

"What's that?" he asked.

"A lei. Didn't you hear?"

"Hear what?"

"She's goin' on that cruise with Winnie!" said Percy, looking relieved. "Sailin' over th' deep blue sea to five ports, an' eatin' eight meals a day, includin' a midnight buffet!"

"No kidding! That's perfect! Fantastic!"

Velma put her hands over her head and wiggled her hips, which wasn't a pretty sight.

"Course, I don't know if they do the hula in St. Thomas."

"I don't think they do," said the rector. "I believe that's more of a limbo kind of place."

"Stand still," said J.C. "I'll take your picture." He raised the Nikon and banged off four shots of Velma standing at the cash register. "Won't be front page, but I think I can work it in next to 'Home Gardenin' Tips.'"

Coot Hendrick put in his two cents' worth from the counter. "You ought to have waited and took a snap of Winnie standin' next to Velma."

"You got to jump on news where you find it," said J.C. "I'm headin' to th' booth, I'm starved!"

"*You're* starved?" said Coot. "I've done had to eat a table leg to keep my strength." He despaired that Velma would ever get back to work and bring his regular order of Breakfast Number One with a fountain Pepsi.

§

Mule looked worried. "How's Barnabas?"

"If pneumonia doesn't set in, he'll be fine, thanks for asking. It was bad. Dooley saved his life."

"Fancy says to tell you she's sorry about what happened."

"Adele says the same."

"Thanks. I'll go out and see him tomorrow."

"Fancy said to ask why you haven't been around, said to call her anytime, she'll work you in." Mule eyed the rector's head as if searching for chicken mites. "Lookin' a little scraggly around the collar."

So be it. He didn't care if he looked like John the Baptist on a bad day, he was never setting foot—

"Th' Randall place is empty, they moved to California to be with their kids," said Mule, dispensing a round of late-breaking real estate news. "Winnie's buyer is breathin' on her pretty heavy, and Shoe Barn sold this week."

"Who to?" asked J.C., spooning yogurt onto half a cling peach.

"Who else? H. Tide."

The editor looked disgusted. "What are they tryin' to do, anyway, make Mitford a colony of Orlando?"

"I've been wondering," said the rector, "what H. Tide stands for."

"Beats me," said Mule. "Maybe High Tide. Or Henry Tide, somethin' like that. Did I hear your deacons got an offer on your house?"

"They're not deacons, they're vestry. And it's not my house."

"They'll sell it out from under you, I reckon, if they get the right price."

"Who knows?" he asked, appearing casual.

"Lookit," said J.C., pulling the *Muse* out of his briefcase. "Hot off th' press, get your own copy on th' street." He turned a couple of pages, folded the paper face out, and laid it on the table.

An entire page of small-space ads . . .

We're stickin' with Esther. Love, Esther and Gene Bolick

We're stickin' with Esther. Hope you do the same.
Tucker, Ginny, and Sue

We're stickin with Esther. She's the best. Sophia and Liza Burton

We're stickin' with Esther. Vote your conscience! The Simpson family

We're stickin' with Esther. She does what it talks about
in Psalm 72:12. A supporter

The rector slapped the table. "This is terrific! Terrific! How much do the ads cost?"

"Forty bucks," said J.C., pleased with himself.

"Where did Sophia get forty bucks?"

J.C. looked uncomfortable. "Don't ask."

"She doesn't have forty bucks."

"So? She wanted to stick up for Esther but didn't have the money. Big deal, I gave 'er the ad free, but if you tell anybody I said that . . . "

Mule gave J.C. a thumbs-up. "I don't care what people say about you, buddyroe, you're all right."

"Look here." J.C. pointed to a couple of the ads.

We're stickin' with Esther. Minnie Lomax, The Irish Woolen Shop

We're stickin' with Esther. Dora Pugh, Mitford Hardware

"Two businesses that aren't afraid to show their politics in front of God an' everybody!" said the editor, approving.

The rector drew a deep breath. Maybe this cloud had a silver lining, after all. He'd certainly drop by and congratulate Minnie and Dora. "You get around town," he said to J.C. "From where you stand, how's the election looking?"

"From where I stand?" J.C. scowled and pushed the yogurt away.

"I'd say that once this edition gets out to th' readers, it'll be runnin' about fifty-fifty."

Something or somebody would have to tip the numbers in Esther's favor, or Edith Mallory would have her claws all over Mitford. This was September fifth, and the election would be hitting the fan less than two months hence. Surely on Sunday he could offer a special prayer, or dedicate the communion service to those who unflaggingly devote themselves to the nobler welfare of the community. And speaking of Psalms, didn't the reading for Sunday say that "the mouth of them that speak lies shall be stopped"?

Ah, well. He remembered that he wouldn't be in the pulpit on Sunday, he'd be sleeping 'til noon, according to his wife's plan, and waking up strong, renewed, and altogether carefree.

"Here," he said, giving J.C. two tens and a twenty. "Run one for me next week and sign it, 'A Friend.'"

§

They stopped at The Local on their way to Meadowgate, to pick up a brisket for Marge Owen. While Cynthia paid their monthly bill, he inspected the contents of the butcher's case.

"Father!" It was Winnie Ivey, carrying a ten-pound bag of flour.

"I'm glad I ran into you, I've made a decision! I decided to go on th' cruise with Velma and not do anything about sellin' 'til I get back. I told the real estate people to wait, just like you said, and I feel like a different person!"

She flushed. "Can you believe I did that?"

"I can! Well done!"

"They didn't like it, they tried to push me, they said I might not get another chance. But then, guess what?"

"What?"

"They offered me another three thousand, but I said no, I'm goin' to wait, and that's that. Besides, thank th' Lord, I'm up seven percent over this time last year!"

"You don't mean it!"

"I do!" He thought Winnie Ivey looked ten years younger, all of which made him feel immeasurably better into the bargain.

"You know what?"

"What?" he asked.

"I'm gettin' to where I don't hardly want to go to Tennessee n'more. Joe said he thought he could get me a job at Graceland, but to tell th' truth, Father, I never cared much for rock an' roll."

§

He didn't have to be George Burns to know that timing was everything.

According to Buddy Benfield, the Malcolms would be getting back to Mitford around eleven o'clock.

He was waiting in front of their house when they pulled into the driveway.

§

Saturday night, and he was looking at a clean slate. No services tomorrow, no arriving early to unlock the church. . . .

Thank God he could rest in the morning. Why did he never know he needed refreshment 'til somebody hit him over the head with a two-by-four?

He ached all over with a weariness he felt even in his teeth.

Yet, how could he lie here like a hog in slop, when there was so much to be thankful for? He ought to be up and shouting and clicking his heels.

"How does it feel?" asked his beaming wife, sitting in bed against a stack of pillows.

"Wonderful. Amazing. *Powerful!*"

"Exactly how I felt!"

"I should have done something like this years ago," he said.

"Maybe. But God's timing is perfect."

"Do you really think we should go ahead with . . . ?"

She nodded. "I think so. It's a nuisance now, but it will pay off down the road."

"Maybe a breezeway someday."

"Maybe. But I'd miss popping back and forth through the hedge, wouldn't you?"

"Ah, the hedge. Where I first laid eyes on my attractive new neighbor."

She laughed happily. "Your doom was sealed."

He sat up and took her in his arms and brushed her cheek with his. "Thank you," he murmured.

"For what?"

"For being the woman you are, for putting up with me, for looking after me."

"You mean you don't think I'm a bossy dame?"

"Sometimes."

"You know what tomorrow is," she said.

"I do. Two years."

"Two *long* years?"

"Not so long," he said, kissing her ear. "But alas, I haven't had a chance to buy—"

"Don't buy me anything," she said, leaning against him. "Don't give me anything you have to wrap."

"You can count on it," he said, feeling the softness of her shoulders, the blue satin gown. . . .

She pulled away, laughing. "Maybe we should try to get some sleep, darling. It's been a long day, a whole string of long days, and besides, now that you're a home owner, you need to save your strength for all those little chores that crop up—like fixing the foundation where it's crumbling, and mending the leak over Dooley's room."

"Aha. The vestry won't be having that done anymore, will they?"

"That's right," she said, kissing him goodnight. "It's just you and me."

"And Harley," he said, brightening.

She turned out the light and rolled on her side, and for a time, he listened for her light, whiffling snore.

He missed his dog and prayed for him, thankful he was mending. He wondered about Dooley, and thought they should call him at school tomorrow, though it might be a trifle soon.

What's more, he was concerned that Father Douglas would leave out The Peace—which he was known, on occasion and for no good reason, to do.

And how would he fix the foundation, anyway? He supposed Harley would know, but what if he didn't? Probably a little mortar; and some new stones where the old had crumbled and fallen out. . . .

He rolled on his back and looked at the ceiling—his ceiling, their ceiling, the first ceiling he had ever owned, as soon as the papers were signed. Now she had a house and he had a house. Bookends. After the work on hers was finished, they would live there and rent this. "To someone with children!" Cynthia hoped.

He had liked handing Ron the check for a hundred and five thousand dollars, though it had taken his breath away to write it. . . .

"Timothy?" she said.

"Yes?"

"You're thinking."

"Right."

"Stop it at once, dearest."

He chuckled. "OK," he said.

He knew the truth, now, of what Stuart Cullen had written to him several years ago:

> *Martha has come in to tell me it is bedtime. I cannot express how wonderful it is to be sometimes told, rather than always doing the telling. . . . There she is again, my friend, and believe me, my wife does not enjoy reminding me twice. That she monitors my energy is a good thing. Otherwise, I would spill it all for Him and have nothing left with which to get out of bed in the mornings. . . .*

He reached for her, and she turned to him, eagerly, smiling in the darkness.

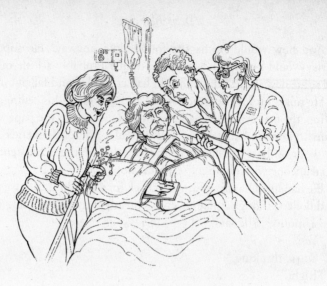

CHAPTER EIGHTEEN

A Cup of Kindness

An early October hurricane gathered its forces in the Caribbean, roared north along the eastern seaboard, and veered inland off Cape Hatteras. In a few short hours, it reached the mountains at the western end of the state, where it pounded Mitford with alarming force.

Rain lashed Lord's Chapel in gusting sheets, rattled the latched shutters of the bell tower, blew the tarps off lumber stacked on the construction site, and crashed a wheelbarrow into a rose bed.

The tin roof of Omer Cunningham's shed, formerly a hangar for his antique ragwing, was hurled toward Luther Green's pasture, where the sight of it, gleaming and rattling and banging through the air, made the cows bawl with trepidation.

Coot Hendrick's flock of three Rhode Island Reds took cover on the back porch after nearly drowning in a pothole in the yard, and Lew Boyd, who was pumping a tank of premium unleaded into an out-of-town Mustang, reported that his hat was whipped off his head and flung into a boxwood at the town monument, nearly a block away.

Phone lines went out; a mudslide slalomed down a deforested

ridge near Farmer, burying a Dodge van; and a metal Coca-Cola sign from Hattie Cloer's market on the highway landed in Hessie Mayhew's porch swing.

At the edge of the village, Old Man Mueller sat in his kitchen, trying to repair the mantel clock his wife asked him to fix several years before her death. He happened to glance out the window in time to see his ancient barn collapse to the ground. He noted that it swayed slightly before it fell, and when it fell, it went fast.

"Hot ding!" he muttered aloud, glad to be spared the aggravation of taking it down himself. "Now," he said to the furious roar outside, "if you'd stack th' boards, I'd be much obliged."

§

The villagers emerged into the sunshine that followed, dazzled by the spectacular beauty of the storm's aftermath, which seemed in direct proportion to its violence.

The mountain ridges appeared etched in glass, set against clear, perfectly blue skies from horizon to horizon.

At Fernbank, a bumper crop of crisp, tart cooking apples lay on the orchard floor, ready to be gathered into local sacks. The storm had done the picking, and not a single ladder would be needed for the job.

"You see," said Jena Ivey, "there's always two sides to everything!" Jena had closed Mitford Blossoms to run up to Fernbank and gather apples, having promised to bake pies for the Bane just three days hence.

"But," said another apple gatherer, "the autumn color won't be worth two cents. The storm took all the leaves!"

"Whatever," sighed Jena, who thought some people were mighty hard to please.

§

Balmy. Like spring. It was that glad fifth season called Indian summer, which came only on the rarest occasions.

He was doing his duties, he was going his rounds, he was poking his nose into everybody's business. How else could a priest know what was happening?

He rang the Bolicks. "Esther? How's it going?"

"I'd kill Gene Bolick if I could catch him, that's how it's goin'!"

"What now?"

"Haven't I been bakin' since the bloomin' Boer War, tryin' to get ready for Friday? And didn't I tell him, I said, 'Gene, don't you mess with these cookies, there's three hundred cookies I just baked, and I'm puttin' 'em in these two-gallon freezer bags this minute, so you'll keep your paws off.' Well, I zipped up those bags and stacked 'em in th' freezer and first thing you know, I came home last night and *who* was sittin' at the table with his head stuck in one of those two-gallon bags, goin' at it like a fox in a henhouse? I ask you!"

"You don't mean it!"

"Frozen hard as bricks and him hammerin' down on those cookies like they'd just come out of th' oven."

"Aha."

"It's a desperate man who'll do a trick like that."

"I agree. But try to forgive him," he said, knowing that Gene Bolick had not had a cookie to call his own since this whole event began brewing several months ago.

He rang off, assuring her that he'd do his part on Friday, down in the trenches with the rest of the troops.

§

He flipped quickly through the *Muse,* looking for another batch of *Stickin'* ads.

"Looks like Esther's pullin' ahead," said J.C., totally convinced that his small-space ad idea had done the trick. It was generally agreed that the full page of Mack Stroupe's face had been a dire mistake by the other camp. It was one thing to look at Mack's mug on a billboard, but somehow seeing it right under your nose had been a definite turnoff, according to the buzz around town.

Along with a growing number of others, the rector was beginning to feel upbeat about the outcome of the election just one month away. The wife of a deacon at First Baptist had planned a preelection Stickin' With Esther tea, and the mayor would also be riding down Main Street in a fire truck during a parade for Fire Awareness Day.

Things were definitely looking up.

§

Coming into the kitchen to make a pot of tea, he noted that Violet had descended from her penthouse atop the refrigerator and was curled up on his dog's bed under the table.

Thank God Barnabas was coming home on Saturday, the day after the Bane. Hal had kept him at Meadowgate nearly a month, just in case.

He'd still have the splint on for a couple of weeks, but the chest wrap had come off. The job of healing could be finished up neatly by close confinement for five or six months, with no running, chasing, or stick-fetching.

"There's certainly a lot of hilarity going on in my house," said Cynthia. She stood at the kitchen door, her head cocked to one side.

"What do you mean?"

She listened intently, as if to the music of the spheres. "Somebody's laughing!"

"What's wrong with laughter?"

She didn't answer, but came and stood by the stove, her brow furrowed, as he put the kettle on.

"Elton used six blocks t' build a model of a staircase that has three steps . . ." Harley's voice drifted up to the kitchen.

"Poor Harley," said Cynthia. "I hope he makes an A this time."

"That B-minus cut him to the quick."

"I think Lace is too hard on him."

"And you're too soft! Delivering his breakfast downstairs on a *tray*, for Pete's sake."

"You're jealous because I don't deliver yours, much less on a tray, but then, dear fellow, you have never, ever once cleaned out and organized my attic so that it looks better than my studio!"

"True."

"Nor have you ever hauled the detritus from said cleanup to the Bane, and brought me back a form which makes it all tax deductible." She turned and went quickly to the door.

"Good Lord, Timothy! Listen!"

He heard a woman's hysterical laughter coming from the little house next door.

They went out to the back stoop. The high-pitched laughter continued, followed by a crash that sounded like breaking glass.

"What on earth?" she asked. Her alarm was evident.

"I'll go and see." He didn't want to go and see; he didn't want anything out of the ordinary to be going on next door.

He darted through the hedge and up the dark steps to the screen door. He looked into Cynthia's kitchen and saw Pauline Barlowe standing at the sink. She was throwing up.

"Pauline," he said.

She retched into the sink again, then turned and stared toward the door, her eyes swollen, wiping her mouth.

"What?" she said. Her voice was cold, coarse; the stench of warm bile and alcohol permeated the room.

He opened the door and went in. "What's going on?" He tried to keep his voice free of anger, tried to make it a simple question, but failed.

"Ask y'r big high an' mighty in there what's goin' on, and if you find out, let me know, that's what *I've* been tryin' to do, is figure out what's goin' on."

She laughed suddenly and sank to the floor, leaning against the cabinets.

He walked down the hall and into the living room, where Buck Leeper sat in a Queen Anne chair, asleep and snoring, an empty vodka bottle on the lamp table and a glass on the floor at his feet.

§

He cleaned the kitchen and swept up a broken glass on the back stoop, while Pauline sat in a chair with her head in her hands. He sensed that she was crying, though she made no sound. Then he turned off the downstairs lights, except for the lamp in the living room and the light in the hallway. Buck didn't stir and he didn't wake him. He would deal with this tomorrow.

He drove Pauline home and they sat in the car in front of the house where her father, son, and daughter were sleeping.

The hilarity and weeping had passed; she was silent as a stone, her face turned away from him.

"We need to talk," he said.

She nodded.

"Sunday afternoon, if you can."

She nodded again. "I'm so sorry," she whispered.

He got out of the car and opened her door and helped her up the sidewalk. The temperature had dropped considerably and she was shivering in a sleeveless dress. "Will you wake anyone?"

"Don't worry," she said, still avoiding his gaze. "I won't let nobody see me like this."

§

When he came in from the garage, Cynthia met him in the hallway.

"It's Esther!" she said. "She had an accident, and they say it looks bad. They want you to come to the hospital at once!"

Esther! He raced to the bathroom, splashed water on his face, took his jacket off the hook in the kitchen, and once again backed the Buick out of the garage, tires screeching.

There were many ways to lose an election. He prayed to God this wasn't one of them.

§

"What happened?" he asked Nurse Kennedy in the hospital corridor.

"She fell off a ladder, broke her left wrist, broke the right elbow, and . . ." Nurse Kennedy shook her head.

"And what?"

"Fractured her jaw. Dr. Harper is wiring her mouth shut as we speak."

"Good Lord!"

"But she'll be fine."

"Be *fine*? How could anybody be fine with two broken limbs and her mouth wired shut?"

"It happens, Father." Nurse Kennedy sighed and continued down the hall.

He wound his way along the corridor to the waiting room, where Gene Bolick sat on a Danish modern sofa in shock.

"Where's Ray?" he asked Gene. Why wasn't Ray Cunningham here? Didn't he know his wife had had a terrible accident?

"Ray who?" queried Gene, looking stupefied.

"Esther's husband!"

"I'm Esther's husband," said Gene, as plainly as he knew how.

"You mean . . . you mean, the mayor didn't fall off a ladder?"

"I don't know about th' mayor, but Esther sure did, and it busted her up pretty bad." He appeared disconsolate.

"Good heavens, Gene, I'm sorry. Terribly sorry." He sat beside his parishioner on the sofa. "How is she?"

"Not so good, if you ask me. She was down at th' parish hall on a ladder, puttin' up signs—you know, *Kitchen Goods, Clothing Items,* such as that, and went to step down and . . ." Gene lifted his hands. "And crashed."

"Where is everybody?" Usually, when someone was rushed to the hospital in Mitford, a whole gaggle of friends and family showed up to pray, make a run on the vending machines, and rip recipes from outdated issues of *Southern Living.*

"They're down at th' parish hall, I reckon, where they've been for th' last forty-eight hours."

"I'll get the prayer chain going," said the rector. He sped along the hall to the phone, where he called his wife to put the chain in motion. "How bad is it?" asked Cynthia.

"There's a break in both arms, and they're wiring her jaws shut."

She gasped. "Good heavens!"

"I'll be here for a while."

"Poor Esther. How awful. Please tell Gene I'm sorry, I'll go see Esther tomorrow, and I'll call the chain right now. Love you, dearest."

"Love you. Keep my place warm."

Hurrying down the hall, he stopped briefly at a vending machine for a pack of Nabs and a Sprite.

§

He'd just finished praying with Gene for Esther to be knit back together as good as new when Hessie Mayhew rushed into the waiting room. He looked at his watch. Eleven o'clock. Hardly anyone in this town stayed up 'til eleven o'clock.

"How is she?" asked Hessie.

"Doped up," said Gene.

"I've got to see her," insisted the Bane co-chair. Given her wide eyes and frazzled hair, Hessie looked as if she'd been plugged into an electrical outlet.

"You can't see 'er," said Gene. "Just me an' th' Father can go in."

"Do you realize that at seven in the morning, the Food Committee's gettin' together at my house to bake twelve two-layer orange marmalades, and we don't even have th' *recipe*?"

Gene slapped his forehead. "Oh, Lord help!"

"I'm sure it's written down somewhere," suggested the rector.

"Nope, it's not," said Gene.

"That's right. It's not." Hessie pursed her lips. "If I've told her once, I've told her a thousand times to write her recipes down, *especially* the orange marmalade, for heaven's sake."

"It's in her head," said Gene, defending his wife.

"Well," announced the co-chair, looking determined, "we'll have to find a way to get it out!"

§

He arrived at the office the next morning, feeling the exhaustion of half a night at the hospital.

At two a.m., he'd left Esther resting, one arm in a cast, the other in a cast and a sling, and unable to speak a word even if she wanted to. Gene slept by her bed on a hospital cot.

How on earth anybody was going to get a cake recipe out of Esther Bolick was beyond him. In any case, Hessie had postponed the baking session until Thursday afternoon, which meant the cakes would be squeaking in under the wire—if at all.

"We *have* to have Esther's orange marmalades," she had said flatly. "People *expect* Esther's marmalades. At twenty dollars per cake times twelve, that's two hundred and forty dollars, which is nothing to sneeze at."

He yawned and sat wearily at his desk.

He was rubbing his eyes as Buck Leeper opened the door and walked in, taking off his hard hat.

"Good morning," said the rector.

Buck stood in the doorway, uneasy. "I need to talk."

"Sit down."

"I can't stay. I came to tell you I'm . . ." Buck looked at the floor, then met the rector's gaze. "I'm sorry. That was bad, what happened. I took a drink, I offered her one, and it went from there."

"Did you know she's an alcoholic? An addict?"

"Yes." Buck's voice was hoarse. "I got to tell you, I talked her into it, I shouldn't have done it, I'm sick to my gut about it."

"There's help, Buck."

The superintendent scraped his work boot on the floor, looking down. "No. I can beat this, I've been beatin' it, this is th' first time in . . . in a while. I wanted to tell you I'm movin' out, one of the crew knows a house for sale, but thinks they'll rent."

"Before we talk about that, let's name the problem. It has a name. It's your alcoholism. Your addiction."

Buck stiffened and turned away, but didn't walk to the door.

"How long have you been drinking, seriously drinking?"

"I was thirteen when my old man started pourin' it down my gullet. The first time, he made me drink 'til I puked." He faced the rector. "Bourbon. Sour mash. He liked it when I got to where I could drink him under the table, not many people could. When he died, I swore I'd never touch th' stuff again."

"But you did, and now you're suffering on your own account as well as Pauline's. Do you care for Pauline?"

"Yeah. I care for her."

"Why?"

"I respect what she's been able to do, to come back like that, out of her hell, and find faith. God, I hate what I did."

"You did it together. It takes two."

"And her kids. They're great kids. Who deserves kids like that? Nobody, not even people who have it all together, who never took a drink! I thought that maybe I could . . . maybe we could . . ."

"You can."

"No." His voice was hard. "It's too late for me."

"What if you had somebody in this thing with you, somebody who'd stick closer than a brother, somebody who'd go to bat for you, help you through it—help you over it?"

"Oh, Jesus Christ!" Buck said with disgust, moving toward the door.

"That's who I had in mind, actually."

Buck's face colored. "That crap don't work for me."

"How long have you hauled the pain of your dead brother in your gut? And how much longer do you want to haul it? Stop, friend. Stop and look at this thing that cheats you out of all that's valuable, all that's precious."

The superintendent turned and stared out the window, his back to the rector.

"You can't beat this alone, Buck. You've tried for years and it never worked. Bottom line, we're not created to go it alone, we're made to hammer out our lives with God as our defender. Going it alone may work for a while, but it never has and never will go the mile."

Buck shrugged his shoulders, still looking out the window. "Pauline knows about God and she couldn't make it."

"No, but she's going to. In any case, we don't come to God to attain perfection, we come to be saved."

"You remember my grandaddy was a preacher. There's no way I could be good enough to get saved or whatever you call it. No way."

"It isn't about being good enough."

Buck turned to him, furious. "So what is it about, for Christ's sake?"

"It's about letting Him into our lives in a personal way. You can do that with a simple prayer you can repeat with me. When we let Him in, He guarantees that we become new creatures."

"New creatures?" Buck laughed bitterly. "Who wants to be a new creature when you can't even get the old one to work?"

"New creatures make mistakes, too, they stumble around and fall in a ditch. But once the commitment is made with the heart, He takes it from there."

"It always sounded like a lot of bull to me."

Father Tim got up and stood beside his desk. "I could tell you all day what you'd gain by making that commitment—but look at it another way: What do you have to lose?"

For a time, the only sound was the ticking of the clock on the bookshelf.

"Listen," said Buck, "I'll be out of the house in a couple of days."

He moved suddenly to the door and opened it, then went down the walk to his truck, not looking back.

"The fields are white . . ."

"Buck!" said the rector. "Wait . . ."

But he didn't wait.

"They want to buy me out and let me run it," said Winnie, looking anxious. "What do you think?"

If he ever had to mess with another real estate deal . . .

"What do *you* think?" he asked.

"It sounds like a good idea. I mean, I do the work and get a regular paycheck, and they have all th' headaches." She sighed. "That might be refreshin'."

"Weren't you going to wait 'til after the cruise to make a decision?"

"They want an answer right away. Soon." She wrung her hands. "At once!"

He didn't feel he had the credentials to counsel Winnie on what amounted to the next few years of her life. "What's God saying to you about all this?"

"I still have that stuck feelin', like I don't know which way to turn."

Definitely not a good sign, but what more could he say?

"Your hair . . ." said Emma.

"What about it?" he snapped.

"Dearest," said Cynthia, "about your hair . . ."

"Don't touch it!" he said. So what if he had hacked on it himself? At least it wasn't draping over his collar like so much seaweed.

"Man!" exclaimed Mule, eyeing him with interest.

"You don't *like* it?" he asked. "I never say anything about *your* hair, I never even *notice* your hair, why you can't do the same for *me* is beyond all *imagining*—"

"Gee whiz," said Mule, looking perplexed. "I was just goin' to ask where you got that blue shirt."

❦

When he walked into Esther's hospital room on Thursday morning, her bed was surrounded by Bane volunteers. One of them held a notepad at the ready, and he felt a definite tension in the air.

They didn't even look up as he came in.

Hessie leaned over Esther, speaking as if the patient's hearing had been severely impaired by the fall.

"Esther!" she shouted. "You've got to cooperate! The doctor said he'd give us twenty minutes and not a second more!"

"Ummaummhhhh," said Esther, desperately trying to speak through clamped jaws.

"Why couldn't she write something?" asked Vanita Bentley. "I see two fingers sticking out of her cast."

"Uhnuhhh," said Esther.

"You can't write with two fingers. Have you ever tried writing with two fingers?"

"Oh, Lord," said Vanita. "Then *you* think of something! We've got to hurry!"

"We need an alphabet board!" Hessie declared.

"Who has time to go lookin' for an alphabet board? Where would we find one, anyway?"

"Make one!" instructed the co-chair. "Write down the alphabet on your notepad and let her point 'til she spells it out."

"Ummuhuhnuh," said Esther.

"She can't move her arm to point!"

"So? We can move the notepad!"

Esther raised the forefinger of her right hand.

"One finger. *One!* Right, Esther? If it's yes, blink once, if it's no, blink twice."

"She blinked once, so it's yes. *One!* One what, Esther? Cup? Teaspoon? Vanita, are you writin' this down?"

"Two blinks," said Marge Crowder. "So, it's not a cup and it's not a teaspoon."

"Butter!" said somebody. "Is it one stick of butter?"

"She blinked twice, that's no. Try again. One *teaspoon*? Oh, thank God! Vanita, one teaspoon."

"Right. But one teaspoon of what? Salt?"

"Oh, please, you wouldn't use a teaspoon of *salt* in a *cake*!"

"Excuse me for living," said Vanita.

"Maybe cinnamon? Look! One blink. One teaspoon of cinnamon!"

"*Hallelujah!*" they chorused.

Esther wagged her finger.

"One, two, three, four, five . . ." someone counted.

"Five what?" asked Vanita. "Cups? No. Teaspoons? No. *Table-spoons?*"

"One blink, it's tablespoons! *Five tablespoons!*"

"Oh, mercy, I'm glad I took my heart pill this morning," said Hessie. "Is it of butter? I just have a feelin' it's butter. Look! One blink!"

"*Five tablespoons of butter!*" shouted the crowd, in unison.

"OK, in cakes, you'd have to have baking powder. How much baking powder, Esther?"

Esther held up one finger.

"One teaspoon?"

"Uhnuhhh," said Esther, looking desperate.

"One *tablespoon*?" asked Vanita.

"You wouldn't use a *tablespoon* of baking powder in a cake!" sniffed Marge Crowder.

"Look," said Vanita, "I'm helpin' y'all just to be nice. My husband personally thinks I am a great cook, but I don't do cakes, OK, so if you'd like somebody else to take these notes, just step right up and help yourself, thank you!"

"You're doin' great, honey, keep goin'," said Hessie.

"Look at that!" exclaimed Vanita. "She's got one finger out straight and the other one bent back! Is that one and a half? It *is*, she blinked once! I declare, that is the cleverest thing I ever saw. OK, one and a half teaspoons of bakin' powder!"

Everyone applauded.

"This is a killer," said Vanita, fanning herself with the notebook. "Don't you think we could sell two-layer triple chocolates just as easy?"

"Ummunnuhhh," said Esther, her eyes burning with disapproval.

Hessie snorted. "This could take 'til kingdom come. How much time have we got left?"

"Ten minutes, maybe eleven!"

"Eleven minutes? Are you kidding me? We'll never finish this in eleven minutes."

"I think she told me she uses buttermilk in this recipe," said Marge Crowder. "Esther," she shouted, "how much buttermilk?"

Esther made the finger and a half gesture.

"One and a half cups, right? Great! Now we're cookin'!"

More applause.

"OK," commanded the co-chair, "what have we got so far?"

Vanita, being excessively near-sighted, held the notepad up for close inspection. "One teaspoon of cinnamon, five tablespoons of butter, one and a half teaspoons of baking powder, and one and a half cups of buttermilk."

"I've got to sit down," said the head of the Food Committee, pressing her temples.

"It looks like Esther's droppin' off to sleep, oh, Lord, Esther, honey, don't go to sleep, you can sleep tonight!"

"Could somebody ask th' nurse for a stress tab?" wondered Vanita. "Do you think they'd mind, I've written checks to th' hospital fund for nine years, goin' on ten!"

"By the way," asked Marge Crowder, "is this recipe for one layer or two?"

He decided to step into the hall for a breath of fresh air.

§

Hammer and tong. That's how one Bane worker said they went at it on Friday.

The weather was glorious, the parish hall was full to overflowing with both goods and people, the lawn was adorned with three white tents, sheltering from any possible bad weather everything from fine antiques and children's toys to hot meals and homemade desserts. Three tour buses stood parked at the curb, signaling the penultimate event of the year.

Parkers filled the two church lots first, then sent traffic up the hill to satellite hospital parking, and down a side street to the Methodists. A stream of cars and pickups also flowed into lots behind the Collar Button, the Irish Woolen Shop, and the Sweet Stuff Bakery.

Mitford Blossoms kicked in ten parking spaces while several Main Street residents, including Evie Adams, earned good money renting their private driveways.

For the Bane workers, it was down in the trenches, and no two ways about it.

For eleven hours running, the rector made change, sorted through plunder for eager customers, dished up chili and spaghetti, boxed cakes, bagged cookies, carried trash bags to Gene Bolick's pickup, made coffee, hauled ice, picked up debris, found Band-Aids and patched a skinned knee, demonstrated a Hoover vacuum cleaner, took several cash contributions for the dig-a-well fund, told the story of the stained-glass windows, and mopped up a spilled soft drink in the parish hall corridor.

Uncle Billy came to supervise, armed with three new jokes collected especially for the occasion.

After five o'clock, vans from area companies and organizations hauled in and out like clockwork, carrying employees who proceeded to eat heartily and shop heavily.

By eight o'clock, the cleaning crew came on with a vengeance, and at eight-fifteen, a small but faithful remnant, despite weariness in every bone, arrived at the hospital, where they gathered around Esther Bolick's bed and sang, "For she's a jolly good fellow."

The marmalades, they reported, had been among the first items to go, with some anonymous donor kicking in sixty bucks—thereby bringing the total to three hundred dollars, or ten feet of well-digging.

It had been the most successful Bane in anyone's memory, and had raised the phenomenal sum of twenty-two thousand dollars. This total not only defeated the Bane's previous record by several thousand, it clearly put every other church fund-raiser, possibly in the entire world, to utter vexation and shame.

§

Pauline came to his office in the afternoon and sat on the visitor's bench, looking proud and strong.

"I'm goin' to AA," she said, "and I'm not seein' Buck anymore. That's the best I can do, Father, and I want to do it, and I'm askin' God to give me strength to do it." She looked at him earnestly. "Will you pray that I can?"

It was the longest speech he'd ever heard her make.

He walked home with Pauline, loving the crisp air, the blue skies.

"Whenever you think you'd like to move into your own place, I'll give you a hand, and so will Harley."

"Thank you. But I don't deserve—"

"Pauline, you've given me one of the richest gifts of this life—the chance to know Dooley Barlowe. I don't deserve that. So, let's not talk about deserving, OK?"

She looked at him and smiled. And then she laughed.

"Mr. Tim!" Jessie ran up the hall and grabbed him around the legs. "I ain't suckin' my thumb n'more. Looky there!" She held her thumb aloft and he inspected it closely.

"Buck got me to quit," she said, grinning up at him. "He give me a baby doll with hair to comb, you want to see it?"

"I do!" he said.

Jessie darted into the living room and returned with the doll. "See how 'er hair's th' color of mine, Buck said he looked at a whole *bunch* of baby dolls 'til he found this 'un. You want to hold it? Her name's Mollie, she don't wet or nothin'." She took him by the hand. "Come and sit down if you're goin' to hold 'er. Buck holds 'er a lot, but he cain't come n'more, Pauline said he cain't."

Jessie popped her thumb in her mouth, then took it out again.

Pauline glanced at the rector and shrugged and turned away, but he'd seen the sorrow in her eyes.

Bane is a Blessing
To Thousands

Last Friday, Lord's Chapel gave their annual Bane and Blessing sale, which netted the record-braking sum of $22,000.

According to Bane co-chair Hessie Mayhew, major funding will be provided to dig wells in east Africa, and buy an ambulance for a hospital in Landon county. Other recipients of Bane funds include mission fields in Bosnia, Croatia, Ruwanda, Harlan County, Kentucky, and food banks throughout our local area.

Mrs. Mayhew said that special thanks are due to co-chai, Esther Bolck, who demanded the best from all voluntears and got it.

A list of voluntears is printed on the back page of today's edition. As Mrs. Bolik is sadly laid up in the hospital with two broken arms and a fractured jaw, you may send a card to room 107, but please, no visits until next Wednesday, doctor's orders. She is allergic to lilies, which kill her sinuses, but likes everything else.

A photograph of a large, fake check for twenty-two thousand dollars was included in the story.

"Who *wrote* this?" asked Father Tim.

"I've hired help," said J.C., looking expansive. "Vanita Bentley!"

"Who keyed it in?"

"I did, Vanita only does longhand. She'll be writin' a special 'Around Town' column every week from here out."

"Congratulations!" said the rector. So what if the *Muse* would never win a Pulitzer? It wasn't like it was *The New York Times,* for Pete's sake.

§

"*Buon giorno,* Father! Andrew Gregory, home at last!"

"Andrew! By George, you've been missed!"

Andrew laughed. The rector didn't think he'd ever heard his friend sounding quite so . . .

"Fernbank has been my fervent contemplation since we last talked," said Andrew. "I'm eager to go up and have a look. How's it faring?"

"Well, for one thing, you have an orchard full of apples, and the roof is holding its own."

"Splendid! Can you let me in to have a look around?"

"Absolutely. What's good for you? How about . . . fifteen minutes?"

"Perfect!" said Andrew, sounding . . . how *was* Andrew sounding, anyway? Was it carefree? Boyish? Relaxed?

Come to think of it, who wouldn't be relaxed after three months of visiting cousins in Italy?

§

When Father Tim arrived at Fernbank, Andrew's gray Mercedes was already parked in the drive, and Andrew stood waiting on the porch with a man and woman.

As he trotted up the steps, he couldn't help but notice that the woman was exceedingly attractive, nearly as tall as the tall Andrew, and with a striking figure. He blinked into the dazzling warmth of her smile, hardly noticing the dark-haired man standing with them.

"Father!"

"Welcome home, my friend!"

They embraced, and Andrew kissed the rector, European-style, on both cheeks.

"Father, first I'd like to introduce you to Anna, my cousin . . ."

Good heavens, this was a *cousin*?

". . . and my wife," said the beaming Andrew.

CHAPTER NINETEEN

Fernbank

Surprised, if not stunned, by joy, the rector could scarcely speak. "Congratulations!" he blurted. "*Mazel tov!* Ah, *felicitaziones!*"

Andrew pumped his hand. "Well done, Father! And this is Anna's brother, Antonio Nocelli."

"Call me Tony!" said Antonio, embracing the rector and kissing him on either cheek. "I have heard much about you, Father."

"While I have heard nothing at all about you and Anna!"

Anna laughed, throwing her head back. "Let me say, Father, that Andrew is our *fourth* cousin, so you must not alarm."

"Yes, for heaven's sake, don't alarm!" said Andrew, chuckling.

Anna shrugged and smiled. "My English? Not perfect."

"Whose is?" asked the rector. "Well, shall we go in? Would you like to take them in while I wait outside?"

"Heavens, no, you must come in, also," said Andrew. The rector thought he'd never seen his friend so tanned, so boyish, so eager.

"Here's the key, then. Fernbank will be yours soon enough, why don't you unlock the door?"

"I am very excited," Anna told her husband.

Tony agreed. "We could not sleep for thinking of the house Andrew has taken into his heart."

Andrew swung the double doors open, and they walked in. There was a moment of hushed silence.

"Ahh, *bella . . ."* said Tony. *"Molto bella!"*

Anna opened her arms to the room. "It is beautiful! Just as you said!"

"A bit damp, my dear, but—"

"But, *amore mio,* sunlight can fix!"

"Anna believes sunlight can fix everything," Andrew told the rector, pleased.

They strolled through the house, savoring each room.

Anna touched the walls, the banisters, the furnishings, often murmuring, "Fernbank . . ."

In the ballroom, he told the story of the painted ceiling and two other Italians, a father and son, who had come all the way to Mitford to paint it, living with Miss Sadie's family for nearly three years.

As angels soared above them among rose-tinted clouds, he felt oddly proud, like a father proud of a child, eagerly savoring the cries of delight.

Someone to love Fernbank! Thanks be to God!

Indian summer had drawn on, offering a final moment of glad weather.

They sat on Miss Sadie's frail porch furniture, which the rector had dusted off. Andrew and Anna took the wicker love seat.

"Now!" said Andrew. "We will tell you everything."

Father Tim laughed. "Easy. I can't handle much more excitement."

"Tony and Anna owned a wonderful little restaurant in Lucera, only a few steps from my *penzione.* The food was outstanding, perhaps the best I've had in my travels around the Mediterranean. I began to go there every day for lunch."

"Soon," said Anna, looking boldly at Andrew, "he came also for dinner."

"Tony cooked, Anna served, we discovered we were cousins, and, well . . ." Andrew smiled, suddenly speechless.

"Shy," said the rector, nodding to the others.

Anna made a wickedly funny face. "He is not shy, Father, he is English!" She put her arms stiffly by her sides, pretending to be a board. "But that is outside! Inside, he is Italian, tender as fresh *ravioli*! If not this, I could not marry him and come so far from home!" She laughed with pleasure, and brushed Andrew's cheek with her hand.

"The building that contained the restaurant was being rezoned," said Andrew, "and Mrs. Nocelli died last year . . ."

Anna and Tony crossed themselves.

"The cousins had moved away, some to Rome, others to Verona; the vineyard had sold out of the family, so there were almost no ties left. Yet, when I asked Anna to marry me, I feared she wouldn't leave Italy."

Anna patted her husband's knee. "Timing is good, Father."

"Don't I know it?"

Andrew smiled easily. "The Nocellis are an old wine-making family in Lucera. We were married by their priest of many years. Fortunately, I was able to squeak in under the wire because of my Catholic boyhood."

"Your children," said the rector, "do they know?"

"Oh, yes. They came to Lucera for the wedding. They are very happy for us."

"Any children for you, Anna?"

"I never had children, Father, and my husband was killed ten years behind by a crazy person in a fast car."

"And so at Fernbank," Andrew said, "Anna and Tony and I will have our home and open a very small restaurant."

"Very small!" exclaimed Anna.

"And very good!" said Tony, giving a thumbs-up. The rector thought Tony was nearly as good-looking—and good-natured—as his sister.

Unable to sit still another moment, Andrew rose and made a proclamation. "We will call the restaurant Lucera, in honor of their lovely village and my mother's girlhood home—and the wine for the restaurant will come from one of the many old vineyards which have produced there since the tenth century."

"*Brava,* Lucera!" said Tony. "*Brava,* Mitford!"

"Good heavens!" The rector felt the wonder of it. "An Italian restaurant in Mitford, wine from old vineyards, and handsome people to live in this grand house! Miss Sadie would be dazzled. We shall all be dazzled!"

Anna stood, nearly dancing with expectation. "I am longing to visit the apples!"

"In those shoes, my dear?" asked Andrew.

"I shall take them off at once!" she said, and did so.

As he walked up Wisteria toward the rectory, he looked at his house in the growing darkness, trying to find the sense of ownership he expected to feel. Oh, well, he thought, that will come when the pipes burst in a hard winter and I'm the one to pick up the tab.

He patted his coat pocket. In it was a check for fifteen thousand dollars, given him at this evening's vestry meeting.

Ron Malcolm had presented it with some ceremony. "Father, we priced the house to allow for a little negotiation. H. Tide wanted it so badly, they didn't try to negotiate, so you paid top price. We all feel that ninety thousand is fair to you and to us, and . . . we thank you for your business!"

Warm applause all around.

He was feeling positively over the top. A two-story residence of native stone, all paid for, and fifteen thousand bucks in his pocket. Not bad for an old guy.

He whistled a few bars from the Pastorale as he ran up the front steps to tell his wife the good news.

He didn't know where Buck had moved, and though he saw the superintendent on the job site, nothing was mentioned of his new whereabouts.

Buck had left the yellow house spotless. This, however, hardly mattered, since the late-starting conversion would be getting under way next week. It would be all sawdust and sawhorses for longer than he cared to think, and Buck would probably leave it in someone else's hands as soon as the attic job was finished.

He didn't want to lose Buck Leeper. In some way he couldn't explain, Buck was part of Mitford now.

§

"Timothy!"

"Stuart! I was just thinking of you."

"Good, I hope?"

"I wouldn't go that far," said the rector, chuckling. "What's up, old friend?"

"*Old* friend. How odd you'd say that. I'm feeling a hundred and four."

"Whatever for? You've just been where people wear bikinis."

Stuart groaned. "Yes, and where I held my stomach in for two long weeks."

"Holding your stomach in is no vacation," said the rector.

"Look, I'm over on the highway, headed to a meeting in South Carolina. Can we meet for coffee?"

"Coffee. Hmmm. How about the Grill? It's close to lunchtime. I'll treat."

"Terrific. Main Street, as I recall?"

"North of The Local, green awning, name on the window. When?"

"Five minutes," said the bishop, sounding brighter.

§

"This," he said, introducing his still-youthful seminary friend, "is my bishop, the Right Reverend Stuart Cullen."

"Right Reverend . . ." said Percy, pondering. "I guess you wouldn't hardly talk about it if you was th' Wrong Reverend."

"Percy!" said Velma.

"Oh, for heaven's sake, don't listen to Timothy, call me Stuart." Stuart shook hands all around, and the rector watched him charm the entire assembly.

"Hold it right there!" J.C. hunkered over his Nikon and cranked off six shots in rapid succession.

"I ain't never seen a pope," said Coot Hendrick, wide-eyed.

"Not a pope, a bishop," said Mule.

Percy looked puzzled. "I thought you said he was a reverend."

"Call me Stuart and get it over with," pleaded the bishop, hastening to a booth with Father Tim.

§

Stuart poured cream in his coffee. "By the way, someone told me that Abraham's route to Canaan now requires four visas."

"Not surprising, since it's a six-hundred-mile trip. I wouldn't mind seeing the real thing one day. I was just remembering from a study we did in seminary that Canaan is the birthplace of the word *Bible*."

"Not to mention the birthplace of our alphabet. So, how would you like a stint on the Outer Banks at some point? I fancy it might be your Plain of Jezreel, at the very least."

"Tell me more."

"Wonderful parish, small Carpenter Gothic church, historic cemetery, gorgeous setting . . ."

"Keep talking."

"There's a rector down there who'd like nothing better than a mountain church. I have just the church, and Bill Harvey, who's the bishop in that diocese, thinks we might work out a trade—you could go down as an interim . . . the summer after you retire."

"I'll mention it to Cynthia. Let me know more. So when are *you* going out to Canaan, my friend?"

"I knew you'd ask, but I don't know. I'm still terrified, just as you were."

"How did I get smarter than you?"

"You're older," said Stuart, grinning. "Much older."

"Remember Edith Mallory?"

"The vulture who tried to get her talons in your hide."

"We have an election coming up, and I feel certain she's been funneling big money to the opposition."

"Who's the opposition?" asked Stuart, taking a bite of his grilled cheese sandwich.

"Not known as the sort who'd be good for this town."

"If I know where you're going with this, the best policy is hands off."

"I agree. Especially since I have no proof."

"Poisonous business. But you know the antidote."

"Prayer."

"Exactly. How's your Search Committee coming along? I haven't had a report recently."

"I'm pretty much out of the loop," said the rector, "but they seem excited. We surveyed the parish, and the consensus is for a young priest with children."

"They can save all of us some heartache by asking the candidates a central question."

"Which is?"

"'Do you believe Jesus is God?'"

"Right. I've talked about that with the committee. Sad state of affairs when we have to point such a question at candidates who took the ordination vows . . ."

The bishop sighed. "Paul said in the second epistle to the good chap you were named after, 'The time is coming when people will not put up with sound doctrine . . . they will accumulate for themselves teachers to suit their own desires, and will turn from the truth and wander away to myths.' Ah, Timothy . . ."

"Eat up, my friend. You've got a long haul ahead of you. Why aren't you flying?"

"I'm driving because I need time to think, I need some time alone."

"A man has to get in a car and hurtle down the interstate to get time alone? Ah, Stuart . . ."

Stuart chuckled. "Two weeks at the beach doesn't solve everything."

"Especially not when you're holding your stomach in," said the rector.

§

"I've done it," Winnie announced.

He couldn't tell whether she was going to laugh or cry.

"Would you take this copy of the contract home and look it over?" she asked. "I had a lawyer look it over, but I don't know how good he is, maybe if you're not too busy, you could do it, I should have asked you before. Course I guess it's too late now, since it's mailed, but still, if you would . . ."

"I don't know what help I can be, but yes, I'll look it over." Dadgum it, why didn't he just go study for a broker's license? He seemed to be spending as much time in real estate as in the priesthood.

"They've about ragged me to death, Father. I guess I'll stay on and run it." She looked white as a sheet, he thought.

"I'm thrilled to hear you'll stay in Mitford. Your business is thriving, you have a legion of friends here—"

"But my family's up there—a brother and sister and two nieces and a nephew."

"I know. But aren't we family? Don't we love you?" Shame on him, trying to win her heart from her own blood kin.

"I'll be glad to go on that cruise next week," she said, not looking glad about anything.

§

Lace was sitting at the kitchen table doing her history homework when Dooley called from school. Father Tim answered the wall phone by the sink. "Rectory . . ."

"I'm on my way to study hall."

"Hey, buddy!"

"Hey, yourself," said Dooley. "What's going on?"

"Not much. What about you?"

"We're having our fall mixer tomorrow night. Man!"

"Man, what?"

"Four busloads of girls are coming, maybe five."

"Man!" He agreed that seemed to say it all.

"How's Barn?"

"Looking good. Eating well. Sleeping a lot."

"I sort of miss him."

"He misses you more. So, what kind of mixer is it?"

"We're having a band, it's gong to be in the field house. I helped decorate."

"Aha."

"We hung a lot of sheets with wires and turned it into a huge tent. It's neat, you should see it."

"When are we coming up for a visit?"

"I'll let you know. I gotta go."

"Want to say a quick hello to Lace? She's here."

"Sure."

He handed the phone to Lace. "Dr. Barlowe."

Her smile, which he had seldom seen, was so spontaneous and unguarded, he blushed and left the room.

§

They were sitting at the table having a cup of tea as Lace organized her books and papers to go home.

"What's interesting in school these days?" Cynthia wanted to know.

"I just found out about palindromes, I'm always lookin' for 'em," she said.

"Like Bob, right?"

"Right. Words that're the same spelled forwards or backwards. Like that," she said, pointing to the contract he'd left lying on the table, "isn't a palindrome, it says H. Tide readin' forwards, and Edith if you read it backwards. But guess what, you can also make a palindrome with whole sentences, like 'Poor Dan is in a droop.'"

"Neat!" said Cynthia.

"See you later," she said, going to the basement door. "'Bye, Harley! Read your book I left on the sink!"

"What did you leave on the sink?" inquired the rector, filled with curiosity.

"*Silas Marner.*"

"Aha. Well, come back, Lace."

"Anytime," said Cynthia.

"OK!"

He pulled the contract toward him.

EdiT .H

His blood pounded in his temples. Edith? Could H. Tide be owned by Edith Mallory?

Is that why H. Tide wanted the rectory so urgently? Edith knew he and Cynthia would be living in the yellow house. Did she want to control the house next door to him in some morbid, devious way?

"What is it, Timothy?"

"Nothing. Just thinking." He took the contract into the study and sat at his desk, looking out the window at the deepening shadows of Baxter Park.

Mack Stroupe. H. Tide. Edith Mallory.

If what Lace just prompted him to think was true, Edith was now trying to get her hands on another piece of Main Street property. The way she had treated Percy wasn't something he'd like to see happen to anyone else, especially Winnie. And what might Edith be trying to gouge from Winnie, who was selling her business without the aid of a realtor?

He glanced at the contract—it was right up there with cave-wall hieroglyphs—and called his attorney cousin, Walter. "You've reached Walter and Katherine, please leave a message at the sound of the beep. We'll return your call with haste."

Wasn't a signed contract legal and binding?

He paced the floor.

Edith Mallory had always held a lot of real estate. But why would she sell the Shoe Barn to her own company? He didn't understand this. Was he making too much of a name spelled backward?

Then again, why had Mack Stroupe swaggered around town, boasting of his influence on H. Tide's buying missions?

Another thing. Could Miami Development have anything to do with all this? Or was that merely a fluke?

He didn't know what the deal was, but he knew something was much worse than he had originally believed.

He knew it because the feeling in the pit of his stomach told him so.

᛫

Walter rang back.

"Cousin! What transpires in the hinterlands?"

"More than you want to know. Legal question."

"Shoot," said his cousin and lifelong best friend.

After talking with Walter, he rang an old acquaintance who worked at the state capitol. So what if it was nine-thirty in the evening and he hadn't seen Dewey Morgan in twelve years? Maybe Dewey didn't even work at the state capitol anymore.

"No problem," said Dewey, who'd received quite a bureaucratic leg up in the intervening years. "I'll call you tomorrow."

"As quickly as possible, if you'd be so kind. And if you're ever in Mitford, our guest room is yours."

"I may take you up on it. Arlene has always wanted to see Mitford."

If all the people he'd invited to use the guest room ever cashed in their invitations . . .

§

At ten o'clock, the phone rang at the church office.

"Tim? Dewey. I looked up the name of the undisclosed partner in H. Tide of Orlando, right? And also Miami Development. It says here Edith A. Mallory—both companies. Hope that's what you're looking for."

"Oh, yes," he said. "Exactly!"

He'd been looking for it, all right, but he hated finding it.

§

He pushed through the curtains to the bakery kitchen without announcing himself from the other side.

"Winnie, I've got to tell you something."

"What is it, Father? Sit down, you don't look so good."

"H. Tide is owned by someone who may not treat you very well, I won't go into the details. The truth is, you probably don't want to sell to these people and be under their management."

"Oh, no!"

"You'd be in the hands of Percy's landlord. I think you should talk to Percy."

"But I've already signed the contract and sent it off."

"And I've just talked with my cousin who's an attorney. Please.

Talk with Percy about his landlord. And if you don't like what you hear, we need to move fast."

She wiped her hands and straightened her bandanna. "Whatever you say, Father."

§

"Don't get 'is blood pressure up 'til we've served th' lunch crowd," said Velma.

She turned to Winnie. "I'm takin' three pairs of shorts, not short short, just medium, three tops, and two sleeveless dresses with my white sweater. Are you takin' a formal for Captain's Night?"

"Oh, law," said Winnie, looking addled, "I don't even have time to think about it, I don't know what I'm takin', I don't have a formal."

"Well, be sure and take a pair of shoes with rubber soles so you don't slip around on deck." Velma had been on a cruise sponsored by her children, and knew what was what.

"Velma," urged the rector, "we need to move quickly. May I ask Percy just one question? How high can his blood pressure shoot if we ask just one question?"

"Oh, all right, but don't go on and on."

Coot Hendrick banged a spoon against his water glass. Ever since Velma got invited on that cruise, she hadn't once refilled his coffee cup unless he asked for it outright.

The rector motioned to the proprietor. "Percy, give us a second, if you can."

Percy stepped away from the grill, slapping a towel over his shoulder, and came to the counter.

Why was he always putting himself in the middle of some unpleasant circumstance? Had he become the worst thing a clergyman could possibly become—a meddler?

"Percy, now, take it easy. Don't get upset. I just need you to tell Winnie about . . ."

"About what?"

"Your landlord."

The color surged into Percy's face. Two hundred and forty volts, minimum.

"Just a sentence or two," he said lamely.

§

He marched down to Sweet Stuff with Winnie, who called H. Tide to say she was withdrawing the contract. She held the phone out for him to hear the general babble that erupted on the other end.

According to Walter, until the contract had been delivered back to the seller by the buyer, either by hand or U.S. mail, it was unenforceable.

When she hung up, he went to a table out front and thumped down in a chair. His own blood pressure wasn't exactly one-twenty over eighty.

"Earl Grey!" he said to Winnie. "Straight up, and make it a double."

Once again, the candy had been snatched from Edith Mallory's hand. She'd lost Fernbank. She'd lost the rectory. And now she'd lost a prime property on Main Street.

In truth, the only property she'd been able to buy was one she already owned.

He was certain she'd make every effort not to lose Mack Stroupe.

Winnie served his tea, looking buoyant. "Lord help, I feel like a truck's just rolled off of me. Now I'm right back where I started—and glad to be there!"

"I have a verse for you, Winnie, from the prophet Jeremiah. 'The Lord is good to those whose hope is in Him, to the one who seeks Him; His compassions never fail. They are new every morning; great is His faithfulness.'"

"Have a piece of chocolate cake!" said Winnie, beaming. "Or would you like a low-fat cookie?"

§

Esther Bolick was at home and mending, Barnabas was gaining strength, the yellow house was full of sawing and sanding, Cynthia's book was finished, and Winnie and Velma had sent postcards back to Mitford.

Percy taped Velma's to the cash register.

Dear Everybody, Wish you were here, you wouldn't believe the colors of the fish, their like neon. Winnie is sunburnt. If you include the ice

*cream sundae party and early bird breakfast on deck, you can eat 11
times a day. I am keeping it to 9 or 10. Ha ha.*
Velma

Winnie had left a sign in her window:

Gone cruisin.' Back on October 30

Percy trotted down the street and taped her postcard next to the sign.

*Hi, folks, sorry I can't be here to serve you, but I am in the Caribbean
soaking up some sun. The Golden Band people had a fruit basket in
our cabin and champagne which gave Velma a rash. Gosh, its beautiful down here, some places there are pigs in the road, though. Well,
you keep it in the road til I get back, I will have you a big surprise in
the bake case. Winnie*

"Father? Scott Murphy!"

He could hear it in Scott's voice. "When? Who?" he asked.

"Last night! Two men who've been showing up every Wednesday,
one with his kids. They said they wanted to know more about God's
plan for their lives, and we talked, and they prayed and it was a wondrous thing, marvelous. Homeless is beside himself. He thinks that
next summer we may be able to do what Absalom Greer did, have
weekly services on the creek bank."

"You must tell me every detail," said the rector. "Want to run together tomorrow morning?"

"Six-thirty, starting from my place?"

"You got it."

Scott laughed, exultant. "Eat your Wheaties," he said.

Andrew rang to find out if Buck Leeper might be available for the
renovation of Fernbank. "I don't think so, but I'll ask him," he said.

"I'll also be looking for a good nursery. I'd like to replace some of
the shrubs and trees."

"I know a splendid nursery, though their trees are fairly small."

"At my age, Father, one doesn't permit oneself two things—young wine and small trees."

The rector laughed.

"I'd give credit to the fellow who said that, but I can't remember who it was—another distinguishing mark of advancing years."

"Come, come, Andrew. You're looking like a lad, thanks to your beautiful bride! I'm smitten with Anna, as everyone else will be. Thanks for bringing Anna and Tony to Mitford. I know they'll make a wonderful difference."

"Thank you, Father, we're anxious to get started on the hill. Anna would like to have a couple of rooms finished by Christmas, though it could take a year to do the whole job properly, given our weather."

"Let me step down to the church and see what's up. If Buck is interested, I'll have him ring you."

He left the office, zipping his jacket, eager to be in the cold, snapping air, and on a construction site where the real stuff of life was going on.

"Early December, I'm out of here," said Buck, stomping the mud off his work boots. "Your house is in good hands and I'll keep in touch, I'll check on it."

"Well, you see, there's another job for you up the hill at Fernbank. I know Andrew Gregory would be a fine person to work with, and certainly Miss Sadie would be thrilled, she was so pleased with what you did at Hope House—"

"I've laid out long enough," Buck said curtly.

Father Tim pressed on. "I believe if you stayed in Mitford, there'd be plenty of work for you. You could grow your own business."

"No way. There's nothing here for me."

He thought of Jessie and the doll . . .

"Well, then," he said, feeling a kind of despair.

"I brought you somethin'!" said Velma.

"Me? You brought *me* something?"

"Lookit," said Velma, taking a tissue-wrapped item from a bag.

She held up a shirt with orange, red, and green monkeys leaping around in palm trees.

"Aha. Well. That's mighty generous . . ."

"You helped Winnie win th' contest, and I got to go free, so . . ."

"I'll wear it!" he said, getting up for the idea.

"Have you seen what Winnie brought home?" asked Percy.

"Can't imagine."

"And don't you tell 'im, either," said Velma. "He gets to find that out for hisself. Go on down there and look and I'll start your order. But hop to it."

Tanned people returning from exotic places seemed to bring new energy home with them. He fairly skipped to the bake shop.

He inhaled deeply as he went in. The very gates of heaven! "Winnie!" he bellowed.

She came through the curtains. Or was that Winnie?

"Winnie?" he said, taking off his glasses. He fogged them and wiped them with his handkerchief. "Is that you?"

"Course it's me!" she said. Winnie was looking ten years younger, maybe twenty, and tanned to the gills.

"Velma said you brought something back."

"Come on," she said, laughing. "I'll show you."

He passed through the curtains and there, standing beside the ovens, was a tall, very large fellow with full, dark hair and twinkling eyes, wearing an apron dusted with flour.

"This is *him*!" crowed Winnie, looking radiant.

"Him?"

"You know, the one I always dreamed about standin' beside me in th' kitchen. Father Kavanagh, this is Thomas Kendall from Topeka, Kansas."

"What . . . where . . . ?"

"I met him on th' ship!"

"In the kitchen, actually," said Thomas, extending a large hand and grinning from ear to ear. "I'm a pastry chef, Father."

"You stole the ship's pastry chef? Winnie!"

They all laughed. "No," said Winnie, "it was his last week on the job, he was going back to Kansas and decided he'd come home with me first. He's stayin' with Velma and Percy."

No doubt about it, he was dumbfounded. First Andrew, now Winnie . . .

"He likes my cream horns," she said, suddenly shy.

"Who doesn't?"

Thomas put his arm around Winnie and looked down at her, obviously proud. "I'm mighty glad to be in Mitford," he said simply.

"By jing, we're mighty glad to have you," replied the rector, meaning it.

§

Esther Cunningham released a special news story to the *Mitford Muse,* which ran the morning before the election.

"When I'm re-elected," she was quoted as saying, "I'll give you something we've all been waiting for—new Christmas decorations!" The single ropes of lights up and down Main Street had caused squawking and grumbling for over a decade. So what if this solution had been forced by economic considerations, when it made the town look like a commuter landing strip?

"Stick with the platform that sticks by the people," said the mayor, "and I'll give you angels on Main Street!"

§

He was among the first at the polls on Tuesday morning. He didn't have to wonder about Mule's and Percy's vote, but he was plenty skeptical about J.C.'s. Had J.C. avoided looking him in the eye when they saw each other in front of Town Hall?

His eyes scanned the crowd.

The Perkinses, they were big Esther fans. And there were Ron and Wilma . . . surely the Malcolms were voting for Esther. Based on the crowd standing near the door, he figured eight or nine out of ten were good, solid, dependable *Stickin'* votes.

So what was there to worry about?

Mack's last hoorah had been another billboard, which definitely hadn't gone over well, as far as the rector could determine.

"Did you see th' pores in his face?" asked Emma, who appeared completely disgusted. They looked like craters on th' moon. If I never set eyes on Mack Stroupe again, it'll be too soon!"

From the corner of his eye, he watched her boot the computer and check her E-mail from an old schoolmate in Atlanta, a prayer chain in Uruguay, and a church in northern England. Emma Newland in cyberspace. He wouldn't have believed he'd live to see the day.

He walked up the street after lunch, leaning into a bitter wind. As Esther Bolick still wasn't going out, he hoped Gene had seen to turning in her proxy vote.

"Good crowd?" he asked at the polls.

"Oh, yes, Father. Real good. Bigger than in a long while."

He adjusted his *Stickin'* button and stood outside, greeting voters, for as long as he could bear the knifing wind.

He hoped his bishop didn't drive by.

§

"You and Cynthia come on over and bring that little fella who lives in your basement," said the mayor.

"Harley."

"Right. I'd like to get him workin' on our RV. Anyway, we're havin' a big rib feast while they count th' votes, Ray's cookin'."

"What time?" he asked, thrilled that his carefully watched food exchange would actually permit such an indulgence.

"Th' polls close at seven-thirty, be at my office at seven thirty-five."

"Done!" he said. He could just see the red splotches breaking out on the mayor.

§

Uncle Billy and Miss Rose were there when he arrived with Cynthia and Harley. Cynthia zoomed over to help Ray finish setting up the food table.

"I've done got a joke t' tell you, Preacher."

"Shoot!" he said. "And tell Harley, while you're at it."

Miss Rose sniffed and stomped away.

"Rose don't like this 'un," said Uncle Billy. "Well, sir, a feller died who had lived a mighty sinful life, don't you know. Th' minute he got down t' hell, he commenced t' bossin' around th' imps an' all, a-sayin' do this, do that, and jump to it. Well, sir, he got so dominatin' that th' little devils reported 'im to th' head devil who called th' feller in, said, 'How come you act like you own this place?'

"Feller said, 'I do own it, my wife give it to me when I was livin'.'"

Harley bent over and slapped his leg, cackling. Father Tim laughed happily. Oh, the delight of an Uncle Billy joke.

"Seein' as you like that 'un, I'll tell you 'uns another'n after we've eat."

"I'll keep up with you," promised the rector.

Aha, there was a fellow clergyman, heedlessly exposing his political views. Bill Sprouse of First Baptist bowled over with his dog, Sparky, on a leash. "Sparky and I were out walking, Esther hailed us in."

"You stuck with Esther at the polls, I devoutly hope."

"Is the Pope a Catholic?"

"You bet," said the rector, shaking his colleague's hand. "Reverend Sprouse, Harley Welch."

"Pleased to meet you, Harley. I heard you're mighty good with automobiles. Here lately, my car's been actin' funny, don't know what th' trouble is, makes a real peculiar sound. Kind of like *ooahoooijigjigooump.* Like that."

Harley nodded, listening intently. "Might be y'r fan belt."

Ray Cunningham strode up, wiping his hands on a tea towel. "Got you boys some ribs laid on back there, I want you to eat up. Harley, be sure and get with me before you leave. I got a awful knock in my RV engine."

"What time do you think we'll know somethin'?" wondered Bill Sprouse.

"Oh, 'bout nine," said Ray, who, after eight elections, considered himself heavily clued in.

The rector backed away from Sparky, who seemed intent on raising his leg on his loafer.

"For th' Lord's sake, Sparky!" the preacher hastily picked up his dog, whereupon Sparky draped himself over his master's arm, looking doleful.

"Esther's got Ernestine Ivory up at th' polls where the countin's goin' on," said Ray. "She'll run down here when it's all over, shoutin' th' good news. Well, come on, boys, and don't hold back, I been standin' over a hot stove all day."

Omer rolled in, flashing a fugue in G major. "Ninth term comin' up!" he said to his sister-in-law, giving her a good pounding on the back.

§

Uncle Billy yawned hugely. "Hit's way after m' bedtime," he said as the clock struck nine. Miss Rose, who even in her sleep looked fierce, was snoring in a blue armchair transported years ago from the mayor's family room. In her hands, Miss Rose clutched several tightly sealed baggies of take-outs.

"Won't be long," announced Ray. "Doll, does Ernestine have the cell phone? She ought to at least be callin' in with a status report."

The phone rang as if on cue, making several people jump.

"Speak of th' devil," said Bill Sprouse, who often did.

The mayor bounded across the room to her desk. "Hello? Ernestine? Right. Right."

Every eye in the room was on Esther Cunningham, as the color drained slowly from her face.

"You don't mean that, Ernestine," she said in a low voice.

Everybody looked at everybody else, wondering, aghast.

Esther slowly hung up the phone.

"Mack Stroupe," she said, unbelieving, "is th' mayor of Mitford."

CHAPTER TWENTY

New Every Morning

In the stunned silence that followed the announcement of Mack Stroupe's win, Ernestine Ivory delivered yet another confounding report:

He had won by one vote.

Esther Cunningham's various red splotches congregated as a single flame as she dialed the Board of Elections bigwig at home and demanded a recount on the following Thursday.

No problem, he said.

Feeling Ray's supper turned to stone in their alarmed digestive systems, and not knowing what else to say or do, nearly everyone fled for home.

Looking ashen, Uncle Billy shook Miss Rose awake. "Esther's lost," he said.

"Esther's *boss*?" shouted Miss Rose. "She's always been boss, and always will be, so what's the commotion?"

§

As the Lord's Chapel bells tolled seven a.m., he left home with Barnabas and turned north on Main Street. Following Hal's orders, they could now cover a couple of blocks of their running route, but only at normal walking speed.

As they passed Sweet Stuff, he saw Thomas, attired in an apron and baker's hat, putting a tray of something illegal in the window. The big, dark-haired fellow looked up and smiled, waving.

This was only the second time he'd laid eyes on Thomas Kendall, yet it seemed as if the jovial baker had always been there. His face was utterly comfortable and familiar.

"Father!"

He was hoofing past the office building and closing in on the Grill when he turned around and saw Winnie. She waved furiously. "Can you come back a minute?"

Barnabas yanked the leash from his hand and galloped toward Winnie, who always smelled like something good to eat. Before she could duck, he lunged up to give her face a proper licking.

"Oh, no!" she whooped.

"The Lord is good to those whose hope is in Him," bellowed the rector, "His compassions never fail!"

Barnabas sprawled on the sidewalk, obedient. He could not, however, resist licking the powdered sugar off Winnie's shoes.

"They are new every morning! Great is his faithfulness!"

Barnabas sighed, desisted, and rolled over on his back.

"Amen!" shouted Winnie. "You said my verse!"

"What's up with you on this glorious day?"

"Can you come in a minute, Father? We were going to call you today, we have somethin' special to tell you." He thought she might begin jumping up and down.

They trooped into the bakery, as Thomas came through the curtains with yet another tray from the kitchen.

"Good morning, Father! Top of the day! It's baclava!" The rector felt his knees grow weak as Thomas displayed the tray of honey-drenched morsels under his very nose; Barnabas salivated.

"Please have one," urged Winnie. "I never made baclava in my life, but Thomas is an expert."

Thomas decided they should all thump down and have a diamond-shaped piece of the flaky baclava. This moment's indiscretion would cramp his food exchanges for a week, mused the rector. How could he be such a reckless gambler when he appeared so altogether conservative?

"Guess what?" said Winnie, unable to wait any longer.

"I can't guess," he replied, although, in truth, he thought he might be able to.

"Thomas isn't going back to Kansas City."

"Aha."

"Not to live, anyway."

"Father," said Thomas, "I'd like to ask you for Winnie's hand in marriage."

"Aha!" Was Thomas Kendall a man of character? Would he be good for Winnie? He'd simply have to trust his instincts, which, as far as he could tell, had no reservations at all.

"He's th' one, Father," Winnie said with conviction. "God sent him."

"Well, then!"

The men laughed, then stood and embraced, slapping each other on the back. The rector pulled out a handkerchief and blew his nose.

"Oh, for gosh sake!" said Winnie, dabbing her eyes with the hem of her apron.

"I'll be gladder than glad to give you her hand in marriage, Thomas, but Winnie, what about your brother? Shouldn't he have the say in this?"

Winnie beamed. "Joe told us to ask you. He said whatever you say is fine with him." She looked proudly at the gentle man beside her.

"Would you perform the ceremony, Father? Sometime in early January? I need to run back to Kansas to see my mother and pack up a few boxes. I've lived on and off a cruise ship for fifteen years, so I haven't accumulated much." Thomas's large hand covered Winnie's.

"Velma will be matron of honor," Winnie said, barely able to contain her joy.

The rector took Winnie's other hand.

"May the Lord bless you both!" he said, meaning it.

§

"Hello, Father Kavanagh here—"

"Town Hall, tomorrow at four o'clock," said Esther Cunningham darkly. "I told th' Lord I'd give up sausage biscuits. *Pray!*"

"I *am* praying!" he exclaimed.

§

"Timothy?" Cynthia looked thoughtful. "About your hair . . ."

Not again.

"You could drive to Charlotte."

"Not in this lifetime."

"You could forgive Fancy Skinner, and—"

"I have forgiven Fancy Skinner, which has nothing to do with the fact that I will never set foot in her chair again."

She eyed him. "That's one way to put it."

"Never," he said, eyeing her back.

§

He was there at three forty-five, as was nearly everyone else, as far as he could see. Even Esther Bolick turned up, with Gene, who looked worried.

Mack Stroupe stood near the door, shaking hands as if the event were in his honor. He frequently stepped outside to smoke, where he flipped the butts into the pansy bed.

Esther Cunningham steamed in with Ray, their five beautiful daughters, and a mixture of grandchildren and great-grandchildren, including Sissy and Sassy, who had come in tow with Puny, straight from day care. He lifted Sissy into his arms and sat next to Puny in the block of seats occupied by the Cunningham contingent.

"This is the most aggravation in th' world," announced his house help. "I had to let your toilets go to come over here and mess with this foolishness."

"You can let my toilets go anytime," he said, jiggling Sissy.

She glared at Mack Stroupe, who was laughing his loud, whinnying laugh and talking with a band of supporters. "If I wadn't a Christian, I'd march over there an' scratch his eyes out!" She examined her nails, as if she might really consider doing such a thing.

Joe Joe Guthrie, Puny's husband and the Cunninghams' grandson, slipped in next to them. "What do you think, Father?"

Joe Joe looked at him the way so many had looked at him over the years, as if he could prophesy exactly how things would turn out. It was not one of the ways he enjoyed being looked at.

§

The recounting was labored, taking nearly three hours. People milled around, going in and out, smoking, muttering, laughing. Some of those accustomed to an early dinner drove over to the highway, wolfed down a pizza, and returned smelling of pepperoni.

Others stayed glued to their seats, counting every vote with the three Board of Elections officials. Sassy fell asleep, while Sissy tore around the hall as if on wheels.

At a little before seven, he moved across the aisle to sit with the Bolicks. "The end is near," said Gene, looking worn.

The votes were running neck and neck. Mack or Esther would pull ahead in the counting, and then the other would catch up and move ahead.

As the stack of ballots slowly dwindled, the laughing and muttering, hooting and yelping died down.

Something had better happen here pretty quick, he thought, as the last three ballots were held up and counted.

"Ladies and gentlemen!" exclaimed the Board of Elections official, "according to the recount, which ya'll have witnessed here with your own eyes . . . it's a tie."

A communal gasp resounded through the hall, followed by murmurs and shouts.

"What we do . . ." the elections official said, trying to speak over the hubbub. The hubbub escalated wildly.

He pounded the mayor's podium with the gavel. "According to th' by-laws, what we do in such a case is . . . we flip a coin."

The rector leaned forward in his chair. Flip a coin? You determine the well-being of a whole town by flipping a coin?

"God help us," said Esther Bolick.

He saw that Esther Cunningham had turned deathly pale. Where were the fiery splotches, the indomitable spirit? Come on, Esther . . .

He prayed the prayer that never fails.

"Ladies first," said the elections official. "Heads . . . or tails?"

Breathless silence.

Esther Cunningham stood and peered into the crowd as if she were about to deliver the Gettysburg Address.

"Heads!" she said in a voice that thundered beyond the back row and bounced off the wall.

The elections official looked toward the door. "Mr. Stroupe?"

Mack Stroupe shrugged.

The official put his hand into his pocket and brought it out again, looking embarrassed. "Ah, anybody got a nickel or a dime?"

Someone rushed to give him a quarter, as the other two officials drew near, ready to verify the outcome.

He took a deep breath, cleared his throat, and bowed slightly over the coin. Then, working his mouth silently as if uttering an official oath, he flipped it.

§

Around Town
—by Vanita Bentley

Last night, in the parish hole of Lord's Chapel, Bane and Blessing co-chairs Esther Bolick and Hessie Mayhe, were feted at a supper in their honor.

Along with nearly eighty volunteers, some from other Mitford churches, Bolck and Mayhew raised $22,000 and were praised for their "heroic endeavor" by Father Timothy Kavanagh.

"Hero simply means someone who models the ideal" said Rev. Kavanagh, "and these volunteers have done this for all of us.

"Also, a hero can be someone who saves lives in a valiant way and these voluntears have almost certainly done that, as well."

The reverend said Bane proceeds have been used for food

and medical supplys to Zaiear, pure well water in several east African villages, and a ambulance for Landon, where two children died last yr for lack of medical ade.

"The Bane has always been a blessing to others," he said. "But this year, thanks to the outstanding organizational skills of two women and their willingness to serve as unto the Lord, we may all celebrate a special triumph for His kingdom."

Bolk and Mayew were presented with plaques and other voluntears were each given a bag of goodies by local merchants.

Mrs. Bvolk whose jaws were wired shut due an accident reported here previously got to request a special dinner of mashed potatoes and gravey to celebrate being able to eat real food again.

§

If time does, indeed, fly, it was the season when it became a Concorde jet, as far as the rector was concerned.

Following the annual All-Church Thanksgiving Feast, which, thankfully, was held this year at First Baptist, events went into overdrive.

Cynthia drove Dooley back to school on St. Andrew's Day, while the rector prepared the sermon for the first Sunday of Advent and began the serious business of trying to juggle the innumerable Advent activities, not the least of which was Lessons and Carols, to be performed this year on a grand scale with the addition of a visiting choir and an organist from Cambridge, England, all of whom would stay over in parish homes for five days and participate in the Advent Walk on December 15, after which everyone would come to the rectory for a light supper in front of the fire.

"Light supper, heavy dessert," said Cynthia, paging frantically through their cookbooks.

He panted just thinking about it all, and so did his wife, who was making something for everyone on her list, and running behind.

"Whatever you do," she told him at least three times, "don't look in *there*." Upon saying this, she would point to the armoire, which he always stayed as far away from as possible.

Then, of course, there was the annual trek into the woods at the north end of the Fernbank property, to hew down a Fraser fir with the Youth Group, which would become the Jesse tree in front of the altar, followed by a visit to the Sunday School to discuss the meaning of the ornaments the children would be making for the tree, and the courtesy call on the Christmas pageant rehearsal, which this year, much to the shock of the parents and the dismay of at least two teachers, would be done in modern dress, inspired by the recent success of the movie *Hamlet* in which Hamlet had worn blue jeans with what appeared to be a golf shirt.

"What will we do with all these *wings*?" wailed a teacher who had voted for traditional costumes, and lost.

He made himself scarce whenever the wrangling over the pageant issue erupted, and gave himself to the more rewarding annual task of negotiating with Jena Ivey for forty-five white poinsettias and the cartload of boxwood, balsam, fir, and gypsophila to be used on Christmas Eve for the greening of the church.

"Why can't you do the negotiating?" he once asked a member of the Altar Guild.

"Because she likes you better and you get a better price," he was told. This notion of improved economics had engraved the mission in stone and caused it to belong, forever, to him.

He had to remember to order the Belgian chocolates for the nurses at the hospital, and meet with the organist and choir director to thrash through the music for the Christmas Eve services, and put in his two cents' worth about the furniture being ordered for the new upstairs Sunday School rooms, and call Dooley's schoolmate's parents to see if they'd bring him to Mitford on their way to Holding, and check to see if anybody was going to visit Homeless Hobbes and sing carols with him this year, and go through what Andrew Gregory didn't want at Fernbank and help Harley haul it to Pauline's tiny house behind the post office so it would look like a home in time for . . .

"We've done it again," proclaimed his wife, shaking her head.

They gazed at each other, spent and pale.

"Next year," she said, relieved, "it will be different."

Next year, he would not be running around like a chicken with its head cut off, because next year, he would not have a parish.

Suddenly his eyes misted, just thinking about it.

Less than twelve months hence, his parishioners would be standing around him in the parish hall, singing "For he's a jolly good fellow," and giving him money, and a plaque of some sort, and tins of mixed nuts.

§

After the wedding, Winnie and Thomas planned to move into her cottage by the creek, while Scott Murphy would move his wok and precious few other possessions into Winnie's present quarters, once the home of Olivia Harper's socialite mother.

"Musical chairs!" said Cynthia.

§

It was the season of good news and glad tidings, in every way. Joe Ivey was moving back to Mitford.

"Hallelujah!" Father Tim said.

Winnie looked pleased as punch. "He said people kept askin' if Elvis was really dead, and he just couldn't take it anymore. He'll barber in that little room behind th' Sweet Stuff kitchen."

"Baking and barbering!" said the jubilant rector. "I like it!" A little off the sides and a fruit tart to go.

§

"Look!" said Jessie. "A baby in a box."

She stood on tiptoes, holding her doll, and gazed into the crèche that had belonged to his grandmother.

He realized she didn't know about the Babe, and wondered how his life could be so sheltered that he should be surprised.

He glanced at his watch and picked her up and stood looking down upon the crèche with her. Standing there in the lamplit study, he told her about the Babe and why He came, as she sucked her thumb and patted his shoulder and listened intently.

Four days before Christmas, and he was running ragged like the rest of crazed humanity. He resisted glancing at his watch again, and set her down gently as the front doorbell gave a blast.

If that wasn't a fruitcake from the ECW, he'd eat his hat. Or, more likely, it was the annual oranges from Walter.

"I came to say . . . so long." Buck Leeper stood in the stinging cold, bareheaded.

He had dreaded this moment. "Come in, Buck!"

"I can't, I'm on my way to Mississippi, I just—"

"Buck!" Jessie came trotting down the hall and grabbed the superintendent around the legs, as Barnabas raced in from the kitchen, barking.

"Please," said the rector, standing back for Buck to come in. "We're keeping Jessie while Pauline shops for pots and pans. Come on back, we'll scare up something hot for the road."

"Well," Buck said, awkward, then stooped and picked Jessie up in his arms.

They walked down the hall and into the study, where a fire simmered on the hearth. Buck stood in the doorway as if in a trance, taking in the tree ablaze with tiny lights and the train running around its base.

Suddenly the rector saw the room with new eyes, also—the freshly pungent garlands over the mantel and the candles burning on his desk, reflected in the window. He had been passing in and out of this room for days, scarcely noticing, enjoying it with his head instead of his heart.

Buck abruptly set Jessie down and squatted beside her on one knee. "Look, you have a good Christmas," he said, speaking with some difficulty.

Her eyes filled with tears. "Buck, please don't go off nowhere!"

"I've got to," he said.

She threw her arms around his neck, sobbing. "Me an' Poo wanted you to live with us!"

Buck held her close and covered his eyes with his hand.

"Don't cry," said Jessie, clinging to him and patting his shoulder. "Please don't cry, Buck."

He stood and wiped his eyes on the sleeve of his jacket. "Thanks for . . . everything. Your job is in good hands. I'll let myself out."

Buck stalked out of the study and up the hall, closing the front door behind him. The rector had been oddly frozen in place, unable to move; Jessie stood at the study door, crying, holding her doll.

The clock ticked, the train whistled and clacked, the fire hissed.

He walked over to her with a heavy heart and touched her shoulder.

She looked up at him, stricken. "Buck shouldn't of done that," she said.

§

Seven-thirty a.m., and he'd already gone through yesterday's mail, typed two letters, and been to see Louella.

Surely he could take ten minutes . . .

He walked to the end of the corridor and opened the door without knocking, just as he'd always done.

"Oh, rats, I might have known that was you," said Esther Cunningham, using both hands to hide something on her desk.

"What's the deal? What're you hiding? Aha! A sausage biscuit!"

"It's no such thing, it's a *ham* biscuit!"

"Sausage, ham, what's the difference?"

"I specifically spoke to th' Lord about *sausage,*" she said, her eyes snapping, "so lay off."

"Esther, Esther."

He sat down and put his feet up on the Danish modern coffee table, grinning.

She grinned in return, gave him a thumbs-up, then threw back her head and roared with laughter.

Ah, but it was good to hear the mayor laughing again.

§

As a bachelor, he had wondered every year what to do on Christmas eve. With both a five o'clock and a midnight service, he struggled to figure out when or what to eat, whether to open a few presents after he returned home at nearly one a.m. on Christmas morning, or wait and do the whole thing on Christmas afternoon while he was still exhausted from the night before.

Now it was all put into perspective and, like his bishop who loved being told what to do for a change, he listened eagerly to his wife.

"We're having a sit-down dinner at two o'clock on Christmas Eve, and we'll open one present each before we go to the midnight service. We will open our presents from Dooley on Christmas morning, because he can't wait around 'til us old people get the stiffness out of our joints, and after brunch at precisely one o'clock, we'll open the whole shebang."

She put her hands on her hips and continued to dish out the battle plan.

"For brunch, of course, we'll invite Harley upstairs. The menu will include roasted chicken and oyster pie, which I'll do while you squeeze the juice and bake the asparagus puffs."

All she needed was a few military epaulets.

"After that, Dooley will go to Pauline's and spend the night, and our Christmas dinner will be served in front of the fire, and we shall both wear our robes and slippers!"

She took a deep breath and smiled like a schoolgirl. "How's that?"

How was that? It was better than good, it was wonderful, it was fabulous. He gave her a grunting bear hug and made her laugh, which was a sound he courted from his overworked wife these days.

§

He reached up to the closet shelf for the camera and touched the box of his mother's things—the handkerchiefs, her wedding ring, an evening purse, buttons . . .

He stood there, not seeing the box with his eyes, but in his memory. It was covered with wallpaper from their dining room in Holly Springs a half century, an eon, ago. Cream colored roses with pale green leaves . . .

He would not take it down, but it had somehow released memories of his mother's Christmases, and the scent of chickory coffee and steaming puddings and cookies baking on great sheets; his friends from seminary gathering 'round her table; and the guest room with its swirl of gifts and carefully selected surprises, tied with the signature white satin ribbon.

He stood there, still touching the box, recalling what C. S. Lewis had said. It was something which, long ago, had expressed his own feelings so clearly.

"With my mother's death," Lewis wrote, "all settled happiness, all that was tranquil and reliable, disappeared from my life. There was to be much fun, many pleasures, many stabs of Joy; but no more of the old security. It was sea and islands now; the great continent had sunk like Atlantis. . . ."

"Mother . . ." he whispered into the darkened warmth of the closet. "I remember. . . ."

§

He wasn't surprised that he hadn't seen Mack Stroupe again at Lord's Chapel. It appeared that even his hotdog stand was closed—perhaps for the holidays, he thought.

He didn't want to consider whether he'd ever see Edith Mallory again.

§

"I do this every year!" said Cynthia, looking alarmed.

"Do what?"

"Forget the cream for tomorrow's oyster pie. And of course no one will be open tomorrow."

It was that lovely lull between the five o'clock and midnight services of Christmas Eve, and he was sitting by the fire in a state of contentment that he hadn't felt in some time. Tonight, after the simplicity of the five o'clock, which was always held without the choir and the lush profusion of garlands and greenery, would come the swelling rush of voices and organ, and the breathtaking spectacle of the nave bedecked, as if by grace, with balsam, fir, and the flickering lights of candles.

He roused himself as from a dream. "I'll run out and find some. I think Hattie Cloer is open 'til eight."

"I'm so sorry."

"Don't be. You cook, I fetch. I get a much better deal." He took her face in his hands and kissed her on the forehead, then went to the kitchen peg for his jacket.

"Man! What's that terrific smell?" He sniffed the air, homing in on the oven.

"Esther's orange marmalade cake! Vanita Bentley gave me a bootleg copy of her recipe. She ran off dozens on her husband's Xerox."

"Where's your conscience, Kavanagh?"

"Don't worry, this is legal. I called Esther and she gave me permission to use it. Have at it! she said."

"Oh, well," he sighed, feeling diabetic and out of the loop.

"You can have the tiniest sliver, dearest. I'm sure your food exchange will allow it."

If she only knew. "Harley!" he called down the basement stairs. "Want to run to the highway?"

"Yessir, Rev'rend, I do, I'm about t' gag on this book about that feller hoardin' 'is gold."

He heard Dooley and Barnabas clambering down from above. "Where're you going?" asked Dooley.

"To the store. Want to come?"

"Sure. Can I drive?"

"Well . . ."

"You said I could when I came home for Christmas."

"Right. Consider it done, then!" Perfect timing! It was just getting dark, and hardly a soul would be out on a cold Yuletide eve.

Harley came up the stairs, wearing a fleece-lined jacket that he'd found, good as new, at the Bane. "I was hopin' f'r a excuse t' lay that book down. It ain't even got a picture in it!"

Barnabas stood in the fray, wagging his tail and hoping to be invited, as the doorbell gave a sharp blast.

"I'll get it!" said the rector, hurrying along the hall.

It was Buck Leeper, standing in the pale glow of the porch light.

"I got as far as Alabama and turned around," he said. "I'm willing to do whatever it takes."

CHAPTER TWENTY-ONE

Lion and Lamb

Buck was shaking as they went into the study. Though the rector knew it wasn't from the cold, he asked him to sit by the fire.

There was a long silence as Buck waited for the trembling to pass; he sat with his head down, looking at the floor. The rector remembered the times of his own trembling, when his very teeth chattered as from ague.

"Does Pauline know you're back in Mitford?"

"No. I came for . . . I came for this." He looked up. "I didn't want to come back."

"I know."

"It was sucking the life out of me all the way. I was driving into Huntsville when I knew I couldn't keep going . . ."

He was shaking again, and closed his eyes. Father Tim could see a muscle flexing in his jaw.

"God a'mighty," said Buck.

Father Tim looked at him, praying. The man who had controlled some of the biggest construction jobs in the Southeast and some of the most powerful machinery in the business couldn't, at this moment, control the shaking.

"I pulled into an Arby's parkin' lot and sat in the car and tried to pray. The only thing that came was somethin' I'd heard all those years in my grandaddy's church." Buck looked into the fire. "I said, Thy will be done."

"That's the prayer that never fails."

The clock ticked.

"He can be for your life what the foundation is for a building."

Buck met his gaze. "I want to do whatever it takes, Father."

"In the beginning, it takes only a simple prayer. Some think it's too simple, but if you pray it with your heart, it can change everything. Will you pray it with me?"

"I don't know if I can live up to . . . whatever."

"You can't, of course. No one can be completely good. The point is to surrender it all to him, all the garbage, all the possibilities. All."

"What will happen when . . . I pray this prayer?"

"You mean what will happen now, tonight, in this room?"

"Yes."

"Something extraordinary could happen. Or it could be so subtle, so gradual, you'll never know the exact moment He comes in."

"Right," said Buck, whispering.

The rector held out his hand to a man he'd come to love, and they stood before the fire and bowed their heads.

"Thank You, God, for loving me . . ."

"Thank You, God . . ." Buck hesitated and went on, "for loving me."

". . . and for sending Your Son to die for my sins. I sincerely repent of my sins, and receive Christ as my personal savior."

The superintendent repeated the words slowly, carefully.

"Now, as Your child, I turn my entire life over to You."

". . . as Your child," said Buck, weeping quietly, "I turn my entire life over to You."

"Amen."

"Amen."

He didn't know how long they stood before the fire, embracing as brothers—two men from Mississippi; two men who had never known the kindness of earthly fathers; two men who had determined to put their lives into the hands of yet another Father, one believing—and one hoping—that He was kindness, Itself.

§

In the kitchen, Cynthia said, "You won't believe this! Look!"

She pointed under the kitchen table, where Barnabas and Violet were sleeping together. The white cat was curled against the black mass of the dog's fur, against his chest, against the healing wound.

Father Tim sank to his knees, astounded, peering under the table with unbelieving eyes.

"It's a miracle," Cynthia told Buck. "They've been mortal enemies for years. You can't imagine how he's chased her, and how she's despised him."

Barnabas opened one eye and peered at the rector, then closed it.

"The lion shall lie down with the lamb!" crowed Cynthia.

"Merry Christmas, one and all!" whooped the rector.

"Merry Christmas!" exclaimed his wife.

"Right," said Buck. "You, too."

"I thought you'd never get finished." Dooley came up the basement steps with Harley. "Hey, Buck, I thought you'd left for Mississippi. How's it goin'?"

"Real good, what are you up to?"

Dooley pulled a pair of gloves out of his jacket pocket. "I'm drivin' to the store! Let's bust out of here, I'm ready."

"Settin' on high idle, is what he is," said Harley.

They trooped to the garage and pushed the button that opened the automatic door. It rose slowly, like a stage curtain, on a scene that stopped them in their tracks.

"Snow!" Dooley shouted.

It was swirling down in large, thick flakes and already lay like a frosting of sugar on the silent lawn.

"Maybe you'd better let me drive," said the rector.

"I can drive in snow! Besides, I won't go fast, I'll go really slow."

"I don't reckon they's any cows out plunderin' around in this, Rev'rend."

Buck and Harley climbed into the backseat, and he slid in beside Dooley. "This isn't Harley's truck, buddy, so there's no clutch. Remember to keep your left foot—"

"I know how," said Dooley.

As they turned right on Main Street, there they were, on every lamppost—angels formed of sparkling lights, keeping watch over the snow-covered streets.

"By jing," said Harley, "hit's another world!"

"Glorious!" said the rector. The Buick seemed to be floating through a wonderland, lighter than air. He turned the radio to his favorite music station. *Hark the herald angels* . . .

"Buck, where are you staying?"

"I'll bunk in with one of my crew for a couple days, then head back. Emil's got me on a big job in Texas startin' January."

"Why don't you bunk in with us? Harley, would you let Buck use your sofa bed? Cynthia's using the guest room as a gift-wrapping station."

"Hit'd be a treat. I sleep s' far down th' hall, I don't reckon I'd keep you awake with m' snorin'."

"And you'll have brunch with us tomorrow, if that suits."

"I'd like that," said Buck. "Thank you."

Dooley braked at the corner. "Let's ride by Mama's, want to?"

"I'll go anywhere you 'uns say," declared Harley.

"We'll just ride by and honk th' horn," said Dooley, "then let's ride by some more places before we go to the store, OK?"

The rector grinned. "Whatever you say, buddy. You're driving."

Dooley turned left at the corner and made a right into the alley. Pauline's small house, nestled into a grove of laurels, was a cheerful sight, with the lights of a tree sparkling behind its front windows and the snow swirling like moths around the porch light.

Dooley hammered on the horn, and the rector cranked his window down as Pauline, Poo, and Jessie appeared at the door.

"Look, Mama, I'm drivin'!"

"Dooley! Father! Can you come in?" She peered at the rear window, but was unable to see anyone in the darkened backseat.

"We're on a mission to the store, but we'll see you tomorrow. Merry Christmas! Stay warm!"

"Merry Christmas, Mama, Jessie, Poo! See you tomorrow!"

"Merry Christmas! We're bakin' the ham you sent, Father, be careful, Dooley!"

"Merry Christmas, Mr. Tim!"

Sammy and Kenny, thought the rector. He hoped he would live to see the day . . .

Dooley put the Buick in low gear and glided off.

"Burn rubber!" yelled Poo.

At the end of the alley, Buck leaned forward, urgent. "Father, I can't . . . I'd like to go back and see Pauline and the kids. Do you think it would be all right?"

Dooley spoke at once. "I think it would."

"Go," said the rector.

In the side mirror, he saw Buck running along the alley, running toward the light that spilled onto the snow from the house in the laurels.

§

"The last time we had snow at Christmas, we burned the furniture, remember that?" he asked, as Dooley turned onto Main Street. It was, in fact, the blizzard the media had called the Storm of the Century.

Dooley cackled. "We were bustin' up that ol' chair and throwin' it in th' fireplace, and fryin' baloney . . ."

"Those were the good old days," sighed the rector, who certainly hadn't thought so at the time.

Dashing through the snow . . .

He was losing track of time, happy out here in this strange and magical land where hardly a soul marred the snow with footprints, where Dooley sang along with the radio, and Harley looked as wide-eyed as a child. . . .

And there was Fernbank, ablaze with lights through the leafless winter trees, crowning the hill with some marvelous presence he'd never seen before. He wanted suddenly to see it up close, feel its warmth, discover whether it was real, after all, or a fanciful dream come to please him at Christmas.

"Want to run by Jenny's?" he asked. "It's on the way to the store."

"Nope," said Dooley. "Let's go by Lace's."

"Excellent! Then we can run over to Fernbank while we're at it."

"And by Tommy's! He'll hate my guts."

"Anywhere you want to run, Harley?"

"No, sir, I've done run to where I want t' go, hit's right here with you 'uns."

They should have brought presents—fruitcakes, candy, tangerines! He was wanting to hand something out, give something away, make someone's face light up . . .

Bells on bobtail ring, making spirits bright, what fun it is to ride and sing a sleighing song tonight! Hey! . . .

They honked the horn in the Harper driveway and shouted their season's greetings, then drove up the long, winding lane to Fernbank, where he would have been contented merely to sit in the car and look at its lighted rooms with a candle in every window.

They circled around to the front steps and honked, as Andrew and Anna came to the door and opened it and waved, calling out felicitations of their own. "Don't mention this to Rodney Underwood!" he said to the couple on the porch.

Andrew laughed. "Our lips are sealed! *Joyeux noël!*"

"Ciao!" cried Anna. "Come soon again!"

They eased down the Fernbank drive and saw the town lying at the foot of the steep hill like a make-believe village under a tree. There was the huge fir at Town Hall with its ropes of colored lights, and the glittering ribbon of Main Street, and the shining houses.

An English writer, coincidentally named Mitford, had said it so well, he could recite it like a schoolboy.

She had called her village "a world of our own, close-packed and insulated like . . . bees in a hive or sheep in a fold or nuns in a convent or sailors in a ship, where we know everyone, and are authorized to hope that everyone feels an interest in us."

Go tell it on the mountain, over the hills and everywhere . . .

After a stop by Tommy's and then by Hattie Cloer's, they headed home.

"Harley, want to have a cup of tea with us before tonight's service?"

"No, sir, Rev'rend, I'm tryin' t' fool with a batch of fudge brownies to bring upstairs tomorrow."

Temptation on every side, and no hope for it.

"Say, Dad, want to watch a video before church? Tommy loaned me his VCR. It's a baseball movie, you'll like it."

If there were a tax on joy on this night of nights, he'd be dead broke.

"Consider it done!" he said.

He sat clutching the pint of cream in a bag, feeling they'd gone forth and captured some valuable trophy or prize, as they rode slowly between the ranks of angels on high and turned onto their trackless street.

Visit America's favorite small town—
one book at a time

Welcome to the next book,

A New Song

CHAPTER ONE

For more works by JAN KARON, look for the

At Home in Mitford
ISBN 0-14-025448-X

A Light in the Window
ISBN 0-14-025454-4

These High, Green Hills
ISBN 0-14-025793-4

Out to Canaan
ISBN 0-14-026568-6

A New Song
ISBN 0-14-027059-0

A Common Life:
The Wedding Story
ISBN 0-14-200034-5

JAN KARON books make perfect holiday gifts.

From Penguin:

The Mitford Years
Boxed set includes: At Home
in Mitford; A Light in the Window;
These High, Green Hills; Out to
Canaan and A New Song.
ISBN 0-14-771596-2

From Viking:

Patches of Godlight:
Father Tim's Favorite Quotes
ISBN 0-670-03006-6

The Mitford Snowmen:
A Christmas Story
ISBN 0-670-03019-8

PENGUIN AUDIO: The Mitford Years Audio

At Home in Mitford   ISBN 0-14-086501-2; A Light in the Window
ISBN 0-14-086596-9; These High, Green Hills ISBN 0-14-086598-5
Out to Canaan ISBN 0-14-086597-7; A Common Life ISBN 0-14-
180274-X; A New Song (Abridged) ISBN 0-14-086901-8; A New
Song (Unabridged) ISBN 0-14-180013-5; The Mitford Years Boxed Set
ISBN 0-14-086813-5

In bookstores now from Penguin Putnam Inc.

Visit the Mitford Web site at www.mitfordbooks.com

To order books in the United States: Please write to Consumer Sales,
Penguin Putnam Inc.
P.O. Box 12289, Dept B, Newark, New Jersey 07101-5289.
VISA, MasterCard and American Express cardholders
call (800) 788-6262 or (201) 933-9292.

New from Viking. . .

JAN KARON'S
In This
Mountain

Father Tim and Cynthia have been at home in
Mitford for three years since returning from
Whitecap Island. In the little town that's home-away-
from-home to millions of readers, life hums along as
usual for the endearing townspeople. Though Father
Tim dislikes change, he dislikes retirement even more.
As he and Cynthia gear up for a year-long ministry
across the state line, a series of events sends shock waves
through his faith—and the entire town of Mitford.

In her seventh novel in the bestselling Mitford
series, Jan Karon delivers surprises of every kind,
including the return of the man in the attic, and an
ending that no one in Mitford will ever forget.

VIKING

PENGUIN BOOKS

A NEW SONG

Jan Karon writes "to give readers an extended family and to applaud the extraordinary beauty of ordinary people living ordinary lives." Other bestselling novels in the Mitford Years series are *At Home in Mitford; A Light in the Window; These High, Green Hills; Out to Canaan; A Common Life: The Wedding Story;* and *In This Mountain.* Her children's books include *Miss Fannie's Hat* and *Jeremy: The Tale of an Honest Bunny.*

Now you can visit Mitford online at
www.penguinputnam.com/mitford or
www.mitfordbooks.com

Enjoy the latest news from the little town with the big heart including a complete archive of the *More from Mitford* newsletters, the Mitford Years Readers Guide, and much more.

Other Mitford Books by Jan Karon

AT HOME IN MITFORD
A LIGHT IN THE WINDOW
THESE HIGH, GREEN HILLS
OUT TO CANAAN
A COMMON LIFE

Children's Books by Jan Karon

MISS FANNIE'S HAT
JEREMY: THE TALE OF AN HONEST BUNNY

The Mitford Years

A New Song

JAN KARON

PENGUIN BOOKS

PENGUIN BOOKS
Published by the Penguin Group
Penguin Putnam Inc., 375 Hudson Street,
New York, New York 10014, U.S.A.
Penguin Books Ltd, 27 Wrights Lane, London W8 5TZ, England
Penguin Books Australia Ltd, Ringwood, Victoria, Australia
Penguin Books Canada Ltd, 10 Alcorn Avenue,
Toronto, Ontario, Canada M4V 3B2
Penguin Books (N.Z.) Ltd, 182–190 Wairau Road,
Auckland 10, New Zealand

Penguin Books Ltd, Registered Offices:
Harmondsworth, Middlesex, England

First published in the United States of America by Viking Penguin,
a member of Penguin Putnam Inc. 1999
Published in Penguin Books 2000

9   10   8

Illustrations by Donna Kae Nelson

Grateful acknowledgment is made for permission to reprint excerpts from the following copy-righted works: "If Once You Have Slept on an Island" from *Taxis and Toadstools* by Rachel Field. Copyright 1926 by The Century Company. Used by permission of Random House Children's Books, a division of Random House, Inc. "God's Way" by Kao Chung-Ming, appearing in *Your Will be Done*, Youth Desk of Christian Conference of Asia, 1986. By permission of the author.

PUBLISHER'S NOTE
This novel is a work of fiction. Names, characters, places and incidents are either the product of the author's imagination or are used fictitiously, and any resemblance to actual persons, living or dead, business establishments, events or locales is entirely coincidental.

THE LIBRARY OF CONGRESS HAS CATALOGED THE HARDCOVER EDITION AS FOLLOWS:
Karon, Jan, date.
A new song/ Jan Karon.
p.   cm.
ISBN 0-670-87810-3 (hc.)
ISBN 0 14 02.7059 0 (pbk.)
1. Mitford (N.C.: Imaginary place)—Fiction. 2. City and town life—North Carolina—
Fiction. 3. Clergy—North Carolina—Fiction. 4. Christian fiction, American.
5. Domestic fiction, American.
I. Title.
PS3561.A678N49   1999
813'.54—dc21   98–55141

Printed in the United States of America
Set in Adobe Garamond
Designed by Francesca Belanger

In memory of my aunt,

Helen Coyner Cloer,

who, when I was ten years old,
typed my first manuscript.

October 4, 1917–October 12, 1998

". . . we shall be like Him . . ."

1 John 3:2

Sing unto the Lord a new song, and His praise from the end of the earth, ye that go down to the sea, and all that is therein, the isles and the inhabitants thereof.

Isaiah 42:10, KJV

Acknowledgments

Gentle Reader,

In the Mitford books, there are nearly as many acknowledgments as there are characters in the story. That's because I try to thank absolutely everyone who helps make the story more authentic. Sometimes I toss in a name out of sheer sentiment, like that of my sixth-grade teacher, Etta Phillips, who comes to my book signings and looks as youthful as ever. Many readers enjoy these acknowledgments because they occasionally find the name of an old school chum, friend, or family member.

Sometimes, they even find themselves.

Warm thanks to:

Brother Francis Andrews, BSG; Rev. Roy M. King; Flyin' George Ronan; John Ed McConnell; Ralph Emery; Dr. Carl Hurley; Loyal Jones and Billy Edd Wheeler; Bonnie Setzer; Mary Richardson; Fr. John Mangrum; Fr. Jeffrey Scott Miller; Dr. George Grant; Austin Gragg; Roger David Craig; Frank Gilbert and his Mustang convertible; the Mitford Appreciation Society; Gwynne Crosley; Rev. Gale Cooper; Sue Yates; Dr. David Ludwig; Dan Blair; Linda Foster; Will Lankenau; William McDonald Parker; Blowing Rock police chief, Owen Tolbert; Officer Dennis Swanson; Bishop Christopher Fitz-Simons Allison; James F. Carlisle, Sr.; Betsy Barnes; Rayburn and

Sheila Farmer; Fr. Scott Oxford; Bishop William C. Frey; Bishop Keith Ackerman; Rev. Stephen J. Hines; Larry Powell; Barry Hubert; Derald West; Sandy McNabb; Donna Kae Nelson for her outstanding cover illustrations for the Mitford series; Captain Weyland Baum, early keeper of the Currituck Light; Billy McCaskill; Major John Coffindaffer; "Bee" Baum; Drs. Melanie and Greg Hawthorne; John L. Beard; Greg and Kathy Fishel; Frank LePore; Garry Oliver; my first-grade teacher, Mrs. Downs; my fifth-grade teacher, Mrs. Sherrill; Dr. Michael C. Ain; Captain Mike Clarkin of *Fishin' Frenzy*; First Mate Matthew Winchester; Dr. Sue P. Frye; Ross and Linda Dodington; Fr. Richard B. Bass; Colonel Ron and Cathey Fallows; Murray Whisnant; Robert Williams; Chris Williams; Michael Freeland; Rabbi David and Barbara Kline; Officer Kris Merithew; Bruce Luke; Johnny Lentz; Judith Burns; Wonderland Books; Tom Enterline; J.W.D.; Loretta Cornejo; Tex Harrison; Jerry Gregg; Officer Tracy Toler; Jeff Cobb; Walter Green; and Anita Chappell.

Special thanks to:

Dr. Bunky Davant, medical counsel to Mitford and Whitecap; Tony DiSanti, legal counsel to Mitford; Grace Episcopal Church, the lovely architectural model for St. John's in the Grove; Fr. Charles Gill, rector of St. Andrews by the Sea; Fr. James Harris, friend and helper; Judy Bistany South, for her warm encouragement over the years; my valued assistant, Laura Watts; Captain Horace Whitfield, master of the *Elizabeth II*; hardworking booksellers everywhere; and, as always, my devoted readers.

Contents

A New Song

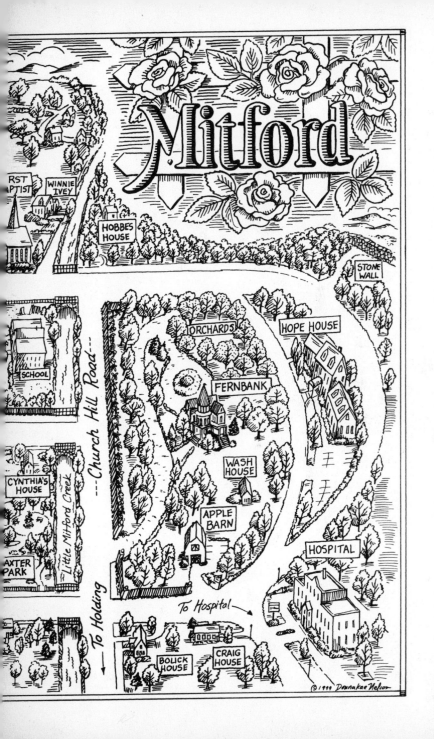

CHAPTER ONE

Angel of Light

Dappled by its movement among the branches of a Japanese cherry, the afternoon light entered the study unhindered by draperies or shades.

It spilled through the long bank of windows behind the newly slip-covered sofa, warming the oak floor and quickening the air with the scent of freshly milled wood.

Under the spell of the June light, a certain luster and radiance appeared to emerge from every surface.

The tall chest, once belonging to Father Tim's clergyman great-grandfather, had undergone a kind of rebirth. Beneath a sheen of lemon oil, the dense grain of old walnut, long invisible in the dark rectory hallway next door, became sharply defined. Even the awkward inscription of the letter M, carved by a pocketknife, could now be discovered near one of the original drawer pulls.

But it was the movement and play of the light, beyond its searching incandescence, that caused Father Tim to anticipate its daily arrival as others might look for a sunrise or sunset.

He came eagerly to this large, new room, as if long deprived of light or air, still incredulous that such a bright space might exist, and especially that it might exist for his own pursuits since retiring six months ago from Lord's Chapel.

As the rector of Mitford's Episcopal parish, he had lived next door in the former rectory for sixteen years. Now he was a rector no more, yet he owned the rectory; it had been bought and paid for with cash from his mother's estate, and he and Cynthia were living in the little yellow house.

Of course—he kept forgetting—this house wasn't so little anymore; he and his visionary wife had added 1,270 square feet to its diminutive proportions.

Only one thing remained constant. The house was still yellow, though freshly painted with Cynthia's longtime favorite, Wild Forsythia, and trimmed with a glossy coat of the dark green Highland Hemlock.

"Cheers!" said his wife, appearing in jeans and a denim shirt, toting glasses of lemonade on a tray. They had recently made it a ritual to meet here every afternoon, for what they called the Changing of the Light.

He chuckled. "We mustn't tell anyone what we do for fun."

"You can count on it! Besides, who'd ever believe that we sit around watching the light change?" She set the tray on the table, next to a packet of mail.

"We could do worse."

They thumped onto the sofa, which had been carted through the hedge from the rectory.

"One more week," he said, disbelieving.

"Ugh. Heaven help us!" She put her head back and closed her eyes. "How daunting to move to a place we've never seen . . . for an unknown length of time . . . behind a priest who's got them used to the guitar!"

He took her hand, laughing. "If anyone can do it, you can. How many cartons of books are we shipping down there, anyway?"

"Fourteen, so far."

"And not a shelf to put them on."

"We're mad as hatters!" she said with feeling. During the past week, his wife had worked like a Trojan to close up the yellow house, do most of the packing, and leave their financial affairs in order. He, on the other hand, had been allowed to troop around town saying his goodbyes, sipping tea like a country squire and trying to keep his mitts off the cookies and cakes that were proffered at every turn.

He had even dropped into Happy Endings Bookstore and bought two new books to take to Whitecap, a fact that he would never, even on penalty of death, reveal to Cynthia Kavanagh.

She looked at him and smiled. "I've prayed to see you sit and relax like this, without rushing to beat out a thousand fires. Just think how the refreshment of the last few weeks will help you, dearest, when we do the interim on the island. Who knows, after all, what lies ahead and what strength you may need?"

He gulped his lemonade. Who knew, indeed?

"The jig, however, is definitely up," she said, meaning it. "Next week . . ."

"I know. Change the furnace filter next door, weed the perennial beds, fix the basement step, pack my clothes . . . I've got the entire, unexpurgated list written down."

"Have your suit pressed," she said, "buy two knit shirts—nothing with an alligator, I fervently hope—and find the bicycle pump for Dooley."

"Right!" He was actually looking forward to the adrenaline of their last week in Mitford.

"By the way," she said, "I've been thinking. Instead of loading the car in bits and pieces, just pile everything by the garage door. That way, I can check it twice, and we'll load at the last minute."

"But it would be simpler to—"

"Trust me," she said, smiling.

Barnabas would occupy the rear seat, with Violet's cage on the floor, left side. They'd load the right side with linens and towels, the trunk would be filled to the max, and they'd lash on top whatever remained.

"Oh, yes, Timothy, one more thing . . . stay out of the bookstore!"

She peered at him with that no-nonsense gleam in her sapphire eyes, a gleam that, for all its supposed authority, stirred a fire in him. As a man with a decidedly old-shoe nature, he had looked forward to the old-shoe stage of their marriage. So far, however, it hadn't arrived. His blond and sensible wife had an unpredictable streak that kept the issues of life from settling into humdrum patterns.

"Anything wonderful in the mail?" she asked.

"I don't know, I just fetched it in. Why don't you have a look?"

His wife's fascination with mail was greater even than his own, which was considerable. William James, in his opinion, had hit the nail on the head. "As long as there are postmen," James declared, "life will have zest."

"Oh, look! Lovely! A letter from Whitecap, and it's to *me*!"

He watched her rip open the envelope.

"My goodness, listen to this. . . .

" '*Dear Mrs. Kavanagh, We are looking forward with great enthusiasm to your interim stay in our small island parish, and trust that all is going smoothly as you prepare to join us at the end of June.*

" '*Our ECW has been very busy readying Dove Cottage for your stay at Whitecap, and all you need to bring is bed linens for the two bedrooms, as we discussed, and any towels and pillows which will make you feel at home.*

" '*We have supplied the kitchen cupboards with new pots, and several of us have lent things of our own, so that you and Father Kavanagh may come without much disruption to your household in Mitford. Sam has fixed the electric can opener, but I hear you are a fine cook and probably won't need it, ha ha.*

" '*Oh, yes. Marjorie Lamb and I have done a bit of work in the cottage gardens, which were looking woefully forlorn after years of neglect. We found a dear old-fashioned rose, which I hear your husband enjoys, and liberated it from the brambles. It is now climbing up your trellis instead of running into the street! We expect the hydrangeas and crepe myrtle to be in full glory for your arrival, though the magnolias in the churchyard will, alas, be out of bloom.*

" '*Complete directions are enclosed, which Marjorie's husband, Leonard, assures me should take you from Mitford straight to the door of Dove Cottage without a snare. (Leonard once traveled on the road selling plumbing supplies.)*

" '*Please notice the red arrow I have drawn on the map. You must be very careful at this point to watch for the street sign, as it is hidden by a dreadful hedge which the property owner refuses to trim. I have thought of trimming it myself, but Sam says that would be meddling.*

" '*We hope you will not object to a rather gregarious greeting committee, who are bent on giving you a parish-wide luau the day following your arrival. I believe I have talked them out of wearing grass skirts, but that embarrassing notion could possibly break forth again.*

" '*When Father Morgan joined us several years ago, he, too, came in* the summer and was expecting a nice holiday at the beach. I'm sure you've been warned that summer is our busiest time, what with the tourists who swell our little church to bursting and push us to two services! We all take our rest in the winter when one must hunker down and live off the nuts we've gathered!

" 'Bishop Harvey was thrilled to learn from Bishop Cullen how greatly you and Father Kavanagh were appreciated by your parish in Mitford! We shall all do our utmost to make you feel as welcome as the flowers in May, as my dear mother used to say.

" 'Goodness! I hope you'll forgive the length of this letter! Since childhood, I have loved the feel of a pen flowing over paper, and often get carried away.

" 'We wish you and Father Timothy safe travel.

" 'Yours sincerely,

" 'Marion Fieldwalker, vestry member of St. John's in the Grove, and Pres. Episcopal Church Women

" 'P.S. I am the librarian of Whitecap Island Community Library (35 years) and do pray you might be willing to give a reading this fall from one of your famous Violet books. Your little books stay checked out, and I believe every child on the island has read them at least twice!' "

His wife flushed with approval. "There! How uplifting! Marion sounds lovely! And just think, dearest—trellises and old roses!"

"Not to mention new saucepans," he said, admiring the effort of his future parishioners.

She drank from her perspiring glass and continued to sort through the pile. "Timothy, look at his handwriting. He's finally stopped printing and gone to cursive!"

"Let me see. . . ."

Definitely a new look in the handwriting department, and a distinct credit to Dooley Barlowe's Virginia prep schooling. Miss Sadie's big bucks, forked over annually, albeit posthumously, were continuing to put spit and polish on the red-haired mountain boy who'd come to live with him at the rectory five years ago.

" 'Hey,' " he read aloud from Dooley's letter, " 'I have thought about it a lot and I would like to stay in Mitford and work for Avis this summer and make money to get a car and play softball with the Reds.

" 'I don't want to go to the beach.

" 'Don't be mad or upset or anything. I can live in the basement with

*Harley like you said, and we will be fine. Puny could maybe come and do
the laundry or we could do stuff ourselves and eat in Wesley or at the Grill
or Harley could cook.*

" 'I will come down to that island for either Thanksgiving or Christmas like we talked about.

" 'Thanks for letting me go home from school with Jimmy Duncan, I
am having a great time, he drives a Wrangler. His mom drives a Range
Rover and his dad has a BMW 850. That's what I would like to have. A
Wrangler, I mean. I'll get home before you leave, Mr. Duncan is driving
me on his way to a big meeting. Say hey to Barnabas and Violet. Thanks
for the money. Love, Dooley.' "

"Oh, well," said his wife, looking disappointed. "I'm sure he
wanted to be close to his friends. . . ."

"Right. And his brother and sister. . . ."

She sighed. "Pretty much what we expected."

He felt disappointed, himself, that the boy wouldn't be coming to
Whitecap for the summer, but they'd given him a choice and the
choice had been made. Besides, he learned a couple of years ago not to
let Dooley Barlowe's summer pursuits wreck his own enjoyment of
that fleeting season.

It was the business about cars that concerned him. . . . Dooley had
turned sixteen last February, and would hit Mitford in less than three
days, packing a bona fide driver's license.

"Knock, knock!" Emma Newland blew down the hall and into the
study. "Don't get up," she said, commandeering the room. "You'll
never believe this!"

His former part-time church secretary, who had retired when he retired, had clearly been unable to let go of her old job. She made it her
business to visit twice a week and help out for a couple of hours,
whether he needed it or not.

"I do it for th' Lord," she had stated flatly, refusing any thanks.
Though Cynthia usually fled the room when she arrived, he rather
looked forward to Emma's visits, and to the link she represented to
Lord's Chapel, which was now under the leadership of its own interim
priest.

Emma stood with her hands on her hips and peered over her
glasses. "Y'all won't believe what I found on th' Internet. Three
guesses!"

"Excuse me!" said Cynthia, bolting from the sofa. "I'll just bring you a lemonade, Emma, and get back to work. I've *gobs* of books to pack."

"Guess!" Emma insisted, playing a game that he found both mindless and desperately aggravating.

"A recipe for mixing your own house paint?"

"Oh, *please*," she said, looking disgusted. "You're not trying."

"The complete works of Fulgentius of Ruspe!"

"Who?"

"I give up," he said, meaning it.

"I found another Mitford! It's in England, and it has a church as old as mud, not to mention a castle!" She looked triumphant, as if she'd just squelched an invasion of Moors.

"Really? Terrific! I suppose it's where those writing Mitfords came from—"

"No connection. They were from th' Cotswolds, this place is up north somewhere. I had a stack of stuff I printed out, but Snickers sat on th' whole bloomin' mess after playin' in the creek, and I have to print it out again."

"Aha."

"OK, guess what else!"

"Dadgummit, Emma. You know I hate this."

She said what she always said. "It's good for you, keeps your brain active."

As far as she was concerned, he'd gone soft in the head since retiring six months ago.

"Just tell me and get it over with."

"Oh, come on! Try at least one guess. Here's a clue. It's about the election in November."

"Esther's stepping down and Andrew Gregory's going to run."

She frowned. "How'd you know that?"

"I haven't gone deaf and blind, for Pete's sake. I do get around."

"I suppose you also know," said Emma, hoping he didn't, "that the restaurant at Fernbank is openin' the night before you leave."

"Right. We've been invited."

She thumped into the slipcovered wing chair and peered at him as if he were a beetle on a pin. Though she'd certainly never say such a thing, she believed he was existing in a kind of purgatory between the inarguable heaven of Lord's Chapel and the hell of a strange parish in a strange place where the temperature was a hundred and five in the shade.

"Will you have a secretary down there?" she asked, suspicious.

"I don't think so. Small parish, you know."

"How small can it be?"

"Oh, fifty, sixty people."

"I thought Bishop Cullen was your *friend*," she sniffed. She'd never say so, but in her heart of hearts, she had hoped her boss of sixteen years would be given a big church in a big city, and make a comeback for himself. As it was, he trotted up the hill to Hope House and the hospital every livelong morning, appearing so cheerful about the whole thing that she recognized it at once as a cover-up.

Cynthia returned with a glass of lemonade and a plate of shortbread, which she put on the table next to Emma. "I'll be in the studio if anyone needs me. With all the books we're taking, we may sink the island!"

"A regular Atlantis," said Father Tim.

"Speakin' of books," Emma said to his wife, "are you doin' a new one?"

"Not if I can help it!"

He laughed as Cynthia trotted down the hall. "She usually can't help it." He expected a new children's book to break forth from his energetic wife any day now. Indeed, didn't she have a history of starting one when life was upside down and backward?

Emma munched on a piece of shortbread, showering crumbs in her lap. "Do you have those letters ready for me to do on th' computer?"

"Not quite. I wasn't expecting you 'til in the morning."

"I'm coming in th' morning, I just wanted to run by and tell you all th' late-breakin' news. But," she said, arching one eyebrow, "I haven't told you everything, I saved th' best 'til last."

His dog wandered into the study and crashed at his master's feet, panting.

"If you say you already know this, I'll never tell you another thing as long as I live. On my way here, I saw Mule Skinner, he said he's finally rented your house."

She drew herself up, pleased, and gulped the lemonade.

"Terrific! Great timing!" He might have done a jig.

"He said there hadn't been time to call you, he'll call you tonight, but it's not a family with kids like Cynthia wanted."

"Oh, well . . ." He was thrilled that someone had finally stepped forward to occupy the rectory. He and Harley had worked hard over the last few months to make it a strong rental property, putting new vinyl flooring in the kitchen, replacing the stair runners, installing a new toilet in the master bath and a new threshold at the front door . . . the list had been endless. And costly.

"It's a woman."

"I can't imagine what one person would want with all that house to rattle around in."

"How quickly you forget! *You* certainly rattled around in there for a hundred years."

"True. Well. I'll get the whole story from Mule."

"He said she didn't mind a bit that Harley would be livin' in the basement, she just wanted to know if he plays loud rock music."

Emma rattled the ice in her glass, gulped the last draught, and got up to leave. "Before I forget, you won't believe what else I found on th' Internet—church bulletins! You ought to read some of th' foolishness they put out there for God an' everybody to see."

She fished a piece of paper from her handbag. " 'Next Sunday,' " she read, " 'a special collection will be taken to defray the cost of a new carpet. All those wishin' to do somethin' on the new carpet will come forward and do so.' "

He hooted with laughter.

"How 'bout this number: 'Don't let worry kill you, let th' church help.' "

He threw his head back and laughed some more. Emma's life in cyberspace definitely had an upside.

"By th' way, are you takin' Barnabas down there?" She enunciated "down there" as if it were a region beneath the crust of the earth.

"We are."

"I don't know how you could do that to an animal. Look at all that fur, enough to stuff a mattress."

Barnabas yawned hugely and thumped his tail on the floor.

"You won't even be able to *see* those horrible sandspurs that will jump in there by th' hundreds, not to mention *lodge in his paws.*"

Emma waited for an argument, a rationale—something. Did he have no conscience? "And th' *heat* down there, you'll have to shave 'im bald."

Father Tim strolled across the room to walk her to the door.

"Thanks for coming, Emma. Tell Harold hello. I'll see you in the morning."

His unofficial secretary stumped down the hallway and he followed.

He was holding the front door open and biting his tongue when she turned and looked at him. Her eyes were suddenly red and filled with tears.

"I'll miss you!" she blurted.

"You *will*?"

She hurried down the front steps, sniffing, searching her bag for a Hardee's napkin she knew was in there someplace.

He felt stricken. "Emma! We'll . . . we'll have jelly doughnuts in the morning!"

"*I'll* have jelly doughnuts, *you'll* have dry toast! We don't want to ship you down there in a coma!"

She got in her car at the curb, slammed the door, gunned the motor, and roared up Wisteria Lane.

For one fleeting moment, he'd completely forgotten his blasted diabetes.

"I'm out of here," he said, kissing his wife.

"Get him to leave something for the island breezes to flow through, darling. Don't let him cut it all off."

"You always say that."

"Yes, well, you come home looking like a skinned rabbit. I don't know what Joe Ivey *does* to you."

Considering what Fancy Skinner had done to him time and time again, Joe Ivey could do anything he wanted.

"Leavin' us, are you?" Joe ran a comb through the hair over Father Tim's left ear and snipped.

"Afraid so."

"Leavin' us in th' lurch is more like it."

"Now, Joe. Did I preach to you when you went off to Graceland and left me high and dry?"

Joe cackled. "Thank God I come to m' senses and quit that fool job. An' in th' nick of time, too. I'm finally about t' clean up what

Fancy Skinner done to people's heads around here, which in your case looked like she lowered your ears a foot an' a half."

"My wife says don't cut it too short."

"If I listened to what wives say, I'd of been out of business forty years ago. Do you know how hot it gits down there?"

If he'd been asked that once, he'd been asked it a thousand times. There was hardly anything mountain people despised more than a "hot" place.

"I'm an old Mississippi boy, you know."

"An th' mosquitos . . . !" Joe whistled. "Man alive!"

"Right there," he said, as Joe started working around his collar. "Just clean it up a little right there, don't cut it—"

Joe proceeded to cut it. Oh, well. Joe Ivey had always done exactly as he pleased with Father Tim's hair, just like Fancy Skinner. What was the matter with people who serviced hair, anyway? He had never, in all his years, been able to figure it out.

"I hear it's a ten-hour trot t' get there," said Joe, clearly fixated on the inconvenience of it all.

"Closer to twelve, if you stop for gas and lunch."

"You could go t' New York City in less'n that. Prob'ly run up an' back."

"There's a thought."

Joe trimmed around his customer's right ear. "I'm gettin' t' where I'd like t' talk . . ."—Joe cleared his throat—"about what happened up at Graceland."

"Aha."

"I ain't told this to a soul, not even Winnie."

There was a long pause.

Father Tim waited, inhaling the fragrance from Sweet Stuff Bakery, just beyond the thin wall. Joe's sister, Winnie, and her husband, Thomas, were baking baklava, and he was starting to salivate.

"You couldn't ever mention this to anybody," said Joe. "You'd have to swear on a stack of Bibles."

"I can't do that, but I give you my word."

Joe let his breath out in a long sigh. "Well, sir, there towards th' end, I got to where I thought Elvis might be . . ."

"Might be what?"

"You know. *Alive.*"

"No!"

"I ain't proud t' admit it. Thing is, I was gettin' in th' brandy pretty heavy when I went up there. My sister's husband, he was laid off and things was pretty tight. Plus, their house ain't exactly th' Biltmore Estate when it comes to room, so ever' once in a while, I'd ride around after supper t' give Vern and my sister a little time to theirselves."

"That was thoughtful."

"I took to lookin' for Elvis ever'where I went, 'specially at th' barbecue place, they all said he was a fool for barbecue. My sister, when she heard I was lookin' to sight Elvis, she started pourin' my brandy down th' toilet. A man can't hardly live with somebody as pours 'is brandy down th' toilet."

"That would create tension, all right." Heaven knows, he'd tried for years to get Joe to quit sucking down alcohol, but Joe had told him to mind his own business. Something, however, had happened in Memphis that sent his barber home dry as a bone.

"Then one night I was drivin' around, I said to myself, I said, Joe, Elvis wouldn't be cruisin' through a drive-in pickin' up a chopped pork with hot sauce, he'd *send* somebody. So I said, if *I* was Elvis, where would I be at?

"Seem like somethin' told me to go back to Graceland, it was about eleven o'clock at night, so I drove on over there and parked across th' street with my lights off. I hate to tell you, but I had a pint in the glove department, and I was takin' a little pull now and again."

Joe took a bottle off the cabinet and held it above his customer's head. "You want Sea Breeze?"

"Is the Pope a Catholic?"

"First thing you know, I seen somethin' at th' top of the yard. There's this big yard, you know, that spreads out behind th' gate an' all. It was somethin' white, and it . . . ."—Joe cleared his throat—"it was movin' around."

"Aha."

Joe blasted his scalp with Sea Breeze and vigorously rubbed it in. "You ain't goin' to believe this."

"Try me."

Joe's hands stopped massaging his head. In the mirror, Father Tim could see his barber's chin quivering.

"It was Elvis . . . in a white suit."

"Come on!"

"Mowin' 'is yard."

"No way!"

"I said you wouldn't believe it."

"Why would he mow his yard when he could pay somebody else to do it? And why would he do it in a suit, much less a *white* suit? And why would he do it at *night*?"

Joe's eyes were misty. He shook his head, marveling. "I never have figured it out."

"Well, well." What could he say?

"I set there watchin'. He'd mow a strip one way, then mow a strip th' other way."

"Gas or push?"

"Push."

"How could he see?" Father Tim asked, mildly impatient.

"There was this . . . *glow* all around him."

"Aha."

"Then, first thing you know . . ."—Joe's voice grew hushed—"he th'owed up 'is hand and waved at me."

Father Tim was speechless.

"Here I'd been lookin' to see 'im for I don't know how long, and it scared me s' bad when I finally done it, I slung th' bottle in th' bushes and quit drinkin' on th' spot."

His barber drew a deep breath and stood tall. "I ain't touched a drop since, and ain't wanted to."

Father Tim was convinced this was the gospel truth. Still, he had a question.

"So, Joe, what's that, ah . . . bottle sitting over there by the hair tonic?"

"I keep that for my customers. You don't want a little snort, do you?"

"I pass. But tell me this . . . any regrets about coming back to Mitford?"

"Not ary one, as my daddy used to say. It's been a year, now, since I hauled out of Memphis and come home to Mitford, and my old trade has flocked back like a drove of guineas. Winnie gave me this nice room to set my chair in, and th' Lord's give me back my health."

Joe took the cape from his customer's shoulders and shook it out. "Yessir, you're lookin' at a happy man."

"And so are you!" said Father Tim. "So are you!"

After all, didn't he have a new haircut, a new parish, and a whole new life just waiting to begin?

He couldn't help himself.

As the bells at Lord's Chapel pealed three o'clock, he turned into Happy Endings Bookstore as if on automatic pilot. He had five whole minutes to kill before jumping in the car and roaring off to Wesley for a bicycle pump, since Dooley's had turned up missing.

"Just looking," he told Hope Winchester. Hope's ginger-colored cat, Margaret, peered at him suspiciously as he raced through General Fiction, hung a right at Philosophy, and skidded left into Religion, where the enterprising Hope had recently installed a shelf of rare books.

He knew for a fact that the only bookstore on Whitecap Island was in the rear of a bait and tackle shop. They would never in a hundred years have Arthur Quiller-Couch's *On the Art of Reading*, which he had eyed for a full week. It was now or never.

His hand shot out to the hard-to-find Quiller-Couch volume, but was instantly drawn back. No, a thousand times no. If his wife knew he was buying more books to schlepp to Whitecap, he'd be dead meat.

He sighed.

"Better to take it now than call long-distance and have me ship it down there for three dollars."

Hope appeared next to him, looking wise in new tortoiseshell glasses.

No doubt about it, Hope had his number.

He raked the book off the shelf, and snatched Jonathan Edwards's *The Freedom of the Will* from another. He noted that his forehead broke out in a light sweat.

Oh, well, while he was at it . . .

He grabbed a copy of Lewis's *Great Divorce*, which had wandered from his own shelves, never to be seen again, and went at a trot to the cash register.

"I'm sure you're excited about your party!" Hope said, ringing the sale. Margaret jumped onto the counter and glowered at him. Why did cats hate his guts? What had he ever done to cats? Didn't he buy his wife's cat only the finest, most ridiculously priced chicken niblets in a fancy tinfoil container?

"Party? What party?"

"Why, the party Uncle Billy and Miss Rose are giving you and Cynthia!"

"I don't know anything about a party." Had someone told him and he'd forgotten?

"It's the biggest thing in the world to them. They've never given a party in their whole lives, but they want to do this because they hold you in the most edacious regard."

"Well!" He was nearly speechless. "When is it supposed to be?"

"Tomorrow night, of course." She looked at him oddly.

Tomorrow night they were working a list as long as his arm, not to mention shopping for groceries to feed Dooley Barlowe a welcome-home dinner of steak, fries, and chocolate pie.

He mopped his forehead with a handkerchief. He'd be glad to leave town and get his life in order again.

"I'll look into it," he muttered, shelling out cash for the forbidden books. "And if you don't mind, that is, if you happen to see Cynthia, you might not mention that, ah . . ."

Hope Winchester smiled. She would never say a word to the priest's wife about his buying more books. Just as she certainly wouldn't mention to him that Cynthia had dashed in only this morning to buy copies of Celia Thaxter's *My Island Garden*, and the hardback of *Ira Sleeps Over*.

$\backsim$

He knocked on the screen door of the small, life-estate apartment in the rear of the town musuem.

"Uncle Billy! Miss Rose! Anybody home?"

He couldn't imagine the old couple giving a party; his mind was perfectly boggled by the notion. Rose Watson had been diagnosed as schizophrenic decades ago, and although on daily medication, her mood swings were fierce and unpredictable. To make matters worse for her long-suffering husband, she was quickly going deaf as a stone, but refused to wear hearing aids. "There's aids enough in this world," she said menacingly.

He put his nose against the screen and saw Uncle Billy sleeping in a chair next to an electric fan, his cane between his legs. Father Tim hated to wake him, but what was he to do? He knocked again.

Uncle Billy opened his eyes and looked around the kitchen, startled.

"It's me, Uncle Billy!"

"Lord if hit ain't th' preacher!" The old man grinned toward the door, his gold tooth gleaming. "Rose!" he shouted. "Hit's th' preacher!"

"He's not supposed to be here 'til tomorrow!" Miss Rose bellowed from the worn armchair by the refrigerator.

Uncle Billy grabbed his cane and slowly pulled himself to a standing position. "If I set too long, m' knees lock up, don't you know. But I'm a-comin'."

"Tell him he's a day early!" commanded Miss Rose.

"Don't you mind Rose a bit. You're welcome any time of th' day or night." Uncle Billy opened the screen and he stepped into the kitchen. The Watsons had cooked cabbage for lunch, no two ways about it.

"Uncle Billy, I hear you're giving . . . well, someone said you're giving Cynthia and me . . . a *party?*"

The old man looked vastly pleased. "Got a whole flock of people comin' to see you! Got three new jokes t' tell, you're goin' t' like 'em, and Rose is makin' banana puddin'."

Father Tim scratched his head, feeling foolish.

"Y' see, th' church give you 'uns a nice, big party an' all, but hit seemed mighty official, hit was anybody an' ever'body, kind of a free-for-all. I said, 'Rose, we ought t' give th' preacher an' 'is missus a little send-off with 'is *friends!*'" The old man leaned on his cane, grinning triumphantly. "So we're a-doin' it, and glad t' be a-doin' it!"

"Well, now—"

"Hit's goin' to be in th' museum part of th' house, so we can play th' jukebox, don't you know."

"Why, that's wonderful, it really is, but—"

"An' me an' Rose took a good bath in th' *tub!*"

He had seen the time when Uncle Billy and Miss Rose could empty two or three pews around their own. . . .

Miss Rose, in a chenille robe and unlaced saddle oxfords, stood up from her chair and looked him dead in the eye. He instantly wished for the protection of his wife.

"I hope you didn't come expecting to eat a day in advance," she snapped.

"Oh, law," said her mortified husband. "Now, Rose—"

She turned to Uncle Billy. "I haven't even *made* the banana pudding yet, so how can we feed him?"

"Oh, I didn't come to eat. I just came to find out—"

"You march home," said Miss Rose, "and come back tomorrow at the right time."

Uncle Billy put his hands over his eyes, as if to deny the terrible scene taking place in front of him.

"And what time might that *be*?" shouted Father Tim.

"Six-thirty sharp!" said the old woman, looking considerably vexed.

His wife went pale.

He felt like putting his hands over his own eyes, as Uncle Billy had done.

"I'm sorry," he said. "I didn't know how to say no. Uncle Billy is so excited. . . . They've never given a party before."

"Why in heaven's name didn't they let us *know*?"

"I think they invited everybody else and forgot to invite us."

"Lord have *mercy*!" said his overworked wife, conveniently quoting the prayer book.

They had collapsed on the study sofa for the Changing of the Light, having gone nonstop since five-thirty that morning. He had made the lemonade on this occasion, and served it with two slices of bread, each curled hastily around a filling of Puny's homemade pimiento cheese.

"I can't even *think* about a party," she said, stuffing the bread and cheese into her mouth. "My blood sugar has dropped through the soles of my tennis shoes."

Ah, the peace of this room, he thought, unbuttoning his shirt. And here they were, leaving it. They built it, and now they were leaving it. Such was life in a collar.

"Timothy, are you really excited about going to Whitecap?"

"It comes and goes in waves. One moment, I'm excited—"

"And the next, you're scared to death?"

"Well . . ."

"Me, too," she confessed. "I hate to leave Mitford. I thought it would be fun, invigorating, a great adventure." She lay down, putting her head on one of the faded needlepoint pillows that had also made it through the hedge. "But now . . ." Her voice trailed off.

"We're pretty worn out, Kavanagh. This is a stressful thing we're doing, pulling up stakes. I've hardly been out of Mitford in sixteen years. But we'll get there and it will be terrific, wait and see. You'll love it. The freedom of an island . . ."

"The wind in our hair . . ."

"Gulls wheeling above us . . ."

"The smell of salt air . . ."

It was a litany they'd recited antiphonally over the last couple of months. It always seemed to console them.

He pulled her feet into his lap. "How about a nap? We've got a tight schedule ahead."

"Tonight," she said, "Puny helps us clean out all the cabinets. . . . Dooley comes tomorrow evening just before the Watson party, and will have supper with his mother. Then a day of shopping with our threadbare boy and moving him in with Harley, followed by your meeting with the new tenant, and Dooley's steak dinner. Then, of course, there's the grand opening at Lucera on Thursday night after we finish packing the car, and on Friday morning we're off. I don't think," she said, breathless, "that we'll have time to celebrate your birthday."

His birthday! Blast! This year, he would be sixty-six, and just think—in four short years, he would be seventy. And then eighty. And then . . . dead, he supposed. Oh, well.

"Don't be depressed," she scolded. "And for heaven's sake, dearest, relax. You're sitting there like a statue in a park."

"Right," he said, guzzling the lemonade.

He had noted over the last few days that the late June light reached its pinnacle when it fell upon the brass angel. Because of the exterior overhang of the room, the direct light moved no higher than the mantel, where the angel stood firm on its heavy base of green marble.

He had found the angel in the attic at Fernbank, Miss Sadie's rambling house at the top of the hill, now owned by Andrew and Anna Gregory. Only months before she died in her ninetieth year, Sadie Baxter had written a letter about the disposition of her family home and its contents. One thing she asked him to do was take something for his own, anything he liked.

As Cynthia rambled through Fernbank seeking her portion of the legacy, he had found the angel in a box, a box with a faded French postmark. Though the attic was filled with a bountiful assortment of inarguable treasures, he had known as surely as if someone had engraved his name upon it that the angel in a box belonged to him.

The light moved now to the angel, to its outspread wings and supplicating hands. It shone, also, on the vase of pink flowering almond next to the old books, and the small silhouette of his mother, which Cynthia had reframed and hung above the mantel.

As long as he could remember, he'd been afraid to sit still, to listen, to wait. As a priest, he'd been glad of every needy soul to tend to; every potluck supper to sit to; even of every illness to run to—thankful for the fray and haste. He'd been frightened of any tendency to sit and let his mind wander like a goat untethered from a chain, free to crop any grass it pleased.

He was beginning to realize, however, that he was less and less afraid to do what appeared to be nothing.

In the end, he wasn't really afraid of moving to Whitecap, either; he'd given his wife the wrong notion. He had prayed that God would send him wherever He pleased, and when his bishop presented the idea of Whitecap, he knew it wasn't his bishop's bright idea at all, but God's. He had learned years ago to read God's answer to any troubling decision by looking to his heart, his spirit, for an imprimatur of peace. That peace had come; otherwise, he would not go.

He inhaled the freshness of the breeze that stole through the open window, and the fragrance of oak and cherry that pervaded the room like incense.

Then, lulled by the sight of his dozing wife, he put his head back and closed his eyes, and slept.

CHAPTER TWO

Social Graces

Rose Watson set out what most people would call an outrageous assortment of cracked, chipped, and broken china, including mis-
matched cups and saucers that teetered atop a tower of salad plates
anchored on a turkey platter.

After standing back and gazing at the curious pile with some satisfaction, she decided to flank the arrangement with a medley of soup
bowls.

The large plastic container of banana pudding sat on the electric
range, bristling with two serving spoons jabbed into its yellow center.
For napkins, Uncle Billy supplied a roll of paper towels, which he
stood on one end next to the pudding.

"Don't set paper on a *stove*!" Miss Rose snatched the roll and
moved it like a pawn on a chessboard to the kitchen table.

"What about spoons?" shouted her husband. He was fairly be-
numbed with the idea of having a swarm of people descend on their
living quarters, though it had been his notion in the first place.

"Pull out the drawer! They can help themselves."

He did as he was told, thinking that his wife sometimes had a good
idea, and wasn't half as crazy as most people thought. Mean-spirited,
maybe, but that was her disease.

He had tried to read about schizophrenia in the Mitford library, one of the few times he had ever stepped foot in the place. He had looked for the oldest volunteer he could find, thinking she would be the boss, and asked her to lead him to a volume on a disease whose name he could not spell. He had then taken the book to a table and sat and asked the Lord to give him some kind of wisdom about what was so terribly, horribly wrong with his wife, but he couldn't understand anything the book had said, nothing.

"That's good thinkin'!" he shouted.

"You say somethin's *stinkin'*?" She turned and looked at him.

"Dadgummit, Rose, I said—"

"It might be your upper lip, Bill Watson." She suddenly burst into laughter.

There it was! The laughter he heard so seldom, had almost forgotten, rushing out like a bird freed from a cage, the laughter of the girl he'd known all those years ago. . . .

He stood, stunned and happy, tears springing to his eyes as suddenly as her laughter had come.

Father Tim found the china assortment fascinating. He could spot several pieces of French Haviland in a pattern his grandmother had owned, and not a few pieces of Sevres.

At least he thought it was Sevres. He picked up a bread-and-butter plate and peered discreetly at the bottom. Meissen. What did he know?

He certainly didn't know what to do about the banana pudding. Everyone except themselves had been asked to bring a covered dish, so there was plenty to choose from. Miss Rose, however, stood like a sentinel by the stove, making sure that all comers had a hefty dose of what had taken her a full afternoon to create.

All those cracks in the china, he thought, all those chips and chinks . . . weren't they a known hideout for germs, a breeding ground? And hadn't he sat by the hospital bed of a woman who had put her feet under Rose Watson's table and barely lived to tell about it?

He could remember the story plainly. "Lord knows, I hadn't hardly got home before my stomach started rumblin' and carryin' on, you never heard such a racket. Well, Preacher, I hate to tell you such a thing, but you've heard it all, anyhow—five minutes later, I was settin' on th' toilet, throwin' up on my shoes."

He had not forgotten the mental image of that good lady throwing up on her shoes. He certainly hadn't forgotten her dark warning never to eat a bite or drink a drop at Rose Watson's house.

"Fill y'r plates and march into th' front room!" Their host's gold tooth gleamed. "Some's already in there, waitin' for th' blessin'."

Cynthia served herself from the pudding bowl as if she hadn't eaten a bite since Rogation Sunday.

"Fall to, darling," she said, happy as a child.

Oh, the everlasting gusto of his spouse! He sighed, peering around for the ham biscuits.

He found that everyone was oddly excited about being in a place as prominent as the town museum. It was a little awkward, however, given that not a single chair could be found, and they all had to mill around with their plates in their hands, setting their tea glasses on windowsills and stair steps.

The jukebox boomed out what he thought was "Chattanooga Shoeshine Boy," and laid a steady rhythm into the bare floorboards.

He and Cynthia made a quick tour of the exhibits, which he'd never, for some reason, taken time to study.

There was a copy of Willard Porter's deed to what had been the Mitford Pharmacy and was now Happy Endings Bookstore. There was also a handwritten list of pharmaceuticals that Willard had invented and patented, including Rose Cough Syrup, named for his then-ten-year-old sister, and their hostess for the evening.

There was the framed certificate declaring the Wurlitzer to be a gift to the town from the owner of the Main Street Grill, where it was unplugged on June 26, 1951. It had been fully restored to mint condition, thanks to the generosity of Mayor Esther Cunningham.

He examined the daguerreotype of Coot Hendrick's great-great-grandfather sitting in a straight-back chair with a rifle across his knees.

It had been Coot's bearded ancestor, Hezikiah, who settled Mitford, riding horseback up the mountain along an Indian trading path, with his new English bride, Mary Jane, clinging on behind. According to legend, his wife was so homesick that Mr. Hendrick had the generosity of spirit to give the town her maiden name of Mitford, instead of Hendricksville or Hendricksburg, which a man might have preferred to call a place settled by dint of his own hard labors.

" 'At's my great-*great*-granpaw," said Coot Hendrick, coming alongside the preacher and his wife. He'd been waiting to catch someone looking at that picture. For years, it had knocked around in a drawer at his mama's house, and he'd hardly paid any attention to it at all. Then somebody wanted it for the town museum and it had taken on a whole new luster.

"He looks fearless!" said Cynthia.

"Had twelve young 'uns!" Coot grinned from ear to ear, which was not a pretty sight, given his dental condition. "Stubs!" Mule Skinner had said, marveling at how he'd seen people's teeth fall out, but never wear down in such a way.

"Six lived, six died, all buried over yonder on Miz Mallory's ridge. Her house sets right next to where him and my great-great-granmaw built their little cabin."

"Well!" said Father Tim.

"Hit was a fine place to sight Yankees from," said Coot.

"I'll bet so."

"There probably weren't many Yankees prowling around up here," said Cynthia, who'd read that, barely a hundred and fifty years ago, an Anglican bishop had called the area "wild and uninhabitable."

"You'd be surprised," said Coot, tucking his thumbs in the straps of his overalls. "They say my great-great-granpaw shot five and give ever' one of 'em a solemn burial."

"I didn't know there were any battles fought around Mitford," said Cynthia, who appeared deeply interested in this new wrinkle of local history.

"They won't. Th' Yankees was runaways from their regiment."

Spying Esther and Gene Bolick making a beeline in their direction, they excused themselves and met the Bolicks halfway.

"We just hate this!" said Esther. Overcome, she grabbed his hand and kissed it, then, mortified at such behavior, dropped it like a hot potato. "Gene and I have run th' gambit of emotions, and we still just hate to see y'all go!"

"We hate to go," he said simply.

"I baked you a two-layer orange marmalade and froze it. You can carry it down there in your cooler." There was nothing else she could do to keep her former priest in Mitford where she was certain he belonged—she had prayed, she had lost, she had cried, and in the end, she had baked.

Her husband, Gene, sighed and looked glum.

This, thought Father Tim, is precisely where a going-away party turns into a blasted wake unless somebody puts on a funny hat or slides down the banister, *something.* . . .

He turned to his wife, who shrugged and smiled and sought greener pastures.

"Gene's not been feelin' too good," said Esther.

"What is it?" asked Father Tim.

"Don't know exactly," Gene said, as Miss Rose strode up. "But I talked to Hoppy and went and got th' shots."

"Got the *trots*?" shouted Miss Rose. Everyone peered at them.

Gene flushed. "No, ma'am. The *shots.*"

"Bill had the trots last week," she said, frowning. "It could be something going around." Their hostess, who was monitoring everyone's plate to see whether her pudding had gotten its rightful reception, moved on to the next circle of guests.

"We reckon you know how hot it gets down there," said Gene.

"Honey, *hot's* not th' word for it!" Fancy Skinner appeared in her signature outfit of pink Capri pants, V-neck sweater, and spike-heel shoes. "You will be boiled, steamed, roasted, baked, and fried."

"Not to mention sautéed," said Avis Packard, who owned the grocery store on Main Street, and liked to cook.

Fancy popped her sugarless gum. "Then there's stewed and broiled."

"Please," said Father Tim.

"Barbecued!" contributed Gene, feeling pleased with himself. "You forgot barbecued."

Fancy, who was the owner of Mitford's only unisex salon, hooted with laughter.

"Did you consider maybe goin' to *Vermont*?" Gene wondered if their former rector had thought through this island business.

"Because if you think your hair's curlin' around your ears *now*," said Fancy, "wait'll all that humidity hits it, we're talkin' a Shirley Temple–Little Richard combo. That's why I liked to keep your hair *flat* around your ears when *I* was doin' it, now it's these chipmunk *pooches* again." Fancy reached out to forcibly slick his vagrant pooches down with her fingers, but restrained herself.

He looked anxiously around the room for Cynthia, who was laughing with the mayor and Hope Winchester.

Omer Cunningham trotted in from the kitchen with a plate piled to overflowing, wearing his usual piano-key grin. Father Tim vowed he'd never seen so many big white teeth as the mayor's brother-in-law had in his head. It was enough for a regular Debussy concerto.

"Lord, at th' traffic I've run into today!"

"On Main Street?"

"I mean air traffic," said the proud owner of a ragwing taildragger. "I been buzzin' th' gorge. You never seen th' like of deer that's rootin' around in there. Seems like ever'body and his brother was flyin' today."

Father Tim had instant and vivid recall of his times in the ragwing with Omer. Once to Virginia to hear Dooley in a concert, with his stomach lagging some distance behind the plane. Then again when they flew over Edith Mallory's sprawling house on the ridge above Mitford, trying to see what kind of dirty deal was behind the last mayoral race.

"I spotted a Piper Cherokee, a Cessna 182, and a Beechcraft Bonanza."

"Kind of like bird-watching."

"That Bonanza costs half a million smackers. You don't see many of those."

"I'll bet you don't."

"Listen, now," said Omer, ripping the meat off a drumstick with his teeth, "you let me know if I can ever buzz down to where you're at to help you out or anything. My little ragwing is yours any time of th' day or night, you hear?"

"Thank you, Omer, that's mighty thoughtful!"

Omer's chewing seemed unusually efficient. "I've flew over them little islands where you're goin' any number of times. Landed on many a beach. If you stay out of th' bad thunderstorms they have down there, it's as calm an' peaceful as you'd ever want t' see."

Omer picked up a ham biscuit and eyed it. "I don't like ham in a cathead biscuit," he said. "Have to dig too far for th' ham."

It was his fault. He was the one who casually mentioned it to Mule Skinner.

In nothing flat, the word of Dooley Barlowe's driver's license had replaced the party buzz about Avis Packard's decision to buy a panel truck for grocery delivery, and the huge addition to Edith Mallory's already enormous house.

Did he imagine it, or were they all peering at him as if to inquire when he was trotting out a car to go with Dooley's license?

Absolutely not. He had no intention of buying a car for a sixteen-year-old boy, then running off and leaving him to his own devices. Fortunately, Dooley had agreed to ride his red bicycle this summer, but he knew the notion of a car was definitely in the boy's mind. After all, didn't everybody's father in that fancy school toss around snappy convertibles and upscale four-wheel drives like so much confetti?

While it was obvious that Dooley couldn't earn enough money for a car by bagging groceries, Father Tim thought a summer of trying would hardly damage the boy's character.

In truth, there was an even more serious concern than Dooley's automobile hormones. And that was the fact he'd have nearly ten weeks to come and go as he pleased. Harley Welch would make a dependable, principled guardian, but Dooley could outwit Harley.

He muddled his spoon in the banana pudding.

As if reading Father Tim's mind, Mule said, "We'll all watch after 'im."

"Right," said Gene, "we'll keep an eye on 'im."

Adele Hogan, Mitford's only female police officer and nearly-new wife of the newspaper editor, caught up with him at the jukebox, as her husband snapped pictures for Monday's edition of the *Muse*.

"Just wanted you to know," said Adele, "we've got cars cruisin' around the clock. We'll keep our eyes open for your little guy while you're gone."

The truth was, there'd be a veritable woof of men to look after the boy, not to mention a fine warp of women, including Puny, and Dooley's mother, and now Adele.

"Thank you!" he said, meaning it.

Adele stood with her thumbs tucked into her belt, appearing for a moment to be hired security. She had come straight from the station in her uniform, wearing a Glock nine-millimeter on her hip. The sight of Adele, who was the new hotshot coach of the Mitford Reds and also the grandmother of three, never failed to astonish and impress him.

"Don't worry about a thing," said Adele.

He was almost inclined not to.

"Right!" agreed Avis. "I'm th' only one that'll drive my delivery truck, except for Lew Boyd's cousin, who's fillin' in on Saturdays. Anyway, I'm goin' to work your boy's butt off this summer. He won't have time to get in trouble." In a spontaneous burst of camaraderie, Avis slapped him on the shoulder.

The mayor barged up and slapped him on the other shoulder. He nearly pitched into the Wurlitzer, which was now playing "One Mint Julep."

"Run out on us, then," said Esther Cunningham. "See if I care."

"You don't need me anymore. After praying you into office eight times in a row, you're hanging it up and going off with Ray in the RV."

Esther narrowed her eyes and peered at him. "I guess you know about th' hurricanes they get down there."

"I do."

"And th' heat . . ."

Would they *never* hush . . . ?

A muscle twitched in the mayor's jaw. "We'll miss you."

"We'll miss you back," he said, putting his arm around his old friend's well-cushioned shoulders. He hated this goodbye business. He'd rather be home yanking a tooth out by a string on a doorknob, anything. "Are you laying off the sausage biscuits?"

"Curiosity killed the cat," she said.

Esther cupped her hands to her mouth and shouted, "Somebody unplug th' box!"

Omer squatted by the Wurlitzer, which couldn't be shut off manually, and pulled the plug.

"Must be Uncle Billy's joke," said Gene Bolick, getting up from the stair step where he was sitting with Mule.

Mule sighed. "I hope it's not that deal about th' gas stove! I've heard that more times than Carter has liver pills."

"Here's one for you," said Gene. "What's a Presbyterian?"

"Beats me."

"A Methodist with a drinkin' problem who can't afford to be Episcopalian."

Mule scratched his head. He had never understood jokes about Episcopalians.

"Come on, everybody!" yelled the mayor, her voice echoing in the vaulted room. "Joke time!"

Uncle Billy stood as straight as he was able, holding on to his cane and looking soberly at the little throng, who gave forth a murmur of coughing and throat-clearing.

"Wellsir!" he exclaimed, by way of introduction. "A farmer was haulin' manure, don't you know, an' 'is truck broke down in front of a mental institution. One of th' patients, he leaned over th' fence, said, 'What're you goin' t' do with y'r manure?'

"Farmer said, 'I'm goin' t' put it on m' strawberries.'

"Feller said, 'We might be crazy, but we put whipped cream on our'n.' "

Uncle Billy grinned at the cackle of laughter he heard.

"Keep goin'!" someone said.

"Wellsir, this old feller an' 'is wife was settin' on th' porch, an' she said, 'Guess what I'd like t' have?'

"He said, 'What's that?'

"She said, 'A great big bowl of vaniller ice cream with choc'late sauce and nuts on top!'

"He says, 'Boys howdy, that'd be good. I'll go down to th' store and git us some.'

"Wife said, 'Now, that's vaniller ice cream with choc'late sauce and nuts. Better write it down.'

"He said, 'Don't need t' write it down, I can remember.'

"Little while later, he come back. Had two ham san'wiches. Give one t' her. She looked at that san'wich, lifted th' top off, said, 'You mulehead, I told you t' write it down, I wanted mustard on mine!' "

Loving the sound of laughter in the cavernous room, Uncle Billy nodded to the left, then to the right.

"One more," he said, trembling a little from the excitement of the evening.

"Hit it!" crowed the mayor, hoping to remember the punch line to the vanilla ice-cream story.

"Wellsir, this census taker, he went to a house an' knocked, don't you know. A woman come out, 'e said, 'How many children you got, an' what're their ages?'

"She said, 'Let's see, there's th' twins Sally and Billy, they're eighteen. And th' twins Seth an' Beth, they're sixteen. And th' twins Penny an' Jenny, they're fourteen—'

"Feller said, 'Hold on! Did you git twins ever' time?'

"Woman said, 'Law, no, they was hundreds of times we didn't git nothin'.' "

The old man heard the sound of applause overtaking the laughter, and leaned forward slightly, cupping his hand to his left ear to better take it in. The applause was giving him courage, somehow, to keep on in life, to get out of bed in the mornings and see what was what.

Uncle Billy and Miss Rose looked considerably exhausted from their social endeavors; the old man's hands trembled as they stood on the cool front porch.

"I'd like to pray for you," said Father Tim.

"We'd be beholden to you, Preacher, if you would," said Uncle Billy, "but seems like we ought t' pray f'r you, don't you know."

Hardly anyone ever did that, he thought, moved by the gesture. "I'd thank you for doing it."

Cynthia slipped into the circle and they joined hands.

"Now, Lord . . ."—the old man drew a deep breath—"I ain't used t' doin' this out loud an' all, but I felt You call me t' do it, an' I'm expectin' You t' help me, don't you know.

"Lord Jesus, I'm askin' You t' watch over th' preacher an' 'is missus. Don't let 'em git drownded down there, or come up ag'in' meanness of any kind. You tell 'em whichaway to go when they need it."

Uncle Billy paused. "An' I 'preciate it. F'r Christ's sake, a-men!"

"Amen!"

Father Tim clasped his arms around his old friend. "Uncle Billy—"

"I hope they give you plenty of fried chicken down there!" squawked Miss Rose. She'd always heard preachers liked fried chicken.

He didn't know how many more goodbyes he could bear.

It wasn't that he and Cynthia hadn't wanted to go to Whitecap to see and be seen. They had carefully planned to go for five days in March, but the weather had turned foul, with lashing rains and high winds that persisted for days along the eastern shoreline.

He had then tried to set a date for April, but most of the Whitecap vestry, who were key players in any approval process, would be away for one reason or another.

"Don't sweat it," Stuart Cullen had said in a phone call. Stuart was not only his current bishop, but a close friend since seminary days. "They know all about you. They're thrilled you'll do the interim. Bishop Harvey agrees it's a match made in heaven, so don't worry about getting down there for the usual preview."

"It's a little on the pig-in-a-poke side, if you ask me."

Stuart laughed. "Believe me, Timothy, they need exactly what you've got to offer. Besides, if you don't like each other, Bill Harvey and I will give you your money back."

"How about telling me the downside of this parish? All Bill Harvey talks about is the church being so attractive, it ends up on postcards."

"Right," agreed Stuart. "He also vows he hears the nickering of wild ponies through the open windows of the nave, though I don't think Whitecap has wild ponies these days."

"What I'd rather know is, who's likely to stab the interim in the back? And who's plotting to run off with the choir director?"

He was joking, of course, but equally serious. He wanted to know what was what in Whitecap, and nobody was telling him.

"Ah, well, Timothy, there isn't a choir director." His bishop sounded strained.

"Really? Why not?"

"Well . . ."

"Stuart!"

"Because the choir director ran off with the organist."

"Is this a joke?"

"I wish."

"Surely you can come up with something slicker than that. Good heavens, man, we had a jewel thief living in the attic at Lord's Chapel, not to mention a parishioner who tried to buy the last mayoral election. Tell me something I can get my teeth into."

"Sorry. But I've just given you the plain, unvarnished truth."

There was a long silence. "What else do I need to know?"

The bishop told him. In fact, he told him a great deal more than he needed to know.

He stepped into the downstairs bathroom and took his glucometer kit from the medicine cabinet. With all the hoopla going on, and the radical changes in his diet, he figured he should check his sugar more often.

Once or twice, he'd felt so low, he could have crawled under a snake's belly wearing a top hat. Other times, his adrenaline was pumping like an oil derrick.

He shot the lance into the tip of his left forefinger and spilled the drop of blood onto a test strip. Then he slid the strip into the glucometer and waited for the readout. 130.

Excellent. He didn't need any bad news from his body. Not now, not ever.

"Thank you, Lord," he murmured, zipping the case shut.

He and Dooley loped across Baxter Park with Barnabas on the red leash, then turned left and headed up Old Church Lane.

They ran side by side until the hospital turnoff, where Dooley suddenly looked at him, grinned, and shot forward like a hare.

As he watched the boy pull away toward the crest of the steep hill, he saw at once the reason for his greater speed. Dooley Barlowe's legs were six feet long.

He huffed behind, regretting the way he'd let his running schedule go. Oh, well. Whitecap would be another matter entirely. All that fresh salt air and ocean breeze, and a clean, wide beach that went on for miles . . .

He would even walk to his office, conveniently located in the basement of the church, only two blocks from Dove Cottage. Nor was he the only one whose physical fitness would take an upturn. Cynthia was sending her old blue Schwinn down with their household shipment, and would leave her Mazda in Mitford. For an island only eleven miles long and four miles wide, who needed a car? Even many of the locals were said to navigate on two-wheelers.

"Better watch your step down there," Omer had advised. "Them bicycles'll mow you down, they ride 'em ever' whichaway."

"Wait up!" he shouted to Dooley.

Dooley turned around, laughing, and for a crisp, quick moment, he saw the way the sun glinted on the boy's red hair, and the look in his blue eyes. It was a look of triumph, of exultation, a look he had never, even once, seen before on Dooley Barlowe's face.

He didn't know whether to whoop, which he felt like doing, or weep, which he dismissed at once. Instead, he lunged ahead, closing the gap between them, and threw his arm around the boy's shoulder and told him what must be spoken now, immediately, and not a moment later.

"I love you, buddy," he said, panting and laughing at once. "Blast if I don't."

They sat on the cool stone wall, looking into the valley, into the Land of Counterpane. There beyond the trees was the church spire, and over there, the tiniest glint of railroad tracks . . . and just there, the pond next to the apple orchard where he knew ducks were swimming. Above it all, ranging along the other side of the valley, the high, green hills outlined themselves against a blue and cloudless sky. It was his favorite view in the whole of the earth, he thought.

"There's something I'd like you to know," he told Dooley. "I believe we'll find Sammy and Kenny."

Father Tim had gone into the Creek with Lace Turner and retrieved Dooley's younger brother, Poobaw. Later, he'd driven to Florida on little more than a hunch, and located Dooley's little sister, Jessie. Now two of the five Barlowe children were still missing. Their mother, Pauline, recovering from years of hard drinking, had no idea where they might be. As far as he could discover, there were no clues, no trail, no nothing. But he had hope—the kind that comes from a higher place than reason or common sense.

"Will you believe that with me?" he asked Dooley.

A muscle moved in Dooley's jaw. "You did pretty good with Poo and Jessie."

Barnabas crashed into the grass at Dooley's feet.

"I believe we're closer to deciding on some colleges to start thinking about."

"Yep. Maybe Cornell."

"You've got a while before you have to make any decisions."

"Maybe University of Georgia."

"Maybe. Their specialty is large animals; that's what interests you. Anyway, that's all down the road. For now, just check things out, think about it, pray about it."

"Right."

"We're mighty proud of you, son. You'll make a fine vet. You've come—we've all come—a long way together."

There was an awkward silence between them.

"What's on your mind?" asked Father Tim.

"Nothing."

"Let's talk about it."

Dooley turned to him, glad for the invitation. "It looks like you could let me borrow the money and I'll pay you back. Working six days a week at five dollars an hour, I'll have sixteen hundred dollars. Plus I figure three yards a week at an average of twenty apiece, I'm countin' it seven hundred bucks because some people will give me a tip. Last year, I saved five hundred, so that's two thousand eight hundred."

He had the sudden sense of being squeezed between a rock and a hard place. . . .

"Nearly three thousand," said Dooley, enunciating clearly. "I could prob'ly make it an even three if I cleaned out people's attics and basements."

Aha. He hadn't counted on three thousand bucks being a factor in the car equation. He gazed out to the view, unseeing.

"This just isn't the summer for it. We can't be here, and that's a very crucial factor. Besides, you know we agreed you'd have a car next summer. If we're still at Whitecap, you'll come there, and everything will be fine." He looked at Dooley. "Call me hard if you like, but it's not going to happen."

Dooley turned away and said something under his breath.

"Tell you what we'll do. Cynthia and I will match everything you make this summer." It was a rash decision, but why not? He still had more than sixty thousand dollars of his mother's money, and was a homeowner with no mortgage. It was the right thing to do.

Dooley stared straight ahead, kicking the stone wall with his heels.

If Dooley Barlowe only knew what he knew—that Sadie Baxter had left the boy a cool million-and-a-quarter bucks in her will, to be his when he turned twenty-one. He knew that part of Miss Sadie's letter by heart: *I am depending on you never to mention this to him until he is old enough to bear it with dignity.*

"Look. We gave you a choice between staying in Mitford and a summer at the beach. That's a pretty important liberty. We didn't force you to do anything you didn't want to do. Give us credit for that. The car is a different matter. We're not going to be around to—"

"Harley's going to be around all the time, he's going to let me drive his truck, what's the difference if I have my own car?"

Well, blast it, what *was* the difference? "But only once a week, as you well know, with a curfew of eleven o'clock."

Father Tim stood up, agitated. He never dreamed he'd be raising a teenager. When he was Dooley's age in Holly Springs, Mississippi, nobody he knew had a car when they were sixteen. Today, boys were given cars as casually as they were handed a burger through a fast-food window. And in fact, a vast number of them ended up decorating the grille of an eighteen-wheeler, not critically injured, but dead. He was too old to have a teenager, too old to figure this out the way other people, other parents, seemed to do.

"Look," he said, pacing alongside the stone wall, "we talked about this before, starting a few months ago. You were perfectly fine with no car this summer; we agreed on it. You even asked me to hunt down your bicycle pump so you could put air in the tires."

He knew exactly what had happened. It was that dadblamed Wrangler. "Is Tommy getting a car this summer?"

"No. He's working to raise money so he can have one next year. He's only saved eight hundred dollars."

This was definitely an encouragement. "So, look here. Harley was going to mow our two yards once a week, but why don't I give you the job? I'll pay twenty bucks a shot for both houses."

"If Buster Austin did it, he'd charge fifteen apiece, that's thirty. I'll do both for twenty-five."

"Deal!"

He looked at the boy he loved, the boy he'd do anything for.
Almost.

It rained throughout the night, a slow, pattering rain that spoke more eloquently of summer to him than any sunshine. He listened through the open bedroom window until well after midnight, sleepless but not discontented. They would make it through all this upheaval, all this tearing up and nailing down, and life would go on.

He found his wife's light, whiffling snore a kind of anchor in a sea of change.

Bolting down Main Street the next morning at seven o'clock, he saw Evie Adams in her rain-soaked yard, dressed in a terry robe and armed with a salt shaker.

"Forty two!" she shouted in greeting.

He knew she meant snail casualties. Evie had been at war with snails ever since they gnawed her entire stand of blue hostas down to nubs. Some years had passed since this unusually aggressive assault, but Evie had not forgotten. He pumped his fist into the air in a salute of brotherhood.

After all, he had hostas, too. . . .

"If I have to say goodbye to you one more time, I'll puke," said Mule.

Actually, Mule was moved nearly to bawling that his old buddy had come by the Grill at all. Father Tim could have been loading his car, or turning off the water at the street, or changing his address at the post office—whatever people did who were leaving for God knows how long.

"Livermush straight up," Father Tim told Percy as he slid into the booth. "And make it a double."

"Livermush? You ain't ordered livermush in ten, maybe twelve years."

"Right. But that's what I'm having." He grinned at the dumfounded Percy. "And make it snappy."

It was reckless to eat livermush, especially a double order, but he was feeling reckless.

Percy set his mouth in a fine line as he cut two slices from the loaf of livermush. He did not approve of long-term Grill customers moving elsewhere. Number one, the Father had been coming to the Grill for sixteen, seventeen years; he was established. To just up and run off, flinging his lunch and breakfast trade to total strangers, was . . . he couldn't even find a word for what it was.

Number two, why anybody would want to leave Mitford in the

first place was beyond him. He had personally left it only twice—when Velma was pregnant and they went to see cousins in Avery County, and when he and Velma went on that bloomin' cruise to Hawaii, which his children had sent them on whether he wanted to go or not.

But worse than the Father leaving Mitford, he was leaving it for a location that had once *broken off from the mainland*, for Pete's sake, and could not be trusted as ground you'd want under your feet. So here was somebody he'd thought to be sensible and wise, clearly proving himself to be otherwise.

As he laid two thick slices on the sizzling grill, Percy shook his head. Every time he thought he'd gained a little understanding of human nature, something like this came up and he had to start over.

J. C. Hogan thumped into the booth. "Man!" he said, mopping his face with a rumpled handkerchief. "It's hot as a depot stove today. I hope you know how hot it gets *down there*."

Father Tim put his hands over his ears and shut his eyes.

"Lookit," said J.C. He tossed the *Muse*, still smelling of ink, on the table. "You made today's front page."

"What for?"

Mule snatched the eight-page edition to his side of the table and adjusted his glasses. "Let me read it. Let's see. Here we go." The realtor cleared his throat and read aloud.

" 'Around Town by Vanita Bentley . . .'

"Blah, blah, blah, OK, here's th' meat of it. *'Father Kavanagh treated everybody as if equal in intelligence and accomplishment, making his real church the homes, sidewalks and businesses of Mitford. . . .*

" 'Whether we had faith or not, he loved us all.' "

Father Tim felt his face grow hot. "Give me that," he said, snatching the newspaper.

"What's the matter?" said J.C. "Don't you like it?"

He didn't know if he liked it. What he knew was that it sounded like . . . an obituary.

He was hunkering down now, trying to cover all the bases.

Thanks be to God, it was nearly over, they were nearly on their way. He'd been going at this thing of leaving as if it were life or death, when in fact it was more like a year to sixteen months, and then he'd be back in Mitford, with half the population not realizing he'd left.

He screeched into Louella's room at Hope House, breathing hard. Miss Sadie's will had provided her lifelong companion with Room Number One, which was the finest room in the entire place.

Louella plucked the remote from her capacious lap and muted *All My Children.*

"You look like you been yanked up by th' roots!" she said, concerned.

"Ah . . . ," he replied, unable to muster anything else.

"An' it yo' *birthday!*" she scolded.

"It is?"

"You sixty-six today!"

"Louella, do I remind you of your age?"

"Honey," she said, looking smug, "you don' know my age."

He'd been coming to see Louella every day since Miss Sadie died. Sometimes they played checkers, but more often they sang hymns. The thought of leaving her made him feel like a common criminal. . . .

"How's your knee?" he asked, kissing her warm, chocolate-colored cheek. "How's your bladder infection? Have you started the potting class yet?"

"Set down on yo' stool," she said. He always sat on her footstool, which made him feel nine years old. A feeling, by the way, he rather liked.

"Now," she said, beaming, "we ain' goan talk about knees an' bladders, an' far as pottin' classes goes, I decided I ain't messin' wit' no clay. What I'm wantin' to do is *sing,* and ain't hardly anybody roun' here can carry a tune in a bucket."

"I'll go a round or two with you," he said, feeling better at once.

"I take th' first verse, you take th' second, an' we'll chime in together on number three."

Louella closed her eyes and raised her hands and began to lift her rich, mezzo voice in song. She rocked a little in her chair.

> *"The King of love my shepherd is,*
> *Whose goodness faileth never;*
> *I nothing lack if I am his,*
> *And he is mine forever."*

He waited two beats and picked up the second verse, not caring if they heard him all the way to the monument.

"Where streams of living water flow,
My ransomed soul he leadeth,
And where the verdant pastures grow,
With food celestial feedeth."

Two nurses stuck their heads in the door, grinning, as he joined his voice with Louella's on the third verse.

"Perverse and foolish oft I strayed,
But yet in love he sought me,
And on his shoulder gently laid,
And home, rejoicing, brought me."

They were silent for a moment. "Now," said Louella, "that feels better, don't it?"

He nodded, sensing the tears lurking in him, some kind of sorrow that he'd noticed for a week or more.

"You pushin' too hard," she said.

"You have to push, Louella." Out there in the world, he wanted to say, it was all about push.

"Maybe you done stepped aroun' th' Lord an' tryin' to lead th' way."

He stood up and looked out the window, into the green valley he called the Land of Counterpane. Maybe she was right.

Louella didn't often get out of her chair these days, but now she rose and stood by him, and put her hand on his shoulder.

"You know I pray for you and Miss Cynthia every mornin' an' every night, and I ain' goin' to stop. Anytime you get in a tight place down yonder, you just think, Louella's prayin' for me, and go on 'bout your business."

As he left Room Number One, he found himself humming. He couldn't remember doing that in a very long time.

"Where streams of living water flow, my ransomed soul he leadeth. . . ."

Maybe the real issue wasn't how Louella would manage without him, but how would he manage without Louella?

He cantered down the hall and found Pauline finishing up in the dining room.

"Pauline?"

"Father!"

He gave her a hug. "What do you hear from Buck?"

"He'll be home the fifteenth of October."

"And we'll roar in on the twenty-fifth, after which I'll personally see to it that you become Mrs. Buck Leeper."

She smiled and looked at her hands. He'd never seen her more beautiful. In fact, the miracle of watching Pauline Barlowe become whole wasn't unlike watching the slow unfolding of the petals on his Souvenir de la Malmaison.

"That is what you want, isn't it?"

"More'n anything. Yes, sir, I do."

"You've waited, and I admire that. How's his job in Alaska?"

"Real good. He says he'll bring it in on time."

"He always does," he said, feeling proud with her. "And Jessie and Poo? How're they feeling about all that's ahead?"

"Excited." She hesitated, then dared to use a word she had never trusted in her life. "Happy!"

He nodded, pleased. "Dooley will be in safe hands with Harley, and I know he'll be coming around to your place often. You might want to . . ." *Watch over him,* he wanted to say.

"I will," she replied, knowing.

He was halfway along the hall when she called after him. "Father!"

He turned around. "Yes?"

"We hate to see you go."

"I'll be back before you know I'm gone."

She smiled and waved, and he saw Dooley in her for a fleeting moment, something about the way she held her head, and the thrust of her chin. . . .

~⊙~

"Law, help!" said Puny, looking exhausted. "I'll be glad to see y'all *go!*"

There! The truth from somebody, at last.

"You never seen th' like of mess Dooley'd squirreled away in his room that we had to drag to th' basement. Harley said if we kept on haulin' stuff down there, he'd have to go to livin' out of his truck." The freckled Puny hooted with laughter.

"Where are my grandbabies?" he wondered. Puny sometimes fetched the twins from church school a little early. Sissy and Sassy even kept a stash of toys at the yellow house, consisting of a red wagon, several dolls, stuffed monkeys, crayons, and other paraphernalia.

"They're dead asleep in th' front room, Miz Hart said they fussed all day."

"Uh-oh."

"But they'll be glad to see their granpaw." Puny smiled hugely. The poor soul standing in front of her would never have had the joy of grandchildren if it hadn't been for her generosity. She'd given him her babies as free-handed as you please, and he'd taken to them like a duck to water. The truth was, Sissy was crazy about her granpaw and often kissed a framed picture of him that Puny had proudly placed in her home.

He patted his pocket. "I'm ready when they are."

"You'll make their little teeth fall out with that candy."

"Once a week, two small pieces? I hardly think so. Besides," he said, "they're going to fall out, anyway."

She shook her head, tsking, happy that someone she loved also loved her twin three-year-olds. It would be different around here with the Father gone, and Cynthia, who was always so bright and helpful. . . .

— ❧ —

Every last scrap of Dooley's tack had made it to Harley's basement apartment, and Father Tim had helped Dooley clean his room at the rectory, top to bottom. In addition, all the books for Whitecap were packed, sealed, and ready for the shipper to pick up tomorrow.

Before he dragged himself upstairs to take a shower, he'd just lie down and put his head on the arm of the sofa, but only for a moment, of course.

If there was ever a birthday when he had no time or energy to read St. Paul's letters to Timothy, this was it. Ever since seminary, he'd made a point of reading the letters on, or adjacent to, the date of his nativity. Perhaps his yearly pondering of these Scriptures was one way of taking stock.

" 'To Timothy, my dearly beloved son,' " he murmured, quoting at random from the familiar Second Epistle. " 'Grace, mercy, and peace, from God the Father and Christ Jesus our Lord . . . watch thou in all things, endure afflictions, do the work of an evangelist, make full proof of thy ministry.' "

He was sinking into the sofa. " 'The cloke that I left at Troas with Carpus,' " he whispered—this was a favorite part—" 'when thou comest, bring with thee, and the books, but especially the parchments—' "

"Timothy!"

It was his wife, calling from the front hall.

"Can you come here a moment?"

He forced himself off the sofa and trotted along the hall, obedient as any pup.

"You rang?" he asked, rubbing his eyes.

She smiled. "Walk out to the porch with me."

"Why?" he asked, peevish.

"Why not?" she said, taking his hand. It occurred to him that she looked unusually . . . expectant, somehow, on the verge of something.

When they stepped to the porch, he noticed it at once. A slick-looking red convertible was parked at the curb, with the top down. Hardly anybody ever parked in front of their house. . . .

"I wonder who *that* belongs to."

"I'm looking at him," said Cynthia.

His wife was lit up like a Christmas tree.

"What do you mean you're—"

"Happy birthday, dearest!" She was suddenly kissing his face—both cheeks, his nose, his mouth.

"But you can't possibly—"

"It's *yours*! To you from me, for our trip to Whitecap, for zooming around like feckless youths in the rain, in the sunshine, in the *snow*, what the heck!"

"But . . ."

Without meaning to, exactly, he sat down hard on the top step.

She laughed and sat with him. "What do you think?"

He stared at it, aghast, unable to think. "But," he said lamely, "it's red."

"So? Red is good!"

"But I'm a priest!"

"All the better!" she crowed. "Now, darling, don't get stuffy on me."

He saw that he might easily wound her to the very depths.

"But the Buick . . ."

"What about it?"

"It's . . . it's still perfectly *good*."

She raised one eyebrow.

He suddenly had another thought, this one worse than the others. "The new priest rolling into town like a rock star . . . what will people think?"

"I never mind what people think—ever! We didn't sleep together 'til we were married, and yet, imagine how the tongues wagged when we were seen sneaking back and forth through the hedge."

"I never sneaked," he said, indignant.

"Timothy. How quickly you forget."

But surely she hadn't *bought* it. "It's a rental! Right?"

"Darling, remember me? I'm Cynthia, I don't do rentals. It's yours. Here's the key." She shoved it into his hand.

She was tired of fooling around, he could tell. He started to stand up, but sat again, weak-kneed.

"I can't believe it," he said, feeling contrite. "Please forgive me. God knows, I thank you. But I mean, the *expense . . .*" Why couldn't he quit babbling about the negatives? What did these things cost, anyway? It was horrifying to contemplate. . . .

She patted him on the knee. "It's not nice to talk about the cost of a gift. Besides, if you really must know, it's three years old and the radio isn't working."

"It looks brand-new!"

"Yet bought with old money. Royalties from *Violet Goes to the Country* and *Violet Goes to School,* tucked into a money market fund long ago. I've worked very hard, Timothy, and been conservative as a church mouse—I wanted to do this."

He was ashamed to ask what make it was. He'd never been able to identify cars, unlike Tommy Noles, who knew Packards from Oldsmobiles and Fords from Chevrolets. Actually, a Studebaker was the only car he'd ever been able to guess, dead-on.

Maybe a Jaguar. . . .

"It's a Mustang GT," said his wife, looking mischievous.

He put his arm around her and drew her close and nuzzled his face into her hair. "You astound me, you have always astounded me, I need to sit here and just look at it for a minute. Thank you for being patient." He felt wild laughter rising in him, as he'd felt the tears earlier. What kind of roller coaster was he on, anyway?

"I don't deserve it," he said. There. He'd finally gotten down to the bottom line.

She lifted her hand to his cheek. "Deserve? Since when is love about deserving?"

"Right," he said. He felt his heart beginning to hammer at the sight of it sitting there so coolly parked at the curb, as if it owned the house and the people in it.

He realized he'd come within a hair of hurting her by persisting in his fogy ways. No, he'd never have believed he'd be driving a red convertible, not in a million years, but he knew it was absolutely crucial that he begin believing it—at once.

He felt the grin spreading across his face, and didn't think he could stop the laughter that was lurking in him.

"Wait'll Dooley sees this!" he said, as they trotted toward the curb.

CHAPTER THREE

Going, Going, Gone

"Timothy!"

His wife was calling him constantly these days. From the top of the stairs, from the depths of the basement, from the far reaches of the new garage.

It was Timothy here, Timothy there, Timothy everywhere.

"Yes?" he bellowed from the study.

"Do we really need this cast-iron Dutch oven?" she yelled from the hallway, where the items to be packed in the car were being severely thinned.

"How else can I make a pork roast?" he shouted.

"I don't think people at the beach *eat* pork roast!" she shouted back.

He hated shouting.

Cynthia appeared in the study, her hair in a bandanna, wearing shorts and a T-shirt. She might have been a twelfth-grade student from Mitford School. Why was his wife looking increasingly younger as he grew increasingly older? It wasn't fair.

"I think," she said, wiping perspiration from her face, "that beach people eat ocean perch or broiled tuna or . . ." She shrugged. "You know."

He took the heavy pot from her, feeling grumpy. "Leave it," he said, toting it to the kitchen.

"And do you really think," she hooted from the study, "that we need those Wellington boots you garden in?"

He stepped back to the study. "What did you say?"

"Those huge green boots. Those Wellingtons."

"What about them?"

"I mean, there's no mud at the beach!"

He sighed.

"Besides, we can't lash anything on top of the car. . ."—she grinned, bouncing on the balls of her feet like a kid—"because we'll have the top *down*."

"Axe the boots."

"And the Coleman stove. Why would we need a Coleman *stove*? We won't be camping out, you know."

If he didn't watch her every minute, they would be roaring down the highway with nothing but a change of underwear and a box of watercolors. Besides, he had thought of maybe cooking out one night on the beach, under the stars, with a blanket. . . .

He blushed, just thinking about it.

"We're taking the stove," he said.

He made a quick sweep of the rectory, looking once more in the kitchen drawers, feeling along the top shelves of the study bookcases, peering into the medicine cabinets.

Clean as a whistle.

Their tenant was moving in tomorrow with what she called "light furnishings," a grand piano, and a cat, and he didn't want any of his jumble lying around to welcome her. Ever since he moved in behind Father Bellwether in Alabama, he was careful to clean up any rectory he was vacating.

Father Bellwether had left behind a 1956 Ford on blocks, several leaf bags filled with old shirts and sweaters, a set of mangled golf clubs, three room-size rugs chewed by dogs, an assortment of cooking gear, several doors without knobs, a vast collection of paperback mysteries, and other litter that couldn't be completely identified. Determined not to whine to the vestry who had called him, Father Tim remembered using a shovel and a hired truck to clean the place out while the movers huffed his own things in.

His footsteps echoed along the hallway to the basement door. He opened it and called down the stairs.

"Harley, are you there?"

Lace Turner appeared at the bottom of the steps, her blond hair in French braids.

"Harley's taking a test," she said.

He thought that each time he saw the fifteen-year-old Lace Turner, she had grown more beautiful, more confident. The hard look he'd once seen on her face had softened.

"But you can come down," she said. "He's almost through."

"What's the test on?" he inquired, trotting to meet her in the basement hallway.

"History. It's his favorite subject."

"Hit ain't no such of a thing!" Harley called from the parlor.

Harley was sitting on the sofa with a sheaf of papers in his lap, using a hardcover book as a writing surface. A fan moved slowly left, then right, on a table next to the sofa.

"It was your favorite last week," she said patiently, as they came into the room.

"Rev'rend, she's got me studyin' Lewis 'n' Clark, how they explored th' Missouri River and found half a dadblame nation. . . ."

"Sounds interesting."

"Oh, hit's in'erestin', all right, but this question she's wrote down here is how many falls is in th' Great Falls of th' Missouri. They won't a soul ever ask me that, I don't *need* t' know it, hit won't *pay* t' know it—"

"Harley . . . ," said Lace, looking stern.

"Two falls!" said Harley.

"No. We talked about it yesterday."

"Six!"

Lace shook her head. "Think about it," she advised. "You don't like to think, Harley."

"Didn't I make eighty-nine on my numbers test you give me?" Harley grinned, displaying pink gums perfectly lacking in teeth.

"Yes, and you can make a hundred on this one if you'll just think back to what you read yesterday."

Father Tim quietly hunkered into a chair.

"I don't give a katy how many falls make up th' Great Falls. I quit, by jing." Harley laid his pencil on the arm of the sofa and put his papers to one side. "I'm goin' to pour th' rev'rend a glass of tea. You can mark up m' score on what I done."

Harley marched to the kitchen, looking as determined as his instructor. He turned at the kitchen door. "An' say some of y'r big words for th' rev'rend."

Lace gazed at Father Tim, her amber eyes luminous and intense. "He's learned an awful lot," she said, defending her practice of coming regularly to educate the man who protected her as she was growing up. It had been Harley who often fed Lace, and hid her from a violent, abusive father. To Lace, it was no small matter that Harley had sometimes risked his life for her well-being.

Lace was now living with Hoppy and Olivia Harper, and adoption procedures were under way. Father Tim considered that her privileged life with the Harpers might have turned the girl's affinities in other directions. But, no. Lace visited Harley often, frequently cooked to encourage his finicky appetite, and protected him fiercely. As for her desire that Harley become a learned man, the Education of Harley Welch was entering its third year.

Lace picked up the test papers and examined them. Her eyes glanced quickly over the pages, and she alternately sighed or nodded.

Father Tim gazed at her, profoundly moved. When he had first met Lace Turner, she was living in the dirt under her ramschackle house on the Creek, foraging for food like a dog. Her transformation was a miracle he'd been privileged to witness with his own eyes.

"Ninety," she pronounced, making a mark with the pencil.

"Why, that's terrific!"

"He spelled the Willamette River correctly."

"Good! I hope you'll give him a couple of extra points for that."

Lace smiled one of her rare smiles. He was dazzled, and no help for it.

"Ninety-two, then!" she said, looking pleased.

"So, how many falls?" he asked.

"Five."

"Aha."

"I'm sorry you're leaving," she said.

"Thank you, Lace. Of course, we won't be gone forever, it's an interim situation."

"What's a interim situation?" asked Harley, coming in with two glasses of tea. "This 'uns your'n," he said to Father Tim, "no sugar."

"It means a time between," said Lace.

"Between what?" Harley wondered.

"Between what I've been doing and what I'm going to do later," said Father Tim, laughing.

Lace held up the test paper. "Harley, you made ninety-two on your test."

Harley's eyes widened. "How'd I git two odd points in there?"

"You spelled Willamette right."

"I got it wrote on m' hand. Naw, I'm jis' kiddin', I ain't." He handed her the tea. "Here's your'n."

"*Yours*," she said. "And thank you."

Harley grinned. "She's like th' *po'*lice, on you at ever' turn." Harley's days in liquor hauling, not to mention car racing, had taught him about police. "Boys, she can go like whiz readin' a book, says words you never heerd of. Did you say one of them big words for th' rev'rend?"

"Omnipresent," said Lace quietly.

"What'n th' nation does that mean?"

"Everywhere at one time."

"That describes my wife's mama near perfect. She had eyes in th' back of 'er head. That woman was a chicken hawk if I ever seen one. Say another'n."

She flushed and lowered her eyes. "No, Harley."

"Look what I done f'r *you*."

"You didn't do it for me, you did it for you."

Harley nodded, sober. "Jis tell th' rev'rend one more, an' I'll not ask ag'in."

"Mussitation."

"Aha."

Lace hurriedly drank the tea, then collected her books. "It's nice to see you, sir. Harley, eat your supper tonight, and thank you for a good job on your test."

"Thank you f'r teachin' me."

"Well done, Lace!" Father Tim called, as she left by the door to the driveway.

Harley glowed with unashamed pride. "Ain't she somethin'? I've knowed 'er since she was knee-high to a duck. She agg'avates me near t' death, but I think th' world of that young 'un."

Father Tim wished his dictionary weren't packed, as he didn't have a clue as to the meaning of "mussitation."

He sat with Harley next to the fan that turned left, then right.

"Lord, at th' rust they've got down there," sighed Harley, shaking his head. "I don't know but what I'd park your new ride in th' garage and drive th' Buick."

"I don't think so."

In the escalating temperature of an official heat wave, the two men spoke as if in a dream. Harley leaned toward Father Tim, to better catch the stream of air on the left; Father Tim leaned closer to Harley to catch the right stream.

Both had their elbows on their knees, their heads nearly touching, gazing at the floor.

"Think you can keep up with our boy?"

"Rev'rend, don't you worry 'bout a thing. Y'r boy'll be workin', I'll be watchin,' an' th' Lord 'n' Master'll be in charge of th' whole deal."

"I don't know, Harley. . . ."

"Well, if *you* don't, who does?"

"Seems like I can trust Him with everything but a teenager."

"That's what you got t' trust 'im with th' most, if you ask me."

Father Tim felt a trickle of sweat between his shoulder blades.

"Don't let Dooley forget to take the livermush to his granpaw."

"Nossir."

"Every other week is how Russell likes to get it."

Harley nodded. "I'll git them hornets' nestes off th' garage come Friday."

"Good. I thank you."

"I ain't goin' t' rake y'r leaves b'fore winter, if you don't mind, hit'll be good f'r th' grass."

"Fine."

"I'll mulch 'em so they'll rot easy. An' I'll mulch up around y'r plants come October."

"And the roses . . ."

"I'll prune 'em back, jis' like you said."

"I wrote the numbers down by your phone in the kitchen; I gave you the church office and home. Call us any time of the day or night, I don't care how late it is or how early."

"I'll do it. And I'll have Cynthia's little scooter runnin' like a top when you come home f'r the' weddin'. In case she gits wore out ridin' that bicycle, she can drive it back."

"Good. But don't soup it up."

"Ain't nothin' t' soup in a Mazda."

He remembered that Harley had once fiddled around with his Buick so it ran like a scalded dog; he had shot by the local police chief in a blur—twice. Not good.

They sat quiet for a time, Father Tim cupping his chin in his hands.

"And don't let Dooley play loud music down here, or we'll run our tenant off."

Harley sighed. "Lord knows I ain't a miracle worker."

He went out into the night, damp with perspiration, leaving his wife sleeping like a child.

Ten to eleven. No moon. Only a humid darkness that sharply revealed its stars as he looked up.

They weren't used to heat like this in the mountains. Mitford was legendary for its cool summers, which brought flatlanders racing up the slopes every May through October, exulting in the town's leafy shade and gentle breezes.

He walked with Barnabas around the backyard of the yellow house, stopping by the maple and hearing the stream of urine hiss into the grass.

The path through the hedge, he saw in the light from the study windows, had nearly grown over. Harley usually came around to the front door these days, and it had been three years or more since he courted his next-door neighbor.

He smiled, remembering the quote from Chesterton: "We make our friends, we make our enemies, but God makes our next-door neighbor."

Once, the depth of their feeling for one another might easily have been judged by the smooth wear on the path through the rhododendrons. Now the branches on either side of the weed-covered path had nearly grown together; one would have to duck to dash through.

As he stepped under the tulip poplar. he felt a sudden coolness, as if a barrier had been formed around the tree, forbidding the day's heat to collect beneath its limbs.

He thumped onto the sparse grass under the poplar, and Barnabas lay at his feet, panting.

Another party tomorrow night. He was weary of parties, of the endless goodbyes that stretched behind him since last December's retirement party in the parish hall. He remembered feeling his head grow light as a feather, and could not imagine the occasion to be anything but an odd and disturbing dream. Then he found himself gone from Lord's Chapel, the parish that had both succored and tormented him, and made him happier than ever before in his life.

Retiring had been precisely what he wanted to do, and yet, when he did it, it had felt awkward and unreal, as it must feel to walk for the first time with a wooden leg.

He rubbed his dog's ear; it might have been a piece of velvet, or a child's blanket that gave forth consolation, as he stared across the hedge at the rectory's double chimneys rising in silhouette against the light of the street lamp.

It seemed an eternity since he'd lived there, quite another person than the one sitting here in the damp night grass.

For many years in that house, he had made it a practice to do what he'd learned in seminary, and that was spend an hour in study for every minute of his sermon. More than twenty hours he had faithfully spent; then fifteen, and later, starting a couple of years ago, ten. Where had the quiet center of his life gone? It seemed he was racing faster and faster around the tree, turning into butter.

On the other hand, wasn't his life now richer and deeper and more solid than ever before? Yes! Absolutely yes. He would not turn back for anything.

God had, indeed, put Cynthia Coppersmith right next door, and given her to him. But marriage, with all its delight and aggravation, seemed to swell like a dry sponge dipped into water, and occupy the largest, most fervent part of his life. Surely that was why some priests never took a spouse, and remained married to their calling.

Barnabas rolled on his side and smacked his lips, happy for the cool night air under the tree.

He loved Cynthia Kavanagh; she'd become the very life of his heart, and no, he would never turn back from her laughter and tears and winsome ways. But tonight, looking at the chimneys against the glow of the streetlight, he mourned that time of utter freedom, when nobody expected him home or cared whether he arrived, when he could sit with a book in his lap, snoring in the wing chair, a fire turning to embers on the hearth. . . .

He raised his hand to the rectory in a type of salute, and nodded to himself and closed his eyes, as the bells of Lord's Chapel began their last peal of the day.

Bong . . .

"Lord," he said aloud, as if He were there beneath the tree, "Your will be done in our lives."

Bong . . .

"Guard me from self-righteousness, and from any looking to myself in this journey."

Bong . . .

"I believe Whitecap is where You want us, and we know that You have riches for us there."

Bong . . .

"Prepare our hearts for this parish, and theirs to receive us."

Bong . . .

"Thank You for the blessing of my wife, and Dooley; for this place and this time, and yes, Lord, even for this change. . . ."

Bong . . .

Bong . . .

The bells pealed twice before he acknowledged and named the fear in his heart.

"Forgive this fear in me which I haven't confessed to You until now."

Bong . . .

"You tell us that You do not give us the spirit of fear, but of power, and of love, and of a sound mind."

Bong . . .

"Gracious God . . ." He paused.

"I surrender myself to You completely . . . again."

Bong . . .

He took a deep breath and held it, then let it out slowly, and realized he felt the peace, the peace that didn't always come, but came now.

Bong . . .

⎯⊙⎯

The tenant was a surprise, somehow. A small woman in her late forties, overweight and mild-mannered, she appeared to try to shrink into herself, in order to occupy less space. He supposed her accent to be French, but wasn't very good at nailing that sort of thing.

They met in the late afternoon in the rectory parlor, now furnished sparingly with her own sofa and two chairs, and a Baldwin grand piano by the window.

The cherry pie he had brought from Sweet Stuff Bakery had been placed on the table in front of the sofa where she sat, her feet scarcely touching the floor. After a day of moving into a strange house in a strange town, he thought she might have been utterly exhausted; to the contrary, she looked as fresh as if she'd risen from a long nap.

". . . very interested in old homes, Father," she was saying.

"Well, you'll certainly be living in one. The rectory was built in 1884, and wasn't dramatically altered until a bishop lived here in the fifties. He closed the fireplace in the kitchen and rebuilt the fireplace in the study—a definite comfort during our long winters. I hope you don't mind long winters."

"Oh, no. We have those in Boston with dismaying frequency."

"Mr. Skinner has shown you around—the attic, the basement?"

"Top to bottom."

"You know you may call him at any time. He'll be looking after everything for us—and for you."

"Thank you, Father, and again, thank you for allowing me to lease for such a short time. It's always good to test the waters, *n'est-ce pas?*"

"Of course."

"Mr. Skinner mentioned that you and Miss Sadie Baxter were dear friends."

"Yes, Miss Sadie meant the world to me. Did you know her?"

"Oh, no. I saw her lovely old home from Main Street and inquired about it. I'm sure she must have left you some very beautiful things."

"I might have taken anything I liked, but I took almost nothing, really. My wife found some needlepoint chair covers she's thrilled with, and so . . ."

He raised his hands, palms up, and smiled. At that moment, a large cat leaped into his lap from out of nowhere, its collar bell jingling.

"Holy smoke!" he exclaimed.

"That's Barbizon," said Hélène Pringle, unperturbed.

He sat frozen as a mullet. Barbizon had taken over his lap entirely, and was licking his white paws for a fare-thee-well. The odor of tinned fish rose in a noxious vapor to his nostrils.

His tenant peered at him. "Barbizon's no bother, I hope."

"Oh, no. Not a bit. Cats don't usually like me."

"Barbizon likes all sorts of people other cats care nothing for."

"I see."

"He was named for my mother's birthplace in France, just south of Paris. I spent my childhood there."

"Well, well."

"Do you speak French, Father?"

"Pathetically."

"I imagine Mr. Skinner told you I'll be giving piano lessons. . . ."

"That's wonderful!" he said. "We need more music in Mitford."

"He's checking to see if I might hang out a sign."

"Aha."

"Only a very small sign, of course."

"Not too small, I hope. We want people to see it!"

" 'Hélène Pringle, Lessons for the Piano, Inquire Within.' " She recited the language of her sign with some wistfulness, he thought.

"Excellent!" He glanced at his watch discreetly, and tried to rise from the chair, thinking the longhaired creature with yellow eyes would pop off to the floor. But no, it clung on with its claws, for which reason Father Tim regained his seat with a strained smile. "I must go. We've a great many things to settle at the last minute, you understand."

Hélène Pringle nodded. "*Parfaitement!* No one could understand better."

"Well, then . . ." He tried to detach the cat from his lap by picking it up, but a single claw was entrenched in his fly. Blast.

"Naughty fellow!" scolded Hélène Pringle, who rose from the sofa and came to him and took the cat, which relaxed its claws at once. He saw, then, the weariness in his tenant's eyes, in her pinched face.

She set the great animal down and it disappeared beneath the Chippendale sofa. "Cats don't like moving, you know."

He sighed agreeably. "Who does?"

"I wish you well on your journey, Father."

"And I wish you well on yours, Miss Pringle. May God bless you, and give you many happy hours here."

"Happy hours . . . ," she said, her voice trailing away.

"Oh, I nearly forgot. The key!" Harley had opened the house for their tenant and the movers.

He placed the key in her hand, and found himself staring at it, lying in her palm. She looked at it, also, and for the briefest moment, something passed between them. He could never have said what, exactly, but he would wonder at the feeling for a long time to come.

He hesitated to put the top down for the haul up the hill to Lucera, thinking it would only agitate Dooley's car lust.

"Put it down, darling!" urged his wife. "That's what it's *for*!"

Oh, well. It *was* a warm June night, and Dooley would just have to grow up and take it like a man. . . .

"Hey, let me drive," Dooley said as they walked to the car he'd been ogling all day. Father Tim thought their charge looked like something out of a magazine in his school blazer, a tie, and tan pants.

"You look great, like something out of a magazine," said Father Tim, rushing around to the driver's side.

"Let me drive," repeated Dooley, staying focused. "It's just up the hill."

Cynthia took her husband's arm and steered him to the passenger side. "Why not let him drive, Timothy? It's just up the hill. But I can't sit in the back, it'll ruin my hair."

Two against one.

What was left of his own hair was flying forty ways from Sunday as they roared up Fernbank's driveway and saw lights blazing from every window in the grand house. He was still combing when they went up the steps and through the open front door.

He blinked. Then he blinked again.

"Wow!" said Cynthia.

"Man!" exclaimed Dooley.

Father Tim remembered flushing Miss Sadie's toilets more than once with rainwater that had leaked from this very ceiling into soup pots and a turkey roaster.

"No way," Dooley muttered, shaking his head in disbelief.

Fernbank's cavernous entry hall had become . . . what? Miraculously warm. Smaller, somehow. Intimate. He fairly shivered with excitement. Was this a dream?

And the music—by jove, it was opera, it was Puccini, he couldn't believe his ears. The last time he'd heard opera was months ago, through the static of his car radio.

"Garlic!" rhapsodized his wife, inhaling deeply.

Along the walls in wooden bins were fresh tomatoes and crusty loaves of bread, bundles of fragrant herbs and great bunches of grapes, yellow globes of cheese and bottles of olive oil. The contents of the bottles gleamed like molten gold in the candlelight.

"Timothy, look! The walls!"

Good grief, there were some of those walls his wife had created in the rectory kitchen a couple of years ago—pockmarked, smoky, primitive—not Miss Sadie's walls at all. Miss Sadie would be in a huff over this, and no two ways about it.

"Father! Cynthia! Dooley! Welcome!"

It was the hospitable Andrew Gregory, coming through the door of the dining room in a pale linen suit.

He felt positively heady with the rush of aromas and sounds, and the sight of Mitford's favorite antiques dealer transformed into a tanned and happy maître d'.

Mule and Fancy dropped by the table where the Kavanaghs and Dooley were seated with the Harpers and Lace Turner.

"How do you say th' name of this place?" Fancy asked in a whisper. "I can't remember for shoot!"

"Lu-*chair*-ah!" crowed Cynthia, glad to be of help.

Fancy stared around the room, disbelieving. "There's people here I never laid eyes on before."

Mule sighed. "This is gonna be a deep-pocket deal," he muttered, following Fancy to their corner table.

Father Tim was fairly smitten with his dinner companions, it all seemed so lively and . . . *fun*, a thing he was always seeking to understand and claim for his own.

Olivia hadn't aged an iota since he married her to the town doctor a few years ago; he remembered dancing at their reception in the ballroom, across the hall from this very table. Her dark hair was pulled into French braids, such as she eagerly wove each day for Lace, and her violet eyes still pierced his heart with appealing candor.

Hoppy grinned at his wife and took her hand. "Where *are* we, anyway?"

"Certainly not in Mitford!" she said, laughing.

"I think we're . . . in a dream," said Lace, so softly that only he and perhaps Dooley could hear.

Enthralled, that was the word. They were all enthralled.

The large dining room, where he'd once eaten cornbread and beans with Miss Sadie and Louella, was crowded with people from Wesley and Holding, with the occasional familiar face thrown in, as it were, for good measure.

There was Hope Winchester waving across the room, and a couple of tables away were the mayor and Ray with at least two of their attractive, deluxe-size daughters, sitting where Miss Sadie's Georgian highboy used to stand, and over in the far corner . . .

His heart pumped wildly, taking his breath away. Edith Mallory. Just as he spotted her, she looked up and gazed directly into his eyes.

He turned away quickly. Any contact at all with his former parishioner was akin to a sting from a scorpion. He had foolishly believed she would somehow drop out of sight, and he'd never be forced to lay eyes on her again. She'd been a thorn in his flesh for years—seeking to manipulate and seduce him, trying to buy the last mayoral race, treating the villagers like pond scum. . . .

Cynthia peered at him. "What is it, dearest? You're white as a sheet."

"Starving," he mumbled, grabbing a chunk of bread.

A couple of years ago, Lace Turner had helped Dooley save Barnabas from bleeding to death when hit by a car. When minutes counted, Dooley and Lace had pitched in to get the job done, and a bond formed between them where only enmity had existed.

But time and distance had strained that bond, and they were now two new and different people.

Father Tim hadn't missed Dooley's fervent appraisal of Lace Turner as she studied her hand-printed menu. He found it more telling, however, that Dooley feigned indifference each time Lace spoke, which wasn't often. Further, he observed, the boy who was known for his appetite picked at his food, laughed nervously, eternally twisted the knot in his tie, and knocked over his water glass.

No doubt about it, Dooley Barlowe was interested in more than cars.

They had feasted on risotto and scallopini, on lamb shank and fresh mussels, on chicken roasted with rosemary from the Fernbank gardens, and on Anna Gregory's freshly made pasta stuffed with ricotta and bathed in a sultry marinara from local greenhouse tomatoes; they had ordered gallons of sparkling water, Coke, and a bottle of Chianti from Lucera, and had all placed their order for Tony's tiramisu.

Hoppy Harper sat back and looked fondly at Lace, who was seated next to him and across from Dooley. "Lace, why don't you tell everyone your good news?"

Lace gazed around the table slowly, half shyly.

Father Tim observed that Dooley pretended to be more interested in drumming his fingers on the table than hearing what Lace had to say.

"I'm going away to school in September."

The fingers stopped drumming.

"Lovely!" said Cynthia. "Where?"

"Virginia. Mrs. Hemingway's." Fresh color stole into the girl's tanned cheeks.

"Oh, man," said Dooley, rolling his eyes. "Gross."

Father Tim bristled. "I beg your pardon?"

"Mrs. Hemingway has geeky girls."

Father Tim could have shaken the boy until his teeth rattled. "Apologize for that at once."

Dooley colored furiously, undecided about whether to stick up for what he had just said, or do as he was told.

He stuck up for what he had just said. "They hardly ever get invited to our school for parties, they're so . . . *smart.*" He said the last word with derision.

"Lace has just told us good news," Father Tim said quietly. "You have just shown us bad behavior. I ask once more that you apologize to Lace."

Dooley tried to raise his eyes to his dinner partner, but could not. "Sorry," he said, meditating on his water glass.

Hoppy slipped his arm around Lace's shoulders. "Dooley's right, actually. The girls at Mrs. Hemingway's are very smart, indeed. Gifted, as well. Lace and several of her classmates will spend next summer in Tuscany, studying classical literature and watercolor—on scholarships. We're very proud of Lace."

Father Tim saw on the girl's face the kind of look he'd seen when he caught her stealing Miss Sadie's ferns—the softness had disappeared, the hardness had returned.

Lace sat straight as a ramrod in the chair, staring over the head of the miserable and hapless wretch opposite her.

Dooley Barlowe had stepped in it, big-time.

While Cynthia trotted off with Dooley to bring the car around, Father Tim went in search of Andrew, seeking the whereabouts of their check.

Andrew Gregory still looked as fresh and unwrinkled as if he'd sauntered through the park, not opened a restaurant and catered to the whims of more than fifty people. He was the only man Father Tim knew who didn't wrinkle linen.

His mind couldn't avoid a momentary flashback to Andrew's earnest courtship of Cynthia. He'd watched their comings and goings from his bedroom window at the rectory, feeling miserable, to say the least. He remembered once thinking of the tall, slender Andrew as a cedar of Lebanon, and of himself, a lowly country parson, as mere scrub pine.

But who had won fair maid?

"I've had quite a visit with your new tenant," Andrew said. "She stayed in Wesley the last few days, waiting for the movers, and came several times to the shop. Very inquisitive about Fernbank, it seems. Wanted to know what was sold out of the house, and so on. Said she had a great interest in old homes."

"Yes, she mentioned that to me."

"She asked me to name the pieces I bought from you, and was eager to learn whether anything was left in the attic. I told her no, it had all been cleaned out and given away. She asked whether relatives had taken anything, and I said I didn't really know."

"Curious."

"I thought so," said Andrew. "And by the way, your money doesn't spend here."

Andrew's wife joined them from the kitchen, looking flushed and happy.

"Put away, put back," said Anna, indicating his wallet. He thought Andrew's Italian bride of two years, who had come from the village of Lucera, bore a breathtaking resemblance to Sophia Loren.

"But . . ."

"It's our gift to you, our farewell present," Andrew insisted.

"Well, then. Thank you. Thank you so much! You've made a great contribution to Mitford, Miss Sadie would be proud to see Fernbank filled with light and laughter. Anna, Andrew—'til we meet again."

"Ciao!" cried Anna, throwing her arms around him and kissing both his cheeks. He loved Italians. "Go with God!"

"Father!" It was Tony, Anna's younger brother and Lucera's chef, running from the kitchen in his white hat and splattered apron. *"Grazie al cielo!* I thought I'd missed you!"

Tony embraced him vigorously, kissed both cheeks, then stood back and gripped his shoulders. Father Tim didn't know when he'd seen a handsomer fellow in Mitford. *"Ciao!"* said Tony, his dark eyes bright with feeling. "God be with you!"

"And also with you, my friend."

"Ciao!" they shouted from the car to Andrew and Anna, who came out to the porch as they drove away from Fernbank, away from the grand old house with the grand new life.

He was driving on the Parkway with the top down, when he looked in the rearview mirror and saw his Buick pulling up behind him.

Who was the driver? It was Dooley, with Barnabas sitting in the seat beside him, looking straight ahead.

Dooley was grinning from ear to ear; he could see him distinctly. Yet, when he looked again, the car was gone, vanished.

He woke up, peering into the darkness.

Two a.m., according to the clock by their bed. He sighed.

"Are you awake?" asked Cynthia.

"I had a dream."

"About what?"

"Dooley. He was driving my Buick."

"Oh. I can't sleep, I can never sleep before a long trip." She sighed, and he reached over and patted her shoulder.

"Maybe I could give Dooley the Buick next year. He could pay something for it, two or three thousand. . . ."

"Umm," she said.

Suddenly he had a brilliant idea. Not everybody could wake in the middle of the night and think so cleverly.

"Tell you what. Why don't I give *you* the Buick, and you let Dooley pay you a few thousand for the Mazda. I think he'd like your car better. It's newer, has more . . . youthful styling."

"Not on your life," she said. "I may be a preacher's wife, but I did *not* take a vow of poverty."

"Cynthia, the Buick drives like a dream."

"Dream on," she said. His wife was stubborn as a mule.

"It never needs any work."

"It is fourteen years old, the paint is faded, and there's rust on the right fender. The upholstery on the driver's side is smithereens, a church fan works better than the air conditioner, and it reeks of mildew."

He sighed. "Other than that, Mrs. Lincoln, how did you like the play?"

She giggled.

He rolled over to her and they assumed their easy spoon position, which someone had called "the staple consolation of the marriage bed." She felt warm and easy in his arms.

"Listen," he said.

"To what?"

"I heard something just then. Music, I think."

They lay very still. The lightest notes from a piano floated through the window.

"A piano," he said.

"Chopin," she murmured.

Moments later, he heard her whiffling snore, found it calming, and fell asleep.

Hammer and tong.

That's how they were going at it in the yellow house.

The plan was to get on the road by eight o'clock, which was when Dooley reported to The Local.

Excited about the idea that had come to him in the dream, Father Tim asked Dooley to help tote the last of the cargo to the curb, where Violet was already in her cage on the rear floor of the Mustang.

The top was down, the day was bright and promising, and Barnabas had been walked around the monument at a trot.

"Ah!" Father Tim inhaled the summer morning air, then turned to Dooley, grinning.

"You're pretty happy," said Dooley.

"I'm happy to tell you that next summer, with only a modest outlay of funds on your part, Cynthia and I would like to make you the proud owner of . . . the Buick."

Dooley looked stunned.

"I ain't drivin' that thing!" he said, reverting to local vernacular and obviously highly insulted.

They were standing on the sidewalk as the Lord's Chapel bells chimed eight.

Puny and the twins were first in line, and he was up to bat.

"Say bye-bye to Granpaw," urged Puny.

"Bye-bye, Ba," said Sissy. She reached out to him, nearly sprawling out of Puny's arms.

He plucked her from her mother and held her, kissing her forehead. "God be with you, Sissy."

Her green eyes brimmed with tears. "Come back, Ba."

He set her down on chubby legs, wondering how he could go through with this. . . .

He hoisted the plump, sober Sassy, who was chewing a piece of toast, and kissed the damp tousle of red hair. "God's blessings, Sassy." Barnabas, who was sitting patiently on the sidewalk, licked Sissy's face.

Puny was openly bawling. Blast. He took it like a man and gave her a hug, feeling her great steadfastness, smelling the starch in her blouse, loving her goodness to him over the years. "You're always in our prayers," he told her, hoarse with feeling.

Puny wiped her nose with the hem of her apron. "We'll miss you."

"We'll be back before you know it."

Puny and the children fled into the yellow house, as Cynthia stood on tiptoe and gave Dooley a hug. "Take care of yourself, you big lug."

"I will."

"And write. Or call. A lot!"

"I will."

Father Tim clasped the boy to him, then stood back and gazed at him intently. "I'm counting on you to help Harley hold things together around here."

"Yes, sir. I will."

"We love you."

"I love you back." Dooley said it fair and square, looking them in the eye. Then he turned and ran to his red bicycle, leaped on it, and pedaled toward Main Street. Before he reached the corner, he stopped, looked back, and waved. " 'Bye, Cynthia, 'bye, Dad!"

They waved as Dooley disappeared around the rhododendron bush.

Father Tim jingled the keys in his hand. "Harley, reckon you can sell the Buick for me?"

Harley looked skeptical, scratched his head, and gazed at the sidewalk.

"Would you . . . like to drive it while I'm gone?"

"Rev'rend, I 'preciate th' offer, but I'll stick to m' truck."

"Aha." Clearly, he had a vehicle he couldn't even give away, much less sell.

"Well, Harley . . ." He put his arm around the shoulders of the small, frail man who was now holding down the fort.

"Rev'rend, Cynthia . . . th' Lord go with you." Harley's chin trembled, and he wiped his eyes with his sleeve.

" 'Bye, Harley," said Cynthia. "We love you."

Father Tim opened the passenger door and put the seat forward. "Come on, fellow, get in."

Barnabas leaped onto the leather seat, sniffed Violet's cage, and lay down, looking doleful.

"Don't even think about crying," he told his wife as they climbed in the car.

"The wind in our hair . . . ," she said, laughing through the tears.

He started the engine. "The cry of gulls wheeling above us . . ."

"The smell of salt air!"

He turned around in a driveway at the end of Wisteria Lane. Man alive, he liked the way this thing handled, and the seat . . . the seat felt like an easy chair.

They waved to Harley, who was rooted to the spot and waving back.

After hooking a right on Main Street, he drove slowly, as if they were a parade car. J. C. Hogan was just trotting into the Grill.

Father Tim hammered down on the horn and J.C. looked up, dumbstruck, as they waved.

Then he stepped on the gas and whipped around the monument, consciously avoiding a glance in the rearview mirror.

CHAPTER FOUR

The Smell of Salt Air

He was loving this.

"You're loving this!" crowed his wife.

He couldn't remember ever having such a sense of perfect freedom; he felt light as air, quick as mercury, transparent as glass.

And hot as blazes.

He looked into the rearview mirror. Barnabas, currently sitting up with his head riveted into the scorching wind, was attracting the attention of all westbound traffic.

"You must stop and get a hat!" his wife declared over the roar of an eighteen-wheeler. "Your head is turning pink!"

"Lunch and a hat, coming up," he said, reluctant to delay their journey, even if it was into the unknown.

They were barreling toward Williamston, through open tobacco country.

"Flat," said Cynthia, peering at the landscape.

"Hard to have an ocean where it isn't flat."

"*Hot,*" she said, reduced to telegraphic speech.

"Don't say we weren't warned. Want to put the top up?"

"Not yet, I'm trying to get the look of an island native." His wife was wearing shorts and a tank top, sunglasses and a Mitford Reds ball cap. All exposed areas were slathered with oil, and she was frying.

"I think we need to get Barnabas under cover before long. We'll put it up at Williamston."

Whoosh. A tractor-trailer nearly sucked them out of the car. He reached up and clamped his new hat to his head.

"Did Miss Pringle say why she left Boston to live in Mitford?"

"No. Didn't say."

"And you didn't ask?"

"Never thought to."

"Why on earth would she pick Mitford? And for only six months! Can you imagine hauling a piano from Boston for only six months? Does she have friends or relatives in Mitford?"

"I don't think so, but I'm not sure."

"Darling, how can you ever *know* things about people if you don't ask?"

As a priest, he usually managed to find out more than he wanted to know, though hardly ever through asking.

She sat thinking, with Violet asleep at her feet on the floorboard.

"Remember that chicken salad we had for lunch?" she inquired.

"Only vaguely."

"It's becoming a distant memory to me, too. I'm starved. Actually, during the entire lunch, I was dreaming of something finer."

"Oh?"

"Esther's cake."

"Aha."

"In the cooler. . . ."

"Umm."

"I've been thinking how moist it is, how cold and sweet, how velveteen its texture. . . ."

"That's Esther's cake, all right."

"And those discreet little morsels of bittersweet rind that burst in your mouth like . . . like sunshine!"

"You're a regular Cowper of cake."

"Don't you think we should have some?" she asked.

"Now you're talking."

"Did you bring your pocketknife?"

"Always," he said, producing it from his pocket.

She got on her knees in her seat and foraged around on the floorboard in back, cranking off the cooler top and fetching out the foil-wrapped mound.

"Oh, lovely. Nice and cold on my legs. Well, now. How shall we do this?" she asked, peeling back layers of foil. "This is the cake that nearly sent you to heaven in your prime. You probably shouldn't have a whole slice."

"If you recall," he said, "it was *two* slices that nearly sent me packing. I'll have one slice, and would appreciate not being able to see through it."

She carefully carved a small piece and put it on a napkin from the glove compartment. "Don't keel over on me," she said, meaning it.

Driving to the beach in a red convertible, eating Esther's cake—how many men wouldn't crave to be in his shoes? The sweetness and delicacy of the vanishing morsel in his hands were literally intoxicating. *Priest Found Drunk on Layer Cake . . .*

"Darling, you talked in your sleep last night."

"Uh-oh."

"You said 'slick' several times; you were very restless."

"Slick?"

"Yes, and once I think you said 'Tommy.' "

"Aha!" The dream flooded back to him instantly. His boyhood friend, Tommy Noles, and that miserable experience that earned him his nickname, a nickname he'd never mentioned to his wife. . . .

"Who is Tommy?" she queried.

"Tommy Noles, my old friend from Holly Springs."

"The one who always knew the make and model of cars."

"Right."

"What were you dreaming?"

As usual, his inquisitive wife wanted to know everything. Should he tell her?

"Well, let's see. I was dreaming about . . . well, about the time when . . ."

"When what?"

Weren't couples supposed to tell each other their fondest wishes, their deepest secrets, their blackest fears? He'd never thought much of that scheme, but so far, it had worked. In fact, he'd found that for every one of his deepest secrets, Cynthia Kavanagh would pour forth two or three of her own; it was like winning at slots.

". . . when I got my nickname."

"Are you blushing or is that the sun?"

"The sun," he said.

"What about when you got your nickname? I never knew you had one."

Tommy Noles had lived right up the road, next to his attorney father's gentleman's farm. Mr. Noles was a history teacher and a packrat. He hauled every imaginable oddity to his seven acres, and parked it around the property as if it were outdoor sculpture. A rusting haymow, an antique tractor, a gas tank from a service station, a prairie schooner, a large advertising sign for tobacco . . .

Mr. Noles mowed around these objects regularly and with great respect, but neglected to trim the grass that grew directly against them, so that each was sheathed in a colorful nest of sedge and wildflowers, which, as a boy, the young Tim had found enhancing.

His father found none of it enhancing, his father who idolized perfection above all else, and no son of his would be allowed to play with Tommy Noles.

But he had, in fact, played with Tommy Noles, wading in the creek, building a fort in the woods, constructing a tree house, fishing for crappie, searching for arrowheads in the fields.

Tommy Noles had wanted to be a fighter pilot in a terrible war, and he, Timothy Kavanagh, wanted to be a boxer or an animal trainer or, oddly enough, a bookbinder, for hadn't he been outrageously smitten with the smell and the look of his grandfather's books?

He remembered training Tommy's dog, Jeff, to catch sticks in midair, and to roll over and play dead. It had been deeply satisfying to finagle another living creature into doing anything at all, and he longed for a dog of his own, but his father wouldn't allow it. Dogs had fleas, dogs scratched, dogs defecated.

He grew uneasy thinking about how it had happened.

Tommy Noles, urged by the others and unbeknownst to him, had put dog poop just inside the double doors of the schoolhouse, two piles of it.

Bust in through those doors, runnin', Tommy said to him, *and we'll give you a nickel.*

Why? he asked. The teachers were in a meeting in the gym, and he smelled trouble brewing.

Just because, just for nothin', just run up th' steps, bust through th' doors, and run down th' hall all th' way to th' water fountain, and we'll give you a In'ian head nickel.

He still didn't know why he did it, he didn't remember wanting the money especially, perhaps he did it because he was the scrawny one, the geek, the one who loved to read and write and think and ponder words and meanings.

Without caring, he just did it; he burst through the doors running, and hit the piles and skidded down the hall as if he'd connected with a patch of crankcase oil. Just outside Miss McNolty's classroom, he lost his balance and crashed to the floor.

He heard the boys screaming with laughter at the front door as he got up, stinking, and tried to scrape the slimy stuff off his shoes. It was slick as grease. . . .

He walked toward them, his heart thundering. He had never picked a fight or been in one; he would have run first, not looking back.

But this was different. His friend had betrayed him.

They watched him coming toward them and backed down the steps.

Hey, Slick! somebody yelled. Three boys who were laughing and holding their noses suddenly turned and ran to the oak tree, where they stopped and peered from behind it. Lee Adderholt and Tommy Noles stood fast near the bottom of the steps, looking awed, mesmerized.

What had they seen on his face? He would never know.

I . . . I'm sorry, Tim, Tommy said.

He felt something building in himself, something . . . towering. He seemed to be suddenly six feet tall, and growing.

I really am! wailed Tommy.

He never remembered what happened, exactly, he just knew that he plowed into Tommy Noles without fear, without trembling, and beat the living crap out of him.

Then he was sitting in the principal's office—thank God it was Mr. Lewis, who was too tenderhearted to whip anybody. Mr. Lewis had looked at him for what seemed a long time, with what appeared to be kindness in his face, but the young Kavanagh couldn't be sure.

He knew, sitting there, that he had liked beating the tar out of

Tommy Noles. But most of all, he had liked making him cry in front of the people who had hooted and laughed, holding their noses.

Your father will never hear this from me, Mr. Lewis said. *But if anyone tells him and he asks, I will, of course, be required to . . .*

For the first time in his life, he had been glad, thrilled, that everyone he knew, his classmates and friends, were terrified of his father, and wouldn't dare speak to him, much less reveal the dark transgression of his son brawling in a fistfight.

What happened, Timothy? asked his mother.

He dropped his head. He had never lied to his mother.

I beat up Tommy Noles.

She studied him. *I'm sure he asked for it,* she said, simply.

Yes, ma'am.

But don't ever do this again.

No, ma'am.

He hadn't ever done it again; he hadn't needed to. It had been the fight of his life, the Grand Inquisition. In his rage, he had taken on the very world with his two hands, and somehow, oddly, won.

The scrawny kid with the scrawny arms and the penchant for reading large books and making straight A's had been suffused with a new aura. They gave him a wide berth when they called him Slick, for they had seen his rage, and witnessed his consuming power, and hadn't understood it and never would. He was Timothy Kavanagh, not to be messed with.

Period.

He grinned, pulling around an RV from Texas. After that incident, Tommy Noles had become the best friend he had in the world, even if he had failed to hand over the nickel. Sometime, when he had nothing else to do, he'd calculate what Tommy would owe him today, given fifty-six years of accumulated interest on a nickel.

"I'm growing older," said his eager wife, "just waiting to hear your nickname."

"Slick," he said, looking straight ahead.

He wasn't surprised that she nearly doubled over with laughter. "Slick! *Slick?*" Clearly, that was the funniest thing she'd ever heard in her life.

"Slick! That's *too* wonderful! I can't *believe* it!"

Ha, ha, ha, on and on. He would nip this in the bud. "So what was *your* nickname, Kavanagh?"

She stopped laughing.

Bingo, he thought.

"Must you know?"

"Cynthia, Cynthia . . . need you ask?"

"You won't laugh?"

"Laugh? I'll kill myself laughing. So tell me."

She sighed deeply and tucked a strand of blond hair under the ball cap. "Tubs."

"Tubs?" Marriage was a wonderful thing. It produced all sorts of ways to get even with somebody without necessarily going to jail. But seeing the look on her face, he couldn't laugh.

"Tubby to begin, then shortened to Tubs. Fatter than fat, that was me."

He couldn't imagine it.

"You couldn't even imagine," she said. "When I was ten years old . . . do you remember those photographers who traveled around with a pony?"

He remembered.

"One took my picture and I waited for weeks for it to come in the mail. When we opened the envelope, I couldn't believe my eyes, nor could anyone else. They all said I was . . . they said I was bigger than the pony."

"No."

"Oh, yes, they raved about it 'til kingdom come, Tubs this and Tubs that. My mother and father loved having their picture taken, so they'd dashed in the house and come out looking like Ginger Rogers and Fred Astaire. I, on the other hand, had been popped onto that sulking pony in a hideous dress, looking precisely like W. C. Fields."

She peered at him. "If you ever mention that hideous name to a soul, I'll murder you."

"If you ever mention mine, same back."

"Deal," she said, shaking his hand.

"Deal," he said, seeing a sign that said *Williamston, 10 miles.*

He was looking at his watch when a raindrop hit the crystal face.

Two-thirty, they should be there around six-thirty or seven o'clock, with plenty of daylight to unload the car and check out their new home.

The suddenness of the downpour was shocking. Without warning, a sheet of wind-driven rain was upon them, thundering out of darkened skies. He veered off the road and careened to a stop, the engine running. Dear God, he knew how to put the top *down* on this thing, but Dooley had been the one who put it up. He fumbled with the button on the console, but nothing happened.

"Timothy!" His wife was drenched, sopping.

"What do we do?" he shouted.

"I don't know!" The wind carried her voice away.

He lunged to the right and felt in the glove compartment for the owner's manual, as Barnabas, quaking with fear, leaped into Cynthia's lap, which was already occupied by Violet.

"Back! Go back!" She was almost wholly concealed by his mass of streaming fur. Barnabas went back.

The force of the rain was unbelievable. It thudded against their skin and heads like so many small mallets. He shoved the manual under the dashboard on Cynthia's side, his glasses running with rain. Index, page 391, not under "Top," not under . . . there it was. "Convertible," page 213. He managed to see the words *Engage the parking brake* before the book absorbed water like a sponge and the instructions ran together in a blur.

He pulled the brake, then pressed the button repeatedly, to no avail. *Dear God, help. . . .*

"The boot!" Cynthia cried.

He leaped out, dangerously close to the highway on which cars were still racing, and fumbled to remove the side edges of the boot clip from under the side belt moldings. It took an eternity, and they were drowning.

Back in the car, he pressed the button, and the top began rising. They were taking on water like a bottomless canoe.

The top rose midway and, like a sail on a boat, was instantly filled with wind and driving rain. The top appeared to freeze in midair.

"We'll have to do it manually!" he shouted above the roar. "Get out!"

Help us, Lord, he prayed, as they hauled the thing over, straining against the terrible force of the wind, then brought it down and opened the doors and sloshed into the brimming seats. They turned the levers and secured the top, and sat back, panting, daunted now by the deafening thunder on the roof.

"The towels!" she shouted. "In the back!"

He strained around and reached behind her seat and found the wrapped bundle of a dozen terry towels, which had been cunningly advertised as "thirsty." They were sodden.

Violet howled in Cynthia's lap.

"If we wring them out, we can mop our seats!"

They wrung the water onto the floorboard at their feet, afraid to open the windows, and swabbed the leather seats. It sounded as if the pounding rain would tear through the canvas and swamp them utterly.

Then the lightning began, cracking over their heads.

Barnabas returned to the front in a single leap, and landed in Father Tim's lap, trembling.

The windows were fogged completely, his glasses were useless. He took them off and put them in his shirt pocket. As he held on to his dog, all he could see from their red submarine were the stabbing streaks of lightning.

The rain that began so violently at two-thirty stopped at three o'clock, then returned around three-thirty to pummel the car with renewed energy, as lightning cracked around them with a vengeance.

Sitting on the shoulder since the last downpour began, they briefly considered trying to get back on the highway and drive to a service station, a bridge, anything, but visibility was zero.

Pouring sweat in the tropical humidity of the car, they found the air-conditioning was no relief. Its extreme efficiency made them feel frozen as cods in their wet clothing.

If only they were driving the Buick, he thought. The feeble air-conditioning his wife had so freely lambasted would be exactly right for their circumstances. In fact, his Buick would be the perfect security against a storm that threatened to rip a frivolous rag from over their heads and fling it into some outlying tobacco field.

The temperature in the car was easily ninety degrees. He remembered paying ten pounds for an hour's worth of this very misery in an English hotel sauna, without, of course, the disagreeable odor of steaming dog and cat fur.

"When life gives you lemons . . . ," he muttered darkly.

". . . make lemonade," said his wife, stroking her drenched cat.

"Four o'clock," he said, pulling onto the highway. "We've lost nearly two hours. That means we'll get into Whitecap around dark."

"Ah, well, dearest, not to worry. This can't go on forever."

He hoped such weather would at least put a crimp in the ridiculous notion of wearing grass skirts tomorrow night.

The aftermath of the storm was not a pretty sight. Apparently, they'd missed the worst of it.

Here and there, billboards were blown down, a metal sign lying in the middle of the highway advertised night crawlers and boiled peanuts, and most crops stood partially immersed.

"Our baptism into a new life," he said, looking at the dazzling light breaking over the fields.

At a little after seven o'clock, the rain returned and the wind with it. No lightning this time, but a heavy, insistent pounding over their heads that clearly meant business.

He stopped and did a glucometer check to make sure he wasn't in a nonketotic hyperglycemic coma, thanks to Esther's cake, and was fairly pleased with the reading.

"What do you think?" he asked, parked by the pump at an Amoco station. "Should we look for supper or keep moving?" When he was tired, he still referred to the evening meal as "supper," as he had in childhood.

"It's a wasteland out there. Where would we find supper unless we catch it off a bank?"

"Now, now, Kavanagh. You were thinking wild asparagus with spring lamb, while I was thinking hot dogs all the way."

"I don't know, darling, I feel we should get there and settle in. After all, we have to make the bed when we arrive, and here we are, hours away, and I'm already dying to be *in* one!"

"No supper, then?"

"Maybe a pack of Nabs or some peanuts while we're here. I mean, look what you've got to drive through for who knows how long."

The Mustang shuddered in a violent crosswind.

"You're right," he said, getting out of the car.

He trudged into the neon light of the service station, feeling like a garden slug in his still-damp clothes.

"This is endless," she said as they crept through the several blinkers of a business district that they presumed to be Roper—or was it Scuppernong? The blinkers danced wildly in the wind, on electric wires strung above the street.

It seemed the wind and rain would hit them for twenty or thirty minutes, slack off or let up altogether, then hit them again with another wallop.

Violet snored in Cynthia's lap, Barnabas snored on the backseat.

Father Tim hunkered over the wheel, staring down the oncoming lights. "Marry a preacher, Kavanagh, and life ceases to be boring."

"I'd give an arm and a leg for a boring life," she said grimly, then suddenly laughed. "But only for five minutes!"

There was a long silence as he navigated through the downpour.

"Dearest, what exactly did you *say* to God in your discussions about what to do in retirement?"

"I said I was willing to go anywhere He sent me."

"Do you recall if He said anything back?"

"He said, 'That's what I like to hear.' Not in an audible voice, of course. He put it on my heart."

"Aha," she said, quoting her husband.

"Look," he said, "there's a sign for Columbia. Do we go on to Columbia, or make a turn somewhere?"

"On to Columbia," she said, squinting at the map.

His wife had never professed to be much of a navigator; he hoped they didn't end up in Morehead City.

When they reached the bridge to Whitecap, the wind and rain had stopped; there was an innocent peace in the air.

A sign stood at the entrance to the bridge, which had been closed off with a heavy chain and a soldierly row of orange cones.

BRIDGE OUT
FERRY 2 Blocks
& Left $10
No Ferry
After 10 P.M.

"Good heavens," said his wife, "isn't it after ten o'clock?"

"Five 'til," he said, backing up. He made the turn and hammered down on the accelerator.

"That's *one* block . . . ," she said.

Going this fast on wet pavement didn't exactly demonstrate the wisdom of the ages. "This is two," he counted.

"Now turn left here. I'm praying they'll be open."

He turned left. Nothing but yawning darkness. Then, a dim light a few yards ahead, swinging.

They inched along, not knowing what lay in their path. A sign propped against a sawhorse revealed itself in the glare of the headlights.

Ferry to Whitecap
Have Your $ Ready

A lantern bobbed from the corner of what appeared to be a small building perched at the edge of the water.

He'd read somewhere about blowing your horn for a ferry, and gave it a long blast.

"Lord, is this a joke?" his wife inquired aloud of her Maker.

A light went on in the building and a man came out, wearing a cap, an undershirt, and buttoning his pants.

Father Tim eased the window down a few inches.

"Done closed."

"Two minutes," said Father Tim, pointing to his watch. "Two whole minutes before ten. You've got to take us across." He nearly said, *I'm clergy*, but stopped himself.

"You live across?"

"We're moving to Whitecap."

"Don't know as you'd want to go across tonight," said the man, still buttoning. " 'Lectricity's off. Black as a witch's liver."

Father Tim turned to Cynthia. "What do you think?"

"Where would we stay over here?"

"Have t' turn back fourteen miles."

Cynthia looked at her husband. "We're going across!"

"Twenty dollars," said the man, unsmiling.

"Done," said Whitecap's new priest.

Leaving the tropical confines of the car and clinging to the rail of the ferry, they looked across the black water, and up to clouds racing over the face of the moon. They were leaving the vast continent behind, and going to what looked like mere flotsam on the breast of the sea.

The ferry rocked and labored along its passage, belching oily fumes. Yet, quite apart from the noxious smell, Cynthia detected something finer, "There it is, Timothy! The smell of salt air!"

"Gulls wheeling above us," he muttered lamely, noting that a few gulls followed the ferry, even in the dead of night.

She leaned against his shoulder, and he put his arm around her and took off her cap and nuzzled her hair. She was his rock in an ocean of change, no pun intended.

"Look at the stars coming out, my dearest. The sky is as fresh and new as the fourth day of Creation. It's going to be wonderful, Timothy, our new life. We're going to feel freer, somehow, I promise."

That was a very nice speech, he noted, as only his wife could make. "Absolutely!" he said, trying to mean it.

Their car had been unchained from its moorings, and the ramp to Whitecap cranked down. The ferry pilot stood by the ramp, a cigarette in his mouth, holding the gas lantern and signaling them off.

"Would you look at our map?" Father Tim leaned out the window. "We're trying to get . . . here." He pointed to the location of Dove Cottage, marked by a red arrow. "Since we're not approaching from the bridge . . ."

The lantern was lifted to light the hand-drawn map. "No problem," said the pilot, leaving the cigarette in place. "I've been around in there a few times. Go off th' ramp, take a left, drive about a mile and a half, turn right on Tern Avenue, go straight for about a mile, then take a left on Hastings. Looks like your place is on th' corner . . . right there."

"Left off the ramp, a mile and a half . . ." Father Tim repeated the litany. "Any idea when the power might be restored?"

"By mornin', most likely. Worst out was three days, back in '89. What line of business you in?"

"New priest at St. John's in the Grove."

The pilot took a heavy drag on his cigarette and pitched it over the rail. Then he reached in his pants pocket, withdrew a ten-dollar bill, and handed it through the window.

"Oh, but—"

"Godspeed," said the ferry pilot, walking away.

A waxing moon drifted above them as they drove along the narrow road.

"They all look alike," Cynthia said, peering at the darkened houses. "White, with picket fences. Some on stilts. Goodness, do you think all these people are really sleeping?"

"I saw something that looked like candles in one window."

"Did we bring candles?"

"What do you think?"

"I think we brought candles! I'm thrilled to be married to such a predictable stick-in-the-mud. I hope you brought extra blades for my razor."

"If I didn't, which I did, you could find them at a store. Whitecap isn't the Australian Outback."

"You know one reason I love you?" she asked.

"I haven't the foggiest."

"Because," she said, "you're steady. So very steady."

A former bishop had once said something like that, calling him a "plow horse." The bishop made it clear, however, that it was the racehorse that clambered to the top of the church ladder and made a fine stall for himself.

Barnabas thrust his head out the window, sniffing. New smells were everywhere, there was nothing known or expected about the smells in these parts.

"Hastings Avenue should be coming up," he said. "There! Do you hear it?"

"The ocean! Yes! Oh, stop—just for a moment."

He slowed to a stop, and realized the great roar was out there somewhere, that just over the high dunes was a beach, and, lying beyond, a vast rink of platinum shimmering under the moon.

" 'Listen!' " he whispered, quoting Wordsworth. " 'The Mighty Being is awake, and doth with His eternal motion make, a sound like thunder, everlastingly.' "

"Lovely!" she breathed.

They moved on slowly, as if already obeying some island impulse, some new metabolism. With only the moon, stars, and headlights to illumine their way in the endless darkness, they might have been the last creatures on earth.

"Let's put the top down!" crowed Cynthia.

"Fat chance," he said, turning off Tern.

He walked back to the car with the flashlight.

"I don't see the half-hidden street sign Marion Fieldwalker talked about. . . ."

"I can't understand it," she said, studying the map under the map light. "We turned right on Tern, we went left on Hastings to the corner. This must be it."

"The overgrown hedges are definitely there."

"Maybe the sign blew away in the storm. Should we . . . retrace our steps and try again, or do you think . . . ?"

It had all become a blasted nuisance as far as he was concerned. And he would never say so to his wife, but it was spooky out here, stumbling around on some godforsaken jut of land in the pitch-dark, miles from home and reeling from what had become a fifteen-hour trip with nothing but a pack of blasted peanuts to . . .

"We did exactly as the map said. I don't think trying to do it all over again would help us. Why don't we investigate?"

He helped her out of the car and shone the flashlight onto the porch. It was an older beach cottage, with a line of rocking chairs turned upside down to keep the wind from blowing them into the yard. A derelict shutter leaned against the shingled wall.

"Gosh," she said, otherwise speechless.

"I don't see a rosebush climbing up anything," He'd been looking forward to that rosebush.

"Maybe the storm . . . ," she suggested.

". . . blew it down," he said.

They went up the creaking steps to the door.

"Look, Timothy, up there."

A sign hung lopsided above the door, dangling from a single nail.

OVE

OTTAGE

"Oh, my," she said quietly.

Surely this wasn't . . . surely not, he thought.

"They said it would be unlocked," whispered his wife. "Should we . . . try the door?"

The door swung open easily. He was afraid to look.

"Aha."

The furnishings sat oddly jumbled in the large, paneled room. A slipcovered sofa faced away from two club chairs, card tables blocked the entrance to what appeared to be a dining room, a faded Persian carpet covered one side of the floor, but was rolled up on the other.

They went in carefully, as if walking on eggs.

Cynthia hugged herself and stared around in disbelief. "How could this *possibly* . . . ?"

He passed the light across one of the tables and saw a half-assembled jigsaw image of the Grand Canyon.

"Look at that lovely old fireplace," she said. "Marion never mentioned a fireplace. . . ."

"Mildew," he said. "Do you smell it?"

"Yes, but how odd. Marion said they'd worked like slaves to clean everything up. Timothy, this can't be Dove Cottage."

"It's certainly where her map led us, and the sign above the door said . . ." He sighed, dumbfounded.

"Let's try a lamp. Maybe the power's back on." It wasn't.

Barnabas sniffed the rugs and the sofa, with special interest in an unseen trail that led to the hallway. They followed him, numb with disappointment and fatigue.

In the kitchen, the refrigerator door stood ajar, as did several cabinet doors.

"Ugh!" she said. "I can't believe they'd do this to us. Surely they didn't think we were coming next week. Remember we originally told them it would be next week. Maybe somehow they got confused and

the cleaning hasn't been done, yet. . . ." Her voice trailed off.

She was trying, but he wasn't buying. He wouldn't live in this dump if they sent the cleaning crew from the Ritz-Carlton in Paris, France. Just wait 'til he got hold of the senior warden. He'd had a round or two with senior wardens in his time; he was no babe in the woods when it came to what's what with senior wardens. . . .

"The phone, there must be a phone around here. We can call the Fieldwalkers, shine the light around."

They found a wall phone on the other side of the cabinets, but the line was dead.

"The bedrooms," she said, desperate.

At the end of the hallway, which was covered by a Persian runner, they found a cavernous bedroom, and surveyed it with the flashlight. Closet doors standing agape . . . windows open . . . curtains blowing . . . the bed made, but sopping wet.

"This can't be right, they wouldn't *do* this to us." He could tell his wife was teetering on the edge of hysteria. "Wait 'til I get my hands on that fine bishop of yours who would send you out to some . . . uninhabited wasteland, after the years of faithful service you've given him.

"That . . . that vainglorious *dog*!"

"Nothing personal," he told Barnabas, who was sniffing the closets.

Because they hadn't known what else to do at nearly midnight on a strange, dark island with no lights and no phone, they made the double bed in the guest room and got in it, Barnabas on the floor on one side and Violet in her open crate on the other, where his inconsolable wife sighed and fumed herself to sleep as he lay staring at the pale circle cast by the flashlight onto the ceiling, muttering words and thinking thoughts he never dreamed he would say or think, and feeling distinctly waterlogged even in a perfectly dry pair of pajamas from his bureau in Mitford, thanks be to God for small favors.

CHAPTER FIVE

A Patch of Blue

He sat up in bed, dazed.

Where in heaven's name . . . ?

Barnabas barked wildly, and someone was knocking on a door. As the room came into focus, he remembered the predicament they were in, and counted it odd that one should wake to, rather than from, a nightmare.

He glanced at his watch—seven o'clock—and bolted into the hallway without robe or slippers. He padded through the dark, paneled living room and opened the door, feeling anger rise in him again.

"Father? Father Kavanagh?"

"Yes!" he snapped, buttoning his pajama top.

"Sam Fieldwalker, sir, your senior warden." The tall, gentle-looking man appeared deeply puzzled.

"Sam . . ." He shook hands as Barnabas sniffed the stranger's shoes.

"We saw your car out front, and . . . well, you see, we waited for you and Mrs. Kavanagh 'til eleven o'clock last night—"

"Waited? Where?"

"In your cottage. Over there." He pointed off the porch.

"You mean . . . this isn't our cottage?"

"Well, no. I'm terribly sorry, I don't know how . . . it must have been the storm and no lights to see by . . ."

"The wrong cottage!" shouted his wife, peering around the hall door in her nightgown. "Thank heaven!"

Sam let Barnabas sniff his hand. "There you are, old fellow, smelling our little Bitsy. My gracious, Father, you all have a dog and a half there!"

"But that sign . . . ," said Cynthia, "that sign above the door . . ."

Sam glanced up, adjusting his glasses. "Oh, my goodness. Of course. Well, you see, this is one of the old *Love* Cottages. . . ."

Cynthia looked fierce. "It certainly doesn't live up to its name!"

"It's owned by the Redmon Love family, who started coming here in the forties. Gracious sakes, Father, Mrs. Kavanagh, I can't begin to tell you how *sorry* . . ."

Father Tim thought Sam Fieldwalker might burst into tears.

"Oh, no, please," he said. "I don't know how we could have thought for a moment . . . well, you see, it was dark as pitch, and we couldn't find the street sign in the hedge, the one Marion told us to look for. . . ."

"Ah, now I'm getting a clear picture!" Sam brightened considerably. "You turned into Love's old driveway, which is wide enough to look like a street—property wasn't so dear in the forties—and, of course, there's a shabby hedge bordering their property, as well. Oh, my, I'm sure Marion never thought of that."

"No harm done! We're glad the mystery is solved. But do the Loves always leave their house unlocked?"

"Hardly anyone on Whitecap locks their doors. And, of course, the Love children and their kids come and go during the summer, though not so much anymore."

"Aha." The sunlight was dazzling, his glasses were by the bed, and he was squinting like a monk at vespers.

"Let me help you move your things, Father. Marion's waiting at Dove Cottage to show you around and cook your breakfast. She's baking biscuits. . . ."

He felt covered with shame. How could he have mistrusted this kind person, believing even for a moment that this was the right cottage? *Lord, forgive me.*

". . . and," Sam continued, looking earnest, "she's found some nice, fresh perch, if . . . if that's all right."

At that moment, Father Tim heard his stomach rumble, and, at the thought of Marion Fieldwalker's fresh perch and biscuits, felt close to tears himself.

⟍⟋

Marion met them on the porch of Dove Cottage, a tall, large-boned woman in an apron, with a pleasant face and snow-white hair like her husband.

"In case you'd taken the ferry," said Marion, "we waited 'til eleven. Then, when you didn't come, we thought the storm had held you up and you'd stayed somewhere for the night."

"When we found the bridge was out, we thought it too far to turn back for a place to sleep," Cynthia said.

"And we nearly missed the ferry!" exclaimed Father Tim, oddly enjoying the account of their travail. "We made it with two minutes to spare."

"Oh, my poor souls! That bridge goes out if you hold your mouth wrong. You know the state bigwigs don't pay much attention to little specks of islands like they pay to big cities. Well, we're thrilled you're here, and I hope you like perch."

"We *love* perch!" they exclaimed in unison.

" 'Where two or more are gathered together in one accord . . .' " quoted the senior warden, laughing. Sam liked both the looks and the spirit of this pair.

In truth, he was vastly relieved that his prayers had been answered, and, as far as he could see, St. John's hadn't been delivered two pigs in a poke.

"Before we go inside," said Marion, "take a look at your rose."

"Ah!" said Cynthia.

They rushed to the trellis and buried their noses in the mass of blooms. "Lovely!" murmured his wife.

"It was running toward the street when we found it, and terribly trampled by the men who worked on the floors. But we loved it along and fed it, and came and watered it every day, and *now* . . ."

"What is it, do you think?"

"I have no idea. Marjorie Lamb and I searched our catalogs and rose books, but we can't identify it to save our lives."

"I believe I know exactly what it is," he said, adjusting his glasses and inspecting the petal formation.

"You *do*?"

"Yes. It's the Marion Climber."

"Oh, Father! Go on!"

"It is, I'd recognize it anywhere."

"The Marion Climber!" crowed Cynthia. "I never thought I'd live to see one. They're rare, you know."

"Oh, you two!" said Marion, flushed with delight.

"What do you think about your kitchen?" asked Sam.

Father Tim was a tad embarrassed to see tears brimming in his wife's eyes. "It's too beautiful for words!" she said.

"We couldn't like it better!"

If last night had been a nightmare, this was a dream come true. The sun streamed through a sparkling bay window and splashed across the broad window seat. Bare hardwood floors shone under a fresh coat of wax.

"One of our parishioners bought this cottage a few months ago and had it completely redone," said Sam. "Otis Bragg—you'll meet him tonight—Otis and his wife offered it to the parish for the new interim."

"You see just there?" Marion pointed out the window. "That patch of blue between the dunes? That's the ocean!" She proclaimed this as if the ocean belonged to her personally, and she was thrilled to share it.

"Come and have your breakfast," said Sam, holding the chair for Cynthia.

On a round table laid with a neat cloth, they saw a blue vase of watermelon-colored crepe myrtle, and the result of Marion Field-walker's labors:

Fried perch, crisp and hot, on a platter. A pot of coffee, strong and fragrant. A pitcher of fresh orange juice. Cantaloupe, cut into thick, ripe slices. Biscuits mounded in a basket next to a golden round of cheese and a saucer of butter, with a school of jellies and preserves on the side.

"Homemade fig preserve," said Marion, pointing to the jam pots. "Raspberry jelly. Blueberry jam. And orange marmalade."

"Dearest, do you think it possible that yesterday in that brutal storm we somehow died, and are now in heaven?"

"Not only possible, but very likely!"

He'd faced it time and again in his years as a priest—how do you pour out a heart full of thanksgiving in a way that even dimly expresses your joy?

He reached for the hands of the Fieldwalkers and bowed his head.

"Father, You're so good. So good to bring us out of the storm into the light of this blessed new day, and into the company of these blessed new friends.

"Touch, Lord, the hands and heart and spirit of Marion, who prepared this food for us when she might have done something more important.

"Bless this good man for looking out for us, and waiting up for us, and gathering the workers who labored to make this a bright and shining home.

"Lord, we could be here all morning only thanking You, but we intend to press forward and enjoy the pleasures of this glorious feast which You have, by Your grace, put before us. We thank You again for Your goodness and mercy, and for tending to the needs of those less fortunate, in Jesus' name."

"Amen!"

Marion Fieldwalker smiled at him, her eyes shining. "Father, when you were talking to the Lord about me doing this instead of something more important, I think you should know . . . there was nothing more important!"

Their hostess passed the platter of fried perch to Cynthia, as Sam passed the hot biscuits to his new priest.

Oh, the ineffable holiness of small things, he thought, crossing himself.

⟶

Marion insisted on cleaning up the kitchen while they sat around the table, idle as jackdaws.

"You're welcome at the library anytime," she said, pouring everyone a last cup of coffee, "as long as it's Monday, Wednesday, or Saturday from nine 'til four!"

"We'll drop in next week," said Father Tim. "And that reminds me, how's the bookstore? I hear you have a small bookstore on the island."

Marion laughed. "It's mostly used paperbacks of Ernie's favorite author, Louis L'Amour!"

"Ernie doesn't sell anything he hasn't read first and totally approved." Sam's eyes twinkled. "I hope you like westerns."

"We've got fourteen boxes of books arriving on Monday," Cynthia announced. "We can open our own bookstore!"

"By the way," said Sam, "Ernie also offers a notary service and UPS pickup, and rents canes and crutches on the side."

"Diversified!"

"Actually, you'll pass Ernie's every morning as you walk to church. It's right up the road."

"Sounds like the place to be."

"Ernie has his quarters on one side of the building, Mona has hers on the other. In fact, they've got a yellow line painted down the center of the hall between their enterprises, and neither one steps over it except to conduct business."

"Aha."

Sam stirred cream into his coffee, chuckling. "Ernie likes to say that yellow line saved their marriage."

Marion looked at the kitchen clock. "Oh, my! We'd better show you how your coffers are stocked, and get a move on!"

She took off her apron and tucked it in her handbag, then opened the refrigerator door as if raising a curtain on a stage.

"Half a low-fat ham, a baked chicken, and three loaves of Ralph Gaskell's good whole wheat . . . Lovey Hackett's bread-and-butter pickles, she's very proud of her pickles, it's her great aunt's recipe . . . then there's juice and eggs and butter, to get you started, the eggs are free-range from Marshall and Penny Duncan—he's Sam's junior warden.

"And last but not least . . ."—Marion indicated a large container on the bottom shelf—"Marjorie Lamb's apple spice cake. It's won an award at our little fair every year for ten years!"

Father Tim groaned inwardly. The endless temptations of the mortal flesh . . .

"What a generous parish you are, and God bless you for it!"

"We've always tried to spoil our priests," said Marion, smiling. "But not all of them deserved it."

Sam blinked his blue eyes. "Now, Marion, good gracious . . ."

"Just being frank," Marion said pleasantly.

"Dearest, I think we should be frank, too."

"In, ah, what way?" inquired Father Tim.

"About your diabetes. My husband likes to think that St. Paul's controversial thorn was, without doubt, diabetes."

"Oh, dear!" said Marion. "That means . . ."

"What that generally means is, I can't eat all the cakes and pies and so on that most folks like to feed a priest."

"But I can!" crowed his wife.

"It helps to get the word out early," he said, feeling foolish. "Cuts down on hurt feelings when . . ."

Sam nodded sympathetically. "Oh, we understand, Father, and we'll pass it on. Well, we ought to be pushing off, Marion. We've kept these good people far too long."

"Everybody's having a fit to get a look at you," Marion said proudly. "We hope you'll rest up this afternoon, and we'll come for you at six. It looks like we've got lovely weather on our side for the luau."

"Is the, ah, grass skirt deal still on?" asked Father Tim.

Marion laughed. "We nixed that. We didn't want to run you off before you get started!"

"Well done! And how do we get to St. John's? I'm longing to have a look."

"Good gracious alive!" said Sam, digging in his pockets. "I nearly forgot, I've got a key here for you."

He fetched out the key and handed it over. "Go out to the front gate, take a left, and two blocks straight ahead. You can't miss it. Oh, and Father, there are a couple of envelopes on the table in your sitting room. From two of our . . . most outspoken parishioners. They wanted to get to you before anyone else does . . ."—Sam cleared his throat—"if you understand."

"Oh, I do," he said.

"If I were you, Father," Marion warned, "I'd visit the church and take a nice nap before you go reading those letters. To put it plainly, they're all about bickering. We hate to tell you, but our little church has been bickering about everything from the prayer book to the pew bulletins for months on end. I've heard enough bickering to last a lifetime!"

They walked out to the porch, into the shimmering light. For mountain people accustomed to trees, it seemed the world had become nothing but a vast blue sky, across which cumulus clouds sailed with sovereign dignity.

"Thank you a thousand times for all you've done for us," Cynthia said.

"It's our privilege and delight. You know, we Whitecappers aren't much on hugging, but I think you could both use one!"

Sam and Marion hugged them and they hugged back, grateful.

The senior warden looked fondly at his new priest. "We'll help you all we can, Father, you can count on it."

He had the feeling that he would, indeed, be counting on it.

His wife notwithstanding, he had eagerly obeyed only a few people in his life—his mother, most of his bishops, Miss Sadie, and Louella. He thought Marion Fieldwalker might be a very good one to mind, so he lay down with Cynthia and took a nap, feeling the warmth of the sun through the large window, loving the clean smell of the softly worn matelassé spread, and thanking God.

Setting off to his new church with his good dog made him feel reborn. But he wouldn't go another step before he toured the garden, enclosed by a picket fence with rear and front gates leading to the streets.

Along the pickets to the right of the porch, a stout grove of cannas and a stand of oleander . . .

By the front gate, roses gone out of bloom, but doing nicely, and on the fence, trumpet vine. Several trees of some sort, enough for a good bit of shade, and over there, a profusion of lacecap hydrangea . . .

He walked around to the side of the house, where petunias and verbena encircled a sundial, and trotted to the backyard. An oval herb garden, enclosed by smaller pickets, a bird feeder hanging by the back steps . . .

He made a quick calculation regarding the grass. Twenty minutes, max, with the push mower Sam had sharpened, oiled, and left in the storage shed.

A light breeze stole off the water, and the purity of the storm-cleansed air was tonic, invigorating. He thought he heard someone whistling as he went out the rear gate, and was amazed to find it was himself.

Zip-a-dee-doo-dah, zip-a-dee-ay . . .

They cantered along the narrow lane, spying the much-talked-about street sign at the corner of the high fence. The fence was thickly massed with flowering vines and overhung by trees he couldn't identify.

It was wonderful to see things he couldn't identify—why hadn't he been more of a traveler in his life, why had he clung to Mitford like moss to a log, denying himself the singular pleasures of the unfamiliar?

He had the odd sense he was being watched. He stopped in the middle of the street and looked around. Not a bicycle, not a car, not a soul, only a gull swooping above them. They might have been dropped into Eden, as lone as Adam.

Ernie's and Mona's, he discovered, sat close to the street, with a dozen or so vehicles parallel-parked in front. Cars and pickups lined the side of the road.

Mona's Cafe
Three Square Meals
Six Days A Week
Closed Sunday

Ernie's Books, Bait & Tackle
Six 'Til Six
NO SUNDAYS

Twelve-thirty, according to his watch, and more than five whole hours of freedom lying ahead. Hallelujah!

He tied the red leash to a bench, and Barnabas crawled under it, panting.

As the screen door slapped behind him, he saw the painted yellow line running from front to back of the center hallway. A sign on an easel displayed two arrows—one pointed left to Mona's, one pointed right to Ernie's.

He read the handwritten message posted next to the café's screen door:

> *Don't even think about cussing in here.*

Should he follow the seductive aromas wafting from Mona's kitchen, or buy a *Whitecap Reader* and see what was what?

He hooked a right, where the bait and tackle shop had posted its own message by the door:

> *A fishing rod is a stick with a hook at one end and a fool at the other.*
> —*Samuel Johnson*

"What can I do for you?" A large, genial-looking man in a ball cap sat behind the cash register.

"Looking for a copy of the *Whitecap Reader*," Father Tim said, taking change from his pocket.

"We prob'ly got one around here somewhere. You wouldn't want to pay good money today since a new one comes out Monday. Roanoke, we got a paper over there?"

Roanoke looked up, squinting. "Junior's got it, he took it to th' toilet with 'im."

"That's OK," said Father Tim. "I'll pay for one. How much?"

"Fifty cents. You can get it out of the rack at th' door."

He doled out two quarters.

"We thank you. This your first time on Whitecap?"

"My wife and I just moved here."

"Well, now!" The man extended a large hand across the counter. "Ernie Fulcher. I run this joint."

"Tim Kavanagh."

"What business're you in?"

"New priest at St. John's."

"I never set eyes on th' old one," said Ernie. "I think Roanoke ran into 'im a time or two."

Roanoke nodded, unsmiling. He thought Roanoke's weathered, wrinkled face resembled an apple that had lain too long in the sun.

"Well, thanks. See you again."

"Right. Stop in anytime. You fish?"

"Not much."

"Need any shrimp, finger mullet, squid, bloodworms, chum . . . let me know."

"I'll do it."

"Plus we're th' UPS station for th' whole island, not to mention we rent crutches—"

"Good, good."

"And loan out jigsaws, no charge."

"I'd like to look at your books sometime."

Ernie jerked his thumb toward a room with a handprinted sign over the open door: *Books, Books and More Books.* "I got a deal on right now—buy five, get one free."

"Aha."

"Can't beat that."

"Probably not. Well, see you around."

He was unhooking the leash from the bench leg as two men walked out of Mona's, smelling of fried fish.

"What kind of dog is that?" one asked, popping a toothpick in his mouth.

"Big," said his friend.

He loved it at once.

St. John's in the Grove sat on a hummock in a bosk of live oaks that cast a cool, impenetrable shade over the churchyard and dappled the green front doors.

The original St. John's had been destroyed by fire during the Revolutionary War, and rebuilt in the late nineteenth century in Carpenter Gothic style. Sam Fieldwalker said the Love family purchased the contiguous property in the forties and gave it to St. John's, so the small building sat on a tract of thirty-five acres of virgin maritime forest, bordered on the cemetery side by the Atlantic.

Father Tim stood at the foot of the steps inhaling the new smells of his new church, set like a gem into the heart of his new parish. St. John's winsome charm and grace made him feel right at home, expectant as a child.

He crossed himself and prayed, aloud, spontaneous in his thanksgiving.

"Thank You, Lord! What a blessing . . . and what a challenge. Give me patience, Father, for all that lies ahead, and especially I ask for Your healing grace in the body of St. John's."

He walked up the steps and inserted the key into the lock. It turned smoothly, which was a credit to the junior warden. Then he put his hand on the knob and opened the door.

Though heavy, it swung open easily. He liked a well-oiled church door—no creaking and groaning for him, thank you.

The fragrance of St. John's spoke to him at once. Old wood and lemon oil . . . the living breath of last Sunday's flowers still sitting on the altar . . . years of incense and beeswax. . . .

To his right, a flight of narrow, uncovered stairs to the choir loft and organ. To his left, an open registry on a stand with a ballpoint pen attached by a string. He turned to the first entry in the thick book, its pages rustling like dry leaves. *Myra and Lewis Phillips, Bluefield, Kentucky, July 20, 1975 . . . we love your little church!!*

He looked above the stand to the framed sign, patiently hand-lettered and illumined with fading watercolors.

> *Let the peace of this place surround you as you sit or kneel quietly. Let the hurry and worry of your life fall away. You are God's child. He loves you and cares for you, and is here with you now and always. Speak to Him thoughtfully, give yourself time for Him to bring things to mind.*

Oh, the balm, he thought, of a cool, quiet church full of years.

He walked into the center aisle, which revealed bare heart-of-pine floorboards. They were more than a handbreadth wide, and creaked pleasantly under his tread. Creaking doors, no, he thought, but floorboards are another matter. He'd never lived in a house in which at least two or three floorboards didn't give forth a companionable creak.

On either side of the broad aisle, eight long oak pews seating . . . three, four, five, six, seven, eight, and four short pews seating four. Here and there, a cushion lay crumpled in a pew, reserving that site as someone's rightful, possibly long-term, territory.

His eye followed the aisle to the sanctuary, where a cross made of ship's timbers hung beneath an impressive stained glass.

In the dimly illumined glass, the figure of Christ stood alone with His hands outstretched to whoever might walk this aisle. Behind Him, a cerulean sea. Above, an azure sky and a white gull. The simplicity and earnestness of the image took his breath away.

" 'Come unto me . . .' " he read aloud from the familiar Scripture etched on the window in Old English script, " 'all ye that labor and are heavy laden, and I will give you rest.' "

These were his first spoken words in his new church, words that Paul Tillich had chosen from all of Scripture to best express his personal understanding of his faith.

Suddenly feeling the weariness under the joy, he slipped into a pew on the gospel side and sank to his knees, giving thanks.

Barnabas strained ahead, his nose to the ground; St. John's new priest-in-charge allowed himself to be pulled hither and yon, as free as a leaf caught in a breeze.

They walked around the church and out to the cemetery, where he pondered the headstones and gazed beyond the copse of yaupon to yet another distant patch of blue. He cupped his hand to his ear and listened, hoping to hear the sweetly distant roar, but heard only a gull instead.

Shading his eyes, he turned and searched toward the Sound, across the open breast of the hummock and into the trees, wondering whether the wild ponies were mythic or actually out there. He hoped they were out there.

Before he and Barnabas headed home, he stood for a moment by the grave site of the Redmon Love family, which was guarded by an iron fence and a tall, elaborately formed angel clothed in lichen. Redmon, his wife, Mary, and a son, Nathan, were the only occupants.

Next to the Love plot was a grave headed by a simple, engraved tablet, which he stopped to read.

> *A loved one from us has gone,*
> *A voice we love is stilled.*
> *A place is vacant in our home,*
> *Which never will be filled.*
>
> *Estelle Woodhouse, 1898–1987*

He took a deep breath and stroked the head of his good dog who sat contentedly at his feet.

All will be well and very well, he thought. He felt it surely.

Dear Father Kavanagh:

I have been baptized, confirmed, and married at St. John's.

I have served on the Altar Guild, sung in the choir, and taught Sunday School (except for the years I was away on the mainland, getting my schooling).

I have ushered, been secretary and treasurer of the ECW for five terms, read the propers each Sunday for seven years, and in 1975, headed the fund-raising drive for the complete restoration of our organ.

The only thing I haven't done in the Episcopal Church is attend my own funeral.

My point is that I know what I am talking about, and what I am talking about is all those people who refuse to do the things of the church with respect and dignity, wishing only to satisfy their whims and confuse our young people.

Would you agree, Father, that you do not list cars for sale in the pew bulletins? Would you agree that you do not switch back and forth from the 1928 prayer book to the 1979, willy-nilly and harum-scarum, on whatever notion happens to strike? Would you agree that holy communion is a time best savored and appreciated in quietude, rather than with the blare and clamor of every odd instrument conceivable, including the harmonica?

I earnestly hope and pray that Father Morgan's favorite instrument, the guitar, will not be making any surprise appearances during your term as interim.

It grieves me that you should come into such a jumble as we've created at St. John's, but Bishop Harvey guarantees that you are without a doubt the one to save us from ourselves.

I fervently hope you will not allow such behavior to continue, and will remind one and all in no uncertain terms how the venerable traditions of the church are to be properly maintained.

Respectfully yours,
Jean Ballenger

He couldn't help but chuckle. If that was the worst squabbling he'd face as interim, he'd be a happy man.

His wife could be heard puttering about in bare feet, humming snatches of tunes, and boiling water to make iced tea. He sat back in his chair and sighed, deciding that he liked this room very much.

Two club chairs, slipcovered in striped duckcloth, flanked a painted green table topped by a reading lamp.

An old parson's table stood against the facing wall, beneath framed watercolors of a country lane, a lake bordered by trees in autumn foliage, ducks on a pond, a small blue and red boat on the open sea, and an elderly man and woman at prayer over an evening meal. An oddly pleasing combination, he thought, nodding approval.

Their books would arrive on Monday, and he would go foraging for bricks and lumber straightaway. By Tuesday evening, if all went well, they would have bookcases in their sitting room, along the now-barren end wall.

The only doubt he entertained about the room was a print of the Roman Colosseum, which had faded, overall, to pale green.

He felt the weariness of recent days in his very bones. Thanks be to God, he wouldn't be preaching in the morning; however, on the following Sunday, it would be fish or cut bait.

He eyed the other letter, propped against the base of the lamp.

Dear Father,

Avery Plummer is a harlot.

Look up the true meaning of this word if you don't already know it which you probably do. Several months ago, she ran off with another woman's husband and God have mercy on the children in this mess, much less the church that helped them do it.

You ask how a church could help anybody commit a sin, and I say the church helps by seeing what is going on and turning its head the other way when certain steps might be taken that would solve the matter once and for all. Read Matthew 18 if you don't already know it which you probably do.

Somebody said that Jeffrey Tolson, our former choir director and the scoundrel that cares for nothing but himself, wants to come back to St. John's because it is where he grew up, and this is to let you know that if he ever sets foot in our narthex again my husband and I will be gone and so will a lot of other people. What this means is that more than half the annual church budget will walk straight out the door and never look back.

We are looking forward to meeting you at the luau at our home this evening.

Regards to you and Mrs. Kavanagh and I hope you have a successful time in Whitecap.

Yours truly,

Marlene Bragg

———

"Here's what you do," said Otis Bragg, waving his fork as he spoke. "If a hurricane's gonna hit, everybody shows up at th' church basement. Built like a oil tanker down there. Everybody in th' parish knows about it, we even got a little stash of canned goods and coffee."

"Thinking ahead," said Father Tim.

"We don't have coffee down there anymore," said Marjorie Lamb. "We ran out for the bishop's brunch last spring and had to use it."

Otis grinned. "Have t' bring your own, then." Otis Bragg was short, thickset, and balding, with a fondness for Cuban cigars. Father Tim noticed he didn't light the cigars, he chewed them.

They were sitting at picnic tables in the Braggs' backyard, behind a rambling house that looked more like a resort hotel than a residence. The water in the kidney-shaped pool danced and glinted in the sunlight.

Cynthia furrowed her brow. "Has a hurricane ever hit Whitecap?"

"You better believe it," said Otis. "*Whop*, got one in '72, *blam*, got a big 'un in '84."

"How bad?" she asked.

"Bad. Dumped my gravel trucks upside down, tore the roof off of my storage buildin's."

Leonard Lamb looked thoughtful. "I believe it was Hurricane Herman that took your roof off, but it was Darlene that set Sam Fieldwalker's RV in his neighbor's yard and creamed half the village."

"Nobody on Whitecap's had any kids named Herman or Darlene in a real long time," said Otis. "By th' way, I hear th' Love cottage over by where you're stayin' has a good basement; same thing at Redmon Love's old place. Hard to dig a good basement around here, but that part of the island's on a ridge just like St. John's. You have t' have a ridge to dig a basement."

Father Tim peered at his wife and knew it was definitely time to change the subject. "Do we get home mail delivery, by any chance?"

Otis helped his plate to more coleslaw and another slab of fresh barbecue. "You mountain people have it soft, Father, we have t' haul to th' post office over by QuikPik." Otis dumped hot sauce on the barbecue. "Th' mail usually comes in about two o'clock, just watch for th' sign they stick in th' window, says 'Mail In.' Course, if th' bridge is out, th' ferry runs it over."

"Is the bridge fixed yet?"

"Prob'ly, don't usually take long. It's one thing or another 'til a man could puke, either the rain causes a short, or the roadbed and bridge expand in th' heat, or the relay switch goes out. I remember th' good old days when my business didn't depend on anybody's bridge, we made our livin' right here."

"What's your business?"

"Commercial haulin'—gravel, sand, crushed oyster shell, you name it. Plus we offer ready-mix cement for all your concrete needs—be it residential or commercial."

"Aha!"

"Today, you've got a Bragg's on Whitecap and Manteo, not to mention five locations on th' mainland."

"Cornered the market!"

"You got it!" said Otis, flushing with pride.

Marlene Bragg was an intense woman with long, fuchsia nails, a serious tan, and a great mane of blond hair with dark roots.

"We're real glad to have you and your wife—and you brought your cool weather with you!"

Father Tim smiled at their hostess, who had just toured him through her home. "Actually," he said, "I believe I did feel a mountain breeze this morning!"

"It's usually awful hot this time of year."

"I've heard that," he said.

"But I know you'll love it on Whitecap, just like we do."

"Have you been on Whitecap long?"

"Seventeen years, we're from Morehead City. My husband has worked very hard, Father, to make a name for himself in this area." She pursed her mouth. "He's been mighty generous with the diocese, not to mention St. John's."

"I'm sure."

She smiled. "We'd like to keep it that way."

"I'm sure," he said. Too bad he'd just said that.

Jean Ballenger was a small woman with bangs that appeared plastered to her forehead. At the dessert table, she looked deeply into his eyes and pressed his hand.

"Thank you for your wise consideration of all the matters contained in my letter," she said.

"You're welcome," he replied.

"Who in the world is *this*?" asked Father Tim. A child who appeared to be around three years old was making a beeline toward him with no adult in hot pursuit.

"This is Jonathan Tolson!" said Marjorie Lamb, beaming.

Jonathan fell against Father Tim's legs and clasped them tight, gazing up as if they were old acquaintances.

He squatted and took the youngster's hands in his. "Hey, buddyroe!"

The blond toddler sucked his lower lip and gazed steadily at Father Tim with blue, inquisitive eyes. Then he turned and raced back the way he'd come.

"He just wanted to tell you hello," piped Marjorie, looking pleased as punch.

The message light on their answering machine was blinking.

"Hey," said Dooley. "I hate answerin' machines. I hope you got there OK. I mowed a yard after work and got fifteen dollars. Avis's truck is cool, it came today.

"Well . . ." Deep sigh. "Harley got the hornet nests down." Long pause. "I miss ol' Barnabas. Talk to you later. 'Bye."

Click. Beep.

"I heard there was a terrible storm down there," said Emma. "I hope it didn't blow you in a ditch. You hadn't hardly left town 'til Gene Bolick keeled over and they had to carry him to th' hospital. I called Esther and th' doctor said he's keepin' him awhile for tests."

Crackling sounds, as if Emma had her hand in a potato chip bag.

"I hear that young interim at Lord's Chapel has been passin' out *song sheets*, they're not even usin' a *book*, plus they say two or three people lifted up their hands while they were singin', I bet I can guess who." She snorted. "I hear your old choir director's lower lip is stuck out so far he could trip over it."

Emma crunched down on a couple of chips.

"I saw that woman tenant of yours the other day, she was scurryin' along like a mouse, oh, an' I saw Dooley at Avis's, he looks even better than when you're here, so don't worry about a thing."

Chewing and swallowing, followed by slurping through a straw.

"Snickers has ear mites, I hope Barnabas is doin' fine in all those sandspurs, I hope to th' Lord you'll check his paws on a regular basis."

Emma was running her straw around the bottom of the cup and sucking with great expectation, but not finding much. He turned the volume down on the answering machine.

"Oh, by th' way, Harold got a real raise, the first one in a hundred years, I wish th' post office would get its act together. Well, got to run, this is costin' a war pension."

Click. Beep.

"Timothy! Bill Harvey here. How do you like the pounding surf? I know you're going to love every minute with the fine people at St. John's. You'll be just what the doctor ordered. All they're looking for is Rite Two, a sermon that doesn't rock the boat, and a little trek across the bridge to Cap'n Willie's Sunday brunch.

"I'll be there on the eighth to plug you in. Barbara's not coming— the grandkids are here from Connecticut—she sends her regrets. I'll bunk in with Otis Bragg and Marlene, as usual.

"Well, listen, call me if you need me, you hear? And be sure and eat plenty of spot and pompano, they're probably running pretty good right now. But I wouldn't eat anything *fried* if I were you; broiled is how I like it, better for the heart. Oh, be sure and do right by Otis, now. He and Marlene are mighty generous donors, wouldn't want to lose *them*, ha ha. Well! Felicitations to your beautiful bride! See you on the eighth."

Click. Beep.

"Let's go find the beach," he said, after returning Dooley's call.

"Now?"

"It's only ten o'clock."

"Nearly everyone in Mitford is sound asleep," said his wife.

"This isn't Mitford." He put his arms around her and drew her close and nuzzled her hair.

"But I'm already in my nightgown."

"Wear it. Nobody's looking."

"And barefoot."

"Perfect," he said.

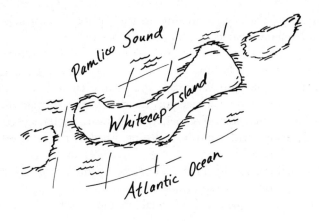

Pamlico Sound

Whitecap Island

Atlantic Ocean

CHAPTER SIX

The Long Shining

Whitecap Island loosely duplicated the shape of a Christmas stocking with a toe full of nuts and candy.

In the toe, Otis Bragg had stationed an extensive system of gravel, rock, and crushed oyster shell inventories, custom cement facilities, and sprawling hangars of grading and construction equipment.

In the heel, the lighthouse stood comfortably surrounded by a hedge of yaupons, an abandoned corral for wild ponies, and a small museum. The remainder of the island was chiefly comprised of high dunes, white beaches, canals and marshes, maritime forest, and a small village of homes, shops, inns, and restaurants, woven together by narrow lanes. The acreage on which St. John's in the Grove sat was located in the top of the stocking.

Increasingly, Whitecap attracted tourists from as far away as Canada and California, swelling the ranks of island churches every summer. While many churches on the mainland cranked down, the churches on Whitecap cranked up, both in numbers and activities.

Even so, a carefree sense of remoteness insinuated itself almost everywhere.

Sandy lanes wound under the heavy shade of live oaks, past summer cottages with picket fences and pleasantly unkempt yards.

Egrets could be seen standing in the marshes, as poised as garden statuary, their black eyes searching the reedy places from which alligators slithered onto banks and sunned themselves.

Early on, St. John's new interim learned that island culture made Mitford look like a beehive of cosmopolitan activity. Time seemed to pass more slowly on Whitecap, and then, even with a calendar, a watch, a phone, and a fax machine, the days began to blend into one another like watercolors. Wednesday might as easily have been Tuesday or Thursday, had it not been distinguished by the midweek celebration of Holy Eucharist.

Sam Fieldwalker chuckled. "This sort of thing soon passes," he said. "You're still in the honeymoon phase."

Father Tim laughed with his affable senior warden. "It all seems like a holiday, somehow, a vacation!"

"You've been going pretty hard, Father, I wouldn't call your first few weeks here a vacation. Truth is, I recommend you take a day off."

Sam looked at his watch. "Good gracious! Got to run by the *Reader* and hand in a story on the Fall Fair, then go across with Marion to the eye doctor and take my fax machine to be fixed. Hope I can get back in time for the planning meeting on the fair."

Even on a small, peaceful island, thought the new priest-in-charge, everybody was going at a trot.

"By the way," said Sam, "glad to hear you're working with Reverend Harmon. The Baptists sure do their part to make the fair the biggest event on the island. We raise a lot of money for needy people."

He went with Sam to the office door that led to the churchyard. "Speaking of needy people," said Father Tim, "I've been counseling Janette Tolson."

"Glad to hear it. When Jeff walked out, Janette didn't feel she could go to Father Morgan, because he was friendly with Jeff. She's gone through the worst of this thing with no priest to turn to."

"She's suffering badly, as you know."

"This has come against us all in a hard way. Not to mention how the choir has fallen into disarray."

Recently, their best tenor had stepped forward to direct the choir and, profoundly disliking such a wrinkle, the lead soprano had quit in disgust and was now teaching Sunday School.

"It'll come right." It was what his mother always said of a rotten situation. "The first thing we need to do is stop thinking of it as a performance choir, and be pleased with how well they lead the congregational singing."

Sam nodded. "Good point."

"You know we're auditioning an organist next week."

"I dislike the thought of a paid organist at St. John's. The Lord has always provided us with somebody in the congregation."

"It may be for the best, Sam. No ties to the church, no axe to grind . . . that's how we handled it at Lord's Chapel for the last few years, and it worked."

"Well, brother . . ."—Sam shook his hand—"hold down the fort while we're across. Oh, my goodness! I forgot the banana bread. I'll just run out to the car. Marion wouldn't be pleased if I come home with it still sliding around in the backseat."

Early on, Father Tim had learned that Marion Fieldwalker was right—the parish really did like to spoil their priests.

He and Cynthia had been treated to brunch at Cap'n Willie's every Sunday, and to dinner at Mona's Café with the Lambs and Fieldwalkers.

They'd received a bushel of hard crabs and clams from the Braggs, and were regularly inundated with bread still warm from parishioners' ovens, not to mention sacks of snap beans and tomatoes.

For performing a baptism, he'd been given a free-range chicken and a pound of butter from the Duncans' little farm, while a wedding ceremony he conducted under the oaks had swelled the Dove Cottage larders with a honey-baked ham.

Thank goodness he was running three days a week, and Cynthia was riding her Schwinn from the post office to the dry cleaner's to the grocery store. She might have been a tanned schoolgirl, wheeling along with carrot tops poking from the grocery sack in her bike basket.

The light on the answering machine blinked as he came in from a meeting with Stanley Harmon at Whitecap Baptist.

"Hey, this is Puny, how y'all doin'? Ever'thing's goin' jis' great up here, hope it's th' same with you. Th' girls wanted to say hey . . . Sissy, come back this minute, come back and say hey to Miss Cynthia and Ba!"

Sounds of small feet storming up the hall, amid shrieks and laughter.

"And there goes Sassy, oh, mercy! Hold on, y'all, 'scuse me. . . ."

Sounds of Puny chasing the girls into another room of her small house. "No, no! Put that down! Ba and Miss Cynthia are waitin' for you to say hey! Oh, Lord help, I can't believe this, come out from under there, Sissy!

"All right, then, I'll let *Sassy* say hey. What a good girl your *sister* is! Come here, Sassy."

Clattering noises along the hallway to the phone.

"Here, now *say hey* to Ba and Miss Cynthia."

Heavy breathing.

"You *wanted* to say hey, you *cried* to say hey . . . now *say hey*!" spluttered a frustrated Puny.

"Kitty?" said Sassy.

"Sassy, honey, stay right there and talk to Ba while I get Sissy! *Sissy!* I see what you're doin', get your hands out of th' toilet this minute!"

Bawling from the bathroom. Heavy breathing on the phone. Puny's footsteps hurrying along the hall.

"Did you say hey yet?"

"Dog!" said Sassy.

"Here, f'r pity's sake, give me th' phone. Well, y'all . . ."

Loud wailing. "Want to say hey! Want to say hey!"

"Not 'til you say somethin' else first," commanded Puny.

"Ple-e-ease!!!"

"All right, here's the phone, say hey and get it over with!"

Deep breath. "Hey, Ba!" Giggling.

"Now go find your cookie! Ba, I mean, Father, I saw your tenant yesterday, she was standin' on 'er tiptoes lookin' in your study window on th' hedge side. I guess I scared her half t' death. I wadn't supposed to go to your house yesterday, but I needed to take in your mail an' all. She said she was lookin' for her cat that run off, and just took a little peek in your window to see how nice it was, said she didn't think y'all'd mind. Well, anyway, Joe Joe says t' tell you hey, and Winnie at Sweet Stuff—

"Sissy, put th' mop down *this minute*! Oh, *law* . . ."

Click. Beep.

The next message was clearly from a dog, who was barking furiously.

"Hush *up*!" shouted Emma. "Go get your sock!

"I guess you know your phone call meant th' world to poor Esther.

I've never seen her like this, practically wringin' her hands, and she's not th' hand-wringin' type, but they still can't find out what's wrong with Gene. They're goin' to run more tests on Monday, you ought to see 'im, he looks bad to me, I hope you're prayin' is all I can say.

"Snickers! Get away from there! Snickers is tryin' to eat th' meat-loaf I just made! Oh, shoot, hold on a minute. . . ."

Growling, huffing, rattling of pots and pans.

"I had to set it on the counter, plus check my beans, I'm havin' string beans and . . . *go get your sock and lie down* . . . mashed potatoes with I Can't Believe It's Not Butter.

"Listen to this. Who just jumped in th' mayor's race against An-drew Gregory? You will *not* believe it. Three guesses! Call me and tell me who you think it is, OK? You will keel over.

"By th' way, I heard it's not even hot where y'all are, they say it's strange th' way th' weather's so cool at th' beaches this year. Oh, I just remembered you got a big box of somethin' from Florida at th' post office, I think somebody sent you grapefruit, do you want me to ship it down there or haul it home with me? Harold loves grapefruit, it would save payin' postage all th' way to that island you're on.

"Speakin' of Harold, here he comes, he does *not* like me talkin' on long-distance."

Click. Beep.

"Father? Otis Bragg here. Wanted to send you a little present by one of my boys. You like bourbon? Scotch? You name it. How 'bout a little Wild Turkey? Somebody said you like sherry, but I must've heard wrong.

"Call my secretary on th' mainland, two-eight-two-four, and let 'er know, OK?"

Click. Beep.

"Hmmm," said his wife, puzzling over who had jumped into Mit-ford's mayoral race.

"Lew Boyd!" he said. "That's who I'd guess. Either Lew or Mule Skinner. Mule's mentioned doing it for years."

Cynthia furrowed her brow. "Would *you* like to see Fancy Skinner as first lady of Mitford?"

"It might add a certain . . ." He was at a loss for words.

"I don't know, I don't have a clue," said his wife, who was usually up for guessing games.

"What do you think about . . . no, no way . . . let's see . . ."

"Or maybe . . . ," said Cynthia, pondering deeply.

"Then again . . . but I don't think so."

"Oh, poop! If you don't call Emma back, I will!"

They raced into the sitting room and took their chairs. He dialed Emma's number.

"Who?" he inquired, when she answered the phone.

"Is this an owl?" asked Emma.

"I guess Lew Boyd!"

"Two more guesses."

He hated that she always made him do three guesses.

"Mule Skinner!"

"Wrong."

"J. C. Hogan!" shouted Cynthia, in a burst of supernatural insight.

"Is it J.C.?" asked Father Tim.

"Are you sittin' down?" inquired his erstwhile secretary.

"We are. Get on with it."

"Coot Hendrick!"

"Coot Hendrick?"

"He says his great-grandaddy founded th' whole town, and it's time he did something that carries on th' family tradition."

"I'll be darned."

"I personally couldn't vote for anybody who has stubs for teeth, but he says he's goin' to work hard to win."

"It's just as well we aren't there. I don't think I could go through another mayor's race," he said, still not fully over the last one.

While he cooked dinner, his wife sat in the kitchen window seat, looking out but not seeing. She was busy twisting a strand of hair around one finger and humming.

He didn't have to be as wise as Solomon to know that every time she got that glazed-over look and twisted her hair and hummed, something was up.

The fresh croaker sizzled in the skillet. "Cynthia?"

No reply. Still humming.

Blast. She definitely had that conjuring-up-a-book look. All of which meant she would soon stop riding her bicycle and lash herself to the drawing board for months on end, getting a crick in her neck and feeling grumpy. When people did what they profess to absolutely love, why didn't they smile and laugh and be carefree and upbeat?

Salt, pepper, a spritz of lemon . . .

Another book would mean this whole beach experience, which might have been relaxing for his overworked wife, would, in fact, be just another nose-to-the-grindstone deal. . . .

"Timothy," she said, "I've been thinking."

He sighed and flipped the croaker, without breaking it apart. He was getting good at this.

"You know how lovely everyone's been to us," she said.

"They have."

"How they've loved us. . . ."

"Right."

"We must do something that loves them back."

"Aha."

She turned to face him, looking fierce. "But *not* a Primrose Tea!" His wife had worked her fingers to the very bone doing two enormous and successful Primrose Teas in Mitford.

"I don't think there's a primrose within two hundred miles of here."

"Absolutely, *positively* not a Primrose Tea!" she said.

"I *hear* you, Kavanagh!"

"It's killing, you know."

"No Primrose Tea."

"Anyway, I'm not sure beach people *drink* tea. Hot tea, I mean, to go with things like scones or shortbread."

"I never thought much about it."

"It seems beach people would be more interested in . . . something *cold*, like lemonade, or a lovely punch with an ice ring of lime sherbet . . . and maybe lots of fresh fruit in a vast, icy watermelon carved with its own handle, to which we could attach a bouquet of flowers from our little garden. . . ."

"There you go!" Out of the pan, onto the plate, and done to perfection.

"And a beautiful cake, three or four layers with white icing—and wedding cookies, don't you think? Except they're so messy, all that powdered sugar falling on your shoes . . ."

"My mouth is watering." He spooned new potatoes onto the dinner plates, cheek by jowl with the fish. Now a dollop of butter, a sprinkle of fresh parsley . . .

"I think we should have everyone here, not at the parish hall," she said. "Parishioners like seeing how their priest lives."

"I'll help. You can count on me."

. . . and a dash of paprika, for color. He felt like a heel for thinking his wife was plotting to write a new book and get a crick in her neck when she was, in fact, intent on doing something exceedingly generous for others. Thank goodness he hadn't opened his big mouth and put his foot in it.

"And I'll probably try something wonderful with peaches, too, I don't know what yet, maybe tarts, very small like this." She made a circle with her thumb and forefinger. "I hear the peaches are lovely this year!"

"Dinner is served," he announced, setting the plates on the table. "Come and get it."

She stared at the plates with surprise. "You *angel*!" She apparently hadn't noticed he was making dinner. "Croaker! And new potatoes and fresh asparagus! Oh, Timothy, I'm so glad you can cook."

"I'm even gladder that you can cook. You have kitchen duty for the next four evenings, I hope you recall."

"Four? Why four?"

"Meetings," he said "Choir practice. The Whitecap Fair Planning Commission. The vestry . . ."

"Umm," she said.

"Umm what?"

"Well, dearest, I've been thinking that maybe . . ."

"Yes?"

"It's so beautiful here, and so liberating, even Violet loves it, have you noticed?"

"I have."

She looked at him in that way he could never resist, with her head tilted slightly to one side and her sapphire eyes gleaming. "I thought I might begin right away . . . working on a new book."

"Let's bow in prayer," he said.

He dialed a number he easily remembered by heart.

"Esther? Is that you?" Esther Bolick didn't sound like herself.

"What's *left* of me."

His heart ached for his old friends; worse, he felt guilty that he wasn't there to go the mile with them.

"How's Gene?"

"Not good." He heard Esther sigh. He couldn't bear it when Esther sighed; Esther was not a sigher, she was a doer.

"We're praying," he said, "and believing Gene's going to be well and strong again. Now tell me about you, Esther, how're *you* doing?"

"I went yesterday to pick out my casket."

"You *what*?"

"It had to be done sometime. All this with Gene reminded me."

"Do you think this is the right time, I mean . . . ?"

"When Louise Parker went to Wesley to pick hers out, Reverend Sprouse went with her."

"Aha."

"There was nobody to go with me."

He felt very uncomfortable. It was the guilt again. "What about your interim? Couldn't he go?"

"Father Hayden? Lord *help*! He's so wet behind the ears, he's still on strained peas and applesauce!"

Father Hayden was forty-five if he was a day. "So what did you pick?" Might as well be upbeat about it.

"Do you know it costs four thousand dollars to get buried in Mitford? Can you believe it? I was goin' to be cremated, but there's nothin' to look at in a jar. I remember when we buried Mama, it was a *comfort* to see her in th' casket."

"Closure," he said.

"So I picked somethin' with a nice iv'ry satin lining. I always looked good in iv'ry."

"I seem to recall that." He honestly did.

"Then you think you're through with th' whole mess, and what happens?"

"What?" He was interested.

"They want to sell you a *liner*! Some bloomin' metal thing you drop th' casket down in, to keep it protected from *dirt*." Esther snorted.

Miss Sadie had been very upset about liners, he remembered.

"Anyway, so I got th' dadblame thing, and now it's all taken care of and if I kick before Gene, everything's done, he can put his feet up! I even filled th' freezer in case I go first."

He didn't like this at all. Clearly, Esther was in denial about Gene's uncertain future; to avoid thinking of his, she was concentrating on her own.

"Lasagna, chicken divan, squash casserole—"

"Esther . . ."

"There's only only one problem," said his former parishioner.

"What's that?"

"I can't decide what to be buried in. Mama had her outfit hangin' in th' closet, ready to go, even panty hose. Course, it hung there so long, th' dress rotted off th' hanger and we had to dive in and come up with another outfit at th' last minute."

"Umhmm."

"So yesterday, Hessie came over and helped me go through th' closet. I laid out my royal blue suit, do you remember my royal blue suit?"

"I think so." He really did think so.

"But Hessie says it's too plain. So I laid out my pink dress with the chiffon sleeves. Do you remember my pink dress with the chiffon sleeves?"

"Ah . . . let's see . . ."

"I wore it to Fancy and Mule's anniversary party in their basement. It's Gene's favorite."

"Right." He felt like dropping onto the floor prostrate, and giving up the ghost.

"Well, that's what we finally decided on. But after Hessie left, it hit me—what if I die in th' winter?"

He hesitated. "I don't understand."

Esther sighed heavily, "Pink is a *summer* color!"

He gave her what was his only word of wisdom in the entire conversation.

"I recommend you surrender all this to the Lord, Esther. He'll be glad to take care of everything when the time comes."

She kissed him goodbye, one of those lingering kisses that he feared might come to a grinding halt when her book began. Seizing the moment, he kissed her back.

"Darling," she said, brushing his face with the tips of her fingers, "I think you need to take a day off."

"Why? We just got here!"

"We just got here six weeks ago, and you've been working nonstop. I mean, racing across to the hospital twice a week, and teaching adult Sunday School, and setting up the men's fall prayer breakfast, and working with Reverend Harmon . . ."

"But it all seems like a vacation, somehow."

"Trust me. You need to take a day off." She kissed him again, drawing him close in that protective way she sometimes had of making him feel both a man and a child.

He sighed. "I can't do it today."

"Rats!"

"But maybe tomorrow. . . ."

"I'll count on it, dearest."

Headed for St. John's, he ran down the steps of the cottage with Barnabas on the red leash.

Another glorious day! If they ever had to pay a price for the ambrosial weather they continually enjoyed, he shuddered to think how steep the cost might be.

Taking out his pocketknife, he stopped at their bed of cosmos and cut several stems for his office bookshelf.

Glory! He gazed at the cumulus clouds scudding overhead, and took a deep breath. The flowers, the everlasting gulls, the patch of blue beyond the dunes—it hit a man in the solar plexus, between the eyes, in the soul.

It was vastly different, this place, from the protected feeling he had in the mountains. There, summer was one long green embrace. Here, it was one long shining, and the sense of endless freedom.

Barnabas suddenly growled, then barked.

Father Tim glanced around for a stray dog or someone walking by. Nothing.

He quickly snipped two more blooms and put the small bouquet in his shirt pocket.

Trotting through the gate and into the narrow lane, he had the strange sense that someone was watching him. He turned to see if Cynthia might be standing on the porch, but she was not.

His parishioners had given him an earful about the uncaring, self-centered, musically gifted choir director who had abandoned his wife and children for St. John's married organist. Speaking of Jeffrey Tolson, a parishioner had quoted John Ruskin: "When a man's wrapped up in himself, he makes a pretty small package."

He had frequently prayed for Jeffrey Tolson, but was unable to dismiss the hardness of heart he often felt when doing it. And, though he'd never laid eyes on St. John's former choir director, he knew precisely who it was when the tall, blond Scandanavian walked into the church office from the side door.

"Jeffrey Tolson," said his caller. He stood by the desk, arms crossed.

He couldn't help but notice that his caller wore leather clogs, and a full-sleeved white shirt in the manner of eighteenth-century poets.

"Jeffrey." *Lord, give me the words, the wisdom, the heart for this, Your will be done. . . .*

"I won't take much of your time."

He wanted to say, *My time is yours,* but could not. It was what he always liked to say to parishioners, no matter what the time constraints.

Jeffrey Tolson removed his billfold from a rear pocket. "I'm back in Whitecap for a few days. I wanted Janette to have this." He withdrew a hundred-dollar bill and handed it to Father Tim.

"You can't give it to her yourself?"

"She's in no mood to deal with me."

He looked at the money and had a fleeting vision of punching Jeffrey Tolson in the nose—squarely, no holds barred. Gone eight months and this was the only offering?

"I'll see that she gets it."

"I know you think hard of me, most people do. But Janette was no angel to live with. Moody, depressed, demanding. I'm a sensitive man, Father. It was like living with a wet blanket."

"How was it living with those children of yours?"

Jeffrey Tolson's face was suddenly hard. "Don't preach to me."

"Far from it, Mr. Tolson."

His heart was pounding, his mouth dry as he stood facing the man who had brought hurt and anger into the midst of St. John's.

Jeffrey Tolson turned and stomped from the office. He jerked open the door to the outside steps, then slammed it behind him.

He awoke to find Barnabas standing by the bed, his black nose barely an inch from his face.

"Don't let him kid you, Timothy, I've already taken him out to the garden."

He rolled over and put his arm around his wife.

A day off! He'd have to swallow down the guilt before he could get up and enjoy it.

"Timothy . . ." He knew that tone of voice; she could read him like a book.

"Umm?"

"I hear your wheels turning already, clickety-clack! You're going over all the things you should be doing today at church."

"Right. You see, we're working with Marion and her staff to organize and catalog St. John's library, which means—"

"I'm hoping you'll rent a bike and go riding with me today."

Barnabas licked him on the ear and wagged his tail, urgent. His dog was never completely satisfied with Cynthia's idea of a morning constitutional.

"But first," she said, "I think you should walk down to Ernie's after morning prayer and look over his books. You've been wanting to do it ever since we came."

"Ernie's . . . I don't know."

"It's six-thirty. You could have breakfast at Mona's and maybe read the paper like you used to do at the Grill . . ."

He *had* missed that sort of thing.

". . . then, meet me back here at nine and we'll go to Mike's Bikes and—"

"I thought I'd make your breakfast," he said.

"You're always looking for something to do for someone." She stroked his cheek. "It might be good if you spent a little time doing . . . whatever it is that men do."

What did men do? He'd never figured it out.

He yawned. "The next thing I know, you'll be packing me off for a day of deep-sea fishing."

She looked at him and burst into laughter. "How did you guess? I can't *believe* it! I just bought you a ticket on Captain Willie's charter boat!"

CHAPTER SEVEN

A Little Night Music

At seven a.m., the day was already sultry; forecasts were for ninety-nine degrees by noon.

He broke a sweat before he reached Mona's, where he found Ernie paying for a sausage biscuit and a cup of coffee at his wife's cash register.

"I'm only allowed over th' yellow line as a payin' customer," said the genial proprietor from next door. "Get your order and come over to my side—chew th' fat awhile."

"Well . . . ," he said, pleased to be asked, "don't mind if I do."

"That'll be two bucks." Mona extended her hand to her husband, who shelled out the tab, mostly in change.

"I'll have what he's having," said Father Tim.

The red-haired Mona had a no-nonsense look behind a pair of glasses with brightly painted frames. "So you're hangin' with the guys this mornin'?"

He nodded, feeling suddenly shy and excited about having someone to hang with.

"They get too rough for you," said Mona, "come on back to where it's civilized."

"Right," he said.

"This yellow line . . . ," said Father Tim, stepping over it, "it must be a real conversation piece."

"Thing was, Mona kept nosin' around my side sayin' old books wouldn't pay th' light bill. Then I'd go over to her side raisin' Cain because she hadn't hiked her prices in four years. We nearly ended up in divorce court."

"Aha."

"We had to learn to mind our own business, you might say. Thing is, I've come to believe all married people ought t' have a yellow line of some kind or another."

Ernie held the screen door open to Books, Bait & Tackle.

"Welcome to where th' elite meet to eat. Boys, watch your language, Preacher Kavanagh's goin' to join us this mornin'."

"Tim," said the preacher, nodding to the assembly. "Call me Tim."

Ernie set his bag on one of the scarred tables by the drink machines. "You remember Roanoke, he don't much like preachers. But he's harmless."

Roanoke nodded curtly and poured a packet of sugar into a Styrofoam cup.

"That's Roger Templeton over there, an' his dog, Lucas. Lucas is blind. Roger's his Seein' Eye human."

"Tim, nice to meet you," said Roger, who was holding what appeared to be a block of wood in his lap. Roger was a tall, slender man, probably in his sixties, with a pleasant face. The filmy eyes of his brown Labrador appeared to rest on the newcomer with some interest.

"Set your sack down," said Ernie, "and pull up a chair. It's not fancy, but it's all we got. Junior, come out here and meet Preacher Kavanagh."

A sandy-haired, bearded young man came through the door of the book room. He wiped his hand on his work pants and extended it with solemn courtesy.

"How you do, sir, glad to meet you."

"Glad to meet you, Junior."

"Junior's off work today, he hauls for Otis Bragg. You know Otis, I reckon."

"Oh, yes. Otis is a member at St. John's."

Roanoke snorted.

Ernie launched into his sausage biscuit with considerable gusto. "Well, boys, we got a lot of work to do to get Junior's ad in before th' deadline. Tim, we're glad you're here, because you're an educated man and know how to put things. Course, Roger's pretty educated hisself. He was runnin' a billion-dollar corporation before him and his wife retired to Whitecap."

Roger smiled as he deftly used a pencil to make marks on the block of wood. "Half a billion."

"Don't sound as good to say half a billion." Ernie gulped his coffee. "Junior, you got your notepad?"

"Right here," said Junior. He removed a ballpoint pen and notepad from his shirt pocket, which was machine-embroidered with the name *Junior Bryson*.

"What's your ad about?" asked Father Tim.

Junior looked at Ernie.

"*You* tell 'im." Ernie said to Junior.

"Well, sir, I'm tryin' to find a wife." Junior's face colored.

"Aha."

"So, me an' Roanoke an' Ernie an' Roger come up with this idea to advertise."

"That's been known to work," said Father Tim, unwrapping his sausage biscuit.

"We recommended advertising off the island," said Roger.

"Right," said Ernie. "Everybody on Whitecap knows Junior, and he knows everybody."

"Does that mean there aren't any candidates on Whitecap?"

"Not to speak of," said Ernie. "Besides, our advice is, get a woman you have to go *across* to see, makes it more . . . more . . ."

"Romantic," said Roger.

Junior beamed and nodded.

"If I was you," said Roanoke, "I'd run me a big ad with a border around it." He drew a cigarette from a pack of Marlboros in his shirt pocket.

"That'd cost more," said Ernie.

Roanoke struck a match. "Might be worth more."

"Read what you have so far," said Roger.

"White male, thirty-six, five foot eleven an' a half . . ."

Roanoke sipped his coffee. "I'd say six foot."

"Right," said Ernie. "Sounds better."

"That'd be a lie," said Junior.

"Put a lift in your shoes," said Roanoke.

"I ain't goin' to lie. Five foot eleven an' a half with kep' beard—"

Ernie shook his head. "I wouldn't mention a beard. Some women don't like face hair a'tall."

"Might as well git things out in th' open," said Junior.

"Keep readin'," said Roanoke.

"Five foot eleven an' a half with kep' beard, likes country music, fishin', and Scrabble, drives late-model Bronco."

Roanoke leaned forward. "What'd you say Scrabble for? You ought t' say poker or gin rummy."

Ernie frowned. "It's th' Bronco I wouldn't say anything about. I'd say more like a . . . like a . . ."

"A Mustang convertible!" suggested Roanoke, unsmiling. "Maybe you could borry the preacher's car."

"Yessir," said Junior, grinning. "I've seen your car around, it's a real sharp ride."

"Thank you."

"We got to hurry up," said Ernie, checking his watch. "If this is goin' to run in th' *Diplomat,* Junior's got t' call it across in thirty minutes."

"Read it again," said Roanoke. He wadded up his biscuit wrapper and lobbed it into a box beside the Pepsi machine.

Junior cleared his throat and ran a hand through his thinning hair. "White male, thirty-six, five foot eleven an' a half with kep' beard, likes country music, fishin', and Scrabble, drives late-model Bronco . . . plus, I'm addin' this . . . lookin' for serious relationship, send photo."

"I wouldn't put nothin' in there about a serious relationship," said Roanoke. "That'll scare 'em off."

Junior gazed helplessly at his advisors. Then he zeroed in on Father Tim. "What do *you* think, sir?"

In truth, he'd hardly been thinking at all. "Well . . ."

Junior's pen was poised above the notepad.

"Actually, I like your idea about getting things out in the open."

Junior nodded, looking relieved. "Well, good! It's wrote, then."

The sweat was trickling down his back as he made a quick sweep through the book room, finding a ragged copy of Conrad Richter's *The Trees.* He knew he'd never read it again, but he recalled his early fondness for it with such reverence that he couldn't resist. Especially not for fifty cents.

He found a cat asleep in one of the numerous book-filled boxes stationed around the room, and nearly leaped out of his running shorts when it sprang up and hissed at him.

"That's Elmo th' Book Cat," said Ernie, standing in the doorway. "He's older'n dirt. That's his sleepin' box, it's full of Zane Grey paperbacks. You ever read Zane Grey?"

"Tried," he said, his eyes roving the shelves. "Couldn't."

"Ever read Louis L'Amour?"

"Never have."

"That's my main man. Listen to this." Ernie grabbed a book off the shelf, thumbed through the pages, and adjusted his glasses.

" 'We are, finally, all wanderers in search of knowledge. Most of us hold the dream of becoming something better than we are, something larger, richer, in some way more important to the world and ourselves. Too often, the way taken is the wrong way, with too much emphasis on what we want to have, rather than what we wish to become.' "

Ernie looked up. "A world of truth in that."

Father Tim nodded. "I'll say."

"This is his autobiography. Looky here." Ernie turned to the back of the book and displayed a long list. "That's some of th' books he read. He read thousands of books and kep' account of every one. Plus he traveled and wandered all over th' world an', with no education to speak of, turned around an' wrote hundreds of books his own self."

Ernie scratched his head. "I guess if I could, I'd just read books and not strike a lick at a snake."

"Sounds good to me!"

The proprietor took a paperback off the shelf. "Here you go, I'm givin' this to you. Take it an' read it, and tell me what you think."

"I'll do it."

"To my way of thinkin', *Last of the Breed* was L'Amour's best book, and if it don't keep you on th' edge of your pew, nothin' will."

"I thank you, Ernie. Thank you!"

"I take you for a big reader, yourself."

"I guess you could say Wordsworth is my main man."

"Wordsworth, Wordsworth . . . ," said Ernie, trying to place the name.

"I'll bring you something, see what you think."

"Good deal," said Ernie, looking pleased.

At the cash register, Father Tim fetched a dollar and change out of his shorts pocket for the Richter book and the eight-page *Whitecap Reader.*

"Seen your neighbor yet?" asked Ernie. "Guess I ought to say heard 'im, is more like it."

"What neighbor is that?"

"Th' one behind th' hedge."

"Didn't know there was one behind the hedge."

"You didn't?" Ernie looked incredulous.

"Should I have?"

"Seems like somebody would've told you."

He waited for Ernie to elaborate, but he didn't. "Maybe you could tell me."

"Well . . . it's what's left of th' Love family, is what it is."

He thought Ernie looked pained, as if regretting that he'd introduced the subject.

"Aha."

"See, there was a whole clan of Loves at one time. Redmon Love, th' grandaddy, bought that big trac' of land up th' road where you are, built him a fine home in there and put a wall around it. Then planted a hedge both sides of th' wall. It's grown up like a jungle th' last twenty years or so."

Father Tim looked at his watch. If he was going to ride bikes this morning, not to mention walk his dog, he'd better get a move on.

"Th' Love house was th' finest thing on any of these islands, a real mansion, but you can't see it's back there 'less you're lookin' for it."

"I'll be darned."

"Mr. Redmon had somebody come in from upstate New York and make him a tropical garden, had palm trees and monkeys an' I don't know what all."

"Monkeys?"

"Well, there ain't any monkeys in there now, but used to be. I used to hear 'em when I was a kid." Ernie paused and gave a loud rendition of what, it might be supposed, was the call of a monkey.

"Like that," said Ernie.

Father Tim nodded, impressed.

"Used to be macaws in there, too, an' some said elephants, but I never went for that."

"Pretty far-fetched," agreed Father Tim, rolling up his newspaper and putting it under his arm.

"Anyway, th' whole clan built around th' mansion. You're livin' up from th' place his second grandson used 'til, oh, I don't know, maybe two or three years ago, then they pretty much stopped comin'.'"

"Right. So who lives behind the wall?"

Ernie looked at him soberly. "I wouldn't say nothin' to your wife."

"Really?"

"No use to make 'er worry."

"*Who?*"

The screen door slammed behind two fisherman. While one examined sinkers and knives, the other ordered bait.

"We need a half pound of shrimp, a dozen bloodworms, and a pound of squid. Better make that a pound and a half."

"Catch you later, Tim," said Ernie. "Come again anytime, you hear?"

———— ⌒⊙⌒ ————

He dropped by St. John's to see how the organization of the church library was developing. Marion Fieldwalker and her volunteers were cataloging, dusting, shelving, and generally making sense of books that had been stacked in a room off the narthex since the time of the early prophets. He cheered them on and made a pot of coffee as his contribution to the effort.

There was no reason at all, of course, for his wife to know he'd taken this little detour. . . .

He was zooming by his desk as the phone rang.

"Hello?"

"Hey!" said Dooley.

"Hey, yourself, buddy! What's going on?"

"The Reds whipped th' poop out of th' Blues last night!"

"Hallelujah! Tell me everything!" He thumped into his groaning swivel chair and leaned back.

"You should of seen ol' Mule, he come t' bat four times with runners on base, got a base hit ever' time!"

Ah, it was music to his ears when Dooley lapsed into the old vernacular.

"I scored four runs on 'is hits. We whipped 'em by seven runs."

"Man alive!" he said, rejoicing with his boy. "Well done!"

"Waxin' th' Blues was great, we cleaned their plows. You should of been there."

He should have, it was true. "Good crowd?"

"Ever'body, nearly. Ol' Coot Hendrick, he was there shakin' hands like he was President of the United States. Ol' Mayor Cunningham, she threw out th' first ball."

"How are Poo and Jessie and your mom?"

"Great. I had supper with 'em Saturday. Poo's gettin' really tall, Jessie's quit suckin' her thumb."

"Have you seen Lace?"

Silence. "A couple of times."

"Really? You took her to a movie?"

"Are you kidding? She hardly looks at me. Anyway, she's not allowed to go out with guys 'til next year. She's still fifteen."

"Aha." He noted that Dooley's speech had returned to the prep school mode.

"But I saw her with some friends a couple of times, like when I took Jenny to a movie."

He rubbed his chin and frowned. That wouldn't have been his agenda for Dooley's summer, but who was he to judge? Jenny was their pretty, soft-spoken neighbor who'd regularly come looking for Dooley, knocking on the back door year after year, summer after summer. What if his own neighbor, his very wife, had not come knocking on the rectory door?

"Is Lace still tutoring Harley?"

"She comes when I'm working, she gave him A-plus on something. I don't know what it was, but he was pretty excited, I think it was math."

"Are you ready to go back to school?"

"I don't want to go back."

"If you're going to be a vet, you have to go to school," he said, stating the obvious.

"Yeah, right. So I'm goin' back, but I'd rather stay home."

"You've got eight days, make the most of it. As we discussed, the Barnhardts will swing by with Joseph to return you to academe."

"*Where?*"

"By the way, Harley says you're doing great with your curfew."

"He said he'd whip my tail if I messed up." Dooley cackled. The thought of the thin, toothless Harley whipping him was clearly a great amusement.

"What are you guys eating these days?"

"Harley made pizza last night, it was great."

"With everything?" He loved the details.

"No anchovies, no onions, tons of sausage and cheese. He could get a franchise."

"How's our tenant?"

"She asked me twice if I'd show her your house, said she wanted to see what y'all did, the addition and all. I said maybe when you come in October, you'd show it to her. Why would she care anything about the addition? She's not going to do one."

"I have no idea."

"Anyway, I think Lace is taking lessons over there before she goes off to school, she leaves in a week. She'll hate that school."

"Please. Keep your opinions on that school to yourself."

"I promise you those girls are weird. They write and draw and read and wear totally weird clothes like lace-up shoes and glasses with wire rims. I mean, they can't even dance, they step all over you."

"How's your bank account?"

"Huge."

"How huge?"

"I made six hundred dollars so far."

"I owe you six to match it, that makes twelve, what's the total?"

"With what I saved last year, that makes seventeen hundred, even."

"You can buy a sharp little ride for what you'll have by the end of summer."

"I don't want an old car, I told you over and over."

"We'll both be old as the hills if we wait 'til you earn enough for a new one."

Dooley sighed.

"Look," he said, feeling guilty, repressed, and prehistoric. "Cynthia and I will kick in another five hundred, that brings you up to twenty-two hundred."

"Thanks! Hey, really! Thanks, Dad."

"You're welcome. Now stay out of trouble."

"I'm stayin' out."

"Good. Well done. If we're still here, you're going to love this place next summer."

"Why?"

"Sand. Water. Girls. Shrimp and hush puppies. I don't know, good stuff."

"And I'll have a car."

"You'll have a car. Right."

"Look, I've got to go."

"Tell Harley hello."

"I miss ol' Barnabas. Tell Cynthia hey, is she OK?"

"She misses you, she looks great, she has a tan and a half."

"Well, I got to go."

"Love you, buddy."

"Love you back."

He sat for a moment at the desk, nodding to himself and smiling. He was proud of that boy. Though there was only about sixty thousand left of the inheritance from his mother, he should have kicked in an extra hundred.

Hot. Hotter than hot.

He walked into Dove Cottage, thankful for the fan whirring in the living room, and was greeted by his dog bounding down the hallway, pursued by a youngster.

"Look who's here!" he said.

"Jon'than!" said Jonathan Tolson.

Cynthia appeared from the kitchen. "Jonathan's come to spend the day with us. I didn't think you'd mind having company. We can go bike riding Saturday."

"Right!"

"Your dog," said Jonathan, hugging Barnabas around the neck. "My dog."

"Right. Any dog of mine is a dog of yours." He squatted down and met the blue-eyed gaze of their blond-haired visitor.

"I went to visit Jonathan's mommy this morning and she wasn't feeling well, so . . ." Cynthia lifted her palms, smiling.

"So, we'll have an adventure," said Father Tim. "We'll take a walk on the beach, then we'll go eat hotdogs, and ice cream after. How's that?"

"Not hotdogs," said Jonathan, wrinkling his nose.

"Pizza, then! Or french fries. I'm easy."

Jonathan nodded eagerly, his curls bobbing. "French fries."

"You're lots more fun with kids around," announced his wife.

"Your big dog can go?" asked Jonathan.

"Absolutely. He loves ice cream."

Cynthia took her husband's hand and pulled him along the hall to the kitchen.

"Janette's terribly depressed," she said in a low voice. "She doesn't want to get out of bed. I went to check on her this morning—I'm not sure Jonathan had been fed recently. He just devoured a whole plate of cheese and crackers, thank heaven I had milk. . . ."

"What about the other children?"

"Gone across to cousins. She said they didn't have room for Jonathan. Apparently, Janette hasn't been working for some time. She takes in sewing, you know."

"Dear Lord," he murmured. He'd recommended medical help for Janette Tolson, but she refused, assuring him she'd be fine. He'd seen the emptiness in her gaze, heard it in her voice, and knew she was in trouble.

"I'll be back," he said, kissing his wife.

"The children . . . ," he said, sitting by Janette's bed.

"I don't . . . care," she whispered.

He remembered Miss Sadie talking about her love for Willard Porter, about caring so much for so long that all caring was at last exhausted.

"God cares. He's with you in this."

She turned her head slowly and looked at him, disbelieving.

He put his right palm on her damp forehead. He remembered his mother's cool hand on his forehead when he was sick, and how much that simple gesture had counted to him.

"I promise," he told her.

She closed her eyes and the tears seeped from under her lashes.

The average view of the Christian life, Oswald Chambers had said, is that it means deliverance from trouble. Father Tim agreed with Chambers that, in fact, it means deliverance *in* trouble. That alone and nothing more, and nothing more required. But the child of God had to face the strain before the strength could be provided. Janette Tolson could not face the strain.

"Let me pray for you," he said.

He kept his palm against her forehead, and with his other hand, held hers.

"I *not* stay," said Jonathan, frowning.

"We'll have pancakes for breakfast," he implored. It was a lame strategy, but the best he could do.

Jonathan shook his head and stomped one foot. "*No!* I want to go *home.*"

"In the shape of ducks!"

"*No.*"

"Babette and Jason are having fun with cousins. Don't you want to spend the night and have fun with Barnabas?"

They couldn't take him home; his mother was in no condition to look after him. He had called Jean Ballenger, who, eager to please her new priest, had agreed to spend the night with Janette. Tomorrow, following the counsel of Hoppy Harper, he would talk with Janette's own doctor, whom she had avoided for months, and take Janette across to the hospital. He dreaded the prospect.

He looked to his wife, who, of all people, should be able to come up with something to entice a three-year-old.

"I don't know how to get little boys to spend the night in a strange house," she said.

Jonathan's eyes were filling with tears.

Hand shadows! He suddenly recalled a family friend in Holly Springs who had kept him engrossed for hours with a kerosene lamp, a bare wall, and two dexterous hands.

"Turn off the lights in the study," he said, feeling desperate.

"Whatever for?"

"Trust me."

"I want to go *home*!" said Jonathan, meaning it.

"Light the big candle in the hurricane globe," he said. Scalpel, sutures . . . "Put it on the table between our chairs."

Cynthia looked at him as if he'd lost his mind and hurried off to the study.

"Movies!" he said to Jonathan. "Picture show!" He thought he could make a dog. At least a pig. He was certain he could make an eagle; he'd made one on his study wall in Mitford only months ago.

"Popcorn?" asked the boy.

"Now you're talking! Cynthia!" he shouted. "Popcorn, and plenty of butter!"

Cynthia appeared from the study.

"Turn off the lights, light the candle, popcorn with plenty of butter . . . where's the division of labor so popular in modern marriage?"

"My dear, I am the *entertainment*, I can't do it all, this takes teamwork!"

"My mommy, my mommy makes popcorn!" said Jonathan, running behind Cynthia to the kitchen.

Lying awake after midnight, he felt the humidity weighing upon them like a blanket. He also felt what he'd dismissed for weeks:

He was homesick.

He was homesick for Mitford and his boy and Harley, for all the countless components that made his mountain village home.

Whitecap had its charms, of course. There was a great deal to be said for the smaller parish, not to mention the general ease induced by sunshine, salt air, and surf. In times past, hadn't doctors prescribed the seashore as a cure-all for nearly anything that ailed?

But he wasn't ailing, and he didn't need curing.

He believed he was making progress in putting the parish into less quarrelsome order. Several rifts had been healed, and he had ignored the petty issues that, he wasn't surprised, were fading away for want of being nursed.

Better still, he saw his wife finding some repose and freedom of spirit after years of toiling like a Trojan. Yes, she'd begun the new book, but overall, he saw her rested, tanned, and vibrant, and flourishing like a kid at summer camp.

Last and certainly not least, St. John's had fallen in love with Cynthia Kavanagh and freely said as much. She stood with him in the churchyard every Sunday after services, giving and receiving handshakes and hugs, and serving in several parish trenches, including the nursery, like paid help.

"But I love doing it!" she'd said only last week, when he thanked her again.

"What don't you love?" he asked.

"Fading eyesight, creeping forgetfulness, and . . . and calendars with no room to enter all the day's events!"

His wife could derail a train of thought in a heartbeat, jump to another track, and run on it with all engines smoking.

Hot.

He drew the sheet off, eased out of bed, and walked down the hall, floorboards creaking.

In the living room, Barnabas left his blanket in the corner and stretched, then came and stood with him at the screen door, looking into the moon-silvered night.

He unlatched the screen and stepped onto the porch. The full moon cast its image on the distant patch of water.

The sight of two moons, voluptuous and shimmering between two sleeping cottages, caused him to shiver in the heat.

What a different world, this immense expanse of sand and shelf that had heaved itself up from the deeps. . . .

He sat on the top step and gazed at the vast dome above, at what James Joyce had called "the heaventree of stars, hung with humid nightblue fruit."

Great beauty was something he had to work up to, he had to take it in slowly, not gulping, but sipping. He put his hands over his eyes and saw the stars dancing behind his hands, another double image in this deep and silent night.

In Mitford, he'd felt tethered; tethered to Lord's Chapel, tethered to the rectory, tethered to the little yellow house. Here, he felt as if he were falling into space, tethered only to God.

He got up and walked down the steps to the garden, restless and excited, like a child who wakes in the night, filled with fervent dreams.

Barnabas lifted his leg against a favorite spot at the picket fence.

If he could, he'd call home and talk with Dooley again. He'd talk even longer than he'd done today, then ask Dooley to pass the phone to Harley. Next, he'd call Esther and check on Gene, even though they'd spoken on Wednesday, and after that, he might ring Louella and they would sing a hymn, right on the phone. . . .

Truth be known, he'd like nothing better than to call Miss Sadie and hear the bright voice that had always made him listen up and step more smartly.

"Miss Sadie," he said aloud to his still-favorite parishioner, "this is a toll-free call. I hope you like it up there and aren't getting in trouble for bossing the angels around. . . ."

He saw the shooting star plummet toward the silhouette of an oceanfront cottage and vanish.

Then he heard the music.

He turned, thinking that somehow a radio had come on in the house.

But the music wasn't coming from the house.

It was Karg-Elert's "Now Thank We All Our God," and it was coming from . . . across the street.

He stood, frozen and alert.

Someone was playing their stereo full blast. It was an extraordinary rendition of one of his sworn favorites for the organ—mighty, dramatic, charged with power.

He walked to the picket fence and looked across the street at the high-grown, moonlit hedge.

Though distant, he could hear each note clearly and, perhaps because the piece was familiar, he was free to hear beneath the notes the terrible urgency of the music behind the wall, under the full and looming moon.

He crept back to bed, thinking of Hélène Pringle and the faint piano music that had floated out on Mitford's night air.

He shivered in the breeze that came suddenly from the water and blew through their open windows.

Sometime before dawn, he felt the bed move near his feet and thought it was Barnabas.

It was Jonathan Tolson. The boy crept toward the head of the bed, silent, and found a place between them. Father Tim heard him sigh and then, in a moment, heard the boy's rhythmic breathing and smelled his damp, tousled hair.

He prayed for Janette and for today's mission before he drifted again to sleep.

On the way to St. John's, he stopped by Mona's for a coffee to go, and ducked into the bait and tackle shop.

"Here's th' latest," said Ernie. "Th' *Democrat* hit th' street last night, Junior's already had an answer to his ad."

"And?" This was pretty exciting stuff, looking for a wife.

"And it was a guy."

"Aha."

"Wanted to know if Junior'd be interested in sellin' his Bronco."

"That's *it*?"

Ernie shook his head, looking gloomy. "I think we need to doctor that ad."

"Maybe so. By the way, you were going to tell me who lives behind the wall."

"Oh, yeah. Right. Well, that's Morris Love that lives back there."

"Morris Love." He searched Ernie's face. "Tell me more."

"Well, Morris is, you know . . ." Ernie pointed to his head and made a circle with his forefinger.

"Like the rest of us," said Father Tim, looking on the positive side.

"Nothin' to worry about. Morris keeps to hisself, never leaves th' place, except he's bad to holler at people sometimes. Kind of hides behind th' wall and hollers crazy stuff. But tell your missus not to worry, he's harmless."

"Why doesn't he leave the place?"

"Don't want anybody to look at 'im."

"Why's that?"

"Well, see, he's got this . . . handicap. There's a woman takes care of him, comes every day or so, does his cookin' an' all, an' th' organ tuner, he comes in his panel truck from Virginia. Not enough traffic in and out of there to keep th' grass off th' driveway."

"Well, well."

"See, there was a big organ put in there by his grandaddy, they say it was world-class in its time, and ol' Morris, he can play th' hair off that thing, but I ain't heard much about him playin' lately. We all take Morris for granted. Most people don't hardly remember he's in there."

"I'll be darned."

"But don't you worry about a thing. He's harmless, just a little mean streak like 'is grandaddy, is all."

"Aha. So, here's the book I promised you."

"Holy smoke! I gave you a used paperback, and this sucker is *leather*."

"Take that and keep it, and I hope you like it."

"You got th' wrong end of th' stick, if you ask me, but I appreciate it." Ernie opened the book, squinted at a random page, and read aloud, slowly:

> *"On his morning rounds th' Master*
> *Goes to learn how all things fare;*
> *Searches pasture after pasture,*
> *Sheep and cattle eyes with care;*
> *And, for silence or for talk,*
> *He hath comrades in his walk;*
> *Four dogs, each pair of different breed,*
> *Distinguished two for scent, and two for speed.*

> *"See a hare before him started!*
> *—Off they fly in earnest chase;*
> *Every dog is eager-hearted,*
> *All th' four are in th' race. . . ."*

Ernie looked up, grinning. "Got a good bit of action to it."

As he left the tackle shop, he glanced in the front window, pleased to see the proprietor giving rapt attention to the little book of pastoral ruminations.

Janette Tolson wept all the way across the bridge to the hospital fourteen miles away. He sat with her through the admission to the psychiatric floor, explaining to the clerk there was no insurance, and giving his word the bill would be taken care of. How, he didn't know; that would be God's job. He waited until her doctor arrived and she was settled in a shared room.

Reluctantly, she let go of his hand as he left. "Jonathan . . ."

"Don't worry," he said.

He clung to Cynthia before leaving for the vestry meeting at St. John's.

Oh, the blessed softness of a wife in a hard world . . .

He kissed her, his hands at her waist. Even with all the bike riding, there was a pleasant little roll there.

He winked. "See you later, Tubs."

She jerked away from him, glaring.

No doubt about it, he thought as he raced for the door, he had stepped over his wife's yellow line.

CHAPTER EIGHT

The Spark in the Flax

The rain began in the night, drumming steadily on the red roof of Dove Cottage.

At six a.m., he tried to think of one good reason to spend a full day at the church office, but couldn't. Didn't clergy usually take two days every single week, and hadn't he taken only one since arriving? He would go in after lunch, that was the ticket.

"Wonderful, darling, you can help me feed Jonathan!" His wife had a positively wicked gleam in her eye.

"No! I don't like it!" Jonathan shook his head vigorously when a bowl of cereal was set before him.

Cynthia proffered buttered toast.

"No!" said Jonathan. "No toast!"

"What if we put jelly on it?" asked Father Tim.

"I've tried that," she said. "It doesn't work. We go through this every morning while you trot happily down the street, whistling." She sighed. "I don't know how to make children eat things they don't like."

"Hasn't he given you any clues?"

"I've tried oatmeal, Froot Loops, buttered grits, bacon, not to mention eggs scrambled and boiled. Nothing will do. He always ends up in tears with crackers and cheese."

"We could call someone," he said brightly, "and *ask* what he likes for breakfast."

"Who could we call?"

"Let's see. Jean Ballenger! She knows the family!" What a great solution. He was a regular Sherlock.

"I got to pee-pee," said Jonathan.

"You just pee-pee'd," said Cynthia, looking frazzled.

Jonathan tumbled from the chair and headed toward the bathroom at a trot.

"Your turn to go with him," said his wife. "And please put the seat down afterward."

⌐◯¬

"I have no idea!" exclaimed Jean when he rang her small cottage next to the library. "I never saw anyone eat anything while I was at the Tolsons'."

After the useless phone inquiry, Cynthia pulled him into the study. "I don't suppose Jean would like to keep Jonathan for a little while?"

"Jean Ballenger? I can't imagine such a thing!" Jean, a fastidious spinster with crocheted antimacassars on her armchairs, would hardly be up for tending a strong-willed three-year-old.

"What are we going to do?" asked Cynthia. "I think he's adorable, truly he is. But he's running me ragged. I'm too *old* for this!"

"I'll be here 'til one o'clock. Go to your drawing board, relax, everything is under control."

So why did she peer at him like that, with one eyebrow up and one down?

⌐◯¬

"Eureka!" he shouted, running along the hall to her studio. "I've found it!"

"Found what?" she asked, not looking up from a watercolor of Violet under a yellow and blue beach umbrella.

"What he likes for breakfast!" He was positively triumphant; he might have located the very Grail.

"I'll never guess, so tell me." She couldn't help grinning at her husband, who looked as if he'd been run through a food processor.

"Guess!" he insisted, playing the mean trick Emma always played on him.

"M&M's?"

"Not even close. Two more."

"Reese's peanut butter cups! That would certainly be *my* preference for breakfast every morning!"

"Cynthia . . ."

"All right, I'm not trying. Here goes, and I'm quite serious this time." She looked out the window. She curled a strand of hair around one finger. She sighed.

"I don't have a clue," she said.

"Spaghetti."

"No."

"Yes!"

"Al dente, I presume."

"A little respect, please. I've just made an important discovery here."

"Yes, dear, and thank you. Plain or with marinara?"

"With butter. No fork, no spoon. Just dump it in a bowl and set it in front of him. Of course, you'll have to bathe him after it's all over."

"Bathe him?" There went that eyebrow again.

"All right, *I'll* bathe him. But just this once."

Why did children keep turning up on his doorstep? Not that he was complaining, but wasn't it odd that he'd lived a full six decades with hardly a youngster in his life except those he encountered in Sunday School? But then, look what it had gained him, after all—Dooley Barlowe. One of the greatest gifts, most of the time, that had ever "come down from the Father of lights," as St. James had put it.

In any case, this was a picnic compared to Father Tracey, who, with his good wife, had adopted fourteen children. Fourteen! It boggled the mind. And then there was Father Moultrie, who had passed into legend, though still living as far he knew. This good fellow had collected twenty-one children of various ages and backgrounds and had managed, so it was said, to keep the lot in good order, though the addition he built to his suburban home had literally fallen down one night after a communal pillow fight; thanks be to God no one was badly hurt.

"And darling . . . ," said his smiling wife as he turned to leave the room.

"Yes?"

"Thank you for mopping the floor under his chair when you've finished."

"No problem," he said, trying to mean it.

He looked out the study window at the incessant rain, then checked his watch.

A quarter 'til twelve.

Mule and J.C. would just be trooping into the rear booth.

He knew it was a busy time at the Grill, but he was missing those guys, and how much trouble could it be for Velma to call somebody to the phone?

He listened as the red phone on the wall beside the grill rang twice. Four times. Six. Seven . . .

He was ready to hang up when Velma answered.

"Velma, it's Tim Kavanagh!"

"Who?"

"Tim Kavanagh."

"What can I do for you, we've got a lunch trade here to take care of."

"Right. Could you, ah, call Mule to the phone? Or J.C.?"

"Hold on."

He heard the receiver being laid on top of the wall unit, then heard it fall, swinging on the cord and knocking against the wall, *blam . . . blam . . . blam.* He held his own receiver away from his ear.

The babble in the Grill sounded a continent away, all the clatter and uproar that had been so familiar for so long seemed so . . . distant. His heart sank.

"I don't serve grits after nine o'clock!" That was Percy.

Clink. Clank. Thunk.

"Dagummit!" Percy again. Must have dropped his spatula.

"Lord help! Lookit what th' President's done now." Sounded like Leonard Stanley, who always sat at the counter opposite the phone. "Oh, boy! *Un*believable."

"I don't read th' paper, makes my stomach wrench. Except for th' funnies, I've plumb quit." Coot Hendrick. "But I like those fliers that come with th' paper—you know, Wal-Mart, Ken's Auto Parts, discount coupons for Domino's Pizza, like that."

Whop. Sizzle.

"We ain't got a special today!" yelled Percy. "I'm over offerin' specials, have t' take it straight off th' menu!"

"So, what'd th' President do?"

"Trust me, you don't want to know. I wonder if there's any Alka-Seltzer in this place." *Rustle, crackle.* Leonard must have sprung for a big newspaper like the *Atlanta Constitution,* considering the racket it made as he turned the pages.

"Can you *believe* it?" He heard Velma stomp by the phone. "Th' front booth wants a 'BLT without lettuce or tomato!' I said right to 'is face, 'How can you have a BLT without *L* an' *T?'* an' he said, *'What?'* That's th' same fool ordered a cheeseburger th' other day an' asked me to hold th' *cheese.*"

"I'd take early retirement if I was you," said Coot.

It was clear that in the lunch-hour rush, Velma had forgotten his phone call.

He yelled into the mouthpiece. "Velma! Percy! *Hello!*"

He heard the front door open and slam, the hiss of a pop-top soda being opened.

"Hello! Somebody! *Anybody!*"

"What's this phone doin' hangin' by th' cord?" asked Percy. "Must have got knocked off th' hook."

Click.

Jonathan poked a chubby finger at the television screen in the guest room. "I want to watch a movie," he said.

"Ah. A movie."

"In a box," said the three-year-old.

He looked at his watch. "In a box." Fifty-seven minutes to go.

"Peter Pan."

"Peter Pan. Right."

"You like Peter Pan?"

"Oh, yes. Very much!"

Jonathan poked his finger at Father Tim's leg. "So, let's watch it then!"

"We could tell a story. I could read to you, how's that?"

"Watch a movie in a box!"

In a box, in a box. He had a box left over from the books. He dashed to the back porch and hauled it in.

"I one time had a *Li'n King* movie," said Jonathan, "an' my daddy, my daddy, my daddy wouldn't let me watch it." Jonathan furrowed his brow.

He set the boy in the cardboard box and turned on the TV. Good grief! He couldn't believe his eyes, and in broad daylight, too. He surfed. Fifty minutes to go.

"Peter Pan!" yelled Jonathan. "In a *box*!"

He trucked to the studio. "For Pete's sake, Kavanagh, what is a movie in a box?"

"A video, dear. We don't have any."

"Why not?"

"We don't have a VCR."

"We don't even have a microwave," he said, perplexed.

He dashed back to the guest room and pulled Jonathan out of the box. "We're going for a walk."

"I don't want to walk!"

"In this life, my boy, you'll be forced to do many things you'd rather not do, so consider this a rehearsal."

He marched Jonathan into the kitchen and dragged Barnabas from under the table. He snapped the red leash on his dog's collar as the phone rang.

He glanced out the kitchen window as he snatched up the cordless from the window seat. Blast! They couldn't go for a walk, he'd forgotten it was raining cats and dogs.

"Hello!" he barked.

"Father? Is that *you*?"

"Esther!"

"You didn't sound like yourself," said Esther, who didn't sound like herself, either. "I've got to talk to you about Gene."

"Shoot!" he said, cantering down the hall after Jonathan, who was making a beeline for the front door.

"He's actin' so strange, I hardly know him. I'm tellin' you, he's just not my Gene, he could be somebody named Hubert or Pete or Lord knows who, he's actin' so peculiar."

"What's he doing?" he asked, grabbing the boy before he dove off the porch.

He carried him back into the house under one arm. "Down!" yelled the boy, squirming and kicking.

"Who in the world is that?" asked Esther.

"That's Jonathan. Tell me what Gene's doing."

"He's counting things. He stares at me and says, 'Seven.' And I say, 'Seven what?' And he says, 'That's seven times you opened the cabinet door over the stove.'"

"Down!" said Jonathan, wriggling out of Father Tim's grasp.

"Aha. I'm listening, Esther, keep talking. You opened the cabinet door seven times . . ."

Johnathan had dropped to all fours and was drinking water from the dog bowl. He transferred the cordless to his left hand and removed the red leash from Barnabas's collar with his right. He snapped the leash to the boy's romper strap and looped the other end over the back of a kitchen chair.

"He looked at me last night, said, 'Eighteen.' I said, 'Eighteen what?' He said, 'Curlers.' We're goin' up to bed, he said, 'Fourteen.' Lord knows, my nerves are shot by this time, he'd been doin' it all day, I didn't even ask fourteen what, an' he said, 'Steps.' I can tell you right now I do not like it, he has been pullin' this dumb trick for months, but it's gettin' worse by th' minute.

"To tell th' gospel truth, I could knock him in th' head. Can you imagine livin' with somebody who walks around goin' *'Sixty-six!* That's sixty-six window panes.' Or, *'Nineteen!* That's nineteen knobs on th' cabinet doors.' The other day I thought, wonder why there's just nineteen knobs and not twenty, an' th' first thing you know, I was countin' knobs *myself.*"

"I'll be darned."

"I'm on th' hall phone, but I can hear him, he's countin' squares in th' kitchen linoleum as we speak!"

"Oh, boy."

"For the umpteenth time!" Esther lowered her voice. "Father, do you reckon he's . . . crazy? It scares th' daylights out of me to even think a word like that."

"Does Hoppy know what's going on?"

"We had all those tests run, you'd think somethin' mental would show up in th' blood work."

"I feel you should talk to Hoppy. When are you seeing him again?"

"Two weeks."

"You may want to give him a ring."

"I can't, he's on vacation. You know he never took one for years, so I reckon he deserves it."

"Talk to his associate, talk to Dr. Wilson."

"Are you kiddin' me? He's green as tasselin' corn."

"I'd talk to Dr. Wilson, Esther."

Esther had started to cry and was trying to hide it. "Only one thing hasn't changed."

"What's that?"

Jonathan was dragging the chair across the kitchen, as Barnabas sat under the table, bewildered.

"He still pats me on the cheek and says, 'Goodnight, Dollface,' just like he's done for forty-two years."

"Horsie!" shouted Jonathan.

"I wish you were here," sobbed Esther.

"I wish I were, too," he said, meaning it.

He put socks on the kitchen chair legs and let Jonathan pull the darned thing all over the house. Cynthia shut her door—in fact, it sounded like she locked it—and Barnabas hid in the corner of the study by the bookshelves. As for himself, he sat in the living room like a country squire, and perused the *Whitecap Reader*.

> Some members of the Wadamo tribe of the Zambezi Valley in Zimbabwe are born with only two toes on each foot, which is an inherited trait. However, these people can walk as well as anyone with five toes on each foot.
>
> ### This Space for Rent
>
> Get Geared Up! Your One Stop Fishing Gear and Auto Supply Store, Whitecap Fishing Gear And Auto Parts
>
> Custom Modular homes, Affordable Quality, Tozier Builders (across from Bragg's in the Toe)
>
> Trivia: Which night precedes May Day? Which island separates the Canadian part of Niagara Falls from the American? Whose army were canned foods developed to feed?
>
> SHEAR CREATIONS: Hairstyling for the entire family, fish sandwiches and pasta to go . . .

Laugh for the week: "I don't mind her being born again,
but did she have to come back as herself?"

He sighed. The *Reader* was the only newspaper he'd ever seen that
made the *Muse* look like the *Philadelphia Inquirer.*

He allowed the boy to exhaust himself until, on the dot of one, he
went down for a nap without a whimper. "Hallelujah!" Father Tim
whispered to his dog as he tiptoed from the guest room and closed the
door.

He got into his car at the rear gate and drew the dripping umbrella
in with him. As he turned the key in the ignition, he noticed a panel
truck parked at Morris Love's entrance. He adjusted his glasses.

L. L. Mansfield, Tuning for Fine Organs.

A driver got out of the truck and went to the iron gate, swung it
open, came back to the truck, and drove through.

He sat for a moment, curious at the first sign of coming and going
he'd seen across the road. He watched the driver trot back and lock the
gate behind him.

Fort Knox! he thought, driving away.

I tell thee what I would have thee do . . .

He sat in the church office, hearing rain peck the windowpanes
like chickens after corn, and read from a sermon of Charles Spurgeon,
delivered at Newington on March 9, 1873.

> *Go to Him without fear or trembling; ere yon sun goes down and ends
> this day of mercy, go and tell Him thou hast broken the Father's
> laws—tell Him that thou art lost, and thou needest to be saved; tell
> Him that He is a man, and appeal to His manly heart, and to His
> brotherly sympathies.*
>
> *Pour out thy broken heart at His feet: let thy soul flow over in His
> presence, and I tell thee He cannot cast thee away . . .*

He jotted in his sermon notebook: *Not that He <u>will</u> not turn a
deaf ear, but that He <u>cannot</u>. Press this truth.* Spurgeon had put into a

nutshell what he wanted to preach on Sunday to the body at St. John's.

> ... *though thy prayer be feeble as the spark in the flax, He will not quench it; and though thy heart be bruised like a reed, He will not break it.*
>
> *May the Holy Spirit bless you with a desire to go to God through Jesus Christ; and encourage you to do so by showing that He is meek and lowly of heart, gentle, and tender, full of pity.*

Bottom line, he would tell his congregation what Nike had told the world:

Just do it.

He finished typing up the pew bulletin and rang the hospital. Janette was down the hall. "Tell her I'll be there tomorrow," he said to the nurse. "Tell her Jonathan's having a wonderful time."

He fished the umbrella from the stand by the downstairs door and prepared to head into the downpour.

"Father Kavanagh, is that you?"

He spun around. "Good heavens!"

"I frightened you, Father, I'm sorry as can be!"

"Mercy!" he said, not knowing what else to say. A tall, thin, stooped woman in a dripping hat and raincoat stood before him, her glasses sliding off her wet nose.

"I came in through the front door and couldn't find a soul, so I helped myself to these stairs. I'm Ella Bridgewater, come to audition!"

He was addled. "But I thought tomorrow . . ."

"I wrote down today in my appointment book, Father, I am very precise about such things, and besides, I couldn't have done it tomorrow, for I'm going across to my niece. I always do that on Saturday, so I would never have—"

"Of course. My mistake, I'm sure." He was very precise about such things, as well. But why quibble?

"Well, Miss Bridgewater, glad to see you!" He took her wet hand and shook it heartily, noting that she appeared considerably older than her letter had stated.

She patted her chest. "I have the music under my coat!"

"Excellent. We'll just pop upstairs and have at it. Thanks for coming out in the deluge."

He followed her up the stairs to the sacristy. She was certainly agile, he thought.

"I've always loved this church, Father. I think I wrote in my letter to you that I played for yoked parishes for many years in these islands."

"Yes. Wonderful!"

"So I certainly know the churches in these parts, though I never stepped foot in St. John's 'til this day." She looked around the sanctuary and nave with some wonder.

"You don't mean it!"

"Not once. Too busy playing elsewhere!"

"I wish you could see it in the sunlight, the way the stained glass pours color into the nave."

Wiry gray curls sprung up as she removed her rain hat. "I believe I *will* see it in the sunlight!"

Mighty perky lady, he thought. And seventy if she was a day. Her letter, however, had said sixty-two, and added "in vibrant good health."

"There's the choir loft, as you can see. I believe you'll find our old Hammond in fine working order. Well, then, let me help you off with your coat, and you can pop up the stairs there. Would you like a cup of coffee? Or tea? Won't take but a moment."

"No, thank you, Father, I'm ready to get on with it. I've been practicing like all get-out for days—you know they say if you fail to prepare, you prepare to fail."

"Perfect line for a wayside pulpit!"

"That's where I got it," she said, with a burst of laughter. "Well, here goes."

She walked briskly up the aisle, clutching her manila envelope, and made short work of the stairs to the loft.

There was a moment's rustling in the loft and, he thought, a mite of hard breathing.

"Great day in the morning!" she shouted down. "This organ is old as Methuselah."

"Manufactured the year of my fourth birthday!"

"Which was a good year, I'm sure. Now . . ."—he heard her clear her throat and heave a sigh—"sit and close your eyes. I'll give you a prelude and fugue, followed by a hymn. Then you're allowed to make one personal request."

"Thank you, Miss Bridgewater." He was glad he didn't mind being told what to do by women; he'd never lacked for direction in that department.

"My, my," he heard her say. "Oh, yes." She fiddled with the stops, pressed the pedals, hummed a little. "Well, then!"

The old organ nearly blasted him out of the pew. Aha! It was Bach's Little Prelude and Fugue in C Major, and she was giving it everything she had. This woman had eaten her Wheaties, and no doubt about it.

At the end, she called in a loud voice, "How was that, Father?"

"Why . . . play on!" he said. Very perky.

"For All the Saints" boomed up to the rafters. Ah. Good to have the organ going in this place, a benediction.

He listened carefully, unable to restrain himself from whispering the words under his breath.

" 'For all the saints, who from their labors rest, who thee by faith before the world confessed, thy Name O Jesus, be forever blessed. Alleluia, alleluia . . .' "

Not especially thrilling, as the rendition of it certainly could be, but better than he might have expected, to tell the truth. He patted his foot and attended each note, keeping an open mind to the very end.

Agreeably workmanlike, he concluded.

"How was that?" she trumpeted.

"Well done!"

"Thank you, Father, honesty is the best policy, and I don't mind saying that all my priests have liked my playing."

Rain blew against the windows, *peck, peck, peck.*

"Miss Bridgewater, is it time for my personal request?"

"It is, and I must say I'm filled with curiosity."

"What about 'Strengthen for Service, Lord'?" A communion hymn worth its salt and then some!

"Excellent, Father! Two-oh-one in the old hymnal, three-twelve in the new. Here we go."

He chuckled. He hadn't encountered such bravado since the last meeting of the youth group.

" 'Strengthen for service, Lord,' " he whispered as she played, " 'the hands that holy things have taken; let ears that now have heard thy songs, to clamor never waken . . .' " *To clamor never waken.* His favorite line.

He looked around the walls and up to the ceiling as if the music were painting the very timbers, bathing them, somehow, and making them stand more firmly.

He was drinking it all in as if starved, and then the audition was over.

He stood and faced the loft and clapped with some enthusiasm.

Huffing slightly and clutching her envelope, she was down the stairs, along the aisle, and standing by his pew in a trice. Her long nose and stooped shoulders gave her the appearance, he thought, of an Oriental crane.

"Well done!" he said again.

"Thank you, Father. I have a confession." She held her envelope like a shield against her chest, looking pained but confident.

"Shall we . . . go to the altar?" he asked.

"Don't trouble yourself, I'll just spit it out right here."

"Sit down," he said. He sat, himself, and scooted over.

She thumped into the oak pew. "I lied about my age."

"Oh?"

"I turned seventy-four last month. I didn't think you'd hire me if I told the truth, and I want you to know I'm sorry. As I was playing your request, the Lord convicted my heart and I asked Him to forgive me. Perhaps you'll do the same."

She looked exceedingly pained.

"Why, certainly, Miss Bridgewater. Of course. And may I say you don't look seventy-four."

She brightened considerably. "Why, thank you, Father. You see, I believe the Lord called me to St. John's. When I heard you had a need, I asked Him about it at once, and He said, 'Ella Jean'—the Lord always uses my middle name—'march over there and ask for that job, they need you.' "

"Aha."

"He doesn't speak to me in an audible voice."

"I understand."

"He puts it in my mind, you might say. As you well know, Father, you have to be quiet before the Lord and keep your trap shut for Him to get a word in edgewise, that's my experience."

"Miss Bridgewater—"

"Call me Ella," she said.

"Ella, if we can agree on your compensation, I think you may be just the ticket for St. John's."

Tears sprang to her eyes. "Do you really think so?"

"I do."

"But," she said, regaining her composure, "you'll have to run it by the vestry."

"Right. I intend to."

"When might that be?"

"Wednesday. I'll get back to you right after the meeting. Shouldn't be any problem. Do you have family?"

"I lived with my mother for many years, she went to heaven last March."

"I'm sorry to hear it. Or glad, as the case may be." Heaven! The ultimate place to escape the clamor . . .

"I'm an old maid," she said, bobbing her head and smiling. "But not the sort of dried-up old maid you see in cartoons."

"Oh?" A priest never knew what he might be told. He shifted uneasily on the pew.

"No, indeed. I fell head over heels in love when I was forty-seven, and truth be told, have never gotten over it. They say you came late to love, yourself."

"Late, yes," he said, smiling. "But not too late."

"Minor was a young explorer with Admiral Byrd, and spent his last years as a maker of hot-air balloons."

"You don't say!"

"Oh, yes. And I went up in one!" Her eyes were bright with feeling. "We sailed up the coast and across Virginia and landed in a cow pasture, where we picnicked on cheese and figs. It was the single grandest thing I ever did."

"I'm happy to hear it," he said. And he was.

Miss Bridgewater adjusted her glasses and peered at him. "And when would I begin if . . . if . . ."

"Sunday after next, I should think."

"Well!" she said, sitting back and beaming. "Well!"

The everlasting rain was still going strong at four-thirty, when he pulled into Ernie's for a gallon of milk.

Roger Templeton sat in the corner by a small pile of wood shavings, and looked up when he came in.

"Tim! Glad to see you! How's your weather?"

"You mean my own, apart from the elements? I'd say . . . sunny!" Hadn't God just delivered an organist to St. John's?

He scratched Lucas behind the ears, then pulled up a chair next to Roger, peering into Roger's lap at what had been a block of wood. The rough form of a duck, though headless, had emerged, its right wing beginning to assume feathers.

"Amazing! May I have a look?"

"Help yourself," said Roger, pleased to be asked.

He took the duck and examined it closely. In principle, at least, this was how David had escaped from Michelangelo's block of marble.

"That's tupelo wood," said Roger. "I get it from up around Albemarle Sound. With tupelo, you can cut across the grain, with the grain, or against the grain."

"It's beautiful!" he said. How had Roger known the wood contained a duck just waiting to get out?

"That's a green-winged teal. It's not much to look at yet; I've rough-edged it with a band saw and now I'm carving in the feather groupings."

"How did you know you could do this?"

Roger took a knife from an old cigar box next to his chair. "I didn't. I'd never done anything with my hands."

"Except make money," said Ernie, walking in from the book room. He thumped down at the table.

"I used to go on hunting trips with my colleagues . . . Alaska, Canada, the eastern shore of Maryland around St. Michael's and Easton. I recall the day I dropped a green-winged teal into the river. When the Lab brought it to me, I saw for the first time the great beauty of it. My eyes were opened in a new way, and I wondered how I'd managed to . . . do what I'd been doing."

"Aha."

"Oh, I'm not preaching a sermon against hunting, Tim. Let a man hunt! I also have a special fondness for a boy learning to hunt. But I quit right there at the river, I said if God Almighty could make just one feather, not to mention a whole duck, as intricate and beautiful as that, who am I to bring it down?"

"He still fishes," said Ernie.

"Why did you start carving?"

Roger shrugged. "I wanted to see how close I could come to the real thing. I thought I'd try to make just one and then quit."

"I see."

"But I never seem to come very close to the real thing, so I keep trying."

Father Tim had never done much with his hands, either, except turn the pages of a book or plant a rosebush. "How long does it take to make one?"

"Oh, five or six weeks, sometimes longer."

"He works on 'is ducks in my place, exclusive," said Ernie, as if that lent a special distinction to Ernie's Books, Bait & Tackle.

"Do you also work at home?"

Roger colored slightly. "I paint at home, but my wife doesn't allow carving."

He'd heard of not being allowed to smoke cigars at home, but he'd never heard of a ban on duck carving.

"Roger, my wife has bought me a chair on Captain Willie's fishing boat. You ever go deep-sea fishing?"

"Does a hog love slop?" asked Ernie, who didn't care to be out of the loop in any conversation.

"Captain Willie has taken me out to the Gulf Stream many times."

"I don't mind telling you I'm no fisherman. I've never spent much time around water."

"That's no liability. Sport fishing is all about relaxing and having fun. It's an adventure."

An adventure! He'd always wanted to have an adventure, but wasn't good at figuring out how to get from A to B. Leave it to his wife to figure it out for him.

"I hear a lot about spending the day with your head over the side."

Roger and Ernie laughed. "Don't listen to that mess," said Ernie. "You stay sober the night before and get a good night's sleep and you'll be fine."

"And don't eat a greasy breakfast," said Roger. "Besides, if it's any comfort, statistics say only twelve percent get seasick."

He was encouraged.

"What'll we see out there?"

"Out in the Gulf," said Ernie, "you'll see your blue marlin, your white marlin, your sailfish, your dolphin—"

"There's wahoo," said Roger, "and yellow tuna—"

"Plus your black tuna and albacore tuna. . . ."

"Man. Big stuff!" He was feeling twelve years old.

Roger whittled. "You can see everything from a thousand-pound blue marlin to a two-pound mahimahi."

"No kidding? But what kind of fish can you actually *catch*?"

"Whatever God grants you that day," said Roger. "Of course, we always release marlin."

"Fair enough. What sort of boat would we go in?"

"Captain Willie runs a Carolina hull built over on Roanoke Island. About fifty-three feet long—"

"—an' eight hundred and fifty horsepower!" Ernie appeared to take personal pride in this fact. "What you might call a glorified speedboat."

"Eight hundred and fifty horsepower? Man!" He was losing his vocabulary, fast.

Roger adjusted his glasses and looked at Father Tim. "Just show up ready to have a good time. That's what I'd recommend."

"And be sure an' take a bucket of fried chicken," said Ernie.

He cooked the requisite bowl of spaghetti while Jonathan sat in the window seat and colored a batch of Cynthia's hasty sketches. Something baking in the oven made his heart beat faster.

"Cassoulet!" said his creative wife. Though she'd never attempted such a thing, she had every confidence it would be sensational. "Fearless in the kitchen" was how she once described herself.

"It's all in the crust, the way the crust forms on top," she told him, allowing a peek into the oven. "I know it's too hot to have the oven going, but I couldn't resist."

"Where on earth did you find duck?"

"At the little market. It was lying right by the mahimahi. Isn't that wonderful?"

He certainly wouldn't mention it to Roger.

Jonathan had clambered down from the window seat. "Watch a movie!" he said, giving a tug on Father Tim's pants leg.

"Timothy, we've got to get a VCR. Could you possibly go across tomorrow, to whatever store carries these things? I don't think I can make it 'til Monday without in-house entertainment!"

"Do we just plug it in?" He'd never been on friendly terms with high technology, which was always accompanied by manuals printed in Croatian.

"Beats me," she said. "That's your job. I'm the stay-at-home mommy."

He put his arms around her and traced the line of her cheek with his nose. "Thank you for being the best deacon in the entire Anglican communion."

⟋

Jonathan had wanted his mother tonight; his tears called up a few of Father Tim's very own.

He thought it must be agony to be small and helpless, with no mother, no father, no brother or sister to be found. He held Jonathan against his chest, over his heart, and let the boy sob until he exhausted his tears.

He walked with him through the house in a five-room circle, crooning snatches of hymns, small prayers and benedictions, fragments of stories about Pooh and Toad and that pesky rabbit, Peter. He didn't know what to do with a child who was crying out of bewilderment and loss, except to be with him in it.

⟋

He covered the sleeping boy with a light blanket, praying silently. Then he closed the door and tiptoed down the hall and out to the porch where Cynthia sat waiting, a rain-drugged Violet slumbering in her lap.

Barnabas followed and sprawled at his feet.

What peace to retire into the cool August evening, after a dinner that might have been served in the Languedoc.

For the first time today, he liked the rain, it was friend and shelter to him, enclosing the porch with a gossamer veil.

They watched the distant patch of gray Atlantic turn to platinum in the lingering dusk.

"Weary, darling?" she asked, taking his hand.

"I am. Don't know why, though. Haven't done much today."

"You do more than you realize. Up at dawn, morning prayer, feed and bathe the boy, help the wife, write the pew bulletin, work on your sermon, hire an organist . . ."

He took her hand and kissed it. Of all the earthly consolations, he loved understanding best. Not sympathy, no, that could be deadly. But understanding. It was balm to him, and he had sucked it up like a toad, often denying it to her.

"Your book—how are you feeling about it?" he asked.

"I guess I don't know why I'm doing another book when I might have the lovely freedom to do nothing. I suppose I got excited about being in a new place, the way the light changes, and the coming and going of the tide. It spoke to me and I couldn't help myself." She smiled at him. "I think I make books because I don't know what else to do."

"You know how to make a ravishing cassoulet."

"Yes, but cassoulet has its limitations. Little books do not."

He nodded.

"Do you think we'll ever just loll about?" she asked.

"I don't think we're very good at lolling."

She put her head back and closed her eyes. "Thank God for this peace."

He heard it first, even through the loud whisper of rain. It was the organ music of their neighbor. He sat up, alert, and cupped his hand to his ear.

"What is it, Timothy?"

"It's Morris Love, in the house behind the wall. Listen."

They sat silent for long moments.

"Wondrous," she said quietly.

The rain seemed to abate out of respect for the music, and they began to hear the notes more clearly.

"Name that tune," she said.

" 'Jesus My Joy.' A Bach chorale prelude." He couldn't help but hear the urgency—in truth, a kind of fury—underlying the music. He told her what he knew about Morris Love, leaving out the part about him shouting through the hedge.

"Is Mr. Love a concert organist?"

"Not unless you consider this a private concert for the Kavanaghs."

"What a lovely thought," she said, pleased.

When the phone rang, he fumbled for it. For a moment, he was at home in Mitford and expected to find it next to the bed. But blast, he was in Whitecap, and the phone was across the room.

It rang again; he bumped into the chair and tried to figure what time it was. The rain had stopped, and a stiff breeze blew through the windows.

As the phone continued to ring, he picked up his watch and glanced at the glowing dial. Twelve-forty. Not good. *Lord, have mercy.* . . .

"Hello!"

"I have a collect call from Harley Welch," said an operator. "Will you pay for the call?"

"Yes!"

"Rev'rend?"

"Harley?" His heart hammered.

"Rev'rend, I hate t' tell you this . . ."

CHAPTER NINE

Home Far Away

"They got Dooley in jail."

"*What?*"

"But he's all right, he ain't hurt or nothin. . . ."

Cynthia sat up. "What is it, Timothy?"

He switched on the lamp. "Dooley."

"Dear God!" she said.

"Tell me, Harley." He once prayed he'd never live to hear what he was hearing now.

"Well, he was comin' home on time, goin' to be here right on th' nickel. . . ."

"And?" His mouth was dry, his stomach churning. *Christ, have mercy. . . .*

"An' he picked up Buster Austin standin' out on th' road. You remember Buster."

Indeed, he did. Buster had called yours truly a "nerd," for which Dooley had mopped the floor of the school cafeteria with him. The last run-in was when Buster stole a pack of cigarettes and talked Dooley into smoking on school grounds. School principal Myra Hayes had nearly eaten one hapless priest alive for "allowing" such a thing to happen, and suspended Dooley for ten days.

"Buster said he needed a ride to git 'is clothes at somebody's house, would Dooley take 'im, an' Dooley said he would but make it snappy. Dooley set in th' truck while Buster took in a empty duffel bag and come out a good bit later. Seems like th' boys was goin' down th' road when two officers drove up behind 'em in a squad car. Pulled 'em over, hauled 'em off to th' station for breakin,' enterin,' an' larceny."

"Larceny?" This was a bad dream.

"You know that empty duffel bag Buster carried in? Hit was full when Buster come out of th' house. Had jewelry, a CD player, money, liquor, I don't know what all in there."

"No!"

"Police said th' house had a silent alarm on it, an' they was on th' boys before they got out of th' driveway good. But Dooley didn't do nothin'."

"I believe that."

"Nossir, he didn't, he was doin' th' drivin' is all, but the police says 'til they know better, he's locked up."

"What can I do?" His legs were turned to water; he sank into the chair by the lamp.

"If I was you, Rev'rend, I'd do what preachers do."

"Pray."

"That's right. I'm down at th' station, an' soon as I hear somethin', I'll call you. I know Dooley don't want you worried an' all. He would of called, but he's upset about worryin' you."

"How is he, Harley? Tell me straight."

"Well, he's scared. He's innocent, but hit's scary bein' th'owed in a cell like that an' locked up."

"Is Rodney there?"

"Last I heard, th' chief was puttin' on 'is britches an' bustin' over here."

"Thank God for you, Harley."

"Now, don't you worry, Rev'rend."

He hung up, trembling, feeling the immutable reality of six hundred miles between Mitford and his racing heart.

At one-thirty, he could bear it no longer and called the Mitford police station.

Rodney Underwood was questioning Dooley and Buster. No, they didn't know when the chief would be through, but he would call when he was.

Jonathan trotted in and clambered onto their bed.

"I think I read somewhere that children aren't supposed to sleep with their parents," he said.

"We're not his parents," explained his wife.

Jonathan bounced down beside Cynthia, looking hopeful. "Watch a movie!"

Cynthia was not amused. "Jonathan, if you so much as utter the M word again, I will jump in the ocean!"

He nodded his head vigorously. "I can swim!"

"Good! Go to sleep."

He poked his chubby finger into Cynthia's arm. "You go to sleep, too."

Father Tim paced the floor, checking his watch.

"I'm hungry," said Jonathan.

"People don't eat during the night."

Jonathan held out both hands. "Give me candy, then?"

Cynthia leaned toward him, shaking her head. "If you weren't so utterly adorable . . ."

"You got bad breath," said Jonathan, wrinkling his nose.

"When I go to the library tomorrow," she told her husband, "I'll see if they have a book on what to do with children."

The phone rang at two o'clock.

"Buster Austin's been askin' for trouble for years," said Rodney. "Now he's gone and stepped in it."

"What about Dooley?"

"Dooley says he rode Buster over to the house and sat in the truck, said he didn't have nothin' to do with it, but Buster says he did. Soon as th' paperwork's done, I'll drive th' boys over to Wesley and take 'em before th' magistrate."

"Good Lord, Rodney. What does that mean?"

"Th' magistrate's th' one signs th' arrest warrant, then I'll serve it. I'm goin' to tell 'im I think Dooley's innocent, he's never been in any trouble, and we'll see where we go from there. He'll set bond, and you'll have to talk to a bondsman if you want Dooley out of jail."

"Right. I know the bondsman in Wesley. Call me the minute you know something. What kind of bond do you think we're talking about?"

"Breakin' and enterin' and larceny is serious business. You might get off for twenty thousand, maybe ten. Th' Austins will probably post a property bond, Buster don't come from fancy circumstances."

He couldn't believe this was happening. It was a nightmare. It was also the ruination of his boy's summer, his last precious days at home. . . . He felt sick in his very gut.

"Where do we go from there?" he asked.

"Th' magistrate will set a court date, two weeks to thirty days away."

"Let me talk with Dooley, if I may." He felt like a Mack truck was sitting on his chest.

"Hey," said Dooley.

"Hey, yourself," he replied, drawing thin comfort from their old greeting.

"I didn't do it."

"I believe you."

"Buster Austin's still th' same lyin', cheatin' geek he always was. I should've known better. I picked 'im up 'cause I thought he was in trouble, I thought maybe his ol' car was broke down an' I was tryin' to help. I could kill 'im, maybe I will."

"I think you did the right thing."

"You do?"

"I do. It was someone you knew, you thought he needed help, and you stopped."

"So how come it turned out like this?" He could hear the barely controlled rage in the boy's voice.

"Sometimes we do good and it turns out badly. I don't know why. But it definitely doesn't mean we're to stop doing the right thing."

"Yeah, well, wait'll Lace an' ever'body hears about it."

"I thought you weren't seeing much of Lace."

"I don't care what she thinks, anyway, but what about ever'body else, like Avis? And what if it gets back to school? I mean, some of th' guys will think it's cool, but th' headmaster, he'll . . . he'll freak."

"If it comes up, tell the truth."

"I want to go home," said Dooley. He sounded exhausted. "I got to work tomorrow."

"Rodney will take you home as soon as the bail issue is settled."

"Did you know I'll have to go to court for this stupid mess?"

"Yes."

"I'll have to come home from school, but I ain't tellin' this to Mr. Fleming, no way. You can say I've got to have an operation or somethin'. Maybe on my kidneys or tonsils or . . . on my brain or spine."

"We'll cross that bridge when we get to it. I'm sorry this happened, I wish we were there. God bless you, everything's going to be fine. I'll call the bondsman as soon I hear back from Rodney, don't be afraid, we love you." He tried to cover all the bases, but his heart felt empty as a gourd.

Rodney called at three a.m.

He'd done everything he could to convince the magistrate that Dooley was a good kid with no previous offenses, emphasizing that his daddy was a clergyman. The magistrate said he was a preacher's kid himself, and based on that alone had a notion to set bail at forty thousand. Bottom line, the magistrate was releasing Dooley on a secured five-thousand-dollar bond, and Rodney was driving him home as soon as the bondsman could get over to the Wesley jail. Buster Austin's parents had refused to post bond, and Buster would not be going home.

He found Ray Porter's number in his black book, and woke him up.

"Ray, Tim Kavanagh. My boy's in the Wesley jail and he's innocent. He's under a five-thousand-dollar secured bond. How fast can you get him out of there?"

"Let me jump in my clothes," said Ray. "I'll have him out in twenty, thirty minutes. Y'all still down at th' coast?"

"Afraid so. How shall I send the fee?"

"Put a check in the mail. You got my address?"

"I have it somewhere."

"Post office box six twenty-one."

"God bless you."

"I've got two boys," said Ray Porter, considering that sufficient empathy.

He was buttering Jonathan's breakfast spaghetti when the phone rang. His hand was on the receiver before it rang again.

"Hello?"

"I hate to tell you this . . . ," said Emma.

"I already know," he said.

"How'd you know?"

"Harley called me last night."

"How'd he know?" she asked, sounding irritable.

"He was *there*."

"I don't know what you're talkin' about," she said, "but I'm talkin' about Gene Bolick havin' a brain tumor."

"*What?*"

"He keeled over again yesterday, they sent him down to Baptist Hospital and did a MRI scan. That's why he's been actin' so peculiar, it was that tumor pressin' on his brain."

"Dear Lord!"

"Here, I wrote down what it is, I have to spell it. M-e-n-i-n-g-i-o-m-a. It's way down deep towards th' base of his brain."

"Is it operable?" He realized he was holding his breath.

"Let's see. Where'd I write that down? Here it is on my shoppin' list. No, they can't operate, it's too far down in there. The doctor said unless it gets bigger, leave it alone."

"Do you know anything else?"

"Nothing except I hear Esther's a basket case. Ray Cunningham drove 'em down to Baptist and called back to give th' report. I know it's none of my business, but . . ."

"But what?"

"Like I say, it's none of my business, but I think you ought to come home."

Come home. Come home.

It went around in his head like a liturgical chant.

But how could he go home? As far as he could figure, there wasn't a soul who could take Jonathan in. Everybody was working, away for the summer, or too old to trot after a three-year-old. And there was Janette, who needed him, or so he believed, and Cynthia's parish tea coming up at Dove Cottage in three weeks, and the vestry meeting, and the Ella Bridgewater issue, and his responsibilities to the White-cap Fair Planning Commission. . . .

"This is home!" he said aloud. But he couldn't force himself to believe it. *Bloom where you're planted,* he'd read on a plaque at Mona's. And wasn't he trying?

In truth, he was longing for Mitford. Longing to see his boy and encourage him and cheer him on and help him pack for school and tuck a few Kit Kats in his suitcase, and sit with Gene and Esther and pray about this terrible thing that had come against them. . . .

He wanted to lay his head on his pillow in the yellow house and walk Barnabas down Main Street and pop into the Grill and surprise everybody. He wanted to dash up to Fernbank and discover what new tricks Anna and Tony were doing with garlic, and visit Uncle Billy and Esther Cunningham, and see his rosebushes, some of which would be more fragrant and richly colored now than in June. . . .

Sleep-deprived and numb with exhaustion, he drove south to the Toe in heat that was ninety degrees and rising.

He didn't know what he expected, but Otis Bragg's office was definitely nothing to write home about. It was, in fact, smaller than his own office in the church basement, and covered with a film of dust from the gravel operation next door. An air conditioner hummed and rattled in the window.

"Well, now!" said Otis. He removed a large cigar butt from his mouth and spit into a wastebasket. "I'd say it's either money or politics that brings you runnin' to th' Toe."

"I didn't know money and politics were necessarily two separate entities."

Otis growled with laughter. "I like a priest with a sense of humor. Seems like the church is a callin' that turns a man sour if he don't watch out."

Father Tim sat down without being asked. "I have come about money."

A strange sadness crossed his parishioner's face. "That's what always sends clergy to my door."

He looked at the short, round man before him, and was oddly moved. He would come back again when he didn't have his hand out; he'd come back just to visit, to say hello.

Otis leaned forward and squinted at him. "What can I do for you, Father? You look like you wrassled alligators half the night."

"There are plenty of alligators out there, only one of which has put Janette Tolson in the hospital with severe depression."

"We heard that. We hear you've got her boy."

"She's having a rough go of it. And there's no insurance in the family. I thought if you'd be willing, I'll see that St. John's matches what you feel led to give."

Otis rolled the cigar butt between his fingers.

"How do you figure St. John's to be dolin' out money for a thing like this?"

"Janette's one of the body, we're her church family. I figure we can put on a fund-raiser, even do something special at the fair—I don't know, but we'll match what you give."

"What if I gave, say, five thousand bucks? Think you could match that?" Otis clamped the cigar in his mouth, narrowing his eyes.

"Well." He was startled. He had expected some largesse, but . . .

"I don't know if we can raise five thousand. I suppose I was hoping for . . . I don't know, maybe a thousand, tops."

"Father, you goin' to rise in this world, you got to think big."

His bishop, Stuart Cullen, firmly held that philosophy; why couldn't he?

"Thanks, Otis. God bless you! Five thousand is more than generous, it will go a long way in helping Janette's children recover their mother."

"I hope I don't ever run across th'—I'll watch my language, out of respect—th' son of a gun. I despised him from the minute I laid eyes on 'im." Otis spit furiously into the wastebasket. "Always struttin' around preenin' hisself, makin' th' choir sing those mid'eval hymns that go back a hundred years."

"Well, there's some good news, Otis. I think we've found our organist."

"Fine, fine, glad to hear it. You just keep up th' good work, you hear?" Otis punched a button on his phone. "Agnes, write th' preacher a check for five thousand, make it to St. John's." He pitched the unlit butt in the wastebasket and stood up. "Now you're in th' Toe, let me show you around my little operation."

Father Tim wanted to decline, but thought better of it. Maybe it wouldn't hurt to see the results of what it means to think big.

❧

"Miz Tolson is not sleeping," said the nurse, clearly displeased. "She just likes to keep her eyes closed." He wanted nothing more than to crash and sleep, himself.

At the door of the room, the nurse whispered, "I hope you'll speak to her about cooperating. She's been acting like she swallows her pills, but we just found out she spits them in her pajama drawer!"

"I'll do my best," he said.

He sat quietly for a time, saying only, "I'm here, Janette." She had her back to him, and didn't move or acknowledge his presence.

His head fell forward twice as he dozed off, then recovered himself. He was here for a purpose, and he'd better get to it. "Janette?"

No answer. Well, then, he would speak to her as if she were listening; he would speak to her heart, her spirit, and let the chips fall where they may. He'd learned a few things about depression, his own as well as that of others. He'd learned that even when the soul seems fallow, there's a vulnerable spot that can be seeded. Whether the seed flourishes was God's job. "I have planted, Apollos watered, but God gave the increase," St. Paul had written to Corinth.

He took the Book of Psalms from the bag.

"I brought you something. You may not be able to read it for a while, but keep it near. It's King David's songs—they're about joy and praise, loss and gain, about his battles with the mortal enemy, and his battles with depression.

"Let me read to you. . . ."

As a child, the most comforting thing he knew was being read to. He figured it worked for everybody.

" 'The Lord is my light and my salvation; whom shall I fear? The Lord is the strength of my life; of whom shall I be afraid?

" 'When the wicked, even mine enemies and my foes, came upon me to eat up my flesh, they stumbled and fell.

" 'Though an host should encamp against me, my heart shall not fear; though war should rise against me, in this will I be confident.' "

He sat silent for a moment.

"David had many foes, Janette, the human kind as well as the foes that have come against you: anger, bitterness, fear, maybe even resentment toward God.

"When I read the psalms, I read them as personal prayers, naming the enemies that come against my own soul.

" 'For in the time of trouble,' " David says, " 'he will hide me in his pavilion: in the secret of his tabernacle shall he hide me: he shall set me upon a rock.'

"Let Him hide you, Janette, until you gain strength. He will set you upon a rock. Please know that."

He listened to her quiet, regular breathing. Maybe she really was asleep. He prayed silently for the seeds to fall on fertile ground.

"I've marked this psalm for you, the thirtieth. Hear this with your very soul, Janette. 'Weeping may endure for a night, but joy comes in the morning.' "

Without turning in the bed, she raised her hand slightly, and he stood, and held it.

He had gone deep into his pockets with the Wesley bondsman, but Dooley was at home with Harley, and that's what counted.

"People look at me different," said Dooley when they talked the following evening. "While I was baggin' their groceries, I could feel their eyes borin' a hole in me."

Dooley's vernacular always returned when he was angry, tired, or frustrated.

"Maybe. Maybe not. Even in a small town, word doesn't travel that fast. Just be yourself. You didn't do anything wrong and you have nothing to apologize for." Couldn't he say something wiser, more profound than that? "Keep smiling!" he said, sounding lame and feeling worse.

"Lace's mama just died," Dooley said.

"I'm sorry to hear it." Lace's mother, ill and failing for years, had never given loving support to her daughter, but had demanded it, instead, for herself. "Have you called Lace?"

"She hates my guts."

"Call her, send her a card, something. She's lost her mother and this will be a blow, no matter what the circumstances were. I'll do the same."

"I wish . . ." Dooley hesitated.

"Wish what?"

"I wish you an' Cynthia would come home. Well, I got to go."
Click.

"Man alive! What's *this*?"

"It's my new iced tea recipe," said his wife. "Do you like it?"

He raised his glass in a salute. "It's the best I ever tasted. I didn't know you could do this."

"I didn't, either. I never knew how to make good iced tea. So, with our parish party coming up, I asked the Lord to give me the perfect recipe."

"That's the spirit!"

"Do you honestly like it?"

"I never tasted better!" he exclaimed, stealing no thunder from his mother, whose tea represented the southern ideal—heavy on sugar, and blasted with the juice of fresh lemons.

"I woke up yesterday morning and was bursting with all these new ideas about tea. It was very exciting."

"Hmm," he said, gulping draughts of the cold, fruity liquid. "Tropical. Exotic." He swigged it down to the last drop. "Two thumbs up," he said. "But I'm not sure everybody would understand where the recipe came from."

She shrugged. "If He gave William Blake those drawings, why couldn't He give me a simple tea recipe?"

"Good point. What's in it?"

"I can't tell you."

"You can't tell me?"

"No, darling, I've decided to do something very southern—which is to possess at least one secret recipe." She looked pleased with herself.

"But you can tell *me*."

"Not on your life!"

"Why not? I'm your husband!"

"Some well-intentioned parishioner would yank it out of you just like that." She snapped her fingers.

"No!"

"Yes. And then I'd be in the same boat with poor Esther, whose once-secret orange marmalade cake recipe is circulating through Mitford like a virus."

"If that's the way you feel," he said, slightly miffed.

"Suicidal," the doctor had said, adding that he had no good idea when she'd be ready to come home.

Father Tim dialed Janette's cousin, long-distance. No, they really couldn't take Jonathan, it was all they could do to squeeze in Babette and Jason, they were sorry and hoped he understood, which he did.

He was definitely into the fray of Whitecap, with back-to-back meetings, hospital treks, home visitation, and a series of three talks to Busy Fingers, the needlework arm of the ECW. He was even pitching in once a week with Cynthia to help tour visitors through the church and grounds.

Because of the hither and yon-ness of it all, he usually took the Mustang. This morning, however, he was walking to church, leaving his dog behind to amuse Jonathan. He heard Jonathan's loud cries from the guest room; the boy definitely wanted his mother.

"I have story hour at the library this morning. It will take his mind off things." Cynthia nudged him down the steps. "He'll be fine, dear, just go!"

He went, not knowing what else to do.

As he passed through the gate into the street, he had the sense, once again, that someone was watching him. He shaded his eyes and peered toward the hedgebound, chest-high wall that surrounded his neighbor's house.

On impulse, he stepped closer to the hedge and called, "Mr. Love! Are you there?"

About two yards to his left, the foliage moved, shook slightly, and was still. What could he lose? If Morris Love was not there, then he was standing here talking to himself. If Morris Love was there, then he was merely being neighborly.

"If you're there, Mr. Love, I'd just like to say that we—my wife and I—enjoy your music very much."

"Out! Out!"

The sudden shout through the hedge was loud, hoarse, and furious. Father Tim stepped back, startled.

"Out!" The command was repeated with even greater ferocity.

The voice sent chills up his spine. Yes, indeed, he'd done the wrong thing in trying to be neighborly.

He trotted quickly down the lane toward Ernie's, without looking back.

"Junior's got mail!" Ernie proudly announced.

"Off and running, then!" Father Tim sat down at the table with Junior.

"Lookit," said Junior, pushing a stack of letters his way. "You can read 'em if you want to."

He removed the lid from his coffee cup. "Anything promising?"

"See this one?" Junior pointed to the pink envelope that crowned the batch. "It's th' best, I'd read that."

"You sure you want me to read it?"

"Sure!" said Junior. "And I'll let you see her picture when you've read th' letter. You ain't goin' to believe it."

Ernie thumped down at the table, grinning. "Read it out loud. I'd like to hear that one again."

"Yes, sir," said Junior, "read it out loud, that's what I did."

"Here goes." He cleared his throat. " 'Dear—' "

The screen door slapped behind Roanoke. "How y'all?" he queried the general assembly.

"Fine," said Ernie. "Set down, th' preacher's readin' Junior's love letters."

Roanoke pulled up a chair and sat, taking the lid off his coffee. He had a cigarette stuck behind his ear. "I hope they ain't too mushy," he said.

Ernie punched Junior on the arm. "We're lookin' for mushy, right, Junior? Go ahead an' read, Tim."

" *'Dear Serious: I couldn't believe my eyes when I saw your ad. I truly love Scrabble and fishing better than anything! But I personally don't like a whole lot of country music except for Loretta Lynn. I have been looking for somebody to go fishing with and have played Scrabble since I was nine years old. It is my favorite. Are you a Christian? This is real important to me. If you are you ought to say so in your ad it could help somebody decide whether to answer or not.*

" *'If you are and if you are really serious like your ad says you will have to meet my daddy before you can take me out. I am not interested in dirty jokes or cussing. Here's my picture. I am named for Ava Gardner the movie star who was born in Smithfield the same town as my mother who died four years ago with cancer.*

" *'Why am I writing a perfect stranger? My sister said to do it especially as Daddy will meet you first. Before it goes that far though send me*

your picture to the Box Number if you are interested. I am 29 and was
married when I was 17 but my husband was killed driving a tractor
trailer which lost its brakes on a bad curve in West Virginia. I have my
own business and believe in hard work.

"*'I also believe that honesty is the best policy.*

"*'Sincerely yours,*

"*'Ava Goodnight.'*"

"Nice letter," said Father Tim. "Very neat handwriting."

"Now lookit," said Junior, taking a photograph out of his shirt pocket.

Father Tim gazed at the photo of a young woman with chestnut hair and a dazzling smile. "I'll be darned. Beautiful!"

"Where's she live at?" asked Roanoke.

"Swanquarter," said Junior, seeming especially proud of this fact.

"That'll be some mighty long distance courtin'."

Junior shrugged as Roanoke peered over Father Tim's shoulder at the photograph. "Looks like you got th' brass ring."

"I don't know. She has her own business an' all, plus she's really . . . nice-lookin'."

"*Good*-lookin' is what I'd say," said Ernie.

"Right. So she prob'ly wouldn't be interested in . . . you know . . . me, or anything."

"Wrong attitude!" said Ernie. "You were rarin' to go 'til you started gettin' feedback, now you want to crawl off an' quit."

"Well, not quit, exactly," said Junior, looking uneasy.

Roanoke blew on his coffee. "With women, you got t' fish or cut bait."

"Right," said Ernie. "Idn't that right, Tim?"

"That's right." Didn't he know? Hadn't he learned? He had cut bait 'til he nearly lost Cynthia Coppersmith for all eternity.

"Write her back," said Ernie. "You don't cuss too bad, and I never heard you tell a dirty joke, so you got that covered. Plus you're both dead set on bein' honest."

"*Are* you a Christian?" asked Roanoke, taking the cigarette from behind his ear. "Seem like that's pretty major in her opinion."

"Well . . ." Junior thought about it. "I guess. I mean, my mama went to church an' all, 'til she died, and I went pretty regular 'til a few years ago."

Roanoke lit his cigarette and inhaled deeply. "That don't necessarily cut it," he said. "I don't know much, but I do know that."

"Anyway," said Junior, "I don't have a picture."

"You got a camera?"

"Somewhere I got a camera I won at the fair."

"Bring it in tomorrow mornin' on your way to the Toe and I'll snap you one or two shots," said Ernie. "I got film over there, we'll use a roll of two-hundred if th' light's not good."

"Should I wear a tie?"

"I wouldn't do that. What you got on'll be fine."

"Maybe I should wear a cap." Junior smoothed his hair, which was thinning in front.

"Honesty is the best policy," said Ernie. "Don't wear a cap. But hold your stomach in an' all."

"I don't think I should wear what I got on, these are my work clothes."

Roanoke blew a smoke ring. "She said she believes in hard work."

Junior was looking increasingly frustrated. Suddenly he turned to Father Tim. "What do you think, sir?"

"Maybe . . . maybe a pair of jeans with a denim shirt and a jacket?"

Junior sighed. "I'll have to wash m' jeans and iron a shirt."

"So?" said Ernie. "Big deal. It ought to be worth a little effort, gettin' a letter like that from a nice girl. Just remember what some of those other letters said."

Junior blushed.

The light on his office answering machine was blinking.

Emma, as usual, did not stand on ceremony.

"Seems like things are fallin' apart up here since you left. I just heard Louella fell and broke her hip, just like Miss Sadie, and she's in th' hospital and Hoppy says it's a good thing she's well padded because it could have been worse. But if you ask me, practically every old person I hear about who breaks a hip . . . well, I don't want to say it, but you know what I mean—

"Snickers, stop that this minute! Hold on, he's chewin' Harold's church shoes." The phone clattered onto the countertop. General mumbling, barking, and door-slamming.

"By th' way, I been meanin' to tell you that Uncle Billy's havin' knee surgery. I think that's what he said, my phone has an awful lot of static since th' storm last week. . . ."

They said their prayers in the darkened room and held each other, talking in low voices lest Jonathan wake up and make his usual midnight invasion.

"I feel we need to run home to Mitford," he said.

"Run home to Mitford? Darling, you don't just *run home* when it's twelve hundred miles round trip and a hundred degrees in the shade. Dooley will be fine, I promise."

"It's not just Dooley. It's also Esther and Gene and Louella and Lace and . . ." He sighed. "I feel helpless."

"You want to help everybody and fix everything. But Timothy, you just can't."

"I've never been able to swallow that down."

"Remember the sign I have over my drawing board at home? 'Don't feel totally, personally, irrevocably responsible for everything. That's my job. Signed, God.' "

"Ummm."

She kissed his cheek. "I love you to pieces," she said.

"I love you to pieces back," he replied, smiling in the dark. He would be in a ditch without Cynthia Kavanagh.

"Listen," she whispered, "you run home to Mitford and I'll hold down the fort, OK? I've got at least two and a half tons of cookies to bake and freeze, not to mention a hundred miniature quiches and six loaves of bread with sun-dried tomatoes."

"You're doing it again, you're not letting anyone help with the party."

"Who can help? Marion is at the library practically every day, poor Jean Ballenger couldn't cook if her life depended on it, Marlene Bragg's fingernails are so long she can barely get ice out of a tray, and everyone else works."

"Who's doing flowers? I know you'll want them in all the rooms."

She sighed. "I'd give my French watercolors for a Hessie Mayhew in this parish. But alas, I suppose I'm doing them myself."

"I'll order flowers for you, have them delivered."

"How sweet, but no, I'll cut what's left in the garden and plunder

Marion's little plot—you know I love that tousled look for flowers, nothing arranged. Anyway, darling, we're getting off the point. Run home to Mitford and see Dooley and make your rounds and come back to me."

"Are you sure?"

"Of course. Go to sleep."

She patted his cheek and turned on her side and he listened for her breathing to become regular, rhythmic. But it did not. He could feel her lying awake, just as he was doing.

"What is it, Kavanagh? Can't sleep?" He reached out and touched her shoulder.

"Cynthia?" Good heavens, she was crying.

He pulled her against him and she turned in his arms and wept quietly.

"My girl, my dearest love, what is it?"

"I'm homesick for Mitford, too, but I've tried and tried to be brave about it and not let you know. I see you wanting to go and take care of things, and, well, so do I. I mean, I like it here, actually I love it here, but I miss Mitford, I miss our home."

"I understand."

"I'm so sorry you've caught me out, Timothy. I feel like a criminal, hiding this from you."

"Thank goodness it's hidden no more. You'll come with me, then, we'll leave first thing next Thursday morning. I'll get Father Jack to supply, I'm sure he'll do it, and we'll head back here on Sunday."

He might have gotten up and danced a jig.

"Best of all," he declared, "we'll have two days with Dooley before he goes off to school."

"Lovely!" she said, forgetting to whisper. "I can't wait to see the big lug. What a dreadful thing he's going through. Of course, we'll have to take Jonathan. . . ."

"Of course! They'll love him in Mitford."

"He can watch a movie, Dooley has a VCR!"

"Thank You, Lord!" he exclaimed, feeling a slow flush happiness.

"Yes, thank You, Lord!" she said, blowing her nose.

CHAPTER TEN

If Wishes Were Horses

He regretted being unable to introduce their new organist around on Sunday, but Sam and Marion said they'd do it for him.

He called Jack Ferguson.

"Happy to!" exclaimed the retired priest, who was fond of peppering his sermons with ecclesiastical jokes. "I'll just pop up with Earlene. Maybe you'll let us stay at your place Saturday night."

"Absolutely! We'll leave the keys under the potted geranium by the front door. You know where the church is . . ."

"Oh, yes, I've supplied St. John's several times, always a pleasure!"

". . . and I'll fax the directions to Dove Cottage."

"Super!" said Father Jack. "By the way, have you heard that Ron Cowper is leaving St. Michael's?"

"I'll be darned. I thought he was rooted in there like a turnip."

"One of the parish told him, said, 'Father Ron, I'm so sorry you're going, we never knew what sin was 'til you came.'"

He chuckled. "Jack, Jack."

"All true, Timothy. And did you hear about Bishop Harvey's big trip to Uganda?"

"Briefly, when he was here in July."

"At the end of a worship service, Bill had a notion to give the blessing in the language of the region. He picked up the printed sheet, made the sign of the cross, then very slowly and solemnly read in Luganda, 'Do not take away the service bulletin.' "

Father Tim laughed heartily. "Thank heaven you don't know anything to tell on me."

"Oh," said Father Jack, "I'll think of something."

There was a new spring in his step; he felt a fresh excitement both at home and at church.

"You're mighty perky," said a member of the Altar Guild, who was trimming candlewicks in the vesting room.

"Darling, you're positively glowing!" said his wife, who appeared to be unusually sunny herself.

"Hit'll be good t' clap eyes on you 'uns," said Harley. "I'll make us a pan of brownies."

"I'm really glad you're comin'," said Dooley.

In the grand anticipation of it all, he made a long-distance "house call" to Uncle Billy.

"I'll be et f'r a tater if it ain't th' preacher!" exclaimed the old man, obviously delighted.

"Just checking on your knee, Uncle Billy."

"My knee? Hit's th' same as ever, ol' arthur's got it, don't you know."

"I thought Emma said you were having knee surgery."

"Nossir, what I had was *tree* surgery."

"Aha. Well. Tell me about it."

"Hit was a big to-do, don't you know, th' town sent a crew t' doctor them old trees out back, they was rotted in some places and about t' fall over. Wellsir, they was there all day Wednesday, then come back again and was there all day Thursday, had a big crane an' all. Hit was like a tent meetin' th' way people turned out t' watch, we could of went t' sellin' corn dogs. Wish you'd been here."

"We'll be there late Thursday for a short visit. I'll get by and see you and Miss Rose on Saturday."

"Hit'll be a treat an' a half t' see you 'uns, I'll ask Rose t' whip up a banana puddin'."

"Don't go to any trouble," said Father Tim, meaning it. "In fact, don't even *think* about it!"

"We're going home, old buddy," he said to Barnabas as they loped toward Ernie's. "We're going to see Dooley, remember Dooley?"

Of course his dog remembered Dooley. Any dog with a penchant for Wordsworth, Cowper, and Keats was a smart dog.

Just four days and he'd be good as new, ready to pour himself back into St. John's and no need to run home again until October for Buck's and Pauline's wedding, which he'd cleared with his bishop early on.

He felt positively on holiday. He would put in five hours at St. John's, and dash home to pack and take Cynthia and Jonathan out for an early dinner. Then, at six-thirty tomorrow morning, they were out of here.

Janette's doctor reported only mild response to the medication. It would take time, he said, for her to feel any meaningful effects; meanwhile, they were monitoring her closely.

He called Janette's room. No answer. He thought he should have her approval to take Jonathan all the way to the other end of the state, but he dreaded the possibility of upsetting her. What if she felt bereft, knowing that her priest and children were all off the island? He recalled that even her doctor was leaving on Friday to play golf in Beaufort.

Marion agreed to go to the hospital after church on Sunday. He caught Jean Ballenger leaving a Busy Fingers class, and asked her to visit Janette on Thursday, Friday, and Saturday.

"Oh, yes!" she said. "I'll go. I enjoy the sick."

"Here," he said, taking out his wallet and giving her five dollars. "If you don't mind, please buy her some oranges, or . . ."

Jean took the bill. "Would you like them maybe in a basket with a little bow on the handle?"

"I'd be much obliged," he said.

"I could put in a pot of African violets for another five," she said, eyeing his wallet.

He had celebrated Holy Eucharist with seven of the faithful remnant and four tourists from Canada, cleared his desk, returned his calls, thoroughly discussed Sunday's music with Ella Bridgewater by phone, and alerted the choir to be on their best behavior. He had also shown a couple from Delaware around the cemetery, typed the pew bulletin, emptied his wastebasket, and stamped the mail.

He was walking out the door when the phone rang.

"St. John's in the Grove!" he said. Then, feeling suddenly inspired to elaborate, he quoted the psalmist. " 'This is the day the Lord has made!' "

There was a brief silence on the other end. "Timothy?"

Sounded like Bill Harvey.

"Speaking."

"That was a very upbeat phone greeting." It was Bill Harvey, all right.

"I'm feeling upbeat, Bishop, how are you?"

"Wanting to have a little talk with you about something." Bill Harvey was not speaking in his let's-go-fishing voice; this was his high-church, gospel-side *vox populi*.

"Shoot!" He may as well walk straight into the wind, head down and hunkered over.

"It comes to my attention that you're making a little trip to Mitford."

"Why . . . yes." He cleared his throat. "Just four days."

"To attend, I believe, to the needs of several former parishioners . . ."

"Well . . . yes." He'd mentioned to one or two people why he was going away, but had said nothing about Dooley.

". . . and dismissing, I presume, your sworn duty to attend to the needs of your current parishioners?"

"I hadn't thought of it that way, Bishop." His stomach did a small turn.

"It's time you thought of it that way, Timothy. You know very well the policy of the church, and that is to be strictly hands-off the old parish while you go about the business of the new. Surely it doesn't escape your memory that Lord's Chapel has a priest of its own to attend these people."

"Certainly." He heard his voice come near to croaking. He didn't think it would help matters to say his boy had been in jail and might like a little cheering up before he went off to school.

Then again, the bishop was right, he wasn't supposed to meddle in the business of Mitford's new priest. But these people were his friends. . . .

"But they're my *friends*," he said, knowing it would avail him nothing.

"Of course they're your friends, you served them for sixteen years."

"It was my wish to . . . I only wished to—"

"If wishes were horses, Timothy, beggars would ride. Let us stick to the point. I believe you're going to Mitford in October to conduct a wedding."

"Yes."

"I strongly caution you against this current jaunt."

Suddenly out of breath, he thumped into his desk chair and stared unseeing at the wall.

His wife gave the entire episcopate a fine tongue-lashing, mincing no words, and got over the whole incident in a trice. While he enjoyed her stinging barbs, they did little to soothe his sense of injury. It was true that, in principle, Bill Harvey was right, but he'd found his tone of voice, his corporate indifference, rude beyond measure. He was accustomed to a bishop whose kindness extended throughout his diocese, with seeming affection for all his deacons and priests; indeed, he was proud to have in Stuart Cullen a bishop who actually wrote important letters "in his own hand," as St. Paul himself had been pleased to do.

"Blast!" he said, looking out the kitchen window. "Double blast!"

"That's right, darling, let it all out!" encouraged his wife, who was buttering Jonathan's spaghetti.

"Blast!" said Jonathan, smacking the table with both hands.

Why hadn't he kept his big mouth shut about going home? He felt like a traitor, a heel, disappointing everyone. And now he had to go back over all the ground he'd plowed, calling everyone and making excuses. . . .

"You need something . . . *vigorous* to do," she suggested.

"I'll take Barnabas and go running," he said testily.

"Isn't your fishing trip coming up soon?"

Fishing trip! The very last thing he wanted to do was go on a fishing trip. A fine spectacle he'd make, knowing almost nothing about a rod and reel, and even less about sliding around on the deck of a boat with an eight hundred and fifty horsepower engine throbbing under his tennis shoes. Didn't he make a fool of himself every Sunday morning of his life? Why do it all over again on a trip that was costing his wife a cool two hundred bucks, not including a bucket of chicken?

Miss Rose answered the phone with a positive shout. *"Hello!"*

"Miss Rose? This is Father Tim."

"Are you here?"

"No, ma'am, I'm *here*," he shouted back. "You see, something's . . . *come up.*"

"What's that? *Bum luck?*"

"Well, yes, in a way. May I speak with Uncle Billy?"

She turned from the phone and squawked, "Bill! Bill Watson! It's our old preacher!"

He thought she might have put it another way.

There was a long silence.

"I'm sorry, son."

Dooley sighed. "I know. It's OK. Really."

"I'm going to try and have the court date set during the time I'm home for the wedding. You'll be home then, too, so I believe everything's going to work out just fine."

"Great," said Dooley, sounding relieved.

"Have fun these last days. How are Poo and Jessie?"

"Really good!"

He heard the sudden tenderness in the boy's voice.

"And your mother?"

"She's really good, too, she got a raise at Hope House."

"Glad news! You're always in our prayers, buddy. God cares about your needs."

"OK, 'bye." said Dooley. "Wait. That woman upstairs . . ."

"What about her?"

"She plays the dern piano mighty loud. Me'n Harley are thinkin' about knockin' on th' ceiling with a broom handle."

And he'd been worried about Dooley's music aggravating his tenant. "I wouldn't do that. Hang in there."

"I got Lace a card."

"Great! I did, too."

"It was hard as heck to pick out, there are millions of cards."

"True. What did it say?"

"Nothin.' It was blank."

"Aha."

"I just wrote in it, 'I'm sorry.' "

"Couldn't be better."

"I signed my whole name, in case she knows anybody else named Dooley."

"Probably not."

"Well, I got to go, Avis wants me to clean out th' butcher case. *Gross.* I told him I'll pick up anything but liver, he has to do that. I mean, you can feel liver all the way through those weird gloves we have to wear."

"Please!" he said, bilious at the thought.

It wrenched his heart to say goodbye. But what were hearts for, in the end? A little wrenching now and then was far, far better than no wrenching at all.

He was trying to forgive Bill Harvey. In the scheme of things, the bishop's attitude was hardly worth his concern. Why couldn't he blow by it, forgive and forget? Of no small concern, however, was the hardness that would come in if he didn't forgive this slight. He was to drag it into the light and expose it before God and get it over with.

He dropped to his knees in the study and prayed silently. The early morning breeze pushed through open windows and puffed the curtains into the room.

There was a tap on his shoulder.

"What are you doin'?" asked Jonathan, standing next to him in rumpled blue pajamas.

He rose from his knees and picked the boy up. They thumped into the chair, Jonathan in his lap. "I was praying."

"Why?" Jonathan snuggled against him.

"That I might find God's grace to forgive someone."

"Why?"

"Because if I don't forgive this person, it will be unhealthy for me, and God won't think much of it, either."

He loved the chunky, vibrant feel of the boy on his lap, the warm, solid weight against his chest. Exactly the way God wants us to come to Him, he thought, his spirits suddenly brightening.

"I don't want p'sketti no more. No p'sketti."

"Good! Hallelujah! What do you want?"

Jonathan pondered this, then looked up at him. "I don't know."

"Well, if you don't, who does?"

Jonathan poked him in the chest with a chubby finger. "You find somethin'."

"Please."

"Please."

"Consider it done."

He and Cynthia had been transplanted, that was all. He knew from years of digging around in the dirt and moving perennials from one corner of the yard to another what transplanting was about. First came the wilt, then the gradual settling in, then the growth spurt. That simple. What had Gertrude Jekyll said to the gardener squeamish about moving a plant or bush? "Hoick it!"

God had hoicked him and he'd better get over the wilt and get busy putting down roots.

He went out to the porch, whistling. Glorious day—his fair wife sitting contentedly in a rocker, Jonathan rigged with a straw hat and playing in the garden with his dog, and an afternoon romp in the ocean on the family agenda.

He sat in one of the white rockers and kicked off his loafers. "Ahhhh!" he sighed.

"Timothy, you have that wilderness look again."

"What wilderness look?" he asked, as if he didn't know.

"That John the Baptist look."

He had been in denial about it for some time, now, until his hair had fanned out over his clerical collar like the tail of a turkey gobbler. He just didn't seem to have what it took to break in a new barber.

"I hear there's a little shop next to the post office, Linda's or Libbie's or Lola's . . . something like that."

"Aha." No, indeed. He'd cut it himself with an oyster knife before he'd put his head in the hands of another Fancy Skinner.

"I'll hold out for a barber, thank you," he said, feeling imperious.

He checked the answering machine when they came in from the grocery store.

"Father? It's me, Puny."

Puny didn't sound like herself.

"I don't know how to tell you this."

This was definitely his least favorite way for a phone call to begin.

"I just got to your house and realized I'd left th' door unlocked for four days!"

"Speak to Ba!" one of the twins pleaded.

"How in th' world I did a dumb thing like that, I don't know, I'm jis' so sorry. But I've looked and looked, and nothin' seems missin', so I think it's all right, but I know how you count on me to take care of things, and I jis' hate lettin' you down on anything."

"It's OK!" he said aloud to the machine. He loved that girl like his own flesh. "Don't worry about it!"

"I know you sometimes don't lock your doors, but I always do because I'm responsible for things here, and I jis' hope that . . . anyway, we're real sorry you aren't comin', we all looked forward to it a lot, and I hope you'll not think hard of me for leavin' your door unlocked."

"Speak to Ba, speak to Ba!"

"Oh, for Pete's sake, Sissy, you'll wake up Sassy, *here*!"

"Ba! Come home, we got puppies. Come home, Ba!"

"Say 'bye, now. Tell 'im you love 'im."

"Love you, Ba."

"Tell 'im you love Miss Cynthia."

"Love Miss Cynthy."

"That was Sissy. Sassy's still asleep," said his industrious house help. "We've got an awful mess of puppies in th' garage, four little speckled things, I don't know what they are, oh, mercy, I'm prob'ly usin' up all your tape, now here's th' good news! Joe Joe's been promoted to lieutenant! That's right under th' chief. How d'you like that?"

He liked it very much indeed.

"We thought you was goin' home," said Roanoke.

"Change of plans. Where's Ernie this morning?"

"Him an' Roger's gone fishin'."

"Captain Willie?"

"Nope. Over to th' Sound."

"You're minding the store?"

"You got it," said Roanoke. Father Tim thought he'd never seen so many wrinkles in one face. Roanoke Clark, it might be said, looked like he'd been hung out to dry and left on the line.

He didn't exactly relish the idea of spending one-on-one time with a man who didn't like preachers. Then again, it was only six-thirty in the morning, and not a darned thing to do at the church office, since he'd already done it all for the trip to Mitford.

What the heck. He thumped down at a table, unwrapped his egg biscuit, and took the lid off his coffee.

"So . . . how's business?"

"We had a big run this mornin', it slacked off just before you come in."

He ate his biscuit while Roanoke read the paper and smoked.

"What about a good barber on the island? Know anybody?"

"Don't have an official barber on th' island. Have t' go across."

"Seems a waste of time to be running back and forth to the mainland just to get your hair trimmed."

Roanoke appeared to be talking to the newspaper he was holding in front of him. "Lola up by th' post office, she'll give you a trim. You won't need t' go back 'til Christmas."

"Who's Lola?"

"Lola sells fish san'wiches, cuts hair, you name it."

He shivered. "Is that where you get your hair cut?"

"Once every two months, whether I need it or not."

He examined Roanoke's haircut. No way.

"So, ah, where do Ernie and Roger get their hair cut?"

"I do it."

"You do it?"

"Keep my barber tools in th' book room over there." Roanoke indicated the book room with a wave of his hand.

"Aha."

"Six bucks a pop," said Roanoke, laying the paper on the table. "Six bucks and fifteen minutes, that's my motto."

"Did you . . . ever cut hair for a living?"

"I cut hair for truckers. When I was haulin' sheet metal, I had a stopover in Concord twice a month; I set up in th' back room of a barbecue joint. They rolled in there from New York City, Des Moines, Iowa, Los Alamos, Calfornia, you name it, they lined up from here to yonder." Roanoke looked proud of this fact, installing a fresh cigarette behind his ear.

"You might say I've cut hair from sea t' shinin' sea."

"I'll be darned." Now what was he going to do? His egg biscuit began to petrify in his stomach.

"You'll have t' set out here, since I got t' watch th' register, but I'll take care of it for you. I didn't want t' say nothin', but I wondered when you was goin' to get it off your collar. I thought maybe that was your religion."

Father Tim laughed uneasily and clapped his hip. He'd paid for his biscuit with pocket change; maybe he'd left his wallet at home. Sometimes he did. He hoped he did.

"You can pay me anytime. I run a little tab for Roger 'n' Ernie."

Oh, well, how bad could it be? He didn't recall that Ernie or Roger looked too butchered; pretty normal, to tell the truth.

"Fine," he said. "Fifteen minutes?"

Roanoke dragged the battered stool from behind the cash register and set it by the front window.

"Couldn't we, ah, move the stool back a little?" He didn't want to be on display for every passing car and truck on the island.

"I need th' light," said Roanoke, squinting at his hair.

Though he'd spent considerable time at morning prayer in his study, he prayed again as he clambered onto the stool.

Roanoke brought a box from the book room, followed by Elmo the Book Cat. It was the first time he'd seen Elmo out in general society. The elderly, longhaired cat sat on the cement floor, flicked its tail, and stared at him, as Roanoke laid his barbering paraphernalia on the window seat.

"Here you go," said Roanoke, throwing a torn sheet around Father Tim's shoulders. The sheet smelled of fish. Maybe that was why the cat was staring at him.

"Back when I was drivin'," said Roanoke, leaning into his work, "I run thirty-seven states and two provinces of Canada. One time I was caught in a tornada, it blowed me over an embankment and totaled my truck, but I walked away without a scratch, which was th' closest I ever come to believin' in God."

Father Tim felt the scissors snipping away, saw the hair thump onto the cement. The cat watched, still flicking its tail.

"I hauled a lot of orange juice outa Florida in my time. If I was haulin' fresh, a load would run around fifty-five hundred gallons. Concentrate, that'd weigh in around forty-seven hundred." *Snip, snip.*

Barbering certainly loosened the tongue of the usually taciturn Roanoke; he'd turned into a regular jabbermouth. Come to think of it, Father Tim had noticed the same phenomenon in Fancy Skinner and Joe Ivey. Clearly, nonstop discourse was very closely related to messing with hair.

"I even hauled chocolate syrup outa Pennsylvania, a lot of chocolate comes outa Pennsylvania, but I never hauled poultry or anything livin', nossir, I wouldn't haul anything livin'."

"Good idea."

"I never got pulled but one time. Now, there's some drivers, they can be wild, they'll run their rigs hard as they can run 'em to git up th' next hill. Regulations say you cain't drive but ten hours a day, but cowboys, that's what we called 'em, they'll go up t' eighteen, twenty hours, drivin' illegal.

"Cowboys is only about two percent of th' drivers out there today, but they give th' rest of us a bad name, you know what I mean?"

"I do!"

Snip, thump. "I do a little roofin' now, a little house paintin', cut a little hair, a man can make a livin' if he's got ambition."

"I agree!"

"Got rid of my car, ride a bicycle now, it's amazin' how much money you can put back when you shuck a car."

"I'll bet."

"I was raised in a Christian home, but I fell away. See, my first wife run off with a travelin' preacher, I brought 'im home, give 'im a good, warm bed an' a hot meal, an' first thing you know, they hightailed it."

"Aha." So that was why Roanoke was never especially thrilled to see him; he'd been tarred with the same brush. He had a sudden, vivid

recall of van Gogh's self-portrait in which he sported only one ear.
Please, Lord . . .

Elmo yawned and lay down, without removing his gaze from the
customer on the stool.

"Now, you take me, I never run around on my second wife,
an' they was plenty of chances to do it. Lot lizards is what we called
'em, they'll pester a man nearly to death. But I stayed true to my wife
an' I'm glad I did, because you never know what you'll pick up on th'
road an' bring home to innocent people."

"Right."

"I never did pills, neither, nossir, th' strongest thing I ever done
when I was drivin' was Sun-drop, it'll knock your block off if you ain't
used to much caffeine in your system. You want a Sun-drop, we got
'em in th' cooler."

"That's OK, I don't believe so. Maybe another time." Boy howdy,
this was an education and a half.

Thump, thump, snip.

"But things is changed. It'd bring a tear to a glass eye to hear what
a owner-operator pays these days to run a big rig."

"How much?"

"More'n sixty cent a mile. You have to be tough to make a livin'
with truckin'."

"I'll bet so."

"I'm goin' to clean your neck up now. How's our time runnin'?"

Father Tim looked at his watch. "You've got a little under one
minute."

"We're goin' to bring you in right on th' dot," said Roanoke, flipping the switch on his electric shaver.

Cynthia waved from the porch. Jonathan and Barnabas were waiting at the gate.

"Look at me!" said the boy, jumping up and down.

"I'm looking. That's a new shirt!"

"And new pants!"

He opened the gate. "Where did those snappy new clothes come
from, buddyroe?"

"UPS!"

"Dearest, where's your hair?" called his wife from the porch.

"In a Dumpster behind Ernie's! What do you think?"

"I love it!" she said, sitting down on the top step. "We've got a surprise for you!"

His wife was herself wearing something new and boggling. Red shorts, which were plenty short, a strapless white top, and espadrilles.

He scratched behind his dog's ears and fairly bounded up the steps.

His sermon was finished and walked through, thought for thought, precept upon precept. In the study, Jonathan had paced to the bookcase at his heels, then to the wall with the painting of the Roman Colosseum. Exhausted at last, Jonathan fell asleep on the rug, where Father Tim stepped over him without missing a beat.

The rest of the day lay ahead, shimmering like silk. They would swim in the ocean, they would go out to dinner in their new duds, and tomorrow they'd hear the organ raising its mighty voice to the timbers.

He felt as young as a curate, as bold as a lion.

"Having a little boy is different," said his wife, drying her hair after their frolic in the ocean. "We're going out to dinner and it's only five-thirty."

"Like a bunch of farmhands," he agreed, pulling on his brand-new shorts and golf shirt. One thing he could say about golf, which he'd never played and never would, he sure liked the shirts.

"I sketched Jonathan today," she said.

"Aha!"

"For the new Violet book. I think he'll weave into it beautifully, just what I've been needing to . . . round it out, I think."

He heard someone knocking, and Barnabas flew at once to the door, his bark as throaty as the bass of St. John's organ.

He zipped his shorts and padded down the hall barefoot, stunned to see Father Jack and Earlene peering through the screen.

Good Lord! He'd completely forgotten to tell Jack Ferguson they weren't going home to Mitford!

Beet-red with embarrassment, he let the eager but surprised couple into the living room, and braced himself for the inept explanations he'd be forced to deliver, not only to the Fergusons but to his *wife*.

Dadgummit, now Father Jack would have a story to tell on him, which would spread through the diocese like fleas in August.

"Welcome to Dove Cottage," he said, trying to mean it.

They had gone to Mona's and eaten fried perch, hard crabs, broiled shrimp, yellowfin tuna fresh off the boat, hush puppies, french fries, and buckets of coleslaw. They had slathered on tartar sauce and downed quarts of tea as sweet as syrup, then staggered home in the heat with Jonathan drugged and half asleep on Father Tim's back.

As they walked, Cynthia did her part to deliver after-dinner entertainment, loudly reciting a poem by someone named Rachel Field.

> *"If once you have slept on an island*
> *You'll never be quite the same;*
> *You may look as you looked the day before*
> *And go by the same old name.*
> *You may bustle about the street or shop;*
> *You may sit at home and sew,*
> *But you'll see blue water and wheeling gulls*
> *Wherever your feet may go."*

"I declare!" said Earlene. "You're clever as anything to remember all that. I wonder if it's the truth."

"What?"

"That part about never being quite the same."

"I don't know," said Cynthia. "We'll have to wait and see."

They sat on the porch and watched the gathering sunset through the trellis, where the Marion Climber had put forth several new blooms.

"Now, Jack," he said, "don't go home and tell this story on me."

"I make no promises." Father Jack chuckled.

He gave a mock sigh. "Is there no balm in Gilead?"

"Not as long as Jack's around," said his wife.

He wondered if Jack had discussed his Mitford trip with the bishop. Very likely they'd talked and Jack had mentioned it, a casual thing.

"Talked to the bishop lately?" he asked.

"Nope. Not a word. Saw him at the convention a while back. He's put on a good bit of weight."

"Who hasn't?" asked Father Tim, feeling relieved.

"I guess you heard what happened at Holy Cross over in Manteo."

"All I know about this diocese is what you tell me, Jack."

"More's the pity. Anyway, Bishop Harvey was making his annual visitation at Holy Cross, got there and saw about eight people sitting in the congregation. He was pretty hot about it, as you can imagine. He got vested, kept looking for somebody else to arrive, they didn't, so he asked Luke Castor, said, 'Father, didn't you tell them I was coming?'

"Luke said, 'No, but obviously they found out somehow.' "

"You have to take Jack with a grain of salt as big as your head," said Earlene.

The sunset delivered a great, slow wash of color above the beach-front cottages and turned the patch of blue to violet, then scarlet, then gold.

"Oh, the blessing of a porch," sighed Earlene. "When Jack and I walk out our front door, we just drop off in the yard like heathens."

"That's one way to put it," said her husband.

Earlene gave her hostess a profound look. "Don't let anybody talk you into a retirement home!"

"Never fear!" exclaimed Cynthia.

"It's not that bad, Earlene," said Father Jack. "You may not have a porch, but somebody else does the cooking three meals a day."

"You've got a point, dear," said Earlene, feeling better about lacking a porch. "And after supper in the dining room, some of us play gin rummy, or sometimes pinochle."

"Lovely!" said Cynthia.

Father Tim peered at his wife, thinking she was holding up gamely, though she appeared to be gripping the arms of her rocker with some force.

Earlene Ferguson did not care for silences in conversation, and was doing her level best to caulk every chink and crack, so he didn't know how long the music had been drifting across the street.

"Listen!" he said, during a chink.

"What's that?" asked Father Jack.

"Just listen." César Franck . . .

There was a brief silence on the porch.

"Goodness!" said Earlene. "Somebody's sure playing their radio loud. That's a problem we have at the retirement home, with so many being half deaf, plus, of course, our walls are thin as paper—"

"Hush, Earlene," said Father Jack.

He'd never quite appreciated the wisdom of having a king-size bed until his wife introduced him to its luxuries on the second night of their marriage. As a bachelor, he'd spent several decades rolled into the middle of a sagging mattress like a hotdog in a bun.

Now, with the addition of a three-year-old in their lives, the chiefest virtues of a large bed were amply demonstrated. He looked in on Jonathan, who was sprawled across Cynthia's pillow, and went to the guest room and tapped on the door.

"Jack? We're going to step down to the beach for a few minutes."

Jack came to the door and cracked it. "How long have you been married?" he asked, grinning.

"Not too long," said Father Tim.

He unrolled the blanket and they spread it on the sand.

"Full moon, my dear, and no extra charge."

"Heaven," she breathed, kneeling on the blanket. "Heaven!"

"Didn't I tell you I'd give you the moon and stars?" He sat next to her and smelled the faintest scent of wisteria lifted to him on the breeze. He would go for months, used to her scent and immune to its seduction, then, suddenly, it was new to him again, compelling.

"How are you holding up being married to a parson?"

"I love being married to my parson."

"The Fergusons didn't throw you too badly?"

"Goodness, Timothy, what kind of wimp do you think I am? I don't know much, but I do know that the wife of a priest must be ready for anything."

"That's the spirit!"

She lay back on the blanket, and he lay beside her, loving her nearness, loving the sense that sometimes, if only for a moment, he couldn't tell where she left off and he began.

Lulled by the background roar and lap of the waves, he gazed up into the onyx bowl spangled with life and light, and took her hand. " 'Bright star,' " he quoted to her from Keats, " 'would I were steadfast as thou art . . .' "

"You've always thought me steadfast," she said, "but I'm not, I'm not at all, Timothy. I'm sometimes like so much Silly Putty."

"You're always there for me, sending off for new clothes, taking in children, drumming up the parish tea, standing with me at the church door. I don't deserve this, you know, it scares me."

"You're all I have," she murmured, drawing him close, "and all I ever wanted. So stop being scared!"

"Yes," he said. "I'll try."

The windows and front doors were thrown open to a fickle breeze, the creaking ceiling fans circled at full throttle. Here and there, an occasional pew bulletin lifted on a draft of moving air and went sailing.

Peering loftward through a glass pane in the sacristy door, he couldn't help but notice that the soprano had returned to the fold and was cooling herself with a battery-operated fan. He also saw that every pew in St. John's was filled to bursting.

Air-conditioning! he thought, running his finger around his collar. Next year's budget, and no two ways about it.

Standing next to him in the tiny sacristy, Marshall Duncan pulled the bell rope eleven times.

. . . bong . . . bong . . .

On the heel of the eleventh bell, Ella Bridgewater, fully rehearsed and mildly fibrillating with excitement, hammered down on the opening hymn as if all creation depended on it.

Marshall opened the sacristy door and crossed himself reverently as the crucifer led the procession into the nave.

Glorious! His congregation was standing bolt upright, and singing as lustily as any crowd of Baptists he'd ever seen or heard tell of.

> *"Lift high the cross*
> *the love of Christ proclaim . . ."*

He threw his head back and, with his flock, gave himself wholly to the utterance of joy on this morning of mornings.

> *". . . till all the world adore*
> *his sacred Name.*
> *Led on their way by*
> *this triumphant sign*
> *the hosts of God in*
> *conquering ranks combine."*

The organ music soared and swirled above their heads like a great incoming tide; surely he only imagined seeing the chandeliers tremble.

"Blessed be God," he proclaimed at the end of the mighty *Amen.* "Father, Son, and Holy Spirit!"

The eager congregational response made his scalp tingle. "And blessed be his kingdom, now and forever!"

He lifted his hands to heaven, and prayed.

"Almighty God, to You all hearts are open, all desires known, and from You no secrets are hid: Cleanse the thoughts of our hearts by the inspiration of Your Holy Spirit, that we may perfectly love You, and worthily magnify Your holy Name; through Christ our Lord."

"Amen!" they said as one.

He didn't sense it every time, no; if only he could. But this morning, the Holy Spirit was moving in the music and among the people of St. John's; He was about the place in a way that left them dazzled and wondering, unable to ken the extravagant mystery of it.

For this moment, this blessed hour, heaven was breathing its perfume on their little handful in the church on the island in the vast blue sea, and they were honored and thankful and amazed.

CHAPTER ELEVEN

Worms to Butterflies

"Father?"

"Puny!"

"Th' most awful thing has happened, I don't know how to tell you. . . ."

He sank into the office chair. "Just tell me," he said, feeling suddenly weary.

"Your angel . . ." Weeping, nose blowing.

"My angel?"

"Th' one on th' mantel! I was runnin' th' dust rag downstairs, you know I run th' dust rag every time I come because of th' work goin' on in th' street, you knew they was relayin' pipes, didn't you?"

"No, I didn't know."

"Well, I was runnin' th' dust rag an' . . ." More nose blowing.

"It's all right. Whatever you're going to tell me is all right." She was dusting and the angel toppled off the mantel and fell to the floor and a wing broke off, or an arm. How bad could it be?

"Well, th' angel . . . it's not *there* anymore, it's gone!"

"Gone?"

"Today I was dustin' downstairs because I dusted upstairs last week, and when I come to th' mantel, I couldn't believe my eyes. It was jis' this empty place where it used to set!"

"Well, now . . ."

"I mean, th' other day when I called you about th' door bein' un-locked, I looked all around an' didn't see nothin' missin', I mean, I thought somethin' seemed different about your study, but I couldn't figure out what it was, I didn't notice anything bein' *gone*, so what I'm sayin' is, maybe it was gone last week, I don't know!"

"Have you talked with Harley? And Puny, stop crying, it's all right. Just sit down, take a deep breath, and tell me everything."

"I talked to Harley, he said he hadn't seen nothin' goin' on at your house, 'cept me goin' in an' out."

"Was anything else missing, anything moved around?"

"No, sir, an' I promise you I really looked, I've went over th' whole house with a fine-tooth comb, even th' closets, an' checked th' win-dows an' basement door, they're locked tight as a drum. I feel terrible about this, Father, I'll pay for th' angel, whatever it cost, me an' Joe will pay ever' cent."

"This is a mystery. I remember having a fifty-dollar bill and a credit card in my desk drawer. I wonder—"

"I'll go look!" she said.

Very odd, he mused.

"Your money and credit card's in th' drawer on th' left-hand side."

Odder than odd. "I wonder if Dooley would know anything."

"I don't think Dooley was in th' house a single time."

"I'll call him at school and ask. I don't know, Puny, I'm as baffled by this as you are."

"I'm real sorry."

"It's OK, I promise. We'll figure it out, don't worry. Just . . . lock up good when you leave."

He sat at his desk for some time, occasionally nodding his head, speaking half sentences aloud and, in general, feeling befuddled.

Harley Welch sounded down and out.

"M'bunk mate's gone, and Lace has went off to school." He sighed deeply. "Hit's a graveyard around here."

"I believe it."

"Seem like I wadn't hardly ready f'r 'em to go off."

"We never are."

"You know, some of th' stuff Lace taught me, it's stickin'! I set here last night and wrote five pages of things that was goin' around in m' noggin'."

"Great! Terrific! I'm proud of you!"

"I got to thinkin' about them great falls of th' Missouri, five of 'em, and how ol' Lewis an' Clark must've felt when they seen such a sight as that."

"Lace is a grand teacher. You're a genuine help and consolation to each other."

But Harley didn't sound consoled. "Both of 'em gone, an' not a soul t' set down an' eat a bite with, hit's jis' mope aroun' an' listen t' y'r head roar. . . ."

"Anytime you feel lonesome, walk up to the Grill, order the special, talk to people. It'll do you good." Heaven knows, that had saved his own sanity a time or two.

"I'm tearin' th' engine out of th' mayor's RV in th' mornin', I ain't got time t' lollygag."

"Puny says you haven't seen anybody around the house, nothing suspicious. . . ."

"Nossir. Course that door bein' unlocked an' all, an' that gang workin' on th' street . . ."

"Seems like they'd have taken something else, though. Well, listen, Harley, you hang in there. We'll be home in October. I'm going to hold you to that pan of brownies."

Harley cackled, sounding like himself again. "I practice on them brownies once ever' week, I'm about t' git it right."

They sat on the porch in the gathering twilight, and watched Jonathan play with a sand bucket and shovel in their end-of-summer garden. The Louis L'Amour paperback lay on the table beside him; Barnabas sprawled at their feet.

His wife knew absolutely nothing about the angel and was as dumbfounded as he. It was bizarre, it was unreal, it was—

"I'll get it," Cynthia said, when the phone rang.

She dashed inside and came back with the cordless.

"Those eggs you gave us last week are wonderful, the yolks are a lovely shade of yellow!"

Covering the mouthpiece, she whispered, "Penny Duncan."

"Oh, really?" She listened intently. "That's wonderful! How good of you, Penny, how thoughtful."

She gazed into the yard at Jonathan. "Oh, he's a handful, all right, but no, thank you so much, we love having him, we're all quite happy together. Yes, I'm sure, but thank you again, you're very dear, Penny. Really? I'd love it if you'd help at the tea. Could you possibly make an ice mold? What a good idea, yes, fresh peppermint would be perfect. Well, then—love to Marshall. See you in church!"

She laid the phone on the arm of the rocker and smiled at him.

"You had an offer for help with Jonathan and turned it down?"

"She has ten days of vacation and offered to keep him, but . . ." She shrugged.

"But what?"

"But I declined."

"Why?" he asked.

She shrugged again. "Because."

"You won't believe this," said Dooley, calling from the hall phone in his dorm.

"Try me."

"Guess what girl's school our first dance is with."

"Mrs. Hemingway's." Who else?

"Can you believe it?"

He thought he discerned a kind of . . . what? Expectation, perhaps, under Dooley's evident disgust.

"I hope you'll ask Lace to dance."

"Not if she's wearing those weird shoes an' all."

"Come on, what do shoes have to do with anything?"

"Plenty," said Dooley, with feeling.

He had pulled whatever strings a clergyman can call to hand, and the court date would fall the day after Buck's and Pauline's wedding, after which Harley would drive Dooley back to school. He gave Dooley the scoop.

"Great! Cool." The boy sounded relieved.

No, Dooley hadn't been in the yellow house, he didn't know anything about the angel, and had never once seen anybody go in or out except Puny.

"Give me a report on the dance," he said.

"May I read you something?"

"I like it when you read," Janette whispered. She sat with him in the cramped space of her semiprivate room, looking toward the wall.

> *"I asked the Lord*
> *for a bunch of fresh flowers*
> *but instead he gave me an ugly cactus*
> *with many thorns.*
> *I asked the Lord*
> *for some beautiful butterflies*
> *but instead he gave me*
> *many ugly and dreadful worms.*
> *I was threatened.*
> *I was disappointed.*
> *I mourned.*
> *But after many days,*
> *suddenly,*
> *I saw the cactus bloom*
> *with many beautiful flowers*
> *and those worms became*
> *beautiful butterflies*
> *flying in the wind.*
> *God's way is the best way."*

Earlier in the visit, he'd been encouraged to see light returning to her eyes, though it was a light that sparked, then waned, like a weak flame in damp wood.

Now she turned her head and looked at him and he searched for the flame, but it wasn't there.

"Someone named Chung-Ming Kao wrote this," he said. "From prison."

She closed her eyes, and he felt the despair of his own helplessness.

In truth, he had no solutions to offer Janette Tolson, not even a burning homily.

In the end, all he had to offer was hope.

"Father—Buck Leeper."

"Buck!" He rejoiced to hear Buck's rough baritone voice. As badly as the superintendent of the Hope House project had once treated him, he now remembered only that night in the rectory, the night Buck had knocked on his door, saying, "I'm ready to do whatever it takes."

What it took, in Buck's case, was a broken spirit and a willing heart. That Christmas Eve night, Buck Leeper prayed a simple prayer and asked Christ to be his Savior and Lord.

They had stood there by the fire, their arms around one another— two old boys from Mississippi, bawling like babies.

He sat forward in his office chair, doubly excited, given that he'd never had a phone call from Alaska.

"How are you, buddy?"

"Scared," said Buck.

"I know. I've been there."

"Yeah, but when you tied th' knot, it was your first time. I've been there three times and messed up."

Buck's three marriages had all ended tragically. His first wife had died of an undiagnosed blood disease, his second wife had committed suicide, and, twelve years ago, his third wife left with his foreman and sued for divorce.

"In those three marriages, you didn't know Him, you didn't have a clue who He really is. St. Paul says that when we give our lives to Christ, we become new creatures. 'If anyone is in Christ, he is a new creation; old things have passed away; behold, all things have become new.'"

There was a grateful silence at the other end.

"I'm praying for you and Pauline and the children. You'll need His grace on this side of the cross as much as you needed it on the other. Pray for His grace, Buck, to carry you and Pauline from strength to strength as you build this new life together."

He listened to static on the line as his friend in Alaska struggled to speak.

"Thanks," said Buck, standing in a phone booth in Juneau, and feeling that a D-8 Cat had just rolled off his chest.

Hoppy Harper called the church office to say that Louella's break was bad, though nothing like Miss Sadie's had been. Louella would be down for the count for a while, but the prognosis looked good.

Gene Bolick's medication was helping, he'd counted the stairs to bed only twice in five nights, and Esther seemed more like her old self. She had, in fact, brought an orange marmalade cake to Hoppy's office.

Hoppy went on to say that a new priest had been called to Lord's Chapel. The interim would finish up the end of October, and the new man, Father Talbot, would be installed on All Saints' Day. Both agreed the call had come pretty quickly; some parishes took up to two years to replace a priest.

He hoofed along the lane toward the Baptist church and the big meeting with the Fall Fair committee.

Thank God things were on the mend in Mitford. He had fish to fry in Whitecap—not the least of which was getting his act together for his wedding anniversary, only three days ahead.

"Father, it's . . . Pauline Barlowe."

"Pauline!"

"I've found something."

He understood at once; she had found some clue, some trail to Kenny and Sammy. He literally held his breath.

"I was gettin' ready to throw out an old pocketbook I hadn't carried in years, and for some reason I looked through it real good, and in th' linin' . . ."

"Yes?"

"In th' linin' I found this little piece of paper, it said . . . Ed Sikes."

"Ed Sikes?"

"Yes. I must have written it down after I gave Kenny . . ." She hesitated, unable to speak the thought. "Th' man that took 'im was named Ed Sikes, that's all I know. I was . . . I was drunk, and didn't ever know where he worked or lived or . . . anything."

He felt the pain under her confession, the pain that might

never heal completely, though Pauline Barlowe had come to know the Healer.

"I'd give anything if you could . . ." She didn't finish.

"I know this man gave you alcohol, but was there any other reason you let Kenny go with him?"

"I don't know . . . he seemed nice, I guess. It seems like I thought he could probably treat Kenny better than I did."

"I'll look into this and let you know if anything turns up. What about Buck? How is he?"

"He just called us, he's doin' real good, he's comin' th' end of September. We're all . . . real excited."

"Dwell on that," he told Dooley's mother.

"Emma, remember when you helped find Jessie Barlowe?"

Emma liked being reminded of the role she played in bringing Dooley's little sister home to Mitford. Emma had gone on-line and nailed the whereabouts of the woman who'd bolted to Florida with Jessie.

On a hunch, he'd piled Cynthia and Pauline into the Buick and driven sixteen hours to Lakeland, Florida, where they miraculously recovered the five-year-old Jessie, now living with her mother and older brother, Poo.

"I'd like you to get on the Internet and look for Ed Sikes. S-i-k-e-s. That could be Edward, Edmund, Edwin—"

"Edisto, even! I had an uncle Edisto we called Ed."

"Whatever. Whatever you can think of."

"Is this about one of Dooley's brothers?" she asked.

"It is."

"I'll get right on it," said his erstwhile secretary, "and I'll pray. Sometimes I pray while I surf."

He slid the Mustang into the gravel area by the church as the heavens burst open in a deluge.

He raced down the basement steps with the *Mitford Muse* under his arm and, sopping wet, trotted to the men's room to dry himself off with paper towels.

"Is that you, Father?" Marion called from the sink at the end of the hall.

"It is! How are you, Marion?"

"Spry! I just made coffee, want a cup?"

"I do!"

A violent clap of thunder crashed overhead as he punched the play button on his office answering machine.

"Father Timothy? Cap'n Willie. We've got a bad storm warnin' for Thursday, and we're cancelin' th' trip. We're right in th' heart of hurricane season, so I guess it's no surprise. I'll make good on your trip anytime, just call to reschedule, four-oh-two-eight." There was an awkward pause. "Thank you for your business, and good fishin' to you."

Hotdog and Hallelujah!

He took the sodden newspaper apart and draped the three double sheets over Sunday School chairs to dry. Another clap of thunder rolled above them. It was comforting, he thought, to be snug in the basement of the old church, the smell of coffee wafting along the hallway, someone nearby to call to, the rain pelting the windows. . . .

Marion bustled in with a mug in either hand.

"There's sugar cookies left from Sunday School," she said, "but I don't suppose you can have any."

"Not a crumb."

Marion settled into the chair by his desk. "Ella Bridgewater's all the talk," she said, nodding her approval. "You did a fine job rounding her up."

"I didn't do the rounding up. Ella was heaven-sent."

Marion smiled. "You and Cynthia were heaven-sent, is what Sam and I think."

He felt his face grow warm. "Now, Marion . . ."

"Well, it's true. How are you all doing, now that you've dug in? Are you happy in Whitecap?" Marion possessed one of his mother's most desirable characteristics—a frank simplicity that invited the truth.

"We are. There are good people at St. John's, we feel very blessed."

"We've got our downside, but I suppose we're no worse than the rest of the lot. You've helped us settle some of our petty squabbles."

"At least the pew bulletin is no longer running classifieds," he said, smiling.

Marion laughed. "And just think—that's where I found my carpet sweeper for nine dollars! In any case, I hope parenting isn't proving too much for you. Goodness, after our grandchildren used to leave, we were pooped for a month of Sundays. And that's when they were old enough to feed and dress themselves!"

"He's a handful, all right."

"Janette's not doing so well, is she? She hardly spoke on Sunday, bless her heart."

"The doctor says the downward spiral has been going on for a long time. The upward spiral takes time, too."

She blew on the steaming coffee. "Thank the Lord I never had trouble with depression. Complaining, that's been my thorn."

"I hadn't noticed," he said.

"I don't suppose most people confide their thorns. Saint Paul only said he had one. I wish he'd gone ahead and told us what it was!"

He laughed. "You'll never hear mine from me!" Self-righteousness, he thought, and no two ways about it.

He enjoyed Marion's company. There was a decided comfort to being in her presence.

"Did you know Janette sews like an angel?" she asked.

"I only know she takes in sewing."

"She sews every bit as well as Jeffrey Tolson sings," Marion said with feeling. "Made all our choir robes and banners, makes all her children's clothes, plus earns a living with it. I guess she'll have to depend on her calling for support 'til she takes him to court. *If* she takes him to court." Marion sipped her coffee, looking concerned. "I saw Jeffrey Tolson the other day."

"Aha."

"I think he's living on the island."

He shook his head. What could he say?

"He thinks this is his church, that it belongs to him because his father and grandfather were members here, as if half the congregation couldn't say the very same thing." She gave a mild shudder. "Oh, how I'd hate to see him come back. Some predict he'll try. It would put us through the wringer."

"Once through the wringer seems quite enough to me," he said, meeting her gaze.

"They say the business with Avery Plummer didn't work out, she left him and went to her mother in Goldsboro." Marion sighed. "I always felt sorry for Janette, being so plain and her husband so handsome. Some people, I won't say who, called her Church Mouse. The boy has his mother's sweet spirit, but looks the spit image of his father, don't you think?"

"I agree."

"Jeffrey always reminded me of an apple I took my sixth-grade teacher, Miss Fox. I'll never forget that apple. I was so proud of it, I polished it on my dress all the way to school; it was the prettiest thing in our orchard. I stood right by her desk and watched her bite into it. I thought she'd say, *Why, Marion Lewis, this is the best apple I ever tasted!* Well! When she bit into it, she had the oddest look on her face."

"Really?"

"Rotten inside! I was embarrassed to death, just mortified."

"Aha."

"We're all excited about the tea," she said, changing a sore subject. "I'm taking a day off from the library to help Cynthia, and Sam and I will loan you our nice canvas folding chairs for the garden. At the ECW meeting, we prayed for sunshine. I don't think that's too pushy, do you?"

" 'Come boldly to the throne of grace!' " he quoted from Hebrews.

"Well, no rest for the weary!" she exclaimed, rising from the chair. "I've got to clean up under the sink, you never saw such a mess of old vases, there's enough oasis under there to capsize a ship. Speaking of ship, when are you going on your big fishing trip with Cap'n Willie?"

"Postponed!"

"Oh, I'm sorry."

"Don't be," he said.

It was nagging him, reminding him of the time years ago when he'd found the lock broken on the church door. He'd found nothing stolen, nothing amiss, and he didn't report it. Then he'd discovered the burial urn filled with precious stones, sitting innocently on the shelf of the makeshift columbarium in the church closet. . . .

"Rodney? Tim Kavanagh, how's business?"

"Slow, thank th' Lord," said Mitford's police chief. "How you doin' down there at th' end of th' world?"

"Pretty well, thanks. Listen, Rodney—an odd thing . . . Puny Guthrie, Joe Joe's wife, you know she's our housekeeper . . ."

"Right."

"She tells me something is missing from our house next door to the old rectory. Just disappeared off the mantel."

"What's th' missin' item?"

"A bronze angel on a green marble base, probably about eighteen inches high, maybe twenty."

"What's th' value?"

"I don't know. But it's a fine piece, very fine. I'd estimate three thousand, at least. Old bronzes aren't cheap."

"What else is missin'?"

"Nothing. And nothing out of place. But Puny had left the door unlocked by mistake, and there's work being done on the street out front, so . . ."

"Any suspects?"

"No, and nobody was seen going in or out. No one even knew the door was unlocked."

"I don't know what we can do but file a report. No suspects, nothin' else missin', no vandalism. That don't leave much to go on. What we probably need to do is go down and take fingerprints."

He remembered that Rodney Underwood loved taking fingerprints.

"Wouldn't it cause an uproar to have your men crawling all over the house? Besides, this was maybe a week or so ago, and Puny dusts pretty faithfully, wouldn't that remove fingerprints?"

"Don't you worry about a thing, you let me take care of it! Now, how do we get in?"

Given the excitement in Rodney's voice, he might have handed the chief the keys to a Harley hog. "Talk to Puny," he said, half regretting he'd brought it up in the first place.

With the newspaper sufficiently dry, he reassembled it and carried it to his desk.

He was surprised to see the gated, well-secluded mountain lodge of Edith Mallory in a photograph. A white arrow pointed to a grove of trees next to Edith's rambling house.

Mallory Property Sight of Tension Over Town History

When the great-great-grandfather of Mitford native and mayoral candidate, Coot Hendrick, settled our town in

1853, he built a dog-trot cabin on Lookout Ridge, and a small trading depot where Happy Endings Bookstore now stands.

Later, as the family of Hezikiah Hendrick grew, our town founder built a spring house, barn, and corncrib on his forty-acre ridge property.

The cabin and outbuildings are long gone, but the stone foundations remains, according to Dr. Lyle Carpenter of Wesley College in our neighboring township. There is also a family graveyard and the graves of five Union soldiers reputed to exist on the property.

"What we discovered on the ridge is a classic example of how our early mountain settlers lived," says Carpenter. "We wish to see this valuable site preserved, perhaps with an eventual replication of buildings, so that residents and visitors can understand and enjoy our mountain frontier heritage."

Dr. Carpenter reports that the Hendrick family dump sight, allegedly located only yards from where the cabin stood, may contain pottery shards, milk buckets, plow shares and other remnants of early highland life.

There is a rub, however. The Hendrick property is now owned by Mrs. Edith Mallory, whose 95-acre ridge-top estate, Clear Day, includes the old homesite. In fact, her house is reported to sit but forty-six feet from the south-facing foundation of the Hendrick cabin.

Mrs. Mallory currently has a town permit to construct an additional 3,000 square feet of residential space, which will intrude on part of the historic sight. She is reported to say she has no intention of halting construction, which is scheduled to begin in September, and has issued a no trespassing warning.

"This is a crucial moment in our local history," says Dr. Carpenter. "We must find a way to preserve this important property, which my colleagues and I have only recently discovered, thanks to the fine work of the Mitford town museum and its archives."

Coot Hendrick, the great-great-grandson of Mitford's founder, says he will fight for the old homeplace to be designated a historic sight.

Dr. Carpenter said that a walking path to the sight from the town, and a nature trail identifying the abundant flora, would also be a fine idea.

The town council is appealing to the State Department of History and Archives for counsel in the matter.

Mrs. Mallory could not be reached for comment.

Edith Mallory, he thought, had the ominous persistence of leaking propane. Just when he thought she had vanished forever in Spain or Florida, she reappeared, and always with malice.

Surely there was some way she could come to terms with the town over this thing.

In the end, had she ever done anything for the benefit of Mitford? Never once, as far as he could remember. Her multimillion-dollar home sprawled along the ridge above the village, looking down on a community of souls who'd been through one tough scrape after another, yet she'd never been forthcoming, even to the library when it was struggling for its very existence.

And hadn't he been sent knocking on her door when the town museum was trying to pull itself together, and hadn't she made her usual seductive, albeit fruitless, overtures and sent him packing? The annual Bane and Blessing had long ago given up asking for contributions, not to mention the volunteer fire department.

Of course, she had given fifteen thousand to add beds to the Children's Hospital, his favorite charity. He'd quickly learned, however, that it was all part of a plan to get him into a bed of her own.

His very skin crawled at the thought of how she'd trapped him in that blasted Lincoln, forcing him to leap from the thing while it was still moving.

He folded the *Muse* and threw it in the wastebasket. As far as he was concerned, the only good news was that J. C. Hogan had evidently installed software with a spell check. Too bad there was no software out there for grammar.

In truth, he was tired of knowing what was going on in Mitford. He didn't want to hear another peep from that realm for a while.

He was going to do what Mona's sign said, and bloom where he was planted.

Somehow, he'd managed to turn the ringer off and didn't hear the phone while he was washing his cup at the sink down the hall.

"I don't know why I keep missin' you," said Emma, when he punched the play button.

"I thought you'd want to know the scoop on Father Talbot, it's what everybody's talkin' about. I didn't lay eyes on him when he was here tryin' out, but Esther Bolick says he's good-lookin' as anything, and *tall. Very* tall. Oh, and thin, she thinks he exercises, maybe with weights. Esther Cunningham said he walked up the street to her office when he was here, said he just wanted to meet the mayor of such a fine town, wanted to shake her hand, wadn't that nice?

"He's comin' in November, is what they're sayin', has a wife that could be th' twin of Meg Ryan, and two kids, both on th' honor roll. Anyway, people are real excited about finally gettin' somebody permanent down at Lord's Chapel, and from a big church, too, I think it was Chicago. They say they saw him on a video and he preaches up a storm and is funny as heck, he had everybody rollin' in th' aisles.

"Let's see, what else . . . somebody, I forget who, said he sings great an' has real white teeth an' looks terrific in . . . whatever it is, maybe his hassock."

Wears a halo, he thought, has wings . . .

"Oh, Lord, here comes Harold back, he must've forgotten his bag lunch."

Click. Beep.

"Timothy?"

"Walter!" His only living cousin, as far as he knew, and lifelong best friend into the bargain. "It's been a coon's age."

"I thought I'd ring down to the boondocks while I'm waiting for a client to show up. How's the fishing?"

"I have no idea."

"Swimming? Doing any swimming?"

"Nope. No swimming."

"Clamming? Crabbing? Duck hunting? *Anything?*"

"Just the same old stick-in-the-mud you've always known me to be." Darn Walter, he was always looking for some big story, some action. So far, the most exciting thing he'd ever done was marry Cynthia Coppersmith. That was such a big one, it got him off the hook with

Walter for a couple of years, but now his attorney cousin was at it again.

"Listen, Potato Head, I've got a new parish to take care of and a yard to mow. That's all the action I can handle right now. How's Katherine?"

"Mean as a snake, skinny as a rail."

"The usual, then!" They laughed easily together. They were both pretty fond of Walter's wide-open wife, her dazzling laughter and unstoppable generosity of spirit.

"And Cynthia?"

"Busy. Doing another book, reading at the library, tending a three-year-old."

"You've taken in another one?"

"Only briefly, his mother's in the hospital."

"How do you like your new parish?"

"I like it. Good people. We're happy here. When can you and Katherine come down? You haven't been my way in years, I was there last, you owe me."

"After you finish this interim, we'll drive down to Mitford for a week, how's that? Slog around in our bathrobes and eat you out of house and home."

"You can't scare me, pal."

"Speaking of scare," said Walter, "we had a little break-in the other night. They took our TVs and my Rolex. We're surprised it wasn't worse."

"We've just had an odd thing happen. Remember the angel I once mentioned, the one from Miss Sadie's attic? It disappeared off the mantel in Mitford. Nothing else was disturbed in the house, no sign of entry, nothing. Just gone, vanished. Very queer."

"Valuable?"

"Probably three thousand or so, maybe more. Bronze. On a heavy marble base. French, I think."

"Life has always been too mysterious to suit my tastes. Well, Cousin, here comes my erstwhile client. It's good to touch base. Love to Cynthia, love to Dooley—how is he?"

"Great!"

"Good. I've got a stock tip for you, so call me, you dog, and let's catch up."

"Consider it done," he said.

He'd written it everywhere but on his hand to make sure he didn't forget. No, indeed, forgetting birthdays and anniversaries did not cut it at his house—nor at any other house, as far as he could tell from his years in clergy counseling.

Headed for the town grocer with the windshield wipers on high, he mulled over the coming event.

They'd already gone to the beach and taken a blanket, but they hadn't gone to the beach and taken a blanket and a Coleman stove.

Just down the strand from the old Miller cottage with the red roof, he would set everything up in their favorite spot.

They would watch the sunset and he would grill fresh mahimahi and corn in the shuck.

He would cut a ripe, sweet melon—he didn't think it was too late in the season to find one—and pour a well-chilled champagne. He noted that he'd have to go across to find a decent label, but while he was there, maybe he could also find something to drink it from, since all they had in the cabinet were what appeared to be top-of-the-line jelly glasses.

For dessert, of course, he'd make her sworn favorite—poached pears—the very thing he'd served Cynthia Coppersmith the first time she came to dinner at the rectory.

All in all, pretty creative thinking for a country parson . . .

As for entertainment, they could search the night sky for Arcturus and Andromeda, maybe Pegasus. He'd bought a book at Ernie's that told very plainly how to find something other than the Big and Little Dippers, which, he'd been disappointed to learn, weren't even constellations.

He went over the list again.

Leonard and Marjorie Lamb had offered to babysit, and were scheduled to arrive at Dove Cottage at six-thirty. . . .

What had he forgotten?

He realized he was holding his breath, and exhaled. All bases covered. Consider the thing done!

Had it been four years ago when he'd raced through the sacristy into the nave of Lord's Chapel, trembling like a leaf in the wind, late for his wedding through no fault of his own, and spied his bride, also late and flushed from running, who appeared like a vision in the aisle?

If ever he'd known the definition of a waking dream, that had been it.

He remembered standing there, terrified that he'd burst into tears with half the congregation, and noted that he'd never seen so many handkerchiefs waving in the breeze. Under the swell of the organ music, there had been a veritable concerto of sniffing and nose-blowing by men and women alike.

And then, there she was, standing with him. He later admitted to his cousin, Walter, that the earth had moved at that moment. He felt it as surely as if the long-inactive fault running from somewhere in the Blue Ridge Mountains to Charleston, South Carolina, had suddenly heaved apart.

He remembered thinking, with a glad and expectant heart, I'm in for it now.

They were out of Jonathan's favorite milk at the grocer's, so back he schlepped to Ernie's, clobbered by rain.

"We had doubles developed," said Ernie, showing him three-by-five glossies of Junior. "These are th' two that went off Friday, what do you think?"

In the first snapshot, Junior had a pained expression, as if he were sitting on a carpet tack. The other was of a red-eyed Junior standing like a statue in front of the drink boxes. He didn't believe Junior had gotten around to ironing his shirt, after all.

"What about these red eyes?" he asked, concerned for the outcome of the whole deal.

"I don't know what that is. Seems like Junior's camera wadn't too swift."

"Well . . ."

"It's been five or six days an' he hadn't heard back."

This didn't look promising. . . .

"Tell me about Junior," he said. "He seems a good fellow. Any family?"

"Junior lost his mama when he was pretty young, and his daddy's not much account. Me an' Roger and Roanoke try to see after him, kind of help raise him."

"Doesn't seem like he'd need much raising at the age of thirty-six."

"Well, but th' thing is," said Ernie, lowering his voice, "Junior's not the sharpest knife in the drawer."

"Who is?"

"We'd like to see him settle down, get married, have a family. He's a hard worker, got money saved, has a little house, and there's not a bigger heart on Whitecap. Helps look after his next-door neighbor, she's blind as a bat. . . ."

"Good fellow!"

Ernie removed his glasses and squinted at Father Tim. "Roanoke told me he barbered you."

"Even my wife was pleased," he said, taking a gallon of milk from the cooler.

"We got a bad storm comin' Thursday."

"I hope it clears out by Friday evening."

Ernie opened the register and gave him change. "Big doin's on Friday?"

"Yep. Fourth anniversary."

"I got one comin' up here sometime, I can't recall when."

"Let it pass and you'll be stepping over something worse than a yellow line."

"You got a point," said Ernie. "By th' way, I'm readin' that Wadsworth book."

"How do you like it?"

"He sure does a lot of runnin' up hill an' down dale. Seems like he takes notice of every little thing, keeps his eyes an' ears peeled. . . ."

"Just like Louis L'Amour!"

"I wouldn't have thought of that," said Ernie, looking pleased.

He hauled the thing from the box.

"A VCR!" His wife was beaming.

He fetched something from a bag. "Not to mention . . ."

"Peter Pan!" she whooped. "Thanks be to God!"

He fetched something else from the bag.

"Babe! I've always wanted to see that."

"Now I've made two people happy," he said, feeling like a hero.

Jonathan flew ahead of them, running at sandpipers, shouting at gulls, squatting to examine a shell.

The sun had looked out an hour ago, and they agreed they should take advantage of it. Barefoot and holding hands on the wide sweep of rain-soaked beach, he knew that what he'd told Marion and Walter was true—they were happy in Whitecap.

He stooped and picked up an old Frisbee and threw it for Barnabas, who loped along the sand in pursuit. Watching the boy and Barnabas tumble for the Frisbee, something came swimming back to him across time. He was nine years old in Pass Christian, Mississippi, and in love with a dog. He'd completely forgotten, and the sudden memory of that summer took his breath away.

"I can feel your wheels turning," declared his wife.

"Pass Christian," he said, as if in a dream. "We drove all the way from Holly Springs to the beach at Pass Christian, it's on the gulf near Gulfport and Biloxi. A wonderful place."

"Tell me everything!" she implored.

"It was the year my father decided I should invite a friend on our summer trek; he thought I was too studious, too much a loner. I wanted to take Tommy Noles, but . . ."

"But the Great Ogre refused."

"Oh, yes. He picked the friend I should take."

"Who was it?"

"Drew Merritt, the son of my father's colleague at his law office."

His wife never liked stories about his father. He should probably keep his mouth shut, but he wanted to talk, he wanted to let go of the constraints he felt he was eternally placing on his memories, on his feelings. If he couldn't talk freely here by the ocean, which lay perfectly open to the sun and the sky . . .

"Drew wasn't someone I wanted to spend two weeks with. He was selfish, short-tempered, demanding. I remember we took a jigsaw puzzle of the nation's Capitol . . . he insisted I do the cherry blossoms and he'd work on the Capitol building. Instead of piece by piece, we worked on it section by section. I didn't want to do cherry blossoms."

"But you did them," she said, "because you're nice."

"Nice has its advantages," he said.

She squeezed his hand. "I love you."

"I love you back."

"Finally, after we'd been there a few days, Drew found a crowd to hang with, and I started wandering off on my own. It was a safe place, of course, plenty of kids came and went, reporting in to parents during the course of an afternoon. We stayed at an old hotel, I wish I could remember the name. Anyway, one day I went down to the beach and met . . . a dog."

She smiled, loving even the simplest of his stories.

"It was a red setter, and he didn't seem to belong to anyone, though he was certainly no maverick. I remember his coat was long and silky, it shone when it blew in the wind. He was like something from heaven, we connected instantly. *Click*—just like that, he was mine and I was his."

"I wouldn't let Barnabas hear you talking this way."

He put his arm around her shoulder, laughing.

"No, Jonathan, don't touch it!" Cynthia cried. The heavy rain had helped the sea disgorge flotsam of great variety.

"We started meeting in the afternoons, I never saw him in the morning. I took a little red ball with me every day and threw it to him. He always brought it back." He was able to recall his sense of freedom, and the unutterable joy of having, at last, the dog that had long been forbidden at home.

"I named him . . . Mick," he said, suddenly uneasy with the confession of a time he'd never mentioned to anyone.

"Mick!" she said. "I love that name!"

"I remember the morning we left to go back to Holly Springs." More than five decades later, his heart could recall the grief of that morning.

"My father decided we should leave a day early, and I . . . hadn't said goodbye. I took a napkin full of biscuits down to the old house where we usually met, but of course he wasn't there, it was too early in the day, so I left the biscuits under the steps."

"I love that you did that."

"Ah, Kavanagh, what don't you love?"

"Husbands who can't talk about their feelings, sand in the bed, and maps that won't refold properly."

"Let's go fold into a rocker on our porch," he said.

"Yes, let's!" She turned and gazed at him, then put her hand to his cheek.

"I'd like to remember you just this way . . . every line of your dear face at this moment."

To his amazement, tears stood in her eyes, and she put her arms around him and kissed him with an odd tenderness.

Jonathan tugged at Cynthia's shorts.

"I got to poo-poo!" said the boy, looking urgent.

The tropical depression moved north from the Caribbean, hung a left toward the Outer Banks of North Carolina, migrated across Whitecap, and dumped six inches of rain inland to Smithfield. Not a hurricane, thanks be to God, but with severe high winds. On Friday morning, it seemed to relish pausing directly over Dove Cottage and unleashing itself for a full two hours.

He padded around the house in his robe the entire morning, working on his sermon, looking over the music for Sunday, scribbling in his quote notebook, reading whatever came to hand. As thunder rolled and wind howled, Barnabas and Violet hid themselves at various points under chairs and beds. Miraculously, Jonathan slept through much of it, while his wife worked at the end of the hall on her new book.

Oh, the ineffable peace of a house darkened by a storm, and the sound of rain at its windows. Though quite unknown to his Irish genealogy, he thought he must have a wide streak of Scot in him somewhere.

So what if his plans for the evening were dashed? Didn't all the world lie before them with, God willing, time to celebrate on the beach even without a special occasion?

He sat in his chair in the study and listened to the rain and wind and the beating of his heart.

Bottom line, wasn't life itself a special occasion?

When the storm abated around six-thirty, they had their anniversary dinner in the kitchen.

Then the entire troop piled onto their bed, Barnabas and Violet at the foot, and Jonathan next to Cynthia, who was propped like a czarina against down pillows.

"And now," he announced, "a movie . . . *in a box!*"

He held the video box aloft for all to see.

"*Peter Pan!*" exulted Jonathan, clapping his hands.

He gave Cynthia a profound look. "You'll never know what you missed tonight."

"It's OK, darling," murmured his contented wife. "I love *Peter Pan!*"

They blew through *Peter Pan* and plugged in *Babe*, adrenaline up and pumping.

"I'm crazy about this movie!" crowed his wife. "But *ugh*, I despise that cat."

"Bad cat!" said Jonathan.

Actually, the cat reminded him of someone. Who was it?

Of course. That cat reminded him of Edith Mallory.

He awoke at two in the morning and listened for the rain. Silence. The storm had passed over, and the room was close and humid.

He went to the window and cranked it open.

The music came in with the sweet, cool breeze that whispered against his bare skin.

CHAPTER TWELVE

Over the Wall

Answering the loud knock, he looked through the screen door and saw Otis Bragg.

Otis was carrying what appeared to be a half bushel of shrimp in a lined basket. "Cain't have a party without shrimp!" Otis said, grinning. His unlit cigar appeared to be fresh for the occasion.

"Otis! What a surprise!" Surprise, indeed. His wife would not take kindly to cooking shrimp fifteen minutes before her big tea, and he wasn't excited about it, either.

"Already cooked, ready to trot. A man over on th' Sound does these for me, all we do is peel and eat. Where you want 'em set?"

"Thanks, Otis. This is mighty generous of you." He hastily cleared one end of the table they'd brought out to the porch and draped with a blue cloth.

"Marlene'll be comin' along in a minute or two with somethin' to dip 'em in." Otis wiped his forehead with a handkerchief. "Maybe I could get a little shooter at th' bar?"

"The bar? Oh, the *bar*! We don't have a bar. But there's tea!"

"Tea." Otis chewed the cigar reflectively.

"Or sherry."

"Sherry," said Otis with a blank stare.

"Good label. Spain, I think." He recalled that Otis had sent him a bottle of something expensive, but couldn't remember where it was. . . .

"Oh, well, what th' hey, I pass. Father Morgan always set out a little bourbon, gin, scotch . . . you know."

"Aha."

Otis squinted at him. "You raised Baptist?"

"I was, actually."

"Me, too," said Otis. "But I got over it."

"Let me get you a glass of tea. Wait 'til you taste it. You'll like it, you have my word." He certainly wouldn't mention where the recipe came from.

The soprano, no worse for wear from her brief career in Sunday School, shook hands vigorously. "Gorgeous day, Father!

"Glorious!" said Sam Fieldwalker. "Good gracious alive, what a day!"

"The best all summer!" crowed Marion, exchanging a hug with her priest.

Also receiving rave reviews were the flowers, the table, the refreshments, the hostess, and even the straggling garden in which he'd labored the livelong morning.

His dog's great size garnered a good share of cautious interest, and Jonathan, dressed in a new sailor suit, was busy eluding all prospects of being dandled on knees or pressed to bosoms.

Father Tim had to admit there was a magical air about Dove Cottage this afternoon; he felt as expansive as a country squire. His wife floated around in something lavender, leaving the scent of wisteria on the breeze and making the whole shebang look totally effortless. The truth was, she'd been up since five a.m., cutting flowers and baking final batches of lemon squares while he installed new lace panels in the living room.

"Lace *belongs* there," she told him. "It filters the morning light and makes patterns on the floor." He had nothing but respect for the miracles wrought via UPS.

Cynthia's workroom was of great interest to the parish children who showed up; eager tour groups processed through the minuscule space, once a large closet, pointing at walls adorned with drawings, book jackets, and—a particular favorite—rough sketches of Violet beneath a beach umbrella. The real Violet positioned herself atop the refrigerator, glowering at anyone who sought her celebrity.

Ella Bridgewater arrived, dressed entirely in black, and looking, he thought, even more like a crane adorning an Oriental screen. She was what his mother would have called "a sight for sore eyes," coming through the cottage gate with a bright rouge spot on either cheek.

Cynthia trotted their new organist around to various groups convened in the garden. "Penny, I don't believe you've met Ella Bridgewater. Ella, meet Penny Duncan. You'll have to see the lovely ice mold she made with fresh peppermint."

"Penny used to be a hippie!" said Jean Ballenger. She proclaimed this as if announcing a former background in brokerage services or marketing. "She grows all their vegetables, raises chickens, and makes goat cheese!"

"Heavenly *days*!" Ella wagged her head in disbelief. "The cleverest thing I ever made was a cranberry rope for the Christmas tree!"

"Penny once made her own shoes," Jean continued, causing everyone to look at Penny's feet, which were shod in pumps for the occasion. "And," said Jean, ending on a triumphal note, "all her children say yes, ma'am!"

He moved away to join Leonard and Marjorie, who had thumped into two of Marion's folding chairs by the crepe myrtle and were busily shucking shrimp and tossing shells into the bushes.

If Violet knew what was going on out here . . .

"Seen anything of your neighbor?" asked Leonard.

"I've seen precisely nothing of my neighbor! But I certainly hear a good deal of him."

"We hope he doesn't make too much racket," said Marjorie.

"Racket! We enjoy it, actually. He's an outstanding musician."

Leonard dunked a shrimp into the sauce that appeared to be setting his lemon square afloat. "Some say he could have been a concert organist. I believe he was schooled at Juilliard. But he never liked the spotlight, as you can imagine. He's a real hermit. I haven't laid eyes on him in years."

"His grandaddy once got in Walter Winchell's column!" said Marjorie. "You remember Walter Winchell?"

"Oh, yes," said Father Tim, feeling suddenly antiquated. "What did he get in there for?"

"Going out with chorus girls in New York City!"

"Aha."

"Joan Crawford came to Whitecap to visit the Loves," Marjorie told him. "And Betty Grable, too, or let's see . . . maybe it was Irene Dunne!"

"It was Celeste Holm!" Jean Ballenger, who enjoyed moving from group to group, plunked into a chair.

"I never much cared for Celeste Holm, Father, did you?" asked Marjorie.

"I don't believe I remember Celeste Holm."

"You see," said Jean, "I told you Father Tim was younger than we thought."

He sucked in his stomach. "What age had you thought . . . exactly?"

"Marjorie said going on seventy."

Seventy!

"Why, Jean Ballenger! I said no such thing! I said with all your wonderful background and experience, Father, you *could* be going on seventy, but in the end, I guessed you to be sixty!"

"Thank you!" he said.

"Who else used to come down here and visit Redmon Love?" wondered Leonard.

Jean smoothed her bangs, which were going haywire in the humidity. "Somebody said Winston Churchill, but I never believed it for a minute. Mr. Churchill certainly had no time to be lollygagging around Whitecap, what with winning Nobel Prizes and putting out wars all over the place."

Leonard licked his thumb. "Well, anyway, we heard the family hid Morris whenever the bigwigs came around. They say Morris spent a lot of time in the attic as a boy. Redmon built him a room up there and put an organ in it, a small version of the big one downstairs. Morris was never allowed to play his music when guests were in the house. I guess they didn't want anybody to know he existed."

"The terrible meanness of people!" said Jean, pursing her lips. "They ought to have been horsewhipped. But, 'Vengeance is mine, saith the Lord.' "

"Did his grandparents raise him, then?" asked Father Tim.

"Pretty much. His parents stayed in Europe most of the time. I went to school with Morris in the fifth or sixth grade, but the kids made it so tough on him, he never lasted to junior high. I'm sure they must have gotten him a tutor."

"What exactly . . . is his problem?"

"You mean you don't know?" asked Leonard.

"Not at all."

"Well, you see—"

"Father!" exclaimed Ella Bridgewater, joining the group. "As I've just said to your wife—your party is delightful, and this tea is *heavenly*." She clinked the ice in her glass, looking appreciative.

"Well, thank you! As for the tea, I couldn't have said it better myself."

Marjorie squinted up at the new arrival. "Miss Bridgewater—"

"Call me Ella!"

"Ella, we hear you live on Dorchester Island." Marion, like the natives, pronounced it *Dorster*. "Lovely over there, quite remote."

"Remote isn't the word for it! I drive ten miles from my little coop by the sea, go over the causeway, come down Highway 20 for fifteen miles, take the bridge to Whitecap, and drive to St. John's at the north end. It's a trek and a half."

"And we thank you for doing it!" said Marjorie. "You nearly took the roof off Sunday. It's been ages since we heard our old organ give forth such a noise!"

"A *joyful* noise," said their priest, wanting no misunderstanding.

"Do come to Dorchester, Father, and bring Cynthia. I'd like nothing better than to behold your faces at my door!"

For the first time, he noticed Ella's gold brooch—it was in the shape of a hot-air balloon.

"We'd like that. We haven't seen much of the area since we came."

"I know how busy your schedule must be with the summer people to shoehorn in, so just pop up whenever—except, of course, Wednesday, that's when I get my hair washed down at Edna's. Louise and I would love seeing you."

"Louise?"

"Louise is my canary. You should hear her sing, Father, you won't believe your ears!"

"I'm sure!"

"Louise is full of years, as they say in the Old Testament. But the older she gets, the sweeter her voice."

"Aha."

"I'll show you around little Dorchester, it's like going back in time. You'll see the oldest live oak on any of these islands, it's right by my house, and we'll visit Christ Chapel, it's hardly big enough to hold the three of us, it has the most glorious rose window above the altar! Then we'll walk over to the graveyard where Mother is resting. Did I tell you how we buried Mother?"

"I don't believe so."

"Holding the 1928 prayer book clasped to her heart."

"A fine way to go."

"You must come for lunch!" Ella's rouge spots appeared to brighten. "Are you fond of sea bass?"

"Fond is an understatement. One of my great favorites!"

"Miss Child taught me how to poach sea bass on TV. I miss Miss Child, don't you? I loved the way she dropped things on the floor and picked them up and went right on, a good lesson for us all, I think!"

"Indeed!"

Sam Fieldwalker joined them as St. John's organist drew herself up to her full height, which was impressive. "I'm a good hand at plum wine, into the bargain!"

He chuckled. "Yet another incentive to visit. Sam, Ella's asked us to Dorchester."

"Oh, my gracious, we love Dorchester. They do a good bit of fishing business up there. It's nice and quiet, without the tourism we get on Whitecap."

"I think you'll like my little house, Father, it's quite historic. Built in 1902 of timbers that washed up from shipwrecks. I like to say I live in a house that once sailed the sea!"

"When you go over to Miss Bridgewater's," Sam suggested, "that could be a good time to visit Cap'n Larkin. He's the old fellow I told you about who was a longtime member at St. John's. He lives with his twin brother now, on Dorchester."

"Their house is just a skip and a jump from mine," said Ella. "They keep an old pickup truck parked at the front door, that's where their dog sleeps."

"You could take him communion," said Sam. "That would thrill him. Father Morgan never . . . got around to doing that."

"Consider it done! Of course, if we come anytime soon, Ella, you may have to entertain a three-year-old, as well. How would that be?"

Ella eyed Jonathan clattering across the porch tailed by two self-appointed Youth Group baby-sitters.

"I have a little garden plot fenced with pickets," she said. "We could stake him out there!"

❧

He saw a group gathered to the right of the porch and walked over to see what was what. Cynthia stood by a lacecap hydrangea, holding Jonathan on her hip and peering into a variety of cameras. "Smile, Jonathan!" she urged.

"I declare," Jean Ballenger said, "that child looks enough like your wife to be her own! Do you see the resemblance?"

He did, actually. Two pairs of cornflower eyes. Two winning smiles. Two heads the color of ripe corn.

"I hope Janette can come home soon."

"It's going to be a while yet. It's . . . a hard thing." It hurt him to think about it. He could scarcely bear to witness deep depression; he had seen it in his father for years.

"Step over there," said Sam Fieldwalker, "and let's get one of you, too!"

Cynthia put her hand over her eyes and squinted in his direction. "Yes, dear, come and let them record your tan."

He hated photos of himself; in a picture in the new church album, he looked as if he'd been dug up by the roots.

Sheepishly, he put his arm around his wife, adjusted his glasses, and peered at the cameras.

"You better smile!" crowed Jonathan.

❧

"First to come, last to go!" Otis Bragg shook his host's hand with vigor. "Look here, they cleaned us out."

Father Tim peered into the depths of the empty shrimp basket. "A grand contribution, Otis. Thank you again and again."

"My pleasure!" he said. "Good to see th' parish turnin' out like this. It's what makes us family."

"I agree. Come back anytime, you and Marlene."

Like the rest of the common horde, his landlord and parishioner definitely had some traits that were unlikable. Yet he was growing to appreciate Otis; he had the odd feeling that if the chips were ever down, he could count on Otis Bragg.

"We ought to go on a little run with Cap'n Willie one of these days." Otis took the cigar from his mouth and eyed it fondly. "You do any fishin'?"

"I hardly know a hook from a sinker, but my good wife has bought me a chair on Captain Willie's boat, and looks like I'll be forced to go before it's over."

Otis pounded him on the back. "Do you good! Clergy has a tendency to think too much, you need a little fun in your life. Nothin' like a good, hard fight with a blue marlin to get a man's blood up!" Otis pounded him again. "Give me a call when you set a date, I'll try to go out with you."

"Well . . . ," he said, not knowing what else to say.

"I'll bring us a bucket of chicken," declared Otis, spitting shreds of Cuban tobacco into the border of cosmos.

While he took a cleanup shift in the kitchen, Cynthia carried Jonathan, now overtired and overwrought, through the house and out to the back stoop.

"Mommy! I want my mommy!" he sobbed.

Father Tim stood at the kitchen window and watched them approach the bird feeder in the backyard, his wife struggling to console and distract the weeping boy.

"I want Babette an' Jason!"

"There, Jonathan, it's all right. You'll see Mommy soon, and Babette and Jason, too, I promise. Oh, look at the bird on the fence, I wonder what it is. . . ."

He watched her holding the boy close, patting his back, and saw him lay his head on her shoulder. When she turned to look toward the house, he could see tears in her eyes, as well. His wife had a natural gift for "rejoicing with them that do rejoice and weeping with them that weep," as St. Paul commanded the Romans to do.

He lifted his hand and waved awkwardly as they passed from view.

Cynthia was growing attached to the boy, no doubt about it. She'd never been able to have children of her own; in fact, her former husband had spent most of his time, she said, "making babies with other women." The barrenness had been a deep hurt to her, a thorn.

He finished washing up as Cynthia carried Jonathan once more around the route they usually traveled when the boy was crying for family. He heard her murmuring softly to him, crooning bits of stories and songs.

This was torture for all alike, he thought, as Cynthia trudged up the porch steps, looking weary. Surely next week Babette and Jason would be back from visiting another set of family in Beaufort, and they could borrow them for an afternoon. . . .

He stood at the door as Cynthia eased the boy onto his bed and Barnabas leaped up and lay at his feet.

He watched her smooth Jonathan's damp blond hair from his forehead, and saw the infinite tenderness in her eyes.

"What a good boy," she whispered. Then she turned and patted Barnabas.

"And what a good dog!" she said.

Feeling an unexpected weariness of his own, he sat by the phone in the study and dialed Emma's number. "Found anything?"

"Oh, law, there's hundreds, maybe *thousands* of Ed Sikeses out there, it's like lookin' for Bob Jones or John Smith! There's two Ed Sikeses right over in Wesley, one Edmund an' one Edward, but Harold knows 'em both and says they couldn't possibly have run off with anybody's kid, one's a deacon at First Presbyterian and th' other one goes frog giggin' with Harold's brother.

"Plus, you don't even want to *know* how many different names Ed stands for."

"How many?"

"I looked it up on th' Internet and found thirteen—Edison, Eddrick, Edgar, Edwin, Eduardo, to name only a few. You know you can find anything you're lookin' for on th' Internet, you ought to be on th' Internet, it would help with your sermons, it seems like preachin' Sunday after Sunday, you'd be *desperately* lookin' for new material. . . ."

Emma Newland had been into the Little Debbies again, he knew sugar-induced hysteria when he heard it.

"So . . . ," he said, seeking an escape.

"So you'll have to come up with another gimmick this time," she announced.

He called Pauline.

"I forgot to tell you somethin'," she said. "He was from Oregon, or he maybe was goin' to Oregon."

"Excellent! Wonderful!"

"Father . . ."

"Yes?"

"I've been . . . I'm really scared about somethin'."

"What scares you?"

"Well . . . you see, I don't feel like I deserve . . . all this."

"All this what?"

She took a deep breath. "This . . . happiness. It don't seem right for me to have it."

"Grace isn't about deserving, Pauline. We can't earn God's grace, there's no way on earth we can earn it. Grace is free, and I believe as sure as I am sitting here that He brought the two of you together. Do you love Buck?"

"More'n anything. Just . . . more'n I can say. He's so good to me and th' children, he's . . . nobody sees it, but he's tenderhearted, you know."

"I know."

"I just pray everything's going to be all right. I've told the Lord I'll work real hard."

"You'll need to," he said. Why not speak the truth?

"Thank you, Father. It always helps when we talk. I feel better."

"Can you think of anything else? Anything else about Ed Sikes?"

"I've been prayin' to think of somethin' else, but there's only one other thing I remember. . . ."

"Yes?" He sat forward in the chair.

"He was losin' his hair in front."

Who isn't? he thought.

He rang Emma again.

"Oregon," he said. "Look up Ed Sikes in Oregon. We may be on to something."

"You should get your church to set you up on the Internet," she said, sounding grumpy. "Especially since they don't give you a secretary, it seems they could at least—"

"Emma, remember how you helped find Jessie? If it hadn't been for you, Dooley's little sister might still be missing."

"That's true!" she said, sounding brighter. "All right, I'll get to it soon as Harold and I go to Atlanta, we're goin' to borrow Avis Packard's RV, you know he never uses it, it just sits in his driveway losin' air in th' tires because he works all the time, he's th' only man I know who's more interested in rump roast than women.

"You and Cynthia ought to get an RV, it would do you good to throw your cares to the wind, after all, you *are* retired. When Harold retires from th' post office, we're goin' to do as we please and not kowtow to another living soul, he's got six years to go, then we might hit Hawaii or Alaska, maybe even Dollywood, have you ever listened to her sing, I mean really *listened*? She is very talented, I know you like Bach and Mozart, but you could at least *try* tunin' in to the real world once in a while, you have no idea what you might be missin'. . . ."

Roughly speaking, he figured the sugar content in a box of Little Debbie fudge rounds possessed the power to jolt the human system for a full eight hours, minimum.

Why the angel?

He was beyond trying to figure out who had entered the yellow house, and wondered only why they would have taken the angel and nothing more.

If he'd been the thief, he would have stolen the books. Books, however, didn't seem to be a popular item with thieves. They liked silver, TV sets, and jewelry, yet none of those items had been touched.

Boggling. Each time he thought about it, he felt as if someone had removed the top of his head and poured in cooked oatmeal.

No word from Rodney, but he didn't want to call and stir that pot any more than he had already.

He looked at his watch. Six-fifteen, and the sun was setting. He didn't feel like running—maybe a long walk with Barnabas instead. If they'd held on to one of the babysitters, he might have talked his wife into coming along. . . .

He trotted down the steps in shorts and a golf shirt, amazed how all evidence of the merriment had vanished, that a lovely moment in the lives of forty-two people had become history—with scarcely a mark in the garden from the folding chairs.

He latched the gate behind him and hunkered into an easy lope, with Barnabas on the red leash. Maybe a trek past Ernie's, hang a left this side of St. John's, another left at the little gray house, and circle back by Morris Love's front gate.

Seventy, indeed, he thought, huffing up the lane.

They were circling toward home when the fattest, sleekest squirrel he'd seen on Whitecap made a dash across the road. The leash was fairly torn from his hand as Barnabas leaped after the creature, leash flying.

"Barnabas!"

His dog was doing sixty miles an hour and barking like thunder as he raced toward Morris Love's rusted iron gate, and, in a flash, slithered under it.

"Barnabas! *Come!*"

Deaf as a doorknob, like any dog chasing a squirrel . . .

He huffed to the gate and examined it. Locked. Not to mention rusted. "Barnabas! Come *now!*"

He wiped the sweat from his eyes and saw his dog disappear into a thicket—no, a kind of loggia to the left of the house, which was barely visible through the trees. The furious barking continued unabated.

He whistled loudly. Dadgummit, his wife was a better whistler than he was. She could shake green apples from the tree.

More barking. More whistling.

What if Barnabas crossed the Love property, went under the fence on the other side, and into the street? He didn't keep his dog on a leash at all times for no good reason. Hadn't Barnabas been stolen by the vilest drug-dealing Creek scum, and kept staked and half starved for weeks on end?

Grasping the top of the wall with his hands, he gained a foothold against the rough surface and managed to heave himself up and over, landing beside the overgrown driveway with a thud.

He stood for a moment, still winded, and looked around.

He had entered another world.

Though he was mere inches beyond the gate, a few feet from the street, and only yards from Dove Cottage—he was no longer in Whitecap.

It was a jungle in here, literally.

The grounds had the density of a rain forest, with trees and vegetation he'd never seen before, save for one enormous live oak, damaged by an old storm. He wouldn't be surprised to hear monkeys and macaws, the trumpet call of an elephant. . . .

He stood still, as if frozen to the spot. Cool in here, and quiet, strangely quiet. He heard his own hard breathing, and remembered his maverick dog.

"*Barnabas!*"

In reply, there was crashing through the underbrush to his left, and a revived fit of barking.

"*Come!* Come, old fella!"

Barnabas bolted into the driveway through a vine-entangled hedge, gave him an odd look, then turned and raced toward the house.

He ran, too, pounding along the weed-grown driveway, until the house came fully into view.

Spanish. Stucco. Tile roof. Moss growing in wide, lush patches on the walls of the loggia or portico; vines covering half the house; the smooth, worn roots of a huge tree gnarling up through a stone semicircle at the front door.

He looked at the windows, which returned only a blank and curtainless stare.

"Barnabas!" he hissed.

Dadgummit, there he came around the right side of the house, galloping like a horse after yet another squirrel, which was fleeing for its life through yet another iron gate on some kind of outbuilding that was nearly obscured by undergrowth.

Enough was enough, by heaven. The party was over.

He dashed after his dog as the squirrel ran through the partially open gate, and Barnabas followed, his long hair catching on the rusted iron and slamming the gate behind him.

As it clanged shut, Father Tim stood for a moment, swallowing down his anger.

It was some kind of ancient, stuccoed enclosure, an old dog run, perhaps, grown up with straggling shrubs and weeds. The squirrel was over the rear wall and gone from sight, leaving Barnabas stranded at the end of the run, barking with impotent fury.

Father Tim jiggled the gate, which appeared to have locked. He'd never seen such an odd contrivance to latch a gate; the rust didn't make it work any better, either. Blast! He hit the thing with the palm of his hand, smarting the flesh and drawing blood.

He could fairly throttle his dog, who now turned toward him with a look of sheepish regret. "Come," he said through clenched teeth.

Barnabas, clearly on the downside of his adrenaline rush, walked slowly toward the gate, head down.

His master punched the gate again, repeated the favorite expletive of his school buddy, Tommy Noles, then gave the blasted thing a stiff kick for good measure.

"Out!"

He heard the bellow as if it were projected on a loudspeaker.

"Out!"

His skin prickled. "Mr. Love," he shouted into thin air, "my dog is locked in your run, and I don't have a clue how to get him . . . *out.*"

"You're a fool to let him *in,*" growled Morris Love.

Father Tim looked to an upstairs window where he thought the voice originated, but saw no one.

"I didn't let him in. He ran in on his own, chasing a squirrel!" He was fairly trembling with the frustration of this escapade, and suddenly angry at the man who refused to show himself, much less proffer a grain of human hospitality.

"Take the pin out," Morris Love yelled.

He slid the pin out. Whoever put this thing together ought to have his head examined. . . .

"Turn the latch to the right!"

He cranked it to the right. Nothing. Dead. Not to mention that something was eating his legs alive.

He was furious. He felt as if he could dismantle the gate with his bare hands, like Samson, and pitch it into the weeds. His blood pressure was probably halfway to the moon.

"It doesn't work!" he shouted, slapping at his bitten legs.

"It works, Father, it has always worked. *Don't push it when you turn it to the right!*"

Morris Love could wake the dead with that huge bellow, as if he were speaking through the pipes of his organ. Father Tim tried again, without pushing. The gate opened as easily as if it had just rolled off the assembly line.

He breathed a sigh of relief and wiped his forehead with the tail of his T-shirt. Blast, what a commotion.

His dog's tail was between his legs as they marched toward the house.

"Thank you!" he shouted to the open upstairs window. "We'll try not to trouble you again."

Silence.

As they swung left into the driveway, he gave one of the gnarled roots an impatient kick.

"Goodbye and good riddance," he muttered under his breath.

Now the duck possessed a portion of its other wing.

He handled it carefully, admiring the lifelike beauty of the emerging creature.

"Do you . . . sell these?" he asked Roger.

"Oh, yes. I haven't kept one for myself in a good while."

"What kind of money do they go for?" Four, maybe five hundred, he thought, and well worth it!

Roger's brown eyes sparkled, as they often did when he spoke of his craft. "I'll probably ask around fifteen hundred for this one."

With what he hoped wasn't obvious haste, he handed it back to Roger.

Ernie thumped into a chair at their table. "Junior's been turned down flat," he said, looking crestfallen.

"How? Who?"

"Ava. She won't go out with 'im, won't even let 'im meet 'er daddy."

"I hate to hear it."

"If you ask me," said Ernie, "it was those pictures that did 'im in. Junior's better lookin' than those pictures."

Roanoke took a cigarette from behind his ear. "His fish done wiggled off th' hook."

Ernie sighed. "We could take 'em again with a better camera. I could get one from th' *Whitecap Reader*, I think they use Nikes."

"Nikons," said Roger, not looking up from his work.

"He ought to start over an' run another ad," said Roanoke. "Leave out th' Bronco business, leave out th' Scrabble business, keep in th' fishin' part, axe th' stuff about a serious relationship—"

"He don't want to run another ad," said Ernie. "He don't want to start over, he wants to meet Ava."

"What did he say in his letter to her? Maybe that's the key."

"Beats me. I tried to tell him what to say, but who knows?" Ernie shrugged, looking disconsolate.

For a while, the only sound was Roger's knife against the tupelo wood.

He threw his cup in the wastebasket by the Pepsi machine and fished around in his shorts pocket for fifty-cents, which he gave Ernie for the *Reader.*

Roanoke had pedaled away on his bicycle, Roger was walking Lucas, and Father Tim figured this was as good a chance as he'd get.

"Ernie," he said, "tell me everything you know about Morris Love."

CHAPTER THIRTEEN

Mighty Waters

He was awake ten minutes before the alarm went off, and heard at once the light patter of rain through the open window.

"Timothy?"

"Yes?"

"Is it four o'clock?"

"Ten 'til. Go back to sleep."

"You'll have a great time, I just know you will."

"I'm sure of it. And remember—don't cook dinner. I'm bringing it home."

"Right, darling. I'm excited. . . ."

She was no such thing; she was already snoring again. He kissed her shoulder and crept out of bed.

He was accustomed to rising early, but four o'clock was ridiculous, not to mention he couldn't get pumped up for this jaunt no matter how hard he tried.

He'd entertained every fishing yarn anyone cared to tell, trying to mask his blank stare with a look of genuine interest. Ah, well, surely the whole business would pleasantly surprise him—he'd return home with a cooler full of tuna, tanned and vigorous from a day on the water, whistling a sea chantey.

Chances were—and this was not a perk to be taken lightly—it could even blow a fresh breeze through his preaching, not to mention make him feel more one-in-spirit with his parish. After all, he'd been on their turf for three months and practically the only thing he'd done that he couldn't have done in Mitford was slap a few mosquitoes and pick sandspurs from his dog's paws.

He dressed hurriedly in the bathroom, brushed his teeth, splashed water on his face, and raced to the kitchen to gulp down a cup of coffee he'd set in the refrigerator last night, figuring cold caffeine to be better than no caffeine at all.

He packed the canvas bag with his lunch, having entirely dismissed the notion of fried chicken. Where on earth anybody would find fried chicken at four in the morning was beyond him. He stuffed in plenty of bottled water and a couple of citrus drinks. No time to eat, he'd do that on the boat, he was out of here.

His dog followed him along the hall, thumped down by the front door, and yawned mightily. "Guard the house, old fellow."

Dark as pitch. He turned the lock, shut the door behind him, and patted his jacket pockets for the rolled-up canvas hat and bottle of sunscreen. All there.

He stood on the porch and drew in a deep draught of the cool morning air; it was scented with rain and salt, with something mysteriously beyond his ken. He didn't think he'd ever again take the ocean for granted. He daily sensed the power and presence of it in this new world in which they were living.

All those years ago when he was a young clergyman in a little coastal parish, the water had meant nothing to him; it had hardly entered his mind. He might have lived in the Midwest for all the interest he took in the things of the sea, except for the several bushels of shrimp and clams he'd surely consumed during his curacy. His mind, his heart had been elsewhere, in the clouds, perhaps; but now it was different. Though he wasn't one for swimming in the ocean or broiling on the beach, he was making a connection this time, something he couldn't quite articulate and why bother, anyway?

The light rain cooled his head as he trotted down the front steps, opened the gate, and got into the Mustang parked by the street.

Goin' fishin'! he thought as he buckled the seat belt. The way he'd worried about this excursion had made it seem like a trek to Outer

Mongolia, but so far, so good. And just think—there were thousands, probably millions of people out there who'd give anything to be in his shoes.

It was still dark when he found the marina where the charter boats were tied to the dock like horses waiting to be saddled.

He pulled into the nearly full parking lot, took his gear from the trunk and locked up, then stood by the Mustang, peering into the murky light. People were huffing coolers as big as coffins out of vans and cars, muttering, calling to each other, laughing, slamming doors.

More than once, he'd heard charter boats called party boats, and fervently hoped this was not one of those deals.

Raining a little harder now, but nothing serious. He wiped his head with his hat and put it back in his pocket, checking his watch. Five o'clock sharp.

He hefted the cooler and started walking, looking for *Blue Heaven* and trying to get over the feeling he was still asleep and this was a dream.

Someone materialized out of the gray mist, smelling intensely of tobacco and shaving lotion.

"Mornin', Father! Let's go fishin'!"

"Otis? Is that you?"

"Cap'n Willie told me you were on board today. I didn't want you goin' off by yourself and havin' too much fun."

Otis was schlepping a cooler with a fluorescent label that was readable even in the predawn light: *Bragg's for All Your Cement Needs.*

A bronzed, bearded Captain Willie stood on the deck wearing shorts and a T-shirt, booming out a welcome.

"Father Timothy! Good mornin' to you, we're glad to have you!" He found himself shaking a hand as big as a ham and hard as a rock. "Step over lightly, now, let me take that, there you go, welcome to *Blue Heaven.*"

"Good morning, Captain. How's the weather looking?" It seemed the boat was lurching around in the water pretty good, and they hadn't even gone anywhere yet.

"Goin' to fair off and be good fishin'." Captain Willie's genial smile displayed a couple of gold teeth. "Meet my first mate, Pete Brady."

He shook hands with a muscular fellow of about thirty. "Good to see you, Pete."

"Yessir, welcome aboard."

"This your first time?" asked the captain.

"First ever."

"Well, you're fishin' with a pro, here." He pounded Otis on the back. "Go on in th' cabin, set your stuff down, make yourself at home. And Father . . ."

"Yes?"

"Would you favor us with blessin' th' fleet this mornin'?"

"Ah . . . how does that work, exactly?"

"All th' boats'll head out about th' same time, then after the sun rises, you'll come up to th' bridge an' ask th' Lord for safe passage and good fishin'. Th' other boats can hear you over th' radio."

"Consider it done!" he said, feeling a surge of excitement.

"We'll have prayer requests for you, like, the last few days, we've all been prayin' for Cap'n Tucker's daughter, she's got leukemia."

"I'm sorry. I'd feel honored and blessed to do it."

"We thank you. Now go in there and introduce yourselves around, get comfortable."

Father Tim stuck his head in the cabin.

Ernie Fulcher, sitting with a green cooler between his feet, threw up his hand and grinned from ear to ear. "Didn't want you runnin' out th' first time all by your lonesome."

"Right," said Roger, looking shy about butting in. "We didn't think you'd mind a little company."

Madge Parrott and her friend Sybil Huffman appeared to be dressed for a cruise in the Bahamas. They were clearly proud to announce they were from Rome, Georgia, and this was their first time on a fishing charter. They were out for marlin, would settle for tuna if necessary, but no dolphin, thank you, they'd heard dolphins could sing and had feelings like people.

Both were widows whose husbands had been great fishermen. this trip was about making a connection with the departed, as they'd heard Chuck and Roy talk about deep-sea fishing like it was the best thing since sliced bread. Madge confessed that even though she and Sybil didn't drink beer, they didn't see why they couldn't catch fish like anybody else.

He noted that the group shared a need to explain what they had in their coolers, some even lifting the lids and displaying the contents, and issuing hearty invitations to dip in, at any time, to whatever they'd brought along.

"You run out of drinks, me'n Roger got all you want right here," said Ernie, patting a cooler as big as a Buick. "Got Sun-drop, Mello Yello, Sprite, just help yourself."

"And there's ham and turkey on rye," said Roger. "I made two extra, just in case, plus fried chicken."

Everybody nodded their thanks, as the engines began to throb and hum. Father Tim was mum about the contents of his own cooler—two banana sandwiches on white bread with low-fat mayo.

"Y'all need any sunscreen," said Madge, "we're loaded with sunscreen. It's right here in my jacket pocket." She indicated a blue jacket folded on the seat, so that one and all might note its whereabouts in an emergency.

"And I've got Bonine," said Sybil, "if anybody feels seasick." She held up her package and rattled the contents.

"Have you ever been seasick?" Madge asked Father Tim.

"Never!" he said. Truth was, he'd never been on the sea but a couple of times, and always in sight of shore, so there was no way he could have been seasick. And for today, he'd done what Ernie and Roger so heartily recommended—he'd stayed sober, gotten a good night's sleep, and didn't eat a greasy breakfast.

"Only twelve percent of people get seasick," Roger said, quoting his most encouraging piece of information on the subject.

Ernie lifted the lid of his cooler. "Oh, an' anybody wants Snickers bars, they're right here on top of th' ice. There's nothin' like a Snickers iced down good'n cold."

Madge and Sybil admitted they'd never heard of icing down a Snickers bar, but thought it would be real tasty, especially on a hot day. Sybil pledged to try one before the trip was over.

Otis announced that anybody who wanted to help themselves to his Kentucky Fried, they knew where it was at. He also had cigars, Johnnie Walker Black, and boiled peanuts, for whoever took a notion.

It was the most instant formation of community Father Tim had ever witnessed. He felt momentarily inspired to stand and lead a hymn.

Captain Willie gunned the engines, and the stern of *Blue Heaven* dug low into the water as they moved away from the dock at what seemed like full speed. Father Tim realized he didn't know how he felt about riding backward, not to mention that the water seemed mighty rough.

Very dadgum blasted rough, he thought as they plowed farther out in an unceasing rain. He looked around the hull of the small cabin, where everyone appeared totally sophisticated about being tossed around like dice in a cup. They were all holding on for dear life to whatever they could grab, and yelling over the roar of eight hundred and fifty horses running wide open.

Otis Bragg was clearly tickled pink to have two women on board who didn't know fishing from frog's legs. He'd already begun a seminar on how to keep your thumb on the fishing line, how to hold the rod, how to hold your mouth, and how to position your feet when reeling in a big one. Father Tim listened as attentively as he could, then finally slumped against the back of the padded bench and peered through the door of the cabin.

Out there, it was rain, churning waters, and diesel smoke. In here, it was earsplitting racket and the worst ride he'd had since Tommy Noles had shoved him down a rocky hillside in a red wagon without a tongue.

The sun was emerging from the water, staining the silver sea with patches of light and color.

Pete Brady came into the cabin, holding a dripping ballyhoo in one hand. "You'll want to go up to the bridge now, sir. Better put your jacket on."

"Right!" he said. He was glad to leave the cabin; only a moment ago, he'd had the odd sensation of smothering. . . .

He stood, holding on to the table that was bolted to the deck, then made his way to the door, praying he wouldn't pitch into Madge Parrott's lap.

"You tell th' Lord we're wantin' 'em to weigh fifty pounds and up, if He don't mind." Otis chewed his cigar and grinned.

Father Tim clung to the doorjamb. "How do I get to the bridge?" he asked Pete.

The first mate, who appeared to be squeezing the guts from a bait fish, jerked his thumb toward the side of the cabin. "Right up the ladder there."

He peered around and saw the ladder. The rungs were immediately over the water, and went straight up. Three, four, five . . .

"*That* ladder?"

"Yessir, be sure'n hold on tight."

He peered into the black and churning sea, and made a couple of quick steps to a chair that was bolted to the cockpit deck. Pete was bustling around without any difficulty in keeping his footing, but Father Tim had the certain feeling that if he let go of the chair, he'd end up at the Currituck Light.

He turned and lunged for the bottom rung of the ladder, but miscalculated and bounced onto the rail. Too startled to grab hold, he reeled against the cabin wall, finally managing to grip the lower rung. Thanks be to God, Pete was baiting a hook and facing seaward, and his cabin mates were oblivious to his afflictions.

Lord Jesus, I've never done this before. You were plenty good around water, and I'm counting on You to help me accomplish this thing.

He reached to an upper rung and got a firm grip.

The spray was flying, the waves were churning, the sun was rising . . . it was now or never. He swung himself onto the ladder and went up, trying in vain to curl his tennis shoes around the rungs like buns around frankfurters.

He hauled himself to the bridge, grabbed the support rail for the hard top, and stood for a moment, awed. The view from the bridge literally took his breath away.

How could anyone doubt the living truth of what the psalmist said? *"The heavens declare the glory of God, the skies proclaim the work of his hands!"* He wanted to shout in unabashed praise.

His shirt whipped against his body like a flag; his knees trembled. This boat was flying, no two ways about it, and beneath their feet, the endless, racking, turbulent sea, and a sunrise advancing up the sky like tongues of fire.

Surely this was the habitation of angels, and life in the cabin a thing to be pitied.

He lurched to the helm, where Captain Willie was holding a microphone, and grabbed the back of the helm chair.

"We're glad to have you with us, Father! Greetings to you from th' whole fleet on this beautiful September day!"

His stomach did an odd turn as he opened his mouth to speak, so he closed it again.

The captain winked. "Got a little chop this mornin'."

He nodded.

"A real sharp head sea."

He felt sweat on his brow as the captain spoke into the microphone.

"We're mighty happy to have Father Tim Kavanagh to lead us in prayer this mornin'. He's from over at Whitecap, where Toby Rider has his boat shop. Anybody with a prayer request, let's hear it now."

The VHF blared. "Father, my little boy fell off a ladder on Sunday, he's, ah, in the hospital, looks like he's goin' to be fine, but . . . his name's Danny. We thank you."

"Please pray for Romaine, he had his leg tore up by a tractor fell on 'im. Thank you."

"Just like to ask for . . . forgiveness for somethin' I done, there's no use to go into what, I'd appreciate it."

Several other requests came in as he bent his head and listened intently, gripping the helm chair for all he was worth.

"That it? Anybody else?"

He fished in his pocket for his hat. Though the rain had stopped, he put it on and pulled it down snugly above his ears. Then he took the microphone, surprised that it felt as heavy as a lug wrench.

"We'd like to pray for th' owner of th' marina and his wife, Angie, too," said Captain Willie. "She's got breast cancer. And Cap'n Tucker's daughter, we don't want to forget her, name's Sarah, then there's Toby Rider, lost his daddy and we feel real bad about it. Course we'd like to ask God's mercy for every family back home and every soul on board. . . ."

Captain Willie turned to the helm, grabbed the red knob, and cranked the engines back to idle.

In the sudden quiet, the waves slammed against the hull, dulling the gurgling sound of the exhaust. They seemed to be wallowing now in the choppy sea; they might have been so much laundry tossing in a washing machine.

His heart was hammering as if he'd run a race. But it wasn't his heart, exactly, that bothered him, it was his stomach. It seemed strangely disoriented, as if it had moved to a new location and he couldn't figure out where.

"Our Father, we thank You mightily for the beauty of the sunrise over this vast sea, and for the awe and wonder in all the gifts of Your creation. We ask Your generous blessings upon every captain and mate aboard every vessel in this fleet, and pray that each of us be made able, by Your grace, to know Your guidance, love, and mercy throughout the day. . . ."

The names of the people, and their needs, what were they? His mind seemed desperately blank, as if every shred of thought and reason had been blown away like chaff on the wind.

Lord! Help!

"For Sarah, we ask Your tender mercies, that You would keep her daily in Your healing care, giving wisdom to those attending her, and providing strength and encouragement. . . ."

More than three decades of intercessory prayer experience notwithstanding, he found it miraculous that the names came to him, one by one. He leaned into the prayer with intensity, feeling something of the genuine weight and burden, the urgency, of the needs for which he prayed.

He wiped the sweat from his forehead. "Oh, Lord, who maketh a way in the sea, and a path in the mighty waters, we thank You for hearing our prayers, in the blessed name of Your Son, our Savior, Jesus Christ. Amen."

The captain took the microphone and keyed it, thanking him.

He noted what appeared to be a look of compassion on the captain's face as they shook hands.

"*Blue Heaven, Salty Dog,* come back."

"*Blue Heaven,* go ahead, *Salty Dog.*"

"Just want to say we really appreciate Father Kavanagh's prayers, and sure hope he doesn't succumb to the torments of a rough sea. OK, *Salty Dog* back to eighty."

"*Blue Heaven* standin' by on eighty."

As the captain gunned the engines, Father Tim careened to the rail and leaned over.

The goodwill and fond hope of *Salty Dog* had come too late.

Twice over the rail should nip this thing in the bud. Already his ribs hurt from the retching; it was probably over now and he could go down the ladder and have something to drink, maybe even a bite to eat—that was the problem, going out on rough seas with an empty stomach. . . .

He was amazed at his agility on the ladder, as if by the earlier practice shot he'd become a seasoned sailor. No big deal, he thought, looking down at the waves hammering the boat.

Good grief! He scrambled off the ladder and leaned over the rail, the bile spewing in a flume from his very core, hot, bitter, and fathomless.

It was his head. He seemed to have lost his head the last time over the rail. He reached up feebly and felt around. No, it was his hat he'd lost. It had slithered off and dropped into the sea, and his scalp was parching like a Georgia peanut.

"Let 'im set there, we ain't findin' any fish," he heard Otis say. He opened his eyes and realized he was sitting in the privileged fighting chair. The fighting chair. What a joke.

"Hat," he said. "Hat."

Nobody heard him, because he found he couldn't speak above a whisper. He had no energy to force audible words through cracked lips.

Fine. He'd just sit here until they dumped him overboard, which he wished they'd do sooner rather than later. He'd never known such suffering in his life, not from mayonnaise that had nearly taken him out at a parish picnic, not from the diabetic coma brought on by Esther Bolick's orange marmalade cake, not from the raging fever he had as a child when he saw his mother as a circus performer who made lions jump through hoops.

"What I don't like about th' Baptists," Otis was saying, "is they won't speak to you at th' liquor store."

Laughing, shuffling around, general merriment—people living their lives as if he weren't there, as if he were invisible, a bump on a log.

"That's th' way it is, some days," said Pete. "You're either a hero or a zero. Yesterday, we were haulin' 'em in faster than I could bait th' hooks; today, I don't know where they are."

"You got to pump 'em," said Ernie. "Like, say you're reelin' in a fifty-pound tuna, you got to raise the rod up real slow, then drop down quick and *crank*."

Conversations came and went; it was all a kind of hive hum, he thought, as when bees returned from working a stand of sourwoods.

"Now, you take tarpon," said Otis. "I was down in th' Keys where they grow too big to mount on your wall. Tarpon you just jump a few times and then break 'em off before you wear 'em out, you wear 'em out too bad, th' sharks eat 'em."

"I never fished any tarpon," said Ernie.

He opened his eyes and shut them fast. Pete was showing Madge and Sybil how he prepped the bait.

"See, you pop th' eyes out like this . . . then you break up th' backbone . . ."

"Oooh," said Madge.

"Don't make 'er faint," said Otis.

"I have no intention of fainting, thank you!"

"Then you squeeze their guts out, see. . . ."

"Lord help," said Sybil.

"Thing is, th' more they wiggle in th' water, th' better they catch."

"Clever!" said Madge. "That is *really* clever."

Without realizing how he got there, he was at the rail again, on his knees.

"On his knees at th' rail," said Madge. "That is very Episcopalian."

"Or Luth'ran," said Sybil. "Can't that be Luth'ran?"

He didn't know who it was, maybe Otis or Ernie, but someone held his head while he spewed up his insides and watched the vomitus carried away on the lashing water.

"We been out every day for forty-one days straight," said Pete, who was currently varying the bait, trying anything.

"Sometimes you just pray for a nor'easter so you can get a break, but if th' weather's good, you have to go."

The weather today is not *good,* he tried to say, but couldn't. Why in blazes did we go today if you don't go when the weather's not good? *Answer that!* Plus, *plus* . . . he wished he could discuss this with Roger . . . his math told him that, discounting the crew, he represented more than any twelve blasted percent.

He declined the fighting chair in case anyone got a strike, and sat feebly in an adjacent chair.

"What do you think the winds are right now?" asked Roger.

"Oh, fifteen, sixteen miles an hour. This ain't nothin'. I know somebody was out all night last night in forty-mile winds."

General, respectful silence. Diesel fumes.

"We need to think positive," said Madge. "Smoked loin of tuna! That's how *I'm* thinkin'!"

"Must be lunchtime," said Otis. "Believe I'll have me a little shooter. Want one?"

"Maybe later."

"Thank you, you go on, but I wouldn't mind shuckin' a few peanuts with you."

He was baking, he was broiling, he was frying, he was cooked. Sunscreen. He remembered the sunscreen in his jacket pocket, but he wasn't wearing his jacket. Someone had helped him remove it earlier.

"Look," said Sybil. "Th' poor man needs something."

"What?" said Madge. "Oh, mercy, look at his head, it's red as a poker. Where's his hat?"

"He went to the rail and came back without it."

"Here you go," Otis was patting sunscreen on his head and followed it with a hat

"Bless you," he managed to whisper.

"What'd he say?"

"He said bless me." He thought Otis sounded touched. "Father, you want some water or Coke? Coke might be good."

"Nossir," said Ernie, "what he needs is ginger ale. Anybody got ginger ale?"

"Fruit juice," said Madge, "that's what I'd give somebody with upset stomach."

"No deal with th' fruit juice," said Pete. "Too much acid."

"How about a piece of ice to just hold in his mouth?"

"I don't know about that. They say when you're real hot you shouldn't swallow somethin' real cold, it can give you a heart attack or maybe a stroke."

"He's moving his lips. What's he saying?"

Otis leaned down and listened. "He's praying," said Otis.

They had veered east, then south, but weren't finding any fish. Neither was the rest of the fleet. Occasionally a boat would get a couple of strikes, radio the news, and everybody would head in that direction. But so far, *Blue Heaven* had taken only two dolphins, and thrown back a few catches that were too small to gaff.

They were currently idling the boat several miles south of Virginia, and trolling a spreader bar. The chop was as bad as, or worse than, before; they were wallowing like a bear in cornshucks. He thought of looking at his watch, but why bother? The misery was interminable. There was no hope that anyone would turn back to shore for a sick man, much less send a helicopter. He was in this scrape to the bitter end.

He denied to himself that he had to urinate, as doing that would require going through the cabin where this thing first snared and suffocated him. He wouldn't go back in that cabin if they tried to drag him in with a team of mules.

Occasionally, a kind soul visited his chair and stood for a moment in silent commiseration.

"Sorry, Tim."

"You're going to make it, buddy."

Even the captain came down from the bridge and laid a hand on his shoulder. "Hang in there, Father." Their concern was a comfort, he had to admit, though he was hard-pressed to get over the humiliation he felt.

At one point, someone assured him he wasn't going to die, which he found altogether lacking in comfort, since he didn't much care either way.

"Did you hear about th' guy got dragged off th' boat reelin' in a marlin?"

"No way."

"It was in th' paper, said th' marlin was four hundred pounds, said it pulled th' guy over th' stern."

"He would've been sucked into th' backwash."

"Wadn't. Somebody went in after 'im, saved 'im. But that's not th' half of it. He got th' marlin."

"Bull. That never happened in this lifetime."

"I'm tellin' you it's th' truth, it was in th' paper."

"I've heard of fish takin' first mates over," said Pete.

"There is no way I want to listen to this mess," said Madge.

He was shocked to find himself kneeling at the rail again, with no power over this thing, none at all. He felt completely out of control, which frightened him utterly; he might have been a piece of bait himself, without will or reason to alter his circumstances.

"Number five," somebody said. "That's th' fifth time."

"Seven. He heaved over th' bridge rail twice."

"You ready to eat? I'm half starved."

"I've been thinkin' about what I made last night. Tuna salad. On French bread! Oh, and there's late tomatoes out of my neighbor's garden. Delicious!" said Madge. "I'll cut 'em up so we can all have a bite."

"Tuna out of a *can*?" asked Otis. "That'd be sacrilegious."

"Are we goin' to just leave 'im out here?" wondered Sybil.

"Father? *Father!*"

Why did people think the sick automatically went deaf?

What? He couldn't say it audibly, so he thought it, which should be sufficient.

"Do you want to go inside?"

"Don't take him inside," said the first mate. "You lose th' horizon when you do that. That's usually what makes people seasick, is losin' th' horizon."

"But he's been sittin' out here since it quit rainin'. I think we should at least put sunscreen on his arms. Look at his arms."

He felt several people pawing over him, and tried to express his gratitude.

"Lookit. He doesn't have socks on. Rub some on his ankles."

"Th' back of his neck," said Ernie. "That's a real tender place, slather some on there."

"He's an *awful* color," said Madge.

He realized he should have been more specific in his will; now it was too late to say that he did *not* want an open casket.

He slept, or thought he might be sleeping. Perhaps he'd slipped into a state of unconsciousness, his mind vacant as a hollow gourd. If there was anything he distrusted, it was an empty mind. He forced himself to open his eyes and saw only glare, a shining that moved and heaved and shuddered and danced and tried to force entry to his stomach. In truth, he'd never been especially aware of his stomach. When it was empty, he put something in it; when it was full, he was happy. Now he felt it as a raw and flaccid thing that swung in him like a sheep's bladder with every swell that tossed the boat.

He wanted his wife. Lacking that consolation, he pulled his jacket around him and squeezed his eyes shut and dreamed a dream as vacant as mist.

Thank God! He might actually be feeling better.

His eyes seemed clear, some strength was returning; but he didn't want to count his chickens, no, indeed. He rubbed Chap Stick on his lips and hunkered down under Otis's hat, wondering about his sugar, which must have dropped straight to the floor of the Gulf Stream. He wished he'd brought his tachometer . . . no, that wasn't it. What was it, anyway? Could he possibly have suffered brain damage from this terrible assault? *Glu*cometer, that's what it was.

Weak . . . terribly weak. He realized he was thinking of Ernie's Snickers bars, iced down cold. A small flicker, a flame of hope rose in his breast. *Thank You, Lord.* . . .

He looked out upon the restless water and saw other boats on the horizon—one there, two there, like family.

"We had the worst nest of yellow jackets in our church wall-l-l!" said Sybil.

"What'd y'all do about it?"

"Swatted 'em with our hymnals and bulletins."

"Why didn't you kill 'em?"

"They only flare up once a year, late April or May, and only on th' side where hardly anybody sits, anyway."

"Yesterday a hero, today a zero," muttered Pete, hauling up bait that looked like a glorified Christmas tree.

Father Tim waved his hand to Ernie, who came over and squatted by the chair.

"What can I do for you, buddy?"

"Snickers," he said, hoarse as a bullfrog.

"Snickers?"

He nodded, feeble but encouraged.

"We got us one!" yelled Ernie. "Otis! Where's Otis?"

"In th' head. You take it!"

Father Tim had heard of total pandemonium, but he'd never seen it 'til now. Six people erupted into a full horde, and swarmed around him like the armies of Solomon.

"We got a fish here! Yee-hah!"

"Got another one right here. Take it, Madge!"

He looked at the throbbing lines crisscrossed over and around the stern like freeways through L.A.

"That's a keeper!" Pete gaffed something and pulled it in.

"Way to go, Roger!"

He saw the rainbow of color that shimmered on the big fish as it went into the box, where it thrashed like a horse kicking a stall. Pete pulled out the gaff and hosed blood from the deck.

The captain was fishing off the bridge; everybody was fishing. He heaved himself from the chair, out of the fray, and huddled against the cabin.

In the fighting chair, Madge was crouched into the labor of hauling in something big.

Otis had his thumb on her line, helping her raise and lower the rod. "You got to pump 'im, now," he said, clenching his cigar in his teeth.

"Oh, law! This must be an eighteen-wheeler I've got on here!"

"Keep crankin'!"

Captain Willie called over the speaker, "Please tend to the left-hand corner, Pete, tend to the left-hand corner, we got a mess over there."

"A fishin' frenzy," muttered Pete, streaking by in a blur.

Madge cranked the reel, blowing like a prizefighter. "This fish is killin' me. Somebody come and take this bloomin' rod!"

"Don't quit!" yelled Sybil, aiming a point-and-shoot at the action. "Keep goin', Chuck would be proud!"

"That ain't nothin' but solid tuna," said Otis. He helped Madge lift the rod as the fish drew closer to the boat.

Father Tim rubberlegged it to the stern and looked over. The black water of the morning had changed to blue-green, and the fish moved beneath the aqua surface, luminous and quick.

He thought it one of the most beautiful sights he'd ever seen.

"Here it comes!"

He stepped back as Pete darted to the right of the fighting chair, lowered the gaff, and hauled the tuna onto the deck.

"Way to go, Madge!"

"Beautiful! *Beautiful!*"

Whistles, cheers, applause.

"That'll weigh in seventy, seventy-five pounds," Otis said, as Madge staggered out of the chair, grinning into Sybil's camera.

The captain was catching fish, Ernie was catching fish, Roger was catching fish.

"Got a fish on th' line!" yelled Pete. "Who'll take it?"

"I'll take it!" As Father Tim thumped into the fighting chair, hoots of encouragement went up from the entire assembly.

He was back from the dead, he was among the living, he was ready to do this thing.

"How was it, darling?"

"Terrific!" he said, kissing her. "Wonderful fellowship, *great* fellowship—fellows in a ship, get it?"

"Got it. And the weather?"

He shrugged. "A little rough, but not too bad."

"What's for supper?" she asked, eyeing the cooler he was lugging.

"Yellowfin tuna and dolphin! Let's fire up the grill," he said, trotting down the hall, "and I'll tell you all about it!" By the time he hit the kitchen, he was whistling.

She hurried after her husband, feeling pleased. He'd come home looking considerably thinner, definitely tanner, and clearly more relaxed. She'd known all along that buying him a chair with Captain Willie was a brilliant idea.

CHAPTER FOURTEEN

Letting Go

"Turn around a minute and don't look," Roger said.

Father Tim turned and faced the book room, where Elmo sat on the windowsill, licking his paws after a meal of thawed finger mullet.

"OK, you can look now."

Roger had positioned the carved head on the body of the green-winged teal; the duck was gazing at him in a way he found positively soulful.

"Aha," he whispered.

"I set the eyes a while back and forgot to show you."

"It'll be as close to th' real thing as you'll ever see in this life!" Ernie Fulcher was grinning as if he were personally responsible for the whole deal. "Fact is, you can compare it to th' real thing right now, if you want to. We got one we keep in th' freezer for when he needs somethin' to go by."

"That's OK," said Father Tim, not eager to see a dead duck in a Ziploc bag.

"Until I set the eyes," said Roger, "it didn't have any character at all, there was no personality. The eyes lying on the worktable are nothing, but set them in place and this piece of wood becomes a duck."

"Amazing! Just amazing."

"I've got to burn all the feathers, now they've been chiseled, then I'll gesso everything and start to paint. See these speculum feathers on the wing? They'll be green, and the under-tail coverts here, they'll be a champagne color."

Roger passed his handiwork to Father Tim, who took it, feeling oddly reverent.

Though he didn't know why, and he certainly didn't know how . . . this was his duck.

He was getting ready to leave when Junior Bryson came in, looking as if he'd lost his last friend.

Lucas's tail thumped the floor in greeting.

"I done it," Junior said.

"Done what?" asked Ernie.

"Talked to Ava's daddy."

"Come and sit down," said Ernie, pulling out a chair. "You want a Pepsi, have a Pepsi! Or get you a root beer."

Junior shook his head at Ernie's offer and thumped down at the table, looking, thought Father Tim, considerably pale around the gills. He changed his mind about leaving and sat down with Junior.

Roger placed the duck in its carry-box.

Roanoke lit a Marlboro.

Silence.

"Well?" said Ernie.

Junior sighed. "Well, I finally worked up th' nerve to call 'er daddy, so I got th' phone book that has Swanquarter, and found a Goodnight listed in it."

"Smart!" said Ernie.

"It wadn't too smart," said Junior. "I was thinkin' her daddy's name would be Goodnight, but then, when th' phone started ringin', it hit me that Goodnight was prob'ly her married name an' she might answer th' phone."

"Right!" said Ernie, hoping for the best.

"I was about to hang up, when a man answered. That kind of th'owed me. I thought it might be, like, you know, a boyfriend. But it was her daddy, Mr. Taylor. He lives at Ava's."

Roanoke blew a smoke ring. Lucas's yawn sounded like a squeak from a door hinge.

"Well, I'd practiced what I wanted to say, but when he answered, I forgot everything."

"Right," said Ernie. "It usually works that way."

"So, anyhow, I said, 'This is Junior Bryson from over at Whitecap, Ava might of mentioned me.' "

"That was a good start."

"He said, 'Are you th' fella plays Scrabble and fishes?' " Junior's face brightened momentarily. "I said, 'Yessir.' He said, I like a fella says yessir, most people've forgot about sayin' yessir.' "

"And what'd you say?"

"I said 'Yessir, you're right about that.' "

"Common ground!" exclaimed Ernie. Roger and Father Tim nodded their agreement.

"So I said I was hopin' Ava might go out with me, I do Sound an' ocean fishin' both, an' have a little boat I take crabbin' an' all, I could offer her a variety of fishin' options."

"That should of done it right there!"

"I said I'm pretty sharp at Scrabble and could prob'ly give her a good run for th' money."

"An' what'd he say?"

"He said she beats th' stuffin' out of him all th' time, not to mention beats her sister an' some of th' neighbors."

Ernie whistled through his teeth.

"I told him about my job, how I was Employee of th' Month back in April an' all. . . ."

"What else?"

"I told him I own my own house an' keep my truck washed an' waxed, that I change th' oil myself an' just put on a new set of Michelins." Junior looked exhausted.

"That's all your cards right there," said Ernie. "You laid 'em on th' table, that's all a man can do. So what'd he say?"

Junior looked at his hands. "He said I sounded pretty decent an' responsible."

Ernie beamed. "Then what?"

"So then I told him I hadn't heard back from Ava, an' wondered if he'd be willin' to give his permission for me to take 'er out an' all."

Father Tim glanced around. Roanoke was cleaning his fingernails with a pocketknife. Roger was pondering the situation intently. Ernie looked nervous.

"So he said, 'Well, son, I like what you're sayin', I really do, and I thought those snapshots showed a fine-lookin' fella, but your letter failed to convince Ava that you're a Christian, and that's a requirement of hers as well as mine.' Then he said she wrote me a note a day or two ago and he guessed I hadn't got it yet."

Ernie looked disgusted. "Shoot, maybe you don't want to go out with somebody that could whip your butt at Scrabble. You thought of that?"

"Just because she whips her daddy don't mean she can whip me."

"So, what can we do here to move things along?" asked Roger.

It appeared that Roger's CEO mode was kicking in.

Junior's gaze searched every face for an answer to this probing question, and at last zeroed in on Father Tim, who knew Junior's look very well.

"Would you like to have a talk?"

Junior nodded.

"Anytime, just let me know."

Junior appeared suddenly hopeful. "How about right now? We could go set in my truck."

Roger and Ernie gave the clergy an approving nod.

"Consider it done," he said.

"If you need air-conditionin', we can roll th' windows up."

Father Tim noticed Junior's hands were trembling. A talk with the clergy sometimes did that to people.

"Not for me. But you might pull over in the shade," he said. *Lord, give me wisdom here. May Your Holy Spirit be with us.* . . . His heart was moved for Junior Bryson.

As Junior started the motor, a shattering blast of country music erupted from speakers the size of drink crates. Junior hit the off button, embarrassed. "I'm really sorry 'bout that."

"No problem," said his passenger, barely able to speak for the adrenaline pumping into his system.

Junior eased the truck under the leafy branches of a nearby tree. "We could ride around if you'd rather do that," said Junior.

"This is fine, we can sit right here. I think we're getting a little breeze."

Junior switched off the ignition and was silent for a moment, looking anguished. "I hate to tell you this, sir."

"What's that?"

"I all of a sudden have to go to th' toilet."

"Go right ahead. I understand."

Junior swung down from the cab and loped across the parking lot.

Junior's uneasiness reminded him, somehow, of himself, as he met with his first bishop all those years ago.

"Why did you decide to become a priest, Timothy?"

"I was called, sir."

"Who called you?"

"God."

The tall, angular Bishop Quayle sat quietly in the leather chair, holding his hands upright before him with all his fingertips touching. Father Tim remembered noting that his fingers formed a sort of steeple, which he thought becoming to a bishop.

"You will have times of doubt."

"Yes, sir."

"Which you can't imagine now, of course."

"No, sir."

"Do you genuinely love Christ with all your heart?"

"Yes, sir, I do."

"What is the chief reason you love Him?"

"Because He loves me."

Their visit had been short, but rewarding. Bishop Quayle prayed with him and made the sign of the cross on his forehead. "I think you'll do, Timothy," he said, smiling. The young priest marked the extraordinary light shining in the bishop's eyes; it was this light that had encouraged him most.

Junior opened the door and slid into the seat looking contrite but refreshed. "I'm sorry, Father. I'm . . . kind of nervous."

"I understand."

"Well," said Junior. "I was hopin' you could help me with what to do about Ava."

"Aha."

"I've got 'er picture right here . . ."—Junior fished it from his shirt pocket, looking proud—"so you could remember what she looks like." He balanced it in a standing position on the volume knob of the radio.

"Here's what I told her in th' letter. I said I went to church when my mama was livin' an' got baptized when I was fourteen. I reckon that makes me a Christian."

He smiled. "*Did* it make you a Christian?"

"I don't know. I mean, seem like bein' baptized was a big deal, th' way I remember it."

"It is a big deal. A very big deal. But it's what happens in our hearts, in our spirits, that's a much bigger deal. What was going on in your heart when you were baptized, do you remember?"

"Nothin' much. Me'n some other people went out to th' creek, th' preacher laid us back in th' water, I come up and dried off, and we all went an' ate catfish at Cap'n Willie's."

"When we ask Jesus to come into our hearts and save us—and if we really mean it—something always happens. Something powerful. Sometimes we sense it the moment we ask, sometimes later. But it never fails to happen."

Junior shrugged and shifted in the seat, which caused his elbow to hit the horn. They both jumped. " 'Scuse me," he said. A few drops of perspiration appeared on his forehead.

"I don't know what Ava's thinking," said Father Tim, indicating the photograph. "Maybe you'll learn more from her letter. But she may be looking for someone who has a personal relationship with Christ."

"I don't see how'n th' world you can have a *personal* relationship with 'im. That don't seem possible to me. That don't seem . . . *possible*."

"That's a hard one to understand, how a God so powerful can be so personal. Yet, when you ask the Son of God to come into your heart, something incredible happens."

"What?"

"He actually comes in."

Junior looked blank.

"He comes in and quickens our spirits so that we're truly alive for the first time. We see with new eyes, we hear with new ears, we're able to receive His love." He thought it was moments like this that he lived for. "The relationship becomes deeply personal, one-on-one."

"I'm sorry, sir, but . . . I just don't get it."

"That's OK. I'll pray for you to get it."

Junior sighed. "What am I goin' to do about Ava?"

"Keep being honest, just as she will be, I'm sure. Whatever happens, honesty is always the best policy."

Junior stared into the vacant lot next door.

"God certainly loves our honesty. You can tell Him anything, Junior, anything!"

"I wouldn't want t' tell 'im *anything*."

He grinned. "Might as well. He knows it anyway."

Junior blushed.

"He not only wants to be your Savior and Lord, He wants to be your best friend. Pretty hard to imagine, but true. Anyway, I think that because you and Ava both admire honesty, everything's going to turn out just fine."

"You think so?"

"I do."

"Thank you, Father. I really thank you."

"Anytime you have questions, anytime you want to just sit and talk, call me or drop by St. John's."

"Yessir, I will. Can I carry you down to church?"

"I'd appreciate it."

Junior removed the photograph from the knob, gave it a furtive glance, and put it back in his pocket. As they wheeled out of the lot, Father Tim couldn't help but see Roger and Ernie peering through the window.

Mother hens! he thought, waving.

The phone on his desk rang twice.

"St. John's in the Grove! Father Kavanagh speaking."

"Hey!" said Dooley.

"Hey, yourself, buddy!" He loved hearing the boy's voice, he could even hear the grin in it. "What's up?"

"I've got . . . like, you know, like a girlfriend."

Whoa. "A girlfriend? Tell me everything."

"Her name's Caroline."

His heart sank. But what business was it of his? "Where did you meet her?"

"I met her at a dance at her school, and we've been writing. You know. Calling each other."

"Aha. What school?"

"It doesn't matter, I mean . . ."

"No, I'd like to know. What school?"

Dooley sounded a little ticked at having it gouged out of him. "Mrs. Hemingway's."

That school where all the girls are geeks, and wear weird shoes and funny glasses? *That* school? "Smart, I suppose . . ."

"Totally smart, straight A's. And really . . . like, you know . . ."

He knew. "Great-looking? Beautiful?"

"Umm, yeah. Yessir. Totally."

He was thrilled that Dooley could confide in him. Who wouldn't be? That pleasure, however, was considerably diminished by wondering what Lace Turner would think of this.

He'd never ask, of course; no, indeed, not for anything.

"Father?" It was Janette's doctor, speaking in his low-country drawl. "I've got a little slip of paper around here somewhere. Janette asked me to give you a message. Let's see, I can't read my own handwriting, I suppose that's no news. . . ."

Father Tim laughed.

"Here it is. Let's see. 'The cactus is beginning to bloom.' "

Tears misted his eyes. "She's coming along, then?"

"Improving. Yes, definitely."

"When do you think she might be coming home?"

"Ten days, maybe two weeks. We want to be absolutely certain the suicidal stuff is behind us."

"Will she be able to care for the children?"

"Yes, we think so. It might help to give her a day or two to settle in, if possible. I understand her cousin is having a time of it, four children in a one-bedroom apartment. . . ."

"We'll do whatever it takes on our end."

"Excellent. Let's just say two weeks, maximum."

"Thanks be to God!" He felt a weight move off his heart. "Thank you, Doctor. Well done!"

"Father Tim?"

"Speaking. Is that you, Rodney?"

"All we could turn up on th' back door an' th' knob was Puny's prints. Then we dusted your mantel and your desk and so on, but didn't find anything. She's rubbed a good bit of lemon oil around in there."

"Right."

"Course we found some of your prints on th' desk drawers, you remember we took your prints a few years ago."

"I do."

"Sorry to be so long gettin' back to you."

Ah, well. He'd done his duty, they'd done theirs, and that was that.

Had Emma Newland vanished from the face of the earth? Whenever she called, he fervently wished she hadn't. When she didn't, he wished she would. Go figure.

Maybe they were still in Atlanta. Maybe Harold had seen the phone bill and laid down the law. Maybe she didn't care anymore what happened to her old boss—out of sight, out of mind.

He dialed her number and charged the call to Dove Cottage.

"Hello!"

"Emma?"

"Is that *you?*"

"It's me, all right. What's up in Mitford? Tell me everything, it's my nickel."

"After we went to Atlanta and saw Jean, we went to New Orleans, Harold had three weeks piled up with th' post office. The food in New Orleans was great, it was unbelievable, you'd never in a hundred *years* believe how much we ate, I think I have gout."

"Gout?"

"From eating all that French food, they say it'll give you gout."

"Does your big toe hurt?"

"My big toe? What does that have to do with anything?"

"With gout, that's usually what's affected. Very painful."

"My toe is fine and dandy, so it must be somethin' else."

"Where did you eat?"

"Sometimes we got carry-out Cajun and ate in th' RV, th' rest of th' time we ate in th' restaurant in th' motel. Meals came with the room, and all for only eighty-eight dollars a day. For *two!*"

"You definitely don't have gout," he said.

"Have they gotten you any help yet? Even *Harold* has help."

"Everybody pitches in." He wondered why on earth he'd called.

"I haven't checked Ed Sikes in Oregon, if that's why you called. We just got in a few days ago, and I'm up to my ears in laundry, plus

Snickers has fleas and they're so bad they're jumpin' on th' counter, I thought I'd spilled pepper. Th' termite man is on his way right now, you wouldn't *believe* what it's goin' to cost and I have to be out of th' house for three hours while they do it, and then come home and *vacuum* for five straight *days*, it's all that rain we had, I'm sure Barnabas is *covered* with fleas. . . ."

"Not that I've seen."

"Well, I don't know why he *doesn't* have fleas, the way th' weather's been, fleas *breed* in weather like we've had."

His erstwhile secretary was positively hopping mad that his dog didn't have fleas.

"Speakin' of fleas, did you hear what Rodney Underwood just got to hunt criminals, you'd never guess."

"True. I wouldn't."

"A rockwilder! You should see people scatterin' when it trots down th' street, Adele Hogan walks it every morning and it drags Joe Joe Guthrie around every evening, I'd hate to be a criminal in this town! Speakin' of criminal, have you heard what Miss Pattie's done now?"

Miss Pattie was a Hope House resident whose mind had been lost some years ago and was found only on the rarest of occasions. Her antics had long been of particular interest to Emma.

"Miss Pattie's too old to get into mischief, I should think."

"Well, think again, she steals everything she can get her hands on in Mr. Berman's room, then goes and throws it out her window."

"No!"

"His money, his bedroom shoes, his good leather belt, you name it. He got undressed the other night and looked around for his pajamas and they weren't there, so he draped himself in a blanket like a red Indian and called the nurse and told her if Miss Pattie didn't stop this mess, his son will sue for a million dollars."

"Can't the staff *do* something?"

"They locked her window, that's the best they can do, they say she's going through a phase."

"What does Mr. Berman say?"

"He says she has a terrible crush on him."

"That makes sense," he said, recalling that Mr. Berman was a very handsome old man.

"Speakin' of crazy people, Coot Hendrick actually believes he's going to win th' election. Can you *imagine* havin' a mayor who's two san'wiches short of a full picnic?"

He suddenly realized that Emma's sluice gate had opened and he was being swept along as if by a raging torrent.

"So, Emma, glad to hear you had a great time in New Orleans. Let me know what you find out about Ed Sikes."

He hung up and wiped his face with his handkerchief.

The search committee was meeting regularly, chatting each other up in the churchyard, whispering among themselves in the parish hall, polling the congregation for general opinion, and basically going about the task of replacement as if eager to unload their interim.

When he laughed with Sam Fieldwalker about their apparent urgency, his senior warden insisted that quite the opposite was true. The committee was hastening to do their job, yes, but in fact, several parishioners had expressed a desire to have their interim remain fulltime. Besides, Father Tim was too young to retire. Hadn't Father Grace served St. John's until he was eighty-seven?

Not every interim was urged by the parish to stay on. In fact, many were viewed with suspicion and some with utter disregard. He remembered what one of his early bishops was fond of saying—that the interim who didn't make enemies was a man who wasn't doing his job. The job, it was popularly supposed, was to stir things up, to throw out the old and make way for the new.

Who could, after all, forget Father Harry?

Father Harry, who was seventy-one when his life as an interim began, thoroughly relished the task of disrupting the comfort level of a parish. His style was to barge in and take command before they knew what hit them.

If the congregation was attached to Rite Two, he celebrated Rite One. If they were stubbornly fond of traditional music, he switched them to praise songs. If they venerated their choir and organ, he had them sing a cappella for weeks on end. If they believed children should be seen and not heard, he invited the small fry to take up collection and read simpler Epistles. If their former priest had avoided the very mention of mammon, Father Harry talked about it at considerable length, with special emphasis on tithing. Further, he enjoyed reinstituting the observance of Morning Prayer, which, if not entirely forgotten by most parishes, was thought to be quaintly antique.

When the incoming priest was finally in place, the congregants were so relieved to be done with the old troublemaker, they went for almost anything the newcomer cooked up.

Father Harry could get the job done, all right. As for himself, Father Tim leaned rather more to what C. S. Lewis had said about worship procedures in *Letters to Malcolm*.

"A good shoe is a shoe you don't notice. . . . The perfect church service would be one we were almost unaware of; our attention would have been on God. But every novelty prevents this. It fixes our attention on the service itself, and thinking about worship is a different thing from worshipping."

He relished a note left on his desk by nine-year-old Margaret Wheeler.

Deer Father Tim when we get a new priest I hope he is just like you. Love, Margaret   PS But I hope he has kids!!!

Mayoral Candidate Agrees with Opponent

Andrew Gregory, one of two mayoral candidates for the election on November 3, says he agrees with his opponent, local native Coot Hendrick.

"Mr. Hendrick is absolutely right to fight for the preservation of early Mitford history, though the hope of winning this particular battle appears lost. If elected, I shall do everything in my power to preserve what is good and positive about Mitford. One of my first projects will be to encourage owners of several local buildings to seek listings on our National Register, and receive federal funding assistance for much-needed restoration.

"For nearly two decades, our incumbent mayor, Esther Cunningham, has set an example of community service that raised the standard of this office for all time. It will be a privilege to try and carry on her remarkable vision."

Gregory said that, if elected, he would also work to bring "sensitive, balanced growth to Mitford, which includes increased lodging, food and retail opportunities."

Gregory, his wife, Anna, and his brother-in-law, Anthony Nocelli, are owners of the popular Lucera Restaurant, located in their private residence known to one and all as Fernbank. Mr. Gregory is also the owner/proprietor of Oxford Antique Shop, a Main Street landmark.

Town Council Meeting Turns Musical

Mrs. Beulah Mae Hendrick, 92-year-old mother of Mitford mayoral candidate, Coot Hendrick, was a surprise visitor at last Monday's meeting of the town council.

Mrs. Hendrick was allowed to open the meeting with a song learned from her grandfather, who was the son of Mitford's founder, Hezikiah Hendrick. Local legend has it that Hezikiah Hendrick shot five Union soldiers running from their regiment, and buried them on what is now property belonging to Ms. Edith Mallory.

State law rules that property containing grave sights can not be be disturbed or developed. Ms. Mallory contends there is no proof or evidence that such graves exist on her 90-acre property. Ms. Mallory is currently beginning construction on a 3,000 sq. ft. extension of her home, Clear Day, near or on the sight of the stone foundations of the old Hendrick cabin.

Mrs. Hendrick, who stood beside her wheelchair to sing the song, said afterward, "It will prove we're right!"
A written copy of the lyrics was sent to Ms. Mallory by certified mail last Tuesday morning.

> *Shot five Yankees*
> *a-runnin' from th' war*
> *Caught 'em in a cornfield*
> *Sleepin' by a f'ar*
> *Now they'll not run no more, oh*
> *They'll not run no more!*
>
> *Dug five graves*
> *With a mattock and a hoe*
> *Buried 'em in th' ground*
> *Before th' first snow*

> *Now they'll not run no more, oh*
> *They'll not run no more!*

Mr. Coot Hendrick said, "Mama has known and sung this song all her life, which right there ought to be proof the graves exist."

At press time, a spokesman reported that the town council has received a letter from Ms. Mallory's lawyer in Florida, stating that no proof of graves exists, and the matter is officially closed. He also said nobody could dig five graves with a mattock and a hoe, and that folk songs do not document real life.

A town council spokesman said, "I think it's a low-down shame to shoot people in their sleep, even if they are Yankees."

Ms. Mallory has issued a firm restriction against any digging or trespassing on her property, and has posted signs to that effect.

New Name, Location For Hair House

Ms. Fancy Skinner, proprietor of Mitford's popular Hair House, is moving her beauty Salon uptown and changing its name.

Ms. Skinner, who currently operates Hair House in her basement off Lilac Road, stated, "It's time to go Main Street!!

"I and my customers agree this calls for a more uptown name. The new name will be A Cut Above."

Ms. Skinner is moving in over the Sweet Stuff Bakery, which means that all hair work in Mitford will now be concentrated in one building, as Joe Ivey barbers on the street level behind the Sweet Stuff Bakery kitchen.

A Cut Above will feature all hair services for both sexes, with cuts starting at $12 and up. Fancy's Face Food, a specialty skincare line with organic ingredients, will be available. "But don't even think about using it," says Ms. Skinner, "unless you want to look and feel ten to fifteen years younger and make an all-around better showing for yourself."

A grand opening will held on Tuesday, beginning at nine a.m. with sugar-free gum for all, and a door prize of acrylic nails.

Congratulations to A cut Above!!!!

Local Laughs
—by Anonymous

Seen the new sign in Percy Mosely's window?

"Shoes are required to eat in the Main Street Grill. Socks can eat anyplace they want to."

Then there's the sign on the door of the labor room at Mitford Hospital:

"Push, push, push."

I guess by now everybody's heard about Evie Adams's midnight snail hunt. Seems she was out with a salt shaker and flashlight hunting down snails in her flowerbed, when one of Chief Rodney Underwood's officers rode by her house on South Main and saw this light bobbing around in her yard. The officer who shall be nameless parked up the street and tiptoed down to Evie's with his pistol cocked. He said the moon was out and he thought it was pretty odd that the burglar was wearing a chenille robe and hair curlers.

After he nearly scared the daylights out of her, Evie handed him an extra salt shaker and made him help finish the flower bed, all of which is to say Evie got the last laugh.

Well, that's it for now!! See you back here next week and don't take any wooden nickels.

Displaying her skills with the ability to fax directly from her computer, he found Emma's note at the office.

<To: Father Tim
<From: Emma Newland
<Date: Monday
<Memo: There is no Ed Sikes in Oregon.

<See you at the wedding. Do you want me to bake a ham so you
   don't have to?
<Love to all.

⟶

He couldn't believe this was happening.

As he approached Morris Love's place on an afternoon walk, his
dog suddenly lurched forward with all the power and muscle of a
horse. The leash jerked from his unsuspecting hand and Barnabas
dove under the gate in a flash. Déjà vu!

His anger erupted with such violence, he was astounded.

"Barnabas!" he thundered.

Was he so dim-witted he couldn't have prepared for this, anticipated it, *expected* it to happen? He would never walk this way again,
Barnabas was confined to the yard and the back porch 'til doomsday.
He'd been treated like a king for years and was now exercising royal
privileges. Father Tim couldn't believe the stubborn, willful, selfish
disobedience of a dog he'd done everything for. . . .

"Barnabas! *Come now!"* He hardly recognized his own voice; it
gave him a positive chill. If he were a dog, he'd either flee the county at
the sound of it or slink back to face the music and get it over with.

Hearing the booming bark fade deeper into the Love jungle, he
scaled the wall and dropped down on the other side, breathing hard. He
didn't want to go through this nonsense again, he really didn't. He certainly didn't want his churlish neighbor ranting at him as if he were some
rum-nosed chicken poacher. So what if Morris Love had had a hard time
of it? Hadn't plenty of other people, and was that any excuse for refusing
to exercise at least a modicum of human kindness toward a neighbor?

He was huffing and blowing as if he'd done the Nags Head Wood
Run instead of a mile-long lap through the neighborhood.

He hadn't, for some time, been forced to use Holy Scripture on his
dog, a ploy that worked best to keep Barnabas from leaping into the
arms of the unsuspecting, or giving their ears and noses a good licking.
Though he had no precedent for the current circumstances, it was
worth a try.

" 'I delight to do thy will, O my God, *yea*, thy law is within my
heart! ' " He fairly bellowed the line from the psalmist; he thought he'd
made the leaves tremble on a bush.

Silence. He felt like a maniac.

Ah, well.

What if he simply gave up and went home? Barnabas would follow eventually; he'd be lying outside their front door in no time flat, looking doleful. But what would that solve? It would only give his dog the dumb notion he could do it again anytime he liked. No, indeed, he was going in after his dog and dragging him home by the collar, and no treats for a week, maybe a *month. . . .*

He stormed down the driveway as if going to a fire, whistling and calling right and left. There was an occasional thrashing in the bushes. Birds started up and flew above him, chattering. A squirrel dashed across his path as he came upon the house.

Beside the drive as it curved toward the front door was something he hadn't noticed before. It was an antiquated verdigris plaque set into a concrete slab and nearly taken by ivy. A house marker, he supposed. He stooped and squinted at the engraving: *Nouvelle Chanson, 1947.*

He wasn't eager to disturb his neighbor, no, indeed, but what could he do? He stood up and let it fly. *"Barnabas!"*

"Is that you again?" Morris Love shouted from an upstairs window.

"Yes, dadgummit, Mr. Love, it is."

"Out! *Out!*"

Please, no more of that drivel. "I can't go out 'til I find my dog. My *dog,* Mr. Love! I'm sorry, for heaven's sake." He stomped through the undergrowth at the side of the house, where he thought he heard a commotion.

"Barnabas! *Come!*" Now there was furious barking at what could be the rear of the house. He suddenly felt the insects chewing on his legs, and if that weren't enough, it was steaming in here. Until he came over the wall, he hadn't noticed the humidity, nor had he realized his desperate thirst.

"Your dog has treed a squirrel off the west side!" Morris Love's hoarse announcement was matter-of-fact.

Father Tim darted into grass that grew to his waist; Lord only knows what was lurking on the ground. He needed a machete, a sling, a hay baler, to get through this stuff. Slogging to the rear of the house, he stumbled over a pile of bricks that had toppled from a chimney and lay hidden in the grass. He fell onto a jagged piece of mortar and hauled himself up. Stubbed toes, skinned knees, cut hands, chewed legs . . . he was biting his tongue.

He forged along the endless rear of the house and rounded the corner, dripping with sweat. Aha, by George, there he was, the impudent beast, sitting on his rear end at the foot of a tree and gazing heavenward as if in prayer.

His dog turned his head and gave him the sort of look that precedes the guillotine.

Speechless, his master pointed to his feet, shod in running shoes. Barnabas thoughtfully considered this gesture for some moments, then arose slowly and, head down, walked toward his master and sat a couple of yards away. Father Tim made the pointing gesture again. Barnabas arose, plodded over, and sat by his master's right foot.

He reached down and plucked the leash from the grass.

"Forgiveness," he said aloud to his dog, "is giving up my right to hurt you because you have hurt me." He didn't know where that particular wisdom had come from, but there it was.

Barnabas sat, looking stoic.

He put his hand through the loop and wrapped the leash around his arm twice. Then, giving his eaten legs a vigorous, overall slapping, he turned to get the heck out of here.

He heard Morris Love laughing behind one of the many shuttered windows on the second floor. It was an odd laughter, to say the least, composed of short explosions of sound.

"Mr. Love," he yelled. "I hope we're entertaining you sufficiently."

"More than sufficiently." Morris Love quit laughing, and the coldness in his voice returned. "You know the way out, Father."

"Yes, indeed, it's becoming all too familiar." His own tone of voice wasn't exactly the one used in greeting people at the church door.

Blast. That high wall ahead must be the back of another wing, though there were no windows. Or perhaps it was the rear of the loggia he'd glimpsed earlier. From the look of things, this meant a longer distance to the front, through a deeper, yet denser thicket.

He had stumbled into some kind of brier patch, or tangle of vines that scratched like a cat. Extracting himself from the snare of this blasted stuff was no easy job. Maybe he shouldn't forge ahead, but retrace his steps. This was maddening, alarming. He felt a moment of panic.

"Go back the way you came." Morris Love was speaking directly above his head.

He tore himself from the vines that snarled about his clothes and stomped back the way he'd come.

Fleas. Emma's suspicion was being confirmed. He yanked up his pants legs and was relieved to find they weren't fleas after all, though something probably worse. He went at a trot, trying to avoid the pile of rubble, and finally made it to the driveway, where he stood and wiped his dripping face with the tail of his T-shirt.

"There's water in the faucet behind you."

Water! He turned and saw the spigot attached to a pipe standing about knee level. He cranked open the tap, letting the sediment flow out, then washed the cut on his hand and splashed his face and head. Cupping his hands, he drank deeply and let Barnabas drink, then drew off his shirt and dried himself and slipped it on again. Good Lord, what a refreshment. He was revived, restored; holy water, indeed!

"God bless you!" he shouted, spontaneous and thankful.

"I don't believe in God." Morris Love's voice contained a positive snarl.

"God believes in you!"

"Then why did He give me such a body?"

"Why did He give you such musical genius?"

"I assure you I think very little of answering a question with a question."

"Sometimes a question is the only answer I have, Mr. Love."

He saw a rusted ornamental lawn chair a few feet to his right, just below the upstairs window where he presumed Morris Love to be standing. He hadn't noticed the chair on his previous safari, nor had he been aware, until now, of his extreme weariness.

He walked to the chair and sat, glad for the chance to catch his breath. What could the lord of the manor do to him anyway—dump a flowerpot on his head?

"I'm sitting down for a moment," he announced, too spent to shout. "I hope you don't object."

He gazed at the view before him, the way the light slanted into the dense tangle of trees and was lost in the foliage. A jungle, indeed. Yet this place had surely been beautiful once, a tropical island within an island, so exotic and unfamiliar that the thought of busy lives just over the wall seemed preposterous.

"Let me ask you, Father, how do you find the conscience to go about practicing the sham of belief?"

He was stunned by the question.

"I don't get your meaning," he said, and he didn't.

"The meaning seems clear enough. You wear a collar, you recite a

creed, you speak of God, and yet, as a man whom I presume to be
more than nominally intelligent, you cannot possibly believe there is a
loving God, or any God at all."

"Quite the contrary, Mr. Love. I find it impossible not to believe in
a loving God."

"I see it is useless to discuss a high truth with you."

"Then you see blindly." Though he didn't wish to be harsh, he had
every desire to be plain.

"Blindness, you may be certain, has never been one of my
handicaps."

"Do you consider your physical condition a handicap?"

"You speak as a fool. Of course I do."

"Many do not, Mr. Love. For example, there are currently several
practicing and highly successful physicians with your precise physical
condition."

"Not my precise condition at all. You deceive yourself grossly, Father, by presuming to know me. You do not know me now, nor will
you ever."

"We're both being presumptuous, Mr. Love. You presume me to be
covertly faithless, I presume you to be more physically proficient than
you think you're able to be. Tit for tat, as my grandmother used to say.
Now let's be done with it, shall we?"

"Out! *Out!*" bellowed Morris Love.

"Yes, indeed, and thank you for your hospitality." He set off at a
trot down the driveway, his dog loping ahead on the leash.

The shouting continued in his wake. "Out! *Out!*"

"Out and away, and never to return!" he muttered, breaking into a
run as he neared the gate.

In the last couple of days, the air had been miraculously devoid of
humidity, and was instead filled with snap and sparkle. Light slanted,
sound intensified, clouds vanished from a sky so cerulean it appeared
enameled.

He was on his knees, weeding and adding fresh pine straw to the
beds, glad to feel his hands in the dirt.

He couldn't, however, ignore the sense of conflict in his spirit—of
loving the new season and at the same time feeling the sorrow it

brought. It had taken years to name the sorrow and, at last, to face it down.

His father had died on October twelfth, more than forty years ago, and every autumn the heaviness surfaced again. During that dark time in the cave, he'd been able to forgive his father once and for all, which had worked wonders in his spirit, in his whole outlook. Yet something of the suffering remained, like a tea stain on linen, and returned each autumn in the changing light, to remind him.

The conflicting feelings experienced at his father's death were so intricately entwined that he'd never been able to disentangle them, and saw no useful purpose in trying again.

Indeed, perhaps it was time to forgive himself—for having felt relief at his father's passing, for anguishing, even now, over never having pleased him, for continuing to wonder, when he could not know, about his father's soul. Oh, how he'd longed to lead Matthew Kavanagh to Christ, to see the hellish torment of his father's spirit transformed by peace and certainty. But it hadn't happened; it was as if his father, in a last effort to thwart his son, had determined to hold himself away from God for all eternity.

Yes! he thought, thrusting the trowel into the dirt. It's time to let go of it, all of it. . . .

He would surrender this thing right now, completely, though he may be tempted again and again to snatch it back.

He sat in the grass like a child, his legs in a V in front of him, and prayed.

When he lifted his head, he knew at once that he was being watched. He looked through the pickets to Morris Love's hedge and, without thinking, threw up his hand and waved.

He'd broken a few lacy tendrils from the sweet autumn clematis, and was coming into the kitchen to wash up and find a vase when he saw Cynthia in the window seat. She was joggling Jonathan on her knee, as the boy laughed and clapped his hands. Seeing the look on her face, he felt a stab of something he couldn't name.

"Hello, darling!" said his wife.

CHAPTER FIFTEEN

Lock and Key

On his way home from a visit with Janette, he stopped by Ernie's.

Roger looked up and nodded, absorbed in burning the speculum feathers of his duck. Roanoke hoisted a forefinger.

"Junior's got good news!" said Ernie. "He got that letter said she wouldn't go out with 'im, but said she was comin' with her sister to see a girlfriend that lives here, an' she's goin' to drop by and say hello. October twenty-second!" Ernie announced the date as if it were right up there with the day the English landed on Whitecap.

"Said she'n her sister would meet Junior for coffee somewhere, so he wrote back and said Mona's, nine-thirty!"

"Bingo!" Father Tim exclaimed, pulling up a chair. "I'm glad to hear it." He liked the smell of Roger's burning wood, it made the place seem positively cozy.

"Junior's goin' to quit drinkin' beer 'til then, see if he can drop ten pounds."

"Aha."

"Yeah, an' goin' to massage his scalp, try to grow some hair," said Roanoke. "But there ain't no way that's goin' to happen."

"If it works, let me know," said Father Tim.

"Plus," said Ernie, "*plus* I sold Elmo's bed—lock, stock, and barrel."

"The Zane Greys?"

"Th' whole shootin' match. Man come in yesterday, bought a couple sinkers, wandered off in there, come back with th' box in his hands. He said how much, I said fifty bucks, he said I'll take it."

"Where did Elmo wind up sleeping last night?" he asked.

"A box of mixed westerns is where I found 'im this mornin'."

Roger didn't look up from his work. "Tell him about *The Last of the Plainsmen.*"

"Fella gave me cash, sat down right over yonder, went through th' whole box one by one, an' found it—a signed hardback first edition! Didn't even know it was there. Worth a fortune, prob'ly two hundred, easy. He said I ain't payin' any more for this, I said I ain't askin' any more, a deal is a deal. But I got to tell you, it broke my heart. Two hundred *bucks!*"

"It'd bring a tear to a glass eye," said Roanoke, tapping a Marlboro from the pack.

Elmo appeared at the door of the book room, looking frazzled and disgusted.

"So, Elmo," said Father Tim, "how are you liking mixed westerns?"

He didn't go home from the office; he went to the beach.

At the bottom of the dune, he took off his socks and stuffed them into his shoes, then rolled up his pants legs and started to walk. No wife, no toddler, no dog, no nothing.

There was a fierceness in him that he didn't completely understand. Maybe he could walk it off, walk it out; maybe it would vaporize over the ocean and descend on Argentina as a minor typhoon. He felt angry at a lot of people for a lot of reasons—at Jeffrey Tolson for being cruel, at Janette Tolson for being passive, at Cynthia Kavanagh for losing her heart to someone else's child, at Morris Love for being imprisoned when he might be free. He was even angry with himself, but for what?

A gull started up from a tidal pool and circled above him, crying. He realized, then, that he was running, running for the way it felt to his bones, his beating heart. He heard the sand churning away from his feet, *chuff, chuff, chuff,* and realized he was the only soul on the beach.

All this vast world, all this great ocean, all this infinite sky, he thought—and Morris Love imprisoned behind a wall in a body he hated.

But, thought Father Tim, hadn't he, too, lived in a prison of his own for years on end, alternately fearing and despising and secretly rebuking his father? As a believer, his freedom in Christ had been severely handicapped for wont of letting go of the old bondage; of the old Adamic bitterness he'd unwittingly nurtured. Chances are, Morris Love's father had been much like Matthew Kavanagh—disappointed and indignant, betrayed by the issue from his own flesh.

And who was praying for Morris Love? Who remembered him at all, except in island legend? Instead of a living, breathing, feeling soul, he'd become apocryphal in the minds of everyone but a housekeeper, an organ tuner, and a retired clergyman who, but for the grace of the living God, would himself be a soul under the Enemy's lock and key.

And another thing—if Morris Love so renounced God, why did he play so much of His music?

Chuff, chuff, chuff . . .

He wondered why he hadn't been praying for Morris Love. How could he continue shirking a mission that had, literally, been dumped in his own backyard?

He muttered aloud as he ran, panting and huffing in a chill breeze coming off the water. That was precisely why he was feeling aggravated with himself: God had found him out for a shirker.

He looked up from the kitchen sink where he was washing tomatoes. His wife, on an errand to pick the last of the basil from the herb bed, suddenly hooted, threw her basket into the air, and began hopping on one foot.

"Ow! Ow! Rats, darn! Hoo! Hoo! *Ha!*"

His wife was a veritable rain dancer, complete with tribal language. What in the world . . . ?

"Timothy! Timothy! *Help!* Oh, ow, ow, *ugh!*"

"Cynthia?" He flew out the back door. *Please, God, not a snake or a terrible cut from broken glass. . . .*

"Yellow jackets!" she shouted, still hopping.

"Here," he said, taking her arm, "I'll help you in."

"I can't put my foot down, Timothy, it's dreadful, it's excruciating, I can't walk!"

"Climb on, then," he said, bending his knees. She threw her arms around his neck and clambered onto his back and he hauled her to the kitchen and thumped her in the window seat like a sack of onions.

"Let's have a look," he said, squatting down. "Aha, two stings, and right between the toes."

"Do something, Timothy, you can't *imagine* how it hurts!" His wife was not a complainer, he knew she meant business.

"Tobacco!" he said. He'd heard that tobacco draws the sting out. He'd seen a cigar butt just the other day. Where was it? "I'll be back!"

Exactly where Otis had thrown it into the bushes when he came by last Tuesday. . . .

He shredded the short stub and mixed it into a paste with water. "Here!" he said, rushing to present it in one of his grandmother's soup bowls. "Put your foot in this."

She did as she was told, shutting her eyes and grimacing. "Ugh! My toes feel exactly like they're being amputated with a handsaw by a doctor in the wilds of Montana, sometime around 1864."

"Really, now." His wife could go a tad over the top.

"It's true, Timothy, that's *exactly* the way it feels."

Jonathan, fully awake from a nap, was pounding him on the back as he squatted by the soup bowl. "You stop!" he shouted. "You stop makin' her cry!"

Truth be told, he was a mite weary of surrogate parenting.

"Look," said his stricken wife, "my toes are swelling up and turning red. How hideous."

"Give it time," he said of his home remedy. "I'll get you a couple of aspirin, then I'll call Marion and see what she recommends."

She drew her breath in sharply and winced. "Have you ever been stung?"

"Not once," he said. "Not a single time."

Even in her suffering, his wife was able to summon an imperious look. "What kind of American boyhood could you possibly have *had*, Timothy?"

He always enjoyed that moment when he could gaze out to his congregation and, as it were, take its pulse. Did it appear eager? Resigned? Grumpy?

Every Sunday, he discovered a different climate of affections, a brand-new meshing of personalities and spiritual longings, all of which assisted in the feeling that what he did was never the same old thing.

There was his buddy, Stanley Harmon, on vacation from the Baptists and seeing what the Anglicans were up to. Stanley would supply St. John's on the twenty-seventh while Father Tim married Pauline and Buck in Mitford.

His wife was beaming at him from the second row of the gospel side, where she sat with Sam and Marion . . .

. . . and there were the Duncans, with their children lined up like so many goslings. Once a month, according to family tradition, the whole lot skipped Sunday School and joined in the service. One, two, three, four hair bows bobbed on dark curls, as the two boys busily colored pew bulletins.

He was dropping his eyes to the opening hymn when he glanced to the rear of the church and saw a face as coldly immobile as if it were carved in stone.

His heart pounded as his gaze locked briefly with Jeffrey Tolson's, in whose countenance he saw anger and arrogance and, yes, defiance.

" 'Ye who do truly and earnestly repent you of your sins, and are in love and charity with your neighbors . . .' "

Because he had long ago committed these words to memory, he wasn't looking at the prayer book, but at his congregation. He noted that some swiveled in their pews and glared at the man in the back row.

" '. . . and intend to lead a new life, following the commandments of God, and walking from henceforth in his holy ways, draw near with faith, and make your humble confession to Almighty God, devoutly kneeling.' "

The parishioners sank to their knees as one, producing a corporate sound of rushing water. Jeffrey Tolson stood and looked for a moment toward the altar, then turned and walked quickly from the nave.

He dreaded his time in the churchyard today, as people poured out into the sunshine. Oliver Hughes withheld his hand, muttering, ". . . to let him come back in here, ransackin' th' church, takin' th' women out one by one like a fox in a henhouse . . ."

". . . carryin' 'em off to his den!" said Millie Hughes, stomping away in disgust.

Marion Fieldwalker gave him a wordless hug. Sam murmured, "My goodness gracious," and laid his hand on his priest's shoulder.

Otis stopped and looked him in the eye, saying only, "We want you to fix this."

Jean Ballenger shook his hand, as usual, but said nothing. Her mouth, which was set in a distinct grimace, said it all.

His wife, who was walking with a temporary limp, came to him and slipped her hand in his.

There were more eloquent ways to express it, but his grand-mother's way covered it sufficiently:

When it rains, it pours.

They were leaving for Mitford in a matter of days, and in the meantime, he must find and talk with Jeffrey Tolson, speak with Stanley Harmon and inform him of the circumstances, and confirm Father Jack as the celebrant when Stanley preached. He also needed to oversee loose ends for the Fall Fair on November ninth, and meet with the indomitable Busy Fingers group who were going hammer and tong to complete nearly a thousand dollars' worth of items for the fair, including aprons, embroidered pillowcases, oven mitts, and an ambitious needlepoint of the Last Supper. Most important, he must get up to Dorchester, with the Eucharist for the captain and his visit with Ella.

Possibly the Dorchester trip could wait, but no, his heart exhorted him otherwise. The old captain had waited long enough—no more excuses, this must be done. And how was he to find Jeffrey Tolson, who, some said, was living on the island, but was as elusive as a trout in a pool?

Worse, what would his parishioners think about their priest vanishing to Mitford in the face of a highly disturbing situation?

He dreaded still more a final thing he must do. Before baring his concerns, however, he imagined their conversation. Perhaps he'd bring it up as they lay in bed.

"Cynthia," he might say.

"Yes?"

"You're growing . . . attached to Jonathan." A simple observation, not a criticism.

"Really? Am I?"

"Yes."

He'd considered the whole issue very carefully and knew it wasn't jealousy. It was fear, fear for her feelings, which ran as deep as the ledges of the continental shelf.

"What is your point, exactly?"

"I see how much you care for him. And you know he'll be going home soon."

"Well, yes, Timothy. Of course. Is there some reason I shouldn't care for him?"

What might he say, then? That he thought it best for her to start letting go, to prepare herself in some way he couldn't fully suggest or understand? Though Jonathan had come to them only weeks ago, his wife had bonded with the boy as if he were her own. But then, hadn't he grown to love Dooley in the very same way? He remembered his dark fears that someone would snatch the boy from him. . . .

In the end, he decided to say nothing at all. Jonathan would be going home, and that would be the end of it.

He was relieved, terribly relieved, that he hadn't brought it up; that he would even think of doing such a thing seemed strange and insensitive.

"Banana bread!" crowed his wife, dumping a panful onto the counter.

"My mommy, my mommy, she makes bread," said Jonathan, nodding in the affirmative.

"One loaf for us, one loaf for the neighbors," she announced. "But wait, I forgot—we don't know the neighbors."

It was true. A couple of times, they'd waved to the people in the gray house, who seemed to come and go randomly, and the family next door hadn't shown up for the summer at all; one of the shutters on the side facing Dove Cottage had banged in the wind for a month.

Neighbors, he mused. It was an odd thought, one that made his brain feel like it had eaten a pickle.

He heard the music as he stepped off the porch into the backyard.

No idea what it might be. But one thing was certain: it was strong stuff. . . .

He listened intently as he trotted to his good deed. The steady advance of the brooding pedal tones appeared to form the basis of a harmonic progress that he found strangely disturbing. Above this, an elusive melody wove its way through a scattering of high-pitched notes that evoked images of birds agitated by an impending storm.

The effect, he thought as he heaved himself up and over the wall, was confused, almost disjointed, yet the music seemed to produce an essential unity. . . .

Clutching the bread in a Ziploc bag, he stood at the foot of the window from which his neighbor usually conducted his audiences, and listened as the music moved toward its climax.

He might be one crazy preacher, but he didn't think so. In fact, he'd come over the wall as if it were the most natural way in the world to go visiting. He was feeling pretty upbeat about his impetuous mission—after all, this was his neighbor for whom he was now praying, and besides, who could refuse a loaf of bread still warm from the oven?

When the music ended, he shouted, "Well done! Well done, Mr. Love!"

Floorboards creaked in the room above. "Father Kavanagh . . ."

"One and the same!"

"Your dog isn't here," snapped Morris Love.

"Yes, and what a relief! I brought you some banana bread. My wife baked it, it's still warm from the oven, I think you'll like it."

Silence.

If his neighbor didn't go for the bread, he'd just eat the whole thing on the way home.

"She said to tell you it's a token of our appreciation for your music."

Silence.

"What was that piece, anyway? It was very interesting. I don't think I've heard it before." He was a regular chatterbox.

Silence.

He began to as feel as irritable as a child. He'd come over here with a smile on his face and bread in his hand, and what did he get for his trouble? Exactly what he should have expected.

"Mr. Love, for Pete's sake, what shall I do with your *bread*?"

"Leave it in the chair," said Morris Love.

"Do what?"

"Leave it in the chair!" he roared.

He considered this for a moment, then determinedly walked over and sat down. He was tired of darting away from his irate neighbor like a hare before the hound. Wasn't the trip over worth a moment of small talk, of mere civility? He'd give it a quick go, then he'd be gone.

"Mr. Love, I couldn't help but notice the sign, *Nouvelle Chanson*. How did the house come by that name?"

"My grandmother gave the house its name. She sang with the Met, and counted Rose Bampton and Lily Pons among her friends. Melchior was my grandfather's close acquaintance."

"Aha."

"When my grandparents built this house in 1947 as a summer home, she hoped for a new beginning for their marriage—a new song, if you will." Morris Love's manner was impatient, though decidedly less hostile. "But it didn't work that way."

Father Tim waited a moment. "How *did* it work?"

"My grandparents could only live the old song."

"The old song . . ."

"Little acts of unspoken violence, Father, and bitter hatred towards one another."

Morris Love was actually talking with him. He realized he'd been holding his breath, and released it carefully. "Who taught you to play the organ?"

"My grandfather. Once he had made his fortune, he began to study the organ. In the forties and fifties, several great organ masters spent summers here, instructing him. By the time I came along, he was respectably accomplished and began to teach me at an early age."

"Someone said he had an organ built especially for you. . . ."

"Yes. When I was six years old."

"Is that the organ you play today?"

"That was a toy, Father, a mere toy. I play my grandfather's custom-built Casavant, which was further customized for me."

"I've never seen a Casavant, though I may have heard one without knowing it. It's among the finest in the world, of course."

"More accurately, it is the most magnificent of instruments. Casavant came here to do an acoustical analysis, and worked with the architect to complete this room. My grandfather was a man of exacting preferences."

"I suppose the key covers are of an exotic wood?" It was a small thing, but he'd always been interested in the key covers on old keyboard instruments.

"Only the sharps, which are ebony. The naturals are purest ivory, and of exceeding beauty in their age."

This was pretty heady stuff; he could imagine the splendid hulk of it reigning over the room above. He dove in headfirst. "I'd like very much to see it sometime, and hear you play . . . without walls between us."

He listened to the beating of his heart in the long pause that followed. He'd stepped in it now, he'd pushed too far, and just when he was getting started.

"That would be . . . inappropriate." There was something wistful in Morris Love's voice, he was sure of it. *Lord, speak to his heart.*

"Mr. Love, may I call you Morris? And please—call me Tim."

"I have never addressed a priest by his first name. I find it a repugnant modern custom."

"You've known priests, then? You went to St. John's?"

"Only for baptism. The priests at St. John's often came here, some to pray over me, others to drink my grandfather's French wines. The only joy I ever found in those visits was their occasional gifts of sheet music purloined from the church."

"Your mother and father . . . were they—"

"Out! *Out!*"

He jumped. The shock of hearing the inevitable made his scalp prickle. The tone and repetition of that furious decree were nearly more than he could tolerate. Feeling an invasive weariness in his spirit, and not knowing what else to say or do, he stood to leave.

"Father . . ."

"Yes?"

"You may call me Morris."

"Morris," he said, suddenly hoarse with feeling. "Please don't let the squirrels get your bread. I hope you like it. Try warming it in the oven for breakfast, that's what we do."

He examined an odd intuition, then addressed a question to the window. "Tourette's?"

"Yes. A mild form."

"I'll come again," he said. But there was no reply.

Marion Fieldwalker looked up from the checkout desk.

"Why, Father Tim! We're tickled to see you!"

"I'm looking for a medical encyclopedia, Marion. Something comprehensive." Given the cost per pound for shipping, he'd decided against dispatching his own to Whitecap.

"You've come to the right place. One of our retirees studied at Harvard Medical School, and gave us a wonderful one. It takes a crane to lift it!"

"Bingo!" he said.

While he was here, he wanted to take a look at Dostoyevsky's *Notes from the Underground*, the memory of which resonated profoundly with what he was learning about his neighbor.

It was a work that made him squirm for its dark despair, yet he flipped through it diligently, sneezing from the dust and mold. Out of curiosity, he turned to the card at the back. Aha! One other reader had visited these pages before him, twelve years ago.

Amused, he inscribed his name on the card, *Timothy A. Kavanagh.* For posterity!

"I am a sick man," wrote Dostoyevsky's fictional diarist. "I am a spiteful man. I am an unattractive man. . . .

"The more conscious I was of goodness and of all that was sublime and beautiful, the more deeply I sank into my mire and the more ready I was to sink in it altogether . . . in despair there are the most intense enjoyments, especially when one is very acutely conscious of the hopelessness of one's position. . . .

"I was rude and took pleasure in being so. . . .

"I might . . . be genuinely touched, though probably I should grind my teeth at myself afterward and lie awake at night with shame for months. . . .

"Now I am living out my life in my corner, taunting myself with the spiteful and useless consolation that an intelligent man cannot become anything seriously, and it is only the fool who becomes anything."

Not light summertime reading. He closed the musty book, relieved to look through the window to the bright and cloudless day.

Seated at the antiquated library table, he ran his finger quickly along the text.

". . . characterized by rapid, repetitive, involuntary muscular movements called 'tics,' and involuntary vocalizations . . .

"Phonic tics are diverse and consist of syllables, words (e.g., 'okay'), short phrases (e.g., 'shut up', 'no, no'), and full sentences. Tics are sudden, involuntary, repetitive. . . .

"Tics intensify during periods of stress and anxiety and are frequently misinterpreted as 'nervous habits.' . . .

"Many suffer depression . . . often become withdrawn and even suicidal . . .

". . . evidence that Tourette's syndrome is not an emotional or psychological problem, but a chronic, hereditary neurological disorder."

"I'd like to check this out," he said, toting the large tome to the desk.

"Oh, my goodness, that doesn't check out. It's reference."

Marion must have noted the disappointed look on his face.

"But we'll make a special exception for clergy," she said, smiling. "Would you like a wheelbarrow to help you carry it to the car?"

He didn't have to go looking for Jeffrey Tolson. Shortly after he unlocked the church on Tuesday morning, Jeffrey Tolson came looking for him.

It wasn't stone from which his face had been carved, thought Father Tim, it was ice. He noted that Jeffrey wore the open-necked white shirt with full sleeves that he'd worn on his earlier visit.

He felt the towering wall between them as they sat in the office. He had no sermon to preach. He'd let Jeffrey Tolson do the talking he'd come to do, then he'd lay his cards on the table, plain and simple.

"I intend to come back to my church," said Jeffrey Tolson. A muscle twitched in his jaw.

"Your church?"

"My grandfather's church, my father's church, and my church. Yes."

"Being born into this church body confers no special distinctions or ownership. You've hurt a great many people here, Jeffrey."

"There is such a thing as forgiveness, Father."

"Are you asking forgiveness from the people of St. John's?"

Jeffrey crossed his legs and moved his left foot rapidly back and forth. "If that's what it takes."

"Then you're admitting you sinned?"

"No. I'm admitting I made a mistake."

Father Tim looked carefully at the man before him. "There's a bottom line to asking forgiveness. And it's something I don't see or sense in you in the least."

"A bottom line?"

"Repentance. Forgiveness isn't some cheap thing to be gotten on a whim. It's purchased with a deep desire to please God. It's about renouncing. . . ."

"I have renounced. We aren't living together anymore."

"You're speaking of the flesh; I'm speaking of the heart."

Jeffrey Tolson's face blanched. "As choirmaster here for fourteen years, I've heard a good deal of Scripture. You aren't the only one equipped with the so-called truth. I seem to recall that St. Paul said, 'Forgive one another as God in Christ forgave you.' "

"Do you believe Christ is the divine Son of God?"

Jeffrey Tolson shrugged. "I suppose so. Not necessarily."

"We're told that everyone who believes in and relies on Him receives forgiveness of sins through His name. It's not really about asking me or the vestry or anyone at St. John's; it's about hammering it out with Him."

Jeffrey drummed the desktop with the fingers of his right hand.

"To repent means to turn, to turn from whatever binds or enslaves you. What, for example, do you intend to do about your family?

"Janette has the house and the car, she has a successful sewing business, and as soon I get work on the island, I'll see that she gets a check every week."

"As soon as you get work?"

"You're not from Whitecap, so it probably never occurred to you that getting work on the island is either difficult or impossible."

He heard the sneer in his visitor's voice, and made every effort to keep his own voice even as he spoke. "You could go across to work, like half the population here."

"I'd prefer to work on the island. Commuting is expensive and inconvenient."

"Let's see if I have this right, Jeffrey. You abandoned your wife and children to enter into an adulterous relationship with a married woman, left the island for several months during which your contribution to your family was a grand total of one hundred dollars; you grieved everyone in the church and your choir in particular, and now you state that you don't necessarily believe Christ to be the Son of God, yet you wish His forgiveness."

Jeffrey Tolson opened his mouth to speak, but Father Tim raised his hand. "In addition, you wish to wait 'til you find work that's convenient, while your wife, currently hospitalized and without income, soldiers on with the fallout as you trot back to God's house, whistling Dixie." He was livid. "When you can return to this place with a humble spirit, confessing your sins and longing for His gift of forgiveness, you'll find a willing heart to hear you." He stood from his desk, shaken.

Jeffrey Tolson stood also, his face white with anger. "I'll come for my son tonight. Have his things ready."

"You'll come for your son? I don't think so. Jonathan was given into our care by Janette. It is Janette who directs his coming and going, and that, you may rest assured, will hold up in a court of law." While he didn't know for certain that it would, it certainly seemed that it should.

He thought he might be punched out on the spot, but didn't care; he felt reckless, invincible.

"You can't stop me from attending St. John's."

"You're absolutely correct, I cannot. But I don't advise it."

Jeffrey Tolson uttered an oath. "Father Morgan, unlike yourself, was a peacemaker. You're no Father Morgan."

"Thanks be to God!" he said, holding his office door open.

"Father, before you take your days off, wouldn't you like to put in your order for a new sport coat?"

He looked at Jean Ballenger's newly trimmed bangs, which were curling upward like the lashes of a film star. "A new sport coat?"

"For Janette, to help her get started back in business when she comes home. I'm going to order a paisley shirtwaist; Marion's ordering a red dress, she says she wears too much navy; and we thought you might like to order a sport coat."

"Well . . ."

"Something blue would be good on you."

He had three blue sport coats, but he didn't say anything.

"Penny Duncan is ordering a wrap skirt, even though she doesn't have gobs of money to throw around and sews like a dream herself! Don't you think that's sacrificial?"

"I do."

"And Cynthia could order a suit in linen or piqué, maybe something with a nice peplum, I think she'd look stunning in a peplum."

"How much is a sport coat?"

"I don't have any idea."

"Why don't you get back to me on that?"

"Oh, I will!" she said, making a note on her pad. "I just think it would be the Christian thing to do, don't you?"

He grinned at the earnest Jean Ballenger trotting down the hall to solicit orders from the Busy Fingers group, which was currently living up to their name, big-time.

It was rather a nice thought, actually, that he'd soon be looking into the nave and seeing his entire congregation turned out in new duds, whether they needed them or not.

The encounter with Jeffrey Tolson had shaken him badly. He sat in the study at Dove Cottage with his head in his hand for longer than his wife liked.

"Timothy, dear, what *is* it?" she demanded on a third inquiry.

"Ahhh," he said, lacking the energy to tell the sordid thing. Besides, did this mean Jeffrey Tolson might be hanging about to forcibly take Jonathan while Cynthia and the boy were alone? He despised even thinking this.

He was just getting into bed when he heard the knock.

What time was it, anyway? He peered at the clock on the nightstand. Past ten.

Through the glass panels in the front door, he saw what appeared to be a flashlight bobbing on the porch. He switched on the porch light and threw open the door.

It was someone in uniform, and someone plenty big, to boot.

"Would you identify yourself, sir?"

"Tim Kavanagh. Why do you ask?"

"I have a civil paper to serve you. You're being sued."

"I beg your pardon?"

"Are you the Reverend Timothy *A.* Kavanagh?"

"I am, yes." His heart was hammering.

"I'm Bill Deal, th' sheriff of this county." Bill Deal pocketed his flashlight and brought out his wallet to display a badge. "I hate to do this to you, I believe you fish with Cap'n Willie."

Speechless, he opened the screen door, took an envelope from the man, and gazed at it, dumbfounded. The sheriff cleared his throat and stepped to the edge of the porch, looking at the sky.

"Prob'ly goin' to get us some rain before long. Well, you take it easy, Reverend." The sheriff lumbered down the steps, walked to the front gate, and got in the car.

He stood there in the chill October air as if mesmerized.

Cynthia called from the hallway. "Timothy, what's going on?"

"I have no idea, I don't know."

Nor did he want to know.

CHAPTER SIXTEEN

Dorchester Island

It wasn't that he couldn't understand the general intent of the papers he'd been served—he could. It was that he wasn't able to make it all come together in any sensible order; each time he read them, it was as if his mind split like an atom. He knew only one thing for certain—he was deeply alarmed.

He went to the study and took his quote book from the shelf, the quote book he'd made entries in for fifteen years. He wanted something St. Francis de Sales had said; he'd copied it into the book just the other day. . . .

Do not look forward to what may happen tomorrow; the same ever-lasting Father who cares for you today will take care of you tomorrow and every day. Either He will shield you from suffering, or He will give you unfailing strength to bear it. Be at peace, then, put aside all anxious thoughts and imaginations, and say continually: "The Lord is my strength and my shield; my heart has trusted in Him and I am helped. He is not only with me but in me and I in Him."

It was after eleven o'clock when he dressed and drove to St. John's, went down the cement steps by the light of the moon, and faxed the papers to his cousin's home in New Jersey. The fax machine was located in Walter's study where he'd be sure to find the papers the following morning, before he left for his law office in Manhattan.

Father Tim scribbled a cover sheet with St. John's phone number and a brief message:

Please call me the moment you look this over. I'll be at the church office by six a.m.

He didn't want to have the conversation with his attorney cousin at home, where his wife was already in a state of trepidation over this ghastly turn of events.

He left Dove Cottage at five forty-five, bundled into a sweater and jacket.

"Layspeak, Walter, layspeak."

He sat at his desk in the chill basement office, drinking a tepid cup of coffee from home and scribbling on a legal pad. "Start at the beginning. I'm writing everything down." *Put aside all anxious thoughts and imaginations. . . .*

"Hélène Pringle is suing you, as trustee, for one-third of the escrow funds of Hope House."

"Right." His voice sounded like the croaking of a frog, and he realized he was again holding his head in his hand.

"She claims to be the illegitimate daughter of Josiah Baxter. . . ."

Miss Sadie's father. This claim seemed so bizarre and extraordinary, his mind couldn't contain it; the whole notion kept flying out of his head, even as he tried to poke it back in.

"But why now, after all these years . . . ?"

"I've no idea. Apparently they're basing the suit on Baxter's holographic will, in which he decreed that a third of his estate would go to Hélène Pringle's mother, Françoise, upon his death. When did Baxter die, anyway?"

He'd tried to work this out in his mind last night. The date was on the urn in the columbarium at Lord's Chapel. He'd seen it numerous times, but couldn't remember exactly. "Sometime in the late forties."

"How old was he at the time of death?"

"Miss Sadie told me once . . . in his seventies, I think. In fact, I believe she said he died soon after an extended trip to France." He knew Miss Sadie's mother had died in 1942, so Josiah Baxter must have been a widower when . . .

"Of course, the domestic statute of limitations has run out by several decades," said Walter.

"Then they don't really have a case?"

"Unfortunately, the suit is based on French law, involving an obscure treaty between France and the U.S., which was adopted at the end of World War II. I don't know much about it, probably something that spun off the problem of occupation troops and paternity issues."

He thought the whole thing a veritable hash of mystery and confusion.

"Looks like Pringle's attorney is French—Louis d'Anjou of d'Anjou and Pichot—and both Pringle and her mother are French citizens. Let me look into it; I know almost nothing about French law. You've got thirty days to file a written response to the allegations."

He shook his head as if to wake himself from a bad dream.

"I'll call her attorney and see what's what, and get back to you in a couple of days—right now, I'm in court on a big one."

"Anything," he said. "Anything you can do . . ."

He hung up, as winded as if he'd run a mile on the beach.

Ava Goodnight was coming day after tomorrow, the day of the Dorchester trip. He'd have breakfast at Mona's, let Roanoke give him a trim around seven-thirty, tend to a couple of things at St. John's, then go back to Ernie's no later than nine-thirty to meet Ava and her sister. So . . . if he and Cynthia and Jonathan left shortly before eleven, they'd arrive at Ella's around noon. They'd visit with Ella, then he'd administer the sacraments to Captain Larkin and they'd head home. Considering all they had to do before Mitford, he'd suggest they tromp through the graveyard another day; heaven knows, the dead weren't going anywhere.

"Our trek to Dorchester is coming up day after tomorrow," he said over the last of their lunch. "We'll try to keep it short. I know you have plenty to do."

"Jonathan may not be able to go," she said. "He has a miserable cough and his nose is dripping like a faucet."

"Allergies?"

"I don't think so, and besides, Timothy, I hear there's a storm front moving in."

"If we had to drop everything each time a storm came our way, we'd get absolutely nothing done around here!"

She looked bleak. "A lawsuit, a sick boy, a ten-hour drive, and a storm front . . ."

"When it rains, it pours," he said. "No pun intended."

Jonathan ran into the kitchen and clambered onto Cynthia's lap. *"Heavens!"* she exclaimed, wiping his nose with the lunch napkin. "Now, *blow!*"

"We're looking forward to seeing you, buddy."

"Me, too. Mama said Buck came in the other day, he's bunkin' with Harley, she says he lost weight an' all for th' wedding. Poo's wearin' a suit, I can't believe Poo in a suit."

"What are you wearing?"

"Umm," said Dooley. "A suit."

"Don't forget your shirt and tie—or, you could borrow one of my ties."

"Your ties are too . . ."

"Too what?"

"Boring."

For someone who was usually in a collar, he'd never thought much about ties. Maybe he needed to buy something . . . upbeat! Something Italian! "What time are you rolling into Mitford?"

" 'Bout eleven Friday morning."

"How are you feeling about the appearance before the judge?"

"Not too good."

"It'll go well, don't worry. And how are you feeling about Caroline?"

Dooley was shrugging; he could practically hear it. The boy was blushing; he could sense it.

"Ah . . ."

"Pretty good?"

"Well, yeah, she's really neat, really interesting. She does these great watercolors, like Cynthia. You should see the one she did of the mountains behind her school, it was exactly like real life, except better."

"I'll be darned."

"She's got this cool laugh, too, sort of like . . . like this." Dooley made an odd sound, something between a snort and a cackle. "That's not right, it's more like . . . I don't know!"

"I can kind of guess."

"Plus she's really funny."

Dooley Barlowe was a goner, as far as he could tell.

"We can't go, dearest, he's burning with fever. I hope it's only the flu. Nearly everyone in story group was croupy and sick on Wednesday; I'd never have taken him if I'd known. I have a call in to his doctor."

He felt the boy's head, he looked at his red eyes and runny nose, he listened to his labored breathing. Convinced that hauling Jonathan to Dorchester would only make things worse, he finally told her. "Jeffrey Tolson may be hanging about. I don't think he's dangerous, but there's no telling what he might do."

"He can do nothing here!" she said, looking fierce. "We'll keep the doors locked and you'll only be away in broad daylight, so there's no use at all to worry. I'll send Ella the lasagna I froze the other day. Single women almost never make lasagna!"

His wife could convince him of anything. Feeling mildly relieved, he went to the study and closed the door and sat in the chair and prayed about it. He had written Captain Larkin the other day to say he was coming, and the last thing he wanted to do was disappoint. Should he go, or move the trip to a later date?

After he prayed, he listened.

God would have him go. He felt certain of it.

The sky was gunmetal from horizon to horizon; it seemed as if a leaden weight had been clamped over Whitecap like a lid on a turkey roaster.

He paced the front porch, unable to think clearly, anxious about leaving tomorrow. Maybe he should skip the Ava business and leave early, but Ernie was as excited about this little gathering as any parent, a fact he didn't feel like treating lightly. Besides, he wanted to see Ava Goodnight, who, let's face it, had accumulated some pretty heavy mystique without even trying.

Cynthia would be fine, she'd insisted on it, and he'd call her from Ella's house at least once, maybe twice.

While he was thinking of it, why didn't he have a car phone? Everyone else seemed to be zooming around at top speed, yammering into one as if their lives depended on it. Yet there was nothing in the thought of a car phone that attracted him. Wouldn't people break into his car and steal it, or did they steal phones anymore? Maybe car phones were now so cheap and run-of-the-mill that no one wanted the hassle of smashing a window. Anyway, if he had one, wouldn't he have to keep the top up on the Mustang? Otherwise, they could just reach in and yank it off its hinge or whatever.

Why was he thinking such nonsense? He was thinking nonsense because he dreaded thinking the real thing; he was trying desperately to hide from the reality of the lawsuit.

He zipped his jacket and sat in his favorite rocker, looking into the gathering dusk.

The lawsuit dogged him like a dark cloud. What on earth could be the possible meaning behind it all? Thank God, Walter was more than a cousin who happened to practice law. Walter was a tough, no-nonsense attorney with a decent reputation and several heavyweight clients; surely he could help him hammer this thing through.

He realized he was wringing his hands, something he'd hardly ever caught himself doing, and stopped it at once.

Yet, even more than the fret and worry of being slammed with a lawsuit was the possibility of losing a third of the escrow, which included part of what Andrew Gregory had paid for Miss Sadie's antiques, and a third of what the money had earned in mutual funds, making Hélène Pringle the possible recipient of around a hundred and fifty thousand dollars. Miss Sadie had trusted him to be a good steward of all she left behind, and he'd never begrudged this enormous responsibility, not for a moment. Now he felt the full weight of it squarely on his shoulders, with no one to turn to but someone he'd known since childhood as Potato Head.

God hadn't given him much family, but God *had* given him Walter; perhaps, just as Mordecai said in the Book of Esther, for such a time as this.

So—he had excellent legal counsel, and he and Cynthia were praying the prayer that never fails. What more could be done, after all?

Aha! His neighbor was at it again, though he didn't recognize the music.

He walked to the north side of the porch and cupped his hands to his ears. Interesting. Very interesting.

He squatted, then sat on the end of the porch, swinging his legs over the side.

Yes! That's it, Morris! What you're doing with the bass, keep it up, great, beautiful, have at it. . . .

He slipped off the porch, trotted to the rear gate and unlatched it, then went into the twilit street, where he stood for a moment, listening.

$\backsim$

His wife would not like him pulling a disappearing act, no, indeed, but he'd be gone only five, maybe ten minutes, she'd never miss him; his dog, however, was another matter. If Barnabas knew he'd gone on a joyride without him . . .

He dropped to the ground on the other side of the wall, and found himself jogging along the driveway.

When he reached the house, he thumped into his chair under the window, and listened.

He alternately nodded enthusiastically and wagged his head. He wagged his head at the foreboding passages in the music, though he knew they gave greater light to the passages of illumination.

Man alive, that Casavant was blowing the roof off.

When the music ended, he felt tears on his cheeks. He waited a few moments.

"Morris?" he shouted.

"It's you, Father."

"Yes."

There was a long, oddly comfortable silence.

"I'm going away for a few days and I came to say . . ." There was a sudden lump in his throat. "I came to say I think the music is . . ." The music is what? Moving? Powerful? How did critics manage to make a living with a language that must often fail them?

"Wonderful!" he shouted. Full of wonder! That was the best he could do for the moment.

"Perhaps you'd like to come in . . . and see the Casavant."

Had he heard right? He wiped his eyes on his shirtsleeve. "Why, yes, thank you, I'd like that." His wife would be frantic, but this was an extraordinary invitation. He was stunned. . . .

"The door is open. Take the stairs. I'll meet you on the landing."

He bolted from the chair, careful not to stumble over the uprooted bricks that once paved the entranceway.

The heavy front door opened easily, and he stepped into a dimly lit foyer. The light appeared to come from a single bulb in a wall sconce, though a large chandelier loomed above his head.

There was definitely a musty smell, but everything looked clean and orderly. Ornately carved armchairs stood on either side of a heavy mirror in which he was startled to see himself. On the floor, a pattern of black and white tiles, and to the right, a curving stairwell and a vast, lighted oil painting on the high wall. The painting was of rolling countryside, somewhere in Europe, perhaps, with a church spire and a procession of people in a lane.

"Father."

He looked toward the landing and saw Morris standing at the rail.

"Morris!"

"Come up."

He went up, as if in a dream. There was absolutely no sense of reality about where he suddenly found himself. He knew only that he needed to be here, was supposed to be here. . . .

Morris held his hands behind his back, apparently declining a handshake, as Father Tim looked directly into his eyes. He noted Morris's prominent forehead and the deep, vertical furrow between his heavy brows.

"You are not surprised," Morris said flatly.

"No, not at all."

"Come with me," said his host.

He was surprised, however, to see that Morris walked with such difficulty. As if sensing his curiosity, Morris turned and said, "Spinal stenosis, aggravated by arthritis. It is not uncommon to my condition. We're in here." Morris stood aside so that he might enter first.

As he stepped over the threshold, he drew in his breath. There, in a room illumined by lamplight, stood the Casavant, regal beneath the rank of elaborately stenciled facade pipes. With its ornamented mahogany casework, he thought the organ possessed the aura of a great throne.

He might have gaped interminably, but turned his gaze to the room itself, which was paneled with walnut. His eyes moved along the intricately detailed dentil moldings and carved inlays, to the open window where Morris must stand when talking with him; it was free of draperies, with only a simple pelmet above, perhaps to enhance the acoustics of the room.

Floor-to-ceiling bookcases, a bare, polished floor, velvet-covered chairs sagging with use, a love seat in a far corner . . .

"Beautiful!" he said, gawking unashamedly. Yet, a prison, nonetheless. He felt the awful weight of the room on his spirit, as if the only thing that ever stirred the air might be the music.

He sensed Morris's eyes on him. "Thank you for asking me in. I'm grateful to be here."

"My housekeeper comes every other day—Mamie has been with me since childhood—and my organ tuner comes as needed. I'm not completely without social intercourse."

"I'm glad. It's one of the things that keeps us soldiering on in this life."

"We strive to keep up appearances in this part of the house, but the grounds are without hope. My grandfather planted a jungle. It cannot be beaten back, and we long ago gave up trying."

Morris's head suddenly wrenched toward his right shoulder, jerking in a manner that seemed uncontrollable. "Out!" he growled. *"Out!"*

Father Tim walked to the organ, making a conscious effort to appear oblivious to what he'd just seen. "The pedals . . ."

"Yes," said Morris, as the tic passed. "Casavant provided a second pedal board for me, elevated one position above the standard pedal board.

"I've considered what I might play for you . . . the Widor Toccata, perhaps. You may know that the Casavant is designed for French voicing. The company founders spent a great deal of time in France, and scaled the pipes to play French repertoire especially well."

Morris slid stiffly onto the bench and pulled the chain of a green-shaded lamp over the keyboards. "You'll find this piece quite vibrant. It demonstrates all the tonal colors of the instrument. Listen to the reed stops, if you will. They're very distinctive, and altogether different from the more mellow English reed stops."

Father Tim stood by the organ, enthralled.

"Please sit," said Morris.

Father Tim hurried to a slipcovered armchair and sat, closing his eyes as the music began. Flashy and flamboyant, upbeat and positive, Widor made the hair stand up along his right arm and leg. Ah, the difference in being in the room with the music rather than sitting outside as a lowly trespasser!

The music so filled him with a nervous and exuberant energy that it flowed out at the climax as laughter.

"Wonderful!" Couldn't he come up with something less tiresome, for heaven's sake? "Marvelous! Bravo!"

Morris reflected for a moment. "And now, perhaps Bach's Great Prelude and Fugue in G Minor. . . ."

As the fugue subject unfolded, he wondered, as he always did when he heard this favorite composition, how a theme in a minor key could express such confident joy and abiding faith. The music soared around the room like a bird set loose from its cage, causing his scalp to prickle.

"Thank you," he said afterward, supremely happy.

Morris labored to rise from the bench, and stood by his instrument. "Thank you for listening, Father. You have an attentive and sympathetic ear."

Father Tim rose from the chair, which gave off the faint odor of old tobacco. "How I wish you might share your gift with . . ." It was hardly out of his mouth before he knew he'd said the wrong thing.

Morris's face grew hard. "Never speak of that again."

"I'm sorry," he said. "You have my word, I'll never speak of it again."

"The wine cellars were depleted years ago. I have nothing to offer you."

"You've given me more than I could possibly wish. Thank you, Morris, thank you. I'll go along, now. My dog will be furious that I've come without him."

Morris did not smile. "I'll walk you to the landing."

At the landing, he had a sudden urge to throw his arms around the man, shake his hand, make the sign of the cross over him—something, anything, to express his deep feeling. "You're faithfully in my prayers," he said.

His host's head jerked toward his shoulder. "Out! *Out!*"

Father Tim's heart pounded as he moved quickly down the stairs, angry with himself for failing to say the right thing, for the terrible alarm those words always ignited in his breast.

In the foyer, he turned briefly to look at Morris, then opened the door of Nouvelle Chanson and stepped into the October night.

He went at a trot—down the dark driveway under a hidden moon, over the wall, across the street, through the gate, up the steps to the back porch, and into the kitchen, panting. She probably had that sheriff out searching for him. He dreaded facing her. How could he have been so thoughtless and insensitive?

"Is that you, dearest?" Cynthia came into the kitchen, rubbing her eyes. "I hope you weren't waiting for me on the porch all this time. I started a new illustration and, well, you know how it is, I forgot." She looked at the kitchen clock. "Good heavens! Eight-thirty! I hope you haven't felt neglected."

"Oh, no, no! Don't even mention it," he said.

Jonathan was on antibiotics delivered from the pharmacy, and Cynthia would spend the day doctoring him for tomorrow's journey to Mitford.

He rose at six a.m., dressed more warmly than usual, and set off for Mona's.

It had definitely been a while since he'd had breakfast like he used to have at the Grill. It gave him a positive thrill to place his order.

"Two medium poached, whole wheat toast, hold the butter, and a side of grits."

"Do you want coffee?" asked the shy waitress, whom he hadn't seen before.

"The hard stuff, no cream, no sugar. Are you new?"

"Yessir, this is my first day. I'm kind of . . . nervous."

"I certainly didn't notice! I'm Father Kavanagh, glad to see you."

"I'm Misty Summers. My name tag says Missy, they got it wrong and have to do it over. Glad to meet you."

"Misty Summers! Now, there's a name for you. Very pretty name."

"Thank you," she said, blushing. "Would you like water? I can get you filtered, Mona serves filtered to special customers, I'm sure you must be special."

"Why on earth would you think so?"

"Your . . ." She indicated his neck. "You know."

"Ah. My collar."

"I've hardly ever met any Catholics."

"I'm Episcopalian."

"Oh," she said. "Well, I'll be right out with your water and your coffee."

"Thank you," he said, pleased to be here with a newspaper and the respite to read it. He really didn't want to make the Dorchester trek, but intended to get this day behind him, no matter what. Besides, when he called last night to say Cynthia and the boy weren't coming, Ella told him she was breaking out the damask tablecloth, which she hadn't used since her mother died and all the neighbors brought food and sat with her.

"There you go!" said Misty, setting a steaming mug before him. She looked like a milkmaid from a storybook, he thought. No makeup, long, chestnut hair caught in a ponytail, and a simple skirt and blouse under the café's signature green apron.

"Where are you from, Misty? Whitecap?"

"Oh, no, sir, Ocracoke. I just moved here two days ago, and was real blessed to get this job right off."

"I'm sure you'll do well. I believe you'll like Whitecap."

"Yessir," she said, pouring his coffee. He couldn't help but notice that her hand shook slightly.

"Try not to worry about getting everything right today," he said.

She lifted her gaze and he noticed her eyes for the first time. Warm. Trusting.

"I'll pray for you."

"Thank you, I really appreciate it. We'll have your order right out. Did you want ketchup?"

"Ketchup?"

"For your hash browns."

"Hash browns?"

She clapped her hand to her mouth. "Oh, gosh, I forgot, you're having grits!"

She fled to the kitchen, flustered.

As relaxed as if he had the whole day in which to do nothing, he opened his newspaper to the editorial page and settled happily into the green vinyl-covered seat of Mona's rear booth.

"Look here!" said Roanoke.

"Look here what?"

"Your hair's growed a good bit more'n I'd expect."

"Olive oil," said Father Tim, propped on the stool like a schoolboy.

"You rub olive oil on your head? I never heard of that one."

"Eat a lot of it on salads."

"Seems like God would've let a man have some say in where 'is hair grows, don't it? I mean, here you got all this hangin' down in back, an' not that much on top."

"Tell me about it."

Snip, snip.

"They say we'll prob'ly get a bad storm tonight," said Roanoke.

"I'm running up to Dor'ster. I hope it holds off 'til I get back."

"Temperature's droppin' pretty steady, too."

There was Elmo, sitting in the doorway to the book room and scowling at him as if he were a mangy hound. "Yo, Elmo!" he said.

At 9:25, according to the clock over Ernie's cash register, the entire room erupted into a bedlam of laughter, fish stories, and adrenaline-driven babble. He figured they wanted Ava and her sister to think this was a busy, prosperous enterprise, not some pokey little deal on a backwater island. Adding to the general vibration was the fact that Roger was nearly through burning, and would soon begin painting.

Father Tim had to admit that Junior was looking good. Instead of washing or ironing anything, however, he'd run across and bought new jeans, a shirt and jacket, and a new cap that read *Go, Bulls.*

"I'd take that off," said Roanoke.

"Why? She's seen my pictures, she knows my hair's a little . . . you know."

"That's not what I mean. I mean she might not like th' Bulls."

Junior looked stubborn. "I don't want to take it off," he said. "It's brand-new."

"Yeah, but what if she likes Carolina? You'd sure wish you was wearin' one that says *Go, Heels.*"

Glowering, Junior snatched the hat off his head and threw it in the corner.

"Now, don't go upsettin' him!" said Ernie, picking up the hat. "If you feel good wearin' th' thing, put it back on."

Junior crammed the hat back on his head and sat stiffly, looking miserable.

"Tim, you ought to tell Junior how you caught that big yellowfin tuna, take everybody's mind off—"

The screen door slammed as Ava Goodnight walked in and stared anxiously at the roomful of men.

The silence was sudden, complete, and absolute.

Ernie appeared turned to stone, Roanoke's hand froze at his shirt pocket where he was reaching for a Marlboro, and Junior's mouth was hanging open.

"You must be Ava!" said Father Tim, walking over and shaking her hand.

"And you must be Father Tim," she said, smiling. "Betty will be here in a minute, Betty's my sister, she's next door in the ladies room." Ava caught her breath and looked as if she might change her mind and run out the way she'd come in.

"And this is Junior. Junior Bryson." As the only one still able to function around here, he guessed the social stuff was up to him.

Junior rose slowly from the table and walked toward Ava as if in a trance. Father Tim wished to heaven that Junior would close his mouth.

"How're you?" asked Junior.

Ava extended her hand. "I'm just fine. How're you?"

"Just fine, an' how 'bout you?"

"And this," he said, pushing on, "is Roanoke Clark. He's a friend of Junior's."

Roanoke grinned and touched his forehead, a remnant gesture, Father Tim supposed, from the days men tipped their hats to women. "Pleasure."

"That's Roger Templeton. . . ."

"How do you do?" said Roger, standing respectfully.

"And I'm Ernie," said Ernie, recovering his speech and bounding over to shake Ava's hand. "We're glad to have you, nice to see you, come and sit down! We know you're goin' next door for coffee, but I could pour you a little somethin' in a cup, like a Cheerwine or a Dr Pepper, but you probably drink Coke, I could open you a Coke, how's that? On th' house!" Ernie was still shaking Ava's hand.

"Oh, no," said Ava, "I don't need a thing. But thanks a lot."

Father Tim figured somebody better make a move or Ava was out of here. "Ava, we're sorry we're a roomful of men. My wife would have come to meet you this morning, but we have a sick boy at home."

"I'm sorry," she said, appearing to mean it.

"Come and sit with us a minute," he said. "Roger, show Ava your duck."

Roger shyly held up his green-winged teal.

"Isn't that a marvel?" asked Father Tim, who was beginning to feel like the Perle Mesta of the Outer Banks.

Ava glanced at the door, looking for Betty. "Really nice! Really pretty!"

"We'd like you to feel welcome on Whitecap," said Father Tim. "Have you been here before?"

"No, sir, I never have. But my friend who lives on Tern Avenue—we've been meaning to get together for a long time."

Junior was currently grinning from ear to ear. He expanded his chest and adjusted his jacket sleeves, which Father Tim judged to be a mite on the short side.

"Oh, law!" said Betty, barging through the screen door. "Are we runnin' late, my watch has stopped, hey, y'all, I'm Ava's sister, her much *old*er sister, who're you?"

"I'm Tim Kavanagh. Glad to see you, Betty." The Lord had sent an icebreaker, and not a moment too soon.

"Hey, Tim, how're you, I hope I don't have lipstick on my teeth, do I have lipstick on my teeth? I dropped my compact in th' ladies room and busted my mirror, but since I already *had* seven years of bad luck, I hope I'm off th' hook!"

She fastened her gaze on Ernie. "An' you must be th' bigwig of this place, you *look* like you're th' bigwig."

"Why, yes, ma'am, I'm Ernie Fulcher, one an' the same. Have a seat and meet everybody. We're glad to have you."

"I don't suppose ya'll'd have a little drop of diet Pepsi or somethin,' I'm dry as a *bone*! I did th' drivin,' since Ava was busy doin' her nails and takin' her rollers out, an' drivin' always makes me thirsty, does it *you*?"

"Oh, yes, ma'am," said Roanoke, glad to be asked. "When I was haulin' lumber, I sometimes drank a whole case of Cheerwine between Asheville an' Wilmington."

"And you're Junior! I declare, you're better-lookin' than your pictures, don't you think so, Ava? A *whole* lot better-lookin' if you ask me, which nobody did!" Betty whooped with laughter and thumped down at a table, hanging the strap of a large shoulder bag over the chair back.

Betty patted the tabletop. "Come on, honey," she said to her sister, "sit down a minute and meet all these nice fellas who've been dyin' to see you, then we'll go next door and have a bite to eat, right, Junior?"

"Now, that's what I call a good-lookin' woman . . . ," said Ernie, dazed and staring at the door.

Without glancing up from his duck, Roger nodded in agreement.

"But seems like she might be too much for Junior."

Roanoke ground his cigarette out in a bottle cap. "You ain't tellin' us nothin' we don't know."

Roger burned a feather. Lucas yawned. The Dr Pepper clock ticked over the cash register.

"Well," said Father Tim, pushing back from the table, "you all can sit here 'til Judgment Day, but I've got fish to fry."

Ernie looked at him, anxious. "D'you think Junior stands a chance?"

"God only knows," he said, meaning it.

The lowering overcast continued—across the bridge, up the coast, and over the causeway to Dorchester. As he hit the island, the rain began.

He turned the heater on, pondering the fact that he could never think rationally when Morris yelled, but at last he understood that the harsh, repetitive command had little to do with him; in his opinion, it meant something else entirely—out of this body, out of this prison, out of this terrible exile. . . .

There . . . a stop sign, and Little Shell Beach Road. He looked at his watch, checked his odometer, and turned right. One and a half miles to Old Cemetery Road . . .

The lawsuit. It swam into his mind relentlessly. *The Lord is my strength and my shield. . . .*

He'd hold off on saying anything to the Hope House Board of Trustees until he talked again with Walter. The irony, he thought, of a stranger moving into his own house to set up shop to sue him. And why had she moved to Mitford to sue, when she might have done it just as well from Boston? It was the most mind-boggling turn of events imaginable.

He prayed as he slowly moved south on the small island of Dorchester—for Junior, Misty Summers, Cynthia, Jonathan, Janette, Morris Love, Buck and Pauline . . .

Old Cemetery Road. He hooked a right, hearing his tires crunch on gravel.

. . . for Dooley's missing brothers, Dooley's appearance before the judge, Busy Fingers' ability to complete the Lord's Supper needlepoint on time . . .

. . . and Jeffrey Tolson. He didn't want to pray for Jeffrey Tolson, but drew a deep breath and did it anyway. Could he personally forgive Janette's husband, even if the man wasn't repentant for the pain he'd caused?

He wanted to, he was required to, and, yes, he would keep trying to—with God's help.

Ella was looking for him. The moment he hit the porch, she opened the door and he blew into her living room with a gust of rain.

"Oh, mercy," she said, shaking his hand, "you're soaked! But come and stand by the piano. I've got the hair dryer ready."

"The hair dryer?"

"To dry you off!" she said, pleased to be helpful.

He had heard of time warps, and was utterly delighted to be in one. Ella Bridgewater's cottage was as pleasant as anything he'd seen in years. He felt instantly at home. In truth, it appeared as if his own mother might have placed Ella's turn-of-the-century furniture and the numerous family photographs in polished silver frames.

Small flames licked up from a single log in the fireplace, and a stack of wood lay by the hearth, ready for anything.

He inhaled deeply of the glorious aroma in the house, which seemed largely composed of salt air, wood smoke, and sea bass with lemon butter. Sitting by the fire as Ella prepared lunch, the clock ticking on the mantel, he felt as contented as a country squire.

This, he presumed, was the place where antimacassars went when they died—they were in evidence everywhere, and starched to beat the band. His mother had used sugar water to starch her own; as a child he'd had an awful desire to eat the one on the piecrust table; it made his mouth fairly water to see it.

Ella brought a small etched glass and a decanter. "There you are!" she said, clearly delighted to have his company. "That's my plum wine, I hope you like it, it won a blue ribbon in 1978! Lunch in ten minutes. And now you're settled, I'll send Louise in."

She went briskly to an adjoining room, out of which a canary momentarily flew. It made a beeline for the piano, where it perched on the bench and cocked its head at him.

"Louise, do sing for Father Timothy, he's come all the way from Whitecap."

To his astonishment, Louise began to warble with great charm and enthusiasm, and finished her rendition perched on an antimacassar atop the piano.

"Amazing!" he said. "Bring her to St. John's for a solo!" They could do worse than sit and listen to one of God's creatures sing from the depths of an unfettered heart.

$\sim$

The rain increased to gusting, wind-driven sheets that made the small house shudder as they sat at the table.

"Minor and I made plans to marry, and then, two weeks before the ceremony was to take place in our little church down the road, he was ballooning over Nova Scotia, and . . . well . . ."

"I'm sorry," he said.

Ella lifted her glass in a salute, and soldiered on as hostess. "Plums are very hard to find nowadays, unless you buy them in a store, and I'm hardly ever tempted to do that. You know what the problem is?"

"I confess I don't."

"Everyone works away from home these days, they don't keep their fruit trees sprayed or pruned, and the poor things simply fall down in the pasture or the yard or wherever, and that's the end of it."

" 'The world is too much with us; late and soon,' " he said, quoting Wordsworth. " 'Getting and spending, we lay waste our powers;/ little we see in Nature that is ours;/ we have given our hearts away, a sordid boon!' "

"Exactly," she agreed. "Amen!"

He was feeling anxious as they finished their dessert. "Do you have a TV we could watch for weather news?"

Ella sighed. "There hasn't been a TV in this house for years! Do you remember when the Dallas Cowboys beat the Denver Broncos in the Super Bowl?"

"I don't believe I do," he said.

"Mother and I were watching the game, sitting right over there, when the screen went black as pitch. I remember to this day what Mother said, she said, 'Ella, do you think this happened because I bet two dollars on the Cowboys with Joe?' Joe was our postmaster. We tried to have it fixed, but it was dead as a doornail, and we never replaced it."

A clap of thunder broke above them so loudly that he started from his chair. "Just . . . looking for a phone!" he said.

He dialed Dove Cottage as Ella stood by, peering at him anxiously. Her mother had taught her never to use a phone in a storm. She was, in fact, eager to unplug everything electrical, including the lamps, though she supposed that wouldn't be proper during a visit by clergy.

Cynthia reported that things were fine at home, and she was praying for him. While his wife implored him to do nothing reckless in such bad weather, he should, nonetheless, hurry home.

He was wanting out of here fast, though he felt compelled by common courtesy to look at a couple of photographs before leaving. There was Minor standing by a hot-air balloon, quite fit and handsome in a flight suit. Glaring from an oval frame, Mrs. Bridgewater appeared sufficiently formidable to wither the hollyhocks that served as background.

"I just hate this storm. I walked down to church last night and raked Mother's grave and dusted the pews . . . but you'll see it all another day." Ella's rouge was two perfectly circular spots. "And I wanted to show you our live oak. It's the oldest on the island as far as anybody knows. Maybe you can get a peep at it as you leave. It's just a few yards from that side of the porch."

"We'll do the full tour another day. I look forward to it."

"Well, then," she said, slipping a parcel into his hand. "This is a smidgen of my plum wine, and a few morsels of sea bass for your Violet. I'd so love to have a c-a-t, but I *can't* have a c-a-t, you know, as long as Louise is with me."

"Aha. Well, I'm off, and can't thank you enough. I've been happy in your home, Ella, and very much like your idea for next Sunday's anthem."

"Thank you for coming, Father, it was an honor. Now, left out of the driveway and two blocks on the right in the old white two-story, that's Captain Larkin. Remember to look for the blue truck in front and beware the dog, they say he bites."

She opened the door and was struck forcibly by a blast of cold wind and rain.

"I'll pray for you!" she called, as he dashed into the deluge.

He'd been out in a few storms, but this one worried him. As soon as they got back from Mitford, he'd have the blasted car radio fixed so he could find a little weather news when he needed it.

Driving at ten miles an hour, he managed to spot what he presumed to be the captain's house, and pulled up behind the blue truck. Any dog that would take the trouble to bite in weather like this was welcome to try, he thought, as he grabbed the wet umbrella and a leather box containing the home communion set.

He slogged to the concrete steps in a driving wind that threatened to invert the umbrella, and opened the screen door to the porch. A scowling face peered through the glass panels of the front door and quickly vanished.

Lord, bless this time, he prayed as he knocked, *and keep us safe from any harm in this storm. . . .*

He nearly leaped from his sodden loafers as a violent clap of thunder rolled overhead and the door opened. An elderly man with the countenance of an angel peered out.

"Hurry in, Father, hurry in!" said Captain Larkin.

CHAPTER SEVENTEEN

Bread and Wine

He stepped into a large parlor that smelled of fireplace ashes and stale bacon, like country houses he remembered from his Mississippi childhood.

His glance took in an afghan-covered sofa, two worn reclining chairs, a television set on a rolling stand, and a bevy of family portraits lining the white beadboard walls. To his right, a stairway with a curved banister, and closed double doors to what was probably a dining room. The house had once been rather fine, if unpretentious, and he was glad for its refuge.

"Where's your oilskins at, Father?" The captain spoke in a loud voice over the din of rain on the tin roof.

"I'm afraid I'm a mountain man, Captain, with nary an oilskin to my name." He shucked out of his damp jacket and hung it on a peg by the door.

"Brother!" shouted his host. "Bring Father a dishrag, if ye don't object."

He thought Captain Larkin was as lively and quick as any Santa Claus, though he walked with a cane and had a distinct limp. The captain also possessed a combination of the pinkest cheeks and bluest eyes he had ever seen.

The old man hobbled to the sofa and straightened the afghan. "Come sit an' make yourself to home. We'll have ye dried off here in a little."

The man who shuffled into the room looked exactly like the captain, yet his countenance was remarkably different; a scowl appeared permanently etched into his face as if by steel engraving. Light and darkness, observed Father Tim—fire and ice, north pole and south!

"This is Twin Brother," said Captain Larkin. "Brother, this is th' Father from down at St. John's."

" 'Bout time you come," said the old man, glowering at him. "We been lookin' out for you since Brother fell four year ago, he could've killed hisself an' it wouldn've mattered to you none."

"I'm sorry I wasn't around then. I came to St. John's in early July."

"Four month ago," said Brother, glaring at him through filmy eyes. He handed over a rag and Father Tim took it, mopping his head, face, and hands. He felt a chill go along his spine as the thunder crashed again, directly over the roof.

"Bad 'un," said Captain Larkin, shaking his head.

"Will you join us, Brother Larkin?"

"No, sir, I'll not!" snapped Brother, leaving the room. Opening one of the double doors, he turned and shouted, "I don't abide with such foolishness."

Father Tim closed his eyes, took a deep breath, and kept a moment of silence that amplified the sound of the lashing wind and rain. A single light bulb, hanging by a long cord from the ceiling, swayed slightly, causing shadows to dance across the pictures on the wall.

"Peace be to this house and to all who dwell in it. Graciously hear us, O Lord, Holy Father Almighty, everlasting God, and send thy holy angel from heaven to guard, cherish, protect, visit, and defend all who dwell here."

Father Tim saw Brother peering at them from behind the door, as he poured wine from a small cruet into an equally small chalice.

Though he knew he might have stood, the captain chose to kneel. Grasping the arm of his recliner and going to his knees with considerable difficulty, he joined Father Tim in the Lord's Prayer, then cupped his hands to receive the wafer.

"Lord," the captain prayed from memory, "I'm not worthy that Thou should come under my roof, but speak th' word only and my soul shall be healed."

"The Body of our Lord Jesus Christ, which was given for you, my brother."

Tears flowed down the pink cheeks of Captain Larkin as he raised his hands to his mouth and took the wafer.

"The Blood of our Lord Jesus Christ, which was given for you, my brother."

The captain drank and wiped his eyes on his shirtsleeve.

Laying his hands on the captain's head, Father Tim prayed, "The blessing of God Almighty, the Father, the Son, and the Holy Spirit, be upon you and remain with you forever, amen."

"Amen," said the old captain.

Father Tim helped him to his feet and they embraced warmly. The tender spirit of this good man flowed out to him with the smell of liniment and unwashed scalp, of shaving talcum and clothes hung too long in a forgotten closet.

"The Lord be with you, Captain."

"And with thy spirit," replied the supplicant, beaming through his tears.

The wind suddenly roared down the chimney and huffed a shower of ashes into the room. He was in too deep with this storm. It didn't appear to be passing over and seemed to be growing worse, moment by moment. Only a lunatic would go out in . . .

"Captain, may I use your phone?"

"We've not had one in a good while. Too much money for too little talkin' is what Brother calls it."

"Ahh." He went to the front door and stood looking out, agonized. He couldn't see his car or the truck parked in front of the porch, only a gray film as if a heavy curtain had been lowered. He shivered in his knit shirt.

The captain reached up and pulled the chain on the light bulb. "B'lieve I'll just switch this off."

In the odd twilight of the storm-darkened room, the old man eased himself into his recliner and sighed.

"Blowin' a gale," he said.

Father Tim thumped onto the sofa.

He'd wait for a letup—every storm had a letup once in a while—then he'd run for it and drive as far as he could go. One way or another, he'd make it home. . . .

"My great-grandaddy come over from Englan' in a little ship called *Rose of Sharon*. It broke up in a bad storm 'bout this time of year, and him an' five other men was warshed up on Dor'ster. We speculate it was about where this road ends at, down past th' church. Back in those days, th' beaches was littered with shipwreck of ever' stripe an' color, an' so they went to work and knocked together a little shack where they could look out for another ship an' git picked up."

What was this stubborn streak that had made him so all-fired determined to come to Dorchester today as if it were some life-or-death, do-or-die endeavor? Worse, how could he have left his wife saddled with a sick boy and a storm warning? Had he bothered to listen to a weather report and check out the particulars? No, he'd shrugged it all off as if it were nothing. . . .

"They wadn't hardly nobody livin' on these little islands back then 'cept Indians, there's some as thinks it was part of Wanchese's crowd. Story goes, my great-grandaddy wadn't more'n twenty year old when he married a Indian woman off of Whitecap, had a head of hair down to her ankles. I been tol' me'n Brother has th' cheekbones and nose of a Indian, but I don't know, I couldn't say."

Please, God, don't let this storm hit Whitecap and take the bridge out, keep the bridge in good working order, the bridge, that's the crux of the matter. . . .

"I built this house for my wife, Dora, back when I was runnin' trawlers. Dora was nineteen year old when we moved in, an' cheery as any angel out of heaven. Then, when we went down to Whitecap to keep th' light, Brother moved in an' managed things for me. When I quit keepin' th' light, I stayed on in Whitecap 'til Dora died, then come back to Dor'ster where I was born an' raised at."

Two thirty-five. An hour's drive in a storm like this would surely double, maybe triple the driving time, so he'd be home by five-thirty, maybe six o'clock, max. . . .

"I've been foolin' with Canada geese a good while, now, ever' fall I pay a neighbor to sow wheat an' winter rye 'round my pond out yonder. This spring, we seen nests as had four to eight eggs apiece. . . ."

He recognized a growing sense of foreboding . . . something that pressed on his chest and worried his breathing. Maybe he wouldn't wait for a break, he'd take his chances. . . .

He bolted off the sofa. "Captain, I've got a wife and boy to get home to, I'm going to run on, it's been a pleasure meeting you, I know how much they care for you at St. John's, God bless you and keep you, I'll be back before Christmas."

The old man looked at him, dumbfounded. "You ain't goin' out in this, are ye?"

"Yes, sir, I am," he said, running to snatch his damp jacket from the hook.

"Brother!" yelled the Captain. "Come an' say goodbye to th' Father, if ye don't object."

The dining room door opened, and Brother peered out, holding a jar of peanut butter with a spoon in it.

"The Lord bless you, Brother Larkin."

The old man scowled at him. "Goin' out in that, you'd do better to bless y'rself."

As he tossed the drenched umbrella into the backseat and slammed the door, he spied the lasagna sitting on the floor behind the passenger seat. Dadgummit, he'd forgotten to give Ella her present. Cynthia had even tied a bow around the foil-covered dish.

He sat for a moment and considered running it in to the twins. Then, feeling the chill of his sodden clothes, he squelched the notion.

He passed what he thought was Ella's house, but didn't see a light. No, indeed, St. John's organist was snug in her cottage with every plug pulled, as disconnected from civilization as any soul on the Arctic tundra.

A mile and a half to the highway . . .

With no yellow line to guide him, he kept his eyes strictly on the right side of the road, but there were long moments when the wipers were of no effect on the streaming windshield and he lost visibility entirely.

At the end of the gravel lane, he had a moment of sheer panic about pulling out to the highway. Pummeled by gusting sheets of wind and rain, he searched for headlights moving toward him from either direction, but saw nothing.

He eased onto the asphalt, praying.

Was this a hurricane? Surely not, or by now he'd be sitting upside down on the mainland in somebody's tobacco field. Besides, he would have heard if a hurricane was predicted; this was merely a heavy storm with high winds, of which they'd seen more than a few since moving to these parts. The thought consoled him, but a subsequent thought of the sea, roiling and churning not far from the highway, gave his stomach a wrench.

In truth, he had no clue about what he should be doing. To cling on in Dorchester seemed wasteful of precious time, but to push ahead seemed potentially hazardous and plain stupid.

He would push ahead.

Twice, he was tempted to pull into what he thought was a service station, but he seemed to be developing a kind of sixth sense for driving in these conditions, a sense that he didn't want to abandon too hastily.

He remembered what Louella said during their last visit. Something like, "You git in any trouble down there, jus' remember Louella's up here prayin' for you."

"Pray for me, Louella!" he shouted, finding comfort in the sound of his own voice.

On either side of the highway, trucks hunkered down like great beasts, waiting out the storm.

Easing south on what he estimated to be the last half of the coastal highway, the Mustang slammed into something unseen. It was a hard hit, and the motor died instantly.

His heart thundering, he leaped from the car and saw a tree limb fallen across both lanes. He pushed against the wind to get back in the car and switch on the emergency lights—he was a sitting duck out here—then, head down, he dived back into the squall to try to move the limb. Blast. The car had rolled over the limb before the motor died.

In the driver's seat, he turned the key in the ignition. Nothing. Again. Nothing. Flooded.

He tried to think calmly. If he could lift the front of the car backward over the limb, he could then push the Mustang onto the side of the road, out of harm's way. He had never lifted a car. . . .

He got out and walked to the right, checking the shoulder. But there was no shoulder; it was a drop-off to a creek, which was quickly rising to the roadway.

His glasses slid off his nose and he caught them and put them in his pocket, half blind. He was a desperate fool, the worst of fools. The rain was hammering him into the asphalt like a nail.

He saw it as he turned from the creek.

It was the lights of a truck bearing down in his lane.

His heart racing, he ran to the rear of the car and threw up both arms, waving frantically. *Dear Jesus, let him see my lights. . . .*

But what if the driver didn't see his lights? He could be chopped liver between the grille of a tractor-trailer and the bumper of his own car.

"Please!" he shouted over the roar and din of the rain. *"Please!"*

He jumped out of the way as he heard the air brakes applied. The massive vehicle rolled to a stop only inches from the Mustang.

His legs were cooked macaroni, warm Jell-O, sponge cake as he walked to the driver's side of the cab and looked up in utter despair.

The window eased down. "What's your trouble?"

"Limb on the road, motor's flooded."

The driver climbed out of the cab in a flash, wearing an Indiana Jones hat with a chin strap, and a brim that instantly shed water like a downspout.

"I'll take a look." The driver bent into the rain and walked to the front of the car, squatted and peered underneath. "Goin' to need a chain. Get in your car, I'm goin' to haul you over th' limb, then we'll roll it off in Judd's Creek."

Sitting in the car, he heard the chain being attached to his rear bumper, and soon after felt the jerk as the big rig reversed its gears and rolled him backward over the limb. He pulled on the emergency brake and returned to the fray.

Together, they heaved, pushed, and rolled the sodden limb off the road and into the creek.

"Where you headed?" the driver shouted.

"Whitecap!"

"I'm runnin' by Whitecap. Come on an' follow me, but not too close or th' spray'll blind you. Just keep your eyes on my taillights and marker lights."

"Done!"

"I'll pull into that vacant lot by th' Whitecap bridge."

"God be with you!" he shouted.

He followed the truck for roughly half an hour in steadily decreasing rain. About four miles north of Whitecap, the storm had blown over, and he turned his wipers off.

In the vacant lot, rainwater stood in deep pools, and he saw a metal sign blown from Jake's Used Cars leaning against the entrance to the bridge.

But, *hallelujah,* there was no sign claiming the bridge was out.

Dodging the pools, the driver pulled the refrigerated rig into the lot, and Father Tim parked alongside.

Leaving the motor running, the driver swung down and shook his hand with an iron grip.

"Tim Kavanagh. I can't thank you enough."

"Loretta Burgess," said the driver. "Glad to help."

"Loretta?" he said, stunned. "I mean . . ." Well, well. Holy smoke.

Loretta Burgess laughed and removed her sodden hat. A considerable amount of salt-and-pepper hair fell around her broad shoulders. "I don't care what they say, Padre, it ain't totally a man's world."

"You're right about that!"

"I'd show you th' pictures of my grandkids if we had time, but I'm runnin' behind th' clock. You take it easy, now."

As Loretta Burgess pulled onto the highway, he turned to get back in the car. He was standing with his hand on the door handle when he sensed something odd and troubling:

The air was strangely, eerily quiet.

And then he heard the siren.

CHAPTER EIGHTEEN

Simple Graces

Three army trucks blew past the vacant lot, tailed by a mainland ambulance with a wide-open siren.

He scratched onto the slick pavement and followed the procession across the bridge without any memory of doing it.

As he came off the bridge, he was clocking seventy, but had no intention of slowing down. Wherever the rescue squad was needed, he could be needed. Instantly he prayed for the need, whatever it might be, and realized he'd been praying, almost without ceasing, since six o'clock this morning. Surely, days on end had been packed into this single half day.

Water rushed across parts of Tern like bold creeks, carving out sections of asphalt. Whatever the vehicles ahead of him plowed through, he plowed through.

As the cavalcade turned left on Hastings, he saw the tree hanging, as if in a sling, on the sagging power lines. Across from the fallen tree was the gray house on the corner, the one Cynthia always admired— another tree had slammed across the roof, caving it in, and scattering bricks from the chimney into the yard. Next door, a section of picket fence dangled in a tree, and over there, a limb had smashed straight down, like an arrow from above, into the hood of a car.

In the rearview mirror, he saw two more troop trucks behind him and, farther back, another ambulance.

A chilling fear was spreading through him like a virus.

In the sullen afterlight of the storm, he had returned to a place he hardly recognized.

Several houses this side of Dove Cottage appeared to have taken a beating, but without any serious damage.

As his house came into view, his heart was squeezed by a kind of terror he'd never known.

Dove Cottage had no porch.

Its facade was oddly blank, like a staring face. He saw that the porch had been blown into the neighbor's yard, partially intact, the rest in smithereens. Pickets from the fence were scattered everywhere. A few had landed on the roof.

The need he'd prayed for only moments ago was partly his own.

He parked at what had been his front gate, as the stream of vehicles behind him blew past. He fled toward the house and stood looking up to the front door, wondering how to get in.

"Cynthia!"

The back porch . . .

He raced around the house and into the kitchen, where he stepped on fragments of china that crunched like bubble wrap under his feet.

"Cynthia! Barnabas!"

He skidded down the hall, and halted at the living room door, where the entire floor had caved in at the middle, in a deep and perfect V.

Their furnishings lay neatly piled along the crotch of the V, and on top of the pile was his mother's Limoges vase; it appeared unharmed, as if it had rolled down one side of the collapsed flooring and, at the last moment, landed conveniently on a chair cushion.

"Cynthia! Please!" He tore along the hall to the bedrooms, which looked as if nothing more than a strong wind had ruffled the bed-covers, as if the porch had not been blown to kingdom come, nor the living room destroyed.

But what if she and Jonathan had been in the living room when . . . ?

He raced out the back door and into the street, thinking he would flag down an ambulance, a neighbor, anybody. But there was no help in sight. Many in the neighborhood worked across, and only a lone pickup truck roared past, the driver refusing to make eye contact.

What had happened? Was it, in fact, a hurricane? Did tornadoes hit the coast? He'd never asked. All his life, he had ignored weather as much as he could, for what could one do about it, anyway?

He would burrow through the furniture like a mole, through the chairs and tables and books and magazines. . . .

Somewhere at the bottom was the rug. If he got to the bottom and found the rug, he'd know she was nowhere in the house. . . .

He called her name unceasingly as he clawed his way through the detritus of their everyday life, terrified that he might find her.

But there was no one, nothing.

And how in heaven's name was he to crawl up the slick, polished floor, from the hole he'd lowered himself into?

"Father! You down there?"

White-faced, Junior Bryson squatted over the threshold of the living room and looked into the pit.

"I'm here, Junior. Have you seen my wife?"

"No, sir, I just drove up from th' Toe an' seen your porch was blowed off. I was goin' to Ernie's. I hear he took a bad hit."

"Can you pull me up?" He'd never been so glad to see a face. He was trembling with feeling and with cold.

"I'm pretty much out of shape, I don't know, but I'll lay down and hook my feet on either side of th' doorway. . . ."

Junior positioned himself and, huffing, reached toward Father Tim.

"OK, you hang on, now, just kind of climb up my arms or whatever."

"This room was built pretty high off the ground, so it's a stretch."

"But don't be pullin' me down in there with you," said Junior, "or we'll both be in a good bit of trouble."

"I can't seem to get any traction with these loafers," he said, breathing hard.

Blast loafers into the next century, he was over loafers.

"It just happened," Junior said, as Father Tim hurriedly changed into dry clothes and pulled warm socks onto his numb feet. "About thirty, forty minutes ago, looks like it tore up th' north end and blew on out to sea, th' rain an' wind just stopped all of a sudden. But we didn't have no damage at th' Toe, not a'tall. Far as I know, 'lectricity's down all over th' island, an' Mr. Bragg's phones went out. How's th' bridge?"

"Still working."

"That's a blessin'," said Junior.

On his way out the back door, he turned and did a final search for Violet, looking under the beds, and hoping she wasn't stranded under the study sofa, which he couldn't get to because of the collapsed living room.

They walked at a trot to the truck and the car.

"Good luck findin' your wife and th' boy. I'm sure they're fine, prob'ly at th' grocery store or post office when it hit."

"Thank you, buddy."

But his wife couldn't have been at the grocery store or the post office; she had no car. She was, he decided, at the church with Jonathan, where she'd gone to work on the Fall Fair. He felt so certain of it, he wanted to shout.

As he drove away from Dove Cottage, he wondered—where was her bicycle? She usually hauled it up the steps and left it on the front porch. Surely she wouldn't have been out on her bicycle. . . .

More cars were on the street now, people coming from across or from the Toe; there was a veritable snake of solid traffic along Hastings, and not a little horn-blowing.

He hated seeing Ernie's. The right wall had crumbled, leaving the framing and a pile of bricks. Glass from the front window was missing as well, and books lay scattered around the parking lot and into the street.

All that unrefrigerated bait, all those books open to the elements, they'd better get a tarp over it, and fast.

But he couldn't think about Ernie's right now.

A camera unit from a mainland TV station blew around him as he wheeled the Mustang into the empty parking lot next to Ernie's, and set off running to St. John's.

"She's leanin' to th' side of my politics, is what it is." Ray Gaskill, who lived in the house closest to St. John's, removed a toothpick from his mouth and surveyed the damage.

Roughly one-third of a live oak had split off and collapsed across the roof of the church, knocking the building askew.

"It's racked to the right," said Leonard Lamb, looking ashen.

"Who was in it?" asked Father Tim.

"Nobody. Sometime after you left for Dor'ster, the women packed up and went over to the Fieldwalkers' to work."

"The organ?"

"It's OK, if we can get a tarp on before it rains again. We can't find Sam, and the phones are down so we can't call Larry to bring a tarp from the ferry docks. Looks like I'll have to go across if th' bridge is working."

"No problem with the bridge."

"Or we could maybe get a tarp from up Dor'ster, maybe at the boat repair."

He felt ridiculously guilty that he hadn't picked up a tarp.

"Trouble is, the plaster's cracked pretty bad and when we set her straight, that'll crack it even worse."

"This ain't nothin' to the' Ash Wednesday storm," said Ray, chewing the toothpick. "Now, that was a storm. This wadn't but prob'ly seventy-five-, maybe eighty-mile-an-hour winds."

He thought St. John's neighbor seemed personally proud of the catastrophe that struck in '62. Though it spared lives, its fury had pretty much battered everything else along five hundred miles of shoreline.

"I've got to find Cynthia," he said. "Do you have any idea . . . ?"

"I don't," said Leonard. "Marjorie's at the Fieldwalkers'. She'd probably be able to say."

Come to think of it, why would Cynthia have taken Jonathan out in a terrible storm, when he was burning with fever and on medication? And she wouldn't have taken Barnabas and Violet to the soiree at the Fieldwalkers'. . . .

His heart was in his throat.

"Looks like some of th' sidin's popped off. That'll expose your studs to water," said Ray.

"What about the basement?" he asked Leonard.

"You don't want to know."

And he didn't. Not until he found Cynthia.

"I'll be back," he said.

When he picked up the Mustang, he spoke with a young police officer in the crowd milling around Ernie's.

"Why is the army in here?" he asked, afraid of the answer.

"They're not any army in here. We use army surplus trucks in storms 'cause saltwater eats up th' brake linin's on our patrol cars. These babies stand way up off th' road."

"Was anyone hurt at Ernie's?"

"No, sir. They think it was all that water in th' ground that did somethin' to part of his foundation, made his wall fall in. Then a big trash can blowed into his front window, an' the' wind scattered books from here to Hatt'ras."

"What about Mona's?"

"One of th' waitresses got her arm burned pretty bad, a deep fryer come off th' stove, fella in a pickup just ran 'er across to ER."

"I've lost my wife," he blurted.

The young man removed his hat. "Gosh," he said.

"I mean, I can't find her," he explained, feeling foolish. Why was he standing here?

Not knowing what else to do, he shook the officer's hand and ran to his car.

Close to tears, he turned the car around in the parking lot and headed onto Hastings, which was covered with water.

He suddenly recalled the time on the beach, only days ago, when she had reached up and stroked his cheek and said she wanted to remember him like this always. Had that been some terrible omen?

With the Whitecap police directing traffic, he made his way back the way he'd come.

The door was not only unlocked at the old Love Cottage, it had been blown open, and most of the furniture overturned. The wind had heaved a rocking chair through a front window; shattered glass was strewn on the sodden floor.

"Cynthia!" There was a basement here, Otis had said so; maybe when the porch had been ripped off their house, she'd come here, fearing worse.

Shaking as with palsy, he searched for the door to the basement, opening closets, finding the water heater, listening for the booming bark of his dog. . . .

"Cynthia! *Please!*"

There! Hidden in the bedroom they'd slept in all those eons ago . . .

He threw open the basement door and peered down into a dark void, unable to switch on a light.

"Cynthia!" he bawled.

Silence.

He turned from the mildewed odor that fumed up at him, and closed the door and put his head in his hands and did what he'd been doing all day.

"Lord," he entreated from the depths of his being, "hear my prayer. . . ."

Maybe there was a note at Dove Cottage.

Maybe there was something on the kitchen counter telling him where they'd gone. If not, he'd drive to the Fieldwalkers' if there were no power lines across the roads. He'd heard that was a problem in some parts of the north end, but so what, he had two feet, and besides, they couldn't have just vanished off the face of the earth. They had to be somewhere. . . .

He parked at the side of Dove Cottage and sprinted across a yard that felt like marsh beneath the soles of his running shoes.

"Father!"

Morris Love . . .

He turned and looked across to the wall. Something odd over there, a blank spot in the sky where a tree had stood. . . .

"They're over here!"

Again, his cognition lapsed, and he wouldn't recall racing from his yard and across the street and through the iron gate, which Morris Love had unlocked and swung back as he dashed onto the familiar turf of Nouvelle Chanson.

"Timothy!"

There had been times of absolute, unfettered joy in his life—his ordination, his wedding, and the day he and Walter stood on a hill in Ireland and looked across to the site of the Kavanagh family castle.

With his wife in his arms, his dog jumping up to lick his face, and Jonathan tugging on his pants leg, he experienced a moment of supreme joy that he felt he may never know again.

"Violet?" he said.

"In the kitchen, having a tin of Mr. Love's sardines."

He regretted that both he and his wife were tearful with happiness, but what could he do?

They saw Morris turn from the reunion in the foyer and stand by the window. There was suffering on his face in profile, something that snatched away the joy in their hearts.

"A nail," said his wife, explaining the bandage on her hand. "Right in the palm."

They sat in the cavernous kitchen lighted by candles in a silver stand, and waited for the teakettle to boil over a can of Sterno. Not seeming to know his kitchen, Morris had been unable to provide anything more than the Sterno and a kettle already filled with water. Cynthia had helped herself to his cabinets and found tea, along with a bag of Fig Newtons, which Morris said belonged to Mamie, but urged them to help themselves. Seeing their reluctance, he ate one himself, out of courtesy.

They all fell to.

"Milk!" said Jonathan. "My mommy, she gives me *milk* and cookies."

"No milk, dear," said Cynthia, hauling the boy onto her lap with one hand. "And no water in the taps, just what we have in the kettle."

"There's apple juice," said Morris.

"I'll get it!" said Father Tim.

"*No*. I'll get it." Morris rose stiffly and went to the refrigerator; he removed a container and poured juice into a glass.

"Say thank you," urged Cynthia.

"Thank you," said Jonathan, gulping it down.

"When the winds became so terrible," she said, "I remembered my bicycle and was afraid it would be blown off the porch like our rockers were last August. So I went out to bring it in the house and it wasn't there, and you know how I love my bicycle. I mean, I could never replace it, it's old as the hills."

"More," said Jonathan.

"More, *please*," counseled his wife.

"More, more, more, please, please, *please*!"

Morris took the glass and got up again, obviously with considerable difficulty, and refilled the glass.

"Thank you," said Jonathan.

Cynthia beamed with pride, and continued her report. "And so, I peered off the porch and saw that my bike had been blown into the side street. I ran down to get it, and all of a sudden, things were flying around in the air, and I realized it was pickets off our fence, they were just showering down, and I raised my hand in front of my face and a picket with a nail in it . . ."

"I'm sorry," he said, taking her bandaged hand.

"Just boom. Nailed. Ugh. Now you finish, Mr. Love."

"Please call me Morris."

"Morris!"

"I had looked out from the music room and seen the tree go over. Fortunately, it fell away from the house, and I had a view of the street. The rain was very heavy and visibility wasn't the best, but I thought I saw your wife, and she appeared to be in distress. I remember you said you were leaving town and I thought she may need . . . help."

"And so he came out to me," said Cynthia, "and at just that moment we saw the porch break off the front of the house. It was awful. I thought—"

Jonathan nodded energetically. "I was, I was *in* th' house!"

"Yes, you were, and so Morris ran to the house with me and we got Jonathan and Violet and Barnabas and he brought us all over here and we stood in his music room, sopping wet, to see if the rest of the house was going, but it didn't, and then Morris saw that I was dripping blood on his carpet. I'm terribly sorry about that, your housekeeper won't be a bit happy—"

"It's a dark Oriental, no one will never know."

"And he washed my wound and put antibiotic cream on it and bandaged me up." His wife beamed at Morris Love, who visibly blanched at the warmth and directness of her feeling.

Father Tim cleared his throat. "Thank you, my friend."

"I was scared," said Jonathan, whose nose was running like a tap. "I was *cryin'.*"

He wiped Jonathan's nose and smoothed his hair, feeling a rush of affection. "And what about the bicycle?" he asked his wife.

"Mr. Love—I mean Morris—went back out into that awful storm and retrieved it. It's under his stairwell."

Morris shifted in the chair, looking uneasy.

"There goes the kettle!" said Cynthia. "Now please sit still, Morris, this is my job."

"I'm hungry," said Jonathan.

"I'm starved," said Cynthia.

His own stomach was growling. "We must get home and see what's up, anyway. What do we have in the refrigerator?"

"Nothing. Zip. A salami, a tomato. We're going to Mitford, and so I didn't want to leave anything."

"A salami and a tomato. It's a start," he said, cheerful.

"You're welcome to look here. I don't know, Mamie brings every-thing. . . ." Morris lifted his hands as if bereft of a solution.

"Bingo!" cried Father Tim.

"Bingo!" repeated Jonathan, slapping the table.

"It just occurred to me, I have just the ticket. Homemade lasagna! Velvety blankets of pasta layered with fresh spinach, fresh ricotta, mozzarella, a thick tomato sauce sweetened with chopped onions, and veal ground from the shank. Precooked, freshly thawed, and ready to roll."

"Mercy!" said his wife. "That sounds like my recipe. Where on earth did it come from?"

"The floor of my car," he replied, feeling as if he'd just hung the moon. "Morris, will you break bread with us?"

"Be thankful for the smallest blessing," Thomas à Kempis had written, "and you will deserve to receive greater. Value the least gifts no less than the greatest, and simple graces as especial favors. If you re-member the dignity of the Giver, no gift will seem small or mean, for nothing can be valueless that is given by the most high God."

Father Tim remembered what the old brother had said as he ate his portion of the lasagna with gusto, and set some on the floor for Barnabas.

He thought it was the best thing he ever put in his mouth. His wife, who had always possessed a considerable appetite, was hammering down like a stevedore. Even Morris Love appeared to enjoy her handi-work, and Jonathan ate without prejudice or complaint.

Further, Ella Bridgewater had saved the day. In the packet with the sea bass, which Violet devoured, was the small jar of plum wine, which, to conserve water and washing up, they poured into their empty tea cups and drank with enthusiasm.

They went across the street with Morris Love's flashlight, and into the cold kitchen of Dove Cottage. He thought their house felt as if all life had gone out of it, as if the terrible assault had wounded it in some way that was palpable.

He was walking into the hall when the floorboards creaked and he saw a shadowy figure coming toward him.

"Good heavens, who's there?"

Jonathan let out a howl.

"It's Otis!" said his landlord, beaming his flashlight up. "You're in a bad fix here."

"Tell me about it."

"Looks like that sorry porch wadn't nailed onto th' house for shoot. I can't tell what all's goin' on 'til I get some daylight and a couple of men out here, but I want you and th' family to come stay at my motel. We'll fix you up with a choice room and king-size bed."

"Oh, no, that's fine, we'll just set up camp right here."

"No water here, no power, no heat, an' I don't know what's under these floors that might go next. When th' porch tore off, looks like a rotted floor joist or somethin' gave way in your front room."

Cynthia looked at him. "Otis is right, dear. Jonathan is sick, and the house is a terrible mess. Besides, we need our rest for tomorrow's trip."

"We won't be going to Mitford," he said.

His parish needed him here. God would work out the details.

Holding the sleeping boy in his arms, he stood on the back steps with Otis while Cynthia did some hurried packing with the aid of a flashlight.

"Not a scratch on my place," said Otis, "save for somebody's deck furniture bobbin' around in th' pool. When I heard what was goin' on up here, I run home lookin' for Marlene and couldn't find her. It like to give me a nervous breakdown, she was supposed to be home. Well, in two or three hours, here she comes, paradin' in like th' Queen of

Sheba, complainin' of th' rain ruinin' her hair. She'd been across havin' her roots touched up."

"Aha."

"Where trees blow down, they sometimes take out th' water lines, and course, th' water lines is takin' out th' roads. Thank th' Lord she was drivin' th' four-wheel."

Jonathan stirred in his arms and put the warm palm of his hand on Father Tim's cheek. "What about power?" he asked Otis. "How long to get everything back up?"

"Th' whole island's lost power. That'll prob'ly take four to five days to get goin' again. Water, I don't know, maybe two days. And it'll take a week of hard haulin' to get th' roads graded and asphalted."

He thought the whole thing seemed a dream. "How long 'til we can hold services?"

"The church looks pretty bad. Shingles are poppin' off like corn. But we got tarps on 'er, three of 'em. I had one, Larry brought one, Sam scrounged one. I've got people comin' tomorrow to look it over, see what it's goin' to take, an' how long." Otis heaved a deep sigh. "Th' water runnin' in turns plaster to mush, then when it dries, it turns to powder."

The tenant echoed his landlord's sigh.

"But this'll bring us together," said Otis, adopting a positive view of what lay ahead for the body of St. John's.

Father Tim felt a drop of rain on his cheek. "Oh, boy," he said, stepping onto the back porch.

He heard his parishioner draw a cigar from his pocket and remove the cellophane. There was a moment of silent consideration.

"Dadgum if I ain't goin' to *smoke* this sucker!"

In the flame of a monogrammed lighter, Father Tim saw the face of a happy man.

Cynthia stood inside the door of Number Fourteen at Bragg's Mid-Way Motel and peered at their room, which was lighted by a kerosene lantern.

"Ugh!" she said vehemently. "Shag carpet!"

CHAPTER NINETEEN

Jericho

His wife looked utterly downcast as he dressed the following morning. She sat on the side of the bed in her nightgown, shod in his leather bedroom shoes, refusing to make any direct contact with the carpet.

"You could take me to church and keep the car," he said, desperate to be helpful.

"I can't be dragging Jonathan around in this rain."

They had eaten a breakfast of cheese sandwiches, which Otis had made himself and delivered at six a.m. with scorching coffee in a thermos. The paper sack included a side of bananas, apples, raisins, and oranges, juice and crackers for Jonathan, and packaged brownies from the convenience store.

"I hate to leave you. You can go to the Braggs', you know. Otis invited us."

"Not in a hundred years," she said, setting her mouth in a profoundly straight line. "Make that a thousand!" Marlene Bragg had suggested his wife stop highlighting her own hair and see a professional; further, she proclaimed that fuchsia wasn't becoming to Cynthia's skin color, and recommended another shade of blusher to bring out the blue of her eyes. This had not set well.

"Marjorie and Sam begged us to come." Sam had shown up at the motel last night at eleven, hoping to rescue them.

"But their guest room has a leak in the ceiling and there's no water. Sam says they're using his grandmother's chamber pot."

"There are worse things than chamber pots," he said, trying to console.

"I can't imagine what."

He didn't want to say it, but how about being trapped in a motel room with no power, no phone, and a three-year-old?

He buttoned his shirt, surveying the scene. The kerosene lantern glowed against the dusk of the rainy morning; the oil-fired heater hissed in the corner; Jonathan slept soundly, clutching a pillow; Barnabas snored in the vinyl armchair; Violet snoozed on a mat in the bathroom. Cozy as it all appeared, he would not want to spend the day here. No, indeed.

"How's your hand?"

"Throbbing."

"Do you think you need to see a doctor?"

"I don't think so. Morris poured something on it that was absolutely scalding before he put on the cream. I think it's fine, dearest, don't worry. I'll have a look under the bandage before you come home with lunch. Ugh! Did I say *home?*"

"Home is anywhere you are, Kavanagh."

She fell against the pillows, sighing.

"What do you think of our neighbor?" he asked, putting on his shoes.

"The strangest, yet loveliest sort of man. I feel that underneath his pain is the deepest tenderness. Then again, is it pain, Timothy? I don't know, perhaps it's something more like anger, a terrible, corrosive anger."

"Odd that he would be so adept at home doctoring."

"He said he learned from Mamie."

"Aha. Well. I'll be back around twelve. Maybe the rain will let up and you can drop me at church and take the car."

"Where would I go?" she asked.

"I don't know. The library?"

"The library isn't open today."

"The grocery store?"

"And watch mold grow in the dairy case?"

He had a great idea. "I could bring you some pot holders to finish up for the Fall Fair." There! Just the ticket to keep her mind occupied.

"Pot holders?"

She looked at him as if he were something that had crawled through the pipes and into the kitchen sink.

As phone service was up in other parts of the village, he drove two blocks and stood in a queue to make calls from a pay booth at the rear of Whitecap Drugs.

When the Hope House switchboard answered, he asked for the dining room.

"Pauline . . ."

"Father! We saw on the news you had a bad storm last night."

"Yes. And Pauline . . ." He'd rather be shot than say it. "I . . . can't come. I can't come for the wedding on Sunday. I'm calling to ask if you can . . . cancel, that is, postpone it for two weeks until we get cleaned up here."

There was a moment of silence. The disappointment on the other end was palpable.

"Or," he said, and he really despised hearing these words out of his mouth, "you could get someone else to officiate, someone else to—"

"Well, no, Father, I mean that's fine, we don't want anybody else, you know we were goin' to keep it really simple, anyway, so it's . . . not much trouble to postpone it."

"I'm sorry, I can't tell you how sorry . . ." He was literally nauseous over the whole thing, especially hating that Jessie's, Poo's, and Dooley's glad excitement would have to be put on hold.

"Well, but don't worry," she said. "We'll set another date. We didn't even run it in th' newspaper, but I did tell everybody in the dinin' room, and Miss Louella, she was goin' to come, but . . . they'll all understand."

"What about Buck? How will this affect his plans?"

"Oh, he's not goin' back to Alaska. He's finished up his part. He's goin' to try an' set up his own business in Mitford."

"Hallelujah!"

"So, I understand," said Dooley's mother, "really I do."

But he could hear the sadness in her voice. He was good at hearing sadness in people's voices. . . .

"Two weeks," he said. "No matter what, we'll be there. And we'll talk again in a few days, all right?"

"Yes, sir. How bad is it down there?"

"No lives lost, as far as we know, but power out, and phones down in places, and no water on the north end. The church has taken a hard hit, part of a big tree fell across the roof and . . ."—he felt suddenly close to tears—"and our cottage had some damage."

"I'm sorry," she said, her voice husky with feeling. He knew that she, too, was good at hearing sadness in others.

He was able to reach Buck in Harley's basement apartment; Buck would go with Dooley to court on Monday, and Harley would return Dooley to school, as planned. They would reschedule the wedding for mid-November.

He took a deep breath and went through yet more telephone rigmarole—access code, the number he was calling, his calling card number, his PIN number, then through the switchboard, where, it was declared, there was no answer in the room, and so up to the fourth-floor nurses' station, and down the hall to the sitting room with the cordless. . . .

"Hello?"

"Janette . . ."

"Oh, Father, I'm so glad to hear your voice, I saw about the storm on TV. Is Jonathan . . . ?"

"He's doing great! A bit of a cold, that's all. Our house is torn up for a few days, but everyone's safe. We're at Otis Bragg's motel in the village."

"Thank heaven! And Father, I'm so happy about coming home."

"We'll be over to get you on Tuesday as we discussed. Around two o'clock. Is that still good?"

"Oh, yes. Perfect! I'll be ready."

"If you'd like to call, we're in Room Fourteen at Bragg's Mid-Way Motel. Uh-oh, I forgot. Phones are out over there, but should be up and humming in a day or two."

"I'll be so happy to see my baby. Has he been . . . good?"

"Better than good!"

Her laughter was music to his ears.

"We'll take you home and get you settled in with something hot for your supper. We can bring Jonathan on Thursday," he said, follow- ing the doctor's advice. "That will give you a chance to—"

"Oh, no, Father, please bring him Tuesday. I've missed my children so much. I can't wait to have my children home."

"Consider it done, then. And when are Babette and Jason coming?"

"They'll be home Wednesday."

"Good, wonderful," he said.

"Have you . . . seen Jeffrey?"

"Not in some time." Taken by surprise, he chose to be vague without being untruthful.

"Jean Ballenger says there's a pile of work waiting for me."

"Including a blazer for yours truly. I haven't had a blazer in years. Cynthia talked me into it and picked out the buttons."

There was a pause. "I'm . . . so very grateful, Father Timothy. For everything."

"So am I," he said. "So am I."

"Emma," he yelled through a lousy connection, "don't bake a ham!"

"What?"

"Don't bake a ham!"

"Spam? What *about* Spam?"

Rats. "I'll call you back!"

When he called back, the line was busy.

He rang Pauline's small house in the laurels, reluctant to wake Dooley, who had arrived late last night from school.

"Dooley . . ."

"Hey!" Dooley said, hoarse with sleep.

"Hey, yourself, buddy. We've got a problem down here."

He went out into the rain and stood beside his car for a moment, dazed and heartsick, finding that everything was finally sinking in—all at once.

On the way to St. John's, he wheeled into Ernie's, which was swaddled front and side with tarps.

Though Books, Bait & Tackle was down for the count, Mona's half of the building was going full throttle, thanks to a serious stash of bottled water, and a generator that had seen the café through the aftereffects of several storms and a hurricane. He stepped into the warmth of Mona's, smelling dripping coffee and frying bacon, and loving the refuge of it.

Every booth was full. "Over here, Tim!" called Roger Templeton.

"Squeeze in," said Roger, moving over to make room.

"Roanoke, Junior, how's it goin'? How's Ernie?"

"Haulin' books to th' Dumpster," said Junior. "We're just gettin' a bite to eat before we pitch in. I took a day's vacation to help."

"Is there any way he can dry the books out?"

"Nope," said Roanoke. "Dead inventory."

"What about Elmo?"

"Seems fine," said Roger, "but he won't come out from under the cash register."

"Junior, I heard you took somebody to ER yesterday. How'd that go?"

"Good mornin', Reverend, what can I get for you this mornin'?" It was Misty Summers, smiling at him and looking prettier, he thought, than the first time he saw her.

"Why, Misty! Did you break your arm?"

"No, sir, it got burned. Hot grease flew off the stove when Ernie's wall fell down."

"Aha." He glanced at Junior, who was lit up like a Christmas tree. "Well, I'm sorry to hear it and hope it heals soon."

"Thank you. It hurts really bad, but the doctor said it's going to be fine. Let's see, now, that was . . . umm, what did you order, sir? I forgot." For some unknown reason, Misty Summers was blushing like a schoolgirl.

"Coffee, no cream, and orange juice," said Father Tim.

"I'll be right back," she said.

"How bad is it at St. John's?" asked Roger.

"Pretty bad. The force of the tree across the roof racked the building to one side. Otis has a crew coming in. Did a good bit of damage."

"When we get Ernie straightened out," said Roanoke, "we'll be down an' give you a hand."

"Why, thanks," he said, touched by the offer.

Walking across the hall to Ernie's, he asked Roger, "By the way, what happened with Ava?"

"Darned if I know. Just out of the picture, it seems. Junior didn't have much to say about her."

"Well, well."

"Looked like a pretty uneven match, anyway."

"Right," said Father Tim, ducking into Ernie's and not liking what he saw.

In the book room, shelves that weren't anchored to the walls had been knocked sprawling, literally scattering books to the wind. The shelves on the fallen wall had crashed with the bricks, piling books among the debris. The smell of wet paper pulp filled the cold, drafty room, which was only loosely protected by the tarp.

Several of Ernie's fishing buddies were stacking ruined books in wheelbarrows.

He embraced the man who, from the beginning, had taken him in like family. "Sorry, my friend."

Ernie tried hard to produce a characteristic smile, but couldn't.

He was standing under the tent Sam had erected in the church-yard, drinking coffee with Leonard and Otis, peering at the endless rain and waiting for the contractor to arrive.

"You th' Rev'ren' Kavanagh?" An elderly man in a cap and slicker stepped under the tent.

"I am, sir."

"Albert Gragg."

Albert Gragg tipped his cap and shyly extended his hand. "I'm from up Dor'ster, Miss Ella sent me."

"I hope there's no trouble. . . ."

"She couldn't get you on th' phone. She's fell and broke her hip."

"No!" he said, stricken by the news. He hated to hear this. He didn't like this at all.

"A fracture or a break?"

"Clean break. She's in th' hospital and can't play y'r organ a'tall, said she'd call soon as she can get through."

"What happened?"

"In th' storm, said she heard somethin' hit her porch real hard, thought it was a limb offa that tree she thinks so much of, but it was th' neighbor's doghouse that was out there blowin' around. Said when she went runnin' out to check, th' rain had made 'er porch slippery as hog grease an' down she went. She got to th' phone, called me, an' I carried 'er to th' hospital."

"I hate to hear this. You're an old friend, Mr. Gragg?"

"Oh, forty years or more I been lookin' out for Miss Ella and 'er mama, doin' whatnot."

"God bless you for it. Who's her doctor?"

"I don't know, she didn't say."

"Tell her I'll be up as soon as I can, we've got a mess on our hands. Tell her she's in our prayers, and she can count on it."

"Yes, sir," said Albert Gragg, tipping his cap.

"And how's the captain and his brother, do you know?"

"What cap'n?"

"Captain Larkin."

"I can't say. I ain't seen him, he don't get out much. His boy carries his groceries in ever' week or two."

"Well, then," he said, feeling helpless. How many times had he wished there were two of him?

⁹⁄

Stanley Harmon stepped under the tent, wiping his bare, bald head with a handkerchief.

"Sorry about this, Tim. Awful sorry."

"Thank you, Stanley. It was a hard hit, all right. Any damage at your place?"

"A few limbs down is all. Y'all are welcome to worship with us on Sunday at eleven, or you could hold your service ahead of ours, at ten o'clock. How'd that be?"

"Terrific. That would be great. Thank you!"

"They say we'll have water by then, so th' commodes'll flush, but far as power goes, bring some candles."

"We'll do it."

"Looks like we won't have power 'til Wednesday. Mildred and I are cookin' on a Coleman stove. Y'all doin' all right over at Mid-Way?"

"Oh, fine, just fine."

"You can come stay with us, and I mean it. Mildred said she'd love to have you. Now the kids are off at school you'd have th' whole base-ment to yourselves, just y'all and our two dogs, Paul and Silas, they wouldn't hurt a fly."

"Thanks, Stanley, we'll hunker down at Mid-Way for a little while, shouldn't be long."

"What else'll you folks need Sunday?"

"I just learned our organist broke her hip."

"Uh-oh. Well, no problem, we've got a crackerjack organist, and come to think of it, he's played a few Anglican services here and there. I'll talk to him and let you know tomorrow. Run by First Baptist in the morning around eight. I'll show you the ropes, give you a key an' all."

"You'll get a crown for this, Stanley!" he called as his colleague dashed into the rain.

Coleman stove! That was the ticket.

Stanley ducked back under the tent. "Oh, shoot, I forgot we can't have organ music without power."

"True enough. How quickly we forget."

"Well, see you in th' morning."

A cappella, then, and no two ways about it.

Less than half the expected crew had shown up at Dove Cottage and, after hauling furniture out of the pit and stuffing it into the study, were tearing out the living room flooring.

According to Otis, the maverick porch had pulled the front wall away, causing the floor joists to collapse. The wall would have to be winched back before they could replace the flooring, and when that was done a crew would come in to do the refinishing. Bottom line, they were looking at a minimum of two or three weeks to complete the job, and the crew couldn't get to the porch before spring.

Hearing this exceedingly unwelcome news, he thought of Earlene Ferguson, who, lacking a porch at the retirement home, simply "dropped off in the yard like a heathen" when exiting her front door.

"Don't worry," said Otis, "I'll have some of my boys from th' Toe put your porch back on. I ain't scared of drivin' a few nails myself."

Shivering in the raw October air, Sam, Leonard, Otis, and Father Tim waited for the contractor, and surveyed the fallen limbs and debris littering the churchyard.

"We ought to stack th' limbs," said Leonard, impatient to get moving.

"No use stackin' limbs in this weather," said Otis.

Rain drummed on the tent roof.

Sam sighed. "Goodness knows, it's sad to see that old tree half ruined."

"It was probably two hundred years old, maybe more. Marjorie and I've seen any number of people married under that tree." Leonard poured coffee from a thermos. "Did you know there are trees still living since before the time of Christ?"

"Where at?" asked Otis.

Leonard blew on his coffee. "I don't know, I forgot. It was in a magazine."

"I ain't believin' it," said Otis.

When the contractor still hadn't arrived at eleven o'clock, Otis bit the end off a cigar, lit it, and, fuming, blew the smoke out his nostrils.

"I'm goin' to be kickin' some butt from here to Chincoteague," he declared, stomping from the tent.

"How'll we let everybody know where we're holding the service?" Marshall Duncan asked Father Tim. "And how will they know it's at ten, not eleven?"

Ray Gaskill hammered down on his toothpick. "Put a sign at th' post office today, so word gets around. Then put one in th' churchyard, people'll be comin' by to see th' damage."

The road crew roared past St. John's in a parade of heavy equipment, waving at the assembly under the tent.

"You want to see the basement?" Leonard asked Father Tim.

"Is it safe?"

"I wouldn't go down there," said Ray. "No, sir, not me."

"I believe I'll pass. Besides, I've got to run to the motel and take lunch to my wife."

"Where you goin' to get lunch?" asked Ray.

"Mona's."

"Not unless you want to stand in line in th' rain. I just come by there, it ain't a pretty sight. You could go to the grocery store, get you some Vienna sausages in a can, tuna in a can, all kinds of things in a can, and a loaf of bread, some mayonnaise . . ."

"Aha."

"And if I was you," said Ray, "I'd keep th' underside of your Mustang hosed off, you're gonna be eat up with rust."

He said nothing to Cynthia about the predicted duration of the job at Dove Cottage. If the thought of three weeks at the Mid-Way was enough to make him crazy, there was no telling what it might do to his wife.

"There's no way to patch it," said Sewell Joiner. "We're talkin' shore up, tear out, strip off, an' set straight—it's goin' to look a lot worse before it looks better."

"Whatever it takes," said Father Tim.

"We'll have to excavate part of th' basement and tear out and rebuild th' wall. You got a bad crack in th' bed joints of th' masonry—"

"We're more in'erested in th' sanctuary right now," said Otis. "What's it goin' to take to get us back in business?"

"First thing we'll do is get some rollin' scaffold inside and tear off th' plaster that's not already fallen off th' ceilin' joists and studs. We'll be tearin' off some sheathin' an' shingles and replacin' that busted roof joist, then we'll use a come-along to straighten th' whole thing up again an' put on a new roof."

"I'd like you to get your boys started in th' mornin'," said Otis.

"Tomorrow's Saturday," said the contractor.

"Go on and get 'em over here, we want to move on this thing. It's depressin' to ever'body not to see some action."

"Fine," said Sewell Joiner. "I can do that."

Otis unwrapped a cigar. "How long to get th' job done?"

"Two, three months if we got th' weather on our side. That'll include gettin' replastered and repainted."

Two or three months? Father Tim's heart sank like a stone.

At three o'clock, a crowd of parishioners had assembled under the tent, looking for a report on the damage, volunteering to help, offering consolation, and fervently commiserating. The rain drew on, shrouding the churchyard in a dusky gloom.

"I've got these little bitty mushrooms growin' between my toes," said Orville Hood, who kept St. John's oil tank filled.

"Let me *see*!" squealed Penny Duncan's youngest.

"I was sittin' in th' livin' room workin' a crossword when I thought th' world was comin' to an end." Maude Proffitt was swaddled in a yellow slicker and rain hat, with only her eyes visible. "Boom, somethin' hit right above my head. Honey, it was the *ceiling*, it just cracked open like a hen egg. Well, don't you know I jumped across th' room, my feet never touched th' floor! Thank th' Lord I didn't stay in that recliner another minute, or I'd've been pushin' up daisies right over yonder."

"Have a brownie," said Marjorie Lamb. "I baked these yesterday before the power went off."

"Law, what I wouldn't give for a cup of coffee to go with this," said Maude, eating the brownie in two bites.

Sue Blankenship's glasses kept trying to slide off her wet nose. "Did you hear th' Father's poor wife was hit by a picket fence?" she asked a baritone in the choir.

"No way! A whole fence?"

"Well, maybe just a picket."

Ann Hartsell, newly arrived from her nursing job across, saw the church and burst into tears. This caused her two youngsters, just fetched from day care, to erupt in a storm of sympathetic weeping.

"Have a brownie!" implored Marjorie, stooping to their level with the plastic tray.

"Th' trouble with this storm," said Ray Gaskill, "is mainly th' trees. It's *trees* that's done th' damage."

" 'Til I moved here, I never knew islands *had* trees," said Edith Johnson, who was an ECW bigwig.

Jean Ballenger shivered in her winter coat. "We nearly got the Last Supper finished, we're just working on the tablecloth. That much white seems to take forever. If you ask me, I don't believe all those men would have *used* a tablecloth."

"Do you think we should still try to have th' Fall Fair?" asked Mildred Harmon, handing around a plate of ham biscuits.

Father Tim turned aside from talking with the contractor. "Yes, *indeed*," he said. "Rain or shine!"

Jean patted her bangs in place. "What a relief! I couldn't bear the thought of all that work lying in a drawer 'til next year."

Early the following morning, the rain stopped.

He drove Cynthia, Jonathan, and Violet to Marion's, popped by First Baptist, and arrived at St. John's at eight-thirty as the five-man work crew blew in, on time and ready to roll.

By eleven o'clock, the sun came out, the temperature rose seven degrees, and a third of the north end regained running water.

"Hallelujah!" shouted Father Tim, tossing his rain hat in the air.

Otis stubbed out his cigar and pocketed the butt. "OK, boys, let's stack limbs."

Father Tim popped into the nave now and again to check the crew's progress. He was over the sick feeling, wanting only to see the work move ahead quickly.

Though pews and pulpit were under tarps, and plaster dust covered everything, the stained-glass window at the rear of the sanctuary was unharmed, with only minor cracking and pulling around the frame. The strong early light illuminated the image sharply, casting color onto the white tarps. *Come unto me....* That was sermon enough for this storm, he thought, or for any storm.

Each time he went inside, he glanced nervously at the choir loft, anxious for the safety and protection of the organ.

"No problem," said Sewell, who, Father Tim learned, was known to constituents as Sew, pronounced *Sue*.

He decided to stop worrying. If he couldn't trust a two-hundred-and-fifty-pound man who could kick in the remaining portion of a concrete-block basement wall, who could he trust?

He'd seen smaller crowds show up for Sunday worship.

By noon, more than half the parish had arrived, many with lunch bags from Mona's, some with family picnics. As the ground was too wet to sit on, they sat in parked cars, doors open, calling to one another, ambling through the tent where Sam had set up a folding table and a forty-two-cup coffeepot powered by a portable generator.

"Doughnut holes!" Jean Ballenger plunked down a box from the shop next door to her mainland hairdresser.

"Lookit!" said Ray Gaskill, who didn't want to miss out on the action. He lifted the lid of a bakery box, exposing half a cake, inscribed *HDAY TO RAY* in lime-green icing. "I was sixty-seven last July . . . that's August, September, October, it ain't but four months old and been in th' freezer th' whole time, help yourself."

Penny Duncan arrived with a gallon of sun tea, made before the rains began, and a freezer bag of thawed oatmeal cookies. Mona Fulcher dispatched Junior Bryson with a vast container of hot soup, a pot of chili, and a sack of cups and plastic spoons. Stanley Harmon dropped by with two thawed loaves of homemade bread from the freezer at First Baptist, along with a quart of apple juice he'd nabbed from the Sunday School.

Not knowing that his priest had already asked a blessing, and feeling his own heart so inclined, Sam Fieldwalker offered a fervent psalm of praise and petition.

"A double shot!" remarked someone who had happily bowed for both prayers.

Leonard Lamb popped a doughnut hole in his mouth. "We need a double shot," he said.

At two o'clock, his adreneline still pumping, he drove to the motel to fetch Barnabas for a run along the beach.

The heater had raised the temperature of the room to that of a blast furnace. He turned the heater off, snapped on the leash, and was out of there with a dog so relieved to be rescued that he slammed his forepaws against Father Tim's chest and gave his glasses a proper fogging.

The beach was more littered than usual, but nothing compared to the pictures he'd seen of Whitecap beaches in the aftermath of worse storms.

His brain felt petrified; he could scarcely think. For a man who'd been accused of thinking too much, it was an odd feeling, as if he were living his life in a dream, reacting to, rather than initiating, the circumstances that came his way.

He did know one thing for certain—he had to get his crowd out of the Mid-Way Motel, pronto.

Dodging the detritus of the storm, he ran easily, chuffing south toward the lighthouse and glancing at a sky so blue it might have been fired onto porcelain. The sea beneath was azure and calm, the water lapping gently at the sand.

He saw it, but thought nothing of it. Then, several yards down the beach, he stopped and looked again.

It was a little plane, bright red against the cloudless sky. He thought of his two jaunts into the wild blue yonder with Omer Cunningham, and the time Omer flew him to Virginia so he could attend Dooley's school concert. Blast, he missed the boy terribly. It had been four months since he saw him vanishing around the corner of Wisteria and Main on his bicycle. " *'Bye, Dad . . .* "

Barnabas skidded to a stop and barked furiously as the plane dipped toward the wide beach, then veered out over the water.

Father Tim stood and watched as it gained altitude and headed south. Did he see someone waving at him from the cockpit?

Probably not, but he waved back, just in case.

He was sitting on the bottom step of the walkway through the dunes, tying a shoelace, when he heard it.

Holy smoke, that plane was not only coming this way again, it was coming in low. Very low.

In fact, it was *landing. . . .*

It blew past him, contacted the sand, and bounced lightly along the beach. As it slowed, farther along the strand, the tail came up, then settled again.

He might have been plugged into an electrical outlet the way his scalp was tingling. It couldn't be, he thought, as he saw the doors open. . . .

But it was.

Barking wildly, Barnabas jerked the leash from under his foot and bounded toward the red plane and the people clambering out of it.

"Omer! Dooley!"

No, indeed, he would not bawl like a baby. He wiped his eyes on the sleeve of his jacket as he sprinted behind his dog. Amazing grace! Hallelujah! Unbelievable!

And it wasn't just Omer and Dooley.

"Pauline!" he yelled to the woman running toward him. *"Buck!"*

Dooley reached him first. "Hey," he said, throwing his arms around Father Tim, who hugged back for all he was worth.

"Hey, yourself, buddy, hey, yourself!"

Dooley cackled. "You're breakin' my ribs! Hey, ol' dog, ol' Barn, ol' buddy." Dooley fell onto the sand with Barnabas, as Pauline shyly gave Father Tim a hug, and Buck and Omer pounded him on the back to a fare-thee-well.

"This is my little Stinson Voyager," said Omer. His proud smile revealed teeth large enough to replace the ivories on an upright. "What d'you think?"

"Beautiful! Handsome! A sight for sore eyes!" said Father Tim.

Buck grinned at him, looking pounds lighter and years younger. "We buzzed over here a little bit ago, checkin' out th' beach. We thought it was you we saw."

"Yeah," said Dooley, "how did you know we were coming?"

"I didn't!"

"Cool."

Omer gave the Voyager's rear tire a swift kick. "Tundra tires. Got those special, since I knew I'd be comin' down on a soft field. By th' way, I had my buddy in Raleigh check it out, he said this end of th' beach was church property, so we could land here, no problem.

"Lookit!" Omer dragged him to the open door and pointed to a storage box behind the backseat. Father Tim smelled something wonderful.

"We're carryin' beef stew, we got fried chicken, we got bottled water, an' . . . what else we got?" he asked Pauline.

"The ham Emma baked for tomorrow!" said Pauline, flushed with excitement. "And Miz Bolick's orange marmalade cake."

"Yeah!" said Dooley. "Three layers! Plus stuff that Tony and Mr. Gregory and Anna sent, but it all smells like garlic."

Omer was busy pulling cargo from behind the seat. "Couldn't haul but forty pounds, what with icin' down th' food and carryin' three passengers, but we got more comin' next trip."

"Let me get a wheelbarrow," said Father Tim. "We're covered up with wheelbarrows at church."

Out of the corner of his eye, Father Tim saw several onlookers gathering.

"You probably don't want to leave it here long. Whitecap is full of nice people, but . . ."

"Oh, I ain't goin' to leave it here long a'tall. I'm makin' a run back to Mitford here in a little bit."

"Back to Mitford?"

"See, tomorrow mornin', I'm haulin' young 'uns."

"Poo and Jessie," said Dooley. "They're comin'."

"Ah," he said, trying to understand.

Dooley adjusted his ball cap. "You better tell 'im, Mama."

"Well," said Pauline. She looked suddenly shy. "Well . . ."

"We tried to call," said Buck, "but we couldn't get through."

"See, what it is," said Dooley, "is Mama and Buck want you to marry 'em tomorrow."

Buck Leeper, who had probably never blushed in his life, turned beet red. "If you don't mind."

"When I heard what was goin' on," said Omer, "I offered to fly 'em down here."

More hand-shaking, back-slapping, and riotous barking as his delirious dog dashed around them in circles.

Hauling a trunk full of food and water, he drove Dooley to the Fieldwalkers', where he let his wife weep the tears he was holding back. That was just one of the many conveniences of marriage, he thought, as Cynthia bawled and clung to Dooley like moss to a log.

On the way to St. John's, he figured Stanley would let him use the sanctuary for the wedding tomorrow afternoon. If that didn't work, surely they'd loan their basement hall. Then, if worse came to worst, there was always the Town Hall—not a pretty sight, but he'd heard of couples getting married there.

Whatever happened would have to happen fast.

Lord, he prayed . . .

They said goodbye to Omer, who was leaving with half the crowd trailing along to see the takeoff.

"What it is," Omer explained as they headed down the lane, "is a complete fabric aircraft. You've got your steel-tube fuselage with a fabric cover . . ."

"Could I go in th' church and look around?" asked Buck.

"Sure, grab a hard hat, I'll go in with you. The crew's packing up to leave. They'll be back on Monday and things will start to get serious around here."

Pauline beamed. "Buck don't have to go far to find a hard hat," she said. "May I come in, too?"

"Come on!" he said. "But watch your step. There's plaster lying forty ways from Sunday."

He called Sew Joiner aside. "Before your men leave, there's something I'd like them to do, if possible. We've just had a very . . . unusual request."

During the impromptu and elaborate meal at the Fieldwalkers', which Marion called a rehearsal dinner, Father Tim proposed a toast to Buck and Pauline. Buck, who was unaccustomed to much society, bobbed his head with awkward appreciation. Pauline smiled and held his hand, saying little, owing to the fullness of a heart overcome with wonder, and what she supposed might even be joy.

Before Tony's tiramisu was passed around, Cynthia and Pauline trundled off to the bedroom with a kerosene lamp to view the wedding frock. Father Tim loved hearing peals of his wife's laughter issuing from the room, as such frivolity had recently been as scarce as hen's teeth.

He put his arm around Dooley, noting that the boy was now a couple of inches taller than himself. He also checked the look on Dooley's face. Was he happy about his mother marrying Buck Leeper? As far as Father Tim could tell, the answer was yes, definitely.

Following an evening made more festive by candles and a crackling fire, Buck and Dooley were dispatched to Room Twenty-two at the Mid-Way. Pauline was invited to bunk in with the Fieldwalkers, who noted that the guest room leak had stopped and another chamber pot had been improvised.

Otis announced that the Kavanaghs would be moving on Tuesday afternoon into the million-dollar home of Martha Talbot, a seasonal resident from Canada who hadn't been in Whitecap for two seasons, due to a series of family weddings from Brazil to Portugal, not to mention Bar Harbor, Maine.

It was all quite breathtaking, thought Father Tim, as he climbed into his pajamas and fell, deeply weary and as deeply grateful, onto the lumpy bed of Room Fourteen.

But he couldn't sleep.

He lay listening to the hiss of the heater and his wife's whiffling snore. Jonathan thrashed and turned, kicking him in the ribs once, then twice.

Numb with exhaustion, he got up and put on his robe and slippers, lit the kerosene lantern, and sat in the worn armchair by the window. A ten o'clock service followed by a one-thirty wedding tomorrow, and here he was at half-past midnight, his eyes as big as the headlights on Loretta Burgess's eighteen-wheeler.

He went to the bathroom and did a glucometer check. Ah, well, no more tiramisu for him for a while; he'd be chopped liver tomorrow.

He took his Bible from the windowsill, opened it in the low light, and closed his eyes and prayed. *Thank you, Lord. . . .*

Let's face it, he could have been fished up from the bottom of Judd's Creek. The nail in the picket could have pierced Cynthia's eye instead of her hand. If Maude Proffitt hadn't jumped when she did, her ceiling would have landed on her head instead of her recliner. The list was endless. St. John's might have been completely demolished, the whole tree could have come down . . .

Jericho.

He jerked awake, realizing he'd dozed off. Out of the blue, a word had come upon his heart.

He saw the word in his mind as if it were inscribed on a blackboard with white chalk, *J E R I C H O.*

"Jericho," he whispered, puzzled. Barnabas stirred at his feet.

Lord, is this of You? Are you telling me something?

He examined his heart, and realized he felt the peace he always required in order to know whether God was in a particular circumstance.

Intrigued, he turned in his Bible to the Old Testament, to the sixth chapter of Joshua, and began to read:

"Now Jericho was securely shut up . . ."

Out of curiosity, Ray Gaskill opened the door of St. John's on Sunday around noon, and gaped at what he saw.

The shattered plaster had been hauled to either side of the nave and covered with tarps. The floor in the middle had been swept perfectly clean, the broken windows covered, and the rolling scaffolds parked neatly at the rear of the nave.

The pulpit had come out from under its tarp and shone with a lustrous coat of lemon wax, as did two pews that were aligned to face the pulpit. Oil-fired heaters, hissing warmth, flanked the pews on either side.

On a table before the altar, which was laid with an embroidered fair cloth and a silver chalice, paten, and candelabra, stood a vase displaying stems of gold leaves and red berries.

Above the wooden cross, the bright autumn noon gave its light through the window where He stood, arms outstretched, waiting.

CHAPTER TWENTY

Dearly Beloved

"Dearly beloved: We have come together in the presence of God, to witness and bless the joining together of this man and this woman in Holy Matrimony."

He knew most of the service by heart, never liking to see a priest's eyes glued to the prayer book instead of the congregation. He spoke the words today with unusually tender feeling.

"The bond and covenant of marriage was established by God in creation, and our Lord Jesus Christ adorned this manner of life by His presence and first miracle at a wedding in Cana of Galilee. It signifies to us the mystery of the union between Christ and His Church, and Holy Scripture commends it to be honored among all people.

"The union of husband and wife in heart, body, and mind is intended by God for their mutual joy; for the help and comfort given one another in prosperity and adversity . . ."

In the front row, Jessie played with the ruffle on her new dress, Poo gave the proceedings his absorbed attention, Dooley looked oddly proud and moved. Cynthia was beaming.

". . . therefore, marriage is not to be entered into unadvisedly or lightly, but reverently, deliberately, and in accordance with the purposes for which it was instituted by God.

"Into this holy union, Pauline Barlowe and Bernard Leeper now come to be joined."

There were enough teeth showing in Omer Cunningham's grin to play the Wedding March.

"Pauline, will you have this man to be your husband; to live together in the covenant of marriage? Will you love him, comfort him, honor and keep him, in sickness and in health; and, forsaking all others, be faithful to him as long as you both shall live?"

Pauline's response was a fervent whisper. "I will!"

Otis Bragg pulled a handkerchief from his plaid sport coat and blew his nose. Marion Fieldwalker dabbed at her eyes; Sam appeared personally pleased, as if the whole lot of Barlowes were, at the very least, first cousins.

"Bernard, will you have this woman to be your wife; to live together in the covenant of marriage? Will you love her, comfort her, honor and keep her, in sickness and in health; and, forsaking all others, be faithful to her as long as you both shall live?"

He saw Buck's eyes mist with tears. Then Buck cleared his throat and spoke in a voice that could be heard to the ceiling joists.

"I will!"

"Will all of you witnessing these promises do all in your power to uphold these two persons in their marriage?"

Dooley spontaneously stood, then sat again, as those assembled chorused in unison, "We *will*!"

He was choking up, himself. He touched his ear, a signal to his wife to pray for him, and step on it.

"Who gives this woman to be married to this man?"

Dooley rose from the pew and came forward, white-faced. Though his heart hammered with anxiety at the responsibility he was about to bear, he felt powerfully certain that this was a good thing; his mother would have someone to care for her, and for the first time ever, his brother and sister would have a real family.

The wedding feast was laid in the basement fellowship hall of First Baptist, where a motley collection of portable generators helped create the welcome aromas of garlic, coffee, hot rolls, and other comestibles, lightly dressed with the scent of gasoline from the generators.

The feast tables were covered with blue paper cloths, and decorated with boughs of red berries purloined from a stand of nandina behind the Sunday School. Votives glimmered on the tables, and along the top of the spinet by the kitchen door.

"Here they come!" someone shouted.

Laughing and excited, St. John's choir, joined by a baritone and soprano from First Baptist, assembled breathlessly in the middle of the room.

As the bride and groom entered, a cheer went up from all who had attended Stanley Harmon's morning service and were thus invited to the feast; then followed the exultant voices of the choir.

> *"Praise, my soul, the King of heaven*
> *to his feet thy tribute bring;*
> *ransomed, healed, restored, forgiven,*
> *evermore his praises sing:*
> *Alleluia, alleluia!*
> *Praise the everlasting King!"*

Pauline Leeper put both hands over her face like an unbelieving schoolgirl, and felt the arm of her husband go around her shoulders. Then she heard the oohs and aahs of her children, who stood beside her. She thought she might never again see, or be blessed with, anything so wondrous.

Following the blessing and subsequent hymn, Father Tim had a moment's thought of Jeffrey Tolson and the earnest choir he had abandoned. His heart felt suddenly moved toward the man; he wondered where he might be, whether he'd escaped harm during the storm, and if he ever longed for his children. Father Tim watched with both sadness and delight as Jeffrey's son made a beeline toward him with an Oreo cookie in each hand, eager to share one. He squatted and proffered the palm of his own hand, eager to receive it.

"Law, where'd this cake *come* from?"

"I don't know, plus, who could bake a cake without electricity? Does anybody know who brought it?"

"I heard it was flown in special."

"I declare, this is th' best cake I ever put in my *mouth*."

"I'd give an arm an' a leg for th' recipe, wouldn't you?"

"If nobody minds, I'm goin' to just scrape off these crumbs that're left and give 'em to Mama—then somebody, meanin' me, can lick th' plate it came on."

He had reserved a piece of the cake, which he wrapped in foil.

He also retrieved a large chunk of lasagna, the drumstick of a baked chicken, four slices of ham, and two biscuits, which he loaded onto a heavy-duty paper plate with a border of irises. He went to the cupboards and found a deluxe-size plastic cup, and stuffed it with potato salad.

Morris Love had been on his mind, and he couldn't shake the thought. He was alone in that dark, rambling house with only candles to light his way, and apparently no clue how to feed himself, unless Mamie was there to do it for him. Even so, she wouldn't have power for cooking, and no Stinson Voyager hauling in victuals.

Aha. A maverick deviled egg. He was tempted to eat it himself, being inordinately fond of deviled eggs, but popped it into a Ziploc sandwich bag. Oh, the infinite resources of a church kitchen . . .

He rummaged around until he found a large, empty jar, took the lid off, and sniffed it. Pickles. He rinsed it out with water from a plastic jug, and filled it with sweet tea.

"I'll be right back," he told his wife. "Looks like this will go on for at least another hour."

"Where on earth . . . ?" she asked, wondering at the bulging plastic grocery bag.

"I'll tell you later." He gave her a jovial kiss, square on the mouth.

Things were different now that the weather had turned cooler. There was no open window to shout to.

At the door, he stood on one foot and then the other, and scratched his head.

Why not ring the bell? That was an original thought!

He pressed the bell, but heard no results from inside. Maybe the bell had a quirk, like most doorbells, and had to be pressed in a certain

way. He pressed again. Nothing. What Morris Love needed was a *dog*,
for Pete's sake.

When he carved out the chunk of lasagna at church, it was still
warm. If he kept standing here, it would be cold.

Hardly believing his audacity, he opened the door and stuck his
head into the dim foyer.

"Morris!" he yelled, loudly enough to be heard upstairs. "Morris,
it's me, Tim Kavanagh! I've brought your *supper*!"

There, that ought to get a rise out of a man who was, for all he
knew, subsisting on Fig Newtons.

"Father . . ."

He nearly jumped out of his skin. Morris Love appeared from behind the stairwell, a ghostly apparition if he'd ever seen one.

"Holy smoke, Morris, sorry I was yelling when you were standing
right there."

"Come in," Morris said, not appearing to mean it.

He followed Morris into the cold and cavernous kitchen, illumined
only by two small windows above the sink, and set the bag on the table.

"The lasagna is still warm," he said. "I hope you'll eat it soon."

He felt like a mother coaxing a child, and stood back from the table, suddenly awkward.

"Thank you," said Morris, standing with his hands in the pockets
of a burgundy bathrobe.

Thank you? A mere *thank you*? He wanted to see the man tear
open the bag and dive in!

Father Tim opened the bag and pulled out the heavy plate and set
it on the table. "It's on a plate," he said, feeling progressively uneasy.
"You can just peel off the aluminum foil. And here's some tea, I put
lemon in it. . . ."

Somewhere in the house, a clock chimed three o'clock.

"Well . . . ," he said, not knowing what else to say.

"Your neighborly kindness will, I'm sure, guarantee your place in
heaven," said Morris.

Father Tim found his scowling countenance formidable in the
dusky light. "Ah, well, it's not kindness that gets us into heaven," he
said, feeling himself in quagmire to his knees.

Morris narrowed his eyes. "I would ask you to consider that I have lived alone without the sap of neighborly interaction for most of my life. And yet, over and over again, you would intrude upon the privacy and solitude I find agreeable. This behavior, which I fail entirely to understand, exhibits the most careless disrespect."

"But . . ."

"I am not a novelty, Father, some bizarre experiment to satisfy your prejudices about the essential spirituality of the human heart. I do not need your kindness, nor do I want your salvation."

"It is not my salvation."

"In addition, I do not desire your friendship, nor do I crave your admiration of my pathetic musical skills."

Father Tim felt an alarming weakness in his legs.

"One further thing. Save your breath, Father, and stop praying for me."

He found his ground, and stood it. "Save your own breath, Morris. I shall pray for you until . . ." His mind raced. *Until the Lord comes with his hosts? Until it suits me to stop?*

". . . until the cows come home!" He delivered this fervent declamation straight up and straight out, meaning it from the depths of his being.

He turned from the kitchen and walked quickly across the foyer, hearing the chilling and inevitable words that cut like knives.

"Out! *Out!*"

Closing the front door behind him, he trotted up the driveway in the late afternoon light that slanted through the canopy of trees.

They were crammed into Room Fourteen like sardines in a tin, seven of them, including Violet and Barnabas.

He thought the least they could do was give the Fieldwalkers and Lambs a break. Not only had their good friends pulled off a feast for more than forty people, they'd come in behind the work crew's cleanup and readied the altar and nave for the wedding.

Though a small and certainly impromptu wedding, he noted it was kicking up a considerable swirl of activity.

Buck had reserved a couple of additional rooms, which were in the process of being cleaned, for Omer and the kids, all of which occasioned the hauling of various sacks, pokes, and grips from Room Fourteen into adjacent quarters, with much trailing of vagrant socks

and sweaters, and leaving open of the door—a feature his dog particularly relished.

As Omer rambled in the village, and the newlyweds inspected the
island in one of Otis's pickup trucks, he and Cynthia put their heads
together about dinner. Should they even have dinner, since they'd
eaten at two-thirty? Children were always hungry, weren't they? Of
course.

But then, Mona's was shut tight as a clam on Sunday, which occasioned searching the yellow pages for what was open across, reminding
them of Cap'n Willie's, which seemed the perfect solution; further, he
learned that Pauline, Buck, and Jessie were flying home first thing in
the morning with Omer, and Harley was arriving this evening to fetch
Dooley and Poo back to Mitford early tomorrow, as Omer couldn't do
another double airlift, given his need to attend a huge going-away
party for his sister-in-law and outgoing mayor, Esther Cunningham,
imminently headed west with her husband in the RV.

Breathless, Father Tim reserved a room for Harley, whose reason
for an early departure tomorrow morning, according to Dooley, was
the emergency overhaul he was doing on the motor in Lew Boyd's
wrecker.

The crowd from next door returned, vibrating with energy.

He hated to bring up the unwelcome subject. "I thought you had
to be in court tomorrow morning."

"Oh," said Dooley. "I forgot."

"Forgot what?"

"Buster Austin went bawlin' to Chief Underwood and said he was
th' one that done it . . . did it . . . not me. He was scared out of his
mind about goin' in front of a judge, so they ain't . . . isn't . . . any
court. Not for me, anyway. Sorry I forgot to tell you. There was so
much goin' on. . . ."

Father Tim sank onto the foot of the bed, feeling as if a great
weight had rolled off his shoulders.

"Oh, somethin' else I forgot. Harley said your cousin Walter called,
said he couldn't get in touch with you down here, said he had somethin' to tell you about a lawsuit, somethin' really important, said to
call him."

The lawsuit!

The weight that had just rolled off, rolled back on and dug in.

"Ahh," he said, wanting nothing more than to seek the opiate of sleep, to put the lawsuit, the storm, the sickening confrontation with Morris Love, out of his mind.

He stood and put on his jacket. "Let's go for a ride," he said to Dooley. "I'll show you around the island."

"Cool," said Dooley. "I'll drive!"

"We want to go, *too!*" shouted Jessie.

Barnabas trotted to the door and sat, looking hopeful.

Poo raced from the bathroom. "Can we go see the lighthouse?"

"I could, I could go, too," said Jonathan, pulling on his hat and grabbing his coat.

Father Tim turned to his wife, who looked decidedly pale around the gills. "Hallelujah," she murmured.

"When we get back to that place we're stayin' at, you can be it," said Jessie.

"It what?" asked Poo.

"Th' husband."

"I don't want to be no husband."

"See, you can marry Jonathan, and I'll say th' words, 'cause I like them words."

"I ain't marryin' no baby," said Poo.

"I'm *not* a baby!" exclaimed Jonathan.

"Well, so Jonathan can be Buck, I can be Mama, and *you* can say th' words, then."

"Say what words?" asked Poo.

"Dearly belove-ud."

"I ain't sayin' that."

Dooley looked into the rearview mirror. "Don't say ain't!" he told his brother.

He lay curled in the fetal position, his back to his wife and Jonathan, feeling a kind of numb pain he couldn't explain or understand. Life was a roller coaster, that simple. Joy and healing here, desperation and demolition there.

With all his heart, he'd desired healing for Morris Love's brokenness, and who was he to think he might give a leg up to such a miracle? There were times when he didn't like being a priest, always on the front line for justice and mercy and forgiveness and redemption; trying to figure out the mind of God; giving the Lord his personal agenda, then standing around waiting for it to be fulfilled. He didn't have an agenda for Morris Love, anymore; he was giving up the entire self-seeking, willful notion. His desperate neighbor belonged to God; it was His responsibility to get the job done. He had schlepped in a paltry sack of victuals when what the man needed was the awesome, thunderstriking power of the Almighty to move in his heart and soul and spirit like a great and consuming fire. . . .

He wiped his eyes on his pajama sleeve.

"So, Lord," he whispered, "just do it."

Though he managed to spend a full half hour with Buck, he had almost no time with Dooley. On Monday morning, he insisted on making the breakfast run to Mona's, and let Dooley drive. They arrived at Mona's as she opened the doors, and waited in the front booth while the kitchen pulled together sacks of sausage biscuits, ham biscuits, fries, Danish, coffee, milk, and Coke for the crowd at Mid-Way.

"How are things with Caroline?" He already knew about Dooley's grades, which were excellent and worthy of all praise. Now he was going for the nitty-gritty.

Dooley reached into the neck of his sweatshirt. Grinning, he pulled forth a small gold ring, set with a single pearl and attached to a chain he was wearing around his neck.

"What does that mean . . . umm, exactly?"

Dooley shrugged. "Just . . . you know."

"Right. Ever see Lace?"

"I ran into her at the drugstore one Saturday. She was in White Chapel with a bunch of girls."

"Did you talk?"

Dooley shrugged again. "Not exactly."

Oh, well. Time would tell.

The boy was becoming handsome, that simple. Father Tim observed sinew gathering on his bones, and noted that his long, slender fingers would be well suited, indeed, to his calling. "Any more thoughts on whether to vet small animals or large?"

"Both," Dooley said with feeling. "I want to vet both."

"Good!" he said. "Good."

"Harley, thanks for making such a long trip. Sorry Omer's plane won't hold but four."

"Don't even think about it, Rev'rend. Hit was good t' git on th' road."

"What do you see of our tenant?"

"Seen 'er twice. She looked kind of hunkered down, like she's scared of 'er own shadow. Somebody said she was lettin' 'er piana students go, an' headin' back up north. She ain't tryin' to run out on th' rent, is she?"

"Oh, no, she's paid up. Well, God be with you, Harley, Poo, Dooley."

" 'Bye, Dad."

" 'Bye, Buddy. See you down here for Christmas, OK?"

"OK!"

"Harley, we want you to come, too."

"Yes, sir, Rev'rend, we'll be here."

"All right, hold her between the ditches."

Feeling a kind of emptiness, he watched the red truck pull out of the motel parking lot and head left on the highway toward Mitford.

"Fella down th' beach said he was sittin' on his deck, said he'd just pulled out his glasses to read th' paper when a book fell in his lap, *whop.*"

"No kidding." He had to get out of here fast; he'd only popped by to see how Ernie's reconstruction was coming.

"I'm tellin' you!" said Ernie, who appeared to be more like his old self. "*Th' Mustangs* by Frank Dobie is what it was. That book come right offa my shelf."

"Amazing," he said, wanting to be respectful.

"Bull," said Roanoke.

"Th' storm was Thursday, th' book dropped in 'is lap Sunday.

Must've blowed somewhere to dry off, then was picked up by a stiff wind and sent south."

Roanoke fired a match head under the tabletop and lit a Marlboro. "I ain't believin' that."

"Told me he liked th' book all right, but wouldn't give two cents for th' endin'."

"That's gratitude for you," said Roanoke.

He didn't want to do this, not at all.

"Walter Kavanagh here."

"Walter . . ."

"Timothy! What in blazes happened down there?"

"Storm. Bad. Busy." Sheer dread had reduced his speech to primitive monosyllables.

"Well," said Walter, "I'm afraid you're not going to like this."

"It never once occurred to me that I might like it."

"D'Anjou says a love letter accompanies the holographic will, which makes the old man's personal feelings and legal intentions perfectly clear and in accordance with the will."

"How do we know it's Josiah's Baxter's handwriting and not some forgery?"

"D'Anjou seems to believe that matter is sufficiently demonstrable in court, he didn't say how. Frankly, I think d'Anjou is behind this thing and pushing hard. He's been minding the family's affairs for years. I get a sense of personal greed here. If it were my case, I wouldn't feel so confident—I mean, no one coming forward for fifty years? But he thinks he can convince the jury."

"What about the money Miss Sadie left to Dooley?" Walter and Cynthia were the only other living souls who knew that Miss Sadie had left Dooley more than a million dollars in trust. "That was her mother's money. Surely this legal action couldn't—"

"No, I don't think so. Don't get ahead of things, Timothy. In any case, it looks like we have to go through with this. I'll work with you on the response to the court; we've got three weeks to pull it together. Can you call me Wednesday night? I have some ideas."

Though he knew full well there was no sorrow in heaven, he hoped, nonetheless, that Miss Sadie wouldn't get wind of this deplorable mess. Shortly before her death, she'd learned of an illegitimate half-sister, born to her mother before she married Josiah Baxter. This dark secret, however, had an exceedingly bright side—Miss Sadie ended up with Olivia Harper as her beloved grandniece, which had been, of course, an inarguable benediction.

But another illegitimate half-sister? It seemed like pure fiction; he hated to think what this lawsuit might have done to his old friend and parishioner if she were still living.

In ways he couldn't yet fully understand, he sensed his life would be entwined with Sadie Baxter for the rest of his days.

At one o'clock on Tuesday, he drove to the Mid-Way from a couple of home visits, and helped Cynthia load Jonathan's things into the car. Jonathan talked endlessly.

"I'm goin' home, Cyn'dy."

"I know, dear."

"Will you come an' see me?"

"Of course."

"An' you can see Babette an' Jason, too."

"Will you come and see us?"

"Maybe I could sometime." Jonathan put on his hat.

"We'll bring your movies later. They're at our house that fell down in the front."

"You could, you could watch 'em again before you bring 'em to my house. That would be OK if you want to."

He glanced at his wife as they piled into the car, and felt her suffering as his own.

He was fairly stunned when he saw Martha Talbot's house, sitting quite alone at the end of an oyster-shell lane. A million smackers rising off the undeveloped bank of the Sound was a pretty impressive sight.

"Wow," Cynthia whispered.

"You must be living right, Kavanagh."

They parked in the two-car garage, simply because it was a luxury to have one, and went up the stairs to the front door.

"Here," he said, giving her the key. "You do the honors."

As the door swung open, they stood looking across the sunlit living room and through the wall of windows to the Sound. The water lay as smooth as a lake, glinting in the sun.

His wife gave a small gasp of wonder and delight.

"Now we're talking!" she said.

They prowled through the spacious house like a couple of kids, amazed at their discoveries. Central vacuum system, enormous fireplace in both living room and master suite, glorious views all around, a room with the right light and location for her work, a room with a comfortable and easy spirit for his study, an intercom system, a large kitchen in which they felt decidedly lost, and a media room that, thanks to its dumbfounding technology and wall-size television screen, caused them to shut the door hastily.

They thumped onto one of two sofas in the living room, thinking to build a fire against the chill.

"Well," he said.

"Well," she said.

He wouldn't have mentioned it for the world, but he wished they had Jonathan to put some life in this place.

"Let's unload the car, then. I'll bring Barnabas and Violet up."

"Wouldn't it be marvelous if we had power?" she mused.

"Just in case, try the lamp."

Sixty watts sprang to life at her touch. "Thanks be to God!" they shouted in spontaneous unison.

They leaped up and dashed to the kitchen and turned on the faucet, which spat and chugged and released a brackish stream of water into the sink.

"Try the phone!" she crowed.

A dial tone!

"The heat . . ." They trotted in tandem, searching for a thermostat.

Having located it at the end of the hallway, they grabbed each other and exchanged a fervent hug as the furnace roared into action.

"Priest and deacon die and go to heaven!" he whooped.

Ah, but no million-dollar house on the Sound could ease the sorrow of his wife's heart.

He lay in the strange bed and held her as she wept.

Maybe the bright, three-quarter moon was keeping him awake. . . .

He got up and looked through the French doors that gave onto the upstairs deck. A ribbon of platinum cascaded across the water. Only a mile and a half from Dove Cottage and they were in another world. A miraculous thing.

He closed the draperies over the doors, patted his sleeping dog at the foot of the bed, and lay down again.

He remembered the sleepless exhaustion that had helped crank his diabetes into high gear.

Hadn't Hoppy advised him to find a good doctor when he arrived? Of course. But had he done it? No way.

No more excuses, he promised himself. He would inquire around first thing tomorrow morning. And he must rid his mind of the lawsuit. It was useless to worry and fret about this alarming thing. He and Walter would do what they could; beyond that, he was dependent upon grace alone.

Be anxious for nothing . . .

He began to mentally recite one of the verses he'd tried to live by for a very long time.

. . . but in everything, with prayer and supplication, with thanksgiving, make your requests known unto God, and the peace that passes all understanding will fill your heart and mind through Christ Jesus.

"Ahhh," he sighed.

Jericho.

Not that again.

Lord, I'm no mind-reader. Reveal to me, please, what You're talking about here.

He tried to open his heart and mind to the answer, but dozed off and fell, at last, into a peaceful slumber.

As twilight drew over the Sound, he heard the front bell ring and trotted to the door, wondering who'd be poking around out here.

He saw a car parked in the circle, and a woman standing at the foot of the steps. Before him on the stoop were two small persons in pirate costumes, and a very much smaller person clad in a sheet and extending a plastic pumpkin in his direction.

"Trick or treat!" said Jonathan Tolson.

Feeling oddly distant from one another as they sat in the chairs that flanked the fireplace, they piled onto a sofa. "You know what I'm craving?" she asked.

"I can't begin to know."

"Your mother's pork roast with those lovely angel biscuits."

"My dear Kavanagh, who was it who refused to tote the Dutch oven on our journey into the unknown?"

"I was wrong and I admit it. Can't you make her roast without it?"

"I never have."

"Does that mean you never will?"

"A pork roast in that oven is a guaranteed, hands-down success. Why should I be tempted to veer off on some reckless tangent, like wrapping it in foil or roasting it on a pizza pan or whatever?"

"You're using your pulpit voice," she remonstrated.

"A thousand pardons," he said, getting up to fiddle with the dials on the home entertainment system and trying to make something, *anything,* happen.

"Julia Child didn't require a Dutch oven to make a pork roast," she said, arching one eyebrow.

"And how did you come by this arcane knowledge?"

"I looked it up in her cookbooks in our new kitchen."

"Well," he said, not knowing what else to say.

"Five pounds of flour . . . ," she murmured, making a list. Cynthia Kavanagh was bound and determined to have biscuits on her dinner plate, whate'er betide.

"Do we really want to buy flour, only to haul it back to Dove Cottage?"

"How long do you expect we'll be here?"

"They said the job will probably take three weeks, four at the most."

"Right. Now, double that prediction, thanks to lumber that doesn't arrive on time or is out of stock altogether, and for the crew who decides to go to another job for a whole week, and the rainy weather that makes the floor too tacky for us to move in for ten days, and . . . you get the idea."

"Two months," he said. "Buy the flour."

Cynthia saluted him with her glass. "Here's to Martha Talbot!"

"And here's to Miss Child, bless her heart!"

He wouldn't admit it, of course, but this was as toothsome a pork roast as a man could want, not to mention their first square meal at Sound Doctrine, the name they found engraved on a plaque at the door.

"Three guesses!" said Emma, munching what sounded like popcorn.

"Andrew won by a landslide!"

"Well, he won, all right, but not by a *landslide*, a lot of people who were born in Mitford voted for Coot. Anyway, guess what else."

"Just tell me and get it over with."

"No, you have to guess. Guess what's going to happen to Coot as soon as Andrew's sworn in."

"He'll be the envoy to our sister village of Mitford, England?"

"No, but I love the idea of a sister village! Somebody ought to recommend that to Andrew, he'd pick right up on it. Guess again."

"I give up." After one guess, she usually let him off the hook.

"Andrew's goin' to appoint him to chair a historical committee!"

What he'd always feared might be true, he now knew for a fact—in appointing Coot Hendrick to chair any committee at all, Andrew Gregory had proved to be a man of far greater largesse than himself.

He'd done his utmost to sever the umbilical cord that typically united a parish to a long-term priest, and felt it was at last a done deal. Indeed, he hadn't heard a word from Esther Bolick or anybody else at Lord's Chapel in a month of Sundays. So, the heck with his interim bishop and two-for-a-penny wisdom, he was calling the Bolicks.

"Esther?"

"Who's this?"

"How quickly you forget. It's your old priest."

"Father Hammond?"

"Esther!"

"Just kidding. How in th' world are you? We hadn't heard from you in a coon's age."

"Lots to do in a new parish, but I think about you and Gene and pray for you faithfully. How is he?"

"Better. I've tried to stop worryin' myself sick."

"I'm very glad to hear it. And you may be glad to hear that your fame now extends to Whitecap. In truth, I'm calling with a total of eleven requests for your marmalade cake recipe. I know you don't give it out, but they implored me to ask."

"Eleven?" He didn't know whether she was pleased with the number or disappointed.

"I'm sure as many more are interested, but I've personally received the names of eleven, including that of the Baptist preacher who's renowned for his lemon meringue pie."

"Oh, all right," she said, "I don't see why not. That recipe's been bootlegged forty ways for Sunday, anyhow."

"They'll be thrilled, and not only that, I'll be a hero."

"Cynthia has a copy I told her she could use. She can pass that around."

"Yes, but it's in Mitford. Do you think you could mail me a copy?"

"I declare, that recipe will pester me to my grave. But I'll do it. What's your address?"

"Just send it to St. John's, post office box fourteen." He gave her the zip code. "Bless you, Esther."

"Father Talbot moved into that big house up th' street from the Harpers. He's th' handsomest thing you'd ever want to see, an' th' whitest teeth, oh, mercy. . . ."

He seemed to recall hearing this before.

"We think he bleaches, you know, wears what they call bleach trays, like people on TV."

"So, I'm glad to know Gene is—"

"And *nice?* You wouldn't want to *see* nicer! Crosses th' street to talk to you, waves at you from his car . . . not to mention has been to visit Gene on a house call, and he was just *installed* two days ago!"

"My goodness," he said, quoting Sam.

"And his children—why, they're meek as lambs and smart as whips, plus you should see his wife, she's a regular movie star. And *preach*? Up a *storm*! Why, he brings th' house down! We're goin' to tie his leg to the altar, is what Gene says. This one's too good to let get away."

"Ahhh," he said, exhaling.

He and Walter had talked for more than an hour, but he felt precious little consolation.

What should he do, if anything, about the rumor she was moving back to Boston? Didn't she owe him the courtesy of telling him she was leaving? On the other hand, what did courtesy have to do with anything—under the circumstances?

Walter suggested he lie low on that one, but go ahead and inform the Hope House board of the lawsuit.

He dreaded this like the plague, for more reasons than one. He would wait until after the weekend, when things were . . . calmer. At the moment, St. John's was under exterior scaffolding front to back, a Bobcat was digging out part of the basement, and a backhoe was on the job, doing God knows what. As anyone in their right mind could see, this was no time to call a board and relay bad news.

As he and Cynthia offered their nighttime prayers, he exhorted the Lord with something from "St. Patrick's Hymn at Evening."

" 'May our sleep be deep and soft,' " he whispered, " 'so our work be fresh and hard.' "

His wife, who was again going at her book hammer and tong, liked St. Patrick's way of putting it.

Nonetheless, he still wasn't sleeping soundly.

And he could scarcely believe what he felt God was writing upon his heart.

"You're sure about this?" he asked aloud, standing on the upstairs deck at sunset. A snowy egret flew over the roof and settled into the tall grasses at water's edge.

"I'd hate to get this wrong," he said.

Then again, if he got it wrong, what did he have to lose?

Nothing.

Nothing to lose, and everything to gain.

He spent much of Monday morning speaking with Hoppy Harper and other members of the board. They were shocked, of course. But he was glad he made the calls, because they were rallying together, and he felt the encouragement of it.

They agreed that it was a blow, but if the suit succeeded, they felt they could replace the money via other avenues.

He felt the encouragement, yes, but in the very pit of his stomach was a sick feeling that appeared to be lodged in for the long haul.

"Barnabas and I are going to walk around the old neighborhood, see what's what." Nine o'clock, now, and a meeting at ten with Sewell Joiner at the church. Perfect timing.

"And please do something about cleaning up the car," said Cynthia. "It looks like a farm wagon."

"Consider it done."

"I don't know what you *do* to cars," she muttered.

"We had a storm, remember?"

"But that was days ago, and the rust is going to leap onto the fenders any minute, mark my words."

"Rust . . ."

"It's a living thing, you know. It *grows.* Have you noticed the cars and trucks running around down here? There's hardly anything left but chassis and steering wheel."

"Surely you exaggerate."

"Surely I do, but please—washed and waxed and whatever else it needs; I must have it tomorrow to go up hill and down dale."

"Tomorrow's supposed to be a beautiful day, you could ride your Schwinn."

"Not if it's under Morris Love's stairwell."

"Good point," he said. "See you for lunch."

After checking the progress at Dove Cottage, he began his first march around the wall of Nouvelle Chanson by walking east from the iron gate, hooking a left on Hastings, and praying as he went.

Staying hard by the wall, he trotted north on Hastings and rounded the corner into the lane that dead-ended in front of Ernie's.

He saw the figure up ahead, crossing the lane toward the Love wall. It was someone tall and slender, dark in color, and, though carrying what appeared to be a grocery bag in either arm, moving gracefully.

"Easy," he said to his dog, who was always curious about who and what crossed their path.

Though trying not to stare, he witnessed the sudden collapse of a paper bag, and saw items go spilling onto the sandy lane. Grapefruits rolled hither and yon.

He sprinted ahead.

"Here, let me help!" he said to the woman. "Barnabas, sit!"

Barnabas didn't sit; he reared on his hind legs so he might greet the stranger who stood looking at him with alarm. Grabbing his dog, Father Tim trotted to a small tree growing outside the wall and fastened the leash around it.

"There. I'm sorry. He's harmless." He went to his knees and began collecting grapefruits and bananas, sticks of butter that had burst loose from their package. . . .

"At least there were no eggs," he said, looking up at the elegant, dark-skinned woman who looked down upon him.

"Thank you kindly." Her voice was soft and lilting—genteel, he thought. "That's a big dog," she said simply.

"He is that. Well, now, what shall we put all this in?"

"I'll go back to the house and get my basket," she said. "I almost never carry groceries without my basket, but this mornin' . . . if you'd watch this for me, I'd thank you."

"Be glad to," he said, taking the other bag from her arm.

She walked toward the house at the opposite side of the lane, a house he'd often noticed and admired for its tidy appearance and large, well-tended garden. He'd exchanged greetings with a man working the garden one summer evening, and had occasionally seen a wash hanging on the clothesline. In a world that seldom displayed its wash on a line, the sight always, and happily, took him back to his boyhood.

He stood guarding the small pile of groceries, organized neatly in the middle of the lane, as she left the house and came toward him carrying a large basket. He thought she moved regally for her age, though he couldn't really determine her age.

"Always, always, I use this basket," she said pleasantly, "and this mornin', wouldn't you know . . ."

Together, they stooped down and loaded the basket.

"May I carry it for you?" he asked.

"No, sir," she said, standing. "I'm just goin' right through there." She pointed to an opening in the thick hedge that camouflaged the wall.

"Ah. Morris Love's place."

"Yes, sir."

"You're Mamie," he said, noting her carefully braided hair and the printed scarf tied round like a headband.

"Yes, sir, I'm Mamie. And you're the preacher whose wife sent Mr. Love that nice banana bread."

"I am!" He was as excited as a child. "So pleased to meet you, Miss, Mrs. . . ."

"Just Mamie is all," she said.

"Sure I can't carry that for you? I'd be happy to."

"Thank you, I've been carrying this basket through there for more years than I care to reckon. Well, I hope you'll tell your wife that Mr. Love enjoyed the taste of lemon in her bread."

"Oh, I will. And thank you. Thank you!" A woman with a strong and lively spirit. . . .

Feeling strangely moved and oddly blessed he watched her disappear along a well-worn path through the opening in the wall.

He looked eagerly for her when he circled the wall on the second day, which was Wednesday, but she didn't appear. What he did see was a small wash, neatly arranged on the clothesline and flapping smartly in the November wind.

He received the welcome sight as a sign, a confirmation, and walked on, praying.

He timed his walk around the wall on Thursday for nine-fifteen, which was when they had met, but Mamie was nowhere to be seen. The sight of smoke puffing from her chimney gave him a curious delight, and he wondered why he had such a strong desire to see her again.

He trotted to the end of the lane and then, as he turned left around the wall, the answer came.

It was as if he'd found someone who'd been lost to him for many years.

"Timothy, ring Harley, he's at Lew Boyd's. I wrote the number by the phone."

"How's the book coming?" he called as he popped into his study at Sound Doctrine.

"Great! I've something to show you after dinner!"

It had taken his wife, who was surprisingly shy about her work, a good two years to open up and really share her work with him. So he was always pleased when . . .

"Lew! Tim Kavanagh here. How's it going?"

"Pretty good, soon as we git this wrecker rollin' again."

"Harley's the one for the job, all right. Is he around?"

"Hold on, and come see us, hear?"

He heard the cash register ring; Lew shouted for Harley; someone asked directions to the restroom.

"Harley speakin'."

"Harley! You called?"

"Yes, sir, I did. Let me get on Lew's cordless."

Static, shuffling around, a horn blowing.

"OK, I'm out at th' grease pit, cain't nobody hear."

He didn't want any bad news, no way. . . .

"Hit looks like I've found y'r angel that was stole."

CHAPTER TWENTY-ONE

True Confessions

"An' you'll not believe where at," said Harley.

"Where?"

"You know that ol' car of Miss Pringle's? Well, she brought it in to git th' fluids changed an' said she'd be travelin' in it pretty soon an' was wantin' it to be safe an' whatnot. Lew was up to th' post office so I said, fine, I'll look after it."

"Right, right."

"She walked up th' street an' I got t' checkin' it out, an' seen 'er tars needed rotatin'. See, I had 'er keys an' all, an' a little time t' do it, so looked like she'd want me to, so I opened up 'er trunk and lifted that panel in there to see if I could find 'er wheel key. Well, see, they's this deep pocket, you might say, on either side under th' panel. I looked in one side an' th' key wadn't in there, an' they was what looked like a sheet stuffed in th' other side."

He was on the edge of his chair.

"So I pulled th' sheet out to look an' Lord help, there was that angel you had on y'r mantelpiece."

He would not jump to conclusions. "About twenty inches high?"

"Yes, sir. An' kind of a dirty gold."

Bronze. "What sort of base?"

"Marble, looked like."

"What color was the marble?"

"Green. An' since she hadn't asked me direct t' do anything but change th' fluids, I didn't do nothin' to 'er tars, or she might figure I found somethin'. When she come back, I jis' said, Miz Pringle, y'r tars need rotatin'."

He sat back in the chair and felt the beating of his heart.

He preferred acting to reacting.

If Hélène Pringle was leaving for Boston, he needed to act fast.

Certainly, he didn't want to focus on this nasty piece of news as he made his fourth trip around the wall. He wanted to keep his mind and heart free of personal anxiety, so he could pray with an unfettered spirit.

God help me, he thought, as he parked the Mustang at the side of Dove Cottage and set off for Hastings with his dog.

Ernie was standing in the parking lot with a couple of fishermen, and hailed him to come in. Without breaking stride, he raised his hand and waved. "I'll be back!" he called.

The glass had been replaced, the side wall was up, and except for some old bricks that hadn't been hauled away, Books, Bait & Tackle was looking fairly normal.

He was only a few yards this side of the passage in the wall when Mamie came through the front door of her house, carrying an empty wicker laundry basket.

"Good morning, Mamie!"

"Good mornin,' Father. How do you like this weather?"

"Oh, I like it. Crisp!"

"My husband built us a good fire again this mornin'. They're calling for frost tomorrow."

As she stepped into the lane with him, he couldn't contain his question another moment. "May I ask where you were educated?"

"Virginia," she said softly. "Mr. Redmon sent me off to a school for young ladies of color. I was sixteen when I left Whitecap, and came home again when I was twenty."

"Ah," he said. Her gentle elegance was balm to his soul.

"Mr. Redmon had his enemies, but he wasn't a bad man, Father, not at all. He gave my mother this house."

"I like your house!" he said, meaning it.

"I remember when Mr. Morris was born, the year before I went to Virginia. I hated to leave him. He couldn't hold his head up 'til he was several months old and couldn't walk 'til he was two and a half. He was . . . special, something told me that."

"His mother . . . ?"

"His mother ran away from her baby. She could never bear to be with him. He had middle-ear infections for the first few years, and used to cry and cry with the pain. Mr. Redmon had all kind of doctors come here, and then Mr. Morris got the base of his skull operated on. There was no end to the suffering, it seemed. No, his mother ran away and stayed most of her life in Europe. Her and Mr. Redmon's other son died in a bad house fire. It was my own mother who took care of Mr. Morris 'til I came home and helped out."

"I see."

"I don't have any idea why I'm standing here talking to you like this, Father, except I believe you to be a kind man. I wouldn't want Mr. Morris to know we talked about such things."

"No, it's between us."

"I've spent many a year trying to help heal the hurt, but there's only One who can heal."

"Yes." He gazed directly into her eyes, finding a kind of refuge he couldn't name. "Morris is blessed to have you."

"I'm blessed to have him. I never dreamed I'd stay on in Whitecap after I saw a little of the world, but I came home and married a good man, and then, when the Lord took Mother . . ."

"Yes?"

". . . I began treading the path through the hedge, just as she'd done for so long."

"Are there any regrets, Mamie?"

"No regrets. Noah and I raised a fine son. He's a doctor in Philadelphia. He looks in on Mr. Morris every time he comes home."

He was happy to hear everything this unusual woman had to tell him, feeling honored, somehow, that she would talk with him at all.

"I see in your face that you understand Mr. Morris, how he's suffered."

He didn't reply. How could he understand?

"He's known a lot of cruelty in this life. Mr. Redmon demanded an awful lot of him. Yet, look at the gift he's been given. Mother was proud of that, and so am I."

"I hope to meet your husband one day. We said hello this summer. And if you ever take a notion to visit St. John's, we'd love to have you."

"Noah and I go across to church. There were never many people of color on Whitecap. Big Daddy Johnson used to take us across in a little fishing boat, then the ferry came, and then the bridge."

"Were you born here?"

"My people washed up on shore like timbers from the old ships. We think our wreck happened sometime around 1860."

"I've kept you far too long, Mamie, forgive me. You're an interesting and gracious lady, and it's a privilege to have this time together."

"I hated that Mr. Morris had nothing to offer when you and your family visited. The next day was grocery day, and what we had on hand, he couldn't heat in the oven."

"By His grace, we had a feast, and food for the soul, as well!"

"I hope we'll meet again," she said, stepping onto the path with her laundry basket.

"The Lord be with you!" he called after her.

She turned and looked back. " 'And with thy spirit!' " she said, quoting the prayer book. "That school I went to in Virginia was an Episcopal school." She smiled, then turned again and vanished along the path.

"You don't know when she's leaving?"

"No."

"Issue a search warrant for her arrest," said his cousin.

"What?"

"Immediately."

"But . . ." Hélène Pringle in *jail*? That meek little woman whose feet didn't touch the floor when she sat down?

"Call your local police chief, that guy you're such buddies with, and describe the angel. Tell him to search her car trunk. If it's not in the car, they'll search the house. You told me the angel has some value?"

"I'm guessing three, maybe even four thousand dollars."

"You can have her arrested for felonious larceny, not to mention felonious breaking and entering. That's a Class H on both counts. If she's convicted, we're talking up to ten years each count. Chances are, she'd get off with three years for each Class H, but for a piano teacher, that's a very long time."

He hung up, stricken over this sordid turn of events.

He and Cynthia would talk and pray about it tonight, and make the decision regarding a search warrant in the morning. He'd never had anyone arrested, and certainly not a woman, but was that the issue here? Wasn't the issue about money being wrongfully gouged out of the Hope House coffers? If it hadn't been for Miss Sadie's meticulous thrift and careful investing, there may not have been any money there at all. Didn't that count for something?

He realized he was once again sitting with his head in his hands.

Whatever the morning's outcome, he could not, would not, miss his fifth walk around the wall.

He called Rodney Underwood at home at eight a.m.

"Rodney, I have a disagreeable piece of business for you."

"I don't guess it's anything as big as th' man in th' attic; prob'ly won't ever get another deal like that." Rodney was talking about the jewel thief who lived in the attic at Lord's Chapel until he turned himself in to local authorities during a Sunday morning worship service.

"I'd like you to take a search warrant to the rectory. I have reason to believe my tenant stole the angel."

The spoken words chilled his blood. He was saying things that couldn't be taken back.

"Unknown to her, Harley Welch found the angel in the trunk of her car while it was at Lew Boyd's."

"You sure it's th' same one? Did he give you a good description?"

"Yes. About twenty inches high, bronze, green marble base."

"You lookin' to search just th' car or you think we ought to have a warrant for the house, too?"

"Both, to be safe."

"It takes a little while to process a search warrant, but I'll personally get right on it."

"What happens if you find the statue?"

"We'll take 'er into custody, take 'er over to th' magistrate in Wesley. He'll prob'ly put an investigative hold on 'er for about twelve hours 'til we get th' statute fingerprinted, get photographs an' all."

"The statue . . ."

"Right, th' statute."

He called Walter. "I didn't like doing it, but it's done."

"Good. When they have the angel in hand, let me know and I'll call her attorney."

In truth, he was only doing what was within the law, but he was literally nauseous over it. So was Cynthia. Oddly, taking legal steps against an unlawful act had made them both feel like criminals.

He didn't want to see Mamie or anyone else this morning. He put his head down and walked quickly, focusing his mind and spirit entirely upon Morris Love and the look on Morris's face as he was ordered from Nouvelle Chanson for what may have been the final time.

He would not exhort God this morning to heal, to bind up, or to transform. He would exhort Him only to bless.

He prayed silently.

Bless the gift You have given him, Lord, to be used to Your glory, bless his spirit which craves You and yet bids You not enter, bless the laughter that is surely there, laughter that has dwelled in him all these years, yearning to be released, longing to spring forth and be a blessing to others. . . .

The laughter of Morris Love—that would be a miracle, he thought, and remembered how he had prayed to hear Dooley Barlowe laugh. That prayer had been answered; he smiled to think of Dooley's riotous cackle.

Thank You for blessing Morris with a quick and lively mind, an inquisitive intellect, and a soul able to form majestic music which ardently glorifies the Giver. Thank You for blessing Morris with Mamie, who, out of all those offered the glad opportunity of loving him, was the only one who came forth to love and serve on Your behalf.

The tears were cold on his face.

Lord, bless him today as he sits at his keyboards, as he breaks bread with Mamie, as he looks out his window onto a world which betrayed him, and which he now betrays. As he lies down to sleep, bless him with Your holy peace. As he rises, bless him with hope. As he thinks, bless him with Your own high thoughts.

Now, Father, I bless You—and praise You and thank You for hearing my prayer, through Christ our Lord who was given to us that we might have new life, Amen.

He walked on.

❧

"It's a done deal," said Rodney, not sounding quite like himself.

"How . . . did it go?"

"We found y'r angel in th' car, like you said, but your tenant broke down pretty bad. . . ." Rodney cleared his throat.

"Broke down?"

"Bawled like I never seen, wrung 'er hands. Me an' th' boys hated to do what we did."

"What did you do?"

"Took her over to th' magistrate an' they're holdin' her 'til everything's nailed down, fingerprints, reports, an' all."

"Then what?" he asked.

"Looks like th' charge'll be felonious breakin' an' enterin', felonious larceny, and felonious possession of stolen property."

He shook his head, hoping to clear it.

"Based on th' evidence, th' magistrate'll issue a warrant for her arrest, an' she'll have to post bond. In two, three weeks, she'll have to show up before a district judge, an' dependin' on how that goes, a grand jury will hear state's evidence which could land 'er in Superior Court."

"What if she leaves and goes to Boston?"

"She can go anywhere she wants to, long as she comes back to court."

"What if she doesn't?" He might as well know the worst-case scenario.

"They'll issue an order for 'er arrest, plus an order of forfeiture on th' bond."

"In other words, she wouldn't want to do that." *Hélène Pringle hunted and pursued . . .*

"Nobody with a lick of sense would want to do that."

Enough. He couldn't go on with this, he was a basket case, let Walter deal with it.

❧

Before services at ten o'clock, he would walk around the wall for the sixth time, and on Monday, seven times consecutively. Then he would have accomplished the thing God had asked him to do.

"I'm a fool for Christ!" he said with St. Paul. Thank heaven nobody had a clue what he was doing; to the world, he was walking his dog, he was getting his exercise, he was increasing his heart rate.

—————

Sunday night on the Sound.

Not a bad life, he thought, sitting on the sofa and holding his wife's hand. He had at last figured out how to work the TV and which of the several remotes it required, and they were watching the Discovery Channel.

"Ugh," said his wife, as a lion bored its head into a carcass, "they're always eating each other."

"That's life," he said as the phone rang.

He muted the sounds of the African plain. "Hello!"

"Father Kavanagh?"

Hélène Pringle. "I am desperate to talk with you."

He thought his hand shook, holding the receiver. "I'd be eager to talk with you, as well, Miss Pringle."

"I cannot go on this way, with so much to confess, so much to make known, it is . . ." She paused. "It is agony."

He heard the great strain in her voice.

"I would give anything to speak with you face-to-face," she said, "but—"

"Just a moment, Miss Pringle." He put his hand over the mouthpiece, as his mind raced over the schedule here—a vestry meeting with Sewell Joiner, Sam would handle it, they could run to Mitford and get back home the morning of the Fall Fair. . . .

"Want to go to Mitford?" he asked his wife.

"Consider us packed!" she said, beaming.

He would walk seven times around the wall tomorrow, first thing—they could be in the car by ten o'clock, and in Mitford by eight on Monday evening. "Miss Pringle, we'll see you at the rectory Tuesday morning at eleven. Will that be convenient?"

Miss Pringle was weeping quietly and, he assumed, unable to speak.

"Take your time," he said. "My time is yours."

He was on his fourth lap when Mamie appeared suddenly on the path from Nouvelle Chanson, startling him.

"Ah, Mamie!"

She laughed easily, her breath making vapor on the air. "I'm just going over home to get mayonnaise. Mr. Morris hardly ever touches it, but this mornin' he has a taste for a little mayonnaise on his grilled cheese."

This seemed to please her very much.

"Mamie, I wonder if I might get my wife's bicycle one day soon. I don't think Morris wants me to come fetch it personally."

Her eyes told him she understood. "I'll roll it down here for you anytime."

"I'll be back around this way in, say . . ."—three and a half laps to go—"twenty, thirty minutes? Would that be good?"

"Fine," she said. "Just fine."

"You could leave it there on the path, where no one can see it. I'd be grateful."

"I used to ride a bicycle—it was a pretty green color with a little bell. I loved my old bicycle."

"Borrow this one anytime," he said.

As they drove into Mitford at eight-fifteen, he felt he was seeing it anew. Though cloaked in fog, the sights he expected to be so familiar seemed fresh and original, almost exotic to his eyes. Lights sparkled in shop windows, street lamps glowed in the heavy mist, the display window of Dora Pugh's Hardware was dressed with pumpkins and shocks of corn stalks.

"I love our town," said his wife, peering out like a kid. Barnabas had his nose flattened against the rear window; even Violet, standing in Cynthia's lap with her paws against the glass, was gazing intently at Main Street.

He realized he was grinning from ear to ear, but when he saw Fancy Skinner's pink neon sign above the Sweet Stuff Bakery, he laughed out loud.

Once they got into the yellow house and turned on the lights and Harley delivered a pan of fudge brownies, it was too late to go visiting in Mitford. Puny, warned of their homecoming, had put roast chicken, potato salad, and tomato aspic in the refrigerator. They fell upon the meal like dock hands.

Afterward, they changed into what he'd been raised to call "night-clothes," and wandered around the house, seeing it all over again, claiming it with their eyes.

"Timothy!" exclaimed his wife. "Doesn't that picture look perfect over the sage-green vase?"

"You must have thought so when you put it there," he said, amused.

"I love our home, Timothy."

"As do I." He thumped down at his desk and idly looked through the drawers.

"What do you think she's going to say tomorrow?"

"I can't imagine, I don't know. I don't think she would have called if she didn't want to make peace. And she spoke of confession. . . ."

"I feel so sorry for Miss Pringle."

He glanced out the study window toward the rectory, where, through the hedge, he saw a light dimly burning in the kitchen.

"As do I," he repeated. "As do I."

Lessons for the Piano, he read on the black and white sign placed in the grass by the front walk, *Inquire Within.*

Hélène Pringle stood in the middle of the rectory living room and looked at him, red-eyed and plaintive. She was dressed simply in a longish dress and worn gray cardigan, and bereft of jewelry or any fanciful adornment. Her hair was swept back severely, as if she'd just dipped her comb in water, and pinned into a chignon.

"I can't tell you how sorry I am . . . and I beg your forgiveness."

He hated that she wrung her hands as she said this. "You are forgiven," he said, meaning it.

"Please sit, Father. I have a long story to relate to you. I pray you aren't in a hurry."

"I'm in no hurry at all." If he did nothing else on this trip, it would be fine with him. Looking around for Barbizon, but failing to spy the outsize mop, he sat in the chair, glad for the ease of it.

"I suppose I should offer you coffee or tea," she said, still standing.

"No, please, Miss Pringle, I have no want of anything. Thank you."

It hurt him, somehow, to witness her terrible anxiety. "Please," he said, smiling.

She sat on the sofa and gazed at her hands in her lap.

"Let me begin, then," she said, "at the beginning."

He was puzzled to realize he scarcely recognized this room, which had been part of his life for more than sixteen years.

"I have two very strong memories of my early childhood," she said, barely speaking above a whisper. "No one ever believed it possible for me to remember the first, for I was still an infant, lying in a pram. I had been rolled outside to the lawn and parked under a tree, and I remember so vividly the color of the leaves above me, almost . . . chartreuse, a delicate and tender shade of green I've seen only once or twice since. I shall never forget the intricate lacework of the leaves, and the sparkle of that wondrous color as they danced in the breeze."

She looked up from gazing at her hands, and he suddenly recognized something vaguely familiar about Hélène Pringle, but he couldn't have said what it was.

"The other early impression that shall remain with me always was when *ma grandmère* looked down upon me as I lay in my little bed in her country home outside Barbizon. I was very sick, and later, as an adult, I thought the whole dreadful episode might have been a feverish dream, but it was not.

"I was perhaps three years old then. She was wearing her lace cap, and the points of the lace appeared to me like the jagged edges of broken glass. I saw every wrinkle in her face; she was suddenly terribly, terribly frightening to me, but I was mesmerized and could not look away. 'You,' she said, 'have no father. I hope you like that piece of news, *ma petite chère*.'" Then she poked me in the chest with her finger, which had a long and hurtful nail, and I wept for the enormous fear I suddenly had of my grandmother, Hélène."

He'd never wanted the ability to feel the pain of others so keenly, but he had it, he had always had it, and there was no help for it. Perhaps it was just as well, for into this empathetic endowment had been lumped the ability to experience his own pain.

"I understand," he said.

She looked at him now with a certain steadiness in her gaze. "At the age of nineteen, my mother, Françoise, went up to Paris to live with her Tante Brigitte. Tante Brigitte was my grandfather's sister, and not a careful person in the least. She was altogether the wrong guardian for my beautiful and innocent mother.

"I think, Father, that aunts and uncles don't always take their roles as seriously as they might."

He saw traces of an old bitterness in her face as she spoke.

"I have always believed that Tante Brigitte conspired to introduce my mother to . . . to . . ." She looked at her hands again.

"Josiah Baxter?"

"Yes. He was a man of wealth, and old enough to be my mother's grandfather."

"Ah," he said.

"It grieves me more than you can know to tell you these things that have lain on my heart for so many years without being spoken."

She wept quietly, placing a handkerchief against her eyes and holding it there.

"Pardon, j'en suis désolée!" she said, at last. "I'm sorry to break down like this."

"Please don't be."

"Mr. Baxter . . . brought many expensive things to the apartment in Paris—paintings, sculpture, beautiful objects . . . my mother has memory of a little hand-carved chair with a needlepoint cushion . . ."

He had seen such a chair in Miss Sadie's bedroom; at the last minute of their negotiations at Fernbank, Andrew Gregory had bought it, along with numerous other pieces of furniture and table linens.

". . . and all those lovely things were shipped to his home in America. The men would come and crate them up, and away they would go across the water, to a place my mother would never know or see.

"I don't mean to imply that he never gave gifts to my mother. He gave her several fine pieces of jewelry which are long vanished, sold to help further my education. And he regularly gave money to Tante Brigitte for the household."

Something about her . . . so familiar . . .

"One day, Mr. Baxter . . ."

He noted that she spoke this name with difficulty, drawing a short breath before she said it.

". . . brought the angel to my mother. She told me that he said, 'Here, my dove, is something to watch over you in my absence.'

"Then he pulled a small key from his waistcoat and gave it to her. 'Unlock the little hiding place in the base of the angel,' he said. My mother examined the base very carefully, but could not find a way to insert a key. He took the key from her then, and turned the angel on its side . . ."

Hélène Pringle sat for a moment as if made of stone. He sensed that she had heard this story many times; her gaze did not take him in at all, but replayed before her eyes the movie she had made of her mother's memories.

". . . and slid out the bottom, which had appeared to be only a piece of felt to keep the statue from marring the furniture. Just inside the lip of the marble base was a very tiny keyhole."

"Ahh," he said.

"Mr. Baxter turned the little key in the hole and the bottom of the base, a thin slab of marble, was released into his hand. 'Now,' he told my mother, 'look inside.'

"She looked inside and found two pieces of paper, folded many times. 'Open this one first,' he told her, and she did. It was his will, written in his own hand and in French, though he spoke and wrote hardly any French at all. He had asked a Paris attorney to translate the wording into the language of my mother, and he had copied it in a very awkward and labored hand. It stated that upon his death he was bequeathing a third of his assets to my mother."

Hélène Pringle drew a deep breath and went on.

"In English, he wrote at the bottom, 'This is a codicil to my final will and testament, which is in the keeping of my solicitor, William Perry, of Philadelphia, Pennsylvania.' It was signed in his handwriting, and dated April 14, 1947. He told her he was traveling back to America with a copy for his solicitor.

"My mother said she felt a strange sort of joy and wonder, yet at the same time a fearful sense of dread. She then withdrew the other folded paper. It was . . . a love letter. I hope you might read it one day."

She sat with the handkerchief pressed to her eyes again, making no sound.

"Afterward," she continued, looking at him, "everything was placed back in the marble base, the key was turned in the lock, and the little slab with the felt bottom was put into place.

"Then Mr. Baxter slipped the key into the pocket of my mother's frock and said goodbye until his next visit, which he supposed would be in the summer, in July.

"That afternoon, the men came to crate the pieces he had bought for his home in America, and Tante Brigitte told them what was to be packed and what was to be untouched. Somehow, the angel was packed and taken away and put on the ship to America. . . ."

He saw the stricken look on her face, as if it happened only yesterday, or last week, and was as near to her in reality as this room in which she was sitting.

"Tante Brigitte sent a man to the docks to look for the crate, but the boat had gone."

She rose from the sofa and walked around the room, anxious and alarmed, then stood in front of the windows and drew the sheer panels apart and looked into the street.

He waited, sick with the weight of her distress.

She turned and came again to the sofa and sat down. "He never returned to Paris. You recall that the will was dated the day of his leave-taking, April 14, 1947. I was born December 12, 1947."

The room might have been contained in a timeless, noiseless bubble. He couldn't hear the ticking of a clock or a car moving in the street; he heard only the beating of his heart.

"When he did not come in July, my mother dispatched a letter to his lumberyard near Mitford, and heard nothing in reply. Several weeks after I was born, a letter was sent again. Two months later, it was returned to us unopened, and stamped *Addressee Deceased.*

"Tante Brigitte wrote a letter to the manager of Baxter Lumber Company, believing she could extort money somehow, and it, also, was returned, with *Out of Business* written on the envelope in longhand. Years later, I would pore over those returned envelopes, pondering the words *deceased* and *out of business*, and their tormenting finality.

"My family had lost all hope of any connection with my . . . with the American visitor to the little apartment in Paris.

"My aunt was not entirely poor, Father, but her means were limited, and there was no family friend or legal counsel to fall back upon. She sent my mother home to Barbizon with a seven-month-old child, to live with *ma grandmère.*"

There was a prolonged silence during which Hélène Pringle stared at the piano, as if it might contain an answer long sought.

"Perhaps to compensate for this terrible strait in the family affairs, Grandmère Hélène created a legacy of bitterness and hatred that I hope never to witness again in this life. Bitterness and hatred, Father, are contagious, did you know?"

"I know," he said.

"She infected my mother with this virulent acrimony, and I, too, became horribly contaminated by it. It was as if . . . as if a venomous liturgy were composed among us, and we recited it, day after day, religiously. It became to us larger than the real world. Our entire focus was upon the bitterness and anger felt toward my father and his money and his fine American home named Fernbank and his deceased wife whom he had called beautiful, and his much-adored Sadie and the fact that she had someone called China Mae to serve her and do her laundry and braid her hair.

"My grandmother would begin the recitation with the arrival of her breakfast tray, telling me how my mother never had *le courage, le cran, le culot,* to pursue the matter to its utmost and final outcome, to claim her portion, no matter what the effort, even if it meant going to America and seeking the thing that contained all our future prospects.

"My mother was once a very beautiful woman, but she sacrificed her beauty to bitterness and sorrow. Do you understand?"

"Yes," he said. "I've seen it happen that way."

"I was never . . . beautiful. I wonder how I could have been born to someone so lovely when I was . . ." She looked away.

"When you were what?" he asked.

"Short and plain, like my father."

Just plain Sadie . . . the thought came to him out of the blue. It was the way Miss Sadie had often referred to herself. Just plain Sadie, whose feet, when she sat on the love seat at Fernbank, had never touched the floor. Of course. That was the familiar thing he had recognized in this lost and lonely woman who had come seeking what she believed to be her brightest hope.

"I developed an image of my father over the years, based upon my grandmother's view of his wicked and profligate conduct, his willful neglect of duty, and his great and selfish wealth. He became monstrous to me, yet I can't tell you how I longed to love him a little, if only a little, but I could not."

He didn't like the ashen look on her face.

"Would you care for some water, Miss Pringle?"

"*Non, merci.* But then, yes, that would be—"

"I know just where it is," he said, sprinting toward the kitchen.

He realized he was shaking his head again, as if to clear it and make some sense of all he was hearing. His kitchen seemed strange to him, as if he'd never stepped foot in it before. *Lord,* he prayed, *may Your peace be upon this house. . . .*

He took a glass from the cabinet and ran the spigot for a moment and filled the glass and went along the hall to the rectory parlor. *And bless this woman in ways I can't think to ask. . . .*

"There," he said, as she drank it down. He took the glass from her as if he were a nursemaid and returned to his chair and sat again, holding it.

"Before my grandmother died fourteen years ago, she contended that a trip to Mitford would be a completely sensible thing to do. She believed the angel would be found sitting on someone's mantel, ripe for the picking."

"And so it was," he said gently.

"I determined that I would do this thing for my mother, who, by the way, married Albert Pringle and went to live in Boston about the time I finished college. They were married for seven years before he died of pneumonia. He was a lovely man. I took his name out of gratitude for his kindness. I think he helped relieve my mother of some of the anger. She became almost . . . almost kind again, and every so often, with Albert, I heard her laugh."

"Ahh."

"I always loved my mother, even when her malice removed her from me over and over again. A year ago, when our finances became so . . . strained, I promised her I would come to Mitford. I didn't tell her I would look for the angel, Father, I told her I would come to Mitford and find it."

"I admire confidence, Miss Pringle."

"I could not believe my good fortune when I discovered that you and Miss Sadie had been dear friends, and that your old rectory was for lease, right next door to your home. I believed then with all my heart that I'd been sent on a mission that would . . . would redeem all the hurt, somehow." She looked at her hands again.

"A mission?"

"Yes. I don't know much about God, Father, that is your forte, but I felt somehow that God had a hand in my coming here. I hope you don't think it's impertinent of me."

"No, Miss Pringle, not impertinent in the least."

"I suppose you wondered why I would bring my furnishings and set up a piano practice with only a six-month lease."

"That did cross my mind."

"I wanted . . . let me say that all my life since I was a young child, I've felt the need of a fresh start, a new beginning. I came here to find the angel, but very deep down, I also hoped I wouldn't find it. I came thinking that perhaps Mitford could be . . ." She sighed and shook her head slowly.

"But then, I've spent my life devoted to the desire for retribution—perhaps there are no new beginnings for someone like me."

"New beginnings are always possible," he said. "What of your mother? What are her circumstances?"

"My mother is in a nursing home outside Boston. Her mental faculties are keener than my own, but a series of health problems causes her to require care I cannot give. Albert left us a bit of money and I've gotten on rather well with my piano lessons, but . . ."

He saw the toll this was taking on her, that it would take on almost anyone to recite a legacy of suffering and loss.

"I'm sorry," she said, "I lost my point, somehow."

"Take a deep breath," he said. "Let's rest for a moment, shall we?"

"Rest?"

There! For one fragile instant, he thought he saw Miss Sadie in Hélène Pringle's face.

"Oh, no, Father, I can't rest until I've told you everything."

He nodded.

"I was very bold that day to look into your window. I stacked one cement block on top of another. Can you imagine my great joy and consternation when I peered into your lovely, sunlit room and spied the angel?"

He nodded.

"It was precisely where my grandmother contended it would be found. I was dumbstruck. I hadn't realized I might have to . . . to thieve something that in a sense didn't belong to me, but which, in quite another sense altogether, was mine."

"Yes," he said. A conundrum if ever there was one.

"Perhaps I deceived myself that if I located it, I could buy it, or . . . I suppose I never thought it through. And so, I began to watch your housekeeper come and go, and one afternoon I saw that she failed to lock the door when she departed. At dusk, I slipped to your house and let myself in. I was as quiet as a breath, and it was all done very quickly.

"My good fortune was alarming, Father; to want something so terribly for so many years, and then . . . it was unthinkable! I began to believe that circumstances had been formed just for me, just for this moment, it was a sign that all I was doing was destined. I brought the angel here."

Relief flooded her face. She seemed immediately stronger as she openly confessed the theft to him.

"I drew all the shades and draperies, and placed it on my bed, where I used the little key to unlock the base, and there . . . there were the papers, never once disturbed for more than a half century. I wept like I had never wept before, to hold something of my father's in my hands. I read the letter, and in it, I found a tenderness of feeling which I'd never hoped he might possess. The letter opened its secrets before me like the petals of a flower, and I discovered my father's true affection—and his humanity. I know that his behavior was very wrong, but you see, for all his wrongdoing, I was able at last to love him a little."

Now he heard a clock ticking somewhere, perhaps in the hallway, as if the bubble had been pierced and life was flowing into them again.

"I sent the papers to my mother's attorney in Boston. I was fearful to have them copied, fearful of being seen using the Xerox machine at the post office, and knowing no other way to proceed, I sent the papers by registered mail to Monsieur d'Anjou. He encouraged me in this thing which others might deem merely a bizarre and frivolous gamble.

"After I sent the papers, I became frightened that the angel would be found here, and so I hid it in the trunk of my car.

"I express to you again my sorrow at having done something that grieved you and the trustees at Hope House."

"It is a cloud," he said, "with a silver lining."

"Do you really believe so?" she asked, anxious again.

"I can't know so, but I do believe so."

"Thank you," she said, looking at him directly. "I went up to Hope House before Monsieur d'Anjou served the lawsuit, and looked around. It is . . . a wonderful place, the sort of place I wish for my mother."

"It was all Sadie Baxter's idea," he told her, "every bit of it, from the rooms overlooking the valley to the Scriptures over each doorway . . . the atrium, the fine medical help, the chaplain, all."

"I know the consequences of my actions, Father. I know that I can go to prison for what I have done. Nonetheless, I must tell you that I'm glad I did it. Very, very glad. I took something from you, yet I gained far more than the temporary possession of an angel on a marble base. There's a surprising sense, now, of owning something deeply precious—I don't yet understand what it is. But I know . . . it is in here." She placed her hand over her heart.

"I've grown to feel almost at home in Mitford. I've never known what it is to feel completely at home anywhere, but here, there's a solace I never found before. And so, I have gained even that."

Now it was he who got up and walked to the window and stood with his hands behind his back, peering without seeing through the sheer panels. It was hard to take it all in, to know what to do with all he had heard, but he knew this:

Something must be done with it. For Hélène Pringle; for Sadie Baxter, who, in heaven, would not be judging wrongdoing on anyone's part; and for himself; for his own peace of mind; and certainly for God, who may, indeed, have brought this woman to a crisis of renewal.

"Miss Pringle," he said, turning around, "I'm prepared to drop all charges against you. That may take some doing. I understand I'll have to meet with the district attorney, who may not take kindly to dropping the charges. But that is what I intend to do."

"Father," she said, standing. "I withdraw the lawsuit."

"Thank you," he said. "And the angel is yours."

"*Non! Ce ne serait pas juste!* That would not be fair. . . ."

"It is completely fair. It was the rightful and intended home for the letter and the will. They are all pieces of God's puzzle, and I believe the pieces must be kept together."

She stood by the sofa, awkward and moved; he wanted to go to her and give her a hug, but clergy had been historically advised to avoid such intimate contact, with no one looking on to approve.

"Well," he said, swallowing hard.

"Thank you, thank you, Father. *Mon Dieu, encore des larmes!*" She

retrieved the handkerchief from her cardigan pocket and pressed it
again to her eyes.

"Miss Pringle," he said, taking a handkerchief from his own
pocket, "we are a pair."

He walked across to the rectory before they left for Whitecap, and
knocked on the door. He hardly recognized Hélène Pringle. She was
holding her shoulders erect; she was looking him in the eye.

"May I have a moment?"

"Please!" she said, opening the door wide.

Aha. There was that blasted cat, curled on the sofa and staring him
down. "I won't come in; I just wanted to give you something."

He handed her an ivory envelope.

"Whatever you find inside, please receive it in the spirit in which it
is given. Promise me that."

She looked dubious for a moment, then smiled. "Well, then. I
shall do it, Father!"

"Good. And Miss Pringle?"

"Yes?"

"We hope you'll stay on in Mitford."

"But . . ."

"I know it's too soon to say, but we trust you'll think about it."

Tears swam in her eyes. *"Oui,"* she said. *"Oui. J'y penserai."*

Passing from the rectory into the bright midday of Mitford, he
looked again at the sign in the yard.

He thought it might as easily have read, *Lessons for the Heart, Inquire Within.*

CHAPTER TWENTY-TWO

A New Song

On the morning of the second Sunday of Easter, seven wild ponies trotted through the open gate of the corral near the lighthouse. Cropping grass with seeming contentment, they were spied by a jogger, who managed to close the rusting gate and then ran on, shouting the news along his route to whoever was up and stirring.

The marvelous sight drew Whitecappers of every age and disposition, all gleeful that the ponies from up Dorchester had escaped the government fence that ran into the Sound and, swimming around it, had struck out for Whitecap.

Penny and Marshall Duncan packed up their brood and drove the derelict Subaru to the corral, where they proffered a thank offering of hay and a large scoop of oats purloined from their lean-to barn. On Monday, the *Whitecap Reader* announced that the government would be coming to cart the ponies back where they belonged, so if anybody wanted to observe their brief homecoming, they'd better hop to it.

In the village, merchants prepared for the wave of tourists that would wash over them only two or three weeks hence. They were eager to see an economy that had slowed to a trickle once again surge like the incoming tide: quite a few prices were discreetly raised and the annual flurry of stocking nearly empty shelves began.

The dress shop reordered Whitecap T-shirts printed variously with images of the lighthouse, the historic one-room schoolhouse moved from the Toe to the village green, and the much-photographed St. John's in the Grove; the grocery store manager decided to dramatically expand his usual volume of hush puppy mix, much favored by tourists renting units featuring a kitchen; and Whitecap Flix, the sixty-two-seat theater rehabbed from a bankrupt auto parts store and open from May 15 through October 1, voted to open with *Babe*, convinced it was old enough to bill as a classic. To demonstrate their confidence in the coming season, Flix scheduled a half-page ad to hit on May 15, and included a ten-percent-off coupon for people who could prove it was their birthday.

Hearing of the advertising boom coursing through the business community, Mona elected to run a quarter-page menu once a month for three months, something she'd never done before in her entire career. Plus, she was changing her menu, which always thrilled a paltry few and made the rest hopping mad. She figured to put a damper on any complaints by offering a Friday night all-you-can-eat dinner special of fried catfish for seven ninety-five, sure to pacify everybody. Due to space too small to cuss a cat, she had resisted all-you-can-eat deals ever since she opened in this location, since any all-you-can-eat, especially fried, was bad to back up a kitchen. All-you-can-eat was a two-edged sword, according to Ernie—who could not keep his trap shut about her business, no matter what—because while you could draw a crowd with it, in the end you were bound to lose money on it since people around here chowed down like mules. In the end, all-you-can-eat was what some outfits called a loss leader. Mona did not like the word "loss," it was not in her vocabulary, but she would try the catfish and see how it worked, mainly to draw attention from the fact there was no liver and onions on her new menu, nor would there ever be again in her lifetime, not to mention skillet cornbread which crowded up the oven, cooked cabbage which smelled to high heaven, and pinto beans. Lord knows, she couldn't do everything, this was not New York City, it was Whitecap, and though she'd been born and raised here, it was not where she cared to spend the rest of her life, she was investing money in a condo in Florida, even if Ernie had expressed the hope of retiring to Tennessee. Tennessee! The very thought gave her the shivers. All those log cabins, all those grizzlies stumbling around in the dark, plus moonshine out the kazoo . . . no way.

Sometime in April, a sign appeared in the window of Ernie's Books, Bait & Tackle:

> Buy Five Westerns
> Any Title, Get a
> Free Zane Grey
> or Louis L'Amour,
> Take Your Pick.

Hardly anyone going in and out of Mona's had ever read Zane Grey, though several had heard of him, and a breakfast regular seemed to remember L'Amour as a prizefighter from Kansas City. Two days after the sign went up, a potato chip rep dropped a hundred and eighty-seven bucks on the special offer and posted Ernie's phone number and address in a chat room devoted to the subject of Old West literature. In the space of eight working days, the book end of the business had blown the bait end in the ditch, and Ernie hired on a couple of high school kids to handle mail orders.

Roanoke Clark was painting one of the big summer houses, and had hired on a helper who, he was surprised to learn, stayed sober as a judge and worked like a horse. He pondered making this a permanent deal, if only for his partner's nearly new pair of telescoping ladders, not to mention late-model Ford truck, an arrangement that would prevent the necessity of renting Chess Doyle's rattletrap Chevy with a homemade flatbed, for which Chess dunned him a flat forty bucks a week.

In the Toe, Bragg's was busy pumping diesel and dispatching tons of gravel and cement to construction sites as far away as Williamston, not to mention an industrial park in Tyrrell County.

At the north end of the small island shaped like a Christmas stocking, St. John's in the Grove was at last divested of its scaffolding. The heavy equipment had vanished, the piles of scrap lumber and roofing had been hauled away, and the errant flapping of loose tarps was heard no more.

Behind this effort had come a parish-wide cleanup. Brooms, rakes, hoes, mattocks and shovels were toted in, along with fresh nursery stock to replace what had been damaged in the general upheaval.

During the windy, day-long workfest, someone discovered that the coreopsis was beginning to bloom, and Father Tim was heard to say that their little church looked ready to withstand another century with dignity and grace.

For months on end, winter weather had delayed work on the reconstruction. He was up to here with plaster dust, drilling, sanding, and sawing. No wonder some of his colleagues resisted the role of "building priest." It probably wasn't the fund-raising they detested, it was the actual putting up and hammering down.

Fortunately, they'd been able to save the old oak, and he was glad for the bonus of increased light that now shone on St. John's.

On a bitterly cold, but bright May morning, he unlocked the front door and stepped across the threshold into a new nave, yet with its old spirit still intact. He sat midway on the gospel side and looked around paternally.

A church, like any other home, had its own singular and individual spirit, and he'd grown to love the unique spirit of St. John's. At Lord's Chapel, he'd felt the bulk and weight of the river stone as a mighty fortress, a sure defense. St. John's, on the other hand, gave him the distinct sense of vulnerability and innocence; it seemed fragile, somehow, as indeed it had been.

Two Sundays hence, the parish would celebrate this glad rebirth with a dinner on the grounds and the first homecoming in more than thirty years. They wouldn't take the long tearing out and putting back for granted, not at all; they would observe it for what it was—a benediction of a high and precious order.

"St. John's in the Grove, Father Kavanagh here."

"Hey, Dad."

"Hey, yourself, buddy!"

"Me and Caroline broke up."

"Ahh. Too bad."

"I'm glad, though. You know what she did?"

"What?"

"Just ran up to me at th' dance and grabbed th' chain around my neck and yanked it so hard, it came apart, and she took her ring back."

"Good grief!" That sounded exactly like something Peggy Cramer might have done.

"Next time, I'm goin' out with somebody more like . . . like . . ."

"Like who?" *Lace Turner!*

"Like, you know, maybe Cynthia."

He could practically feel his chest expand. "Now you're talking!" he said.

"I really liked it down there at Christmas."

"It was great, and we're looking forward to spending the summer together."

"Me, too, and when are we goin' to talk about my Wrangler?"

"I've got Harley checking around for the best deal. We'll get back to you as soon as we find something."

"Not too old," said Dooley, meaning it.

"Right. Not too old. We're looking for mint condition, low mileage, so don't worry about it."

He wasn't going to worry about it, either. This summer, Dooley would be living at the beach with a sharp little ride and a job at Mona's. Father Tim felt the excitement of it as his own.

"So, tell me, why did Caroline do . . . what she did?" Dooley Barlowe seemed to bring out mighty strong feelings in the opposite sex. He remembered the time Lace Turner had nearly knocked Dooley's head off for stealing her hat.

"I don't know, it was weird. Somebody said I was supposed to be dancin' with Caroline, and that I forgot and talked the whole time to Lace, but that's not true, I hardly talked to Lace more than five minutes—I don't know, maybe fifteen."

"Aha. Well." *Well, well, well.*

He sat in his office, mildly addled by the persistent smell of fresh paint and new carpet, and struggled without success to keep his mind on his sermon outline.

Finding Jessie Barlowe had been a fluke, but finding Sammy and Kenny would take a miracle.

There was no way he could trace Kenny via the clues of "thinning hair" and "headed for Oregon."

As for Sammy, Buck had called to say that someone saw Sammy with the road crew who worked on the highway from Holding to New Hampton more than six years ago. The boy's father had once worked on that road crew; maybe Sammy had been taken by his father. It disturbed him that he might one day have to confront Dooley's father; it wasn't a pleasant thought at all, yet he couldn't shut it out of his mind.

When they returned to Mitford, he would have to pursue this fragile thread, this vapor upon the air.

Before lunch, he went down his list of calls.

"If I was going to pass from a broken hip, I'd already have passed," said Ella Bridgewater.

"Absolutely!"

"I'm not ready to be carried down the road in a box just yet!"

"Amen!"

"I am going to the graveyard, though, to plant a little something on Mother's grave. We'll see how this hateful contraption works on gravel."

Ella Bridgewater hobbling down an isolated gravel lane on an aluminum walker? Wearing a long, black dress and toting a spade and a bush?

"I'll come up next week and go with you."

"Now, Father," she said, obviously pleased, "you don't have to do that!"

"I know I don't *have* to, which is another reason I'm happy to."

"You beat all!"

"Worse has been said," he told her.

"Louella!"

"Who that talkin'?"

"Father Kavanagh."

"Honey, how you doin'?"

"I can't complain. But how about you, how's the hip?"

"That hip ain't keepin' me down. This mornin' I rolled to th' kitchen an' made a pan of biscuits."

"Buttermilk?"

"Thass all I use."

"Wish I could have one." He sounded positively wistful. "With plenty of butter and . . . what kind of jam, do you think?"

"Huckleberry!" said Louella.

"Bingo!"

"When you an' Miss Cynthia comin' home?"

"I don't know. Maybe by the end of the year. Soon!"

"Not soon enough. We miss you aroun' here. I go an' pray with Miss Pattie, poor soul. Law, law, that Miss Pattie . . ."

"What's Miss Pattie done now?"

Louella gave forth with her rich, mezzo laughter.

"Miss Pattie have eyes for Mr. Berman, you know he's a mighty handsome man. Now she quit throwin' 'is clothes out th' window, she likes to wear 'is shoes."

"How on earth does she get around in his shoes?"

"Oh, she in a chair, you know, like me; she can't walk a step. She put those shoes on, climb up in that buggy, an' off she go, pleased as punch."

"Aha."

"Mr. Berman is *sweet*, honey, he gave her a pair of alligator loafers, said to Nurse Lola, let 'er have 'em, a man can't wear but one pair of shoes, anyway. Ain't that nice?"

"I'll say!"

She sighed. "Not a soul to sing with up here."

He sighed. "Not a soul to sing with down here."

"You hit one and I'll join in," she said, chuckling.

He didn't think he'd ever sung four verses of anything over the phone before, but when he finished, he was definitely in improved spirits.

His wife set freshly made chicken salad before him, with a hot roll and steaming mug of tea. She stood holding his hand as he asked the blessing.

"What do you think of me coming home for lunch?" he asked. "I've known some who don't take kindly to husbands falling in to be fed." Might as well learn the truth, which his wife seemed generally enthusiastic to deliver.

"I love that you come home for lunch, Timothy, you're my main social contact now that I'm working so hard to finish the book." She set her own plate on the table and kissed the top of his head.

"How's it coming?"

"Peaks, valleys, highs, lows," she said, sitting down.

"Life," he said.

"Oh, gosh, that reminds me, I need the car this afternoon. I'm running over to the Sound to sketch a blue heron."

His wife needed live fodder, flesh and blood; no Polaroids for her, thank you—she was *plein air* all the way. Except for an occasional beach umbrella or background bush that might be lifted from memory, she went looking for the real thing. Violet, who was certainly the real thing, was the fourth or fifth white cat in an unbroken chain of actual Violets adopted by his wife over the years. He had, himself, been recruited to appear as a wise man in her book *The Mouse in the Manger*. He didn't think he'd looked very wise in her watercolor—more idiotic, truth be told—but she'd been pleased.

They'd once gone to the woods together, where he tried to enter her world of absorption as she fixed her gaze on lichen—but his mind had wandered like a free-range chicken, and he ended up thinking through a sermon based on Philippians four-thirteen.

"Oh, and after the Sound, I'm running by Janette's and taking the children out for ice cream."

"Good deal." He thought her eyes were as blue as wild chicory.

"By the way, just before you came in, Roger Templeton called. He said he didn't reach you at church."

"Aha."

"Wants you to give him a ring."

"Will do."

They ate quietly, the clock ticking over the stove.

"Timothy . . ."

"Yes?"

"Don't ever leave me."

Every so often, quite out of nowhere, she asked this plaintive thing, which shook and moved him. He put his fork down and took her hand. "I would never leave you. Never."

"Even when I'm old and covered with crow's-feet?"

"I love your crow's-feet, Kavanagh."

"I thought you once said I didn't have any crow's-feet." He was relieved to see her veer away from the fleeting sadness, and laugh.

"You've nailed me," he said, grinning.

He lifted her hand and kissed her palm and held it to his cheek. "You mean everything to me. How could I ever thank you for what you are, day and night, a gift, a gift. . . ."

She looked at him, smiling. "I love it when you talk like that, dearest. You may come home for lunch whenever you wish."

Roger met him at the church office on Wednesday morning, carrying a paper bag closed with a twist-tie, and looking bashful.

"Face your desk and close your eyes," said Roger.

Father Tim did as he was told, hearing the rustle of the paper bag being opened.

"Okay, you can turn around now."

The green-winged teal in Roger's outstretched hands looked him dead in the eye.

Newly painted in all its subtle and vibrant colors, he found it beautiful, breathtaking, alive. He opened his mouth to speak, but found no words.

"It's yours," said Roger.

"You can't mean that."

"It's yours. It's been yours all along. I saw the look on your face when you watched what I was doing. I know that look; it's yours."

He took it reverently, moved and amazed.

"Turn it over," said Roger, flushing with pleasure.

He turned it over. On the flat bottom was burned the name of the island, today's date, and a message:

> *Green Winged Teal*
> *For Tim Kavanagh*
> *From Roger Templeton*
> *Fellows in a ship*

Clutching the prized possession in his left hand, he embraced Roger Templeton and pounded him on the back.

"Thank you," he said, just this side of croaking.

"I've only given away a few. Ernie has one, and my son and his wife, and . . ." Roger shrugged, awkward and self-conscious.

"I can't thank you enough, my friend. I'll treasure it more than you know."

He set it on his desk and gazed at it again, marveling.

A few months ago, he'd relinquished an angel; today, he'd been given a duck. He'd come out on the long end of the stick, and no two ways about it.

He stood in the sacristy, vested and waiting with the anxious choir, and the eager procession that extended all the way down the steps to the basement.

There was new music this morning, composed by the organist, something wondrous and not so easy to sing, and choir adrenaline was pumping like an oil derrick. Adding voltage to the electricity bouncing off the walls was the fact that the music required congregational response, always capable of injecting an element of surprise, if not downright dismay.

He peered through the glass panels of the sacristy door into the nave, able to see only the gospel side from this vantage point. He spied quite a few faces he'd never laid eyes on, given that today was Homecoming.

Some of the faithful remnant had been beaten to their pews by the homecomers, so he had to search for Otis and Marlene and the Duncan lineup, on the far right. Down front was Janette with Jonathan on her lap, flanked by Babette and Jason, *thank You, Lord.* And two rows back was Sew Joiner, gazing at the work on the walls and ceiling, and generally looking like he'd hung the moon.

At the sound of the steeple bell, the crucifer burst through the door and into the nave with her procession, the organ played its mighty opening notes, and the choir streamed forth as a rolling clap of thunder.

Carried along by the mighty roar and proclamation of the organ, the choir processed up the aisle with vigor.

> *"Sing to the Lord a new song*
> *And His praise from the ends of the earth*
> *Alleluia! Alleluia!*
> *You who go down to the sea, and all that is in it*
> *Alleluia! Alleluia!"*

The congregation joined in the first two alleluias as if waking from a long sleep; at the second pair, they hunkered down and cranked into high gear, swept along by the mighty lead of the choir.

> *"Let them give glory to the Lord*
> *And declare His praise in the coastlands*
> *Alleluia! Alleluia!"*

As the choir passed up the creaking steps to the loft, the organ music soared in the little nave, enlarging it, expanding it, until it might have been o'ercrossed by the fan vaulting of an English cathedral.

Quickly taking their places by the organ, the choir entered again into the fervent acclamations of Isaiah and the psalmist.

> *"Sing to Him a new song*
> *Play skillfully with a loud and joyful sound*
> *Alleluia!*
> *For the work of the Lord is right*
> *Alleluia!*
> *And all His work is done in faithfulness!*
> *Alleluia!"*

A full minute of organ music concluded the first part of the new work, celebrating God's grace to the people of St. John's, and the joyful first homecoming in three decades. Many of the congregants, marveling at the music that poured forth from the loft, turned around in their pews and looked up in wonderment.

> *"Alleluia! Alleluia!"*

In the ascending finale, which was sung a cappella, the soprano reached for the moon and, to the priest's great joy and relief, claimed it for the kingdom.

"When trees and power lines crashed around you, when the very roof gave way above you, when light turned to darkness and water turned to dust, did you call on Him?

"When you called on Him, was He somewhere up there, or was He as near as your very breath?"

He stood in front of the pulpit this morning, looking into the faces of those whom God had given into his hand for this fleeting moment in time.

"What some believers still can't believe is that it is God's passion to be as near to us as our very breath.

"Far more than I want us to have a bigger crowd or a larger parish hall or a more ambitious budget . . . more than anything as your priest, I pray for each and every one of you to sense and know God's presence . . . as near as your breath.

"In short, it has been my prayer since we came here for you to have a personal, one-on-one, day-to-day relationship with Christ.

"I'm talking about something that goes beyond every Sunday service ever created or ever to be created, something you can depend on for the rest of your life, and then forever. I'm talking about the times you cry out in the storm that prevails against you, times when your heart and your flesh fail and you see no way out and no way in, when any prayer you utter to a God you may view as distant and disinterested seems to vanish into thin air.

"There are legions who believe in the existence of a cold and distant God, and on the occasions when they cry out to Him in utter despair and hear nothing in reply, must get up and stumble on, alone.

"Then there are those who know Him personally, who have found that when they cry out, there He is, as near as their breath—one-on-one, heart-to-heart, savior, Lord, partner, friend.

"Some have been in church all their lives and have never known this mighty, marvelous, and yet simple personal relationship. Others believe that while such a relationship may be possible, it's not for them—why would God want to bother with them, except from a very great distance? In reality, it is no bother to God at all. He wants this relationship far, far more than you and I want it, and I pray that you will ponder that marvelous truth.

"But who among us could ever deserve to have such a wondrous and altogether unimaginable thing as a close, personal, day-to-day relationship with Almighty God, creator of the universe?

"It seems unthinkable, and so . . . we are afraid to think it.

"For this fragile time in history, this tender and fleeting moment of our lives, I am your priest; God has called me to lead this flock. As I look out this morning, my heart has a wish list for you. For healed marriages, good jobs, the well-being and safety of your children; for

Eleanor, knees that work; for Toby, ears that hear; for Jessie, good news from her son; for Phillip, good news from his doctor. On and on, there are fervent desires upon my heart for you. But chief among the hopes, the prayers, the petitions is this: *Lord . . . let my people know.* Let them know that the unthinkable is not only real, but available and possible and can be entered into, now, today—though we are, indeed, completely undeserving.

"It can be entered into today, with only a simple prayer that some think not sophisticated enough to bring them into the presence of God, not fancy enough to turn His face to theirs, not long enough, not high enough, not deep enough. . . .

"Yet, this simple prayer makes it possible for you to know Him not only as Savior and Lord, but as a friend. 'No longer do I call you servants,' He said to His followers in the Gospel of John, 'but friends.'

"In the storms of your life, do you long for the consolation of His nearness and His friendship? You can't imagine how He longs for the consolation of yours. It is unimaginable, isn't it, that He would want to be near us—frail as we are, weak as we are, and hopeless as we so often feel. God wants to be *with us.* That, in fact, is His name: Immanuel, God with us. And why is that so hard to imagine, when indeed, He made us for Himself? Please hear that this morning. The One who made us . . . made us for Himself.

"We're reminded in the Book of Revelation that He created all things—for His pleasure. Many of us believe that He created all things, but we forget the very best part—that He created us . . . *for His pleasure.*

"There are some of you who want to be done with seeking Him once a week, and crave, instead, to be with Him day after day, telling him everything, letting it all hang out, just thankful to have such a blessing in your life as a friend who will never, under any circumstances, leave you, and never remove His love from you. Amazing? Yes, it is. It is amazing.

"God knows who is longing to utter that simple prayer this morning. It is a matter between you and Him, and it is a prayer which will usher you into His presence, into life everlasting, and into the intimacy of a friendship in which He is as near . . . as your breath.

"Here's the way this wondrous prayer works—as you ask Him into your heart, He receives you into His. The heart of God! What a place to be, to reside for all eternity.

"As we bow our heads to pray under this new roof and inside these new walls, I ask that He graciously bless each and every one of us today . . . with new hearts."

He bowed his head and clasped his hands together and heard the beating of the blood in his temples. Ella Bridgewater, sitting next to the aisle with her walker handy, looked on approvingly. Captain Larkin, seated to her right, bowed his head in his hands.

"Sense, feel God's presence among us this morning . . ."

He waited.

". . . as those of you who are moved to do so, silently repeat this simple prayer:

"Thank You, God, for loving me . . .

". . . and for sending Your Son to die for my sins.

"I sincerely repent of my sins . . .

". . . and receive Jesus Christ as my personal savior.

"Now, as Your child . . .

". . . I turn my entire life over to You.

"Amen."

He raised his head, but didn't hurry on. Such a prayer was mighty, and, as in music, a rest stop was needed.

The recitation of the Nicene Creed was next in the order of service, and he opened his mouth to say so, but closed it again.

He looked to the epistle side and saw Mamie and Noah; Mamie was smiling and nodding her head. Behind them were Junior Bryson and Misty Summers; he thought Junior's grin was appreciably wider than his tie.

"If you prayed that prayer and would join me at the altar, please come." He hadn't known he would say this; he had utterly surprised himself.

Some would be too shy to come, but that was God's business; he hoped he wouldn't forget and leave out the Creed altogether.

"If you'd like to renew your baptism vows in your heart, please come. If you'd like to express thanksgiving for all that God has fulfilled in your life, please come. If you'd like to make a new beginning, to surrender your life utterly into His care, please come."

Though this part of the service was entirely unplanned, he thought it might be a good time for a little music. His choir, however, was stricken as dumb as wash on a line.

From the epistle side, four people rose and left their pews and walked down the aisle.

On the gospel side, five parishioners and a homecomer stood from the various pews and, excusing themselves, stepped over the feet of several who were furiously embarrassed and looking for the door.

Father Tim opened a vial of oil, knelt for a moment on the sanctuary side of the rail, and prayed silently. One by one, the congregants dropped humbly to their knees, at least two looking stern but determined, others appearing glad of the opportunity to do this reckless thing, to surrender their hearts in an act of wild and holy abandon and begin again.

He dipped his right thumb in the oil and touched the forehead of the first at the rail, making the sign of the cross and saying, "I anoint you, Phillip, in the name of the Father, and of the Son, and of the Holy Spirit . . ."

In the choir loft, the organist rose from the bench, and walked stiffly down the stairs and along the center aisle with the aid of a cane.

Madeleine Duncan scrambled to her knees in the pew and whispered in her mother's ear, "Look, Mommy, it's a little tiny man with a big head."

Observing the penitent who now approached the altar, Leonard Lamb didn't realize he was staring with his mouth open, nor that tears suddenly sprang to his eyes.

Marion Fieldwalker poked Sam in the ribs. "Who's that?"

"Good gracious alive!" Sam whispered, as if to himself.

As Father Tim touched the forehead of the man kneeling before him, it seemed that an electric shock was born from the convergence of their flesh, it arced and flashed along his arm like a bolt.

"I anoint you, Morris, in the name of the Father, and of the Son, and of the Holy Spirit, and beseech the mercy of our Lord Jesus Christ to seal forever what is genuine in your heart. May God be with you always, my brother."

"The Lord drew me up
out of an horrible pit,
out of the miry clay,

Alleluia!
and set my feet upon a rock,
Alleluia!
steadying my steps and
establishing my goings,
Alleluia!
And he has put a new song
in my mouth, a song of praise
to our God!
Alleluia! Alleluia! Amen!"

" 'No one,' " he told Barnabas as they walked down the lane to the beach, " 'appreciates the very special genius of your conversation as the dog does.' "

His dog did not reply.

"Christopher Morley said that."

Barnabas plodded ahead.

"Don't you think there's a certain truth in it?"

What if someone heard him out here talking to his dog? Then again, why couldn't a man talk to his dog whenever he took the notion?

"Ah, my friend, what a sunset this is going to be." He felt positively jaunty, as if spring were luring something out of him that hadn't emerged in a very long while.

He'd asked his wife to come along, but she had a far more important and monumental thing to do than watch a spectacular sunset on a glorious evening; indeed, she was washing her hair.

He'd experienced this feeling of lightness only once before since coming here. It was the day he walked to Ernie's for the first time, free as a bird. Whole hours of freedom had lain before him in a strange new place with secrets yet to be revealed. Why couldn't all of life give one that feeling, the feeling of being on the brink of discovery? Wasn't every moment a revelation? Who ever knew, after all, what lay around the bend?

Ah, well, he'd probably be moping around like the rest of the common horde in a day or two. He'd better sop up this carefree business while he could.

He found himself whistling the organ piece from yesterday's service; difficult though it was, it contained an inner melodic line that he found thoroughly fascinating. What a miracle it had all been; he shook his head with the wonder of it, remembering the stunned delight of his congregation, and Mamie's soulful joy. Indeed, there had been enough gladness in the day to make memories for a month of Sundays.

They left the pavement and went along the boardwalk through the dunes. "Sit," he said, standing on the walk before they trotted down the steps. Watching the color begin to wash over the water, it suddenly occurred to him that St. John's should haul some chairs out here for an early Sunday service.

What a nave, what a sanctuary! And the ceiling beat any fan vaulting he'd ever laid eyes on, hands down. Why on earth they hadn't held this year's sunrise service right here was beyond him; he must be as dumb as a rock.

Well, then, maybe next year. If there was a next year. Very likely, St. John's would call their priest by winter.

They went down the steps and along the beach, not running, not jogging, but strolling. About a quarter of a mile into the walk, he let Barnabas off the leash.

That sunset is smokin', he thought, sitting on the sand to take off his shoes and socks. He remained sitting, looking, wondering.

It had been a joy to see Janette Tolson in church with her children yesterday, her life restored and settled. But it wasn't a joy to see the toll it was taking on her to go it alone, sewing until two in the morning, and rising early to get the children ready for school and Jonathan off to day care.

He dropped by to see her more often than he should, perhaps, but generally stayed only long enough to assure her of his prayers and encourage her in her work. Single parents were a dime a dozen in today's world. Such a thing rolled off the back of modern society like water off a duck; it had become the common run of so-called civilized life.

But it hadn't become common to him, not in the least. It always hurt him to see the damage and confusion and, too often, the utter desperation of those forced to go it alone. In short, it was a hard row to hoe, and fraught with unique assaults by the Enemy.

The last time he visited, she mustered the courage to ask again, "Have you seen him?" He hadn't, nor had anyone else, as far as he knew. "He could be dead," she said, looking across her sewing machine and out the window. "The storm . . ."

It was true. Nobody knew where he was living on the island, or in what sort of circumstances. If the ceiling plaster had narrowly missed Maude Proffitt, who was to say whether the storm had left its fatal mark elsewhere?

But hold on. He was doing the thing he had a made a resolution only yesterday to try to consciously avoid—he was thinking too much. "That young Timothy," an elder in his mother's church once said, "he thinks too much."

He never forgot that offhand remark, though he couldn't have been more than seven or eight years old. How much thinking was too much, he had wondered, and who was to say? Should he quit thinking anything at all once in a while, and go around with an empty mind? He tried to empty his mind and found it completely impossible to do. Or maybe other people could empty their minds and he was the only one who could not. This was disturbing. On the other hand, were there people who thought too little? As an adult, he occasionally considered that he might know a few. . . .

He whistled for his dog, who bounded out of the surf and stood before him, shaking salt water forty ways from Sunday.

"Sit," he said. Barnabas sat.

He remembered the time when the only thing he could get his dog to do was eat. It was years before he sat when asked, or came when called. Old age, that's what it was. Old age and wisdom! If Barnabas had been, say, two years old when he came to the rectory—and that was seven years ago—then in dog years he was . . . sixty-three. About the same age as his master. OK, then, it wasn't old age at all, no indeed, it was merely wisdom.

So thinking, he got up and ran down the beach, his dog loping beside him.

They had turned into the lane when Barnabas stopped and growled low in his throat.

It was dark now; a single street lamp burned just up the road. He saw that someone approached them, thrown into silhouette by the light.

"Who is it?" he asked. "Who's there?"

"Father Kavanagh?"

He recognized the voice at once. "Yes."

"I'm sorry to startle you." Though the figure walked closer, Barnabas stopped growling. In fact, his tail was wagging.

The white shirt gleamed like a pearl. "I've been hoping we could talk."

"I've been hoping that, too."

"If you have time."

Father Tim reached out, extending his hand into the darkness. "My time," he said, "is yours."

For more works by JAN KARON, look for the

At Home in Mitford
ISBN 0-14-025448-X

A Light in the Window
ISBN 0-14-025454-4

These High, Green Hills
ISBN 0-14-025793-4

Out to Canaan
ISBN 0-14-026568-6

A New Song
ISBN 0-14-027059-0

A Common Life:
The Wedding Story
ISBN 0-14-200034-5

JAN KARON books make perfect holiday gifts.

From Penguin:

The Mitford Years
Boxed set includes: *At Home in Mitford*; *A Light in the Window;*
These High, Green Hills; Out to Canaan and *A New Song.*
ISBN 0-14-771596-2

From Viking:

Patches of Godlight:
Father Tim's Favorite Quotes
ISBN 0-670-03006-6

The Mitford Snowmen:
A Christmas Story
ISBN 0-670-03019-8

PENGUIN AUDIO: The Mitford Years Audio

At Home in Mitford ISBN 0-14-086501-2; *A Light in the Window*
ISBN 0-14-086596-9; *These High, Green Hills* ISBN 0-14-086598-5
Out to Canaan ISBN 0-14-086597-7; *A Common Life* ISBN 0-14-
180274-X; *A New Song* (Abridged) ISBN 0-14-086901-8; *A New
Song* (Unabridged) ISBN 0-14-180013-5; *The Mitford Years Boxed Set*
ISBN 0-14-086813-5

In bookstores now from Penguin Putnam Inc.

Visit the Mitford Web site at www.mitfordbooks.com

To order books in the United States: Please write to Consumer Sales,
Penguin Putnam Inc.
P.O. Box 12289, Dept B, Newark, New Jersey 07101-5289.
VISA, MasterCard and American Express cardholders
call (800) 788-6262 or (201) 933-9292.

New from Viking...

JAN KARON'S

In This Mountain

*F*ather Tim and Cynthia have been at home in Mitford for three years since returning from Whitecap Island. In the little town that's home-away-from-home to millions of readers, life hums along as usual for the endearing townspeople. Though Father Tim dislikes change, he dislikes retirement even more. As he and Cynthia gear up for a year-long ministry across the state line, a series of events sends shock waves through his faith—and the entire town of Mitford.

In her seventh novel in the bestselling Mitford series, Jan Karon delivers surprises of every kind, including the return of the man in the attic, and an ending that no one in Mitford will ever forget.

VIKING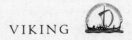

A
Common
Life

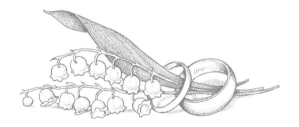

PENGUIN BOOKS

A COMMON LIFE

Jan Karon says she writes "to give readers an extended family, and to applaud the extraordinary beauty of ordinary lives." Other bestselling novels in the Mitford Years series are *At Home in Mitford*; *A Light in the Window*; *These High, Green Hills*; *Out to Canaan*; and *A New Song*. Coming in 2002 is her seventh novel in the series, *In This Mountain*. Her children's books include *Miss Fannie's Hat* and *Jeremy: The Tale of an Honest Bunny*.

A Common Life

The Wedding Story

JAN KARON

PENGUIN BOOKS

PENGUIN BOOKS
Published by the Penguin Group
Penguin Putnam Inc., 375 Hudson Street,
New York, New York 10014, U.S.A.
Penguin Books Ltd, 80 Strand, London WC2R 0RL, England
Penguin Books Australia Ltd, 250 Camberwell Road,
Camberwell, Victoria 3124, Australia
Penguin Books Canada Ltd, 10 Alcorn Avenue, Toronto,
Ontario, Canada M4V 3B2
Penguin Books India (P) Ltd, 11 Community Centre,
Panchsheel Park, New Delhi – 110 017, India
Penguin Books (N.Z.) Ltd, Cnr Rosedale and Airborne Roads,
Albany, Auckland, New Zealand
Penguin Books (South Africa) (Pty) Ltd, 24 Sturdee Avenue,
Rosebank, Johannesburg 2196, South Africa

Penguin Books Ltd, Registered Offices: Harmondsworth, Middlesex, England

First published in the United States of America by Viking Penguin,
a member of Penguin Putnam Inc. 2001
Published in Penguin Books 2002

1 3 5 7 9 10 8 6 4 2

Illustrations by Laura Hartman Maestro

THE LIBRARY OF CONGRESS HAS CATALOGED
THE HARDCOVER EDITION AS FOLLOWS:
Karon, Jan, date.
A common life : the wedding story / Jan Karon.
p. cm.—(The Mitford years)
ISBN 0-670-89437-0 (hc.)
ISBN 0 14 20.0034 5 (pbk.)
1. Weddings—Fiction 2. Mitford (N.C. : Imaginary place)—Fiction.
3. North Carolina—Fiction. 4. City and town life—Fiction I. Title.
PS3561.A678 C6 2001
813'.54—dc21   00-031984

Printed in the United States of America
Set in Fournier MT / Designed by Francesca Belanger

For my much-appreciated
nieces and nephews,
with love

David Craig, Jennifer Craig,
Lisa Knaack, Courtney Setzer, Monica Setzer,
Randy Setzer, and Taja Setzer

Give them wisdom and devotion in the ordering of their common life, that each may be to the other a strength in need, a counselor in perplexity, a comfort in sorrow, and a companion in joy.

Amen.

—*The Book of Common Prayer*

Contents

Acknowledgments

Warm thanks to Viking Penguin Chairman Susan Petersen Kennedy; my agent, Liz Darhansoff; my editor, Carolyn Carlson; Paul Halley; Ruth Bush; Kay Auten; Betty Cox; Bishop Keith Ackerman; Father Charles L. Holt; Father Terry Sweeney; Harvey Karon; Martha J. Marcus; Gail Mayes; James Harris Podgers; Betty Pitts, and the late Hayden Pitts.

Special thanks to Father James Harris, a faithful friend to Mitford; to *Victoria* magazine for excerpts from Mitford fiction that appeared in its pages; and to the lovely Carolyn Clement, our own Hessie Mayhew, who gathered and arranged the wedding flowers which are captured in pastels by Donna Kae Nelson for the jacket of this book.

A
Common
Life

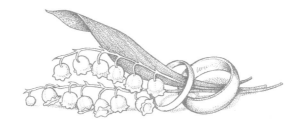

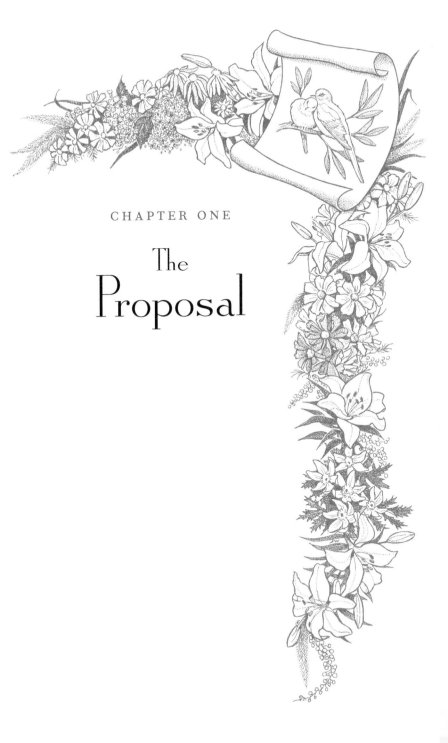

CHAPTER ONE

The

Proposal

*F*ather Timothy Kavanagh stood at the stone wall on the ridge above Mitford, watching the deepening blush of a late June sunset.

He conceded that it wasn't the worst way to celebrate a birthday, though he'd secretly hoped to celebrate it with Cynthia. For years, he'd tried to fool himself that his birthday meant very little or nothing, and so, if no cards appeared, or cake or presents, that would be fine.

Indeed, there had been no card from Cynthia, though he'd received a stack from his parishioners, and certainly she'd given no promise of cake or candles that definitively pronounced, *This is it, Timothy, the day you appeared on earth, and though I know you don't really care about such things, we're going to celebrate, anyway, because you're important to me.* He was deeply ashamed to admit that he'd waited for this from her; in truth, had expected it, hoped for it.

He'd known suffering in his thirty-eight years in the priesthood, though nearly always because of someone else's grief or affliction. Now he suffered for himself, for his maddening inability to let his walls down with her, to cast off his armor and simply and utterly love her. He had pled with God to consume his longing and his love, to cast it out as ashes and let nothing interfere with the fulfillment of the vows he'd made years ago as an ordinand. Why should such a flame as this beat up in him now? He was sixty-two years old, he was beyond loving in the flesh! And yet, as desperately as he'd prayed for his longing to be removed, he craved for it to be satisfied.

He remembered the times she had shut herself away from him, guarding her heart. The loss of her ravishing openness had left him cold as a stone, as if a great cloud had gone over the sun.

What if she were to shut herself away from him once and for all? He paced beside the low stone wall, forgetting the sunset over the valley.

He'd never understood much about his feelings toward Cynthia, but he knew and understood this: He didn't want to keep teetering on the edge, afraid to step forward, terrified to turn back.

The weight on his chest was palpable; he'd felt it often since she moved next door and into his life. Yet it wasn't there because he loved her, it was there because he was afraid to love her completely.

Perhaps he would always have such a weight; perhaps there was no true liberation in love. And certainly he could not ask her to accept him as he was—flawed and frightened, not knowing.

He sank to his knees by the stone wall, and looked up and opened his mouth to speak, but instead caught his breath sharply.

A great flow of crimson and gold was spilling across the sky like lava, running molten from west to east. He watched, awestruck, as the pyre consumed the blue haze of the firmament and bathed the heavens with a glory that shook and moved him to his very depths.

"Please!" he whispered.

It was then that he felt a sensation of warmth welling in him, a kind of liquid infilling he'd never experienced before. Something in his soul lifted up, as startling as a covey of quail breaking from the underbrush, and his heart acknowledged, suddenly and finally, that his love for her could not, would not be extinguished. He knew at last that no amount of effort, no amount of pleading with God would enable him to sustain any longer the desperate, wounding battle he had launched against loving her.

In a way he couldn't explain, and in the space of the

merest instant, he knew he'd come fully awake for the first time in his life.

He also knew that he wanted nothing more than to be with her, at her side, and that after all the wasted months, he couldn't afford to waste another moment. But what if he'd waited too long, come to his senses too late?

He sprang to his feet, as relieved as if he'd shaken off an approaching illness; then, animated by a power not his own, he found himself running.

"There comes a time," his cousin Walter had said, "when there's no turning back."

He felt the motion of his legs and the breeze on his skin and the hammering in his temples, as if he might somehow implode, all of it combusting into a sharp inner flame, a durable fire, a thousand hosannas.

Streaming with sweat, he raced down Old Church Lane and into the cool green enclosure of Baxter Park, his body as weightless as a glider borne on wings of ether, though his heart was heavy with dread. She could have gone away as she'd done before . . . and this time, she might never come back.

The dark silhouette of the hedge separating the park from Cynthia's house and the rectory appeared far away, another country, a landmark he might never reach.

As he drew closer, he saw that her house was dark, but his own was aglow with light in every window, as if some wonderful thing might be happening.

He bounded through the hedge; she was standing on his stoop. She held the door open, and the light from the kitchen gleamed behind her.

She stood there as if she'd known the very moment he turned into the park and, sensing the urgency of his heart, felt her own compelled to greet it.

He ran up the steps, his chest heaving, as she stepped back and smiled at him. "Happy birthday!" she said.

"I love you, Cynthia!" His lungs seemed to force the declaration onto the night air as if by their own will. He stood with his mouth open, marveling, while she raised her hand to her cheek in a way that made her appear dubious, somehow, or amused.

Did she think him mad? He felt mad, riotous, he wanted to climb on the roof, baying and whooping—a sixtysomething bachelor priest, mad with love for his next-door neighbor.

He didn't consider the consequences of this wild skidding out of control; it was now or never.

As she backed into the kitchen, he followed. He saw the cake on the breakfast table and the card propped against a vase of flowers, and he fell to one knee beside the table and gathered her hands in his.

7

"Will you?" he croaked, looking up at her.

"Will I *what*, dearest?"

"You know."

"No, I don't know."

He knew that she knew; why wouldn't she help him with this thing? He was perfectly willing to bring the other knee down if only she would help him.

And why was he crouching here on the linoleum, sweating like a prizefighter, when he might have been dressed in his best suit and doing this in the study, or in the Lord's Chapel garden by the French roses?

He tried to scramble to his feet and run upstairs, where he would take a shower and brush his teeth and get dressed and do this the right way, but his strength failed and he found he couldn't move; he might have been glued to the linoleum, one knee up and one knee down, frozen as a herring.

"Hurry, Timothy!" she said, whispering.

"Will you marry me?"

"Yes! A thousand times yes!"

She was helping him to his feet, and then he was kissing her and she was kissing him back. She drew away and looked at him with a kind of awe; he found her radiance dumbfounding. "I thought you'd never ask," she said.

It was done. He had jumped over the barbed wire.

He buried his face in her hair and held her close and bawled like a baby.

He was a muddle of happiness and confusion, as if his brain had been stirred like so much porridge. He was unable to think straight or put one thought logically after another; he felt the magnitude of the thing he'd done, and knew he should do something to carry through, though he wasn't sure what.

They had sat on his sofa, talking until three in the morning, but not once had they mentioned what they would do today; they had talked only about how they felt and how mindlessly happy and grateful they were that this astonishing benediction should come to them, as a wild bird might come to their outstretched palms.

"To have and to hold," she had murmured.

"'Til death do us part," he had said, nuzzling her hair.

"And no organizing of church suppers or ironing of fair linens, and positively *nothing* to do with the annual Bane and Blessing."

"Right," he said.

"Ever!" she said.

He hadn't a single rule or regulation to foist upon

her; he was chopped liver, he was cooked macaroni; he was dragged into the undertow of the great tsunami of love he'd so long held back.

They had prayed together, at last, and fallen asleep on the sofa, her head on his shoulder, his head against hers, bookends, then waked at five and scrambled to the back door, where Cynthia kissed him and darted through the hedge, devoutly hoping not to be seen.

He'd bounded up the stairs to his room with a vigor that amazed him, murmuring aloud a quote from Wordsworth:

"'Bliss it was in that dawn to be alive, But to be young was very heaven!'"

Bliss, yes, as if he'd suddenly become lighter than air, as if the stone were at last rolled away from the tomb. He thought he might spring upward like a jack-in-the-box. Was any of this familiar to him, had he ever felt it before? Never! Nothing in his supposed love for Peggy Cramer, all those years ago, had prepared him for this.

In a misting summer rain, he headed for the church office at nine o'clock with Barnabas on the red leash.

He should tell Emma, he supposed, who had served him faithfully for nearly thirteen years. And Puny, the best house help a man could ever have, Puny would want to know.

He could see them both, Emma wincing and frowning, then socking him on the arm with approval, and Puny—she would jump up and down and hoot and shout, and great tears would stream down her freckled cheeks. Then she'd go at once and bake a cake of cornbread from which he, due to his blasted diabetes, might have one unbuttered, albeit large, slice.

Aha! And there was Miss Sadie, of course! Wouldn't her eyes sparkle and gleam, and wouldn't she hug his neck for a fare-thee-well?

And wouldn't Louella break out a coconut cake or a chess pie and wouldn't they have a party right there in the kitchen at Fernbank?

On the other hand, wasn't Cynthia supposed to be along when he broke the news to everybody?

He sighed. He was in the very business of life's milestones, including the occasional overseeing of engagements, yet he seemed to have forgotten everything he ever knew— if, indeed, he ever knew anything.

Besides, he wasn't sure he was up for hooting and hollering and being punched in the arm or any of the other stuff that usually came with such tidings.

Then there was J.C. And Mule. And Percy.

Good Lord, he dreaded that encounter like a toothache. All that backslapping and winking and cackling, and the word spreading through the Grill like so much wildfire, and spilling out the door and up Main Street and around the monument to Lew Boyd's Exxon. . . .

He felt his stomach do a kind of dive, as it always did when he took off or landed in a plane.

If Barnabas hadn't suddenly jerked the leash, he would have walked straight into a telephone pole outside the Oxford Antique Shop.

Bottom line, he decided, Dooley Barlowe should be the first to know. And it was clearly right that they tell Dooley together. He was frankly relieved that Dooley had spent the night at Tommy's and hadn't been there to see him skid through the back door and drop to his knee. Not a pretty sight, he was sure of it.

He could just see the face of his thirteen-year-old charge when he heard the news. The boy would flush with embarrassment or relief, or both, then laugh like a hyena. He would very likely exclaim, *Cool!* then race upstairs with a joy that he dare not freely display.

Still, telling anyone at all seemed hotheaded and premature. This was between Cynthia and himself; it was their secret. It was somehow marvelous that it was yet unknown to anyone else in the world.

At the corner, he stopped at a hemlock to let Barnabas lift his leg, and suddenly knew he couldn't contain the secret any longer, he was full to bursting with it.

"Make it snappy," he said to his dog. "I have something to tell you."

Barnabas did as he was told, and when they crossed the street, the rector of the Chapel of our Lord and Savior paused in front of the church office and said under his breath, "I've just decided . . . that is, Cynthia and I are going to get . . ."

His throat tickled. He coughed. A car passed, and he tried again to tell his dog the good news.

But he couldn't say it.

He couldn't say the *m* word, no matter how hard he tried.

As he opened the office door, he realized with complete clarity where he should begin.

His bishop. Of course. How could he have forgotten he had a bishop, and that such a thing as this thing he was going to do would be of utmost importance to Stuart Cullen?

But, of course, he couldn't call Stuart this morning, because Emma Newland would be sitting at her desk cheek-by-jowl with his own.

He greeted his longtime, part-time secretary as

Barnabas collapsed with a sigh onto his rug in the corner.

Desperate to avoid eye contact, he sat down at once and began to scribble something, he knew not what, into his sermon notebook.

Emma stared at him over her half-glasses.

He put his left elbow on the desk and held his head in his hand, as if deeply thoughtful, feeling her hot stare covering him like a cloak.

Blast, he couldn't bear that look. She might have been examining his tonsils or readying him for colon surgery.

"For heaven's sake," he said, swiveling around in his squeaking chair to face the bookcases.

"I'd leave heaven out of this if I were you," she said, sniffing.

"What's that supposed to mean?"

"I mean, I can't imagine heaven wantin' anything to do with you this morning."

Church secretaries had been fired for less, much less, he thought, grinding his teeth. The office was suddenly doing that bizarre thing it sometimes did—it was growing rapidly and infinitely smaller; it was, in fact, becoming the size of a shoe box.

He bolted to his feet and half stood behind his desk, trying to get a deep breath.

"Your collar's too tight," she said.

"How do you know?"

"Your face is red as a beet."

"It's possible that I'm having a heart attack," he snapped.

"I'm telling you it's your collar. Are you wearin' one of those Velcro deals?"

"Yes."

"Let it out a little."

Dadgummit, she was right. He realized he was nearly choking to death. He adjusted the Velcro, disgusted with himself and everybody else.

What had happened to the soft, circumcised heart God had given him only last night? Where had the lighter-than-air spirit of this morning fled? Why was he grumping and grouching when he ought to be leaping and shouting?

Barnabas yawned and rolled on his side.

"I'm getting married!" he blurted uncontrollably. Then he sat down, hard, in his chair.

He would never be able to explain the mysteries surrounding love, only one of which surfaced when he confessed his news to Emma.

By the involuntary utterance of those three amazing words, his frozen Arctic tundra had been transformed into a warm tropical lake. Something in him had actually melted.

In the space of a few moments, he had become jelly. Or possibly custard. Then a foolish smile spread across his face, which seemed destined to remain there for the rest of his life.

When Emma left for the post office, vowing not to say a word to anyone, he prayed at his desk, went to the toilet and did a glucometer check, then positively swaggered to the phone to call his bishop.

Stuart's secretary said he was either in the loo or in a meeting, she wasn't sure which, but she would find out and have him call back.

He slumped in the chair, disappointed.

But wait. *Walter!* Of course, he must call Walter and Katherine at once.

The names of those with special interest in his good fortune were being revealed to him, one by one, in the way some are given inspiration for their Christmas card list.

Since Cynthia had never met Walter, his first cousin

and only known living relative, he supposed he was on his own for spilling the beans to New Jersey.

"Walter!"

"Cousin! We haven't heard from you in the proverbial coon's age."

"Which phone are you on?" asked the rector.

"The kitchen. Why?"

"Is Katherine there?"

"Just blew in from the nursing home, she's teaching them to finger paint. What's up, old fellow?"

"Tell her to get on the phone in the study."

"Katherine!" bellowed Walter. "Pick up in the study! It's clergy!"

"'Lo, Teds, darling, is that really you?" He could see the tall, thin-as-a-stick Katherine draped over the plaid chaise, with the cordless in one hand and her eternal glass of ginger ale in the other.

"Katherine, Walter," he said. "Are you sitting down?"

"Good heavens, what is it?" asked Walter, clearly alarmed.

"Teds . . . those tests you were going to have weeks ago . . . is it . . . ?"

"Dooley, is it Dooley?" asked Walter. "Or Barnabas? We know how you feel about—"

"I'm getting married," he said.

There! Twice in a row, and already it was getting easier.

The other end of the line erupted into a deafening whoop that could have filled Yankee Stadium. He held the receiver away from his ear, laughing for the first time this morning, as Barnabas leapt from the rug and stood barking furiously at the clamor pouring forth from New Jersey.

When Stuart hadn't called back in twenty minutes, he phoned again and was put through to the bishop's office.

"Stuart? Tim Kavanagh here. Are you sitting down?" He was truly concerned that no one go crashing to the floor in a faint.

"For the first time today, actually! What's up?"

"Remember the woman I once brought to visit you and Martha?" That wasn't what he wanted to say. "When we, ah, gave you the bushel of corn? *Cynthia!* You remember. . . ."

"I remember very well, indeed!"

"Well, you see, it's like this. . . ." He swallowed.

He heard his bishop chuckling. "Like what, Timothy?"

"Like . . ."

He was momentarily frozen again, then the custard triumphed.

". . . we're getting married!"

"Alleluia!" shouted his bishop. *"Alleluia!"*

Tears sprang suddenly to his eyes. He had been friends with his bishop since seminary, had confided his heart to him for years. And now came this greatest confidence, this best and most extraordinary of tidings.

"Martha will be thrilled!" said Stuart, sounding as youthful as a curate. "We'll have you for dinner, we'll have you for tea . . . we'll do it up right! This is the best news I've heard in an eon. Good heavens, man, I thought you'd never screw up your courage. How on earth did it happen?"

"It just came to me that . . . well . . ."

"What came to you?"

"That I didn't want to go on without her, that I couldn't."

"Bingo!" said his bishop.

"I, ah, went down on one knee, couldn't help myself."

"You should have done the full kneel, Timothy, she's a prize, a gem, a pearl above price! You dog, you don't deserve such a one!"

"Amen!" He said it the old Baptist way, with a long *a*, the way he was raised to say it.

"Well, now, thanks be to God, what about a date?" asked Stuart.

"We're thinking September, I know that's a busy month for you, but . . ."

"Let's see, I have my calendar right here." Deep sigh, pondering. "Alas, alack." Stuart's fingers drumming on his desktop. "Good heavens, I'd forgotten about that. Hmmm. Ahh." Tuneless, unconscious humming. "No, certainly not then."

If Stuart couldn't do it, they'd get it done somehow, they were definitely not waiting 'til October. . . .

"Oh, yes, look here! I've got September seventh, how's that? Otherwise, I can squeeze you in on—"

"I'm not much on being squeezed in," said the rector.

"Of course not! Will the seventh work for you, then?"

"We're willing to take whatever you have open."

"Then it's done!"

"Perfect!" said the rector.

"Now," said Stuart, "hang up so I can call Martha."

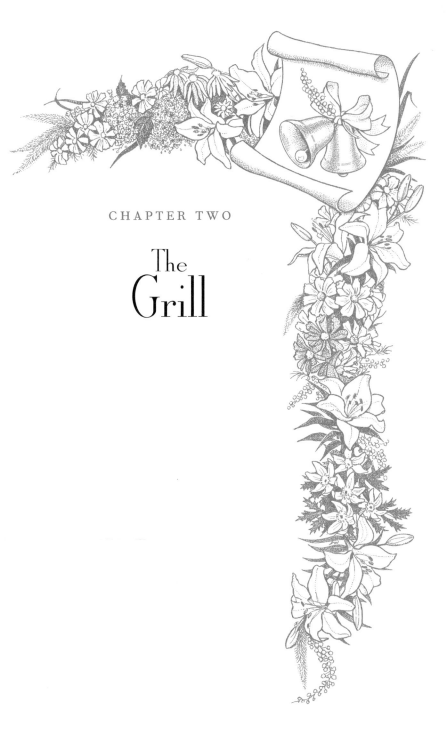

CHAPTER TWO

The
Grill

*Y*ou goin' to have babies?" asked Dooley.

"Not if I can help it," said Cynthia.

Searching the boy's face, Father Tim felt sure their news was a go, but wanted to hear Dooley declare it. He put his arm around Dooley's shoulders. "So, buddyroe, what do you think about all this?"

"Cool!" said Dooley.

Hallelujah! Dooley Barlowe had been buffeted by every violent wind imaginable before he came to live at the rectory over two years ago. Abandoned by his father and given by his alcoholic mother to his disabled grandfather, the boy had known only upheaval and change.

"Nothing will change," the rector promised. "You'll keep your same room, everything will flow on as usual. The only difference is, Cynthia will live here . . . instead of there." He gestured toward the little yellow house next door.

"I like her hamburgers better'n yours, anyway."

"Yes, but she doesn't have a clue how to fry baloney the way you like it. That's my little secret." He loved the look of this red-haired, earnest boy he'd come to cherish as a son, loved the rare surprise and delight shining in his eyes. Dooley and Cynthia had gotten on famously from the beginning, and Dooley's stamp of approval was more important than that of any bishop.

Not wishing to waste time gaining ground, Dooley gave Cynthia his most soulful look. "Since I'm goin' off t' 'at ol' school pretty soon, I bet *you'll* let me stay up 'til midnight."

Ah, politics! thought the rector, happily observing the two. They're everywhere.

Both Dooley and Emma had promised to keep mum, but truth be told, they were only human.

Before there was a leak, however unintentional, the news must go in Sunday's pew bulletin, thereby giving his parish the dignity of hearing it in church instead of on the street. As this was Friday, he supposed he should tell the guys at the Grill before they heard it from a parishioner. But would they keep it quiet until Lord's Chapel got the news on Sunday?

Then there was Miss Sadie. She definitely wouldn't like reading it in a pew bulletin.

He went home at eleven, changed hurriedly into his running clothes, and jogged up Old Church Lane with Barnabas.

He had just run down this hill to do the thing that resulted in why he was now running up it. Life was a mystery.

Huffing, he zigged to the left on Church Hill Road. Then he zagged to the right and ran up the driveway instead of cutting through the orchard like a common poacher.

Miss Sadie and Louella were sitting on the porch, fanning and rocking.

Each time he came to Fernbank's front porch, the years automatically rolled away. With these two old friends, he felt twelve, or possibly ten. Fernbank was his fountain of youth.

His heart pounding, he sat on the top step and panted. Barnabas lay beside him, doing the same.

"Father," said Miss Sadie, "aren't you too old for this running business?"

"Not by a long shot. I do it to keep young, as a matter of fact."

"Pshaw! Too much is made of running up hill and down dale. I've never done such a thing in my life, and I'm coming up on ninety and healthy as a horse."

Louella rocked. "That's right."

"Is that lemonade?" asked Father Tim, eyeing the pitcher on the wicker table.

"Louella, what's happened to our manners?" asked Miss Sadie.

"I don't know, Miss Sadie. I 'spec' we don' get enough comp'ny t' hardly need manners."

Louella put ice in a glass and handed it to Fernbank's mistress, who, ever conserving, poured the glass half full.

He got up and fetched the lemonade from her, wondering what on earth they would think about his announcement. He'd envisioned them as happy about it, but now he wasn't so sure. He drank the lemonade in two gulps and stood on one foot, then the other.

"You itchy," said Louella.

They could read him like a book.

"Miss Sadie, Louella, are you sitting down?"

The two women looked at each other, puzzled.

Of course they were sitting down, how stupid of him to ask such a thing, it had flown out of his mouth. "Joke!" he said feebly.

"Father, why don't *you* sit down? Get in this chair next to me and start rocking!"

He did as he was told. "Yes, ma'am." Eight years old.

"Louella and I like to rock in harmony, you pay a penny if you get off track."

"Who's leading?"

Miss Sadie looked at him as if he were dumb as a gourd.

"Honey, Miss Sadie always lead."

"Here we go," said Miss Sadie, looking bright and expectant. Since her feet barely touched the floor, this would be no small accomplishment.

After a ragged start, they nailed their synchronization, then worked on building momentum. Miss Sadie was flying in that rocker. . . .

Lord knows he couldn't sit around on porches all day like some jackleg priest, he had things to do, people to see, and besides, he was getting married. . . .

"Miss Sadie, Louella, I have great news."

The two women looked at him eagerly, never missing a beat.

"I'm getting married!" he shouted over the roar of six wooden rockers whipping along on aged white pine.

Miss Sadie's feet hit the floor, Louella's feet hit the

floor. Their rockers came to a dead stop. His was still going.

"To Miss Cynthia?" asked Louella, who was generally suspicious of good news.

"The very one!" he said, feeling a stab of happiness and pride.

Louella whooped and clapped her hands. "Thank you, Jesus! Thank you, *thank* you, Jesus!"

Miss Sadie dug a handkerchief from the sleeve of her dress and pressed it to her eyes. "This is a happy day, Father. I can't tell you how happy we are for you. Cynthia is the loveliest imaginable lady, so bright and positive, just what you need. I hope you've been on your knees thanking the Lord!"

He had, actually.

Louella was beaming. "Miss Sadie, I'm goin' t' cut us all some pie." As she opened the screen door to go inside, she turned and said, "An' remember you owe me five dollars!"

They heard Miss Sadie's longtime companion shuffling down the hall in her slippers. "Why, may I ask, do you owe Louella five dollars?"

She looked at him, barely able to conceal her mirth. "Because, Father, I bet five dollars you didn't have it in you to marry that lovely woman!"

Knowing how dear five dollars was to Sadie Baxter,

he smiled at his favorite parishioner and said, "I suppose I could say I'm sorry you lost."

She patted his arm fondly. "Actually, Father, your good news declares that we've all won."

⊙⊙

He typed it on his aged and finicky Royal manual and passed it to Emma, who would do whatever she did to work it into the bulletin:

> ii publish the banns of marriiage between Cynthiia clary Coppersmiith of thė pariish of the Chapel of our Lord and Saviior and father Tiimothy andrew Kavanagh, rector of thiis pariish. iif any of you know just cause why they may not be joiined together iin Holy Matriimony, you are biidden to declare iit.

⊙⊙

Mitford Muse editor J. C. Hogan slammed his over-stuffed briefcase onto the seat in the rear booth and thumped down, huffing.

Mule Skinner, local realtor and longtime Grill regular, slid in beside Father Tim.

"So, what are you roughnecks havin' today?" asked Velma, appearing with her order pad.

Mule jerked his thumb toward the rector. "I'm havin' what he's havin'."

"And what might that be?" This was not her favorite booth; at least two of these turkeys could never make up their minds.

"Chicken salad sandwich," said the rector, always prepared, "hold the mayo, and a side of slaw."

"I don't like slaw," said Mule.

"So sue me," said the rector.

"Make it snappy. You want what he's havin' or not?"

"I don't like slaw," Mule repeated. "I'll have what he's havin', except hold the slaw and give me mayo."

Velma pursed her lips. It was definitely time to retire. Some days, she'd rather work a canning line at the kraut factory than come in here and put up with this mess.

"I'll have th' special," said J.C., wiping his perspiring face with a square of paper towel.

"What special?" asked Mule. "I didn't know there was a special."

"Th' sign's plastered all over th' front door," said Velma, thoroughly disgusted. How Mule Skinner ever sold anybody a house was beyond her.

"So what is it?" asked Mule.

"Raw frog's liver on a bed of mashed turnips."

The rector and the editor roared; the realtor did not.

"I don't like turnips," said Mule.

J.C. rolled his eyes. "Just bring 'im th' frog's liver."

"Dadgummit, give me a BLT and get it over with."

"You might try sayin' please," snapped Velma, who had to talk to some people as if they were children.

"*Please*," said Mule through clenched teeth.

"White or wheat?" Velma inquired.

"Wheat!" said Mule. "No, make it white."

"Toasted or plain?"

"Ahhh . . ."

"Bring 'im toasted," said J.C.

Velma stomped off and came back with the coffeepot and filled their cups, muttering under her breath.

"What'd she say?" asked Mule.

"You don't want to know," said Father Tim.

He stirred his coffee, though there was nothing in it to stir. Maybe he shouldn't say anything until everyone had eaten lunch and felt . . . happier about life in general. After all, Mule was scowling, and J.C. had his nose stuck in the Wesley newspaper, checking to see if any *Muse* advertisers had defected to the *Telegram*.

He hoped the ensuing discussion wouldn't collapse into a mindless lecture on his advanced age. Age had nothing to do with it, nothing whatever. No one else had bothered to bring it up, and even if they'd thought it, they had the common decency not to mention it.

Then again, why wait to spill the beans? Maybe there was no such thing as the right time with this crowd.

"I've got some great news."

J.C. glanced up and took a sip of coffee. Mule swiveled toward him and looked expectant.

"Cynthia and I are getting married."

The coffee came spewing out of J.C.'s mouth, which was not a pretty sight.

Mule put his hand to his ear. "What's that? I can't always hear out of—"

J.C. wiped his shirtfront with a napkin. "He's gettin' *married*."

"Don't shout, for heaven's sake!" snapped the rector. He might as well have blared it up and down Main Street from a flatbed truck.

"Who to?" asked Mule.

"Who do you think?" asked J.C., who had apparently appointed himself the rector's official spokesman.

"Cynthia," said Father Tim, wishing to the Lord he'd never mentioned it. "And I have to ask your complete confidence, you're not to tell a soul until it comes out in the pew bulletin on Sunday. I need your word on this," he insisted.

"You want me to swear on th' Bible?" asked Mule.

"No, just promise me. I didn't want you to hear it on the street, I wanted to tell you in person. But I don't want my parish to hear it on the street, either."

"Done," said J.C., shaking hands across the table.

"You've got my word," said Mule.

"Son of a gun. Married." J.C. shook his head. "I thought you had good sense."

"I do have good sense. Look who I'm marrying." His chest actually felt more expansive as he said this.

"Now, that's a fact," agreed J.C. "Cynthia Coppersmith is one fine lady, smart as a whip and good-lookin' into the bargain. What she sees in you is a mystery to me."

"You sure about this?" asked Mule. "Is it a done deal?"

"Done deal. We'll be married in September."

Mule scratched his head. "Seems like you're a little . . . *old* for this, seein' it's the first time and all. I mean, sixty-five—"

"Sixty-two," said the rector. "Sixty-*two*."

J.C. looked grim. "I wouldn't get married if somebody gave me a million bucks. *After* taxes."

"You all are a real encouragement, I must say." The rector heard a positive snarl in his voice.

"Hold on," said Mule. "We're glad for you, cross

my heart an' hope to die. It just shocked me, is all, I'll get over it. See, I'm used to you th' way you *are*. . . ."

"Right. Emerson said it was a bloomin' inconvenience to have to start seeing somebody in a new light. But here's to you, buddyroe." The editor hoisted his coffee cup as Velma delivered their lunch.

She carried a plate in each hand and one in the crook of her right arm. "Take this offa my arm," she said to Mule. He took it.

She set the other two plates down and stomped off.

"I didn't order this," said Mule.

"That's mine," said J.C., snatching the plate.

"If I'd known that's what you were havin,' I'd of had that. Country-style steak is practically my favorite." Mule gazed with remorse at his sandwich, which featured a dill pickle on the side.

"I don't like pickles, you want my pickle?" he asked the rector, who hadn't felt so generally let down since the choir and the organist got the flu simultaneously and the congregation had to sing a cappella.

It was all rushing by in a blur. He didn't want to lose this moment so quickly. He wanted to savor it, rejoice in it, be thankful in it.

He put on his pajamas and pondered what was happening.

It gladdened him that he wanted to see her at the slightest opportunity; he yearned toward his neighbor as if a magnet had been installed in him on the night of his birthday, attracted to some powerful magnet in her.

How he wished the magnet had been installed sooner. He didn't want to think of the time he'd wasted trying to make up his mind. But no, it hadn't been his mind that was slow to make up, it was his heart. His heart had always pulled away when he felt happiness with her; each time the joy came, he had retreated, filled with the fear of losing himself.

He remembered the dream he'd had when she was in New York, when their letters had helped thaw the frozen winter that kept them apart. He dreamed he was swimming toward her in something like a blue lagoon, when his strength failed and he began to sink, slowly, as if with the weight of stones. He felt the water roaring in and the great, bursting heaviness of his head. He had come awake then, gasping for air and crying out.

Now there was the custard feeling, which would terrify most people if they didn't recognize it for what it was—it was love unhindered.

This, too, took his breath away, but by the grace of

God, he was easy with it, not enfeebled or frightened by it.

No wonder he had counseled so many men before their walk down the aisle; the true softening of the heart and spirit toward a woman was usually an alarmingly unfamiliar feeling. How might a man wield a spear and shield, preserve his very life, if he were poured out at her feet like so much pudding?

He turned off the lamp and went to his knees by his bed, praying aloud in the darkened room.

"Father, we bless You and thank You for this miracle, for choosing us to receive it.

"May we treat the love You've given us with gratitude and devotion, humor and astonishment.

"May it be a river of living water to bring delight and encouragement to others, Lord, for we must never hold this rare blessing to ourselves, but pour it out like wine.

"Protect her, Lord, give her courage for whatever lies ahead, and give me, I pray, whatever is required to love her well and steadfastly all the days of our lives."

There was something else, something else to be spoken tonight. He was quiet for a time in the still, dark room where only the sound of his dog's snoring was heard.

Yes. There it was. The old and heavy thing he so often ignored, that needed to be said.

"Father—continue to open me and lay me bare, for I have been selfish and closed, always keeping something back, even from You. Forgive me. . . ."

The clock ticked.

The curtains blew out in a light breeze.

"Through Jesus Christ, our Lord.

"Amen."

CHAPTER THREE

The
Fanfare

The tidal wave, the firestorm, the volcanic spew—all the things he'd dreaded had come at last, and all at once.

People were pounding him on the back, kissing him on the cheek, slapping him on the shoulder, pumping his hand. One of his older parishioners, a mite taller than himself, patted his head; another gave him a Cuban cigar, which Barnabas snatched off the kitchen table and ate in the wrapper.

Well-wishers bellowed their felicitations across the street, rang his phone off the hook at home and office, and generally made a commotion over the fact that he had feelings like the rest of the common horde.

Cynthia's phone got a workout, as well. In approximately three days since the news had hit the street, a total of five bridal showers had been booked, not to mention a luncheon at Esther Cunningham's and a tea at

Olivia Harper's. Emma Newland was planning a sit-down dinner with the help of Harold's mother, and the ECW was doing a country club event.

He was stopped on the street by Mike Stovall, the Presbyterian choirmaster, who offered to throw in sixteen voices for the wedding ceremony, which, including the voices at Lord's Chapel, would jack the total to thirty-seven. "A real tabernacle deal!" enthused the choirmaster. "And tell you what, we'll throw in a trumpet! How's that?"

(He'd hardly known what to do about the Anglicans from Wesley, who offered to throw in a handbell choir.)

Had he agreed to Mike Stovall's ridiculous offer? He didn't think so. He might have mumbled something like "Great idea," which it was, but would Mike take that to mean he'd accepted? Thirty-seven people in the choir would barely leave room for the bride and groom to squeeze to the altar.

His head was swimming, his stomach was churning, his palms were sweating, he felt like . . . a rock star. That heady notion was soon squelched, however, when he was forced to dash to the toilet at the church office and throw up. He flushed three times, trying to disguise the wretched indignity of the whole appalling act.

"Something I ate," he said to Emma, who knew a lame excuse when she heard one. He snatched a book off the shelf and sat with his back to her, numb as a pickled herring.

"I'm sorry," he told Cynthia one evening at the rectory.

"Whatever for?"

"For . . . you know . . . the ruckus, the . . . the *tumult*!"

"But dearest, I love this! There's never been such ado over any of my personal decisions. It's wonderful to me!"

"It is?"

"And can't you see how happy this is making everyone? Sometimes I think it really isn't for us, it's for them!"

"Wrong," he said, taking her hand in his. "It's for us."

"Then please relax and enjoy it, darling. Can't you?"

She looked at him so searchingly, with such a poignant hope, that he was weak with a mixture of shame for his current dilapidation and love for her bright spirit.

"Of course. You're right. I'll try. I promise."

"Please. You see, this will only happen to us once."

There! She'd nailed it. What made him uneasy was that it was happening *to* them; he preferred having some say-so, some . . . *control*.

"Let God be in control," she said, smiling. He was

unfailingly astonished that she could read his mind. "Af-ter all, He's done a wonderful job so far."

The tension flowed out of him like air from a tire.

"Ahhhh," he said, sitting back on the sofa and un-snapping his collar.

The bishop rang him shortly after dawn.

"Timothy! I know you're an early riser. . . ."

"If I wasn't, I am now."

"Martha and I want the two of you to use our old family camp in Maine, it's on a lake, has a boathouse and two canoes, and an absolutely glorious view! We're thrilled about all this, you must say yes, we'll call at once and make sure it's set aside. . . ."

His bishop was gushing like a schoolgirl.

"And wait 'til you hear the loons, Timothy! Mesmer-izing! Magical! Our family has gathered at this house for nearly fifty years, it might have been the set of *On Golden Pond*! Trust me, you'll be thrilled, you'll think you've expired and shot straight up!"

"Thanks, Stuart, let me get back to you on that, we haven't really discussed what we're going to do."

"Don't even think about Cancún, Timothy!"

He hadn't once thought of Cancún.

"And get any notion of southern France out of your head . . ."

He hadn't had any such notion in his head.

". . . it's all the rage, southern France, but you'll like Maine far better! It's where Martha and I spent *our* honeymoon, you know."

He hardly knew what to say to all the offers pouring in; Ron Malcolm had offered the services of a limousine following the wedding, but he'd declined. Why would they need a limo when they were only going a block and a half to spend their wedding night?

Esther Bolick sat in the den that opened off her kitchen and stared blankly at *Wheel of Fortune;* it was nothing more than flickering images, she didn't give a katy what a five-word definition for *show biz* might be.

She glanced irritably at Gene, who was snoring in his recliner after a supper of fresh lima beans, new potatoes, fried squash, coleslaw, and skillet cornbread. They'd also had green onions the size of her fist, which Gene took a fit over. "Sweet as sugar!" he declared. She had never trusted a man who wouldn't eat onions.

She was thinking that she was happy for Father Kavanagh, happy as can be. But it had been *days* since she heard the good news and not *one word* had anybody said to her about baking the wedding cake. She knew Cynthia was very talented; she could do anything in the world except cross-stitch, so she could probably bake her own cake.

Well, then, that was it, she thought with relief. That was why nobody had said doodley-squat about her famous orange marmalade being the center of attraction at one of the most important weddings in Mitford in . . . maybe *decades*.

On the other hand, why would anybody in their right mind take time to bake their own wedding cake when all they had to do was dial Esther Bolick at 8705?

She had designed that cake over and over in her mind. Considering that the color of the icing was white, she might crown the top with calla lilies. Jena Ivey at Mitford Blossoms could order off for callas in a heartbeat. She'd even thought of scattering edible pearls around on the icing; she'd never used edible pearls before, and hoped people's fillings wouldn't crack out and roll around on the parish hall floor.

She also considered wreathing the base of the cake with real cream-colored roses, plus she'd have icing roses tumbling down the sides—after all, she'd seen a few magazines in her time, she was no hick, she knew what was what in today's cake world. And would she dun the father for all that work? Of course not! Not a red cent, though Lord only knows, what they charged for ingredients these days made highway robbery look law-abiding.

Esther pursed her lips and stared, unseeing, at a spot on the wall.

The thing was, it didn't make a bit of sense for somebody to bake their own wedding cake . . .

. . . so, maybe somebody else had been asked to bake the cake.

The thought made her supper turn to a rock in her digestive system. She balled up her fist and rubbed the place between her ribs, feeling the pain all the way to her heart.

How could they ask anybody else to bake the father's wedding cake? He had raved about her orange marmalade for years, had personally told her it was the best cake he had ever put in his mouth, bar none. *Bar none!* So what if two pieces of it had nearly killed him? It was his own blamed fault for stuffing himself!

And how many orange marmalades had she carried to the doors of the downtrodden, the sick, the elderly, and the flat broke? And how many hundreds of miles had she walked from fridge to oven to sink, getting varicose veins and bad knees, not to mention bunions? Well, then—*how many?*

She remembered the rueful time she baked marmalades the livelong day and finally dragged herself to her electric-powered recliner, where she pressed the button on her remote and tilted back to what Gene called "full sprawl." All she lacked of being dead was the news getting out, when, *blam!* the most violent and sudden storm you'd ever want to see hit square over their house and the power went out. There she was, trapped in that plug-in recliner, clutching a dead remote—with no way to haul herself up and Gene Bolick out to a meeting at the Legion hut.

She recalled the shame of having to pitch herself over the side like a sailor jumping ship; landing on the floor had caused her right leg to turn blue as blazes, then black, then brown, not to mention her hip, which, as she'd told the doctor, had given her sporadical pain ever since. And all that for what? For four orange marmalades to help raise money for a new toilet at the library!

Trembling slightly, Esther picked up the TV remote and surfed to a commercial with a talking dog. She and Gene had never had a dog and never would, they were too much trouble, but she liked dogs. She tried to occupy her mind with dogs so she wouldn't think about a shocking idea that suddenly occurred to her. Her attention wandered, however, and there it was, the bald truth, staring her in the face:

Winnie Ivey!

Winnie Ivey was exactly who they'd turned to for this special, once-in-a-lifetime deal—Winnie Ivey, who was a *commercial* baker; Winnie Ivey, who'd never made just *one* of anything in her life!

She sat bolt upright and tried to get her breath. Commercial flour! Commercial butter! And, for all she knew, powdered eggs.

Her blood ran cold.

"Of all th' dadblame things to do!" she said, kicking one of her shoes across the room.

"What?" Gene raised his head and looked around. "Was that you, dollface?"

"Do you know who they've asked to bake the weddin' cake?"

"What weddin' cake?"

"Why, the father's, of course!"

"Who?" asked Gene, genuinely interested.

"Winnie Ivey."

Gene burped happily. "Well, I'll say."

"You'll say what?" she demanded.

When his wife stood up and leaned over his recliner as she was now doing, he thought she looked ten feet tall. "I'll say that was a dirty, low-down trick not to ask you to bake it!"

There. Gene Bolick knew what side his bread was buttered on.

She was stomping into the kitchen, mad as a hornet, when the phone rang.

"Hallo!" she shouted, ready to knock somebody's head off.

"Esther? This is Cynthia Coppersmith, I'm so glad you're home, I thought you and Gene might have gone bowling tonight. Timothy and I agree we'd like nothing better than to have one of your fabulous three-layer marmalades as our wedding cake. We hope you'll be able to do it, Timothy said we'll pay top dollar!"

Cynthia was astounded to hear Esther Bolick burst into tears, followed by a pause in which there was considerable murmuring and shuffling about.

"Hello!" Gene bawled into the phone. "Esther said tell you she'd love to bake your weddin' cake! And no charge, you tell th' father no charge!"

Now his choir was upset because the crowd from down the street had horned in.

Had he actually agreed to such a plan? He remembered only that Mike had brought it up, nothing more. He called Mike Stovall.

"I believe we talked about your choir joining our choir for—"

"Right! And everything's going great, just great! We've got a couple of ideas for the music—"

"The music, of course, is entirely Richard's domain, Richard's and Cynthia's, so—"

"Well!" Mike Stovall sounded annoyed.

"In any case, given the small quarters of our nave and chancel, I think it might be best to—"

"Oh, we've thought that through, Father, here's the deal. Your choir in the chancel, ours in the rear, what do you think?"

He couldn't think. He needed a job foreman, somebody in a hard hat. . . .

"It *will* be September, you know."

Hessie Mayhew—*Mitford Muse* reporter, Presbyterian mover and shaker, and gifted flower arranger—had come to consult with Cynthia in the rectory living room. As Father Tim served them lemonade and shortbread, he couldn't help but listen. After all, wasn't he a gardener? Wasn't he interested in flowers?

He crept to a corner of the room with a glass of lemonade and appeared to be wholly absorbed in scratching his dog behind the ears.

"And in September," said Hessie, "there's precious little that's worth picking." Hessie had staked her reputation on what she foraged from meadow and pasture, roadside and bank. Her loose, informal bouquets were quite the hit at every spring and summer function, and her knowledge of where the laciest wild carrot bloomed and the showiest hydrangeas grew was both extensive and highly secret. However, as autumn drew on and blooms began to vanish, she hedged her bets—by dashing cold water on her clients' heady expectations, she was usually able to come up with something agreeably breathtaking.

"What does this mean?" asked Cynthia, looking worried.

"It means that what we mostly have to deal with is pods."

"Pods?" His fiancée was aghast.

Hessie shrugged. "Pods, seeds, berries," she said, expanding the list of possibilities. "Unless you'd like *mums*." Hessie said this word with undisguised derision.

Mums. He noted that the very word made his neighbor blanch.

Cynthia looked his way, imploring, but he did not make eye contact. No, indeed, he would not get in the middle of a discussion about pods and berries, much less mums.

"Pods and berries *can* be wonderful," Hessie stated, as if she were the full authority, which she was. "Mixed with what's blooming and tied in enormous bunches, they can look very rich hanging on the pew ends. Of course, we'll use wide ribbons, I'd suggest French-wired velvet, possibly in sage and even something the color of the shumake berry." As a bow to tradition, Hessie enjoyed using the mountain pronunciation for sumac.

He stole a glance at Cynthia from the corner of his eye. How had that gone down? She seemed uncertain.

"Why can't we just order dozens of roses and arm-loads of lilacs and be done with it?"

Hessie sucked in her breath. "Well," she said, "If you want to spend *that* kind of money . . ."

And let the word get out that his bride was a spendthrift? That was Hessie's deeper meaning; he knew Hessie Mayhew like a book. He knew, too, that Hessie considered the ordering of lilacs in September to be something akin to criminal—not only would they cost a royal fortune, they were *out of season in the mountains*!

"Not to mention," said Hessie, pursing her lips, "they're out of season in the mountains."

"Excuse me for living," said his fiancée. "Anyway, we *don't* want to spend that kind of money." In truth, his bride-to-be had the capability to spend whatever she wished, being a successful children's book author and illustrator. Besides, thought the rector, wasn't it her wedding? Wasn't it their money to spend however they liked? He hunkered down in the chair, anonymous, invisible, less than a speck on the wall.

Cynthia heaved a sigh. "So, Hessie, whatever you think. Sage and burgundy . . . or let's call it claret, shall we? Burgundy sounds so . . . *heavy*. Do you think we should intermix the ribbon colors along the aisle or put sage on one side and claret on the other?"

The color deepened in Hessie's ample cheeks. "Sage for the bride's side and claret for the groom's side, is my opinion!"

"Of course, I don't have any family for the bride's side. Only a nephew who isn't really a nephew, and the last I heard, he was in the Congo."

His heart was touched by the small sadness he heard in her voice, and so, apparently, was Hessie's.

"Oh, but you *do* have family!" Hessie threw her head back, eyes flashing. "The entire parish is your family!"

Cynthia pondered this extravagant remark. "Do you really think so?"

"*Think* so?" boomed Hessie. "I *know* so! Everyone says you're the brightest thing to happen to Lord's Chapel in an *eon*, and you must *not* forget it, my dear!" Mitford's foremost, all-around go-getter patted Cynthia's arm with considerable feeling.

Click! Something wonderful had just taken place. Hessie Mayhew, sensitive to the bone underneath her take-charge manner, had for some reason decided to be his fiancée's shield and buckler from this moment on; and nobody messed with Hessie.

"We'll fill every pew on the bride's side," Hessie predicted. "We'll be falling over ourselves to sit there! It's certainly where *I'm* sitting—no offense, Father."

Cynthia took Hessie's rough hand. "Thank you, Hessie!"

Thank you, Lord, he thought, forsaking his invisibility by bolting from the chair to refill their glasses all around.

"And what," inquired Hessie, "are you planning to do, Father, other than show up?"

Hessie Mayhew was smiling, but he knew she was

dead serious. Hessie believed that every man, woman, and child, including the halt and lame, should participate in all parish-wide events to the fullest.

"I'm doing the usual," he said, casting a grin in the direction of his neighbor. "I'm baking a ham!"

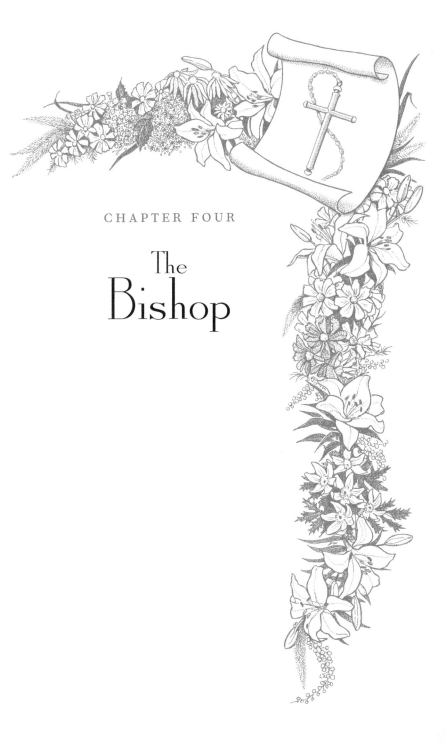

CHAPTER FOUR

The
Bishop

*G*one to seed" is how the rector once fondly described his rectory home of more than thirteen years. Puny's eagerness to keep the place fastidious had, he was certain, worn away at least a stratum of walnut on the highboy, a gram or two of wool on the Aubusson, and a millimeter of sterling on the tea service.

She was now feverishly removing another layer from the whole kaboodle, in preparation for any celebration that may be held in the rectory, since, she said, Cynthia's house was too small to cuss a cat, no offense to Violet.

Nearly overcome by the odor of Lemon Pledge, he went to the phone and dialed his neighbor. "Want to bring your notebook and go to the park?"

"I'll race you!" she said.

They sat on the bench and listened for a moment to the birds and a light wind that stirred the leaves in Baxter Park. He kissed her, lingering. She kissed him back, lingering still more. She drew away and fanned herself with the notebook, laughing.

"On to more serious matters!" he exclaimed. "First order of business—pew bulletin or invitations, what do you think?"

"Pew bulletin! That way everyone knows, and those few who aren't in the parish, we'll call. I'll try to reach David, though I can't imagine he'd trek all the way from the Congo to Mitford!"

"Where shall we put Walter and Katherine? Your place or mine?"

"First things first," she said. "We need to know where we're spending our wedding night."

"The rectory?"

"But darling, your bed is so small."

"Yes, but your bed is so *big*." In his view, they could hold a fox hunt on the vast territory she called a bed.

"Draw straws!" she said, leaning from the bench to pluck two tall spears of grass. She fiddled with them a moment, asked him to close his eyes, then presented them in her fist.

"Gambling again," he said.

"Long one, my house, short one, your house."

He drew the short one.

"Rats in a poke!" fumed his neighbor.

"Watch your language, Kavanagh."

"Isn't it a tad early to call me Kavanagh?"

"I'm practicing."

"Anyway, there's your answer. Walter and Katherine spend the night at my house."

"Done!" He checked the topic off his list. "Have you thought any more about flower girls?"

"Amy Larkin and Rebecca Owen!"

"Perfect. Music?"

"Richard and I are just beginning to work on it—let's definitely ask Dooley to sing."

"Splendid. Should have thought of it myself."

"A cappella."

"He doesn't go for a cappella."

"He'll get over it, darling, I promise, and it will be wonderful, a true highlight for everyone. 'O Perfect Love,' what do you think?"

"There won't be a dry eye in the house. By the way, we're scheduled for the bishop on Wednesday at eleven o'clock."

"What are you wearing?" she asked.

"Oh, something casual. A pink curler in my hair, perhaps."

She swatted his arm over this old joke.

"I love you madly," she said.

"I love you madlier."

"Do not!"

"Do, too!"

"Prove it!"

"I shall. I'm serving you dinner tonight, Puny made chicken and dumplings."

"Chicken and dumplings!" she crowed.

"With fresh lima beans."

"I'm your slave!"

"I'll remember that," he said.

He felt the same age he usually felt at Miss Sadie's house.

Here he was in his bishop's office, seated next to his sweetheart, and only minutes away, they'd be talking about sex. He felt the blood surge to his head, coloring his face like a garden tomato. Though he was the priest, presumably competent to discuss a wide variety of personal issues, it was, in fact, Cynthia who felt perfectly at ease talking about anything to anybody, anytime.

They were currently in the touchy area of Financial, always the leading subject on Stuart's program for premarital counseling. Thus far, they were in good shape, having discussed some days ago what Stuart called his bottom-line on the issue:

Consult with the other about significant purchases, be open about your assets and willing to share equally, and agree on a budget that puts God first.

"And how do you feel, Timothy, about having a wife whose income is significantly greater than your own?"

Blast. Why couldn't Stuart have the discretion to avoid this issue? He and Cynthia had discussed it, but he hadn't been completely candid with her. He hesitated, hating this moment for both of them. "Not good," he said at last.

Cynthia looked at him. Did he see hurt or surprise, or both?

"God brought us together," he said. "He knew what He was doing. And if He doesn't mind the inequity in what I bring to the marriage, then I know I'm not to mind it, either. But—sometimes I do.

"Please understand that I don't resent her greater assets, not in the least—Cynthia Coppersmith is the hardest-working, most deserving woman I've ever known. The problem, if there is one, is that . . ." He paused. What *was* the problem? Hadn't he pondered this on several sleepless nights?

"The problem," said Cynthia, "is loss of control! Isn't that it, dearest? You've feared a loss of control all along, from the beginning. And now I'm the one who could buy a new car or take us to Spain—"

"I don't want to go to Spain," he said, feeling suddenly vulnerable, close to tears. He also didn't want a new car; he was perfectly happy with the old one.

Stuart smiled.

"If you're all that God wishes you to be in marriage, you will be one flesh. The money must belong to you equally, Timothy. In your heart you must be able to accept it, not as money you've worked for and earned, but as money God means you to have in stewardship with your wife."

Cynthia leaned over and kissed him on the cheek. Tears sprang instantly to his eyes and escaped to the sides of his nose before he could press them with a handkerchief.

"I think," he said, "that I'm overwhelmed on every side. I still can't think why God should give me this tremendous blessing—a gracious and loving soul who comprehends the depths of my own soul completely—and then to add financial resources beyond my wildest dreams . . .

"In truth, money means very little to me. I've lived simply all my life, and can't imagine doing otherwise."

"You've been exceedingly generous to others," said Stuart. "For example, you've poured your personal revenues into the Children's Hospital for years. Now, Timothy, you must allow someone to be generous with you, if she so chooses."

"I so choose!" Cynthia patted the rector's arm.

Relieved, they all had a sip of water from glasses waiting on a tray.

"Another crucial issue," said Stuart, "is in-laws."

"We won't have any!" exclaimed Cynthia.

Stuart smiled paternally. "In truth, you will."

"We will?"

"According to the Lord's Chapel membership register, there are one hundred and eighty-three of them, which roughly translates to a mere hundred and twenty-five *active* in-laws."

His fiancée appeared vexed, to say the least. "Yes, and there are some who can't bear the sight of me anymore. Everything was just fine until—"

"Until they learned you were getting married," said Stuart. "Then the jealousy flooded in. They were there first—they got his undivided attention for years—now it must be divided."

"Ugh," she said.

"What I hope you'll be able to live with is that his attention to you will also be divided. Like them, you'll have to share your priest. Unlike them, you must also share your beloved, your sweetheart." Stuart looked fondly at Cynthia. "If anyone can do this, you're the one."

"Thank you," she said. "Pray for me."

"Martha and I have prayed for you since the day Timothy brought you to lunch. We both thought you possessed the most extraordinary light, it reflected upon our friend like a beacon. We thank you for that."

The rector noted with a pang of tenderness that his fiancée blushed deeply, something he rarely witnessed.

"I've always felt it takes especially noble character to be a clergy spouse," said Stuart. "In any case, you and they will soon grow accustomed to sharing him; it's all a process—a matter of time and patience and love. I know you're willing."

"Yes!" she said. "Oh, yes!"

The bishop folded his hands across his lean midsection and gazed at his visitors.

Here it comes, thought the rector.

"Do you pray together?" asked Stuart.

"Yes!" they said in unison.

"Every evening," volunteered Father Tim.

"Excellent! I'm reminded of what our friend Oswald Chambers said, that prayer doesn't fit us for the greater work, prayer is the greater work. Praying together affirms you as one flesh, and, among the endless benefits it bestows, it can greatly enhance your sexual communication."

A patch of light danced upon the worn Persian carpet, reflecting the branches of a dogwood tree outside the window.

"The highest form of prayer is one in which we don't beg for ourselves," said Stuart, "but seek to know what we can do for God. This delights God immensely! As you seek to know what you can do for the other, you will surely receive your own inexpressible delight."

The rector took Cynthia's hand.

"To put it simply, making love confirms your spiritual relationship, and your spiritual relationship will deepen your lovemaking. It all moves in a wondrous circle."

The rector and his neighbor drew a deep breath at precisely the same moment and looked at each other, laughing.

"Now!" said Stuart.

"Now, what?" asked Father Tim.

"Conflict resolution."

"Do we have to?" asked Cynthia.

"Have you had any conflicts?"

The two looked at each other. "His car," she said.

"What about my car?" queried the rector.

"Don't you remember? I said it was a gas guzzler, has rust, and the seat covers look like Puny's dishrags."

"And I said I'm perfectly satisfied with it." There! The bishop wanted conflict, he got conflict. The rector felt his collar suddenly tighten.

"And so," Cynthia told Stuart, "when we drive on the Parkway or visit our bishop, we take my car."

"How do you feel about that?"

She wrinkled her nose. She stared briefly at the ceiling. She smiled. "I can live with it."

Stuart chuckled. He had his own opinion of his priest's car, but far be it from him to comment. "It's terrific that you're willing to name the conflict, my dear. This equips us to attack the problem instead of attacking the other person."

Stuart sat back in his chair. "So, Timothy, how do you feel about driving her car instead of yours?"

"Good!" he said, meaning it. "I can live with it." He pressed Cynthia's hand and turned to look at her. She appeared to sparkle in some lovely way he'd never seen before. After his brief moment of righteous indignation, he was custard again.

On the way home in her Mazda, he noticed that she looked at him fondly more than once.

"Sweetie pie," she murmured, patting his knee.

Sweetie pie! As a kid, he was called Slick; Katherine called him Teds; one and all called him Father. He liked this new appellation best of all. Maybe one day—*maybe*—he'd look into trading his Buick for a new model. But certainly nothing *brand*-new, no; no, indeed.

CHAPTER FIVE

The Joke

$\mathcal{H}$e drove to the Wesley mall and looked in the jewelry store display cases.

His heart sank like a stone. There was absolutely nothing that measured up to the fire and sparkle, the snap and dazzle of his neighbor.

He would have a ring made, then, fashioned exclusively for Cynthia Coppersmith Kavanagh. He saw their initials somehow entwined inside the band—*ccktak*. But of course he had no earthly idea who to call or where to turn. When someone left a Ross-Simon catalog on the table at the post office, he snatched it up and carried it outside to his car, where he pored over the thing until consciousness returned and he realized he'd sat there with the motor running for a full half hour, steaming in his raincoat like a clam in its shell.

"I'm sorry," he said, looking at her bare ring finger.

"If I'd done things right, I would have given you a ring when I proposed."

"I don't really want an engagement ring, dearest. Just a simple gold band would be perfect."

"You're certain?"

"Yes!" she said. "I love simple gold bands."

The image of his mother's wedding band came instantly to mind. It was in his closet, in a box on the shelf, tied by a slender ribbon. He would take it to the store and have it cleaned and engraved and present it at the altar with unspeakable joy and thanksgiving.

He felt he was at last beginning to get things right.

Uncle Billy Watson brushed the leaves and twigs from last night's storm off the seat of a rusting dinette chair and sat down in the backyard of the Porter house, a.k.a. Mitford's town museum.

He gazed dolefully into the sea of towering grass that extended to the rear of the house and then beyond his view. The town crew was supposed to mow the grass once every twelve days; by his count, it was fourteen going on fifteen, and a man could get lost out here and not be heard from again; it was a disgrace the way the town put every kind of diddledaddle ahead of mowing something as proud and fine as their own museum. If he could do it himself, he would, but his arthritis hardly allowed him to get up and down the steps, much less scour a full acre and a quarter with a rusted push mower. He hoped that when he got to Heaven, the Lord would outfit him with a new body and give him a job that *required* something of a man.

But he hadn't come out here to get his dander up. He'd come out to noodle his noggin about a joke to tell at the preacher's wedding, back in that room where they'd all eat cake and ham after the ceremony. Though nobody had said a word about it, the old man knew the preacher would be expecting a joke, he'd be counting on it, and it was his responsibility, his civic duty to tell the best joke he could come up with.

He would never say this to a soul, but it seemed like the preacher getting married so late in life was sort of a joke in itself. It would be a different thing if the father had been married before and had some practice, but as far as anybody knew, he hadn't had any practice.

But who was he to judge other people's setups? Half the town thought he was crazy as a bedbug for living with Rose Watson; even his uncle—who'd come to see them years ago when Rose was still as pretty as a speckled pup—his uncle had said, "They ain't no way I'm understandin' how you put up with this mess."

Her illness seemed to start right after they married, though he'd witnessed, and ignored, warning signs from the day they met. For years, he'd told himself that it was something he'd done wrong, that he hadn't cherished her like the vows said, and maybe God was punishing them both for his ignorance and neglect. Then the doctors found out about the disease he couldn't spell and could barely pronounce, schizophrenia.

On the worst days, he squeezed his eyes shut and remembered the girl he'd seen in the yard of this very house, more than—what was it?—forty-five, maybe fifty years ago. She was barefooted and had her hair tied back with a ribbon. Ragged and dirty from working in the fields since daylight, he'd come up from the valley with a wagonload of tomatoes and roasting ears, carrying a sack of biscuits and fried side meat for his dinner. He'd gone around the village looking for a spot to park his wagon and sell his produce, and saw her standing in her yard. At first he thought she was a statue. Then she moved and the light fell on her in a certain way and he called out, "Would you let a man park his wagon on your road?" And she'd walked out to him and smiled at him and nodded. "Get on down," she said. He'd always remember her first words to him: *Get on down*. He was ashamed that he wasn't wearing shoes, but then he saw that she wasn't, either. She had hung around, looking at him in a way that made him feel uneasy, then happy, and he'd shared his biscuits and side meat with her and she'd gone in the house and brought out a Mason jar of tea so cold and sweet it hurt his teeth. Between times when customers came and went, she talked about herself more than a little. Her beloved brother, Willard, was dead in the war, buried across the ocean in France, and she was looked after by a woman who paid no attention to her. By early afternoon, he'd sold everything but two tomatoes, which he gave to Rose, who said she'd allow him to park his wagon there next week.

They married eighteen months later, against the wishes of his family in the valley, whom he never went back to visit. And there he was, a rough valley boy with no education to speak of, married to a girl with a big inheritance including the finest house in Mitford, and him caning chairs and making birdhouses and doing whatever else he could to hold up his end of the bargain.

But he wouldn't go back and do it any different. Nossir. He'd loved that long-legged girl with the wild eyes more than anything in this world, and could never forget how she used to cling to him and call him Billy Boy and Sweet William, and kiss him with all the innocence of a woods violet.

His chin dropped to his chest and he jerked awake. Here he was sleeping when he had a job to do.

What was the job? For a moment, he couldn't remember. Then it came to him.

His hand trembled as he propped his cane against the tree. "Lord," he said aloud, "I hope You don't mind me askin' You to provide a good joke for th' preacher, don't you know. . . ."

Mayor Esther Cunningham couldn't help herself. Every time she thought about Father Tim getting married, she thought about the way she and Ray had met and courted, and her eyes misted. She did not like her eyes to mist; she had quit crying years ago when her daddy passed. Whenever she felt like crying, she had learned to turn it inside, where it sometimes felt like a Popsicle melting. She had read an article in a magazine at Fancy Skinner's which said that if you turn sorrow in, it will come out—as cancer or something worse, though she couldn't think of anything worse. The article had gone on to say that intimacy with your husband was good for your health, and no matter what else might happen in this life, she and Ray had that in spades; forty-seven years later, they were still holding hands just like on their first date.

Before Ray, Bobby Prestwood had tried everything to get in her good graces, including making a fool of himself in Sunday School when he stood up one morning and told what he was thankful for. "I'm thankful for my Chevy V-8, my mama and daddy, and Esther Lovell!" She didn't give a katy what Bobby Prestwood was thankful for, and told him so at the picnic, which was where she met Ray. Ray had come late with his cousins, carrying a basket of fried chicken and coleslaw, which he'd made himself. She couldn't believe that anybody that big and tall and good-looking could cook, much less chop cabbage; it just amazed her. She had eyed him up and down to see if he was a sissy, but found no evidence of this. When the cousins invited her to sit with them, she accepted, ate three pieces of Ray's fried chicken with all the trimmings, and took home a wing wrapped in a napkin. Two months later, they were married.

To this day, she'd never met another woman whose husband rubbed her feet, or maybe people just never mentioned it. And not only did Ray rub her feet after she'd worked like a dog all day and half the night in meetings at town hall, he'd have her supper in the oven, which she sometimes took to bed and ate sitting up watching TV, with him lying there patting her leg. "Little darlin'," he might say while he patted.

If she ever had to climb in a bed without Ray Cunningham in it, she would die, she would *go morte*, as Lew Boyd liked to say.

She picked up the phone and dialed home.

"Ray . . ."

She heard Teensy barking in the background. "Hey, sugar babe! It's hot as blazes today, I'll run you up a jar of lemonade in a little bit. What else you need?"

She wouldn't have told him that all she needed was to hear his voice.

Uncle Billy shuffled to the dining room and rifled through stacks of newspaper that the town inspector had threatened to haul off, but had forgotten to do. He was after some copies of *The Farmer's Almanac* that he'd saved for the jokes.

Sweat beaded his forehead and upper lip as he worked through the piles, but not a trace of a *Farmer's Almanac* with its red cover could he find. Dadgummit, he'd hid things in here for years and always managed to find them, and now, not a trace.

He worked his hand around in the pile of *Mitford Muse*s, which occupied a space next to the kitchen door, and felt for the familiar shape of an almanac. What was that? He pulled it out and looked. A twenty-dollar bill! He wanted to whoop, but knew better.

If Rose got wind of this twenty, she'd connive every

way in creation to yank it out of him. No, by jing, he'd do something he hardly ever did, but often thought about: he'd walk down to the Grill and get an order of fries and bring Rose a surprise milkshake. Besides, he'd gotten two or three of his best jokes at the Grill—maybe that was where he'd find this one.

Careful to put the twenty in the pants pocket without the hole, he abandoned the search for the almanacs and instituted a hurried quest for any other currency he'd once hidden in the vicinity.

Louella Baxter Marshall sat by the window in the sewing room, now her bedroom at Fernbank, looking at the catalog.

The light was good in here and she could clearly see the picture of the dress she'd be wearing to the wedding.

After two days of praying about it and going back and forth from page 42 to page 47, she had showed Miss Sadie her pick. "Green or lavender?" she asked her life-long friend and sister in Christ.

Miss Sadie didn't hesitate. "Lavender!" she said. "You always looked good in lavender."

Miss Sadie was a little bit like a mama, for it was Miss Sadie who knew Louella's history, who said things like,

"When you were a baby, you hated apple butter," or "I remember the time I pulled you to town in the wagon— you hopped out and chased Perry Mackey down the street for a lick on his peppermint stick. You nearly scared him to death!"

Louella didn't remember any of the events Miss Sadie liked to recall, but she'd heard them so often, they'd become as good as real memories. She savored the image of chasing a little white boy down the street to lick his candy, and wondered why on earth she loved apple butter now if she hated it then.

"How you know I *always* look good in this color?"

"When you were about six years old, Mama made you a lavender dress with smocking on the bodice. Don't you remember it, with little pearl buttons? It was such a pretty dress I was half jealous!"

She was disgusted with herself for not remembering. "Don' you think this big white collar too fancy for my face?"

"Posh tosh! Your face may be too fancy for that collar!"

They had both laughed and laughed, then they'd zeroed in on the business of Miss Sadie's final choice. Page 36 was too drab; page 37 was too high in the waist; page 40 was not only shapeless, it had three-quarter-length sleeves, which, as anybody knew, were unflattering all the way back to the pharaohs. Page 41, however, showed promise.

"I like the way it's cut," said Miss Sadie, peering at the dress through a magnifying glass, "but I'm too gray-headed for this color."

"Why, listen at that! Gray-headed is what look *good* wit' blue."

"But it's a pale blue, and it might wash me out."

"No, honey, you might wash *it* out!"

They had laughed again, like children, and decided on the pale blue French crepe with smocked bodice.

Louella held the catalog closer to the window and squinted at the picture.

She wished Moses Marshall could see her all dressed up for the father's wedding. He would look at her and be so proud. Oh, how she'd loved that man from the day she laid eyes on him!

She closed her eyes to rest them and held the picture against her heart, and saw her husband-to-be walking into the kitchen of the Atlanta boardinghouse.

She was fifteen years old, with her hair in cornrows and the sense that something wonderful was about to happen.

Moses Marshall flashed a smile that nearly knocked her winding. She had never seen anybody who looked like this when she was growing up in Mitford. The only people of color in Mitford were old and stooped over.

"Who's th' one baked them good biscuits for supper?" he asked.

She'd been scarcely able to speak. "What you want to know for?"

"'Cause th' one baked them good biscuits, that's th' one I'm goin' to marry."

She had looked at old Miss Sally Lou, who had to stand on tiptoe to peer into a pot on the stove. She was so little and dried up, some said she was a hundred, but Louella knew she was only eighty-two, and still the boss cook of three meals a day at the boardinghouse.

She had pointed to Miss Sally Lou, afraid to say the plain truth—that she, Louella Baxter, had baked the biscuits herself, three pans full and not one left begging.

Moses Marshall looked his bright, happy look at Miss Sally Lou and walked over and picked her up and swung her around twice before he set her down like a doll. "Fine biscuits, ma'am. Will you jump th' broom wit' me?"

"Git out of my way 'fore I knock you in th' head!" said Miss Sally Lou. "Marry that 'un yonder, she th' one do biscuits, I does yeast rolls."

She was sixteen when they were married at her grandmother's house in Atlanta, where she'd gone to live after leaving Mitford. Her grandmother had cooked the wedding feast, which was topped off with fresh peach cobbler. "Why eat cake when you can eat cobbler?" was what her grandmother always said.

Her years with Moses had been the happiest years of her life, next to those with Miss Sadie. But the Lord had taken Moses home when he was just thirty-nine, and then He'd taken her precious boy in a terrible wreck, leaving her a grandson living in Los Angeles. . . .

She looked out to the green orchard and nodded her head and smiled. "Moses Marshall," she said, "I invite you to sit wit' me at th' weddin,' an' don' be pinchin' and kissin' on me in front of th' good Lord an' ever'-body. . . ."

Dooley Barlowe was trying to be happy, but he figured he didn't know what that was supposed to mean. He felt around inside himself, around the area of his heart, maybe, and tried to see if he could make things seem good and right about Father Tim and Cynthia getting married. He'd seen what happened when people lived together under the same roof: They yelled and screamed and fought and said terrible things to each other. He'd seen his daddy go at his mama with a butcher knife more than once, and after his daddy ran off, he'd seen his mama leave for two and three days at a time and depend on him to mind the kids and feed them without any money to buy stuff with.

He remembered stealing a pork loin from the grocery store and getting it home and not knowing how to cook it. He had dropped it in a pot of boiling water with oatmeal and let it cook 'til the water boiled out on the stove, then he carved the meat in five chunks and they tried to eat it and got so sick, he thought they'd all die in the night. Once he'd stolen five cans of creamed corn, so they could all have exactly the same thing and not fight over who got what and how much, and the store manager had caught him and jumped on him really bad, but he'd let him have the corn, saying if he ever did it again he'd be sent to the penitentiary. A woman who overheard the commotion had gone and gotten a can of Harvard beets, a loaf of Wonder bread, a pound of M&Ms, and a quart of buttermilk and gave the items to him in a plastic bag. He remembered that he couldn't stomach buttermilk and the kids wouldn't drink it, either, but they couldn't bear to throw it out and it sat in the refrigerator for maybe a year.

He didn't like to think about these things, he wanted to forget everything that had ever happened before he came here, but sometimes he couldn't. He especially wanted to forget about his little sister, Jessie, because thinking of her being gone and nobody knowing where made him want to cry, and he tried to keep his face as hard and tight and straight as possible so nobody would ever be able to tell what he was thinking.

Sometimes, at night especially, he remembered trying to help his mama when she was drunk, and would suddenly feel a great love for her welling up in him. Then he'd be angry with himself for being stupid, and feel the old and shameful desire for her to die.

Things were just fine for him and Father Tim; he felt safe, finally, like things would be all right. But now he didn't know what would happen. He liked Cynthia, but what if she didn't like him, what if she tried to get him to leave or go back to his mother, if anybody could even find his mother? Or what if Cynthia tried to be his mother? His heart felt cold at such a thought. He wanted his own mother, even if he did hate her and wish he would never see her again as long as he lived.

He was glad that Barnabas came to his room and jumped on the foot of his bed, because it felt good to have a friend. Besides, Barnabas would never tell anyone that he was crying and couldn't stop.

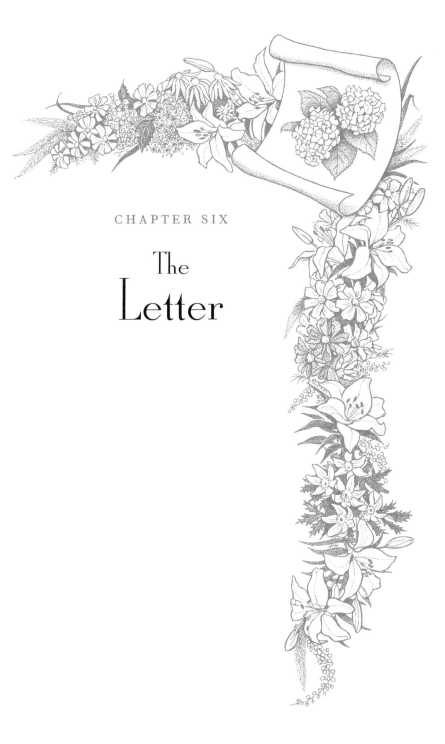

CHAPTER SIX

The
Letter

His heart was nearly bursting with a kind of longing, though he had no idea why. After all, he was blessed with everything this life could afford, everything and more.

He sat at his desk in the study and looked out the window into the gloaming as it settled over Baxter Park. Cynthia was working on an illustration that had to go out tomorrow by FedEx, or he would have been at her side, as magnetized to her living presence as his grocery list to the refrigerator.

He drummed his fingers on the desktop.

He didn't want to work on his sermon. He didn't want to take a shower and crawl into bed with a well-loved book from his well-stocked shelves, and he most certainly did not want to turn on the TV and have the clamor pour into this quiet place like some foul Niagara.

He was unable to think of anything he wanted to do; there was no seduction in any of the usual pursuits.

Aha. His fingers grew still upon the desktop.

There it was, plain as day:

He wanted to record, somehow, the joy of this breathless thing that had swept him up and overpowered and mesmerized him. Perhaps for most people, people who had been in love again and again, it would not be such a beauteous experience, but it was new to him and dazzling. Yet even in its newness, he felt it slipping away, becoming part of a personal history in which the nuances, the shading, would be lost forever; buried within the consciousness, yes, but paled by time, and then, he feared, vanished altogether.

He opened the desk drawer and took out a writing pad and one of the commercial pens he'd grown to prefer. Though the ink had a noxious odor, he liked the way it flowed onto the page—black, bold, and able.

He knew now what his soul was driving him to. He knew, and he liked the idea immensely.

He would write a poem.

In it, he would tell her everything, he would confess the all of his love, which, by its great and monumental force, had heretofore rendered him dumb as a mackerel.

With her, he experienced a galaxy . . . no, an entire

universe of feelings, yet they continually displayed themselves as the western portion of the state of Rhode Island:

YouarebeautifultomeIshallloveyoueternallywillyou marrymeandmakemethehappiestmanwhoeverdrewbreath, period, end of declaration.

He was amazed at how far he'd gotten with this extraordinary woman by the utterance of the most rudimentary expressions of love, all of them sincere beyond measure, and yet, they were words too simple and words too few; not once had they been equal to the character, the beauty, or the spirit of the one to whom they were addressed.

He knew, now, why people wanted to shout from rooftops, yet he couldn't imagine it to have great effect, in the end. One would clamber onto the roof and, teetering on some gable or chimney pot, bellow until one was hoarse as a bullfrog, "I love! I love!"

And what would people on the street do? They would look up, they would shrug, they would roll their eyes, they would say:

So?

He bounded happily from the chair and went to the kitchen to put the kettle on. Clearly, shouting from the rooftops had been a fleeting thing in the history of the lovestruck, not long enjoyed as a certified expression of ardor. Indeed, what had done the trick each and every time? Poetry! And history had proved it!

"'I love thee,'" he recited as he filled the kettle, "'. . . to the level of every day's Most quiet need, by sun and candlelight . . . I love thee freely, as men strive for Right . . .'"

There! That was getting down to it. The only problem was that E. B. Browning had already written it.

He stood musing by the stove in a kind of fog that made him forget momentarily where he was and what he was up to, until the kettle whistled and he awoke and found himself oddly joyful to be dropping the bags into the teapot and pouring the steaming water therein.

He clamped the lid on the pot and, leaving it to the business of steeping, returned to the study and visited his bookshelves. He couldn't readily put his hand on a volume of love poetry, but surely he'd find something here to spark a thought, to get his blood up. He chose a small blue volume that he'd used a time or two in marital counseling, and opened it at random.

"'I feel sad when I don't see you,'" he read aloud from a letter by a nineteenth-century American suitor. "'Be married, why won't you? And come to live with me. I will make you as happy as I can. You shall not be obliged to work hard, and when you are tired, you may lie in my lap and I will sing you to rest . . .'"

There's a good fellow! he thought.

"'. . . because I love you so well, I will not make you bring in wood and water, or feed the pig, or milk the cow, or go to the neighbors to borrow milk. Will you be married?'"

He shoved the book upon the shelf, took down another, and thumbed through the section on all things marital.

"'I love you no longer; on the contrary, I detest you . . .'" Napoleon Bonaparte to Josephine, wrong section.

Ah, well, here was one for the books, something Evelyn Waugh had trotted out in a letter of proposal. "'I can't advise you in my favour because I think it would be beastly for you, but think how nice it would be for me!'"

Would it be beastly for Cynthia? Living with him, an old stick in the mud? He shook the thought away and licked his right forefinger and turned to another page.

"'You have set a crown of roses on my youth and fortified me against the disaster of our days. Your courageous gaiety has inspired me with joy. Your tender faithfulness has been a rock of security and comfort. I have felt for you all kinds of love at once. I have asked much of you and you have never failed me. You have intensified all colours, heightened all beauty, deepened all delight. . . .'" Duff Cooper, writing to his future wife in the war-dark year of 1918, had known how to get down to brass tacks, all right. Maybe he could do something with the idea of courageous gaiety; he had always thought Cynthia courageous.

He sighed deeply. In truth, this was going nowhere. It was a waste of precious time to try and glean from another man's brain. There'd be no more lollygagging.

He dashed again to the kitchen and poured a mug of tea, then added a little milk and stirred it well, and returned to his desk and sat, gazing at the mug, the pad, and the pen, and the nightfall dark against his window.

He considered that he had written hymns to God, several in his time, but he'd never done anything like this, never! He knew that God was familiar with his very innards and that He perceived the passion of his heart full well; thus he had not sweated greatly over lines that were awkward here or a tad sophomoric there, but this . . .

"Write!" he bellowed aloud.

Barnabas bolted from the rug by the sofa and trotted to his master and stood by the desk. The rector turned his head slowly, and for a moment each looked soulfully into the other's eyes.

Dearest love . . . , he wrote at last, *tender one . . . my heart's joy . . .*

He drew a line through the feeble words and began again:

Loveliest angel of light and life . . .

What about something from the Song of Solomon? On second thought, scratch that. The Song still made him blush. Whoever drummed up the notion that it was about Christ and the church . . .

He nibbled his right forefinger and mused upon lines from Shakespeare; he chewed his lower lip and called to mind Keats; he sank his head onto his arms on the desktop and contemplated Robert Browning's fervent avowal, "All my soul follows you, love . . . and I live in being yours."

Blast and double blast. The good stuff had already been written.

He talked to himself with some animation as he trotted up Main Street from Lord's Chapel. What if Shakespeare had never put pen to paper because the good stuff had already been written? In truth, what if he refused one morning to preach because all the good sermons had already been preached?

Ha!

On the other side of the Irish Shop's display window, Minnie Lomax examined the bent head and hunched shoulders of the village priest as he blew past, his mouth moving in what she supposed was prayer.

He didn't look at all like a man besotted with love, not in her view.

Why was he staring at the sidewalk when he might be looking into the heavens, or whistling, or waving to her through the window as he usually did? He was scared of what he'd let himself in for, that's what! Sixty-something and getting married for the *first time*? The very thought gave her the shivers.

She had never married, and never wanted to. Well, not never, exactly. She had wanted to once, and look what happened. She sniffed and smoothed her cardigan over her thin hips and took a Kleenex from her pocket and blew her nose, then turned around to the empty store, wondering what she might do to lure traffic through the door today. Boiled wool had a terrible go of it during the summer; next year she would advise the owner to put in more cotton and linen, for heaven's sake, and get shed of the entire lot of those hideous crocheted caps.

∞

He would choose each word as carefully as his mother had chosen peaches off Lot Stringman's truck. "Let me pick them out for you, Miz Kavanagh." "No, thank you, Mr. Stringman," she would say, "I like the doing of it myself."

Finally despairing that writing a poem was beyond his endowment, he had decided to be content with writing a letter.

Peach by perfect peach, that is how he would choose his words. . . .

Sunday afternoon, four o'clock, a breeze stirring through the open windows

My Own,

Consider how these two small words have the power to move and shake me, and take my breath away! I am raised to a height I have never before known, somewhere above the clouds that hide the mountain-rimmed valleys and present a view of floating peaks. I have been comfortable for years, haplessly rooted in myself like a turnip, and now am not comfortable at all, but stripped of everything that is easeful and familiar, and filled with everything that is tremulous and alive; I am a spring lamb upon new legs. Every nerve is exposed

to you, my dearest love, and my thankfulness for
this gift from God knows no bounds, no bounds!
Indeed, He has saved the best for last, and that He
should have saved it at all, set it aside for me, is a
miracle. A miracle! Let no one ever say or even
think that God does not work miracles, still; every
common day, every common life is filled with
them, as you know better than anyone I have ever
met. You, who see His light and life in the dullest
blade of grass, have taught my own eye to look for
and find His magnitude abounding everywhere.

Though you are merely steps away, beyond the
hedge, I long for you as if you were in Persia, and
yet, your presence is with me, your very fragrance
clings to the shirt I wear.

I have given my heart completely only once,
and that was to Him. Now He has, Himself, set
aside in my heart a room for you. It is large and
open and suffused with light, with no walls or
boundaries to stifle us, and He has graciously fash-
ioned it to give us warmth and shelter and joyous
freedom until the end of our days.

May this be only the first of many times I
thank you for all you are to me, and for the pre-
cious and inimitable gift of your love.

Please know that I shall set a watch upon my-

self—to make every effort to bring you the happiness you so richly deserve, and, by His grace, to place your needs before my own.

May God bless you with His greatest tenderness now and always, my sweetheart, my soon-to-be wife.

Timothy

He sat as if drained; there was nothing left of him, nothing at all, he was parchment through which light might be seen.

"Barnabas," he murmured.

His good dog stirred at his feet.

"I have a mission for you, old friend." He folded the letter, regretting that he'd written it on paper from a mere notepad. Ah, well, what was done was done. He placed the letter in an envelope and thought carefully how he might address it.

In a letter hidden inside an envelope, one might say whatever one wished, but the outside of the envelope was quite another thing, being completely exposed, as it were, to . . . to what? The hedge? The sky?

My love, my blessing, my neighbor, he scrawled with some abandon.

He licked the flap and pressed it down and sat for a moment with it under his hand, then took it to the kitchen and found a length of twine, which he looped around the neck of his patient dog. Lacking a hole punch, he stuck the tip of a steak knife through the corner of the envelope and ran the twine through the hole and tied it in a knot.

"There!" he said aloud.

He walked with Barnabas down the back steps and across the yard to the hedge. "OK, boy, take it to Cynthia!"

Barnabas lifted his leg against a rhododendron.

"Take it to Cynthia!" he said, wagging his finger in the direction of the little yellow house. "Over there! Go see Cynthia!"

Barnabas turned and looked at him with grave indifference.

"Cat!" he hissed. *"Cynthia's house! Cat, cat, cat!"* That ought to do it.

Barnabas sniffed a few twigs that lay in the grass, then sat down and scratched vigorously.

Rats, what a dumb idea. In the old days, a fellow would have sent his valet or his coachman or some such, and here he was trying to send a dog—he deserved what he was getting.

"Go, dadgummit! Go to Cynthia's back door, that's where you love to go when you're not supposed to!"

Barnabas gazed at him for a moment, then turned

and bounded through the hedge and across her yard and up the steps to her stoop, where he sat and pressed his nose against the screen door, peering in.

He suddenly felt ten years old. Why couldn't he think straight for five minutes in a row? His dog might sit at that door 'til kingdom come, with Cynthia having no clue Barnabas was out there. Should he run to the door and knock to alert her, then run away again?

This was suddenly the most ridiculous mess he'd gotten himself into in . . . ever. His face flamed.

"Timothy?" It was Cynthia, calling to him through her studio window. He'd utterly forgotten about her studio window.

"Umm, yes?"

"Why are you hiding behind the hedge?"

He was mortified. *I have no idea,* he wanted to say. "There's a *delivery*"—he fairly thundered the word—"at your back door."

"Oh," she said.

He waited, covering his face with his hands.

"My goodness!" he heard her exclaim as she opened the screen door. "A letter on a string!"

Surely he would regret this.

"'My love, my blessing, my neighbor'!" she crowed.

Did she have to inform the whole neighborhood?

"Go tell your master that I've received his most welcome missive . . . which I can barely get off the string. Ugh! . . . Oh, rats, wait 'til I get the scissors."

His dog waited.

"And further," she said, coming back and snipping the letter off, "do tell him I shall endeavor to respond promptly. However, my dear Barnabas, do not harbor, even for a moment, the *exceedingly* foolish hope that it will be delivered by Violet."

The screen door slapped behind her.

The deed done, his dog arose, shook himself, and came regally down the steps, across the yard, and through the hedge, where, wearing the remains of the twine around his neck, he sat and gazed at his master with a decided air of disdain, if not utter disgust.

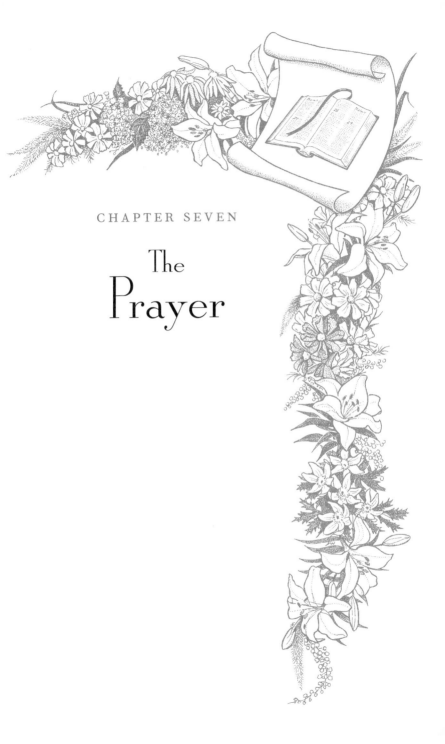

CHAPTER SEVEN

The
Prayer

*S*he pressed the letter to her heart, wishing the power of its message to enter her very soul and cause her to believe with the writer what an extraordinary benediction had come to them.

Yes, she loved him; in truth, more than life itself. And yet, the fear was beginning to creep in, the fear she had at last grown wise enough to recognize—that she could not please him and give him the joy that he above all others, deserved; the fear that Timothy, like Elliott, would not find her valuable enough for any true purpose; the fear that her priest, her neighbor, and now her betrothed, might discover in her some "terrible lack," as Elliott had called her inability to bear children.

Only weeks earlier, she had wept in despair that Timothy Kavanagh would ever be able to abandon his own raw fear and surrender his heart.

Now she bowed her head and wept because, at last, he had.

She stood at the kitchen sink, spooning an odorous lump of congealed cat food into Violet's dish.

Drawing her breath sharply, she stared at the cat bowl that she had just filled without knowing it.

She felt stricken. What had she done when she accepted his proposal with such unbearable eagerness and joy? Had she rashly agreed to something in which she might prove a bitter disappointment to both Timothy and herself?

And another thing—could she, who had often felt thrown away, be a friend and guide to a thrown-away boy? She thought she could, she knew she wanted to—for Dooley's sake and her own.

She put the bowl on the floor and walked down the hall to her studio and stood at the window, gazing across the hedge to the rectory. There was his stone chimney, his slate roof, his bedroom window beneath the gable. . . .

How often she had found solace in merely looking upon his house, the place where he would be working in his study, snoring by his fire, brushing his dog, commandeering his wayward boy, living his life.

She'd begun by having the most terrific crush on him, like a pathetic schoolgirl; it had been the sort of thing that made her blush at the sight of him, and caused her skin to tingle when she heard his voice. Worse, there had been long lapses in concentration that afflicted her for months on end.

She had plotted ways to meet him on the street, and once thumped onto the bench in front of the Main Street Grill, affecting a turned ankle that delayed her jaunt to The Local. He had, indeed, come by, just as she'd hoped, and sat with her and smiled at her in a way that made her nearly speechless until, finally, she fled the bench, forgetting to limp, and avoided him altogether for several weeks.

She remembered, too, the day she had prayed and marched boldly to his back door. Her heart thundered under her jumper as she asked to borrow a cup of sugar to make a cake. Having no intention of making a cake, she worried whether, in some priestly way, he might see through such guile and find her out. But he had invited her in and fed her from the remains of his own supper and she had seen something in his eyes, some kindness that had nearly broken her heart with its plainness and simplicity. And then his dog, attached to the handle of the silver drawer by a leash, had yanked the drawer out, sending forks, knives, and spoons clattering about the kitchen and skidding into the hallway. They had dropped to their knees as one, hooting with laughter as they collected the errant flatware. Even then, she knew that something had been sealed between them, and that it was laughter that had sealed it

It had been years since Elliott walked out—the divorce papers arrived by certified mail the following day—and in those years, not one soul had made her mouth go dry as cotton and her knees turn to water. Oh, how she had despised the torment of loving like a girl instead of like . . . like a sophisticated woman, whatever that might be.

That early, awkward time had also been irresistibly sweet. But now this—confusion and distress and alarm, and yes, the oddly scary thoughts of the women of Lord's Chapel who for years had stood around him like a hedge of thorns, protecting him as their very own; keeping him, they liked to believe, from foolish stumbles; feeding him meringues and layer cake at every turn; mothering and sistering him as if this were their life's calling. She saw, now, something she'd only glimpsed before, and that was the way an unmarried priest is thought to belong to the matrons of the church, lock, stock, and barrel.

More than once she'd waited at his side, feeling gauche and adolescent, as they clucked over him—inquiring after his blood sugar, flicking an imaginary hair from his lapel, ordering him to take a week off, and coyly insisting he never stray beyond the town limits. They were perfectly harmless, every one, and she despised herself for such cheap and petty thoughts, but they were real thoughts, and now that the word was out, she felt his flock sizing her up in a fresh, even severe way.

Yet, for all their maternal indulgence of their priest, she knew they underestimated him most awfully. She had heard a member of the Altar Guild wondering how anyone "so youthful and sure of herself" could be attracted to their "dear old priest who is going bald as a hen egg and diabetic to boot."

Indeed, he wasn't merely the mild and agreeable man they perceived him to be; he was instead a man of the richest reserves of strength and poise, of the deepest tenderness and most enormous wit and gallantry.

From the beginning, she found him to possess an ardor for his calling that spoke to her heart and mind and soul in such a deep and familiar way, she felt as if he were long-lost kin, returned at last from a distant shore.

He had felt this, too, this connection of some vital force in himself with her own vitality, and he had been knocked back, literally, as if by the thunder-striking power of a summer storm.

She had known she would never again be given such a connection, and she had moved bravely toward it, toward its heat, toward its center, while he had drawn back, shaken.

"'Love bade me welcome,'" he had once quoted from George Herbert, "'but my soul drew back.'" She found a delicate irony in the fact that George Herbert had been a clergyman.

She looked at the handwritten sheet pinned above her drawing board, something she had copied at the Mitford library from an old book by Elizabeth Goudge:

> She had long accepted the fact that happiness is like swallows in spring. It may come and nest under your eaves or it may not. You cannot command it. When you expect to be happy you are not, when you don't expect to be happy there is suddenly Easter in your soul, though it be midwinter. Something, you do not know what, has broken the seal upon that door in the depth of your being that opens upon eternity.

Eternity!

She moved from the window and walked quickly to the kitchen. She would do something that, if only for the briefest hour, had the power to solve everything, to offer certain and absolute consolation.

She would cook.

She removed the chicken from the refrigerator, already rubbed with olive oil and crushed garlic, with half a lemon tucked into its cavity. She misted olive oil into her ancient iron skillet, placed the bird on its back, and ground pepper and sea salt onto its plump flesh. From a glass of water on the windowsill she removed a pungent stalk of fresh rosemary and stuck it under the breast skin. The top of the green stalk waved forth like a feather from a hat band.

She turned the stove dial to 450, where it would remain for thirty minutes before being set at 350 for an hour, and slid the raw feast onto the middle rack.

The wrenching thing, she knew in her heart, was having no one to talk with about it all, and whose fault was that but her own? Had she not worked like a common stevedore since coming to Mitford, making a way for her work instead of making friends? Oh, yes, she was liked well enough, she really was, but there was no trusted friend to whom she might pour her heart out. There was no one, not a soul.

Except . . . she smiled at the thought . . . the priest himself. Her heart warmed suddenly, and lifted up. Hadn't she confessed something to him only yesterday?

"They don't like me," she had said, despising the whine she heard in her voice. "They did, of course, until they learned you were actually going to marry me, but now . . ."

"Nonsense!" he'd said with feeling. "They think the *world* of you!"

That was apparently the most profound compliment a Southerner could pay, to insist that one was thought the "world" of!

She realized she wouldn't finish the illustration as she'd promised her editor; she would finish it tomorrow, instead. She, who was ever loath to break a promise, would break this one.

"Timothy?" she said when he answered the phone. "Can you come over?" Her heart was pounding, and there was a distinct quaver in her voice; she was warbling like a canary.

"I'm scared, dearest, scared to death."

She loved the way he sat with her, not saying anything in particular, not probing, not pushing her, just sitting on her love seat. Perhaps what she liked best was that he always looked comfortable wherever he was, appearing glad to live within his skin and not always jumping out of it like some men, like James, her editor, who was everlastingly clever and eloquent and ablaze with wild ideas that succeeded greatly for him, while with Timothy the thing that succeeded was quietude, something rich and deep and . . . nourishing, a kind of spiritual chicken soup simmering in some far reach of the soul.

"Tell me," he said at last. "Tell me everything. I'm your priest, after all." She thought his smile dazzling, a dazzling thing to come out of quietude. She had pulled a footstool to the love seat and sat close to him.

"I'm terribly afraid I can't make you happy," she said.

"But that was my fear! I finally kicked it out the back door and now it's run over here."

"It's not funny, Timothy."

"I'm not laughing."

He took her hands in his and lightly kissed the tips of her fingers and she caught the scent of him, the innocence of him, and her spirit mounted up again.

"Why don't we pray together?" he said. "Just let our hearts speak to His. . . ."

Sitting at his feet, she bowed her head and closed her

eyes and he stroked her shoulder. Though the clock ticked in the hallway, she supposed that time was standing still, and that she might sit with him in this holy reverie, forever.

"Lord," he said, simply, "here we are."

"Yes, Lord, here we are."

They drew in their breath as one, and let it out in a long sigh, and she realized for a moment how the very act of breathing in His presence was balm.

"Dear God," he said, "deliver Your cherished one from feeling helpless to receive the love You give so freely, so kindly, from the depths of Your being. Help us to be as large as the love You've given us, sometimes it's too great for us, Lord, even painful in its power. Tear away the old fears, the old boundaries that no longer contain anything of worth or importance, and by Your grace, make Cynthia able to seize this bold, fresh freedom. . . ."

"Yes, Lord," she prayed, "the freedom I've never really known before, but which You've faithfully shown me in glimmers, in epiphanies, in wisps as fragile as . . . light from Your new moon!"

He pressed her hand, feeling in it the beating of her pulse.

"Father, deliver me from the fear to love wholly and completely, I who chided this good man for his own fears, his own weakness, while posing, without knowing it a pose, as confident and bold. You've seen through that, Lord, You've . . . You've found me out for what I am . . ."

There was a long silence, filled by the ticking of the clock.

". . . a frightened seven-year-old who stands at the door looking for a father and mother who . . . do not come home.

"Even after years of knowing You as a Father who is always home, I sometimes feel—I feel a prisoner of old and wrenching fears, and I'm ashamed of my fear, and the darkness that prevents me from stepping into the light. . . ."

"You tell us in Your Word," he prayed, "that You do not give us the spirit of fear—"

"But of power and of love and a sound mind!" she whispered, completing the verse from the second letter to Timothy.

"And so, Lord, I rebuke the Enemy who would employ every strategy to deny Your children the blessing of Your grace."

"Yes, Lord!"

"Help us to receive Your peace and courage, Your confidence and power," he said.

"Yes, Lord!"

"Thank you for being with us now, and in the coming weeks and coming years."

"And Father," she said, "please give me the grace to love Dooley as You love him, and the patience to encourage and support and understand him, for I wish with all my heart that we might grow together in harmony, as a true family." She took a deep and satisfying breath. "And now, Lord . . ."

As the prayer neared its end, they spoke in unison as they had recently begun to do in their evening prayers.

". . . create in us a clean heart . . . renew a right spirit within us . . . and fill us with Your Holy Spirit . . . through Christ our Lord . . . amen."

He helped her from the footstool and she sat beside him on the love seat and breathed the peace that settled over them like a shawl.

"There will be many times when fear breaks in," he said, holding her close. "We can never be taken prisoner if we greet it with prayer."

"Yes!" she whispered, feeling a weight rolled away like the stone from the sepulcher.

"I smelled the chicken as I came through the hedge."

"Dinner in twenty minutes?" she murmured.

"I thought you'd never ask," he said.

CHAPTER EIGHT

The
Preamble

$\mathcal{O}$n the morning of September seventh, in the upstairs guest room of the rectory, Bishop Stuart Cullen checked his vestments for any signs of wrinkles or unwanted creases, found none, then took his miter from the box and set it on the bureau, mindful that his crozier was in the trunk of the car, as were his black, polished shoes and an umbrella in case of rain.

Rummaging about the room in a pair of magenta boxer shorts given him by his suffragan, he hummed snatches of a Johnny Cash tune as Martha Cullen sat up in bed and read an issue of *Country Life* magazine that Puny had placed on the night table three years ago and faithfully dusted ever since. Studying a feature on knot gardens, she was utterly unmindful of the bishop's rendition of "Ring of Fire" as he enjoyed a long, steaming shower that caused water in the shower across the hall to trickle upon the rector's head in a feeble stream.

Under the miserly drizzle, the rector counted his blessings that the bishop would be preaching this morning and he celebrating, a veritable holiday in the Caymans, as far as he was concerned. In truth, he feared that if he opened his mouth to deliver wisdom of any sort, it would pour forth as some uncertified language, resulting not from the baptism of the Holy Spirit but of something akin to panic, or worse. He despaired that the custard had vanished in the night, and fear and trembling had jumped into its place with both feet.

In his room across the hall, Dooley sat on the side of his bed and felt the creeping, lopsided nausea that came with the aroma of baking ham as it rose from the kitchen. He said three four-letter words in a row, and was disappointed when his stomach still felt sick.

He hoped his voice wouldn't crack during the hymn. Though he'd agreed to sing a cappella, he didn't trust a cappella. If you hit a wrong note, there was nothing to cover you. He wished there were trumpets or something really loud behind him, but no, Cynthia wanted "Dooley's pure voice." Gag.

"God," he said aloud, "don't let me sound weird. Amen." He had no idea that God would really hear him or prevent him from sounding weird, but he thought it was a good idea to ask.

He guessed he was feeling better about stuff. Yesterday, Father Tim spent the whole day taking him places, plus they'd run two miles with Barnabas and gone to Sweet Stuff after. Then, Cynthia had given him a hug that nearly squeezed his guts out. "Dooley," she said, "I really care about you."

When he heard that, he felt his face getting hard. He didn't want it to, but it was trained that way. He could tell she really meant it, but she'd have to prove she meant it before he would smile at her; he knew she wanted him to smile. Maybe he would someday, but not now. Now he was trying to keep from puking up his gizzard because he had to sing a song he didn't even like, at a wedding he still wasn't sure of.

In the kitchen of the little yellow house beyond the hedge, Cynthia Coppersmith stood barefoot in her aging chenile robe, her hair in pink foam curlers, eating half a hotdog from the refrigerator and drinking coffee so strong it possessed the consistency of tapioca.

On arriving home last night from the country club dinner party where, out of courtesy, she'd picked at a salad, she had boiled a hotdog and eaten the first half of it in a bun with what she thought was mustard but was, in fact, horseradish, loosely the age of her expiring Boston fern. It was the first true nourishment she'd recently been able to take, except for a rock shrimp and three cherry tomatoes at Friday's bridal luncheon. She ate the remains of the hotdog in two bites and, feeling her lagging appetite suddenly stimulated, foraged in the refrigerator until she found a piece of Wednesday's broiled flounder, which she spritzed with the juice of a geriatric lemon and, standing at the sink, consumed with gusto.

Two blocks south, Esther Bolick peered out her kitchen window as a straggle of rain clouds parted to reveal the sun. "Happy is th' bride th' sun shines on!" she announced with relief.

Going briskly to the oven, she removed three pans of scratch cake layers to a cooling rack, and stood with her hands on her hips in a baby doll nightgown and bedroom shoes with the faces of bunnies. She gazed with satisfaction at the trio of perfect yellow moons, then trotted across the kitchen for another cup of decaf, the black pupils of the bunnies' plastic eyes rolling and clicking like dice.

She would go to Sunday School and the eleven o'clock, then come home and ice the cake and let it sit 'til she carried it to church at four. She and Gene would do what they usually did when hauling around a three-layer—put newspaper on the floor of the cargo area, and while Gene drove, she would sit back there on a stool and hold the cake to keep it from sliding around in its cardboard box. Without a van, there was no way on

God's green earth to follow her calling unless you were making sheet cakes, which she utterly despised and would not be caught dead doing. The icing would go on at home, but she'd put the pearls and lilies on at church in one of the Sunday School rooms. Then she'd take the shelves out of the church fridge and pop the whole thing in 'til just before the thundering horde hit the reception.

She removed the hair net from her head and stuck it in the knife drawer.

Four blocks north, Uncle Billy Watson took the wire hanger from the nail on the wall and squinted at the black wool suit, inherited from his long-dead brother-in-law. Its heaviness had bowed down the arms of the coat hanger, giving the whole thing a dejected appearance.

"Dadgummit," he said under his breath. There was a spot on the right lapel as big as a silver dollar; it looked like paint—or was it vanilla pudding? In his pajamas, he shuffled to the kitchen, where he could see in a better light.

Miss Rose was sitting in her chair by the refrigerator, peeling potatoes with a knife too dull to cut butter. "What are you doing, Bill Watson?"

"Cleanin' my coat."

"You'll not be getting *my* goat!" she said, indignant.

His wife was going deaf as a doorknob, and there

wasn't a thing he could do about it. She wouldn't even discuss hearing aids, let alone ask the county to buy her a pair.

"What are you wearin' to the weddin'?" he shouted.

"What wedding?"

"Th' preacher's weddin' this evenin' at five o'-clock!"

"Five o'clock!" she squawked. "That's suppertime!"

"Well, I cain't help if it is, hit's th' preacher's wed-din' an' we're a-goin'." Hadn't he talked about this wedding 'til he was blue in the face, even picked out three dresses she had bitterly rejected? And now this.

He wagged his head and sighed. "Lord have *mercy*."

"What about Percy?" she demanded.

The old man scrubbed at the lapel with a wet dishrag. Some days he could put on a smiley face and go about his business just fine, some days Rose Watson tested his faith, yes, she did. He'd have to trot to church this morning and sit there asking forgiveness for what he was thinking. He'd also be thanking the Lord for the joke. Don't tell him that God Almighty didn't answer foolish prayers!

Four blocks northwest, Hessie Mayhew lay snoring in her double bed with the faded flannel sheets and vin-tage Sears mattress. She had taken two Benadryl caps last night to dry up her sinuses after a day of messing with lady's-mantle and hydrangeas. Hydrangeas always did something to her sinuses, they had drained like a tap as she plowed through people's yards, taking what she wanted without asking. She'd even ducked behind the Methodist chapel, where a thick hedge of hydrangeas flowered magnificently every year, and took her pick of the huge blooms.

People knew who she was, they knew whose wedding this was; if she'd stopped to ask permission, they'd have said help yourself, take all you want! So why stop and ask, that was her philosophy! People should be proud for her to rogue their flowers, seeing they made so many people happy. *I declare,* she once imagined someone saying, *Hessie Mayhew stripped every peony bush in my yard today, and I'm just* tickled *about it!*

For her money, the hydrangeas were a week shy of the best color, but did people who set wedding dates ever stop and think of such things? Of course not, they just went blindly on. If she lived to marry again, which she sometimes hoped she would, she'd do it in May, when lily of the valley was at it peak.

On her screened porch, a decrepit porcelain bathtub boasted a veritable sea of virgin's bower and hydrangeas.

In her double kitchen sink, Blue Mist spirea, autumn anemone, Queen Anne's lace, artemisia, and knotweed drank thirstily. Inside the back door, buckets of purple coneflowers, autumn clematis, cosmos, and wild aster sat waiting. On the counter above the dishwasher, a soup pot of pink Duet and white Garden Party roses mingled with foxtail grass, Jerusalem artichoke, dog hobble, and panicles of the richly colored pokeberry. A small butterfly that had ridden in, drugged, on a coneflower, came to itself and visited the artemisia.

At seven-thirty, Hessie Mayhew turned on her side, moaning a little due to the pain in her lower back, and though a team of helpers was due to arrive at eight, she slept on.

In her home a half mile from town, Puny Guthrie crumbled two dozen strips of crisp, center-cut bacon into the potato salad and gave it one last, heaving stir. Everybody would be plenty hungry by six or six-thirty, and she'd made enough to feed a corn shuckin', as her granpaw used to say. She had decided to leave out the onions, since it was a wedding reception and very dressy. She'd never thought dressing up and eating onions were compatible; onions were for picnics and eating at home in the privacy of your own family.

Because Cynthia and the father didn't want people

to turn out for the reception and go home hungry, finger foods were banned. They wanted to give everybody a decent supper, even if they would have to eat it sitting on folding chairs from Sunday School. What with the father's ham, Miss Louella's yeast rolls, Miss Olivia's raw vegetables and dip, her potato salad, and Esther Bolick's three-layer orange marmalade, she didn't think they'd have any complaints. Plus, there would be ten gallons of tea, not to mention decaf, and sherry if anybody wanted any, but she couldn't imagine why anybody would. She'd once taken a sip from the father's decanter, and thought it tasted exactly like aluminum foil, though she'd never personally tasted aluminum foil except when it got stuck to a baked potato.

She thought of her own wedding and how she had walked down the aisle on Father Tim's arm. She had felt like a queen, like she was ten feet tall, looking at everything and everybody with completely new eyes. Halfway down the aisle, she nearly burst into tears, then suddenly she soared above tears to something higher, something that took her breath away, and she knew she would never experience anything like it again. Later, when she called Father Tim "Father," she was struck to find she said it as if he really were her father, it wasn't just some religious name that went with a collar. Ever since that moment, she'd felt she was his daughter, in a way that no one except herself could understand. And hadn't he been the one to pray that parade prayer that brought Joe Joe to the back door and into her life forever? She had been cleaning the downstairs rectory toilet when Joe Joe came to the back, because she hadn't heard him knocking at the front. When she saw him, her heart did a somersault, because he was the cutest, most handsome person she'd ever seen outside of a TV show or magazine.

"Father Tim said he might have a candy wrapper in the pocket of his brown pants, if you could send it, please."

She knew immediately that this policeman had been raised right, saying "please." Not too many people said please anymore, much less thank you, she thought it was a shame.

She had invited him in and given him a glass of tea and he perched on the stool where Father Tim sat and read his mail, and she went upstairs and looked in the father's brown pants pockets and there it was, wadded up. Why anybody would want to carry around a wadded-up candy wrapper . . .

"'Scuse my apron," she remembered saying. She would never forget the look in his eyes.

"You look really good in an apron," he said, turning beet red.

She'd never been told such a thing and had no idea what to say. She handed him the candy wrapper and he put it in a little Ziploc bag without taking his eyes off her.

She thought she was going to melt and run down in a puddle. Then he bolted off the stool and was out the door and gone and that was that. Until he came back the very next day when she was cooking lima beans.

"Hey," she said through the screen door as he bounded up the steps. By now, she knew that the whole police force was working on the big jewel theft at Lord's Chapel.

"You're under arrest," he said, blushing again.

For a moment, she was terrified that this might be true, then she saw the big grin on his face.

"What're th' charges?"

"Umm, well . . ." He dropped his head and gazed at his shoes.

She thought it must be awful to be a grown man who blushed like a girl.

He jerked his head up and looked her in the eye. "You're over the legal limit of bein' pretty."

She giggled. "What're you goin' to do about it?" Boy howdy, that had flown right out of her mouth without even thinking.

"Umm, goin' to ask you to a movie in Wesley, how's that?"

"Is it R? I don't see R."

"I don't know," he said, appearing bewildered.

"You could look in the newspaper, or call," she said. She could scarcely get her breath. She had never noticed before that a police uniform looked especially good, it was like he was home on leave from the armed forces.

"Will you see, umm, PG-13?"

"Depending." Why on earth was she being so hard to get along with? Her mouth was acting like it had a mind of its own.

"My grandmother's th' *mayor*!" he exclaimed.

"That's nice," she said. This was going nowhere. She felt she was fluttering around in space and couldn't get her toes on the ground. Suddenly realizing again that she was wearing her apron, she snatched it up and over her head and stood there, feeling dumb as a rock.

"So, just trust me," he said. "We'll find a good movie if we have to go all th' way to . . ." He hesitated, thinking. *"Johnson City!"*

"Thank you," she said, "I'd enjoy goin' to th' movies with you."

After he left, she felt so addled and weak in the knees that she wanted to lie down, but would never do such a thing in the father's house; she didn't even *sit* down on the job, except once in a while to peel peaches or snap string beans.

She walked around the kitchen several times, trying to hold something in, she didn't know what it was. She ended up at the back door, where it suddenly came busting out.

It was a shout.

She put the plastic cover on the potato salad bowl and smiled, remembering that she'd stood at the screen door for a long time, with tears of happiness running down her cheeks.

Having had their flight canceled on Saturday due to weather, Walter and Katherine Kavanagh arrived at the Charlotte airport at 11:35 a.m. Sunday morning, following a mechanical delay of an hour and a half at La Guardia. They stood at the baggage carousel, anxiously seeking her black bag, which contained not only her blue faille suite for the wedding, but the gift they'd taken great pains to schlep instead of ship.

"Gone to Charlottesville, Virginia!" said the baggage claim authority, peering into his monitor. "How about that?"

From her greater height of six feet, Katherine surveyed him with a look capable of icing the wings of a 747.

"Sometimes they go to Charleston!" he announced, refusing to wither under her scorn. He was used to scorn; working in an airline baggage claim department was all about scorn.

Miss Sadie Baxter sat at her dressing table in her slip and robe, near the open window of the bedroom she'd occupied since she was nine years old. The rain clouds had rolled away, the sun was shining, and the birds were singing—what more could any human want or ask for?

She carefully combed the gray hair from her brush, rolled it into a tidy ball, and let it fall soundlessly into the wastebasket that bore the faded decal of a camellia blossom.

Where had the years gone? One day she'd sat here brushing hair the color of chestnuts, and the next time she looked up, she was old and gray. She remembered sitting on this same stool, looking into this same mirror, reading Willard Porter's love letter and believing herself to be beautiful. . . .

"Willard!" she whispered, recalling the letter she had committed to memory, the letter he wrote on her twenty-first birthday:

You may know that I am building a house in the village, on the green where Amos Medford grazed his cows. Each stone that was laid in the foundation was laid with the hope that I might yet express the loving regard I have for you, Sadie.

I am going to give this house a name, trusting that things may eventually be different between us. I will have it engraved on a cedar beam at the highest point in the attic, with the intention that its message may one day give you some joy or pleasure.

Perhaps, God willing, your father will soon see that I have something to offer, and relent. Until then, dear Sadie, I can offer only my fervent love and heartfelt devotion.

Soon afterward, Willard had been killed and buried in France, and many years went by before she learned the name he had engraved on the beam.

"'For lo, the winter is past . . . ,'" she murmured, gazing from her window into the orchard. Learning the name, Winterpast, had indeed given her much joy and pleasure.

"'. . . the rain is over and gone. The flowers appear on the earth; the time of the singing of birds is come. . . .'"

The time of the singing of birds had come for the father and Cynthia.

Miss Sadie looked into the mirror and smiled. Yes, it was their time, now.

At four-fifteen, Cynthia urged Katherine to give her a few minutes alone. So much had gone on in the last days and weeks, she said, that she was quite breathless.

"What if you should fall down the stairs?" Katherine inquired. "And your hair, it's still in curlers!"

Cynthia had known Katherine for just under two hours, but already reckoned her to be a woman who minced no words.

"I'm not going to fall down the stairs," she said. "And the curlers come out in a flash. I must say you look smashing in Olivia's suit, really you do, the color is wonderful on you."

"I've never worn anything this short in my life!" fumed Katherine, peering into the full-length mirror and tugging at her skirt. "I look exactly like Big Bird, I had no *idea* I was so knock-kneed. I'll scandalize the church, your friends will think we're riffraff."

"They'll think no such thing, they've all been dying to meet you." Cynthia urged Katherine toward the door of her bedroom, the bedroom that would, tonight, belong to Walter and Katherine, who currently had no room of their own at all, poor souls.

"I'll take your bouquet out of the parish hall refrigerator," said Katherine, "and see you in the narthex." What could she do with a bride who wanted to be alone? As for herself, she had sprained her ankle twenty minutes before her own wedding and if friends hadn't surrounded her, she might still be lying by the fish pond at that dreadful hotel in the Poconos.

At five 'til five, Father Tim shot his French cuffs and exchanged meaningful glances with Walter and the bishop.

They were cooped into the six-by-eight-foot sacristy like three roosters, he thought, and not a breath of air stirring.

He walked to the door and pushed it open. Avis Packard's cigarette smoke blew in.

"'Scuse me," said Avis, peering into the sacristy at what he considered a sight for sore eyes. There was their pope, dolled up in a long white robe and the oddest-looking headgear he ever laid eyes on, not to mention that long stick with a curve at the end, which was probably for snatching people up by the neck when they dozed off in the pew. Avis took a deep drag off his filtered Pall Mall and threw it in the bushes.

At precisely five o'clock, Father Tim heard the organ. What was going on? Why hadn't anyone come to the outer sacristy door to tell them the bride had arrived?

"Don't go out there!" he nearly shouted, as the bishop's hand went for the door that led to the sanctuary. "Walter, please find Katherine, find out what's going on." Somebody had missed a signal, somehow. He felt oddly uneasy.

At five after five, Walter reappeared, looking mystified. "Katherine can't find Cynthia. She was supposed to meet her in the narthex at five 'til."

Ten minutes late! Cynthia Coppersmith was the very soul of punctuality.

He had a gut feeling, and it wasn't good. "I'll be back," he said, sprinting through the open door.

"I'll come with you!" said Walter.

"No! Stay here!"

He dashed up Old Church Lane, cut through Baxter Park, and hit her back steps running.

"Cynthia!" He was trembling as he opened the unlocked door and ran into the hall. He stood for a moment, panting and bewildered, as Violet rubbed against his pant leg. He wished he could find cats more agreeable.

He took the stairs two at a time and hung a left into her bedroom. "Cynthia!"

"Timothy!"

She was beating on her bathroom door from the inside. "Timothy! I can't get out!"

He spied the blasted doorknob lying on the floor. He picked it up and stuck the stem back in the hole and cranked the knob to the right and the door opened and he saw his bride in her chenile robe and pink curlers, looking agonized.

"Oh, Timothy . . ."

"Don't talk," he said. "Don't even tell me. How can I help you, what can I do?"

She raced to the closet and took out her suit. "I already have my panty hose on, so I'm not starting from scratch. Stand outside and I'll do my best. Pray for me, darling! Oh, I'm so sorry, I should have borrowed something blue for good luck, what a dreadful mess. . . ."

He stood in the hall and checked his watch. Five-seventeen.

Violet rubbed against his ankle. He felt his jaws beginning to lock.

"OK, you can come in now, I have my suit on, where are my shoes, oh, good grief, how did they get there, I can't believe this, Timothy, I couldn't help it, the knob just *fell off,* I yelled out the window and nobody heard, it was awful—"

"Don't talk!" he said, coming into the room. Why was he commanding her not to talk? Let the poor woman talk if she wanted to! Helpless—that's what he felt.

She thumped onto the bench at her dressing table and powdered her face and outlined her lips with a pencil and put on lipstick.

Five-twenty.

Then she did something to her eyebrows and eyelids.

Five-twenty-two.

She sprayed the wisteria scent on her wrists and rubbed them together and touched her wrists to her ears.

He could see Stuart pacing the sacristy, Katherine wringing her hands, Walter going beserk, the entire congregation getting up and walking out, the ham, covered by Saran Wrap, abandoned in the refrigerator. . . .

"Cynthia . . ."

"Oh, dreadful, oh, horrid!" she cried, finishing her mascara with a shaking hand. "And I just remembered, you're not supposed to see the bride before the ceremony!"

"Too late!" he said, eyeing his watch. "Five twenty-four."

"I'm coming, I'm coming!"

She got up and dashed toward him.

"Curlers," he said, his jaws cranking still further into the lock position.

"Rats!"

She plucked curlers from her head like so many feathers from a chicken, and tossed them into the air. They literally rained around the room; he'd never seen anything like it.

"No time to brush!" She looked into the mirror and ran her fingers through her hair. "There! Best I can do. God help me!"

She turned to him now, and he felt a great jolt from heart to spleen. She was so astonishingly beautiful, so radiant, so fresh, it captured his very breath. Thanks be to God, his custard was back. . . .

She grabbed her handbag from the chair. "We can take my car!"

"No place to park!"

"So," she cried, as they headed for the stairs, "race you!"

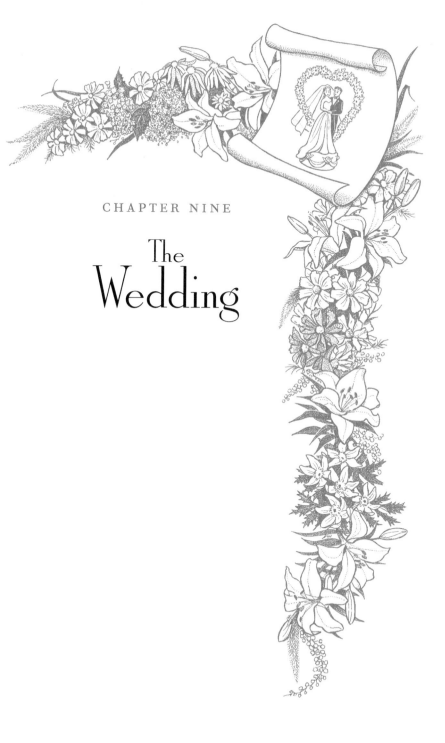

CHAPTER NINE

The
Wedding

*I*n the ninth row of the epistle side, next to the stained-glass window of Christ carrying the lost lamb, Hope Winchester blushed to recall her once-ardent crush on Father Tim. She'd taken every precaution to make certain he knew nothing of it, and now it seemed idiotic to have felt that way about someone twice her age.

She remembered the fluttering of her heart when he came into the bookstore, and all her hard work to learn special words that would intrigue him. She would never admit such a thing to another soul, but she believed herself to be the only person in Mitford who could converse on his level. When she'd learned about Cynthia months ago, she had forced herself to stop thinking such nonsense altogether, and was now truly happy that he and his neighbor had found each other. They seemed perfect together.

Still, on occasion, she missed her old habit of looking for him to pass the shop window and wave, or stop in; and she missed pondering what book she might order that would please and surprise him.

It wasn't that she'd ever wanted to marry him, for heaven's sake, or even be in love with him; it was just that he was so very kind and gentle and made her feel special. Plus he was a lot like herself, deep and sensitive, not to mention a lover of the romantic poets she'd adored since junior high. Early on, she had made it a point to read Wordsworth again, weeping over the Lucy poems, so she could quote passages and dig out morsels to attract his imagination.

"Come in out of the *fretful stir*!" she once said as he popped through the door at Happy Endings.

He had looked up and smiled. "Wordsworth!" he exclaimed, obviously pleased.

How many people would recognize two little words among a poet's thousands? She had felt positively thrilled.

Opening her purse, she examined the contents for the Kleenex she'd stuffed in at the last minute. Though she thought it fatuous to cry at weddings, she deemed it wise to be prepared.

In the fourth row of the epistle side, Gene Bolick wondered what on earth was going on. His watch said five-fifteen. He knew Richard well enough to know he was looking pale after hammering down on the organ all this time with nothing happening.

He glanced again at the bishop's wife, whose head was bowed. Was she praying that the father hadn't chickened out at the last minute? Wouldn't that be a corker if their priest was on a plane bound for the Azores? He didn't know where the Azores were located, but figured it was a distance.

Realizing his fists were clenched and his palms sweaty, he forced his attention to the three-layer orange marmalade sitting in the parish hall refrigerator, looking like a million bucks. He hoped to the Lord the temperature was set right and hadn't accidentally been switched to extra cool, which had once frozen two hundred pimento cheese sandwiches as hard as hockey pucks. He nudged Esther, who appeared to be sleeping under the brim of the hat she wore only to weddings and funerals.

Esther was not sleeping, she was thinking, and ignored the nudge. Didn't she deserve to sit and catch her breath until these people got their act together and got on with it? She was thinking that maybe she'd put in too much sugar, she knew Father Tim didn't like too much sugar, but why, after all these years and hundreds of cakes later, did she still worry and fret over her work as if she'd never baked a cake in her life? The Expert is what some called her, but who could feel like an expert at something as willful and fickle as a cake, cakes having, as she'd always feared, a mind of their own? Use the same ingredients in the same amounts, time after time after time, and were her cakes ever the same? Not as far as she could see.

She'd always depended on Gene to be the judge and he hadn't failed her yet. Gene would take a taste of the batter and his eyes would wander around the room, as if that little taste had transported him on some round of roving thoughts and idle speculation. After a while, he'd come back to himself. "Best yet!" he might say, or, "Couldn't be better!"

Whatever he said, he would have reasoned it out, thought it through, and she could depend on the answer—which was more than most wives could say of their husbands. Now, you take Father Tim, his wife would be able to depend on him—the only question was, was she deserving of such a prize? She thought she was, she hoped she was; she was crazy about Cynthia, but hadn't her senator husband, or was he a congressman, run around with other women? What did that mean? Cynthia didn't look like a cold fish—the opposite, more like it.

Anyway, didn't their rector have enough sense to come in out of the rain and choose who he wanted to spend the rest of his life with? And in the last few months, hadn't she and everybody else in the parish heard him laugh and joke like never before?

Lord help, it must be virgin's bower that was making her eyes burn and her sinuses drain. Virgin's bower mixed with lilies, the bane of her existence, and nobody with the simple courtesy to remove the pollen from the anthers, which means it would be flying around in here like so much snuff, and her with no Sinu-Tabs in her pocketbook and too late to do anything about it.

Pete Jamison made his way into the nave of Lord's chapel, where a robed and expectant choir overflowed from the narthex. Embarrassed at being late, he dodged through the throng to the rear wall and stood, reverent and shaken, feeling at once a stranger here and also oddly at home. He realized his breath was coming in shallow gasps, probably because he'd run more than a block from the Collar Button where he'd parked—or was it from the excitement he felt in being here for the first time since his life had been changed forever?

Two rows from the front, on the gospel side, Miss Sadie sat holding hands with Louella, oblivious of the time and enjoying the music. She felt certain that the emotions stirring in her breast were those of any proud mother.

After all, Father Tim wasn't merely her priest, her

brother in Christ, and one of the dearest friends of this life, he was also like a son. Who else would run up the hill after a hard rain and empty the soup kettle sitting brimful under the leak in her ceiling? And who else would sit for hours listening to her ramble, while appearing to be genuinely interested? God in His Providence had not seen fit to bless her with children, but He'd given her Olivia Harper and Timothy Kavanagh! And, since she'd helped raise Louella from a baby, she could almost count her pewmate as her child—Lord knows, she wasn't but ten years old when she'd begun diapering and dressing that little dark baby as if it were her own!

Miss Sadie wiped a tear with the handkerchief she had carefully chosen for the occasion, a lace-trimmed square of white Irish linen monogrammed with her mother's initial, and turned and smiled proudly at Louella, who looked a perfect blossom in the lavender dress.

Dooley Barlowe swallowed hard. It would have been fine if everything had started when it was supposed to, but here it was twenty minutes after five and who knew where Cynthia and Father Tim were, like maybe they both got scared and ran off, or had a fight and weren't going through with it. He felt foolish sitting here in the front row, all of them tricked into waiting like a bunch of stupid goats, listening to organ music. He was about to die to go to the toilet, but if he tried now to make it to the parish hall, everybody would know where he was going.

He crossed his legs and squeezed his eyes shut and jiggled his foot and went through the verses again.

Reverend Absalom Greer had purposely followed Sadie Eleanor Baxter into the nave, though he tried to appear as if he had no idea she was anywhere around. He followed her so he could sit behind her and look at her again. Who knows when the Lord might call him Home and this would be his last chance on earth to see her face?

The way it fell out was, he was the first to go into the pew behind her, which meant he had to sit all the way to the end, by the window of Jesus washing the disciples' feet. He thought this location was a blessing from above, seeing as he could look at her in profile instead of at the little gray knot on the back of her head.

Absalom felt such a stirring in his breast that he might have been fourteen years old, going up Hogback to see Annie Hawkins, carrying two shot quails and a mess of turnips in a poke. Annie's mama was dead of pneumonia and her daddy not heard of since the flood, and as Annie was left to raise a passel of brothers and sisters, he never went up Hogback without victuals;

once he'd killed a deer and helped her skin it and jerk the meat.

It had taken him three years to get over big-boned, sassy-mouthed Annie Hawkins, but he'd never gotten over Sadie Baxter. Sadie had filled his dreams, his waking hours, his prayers for many a year; he'd earnestly hoped she would forget Willard Porter and marry him. Finally, the burning hope had fizzled into a kind of faint glow that laid on his heart like embers, making him smile occasionally and nod his head and whisper her name. He'd confessed this lingering and soulful love only to the Almighty and never told another, though sometimes his sister, Lottie, suspicioned how he was feeling and derided him with a cool stare.

Reverend Greer settled stiffly into the creaking pew and nodded to those around him and bowed his head and prayed for his dear brother in the Lord, Tim Kavanagh, as fine a man as God ever gave breath to, amen. When he lifted his head and looked at Sadie's profile and the tender smile on her face, the tears sprang instantly to his eyes and he fetched the handkerchief from his pocket, the handkerchief Lottie had starched and ironed 'til it crackled like paper, and thanked the Lord Jesus that he still had eyes to see and tears to wipe, hallelujah.

Pete Jamison, though six-foot-three, eased himself up on the balls of his feet so he could see down front to the gospel side. He found the pew where he sat the day he had wandered, alarmed and desperate, into the darkened church. It had been sometime around Thanksgiving and there was snow on the ground; he remembered noticing his incoming tracks as he left the church a different man, one to whom everything seemed fresh and new.

He'd knelt that day and cried out to God, asking a simple question: *Are you up there?* He wasn't trying to get anything from God, he wasn't begging for money or success, though at the time he urgently needed both, he just wanted to know more desperately than he'd ever wanted to know anything in his life, if God was up there—no more ifs, ands, or buts, just *yes or no.* Now he knew the answer more completely than he could ever have hoped or imagined.

He felt tears smart his eyes, and his heart expand. The music was beginning to enter him; he was beginning to hear it over the pounding of his heart, and was glad to feel the joy of this time and place as if it might, in some small way, belong also to him.

Standing outside the church door in the warm September afternoon, Katherine Kavanagh saw the bride and groom literally galloping down the street, and suppressed a shout of relief. She tugged on her skirt for the umpteenth time and tried to relax her tense shoulders so the jacket would fall below her waistline. In the desperate half hour she'd waited for Cynthia to show up, she had decided what to do. The minute she returned home, she was suing the airline, who had gotten away with their criminal behavior long enough.

Though wanting very much to dash across the churchyard and meet Cynthia, she realized this impetuous behavior would cause her skirt to ride up. She stood, therefore, frozen as a mullet as she watched the bride sprinting into the home stretch.

Next to the aisle on the epistle side, Emma Newland nearly jumped out of her seat as the organ cranked up to a mighty roar. The thirty-seven-voice ecumenical choir was at last processing in, sending a blast of energy through the congregation as if someone had fired a cannon.

The congregation shot to its feet, joining the choir in singing hymn number 410 with great abandon and unmitigated relief:

Praise my Soul the King of Heaven;
To His feet thy tribute bring;
Ransomed, healed, restored, forgiven,
Evermore His praises sing;
Alleluia, alleluia!
Praise the everlasting King!

Dooley Barlowe felt something happen to the top of his head. He had opened his mouth with the rest of the congregation and heard words flow out in a strong and steady voice he scarcely recognized as his own.

Praise Him for His grace and favor;
To His people in distress;
Praise Him still the same as ever,
Slow to chide and swift to bless.
Alleluia, alleluia,
Glorious in His faithfulness.

Dooley thought Father's Tim's voice carried loud and clear from where he stood with the bishop and Walter at the rail. The bishop was decked out in a really weird hat, but looked cool as anything otherwise. As for Father Tim, he'd never seen him in a tuxedo before and thought he looked . . . *different,* maybe sort of handsome.

The tremor in his stomach subsided; he felt suddenly tall and victorious and forgot about having to go to the toilet.

Hessie Mayhew gazed at Stuart Cullen, whom she found exceedingly good-looking, and thought it was a darned good thing that Episcopal clergy were allowed to marry, otherwise it could cause a rumpus. She'd never chased after clergy like some women she knew, but she couldn't dismiss their powerful attraction, either. Anyway, who'd want to tie the knot with a preacher and end up with a whole churchful of people pulling you to pieces day and night? *Head this, chair that!* No, indeed, no clergy for her, thank you very much.

She fluffed her scarf over the odd rash that had appeared on her neck, dismissing it as one of the several hazards of her calling, and hoped the bishop was noticing the flowers and that someone would tell him about Hessie Mayhew, who, even if she was Presbyterian, knew a thing or two about the right and proper way to beautify a church.

> *Angels, help us to adore Him;*
> *Ye behold Him face to face;*
> *Sun and moon, bow down before Him,*
> *Dwellers in all time and space.*
> *Alleluia, alleluia!*
> *Praise with us the God of grace.*

Jena Ivey could not carry a tune in a bucket and preferred to look at the stained-glass window for the duration of the processional hymn. The window was of Christ being baptized while John the Baptist stood onshore in his animal skin outfit. It seemed to her that St.

John could have presented himself better, seeing it was the Lord Jesus who was getting baptized; like it wasn't as if St. John didn't know He was coming, for Pete's sake. Look at the three wise men, who always appeared nicely groomed, though they'd been riding camels for *two years*.

She was startled by the sound of the trumpet only a few feet away, causing, simultaneously, an outbreak of goose bumps and a wild pounding of her heart.

Then, suddenly, there was the matron of honor charging down the aisle; Jena didn't have a clue who this woman might be, she was tall as a giraffe. That's the way it was with weddings, they turned out people you'd never seen before in your life and would never see again.

Emma thought the matron of honor blew past like she was going to a fire, canceling any opportunity to study the skimpy cut of Katherine Kavanagh's suit, or to check out the kind of shoes she had on. She did, however, get a whiff of something that wasn't flowers, it was definitely perfume, possibly from Macy's or some such.

Then came Rebecca Jane Owen and Amy Larkin, wearing velvet hair bows the color of green Baxter apples. As far as Emma could tell, they were fairly smothered with flowers; you'd think Hessie Mayhew would scale down for children, but oh, no, Hessie scaled up, these two infants were fairly tottering under the weight of what looked like full bushes of hydrangeas.

Jabbing Harold to do the same, Emma swiveled her head to see the bride trotting behind the small entourage.

Cynthia Coppersmith was flushed as a girl—her eyes shining, her face expectant, her hair curled damply around her face as if she'd just won a game of tag. Emma thought she looked sixteen years old if she was a day, and her suit was exactly the color of a crayon Emma had favored in first grade, aquamarine. She appeared to be moving fast, but that was all right—hadn't she herself run lickety-split to marry Harold Newland, starved to death for affection after ten years of widowhood and thrilled at the prospect of someone to hug her neck every night?

Emma leaned over the arm of the pew so she could see Father Tim as his bride approached the altar. The look on his face made her want to shut her eyes, as if she'd intruded upon something terribly precious and private.

"Dearly beloved, we have come together in the presence of God to witness and bless the joining together of this man and this woman in Holy Matrimony. The bond and covenant of marriage was established by God in creation, and our Lord Jesus Christ adorned this manner of life by His presence and first miracle at a wedding in

Cana of Galilee. It signifies to us the mystery of the union between Christ and His Church, and Holy Scripture commends it to be honored among all people.

"The union of husband and wife in heart, body, and mind is intended by God for their mutual joy; for the help and comfort given one another in prosperity and adversity; and, when it is God's will, for the procreation of children and their nurture in the knowledge and love of the Lord. Therefore marriage is not to be entered into unadvisedly or lightly, but reverently, deliberately, and in accordance with the purposes for which it was instituted by God.

"Into this holy union, Cynthia Clary Coppersmith and Timothy Andrew Kavanagh now come to be joined. . . ."

Uncle Billy Watson hoped and prayed his wife would not fall asleep and snore; it was all he could do to keep his own eyes open. Sitting with so many people in a close church on a close afternoon was nearabout more than a man could handle. He kept alert by asking himself a simple question: When it came time, would he have mustard on his ham, or eat it plain?

"Cynthia, will you have this man to be your husband; to live together in the covenant of marriage? Will you love him, comfort him, honor and keep him, in sickness and in health; and, forsaking all others, be faithful to him as long as you both shall live?"

Winnie Ivey clasped her hand over her heart and felt tears burn her cheeks. To think that God would give this joy to people as old as herself and no spring chickens . . .

The bride's vow was heard clearly throughout the nave. "I will!"

"Timothy, will you have this woman to be your wife; to live together in the covenant of marriage? Will you love her, comfort her, honor and keep her, in sickness and in health; and, forsaking all others, be faithful to her as long as you both shall live?"

"I will!"

"Will all of you witnessing these promises do all in your power to uphold these two persons in their marriage?"

"*We will!*"

At the congregational response, Dooley Barlowe quickly left the front pew by the sacristy door and took his place in front of the altar rail. As he faced the cross and bowed, one knee trembled slightly, but he locked it in place and drew a deep breath.

Don't let me mess up, he prayed, then opened his mouth and began to sing.

Oh, perfect Love, all human thought transcending,
Lowly we kneel in prayer before Thy throne,
That theirs may be the love which knows no ending,
Whom Thou forevermore dost join in one.

It all sounded lovey-dovey, thought Emma, but she knew one thing—it would never work if Cynthia sat around drawing cats while her husband wanted his dinner! Oh, Lord, she was doing it again, and this time without intending to; she was running down a person who didn't have a mean bone in her body. She closed her eyes and asked forgiveness.

She'd held on to her reservations about Cynthia like a tightwad squeezes a dollar, but she felt something in her heart finally giving way as if floodgates were opening, and she knew at last that she honestly approved of the union that would bind her priest's heart for all eternity. Disgusted with herself for having forgotten to bring a proper handkerchief, Emma mopped her eyes with a balled-up napkin from Pizza Hut.

Oh, perfect Life, be Thou their full assurance
Of tender charity and steadfast faith,
Of patient hope and quiet, brave endurance,
With childlike trust that fears nor pain nor death.

Pete Jamison pondered the words "childlike trust that fears nor pain nor death," and knew that's what he'd been given the day he'd cried out to God in this place and God had answered by sending Father Kavanagh. He remembered distinctly what the father had said: "You may be asking the wrong question. What you may want to ask is, Are You down here?"

He'd prayed a prayer that day with the father, a simple thing, and was transformed forever, able now to stand in this place knowing without any doubt at all that, yes, God is down here and faithfully with us. He remembered the prayer as if he'd uttered it only yesterday. *Thank you, God, for loving me, and for sending Your son to die for my sins. I sincerely repent of my sins, and receive Christ as my personal savior. Now, as Your child, I turn my entire life over to You.* He'd never been one to surrender anything, yet that day, he had surrendered everything. When the church was quiet and the celebration over, he'd go down front and kneel in the same place he'd knelt before, and give thanks.

Gene Bolick wondered how a man Father Tim's age would be able to keep up his husbandly duties. As for himself, all he wanted to do at night was hit his recliner after supper and sleep 'til bedtime. Maybe the father knew something he didn't know. . . .

Louella heard people all around her sniffling and

blowing their noses, it was a regular free-for-all. And Miss Sadie, she was the worst of the whole kaboodle, bawling into her mama's handkerchief to beat the band. Miss Sadie loved that little redheaded, freckle-face white boy because he reminded her of Willard Porter, who came up hard like Dooley and ended up amounting to something.

Louella thought Miss Cynthia looked beautiful in her dressy suit; and that little bit of shimmering thread in the fabric and those jeweled buttons, now, that was something, that was nice, and look there, she wasn't wearing shoes dyed to match, she was wearing black pumps as smart as you please. Louella knew from reading the magazines Miss Olivia brought to Fernbank that shoes dyed to match were out of style

It seemed to her that the sniffling was getting worse by the minute, and no wonder—just *listen* to that boy sing! Louella settled back in the pew, personally proud of Dooley, Miss Cynthia, the father, and the whole shooting match.

Finally deciding on mustard, Uncle Billy abandoned the game. He'd better come up with another way to noodle his noggin or he'd drop off in a sleep so deep they'd have to knock him upside the head with a two-by-four. He determined to mentally practice his main joke, and if that didn't work, he was done for.

Grant them the joy which brightens earthly sorrow,
Grant them the peace which calms all earthly strife,
And to life's day the glorious unknown morrow
That dawns upon eternal love and life.
Amen.

Dooley returned to his pew without feeling the floor beneath his feet. He was surprised to find he was trembling, as if he'd been live-wired. But it wasn't fear, anymore, it was . . . something else.

Father Tim took Cynthia's right hand in his, and carefully spoke the words he had never imagined might be his own.

"In the name of God, I, Timothy, take you, Cynthia, to be my wife, to have and to hold from this day forward, for better for worse, for richer for poorer, in sickness and in health, to love and to cherish, until we are parted by death.

"This is my solemn vow."

They loosed their hands for a moment, a slight movement that caused the candle flames on the altar to tremble. Then she took his right hand in hers.

"In the name of God, I, Cynthia, take you, Timothy,

to be my husband, to have and to hold from this day forward, for better for worse, for richer for poorer, in sickness and in health, to love and to cherish, until we are
parted by death.

"This is my solemn vow."

As Walter presented the ring to the groom, the
bishop raised his right hand. "Bless, O Lord, these rings
to be a sign of the vows by which this man and this
woman have bound themselves to each other; through
Jesus Christ our Lord, Amen."

"Cynthia, I give you this ring as a symbol of my
vow, and with all that I am, and all that I have, I honor
you, in the name of the Father, and of the Son, and of
the Holy Spirit."

She felt the worn gold ring slipping on her finger; it
seemed weightless, a band of silk.

Katherine stepped forward then, delivering the
heavy gold band with the minuscule engraving upon its
inner circle: *Until heaven and then forever.*

"Timothy . . . I give you this ring as a symbol of my
vow, and with all that I am, and all that I have, I honor
you, in the name of the Father, and of the Son, and of
the Holy Spirit."

Hessie Mahew was convinced the bishop looked
right into her eyes as he spoke.

"Now that Cynthia and Timothy have given themselves to each other by solemn vows, with the joining of hands and the giving and receiving of rings, I pronounce that they are husband and wife, in the name of the Father, and of the Son, and of the Holy Spirit.

"Those whom God has joined together . . . let no man put asunder."

Dooley felt the lingering warmth in his face and ears, and heard the pounding of his heart. No, it wasn't fear anymore, it was something else, and he thought he knew what it was.

It was something maybe like . . . happiness.

CHAPTER TEN

The
Beginning

enry Oldman met them at the airport in the Cullen camp car, a 1981 turquoise Chevy Impala that made the rector's Buick look mint condition, showroom.

It was theirs to drive for the week, and they dropped Henry off at his trim cottage with a two-stall cow barn and half-acre garden plot. While Cynthia chatted with Mrs. Oldman, Henry gave him the drill.

"New tires," Henry said, delivering a swift kick to the aforesaid.

"Wonderful!"

"New fan belt."

"Great!"

"Miz Oldman washed y'r seat covers."

"Outstanding. Glad to hear it."

"Mildew."

The handyman who'd served the Cullens for nearly

fifty Maine summers was sizing him up pretty good, he thought; trying to figure whether he'd be a proper steward for such fine amenities.

"You'll be stayin' in th' big house, what they call th' lodge. Miz Oldman put this 'n' that in y'r icebox. Juice an' cereal an' whatnot."

"We thank you."

Henry pulled at his lower lip. "Washin' machine door come off, wouldn't use it much if I was you."

"I suppose not."

"Downstairs toilet handle needs jigglin' or it's bad to run. Ordered th' part t' fix it, but hadn't got it yet."

"We'll remember."

"You got a pretty big hole in y'r floor. Last year or two, we've had more'n one snake come in."

"*Which* floor exactly?"

"Dinin' room. I set a barrel over it, Bishop said it'd be all right 'til I can get somethin' to fix it. Had a rag in th' hole but somethin' chewed it out."

Now we're getting down to it, he thought.

"Got rid of y'r ants, but not much luck with th' mice, mice're smarter'n we give 'em credit for."

His wife didn't need to know this. Not any of this.

Henry kicked the tire again for good measure. "Attic stairs, you pull 'em down, they won't go up ag'in."

The rector shrugged. He'd rather have a root canal without Novocain than stand here another minute.

"Course you know there's no electric at th' Cullen place."

No electric? His blood pressure was shooting up; he could feel the pounding in his temples. "What *lights* the place? *Pine torches?*"

"Only two places hereabout still has gas-lit."

He hadn't fared so badly since trucking off at the age of nine to Camp Mulhaven, where he entertained a double-barreled dose of chiggers and poison ivy. What would Cynthia think? What had he gotten them into? He'd wring his bishop's neck, the old buzzard; his so-called honeymoon cottage was a blasted tumbledown shack! He'd call the moment they arrived and give Stuart Cullen a generous piece of his mind. . . .

"Wouldn't keep any food settin' on th' porch." Henry removed a toothpick from his shirt pocket and pried the circumference of his left molar.

"Why's that?" He couldn't remember ever leaving food on a porch. Why would anyone leave food on a porch?

"Bear."

Bear?

He craned his neck to peer at his wife, standing with

Mrs. Oldman by a flower bed. Thank heaven she hadn't overheard the last pronouncement.

"Well!" said the rector, putting an end to the veritable Niagara of bad news. "We'll see you when we bring the car back."

"You'll see me tomorrow," said Henry. "Bishop called today, asked me to come check th' water, see if it's runnin' muddy. Bishop's daddy, he tried to dig a new well before he passed, but . . ." Henry raised both hands as if he had no responsibility for the failure of this mission, it was some bitter destiny over which he'd lacked any control. "Bishop said bring you some speckled trout, you know how to clean trout?"

"Ahhh," he said, wordless. He'd never cleaned trout in his life.

Henry raised an eyebrow. "I'll have Miz Oldman do it for you."

He could hardly wait to get in the car, if only to sit down.

These were the days of heaven. . . .

He walked out to the porch, loving the feel of old wood, silken with wear, under his bare feet.

The view took his breath away. Early morning mist

hovered above the platinum lake, and just there, near its center, a small island with a cabin on its narrow shore. . . .

Nothing stirred except waterfowl: He saw a merganser and a string of young ply the water with great determination. Next to the lodge, cedar waxwings dived and swooped in the seed-dowered garden.

It would definitely take some getting used to, but he was liking this place better with every passing moment.

He expanded his chest and sucked in his stomach and circled his arms like propellers, awash in happiness, in contentment—in a kind of energized sloth, if there could be such a thing.

Though they'd slept at his house the first night and at hers on the second, last night had somehow marked the true beginning.

At the rectory, his antediluvian mattress had rolled them into the middle of the bed like hotdogs in a bun. At her house, circumstances were considerably improved, though the alarm clock had, oddly, gone off at three a.m. Odder still, the clock wasn't in its usual place on her bedside table. Failing to turn on a lamp, they leapt up to locate the blasted thing and, navigating by moonlight alone, had crashed into each other at the bookcase.

But last night had been everything, everything and more.

He cupped his hands and drew them to his face and smelled her warm scent, now and forever mingled with his own. In truth, he had entered into a realm that had little to do with familiar reason and everything to do with a power and mystery he'd never believed possible. Perhaps for the first time in his life, there was nothing he craved to possess, nothing he felt lacking; he was only waiting for his coffee to perk.

He had schlepped the coffee in his suitcase, for which effort his underwear smelled of decaf Antigua and his socks of full-bore French Roast. Eager to begin their honeymoon on a note of thoughtfulness, if not downright servitude, he had gone to the kitchen to concoct the coffee, to be followed by a breakfast of . . . he opened the cabinets and checked the inventory . . . a breakfast of raisin bran in blue tin bowls.

He'd never messed with gas stoves. While chefs were commonly known to prefer cooking with gas, he'd always feared it might blow his head off. Dangerous stuff, gas, he could smell it in here more strongly than in the rest of the house. If he lit a match, they could be spending their honeymoon in Quebec. . . .

But come on, for Pete's sake, wasn't he up for a little excitement on this incredibly beautiful, endlessly promising day? Wasn't all of this an adventure, a new beginning?

He withdrew a kitchen match from the box and studied it soberly, then walked to the gas-powered refrigerator and retrieved the coffee. Now. Where might the coffee pot be lurking?

Aha. That must be it on the shelf above the stove. Then again, surely not. He took it down and inspected it. Campfires. Many campfires. He lifted the lid. Oh, yes, just like his mother once used, there was the basket on its stick. . . .

Thinking he should try and clean the pot, he removed the basket and peered inside. Hopeless! He rinsed it out under a trickle of cold water. That would have to do; this was not, after all, a military kitchen.

He filled the basket with some satisfaction, thankful he'd brought preground, otherwise they'd be chewing beans. . . .

His wife appeared, looking touseled and teenaged in her nightgown. She slipped her arms around his waist and kissed him. "I love campfire coffee!"

Using the flat of his hand, he hammered down on the lid, which, once round, had somehow become oval with age. "What don't you love, Kavanagh?"

"Ducks that cry all night, beds with creaking springs, and feather pillows with little gnawing things inside."

"My sentiments exactly." He smiled at his bride, set the pot on the stove, and struck the match.

"Stand back!" he warned.

⊙⊙

"Those weren't ducks calling last night."

They were rocking on the porch, side by side. He had never felt so far from a vestry in his life. "They're loons."

"Loons!" she said, marveling.

The ensuing silence was punctuated with birdsong.

"Related to the auks."

"Who, dearest? The Cullens?"

"The loons."

"Of course."

"They mate for life."

"Lovely! Just like us."

They watched the navigation of yet another duck family, thought they spotted a bald eagle, counted three kingfishers, sipped a second cup of coffee.

He relished their easy quietude this morning; it held a richness to be savored. Surely he was blessed beyond all reckoning to have a highly verbal wife who could also be quiet. He had always valued that in a woman, in a man, in a friend. Though his mother had possessed a sparkling way with people and was bright and eager in conversation on many subjects, she also had a gentle quietude that made her companionship ever agreeable.

"God is mercifully allowing me to forget the dreadful experience of getting here," Cynthia said of yesterday's journey.

"You mean the four-hour mechanical delay, the two-hour layover, and the forty-five minutes on the runway with no air stirring in the cabin?"

"The same!" she said.

"The usual," he said.

He wondered what his dog might be doing at the moment. And how about his boy—how was he faring? He'd call home tonight. On second thought, he could forget calling anybody. His bishop had conveniently forgotten to say there was no phone at Cullen camp.

"I love this place, Timothy. It's so wonderfully simple."

"What would you like to do today?"

"Nothing!"

He was thrilled to hear it.

"Of course," she said, "we might pop down to the village and peek in the shops."

He hated to be the bearer of bad news. "Umm . . ."

"There are no shops!" she said, reading his mind.

"Right. Only a service station, a small grocery store with a post office, and an unused church."

"So we can poke through the graveyard. I love graveyards!"

He grinned. "Of course you love graveyards. But I don't think there's a graveyard at this particular church. Stuart mentioned that the flock was buried elsewhere."

She leaned back in the rocker and turned her head and looked into his eyes, smiling. "Well, then," she murmured.

He took her hand and lightly kissed the tips of her fingers. "Well, then," he said.

Henry had come on Wednesday with fresh trout and a blackberry pie baked by Mrs. Oldman, and on Thursday with a free-range chicken, a quart of green beans, a sack of beets and potatoes, and a providential lump of home-churned butter.

In truth, they were savoring unforgettable meals at an oilcloth-covered table on the porch, lighted in the evening by a kerosene lantern. One evening had been crisp and cold enough for a fire; they'd hauled the table indoors and dined by the hearth on a hearty vegetable stew, sopping their bowls with bread toasted over the fire and slathered with Oldman butter. Each dish they prepared was such a stunning success that he now dreaded going home to four pathetic electric eyes, albeit on a range of more recent vintage.

In the four days since arriving, they'd clung to the porch like moss to a log, celebrating the sunrise, cheering the dazzling sunsets. Their off-porch expeditions had been few—a walk around the lake, twice, and a canoe excursion to the island. Not being water lovers, they made the island foray with considerable temerity. Finding the cabin empty, they picnicked under a fir tree on a threadbare Indian blanket and, setting off for home, found the trip across had so bolstered their confidence that they paddled north for a couple of miles, only to be drenched by a downpour.

Yesterday, they'd climbed through the window of another cabin in the Cullen camp. Sitting on the floor of a room built in 1917, according to the date carved on a rafter, they drank Earl Grey tea from a thermos and told all the jokes they could remember from childhood.

Finding themselves on a roll, she suggested they draw broomstraws to see who'd entertain the other with a retelling of Uncle Billy's wedding joke.

The rector was not pleased to draw the short straw. After all, who but Uncle Billy could tell an Uncle Billy joke? He returned the straw. "Sorry," he said, "but this joke can't be done without a cane."

She got up and went to the fireplace, whipped the broom off the hearth, and handed it over.

"Is there no balm . . . ?" he sighed.

"None!" she said.

Using the hearth for a stage and the broom for a cane, he hunkered down and clasped his right lower back, where he thought he might actually feel an arthritic twinge.

"Wellsir, two fellers was workin' together, don't you know. First'n, he was bright 'n cheerful, th' other'n, he didn't have nothin' to say, seem like he was mad as whiz. First'n said, 'Did you wake up grouchy this mornin'?' Other'n said, 'Nossir, I let 'er wake 'er own self up.'"

Hoots, cheers, general merriment.

"That's just m' warm-up, don't you know, hit ain't m' main joke."

The audience settled down and gazed at him raptly.

"Wellsir, Ol' Adam, he was mopin' 'round th' Garden of Eden feelin' lonesome, don't you know. So, the Lord asked 'im, said, 'Adam, what's ailin' you?' Adam said he didn't have nobody t' talk to. Wellsir, th' Lord tol' 'im He'd make somebody t' keep 'im comp'ny, said hit'd be a woman, said, 'This woman'll rustle up y'r grub an' cook it f'r you, an' when you go t' wearin' clothes, she'll wash 'em f'r you, an' when you make a decision on somethin', she'll agree to it.' Said, 'She'll not nag n'r torment you a single time, an' when you have a fuss, she'll give you a big hug an' say you was right all along.'

"Ol' Adam, he was jist a-marvelin' at this.

"The Lord went on, said, 'She'll never complain of a headache, an' 'll give you love an' passion whenever you call for it, an' when you have young'uns, she'll not ask y' to git up in th' middle of th' night.' Adam's eyes got real big, don't you know, said 'What'll a woman like 'at *cost* a feller?' Th' Lord said, 'A arm an' a leg!'

"Adam pondered a good bit, said, 'What d'you reckon I could git f'r a rib?'"

Generous applause, ending with the whistle his wife learned as a ten-year-old marble player.

Crawling out the way they'd come in, they left the cabin before dusk and trekked to the lodge on an over-grown path.

During these jaunts, he faithfully looked for bear and stayed alert to protect his wife, though he saw nothing more suspicious than a raccoon seeking to purloin Wednesday's chicken bones.

Today, Cynthia had hauled out sketch pads and pencils and abandoned any notion of leaving the porch. She vowed she'd seen a moose swimming in the lake and was not keen to miss further sightings. He, meanwhile, lay in a decrepit hammock and read G. K. Chesterton.

Peace covered them like a shawl; he couldn't remember such a time of prolonged ease. There were, however, moments when Guilt snatched him by the scruff of the neck, determined to persuade him this was a gift he had no right to unwrap and enjoy, and he'd better watch his step or *else*. . . .

"Listen to this," he said. "'An adventure is only an inconvenience rightly considered. An inconvenience is only an adventure wrongly considered.'"

She laughed. "I didn't know G.K. had been to Cullen camp."

"And this: 'The Christian ideal has not been tried and found wanting. It has been found difficult, and left untried.' Does that nail it on the *head*?" He fairly whooped.

"I love seeing you like this," she said.

"Like what?"

"Happy . . . resting . . . at ease. No evening news, no phones, no one pulling you this way and that."

"Stuart knew what he was doing, after all."

"I have a whole new respect for your bishop," she declared.

A loon called, a dragonfly zoomed by the porch rail.

"I heard something in our room last night," she said.

"Something *skittering* across the floor. What do you think it was?"

"Oh, I don't know—maybe a chipmunk?" Right there was proof positive that his brain was still working.

"I love chipmunks!"

He put the Chesterton on the floor beside the hammock and lay dazed and dreaming, complete. "'Blessed be the Lord . . . ,'" he murmured.

"'. . . who daily loadeth us with benefits!'" she exclaimed, finishing the verse from Psalm Sixty-eight.

A wife who could read his mind and finish his Scripture verses. Amazing. . . .

When he awoke, he heard only the faint whisper of her pencils on paper.

"Dearest, could you please zip to the store for us?"

"That car will not *zip* anywhere," he said.

"Yes, but we can't go on like two chicks in the nest, with poor Henry our mother hen. We must have *supplies*."

"I suppose it would be a good thing to keep the battery charged."

"A quart of two-percent milk," she said, without looking up from her sketch pad, "whole wheat English muffins, brown eggs, an onion—we can't make another meal without an onion—and three lemons—"

"Wait!" He hauled himself over the side of the

creaking hammock and trotted into the house for a pen and paper.

She held up the sketch and squinted at it. "Oh, and some grapes!" she called after him. "And bacon! Wouldn't it be lovely to smell bacon frying in the morning? I do love raisin bran, Timothy, but *really*. . . ."

Though the late afternoon temperature felt unseasonably warm when he left the car, it was refreshingly cool as he entered the darkened store.

A man in a green apron was dumping potatoes from a sack into a bin; he looked up and nodded.

The rector nodded back, wondering at his odd sense of liberty in being untethered, yet wondering still more about his desire to hurry back to his wife. This was, after all, the first time they'd been apart since the wedding; he felt . . . barren, somehow, *bereft*. Perhaps it was the sixtysomething years for which, without knowing it, his soul had waited for this inexpressible joy, and he didn't want to miss a single moment of it. Then again, his joy might owe nothing to having waited, and everything to love, and love alone.

He didn't understand these things, perhaps he never

would; all he knew or understood was that he wanted to inhale her, to wear her under his very skin—God's concept of "one flesh" had sprung to life for him in an extraordinary way, it was food, it was nectar; their love seemed the hope of the world, somehow. . . .

He chose a package of thick-sliced market bacon. This was living on the edge, and no two ways about it.

But perhaps he was happiest, in reflection, about the other waiting, the times when the temptation to have it all had been nearly unbearable, but they had drawn back, obeying God's wisdom for their lives. The drawing back had shaken him, yes, and shaken her, for their love had exposed their desire in a way they'd never known before. Yet, His grace had made them able to wait, to concentrate on the approaching feast instead of the present hunger.

He set his basket on the counter.

"You over on the lake?" the man asked.

"We are."

"Looks like you'll have a fine sunset this evenin'."

He peered through the store windows toward the tree line. *Holy smoke!* If he hurried, he could make it back to the lodge in time. . . .

"Anything else I can round up for you?"

"This will do it."

"You sure, now?"

As he took out his wallet, he realized he couldn't stop smiling.

"Thank you, this is all," he said. "I have absolutely everything."

COMING IN SUMMER 2002

New from Viking. . .

JAN KARON'S

In This
Mountain

Father Tim and Cynthia have been at home in
Mitford for three years since returning from
Whitecap Island. In the little town that's home-away-
from-home to millions of readers, life hums along as
usual for the endearing townspeople. Though Father
Tim dislikes change, he dislikes retirement even more.
As he and Cynthia gear up for a year-long ministry
across the state line, a series of events sends shock waves
through his faith—and the entire town of Mitford.

In her seventh novel in the bestselling Mitford
series, Jan Karon delivers surprises of every kind,
including the return of the man in the attic, and an
ending that no one in Mitford will ever forget.

VIKING

For more works by **JAN KARON**, look for the

At Home in Mitford
ISBN 0-14-025448-X

A Light in the Window
ISBN 0-14-025454-4

These High, Green Hills
ISBN 0-14-025793-4

Out to Canaan
ISBN 0-14-026568-6

A New Song
ISBN 0-14-027059-0

*A Common Life:
The Wedding Story*
ISBN 0-14-200034-5

JAN KARON books make perfect holiday gifts.

From Penguin:

The Mitford Years
Boxed set includes: *At Home in Mitford; A Light in the Window; These High, Green Hills; Out to Canaan* and *A New Song.*
ISBN 0-14-771596-2

From Viking:

*Patches of Godlight:
Father Tim's Favorite Quotes*
ISBN 0-670-03006-6

*The Mitford Snowmen:
A Christmas Story*
ISBN 0-670-03019-8

PENGUIN AUDIO: The Mitford Years Audio

At Home in Mitford   ISBN 0-14-086501-2; *A Light in the Window*
ISBN 0-14-086596-9; *These High, Green Hills* ISBN 0-14-086598-5
Out to Canaan ISBN 0-14-086597-7; *A Common Life* ISBN 0-14-180274-X; *A New Song* (Abridged) ISBN 0-14-086901-8; *A New Song* (Unabridged) ISBN 0-14-180013-5; *The Mitford Years Boxed Set*
ISBN 0-14-086813-5

In bookstores now from Penguin Putnam Inc.

Visit the Mitford Web site at www.mitfordbooks.com

To order books in the United States: Please write to Consumer Sales,
Penguin Putnam Inc.
P.O. Box 12289, Dept B, Newark, New Jersey 07101-5289.
VISA, MasterCard and American Express cardholders
call (800) 788-6262 or (201) 933-9292.